THE WAGES
of
FAME

By Thomas Fleming from Tom Doherty Associates

Remember the Morning
The Wages of Fame

THE WAGES

of

FAME

Thomas Fleming

A TOM DOHERTY
ASSOCIATES BOOK
New York

THE WAGES OF FAME

This book is printed on acid-free paper.

A Forge Book
Published by Tom Doherty Associates, Inc.
175 Fifth Avenue
New York, NY 10010

Forge® is a registered trademark of Tom Doherty Associates, Inc.

Library of Congress Cataloging-in-Publication Data

Fleming, Thomas J.
    The wages of fame / Thomas Fleming.—1st ed.
        p.   cm.
    "A Forge book"—T.p. verso.
    ISBN 0-312-86309-8
    I. Title.
  PS3556.L45W3   1998   98-23446
813'.54—dc21   CIP

First Edition: September 1998
Printed in the United States of America
0 9 8 7 6 5 4 3 2 1

To Tom and Susan

The history of every country begins in the heart of every man or woman.

—WILLA CATHER

CHRONOLOGY

1800—Thomas Jefferson elected president. "Second American Revolution" attacks elitism in national life.

1803—Jefferson purchases Louisiana Territory from France, vastly expanding the national domain.

1804—Aaron Burr kills Alexander Hamilton in duel.

1804—Jefferson reelected president.

1808—James Madison, Jefferson's secretary of state, elected president.

1812—Madison reelected. War of 1812 with England begins. Americans badly defeated in Canada.

1814—British burn Washington, D.C.

1815—General Andrew Jackson rescues America from humiliation by inflicting a shattering defeat on an invading British army at New Orleans.

1816—James Monroe, another disciple of Jefferson's, elected president.

1818—General Jackson invades Florida in a punitive expedition against raiding Indians. He hangs two British traders who are supplying the Indians with weapons.

1820—James Monroe reelected president.

1824—John Quincy Adams elected president by House of Representatives. "Corrupt bargain" between Adams and Henry Clay excludes Andrew Jackson, who received the largest popular vote.

1826—Thomas Jefferson and John Adams die. Symbolic farewell of the generation that founded the nation.

1828—Andrew Jackson defeats President John Quincy Adams in a landslide. The Democratic Party is born.

1832—Andrew Jackson reelected in another landslide.

1832–33—South Carolina secedes from the Union. President Jackson's threat to use force and lack of support from other Southern states bring a quick end to the crisis.

1836—Texas defeats Mexico and declares its independence. It expects to be admitted to the United States but its status as a slave state causes problems.

1836—Martin Van Buren, Jackson's vice president, elected president, defeating William Henry Harrison, candidate of the new Whig Party.

1840—William Henry Harrison defeats Van Buren for the presidency in the "log cabin" campaign—the first to use slogans and imagery.

1841—Harrison dies after only a month in office. John Tyler of Virginia becomes president. Essentially a Democrat, he vetoes most of the Whig program.

1842—Tyler's wife, Letitia, dies. In 1844 he marries Julia Gardiner and together they launch a campaign to admit Texas to the Union.

1844—James Polk elected president.

1845—Congress votes to admit Texas on President Tyler's last day in office.

1845—Andrew Jackson dies at his Tennessee home, the Hermitage.

1846—Mexican War begins when Mexico attacks U.S. Army on the Rio Grande. General Zachary Taylor wins two quick victories at Palo Alto and Resaca de la Palma. He captures Monterrey in September 1846 and becomes a presidential candidate.

1847—Taylor wins another battle at Buena Vista in February. President Polk puts General Winfield Scott in charge of the war and he begins drive on Mexico City from Vera Cruz. After hard fighting he captures the capital in September.

1848—Treaty of Peace with Mexico is approved. United States acquires New Mexico and California, adding five hundred thousand square miles to the national domain.

1848—Whig candidate Zachary Taylor elected president. Violent battle in Congress over whether slavery should be permitted in the newly captured territories.

1849—Ex-president Polk dies three months after leaving office.

1850—President Taylor dies. Millard Fillmore becomes president. He signs Compromise of 1850, temporarily defusing confrontation between North and South.

1852—Democrat Franklin Pierce elected president. Turmoil over slavery subsides but South remains restive and seeks expansion, either by acquiring Cuba or territory in Central America.

1854—Kansas-Nebraska Act makes concessions to the South—offers "squatter sovereignty" in the territories—slavery will be banned or permitted by majority vote. Abolitionists and pro-slavers fight civil war in Kansas.

1856—Republican Party organized on a platform of no slavery in the territories.

1856—Democrat James Buchanan narrowly elected president. Turmoil over Southern desire for expansion continues. "Filibustering" expeditions attempt to seize Cuba.

1860–61—Republican Abraham Lincoln elected president with only 39.8 percent of the popular vote. In ten Southern states he does not receive a single vote. Southern states secede. The Civil War begins.

THE WAGES
of
FAME

A WORD TO READERS
OF THE FUTURE

As I begin this book, my heart is filled with dread that I may be inflicting a wrong on my friend George Stapleton. But write it I must, not merely because it is a look behind the veils that men draw across the history of their time. It is also an attempt to do justice to all the actors in the story, not least of them myself.

To remove even the taint of partisanship, I have reduced myself to one of the many characters. Who of us would deny that when we look back fifty years, the self we discover is a semi-stranger, perhaps better described in the third person?

Although the narrative begins in 1827, when George Stapleton and I were in our early twenties, the story extends deep into the years that preceded those days of our youth. Thanks to the Stapletons and their profound sense of involvement in America's meaning and destiny, we are in intimate touch with the thoughts and the feelings of men and women who knew Washington and Jefferson and Hamilton as friends—or enemies. Their political and personal passions vibrate through the decades. America has never been a dusty package of economics and abstract issues. From the start it involved fervid partisans challenging one another for power and fame, each intensely convinced that justice and history were on his side.

I hope this vital truth has enabled me to avoid the habit of so many memoirists, to coat the days of youth in a glow of golden unreality. We sensed the tensions, the regrets, the sorrows, swirling through the lives of the older generation. But I must confess, like most Americans, we faced the future with a confidence that we would somehow avoid the pitfalls and tragic paradoxes of age. America of the 1820s was charged with hope and heartbreaking innocence.

Perhaps you will say we should have known better. Beyond the founders, the Stapletons' reach extended to those dim days when white men and red men, Frenchmen and Englishmen, fought for possession of a primeval continent and the first blacks arrived in slave ships from Africa to confront America with a moral challenge that continues to torment her. But Americans, their eyes turned resolutely to the future, managed to avoid this somber reality for a long time. In our story you will witness the gradual realization that this baffling tragedy has at its heart a terrific conflict between good and evil.

Evil becomes a presence in this story the way it often infiltrates people's lives—silently, stealthily, while the eyes are averted, while the heart is groping for love or the self for recognition. Evil does not negate the human—it surrounds it little by little with a web of compromises and half-truths until the moment of terrible realization is reached, the moment when a life is ultimately entangled—or freed.

As I wrote this narrative, I watched myself succumb to evil. I watched my friend George Stapleton confront it and struggle fiercely in its deadly strands. Above all I have pondered the angry humanity, the inexplicable vulnerability, the hidden anguish of that formidable woman who is at the heart of the story—my enemy, Caroline Kemble Stapleton. How she tormented me over the decades! Even when we were hundreds of miles apart, when we did not speak for years, I lived in her mind, even at times in her body, to the detriment of my own life. She was a kind of vortex, draining my emotions and thoughts into her imperious soul, the way a planet seizes a wandering asteroid in its voracious, invisible gravity.

Was she admirable? Pitiable? In the wake of a war that has left six hundred thousand Americans dead, such personal questions seem absurd. Perhaps it is better to fling into history's face the words she hurled into mine: *I regret nothing.* Even if those words are a lie. These days, the truth often seems no more than a haunted lie.

Jeremy Biddle
Washington, D.C., July 4, 1870

BOOK

ONE

ONE

ABOVE THE HUDSON RIVER AND THE ever multiplying rooftops of New York, the September sky was crystal blue, dotted by scudding clouds. A brisk west wind invoked apostrophes to Shelley—and to the vast continent that receded over the horizon on the other side of the broad river. On such a perfect day, Jeremy Biddle had no trouble persuading George Stapleton and John Sladen to join him for an amble to the steamboat dock beside the Bowling Green at the tip of Manhattan to meet his Ohio cousin Caroline Kemble.

In their years at Columbia, the three had become more or less inseparable. Jeremy, sentimental about friendship, called them the *frères trois*. He took not a little credit for this harmony. In those days he was fond of considering himself a third—an expert at softening the collisions and clashes that our very different natures seem to make inevitable in this world. Between Sladen and Stapleton, a third was urgently needed. Slim and swarthy, with something of the aura of a fallen angel, John Sladen had a reserved, caustic personality, its edges sharpened by poverty and family disappointment. George Rensselaer Stapleton was his opposite, a big, easygoing paragon of amiability and optimism, thanks to his family's wealth and his view of life as a romantic adventure.

Jeremy, with his thick glasses and unruly mass of red hair and mouth full of uneven teeth, was anything but handsome. Interest in his Ohio cousin was minimal, on the unspoken assumption that there was likely to be a family resemblance. There was another reason why Stapleton had abandoned his books of poetry and Sladen had put aside his newspapers crammed with acrimonious political prose. Aboard the good ship *Hercules* arriving from Perth Amboy was the ex-president of the United States, James Monroe, who had vacated the executive mansion in Washington some two years ago.

Columbia, not yet driven from its ancient buildings on Murray and Chapel Streets by the real estate developers, was only a brisk walk from their destination. A moderate crowd had assembled on and around the dock by the time the *frères trois* arrived. *Hercules* was a spanking new steamer, well over a hundred feet long, with powerful paddle wheels on both sides. She churned smartly up to the dock and reversed her engines with a blast of her whistle that caused many ladies and a few men to cover their ears.

Down the gangplank soon stumped the ex-president. To the young eyes of the *frères trois,* he was a curious figure. The collegians wore the pantaloons, tall hats, and flowing coats of their era, which had profited from the liberating influences of the French Revolution. The president was wearing the constricting style of 1776—knee breeches, lung-binding waistcoat (vest), and tight coat that sloped away to two narrow tails in the back. On his gray head was a cocked hat such as George Washington wore. For a moment they could do nothing but goggle. It was like seeing a piece of history, alive and walking among them.

George Stapleton's eyes grew damp. He hoped to write a chant to the Revolution in Homeric hexameters. Seeing Monroe stirred his admiration of the heroes of that era, so different from their puny contemporary politicians. Beside him, John Sladen had a different reaction. "He looks like an even bigger fool than they say he is," he muttered.

Down the gangplank behind Mr. Monroe strode a young woman in a simple, high-waisted, blue dress and carelessly draped blue cloak. Raven black hair fell in a cascade to her shoulders. The broad, open forehead, the brows firmly arched without a hint of heaviness, the chiseled nostrils, and perfect mouth cast in the softest feminine mold reminded the *frères trois* of some supreme work of art. With all its purity of outline, the face was not severe or coldly statuesque but superbly serene. To its perfect glory was added a pink coral tint that flushed faintly through the pale cheeks, while the lift of the long, trailing lashes revealed the magnificent eyes.

"Who's that adorable creature?" John Sladen murmured.

Having no idea, Jeremy and George could only stare as the ex-president, once he had reached the bottom of the gangplank, turned and gallantly assisted the black-haired beauty to the dock. "Mr. Monroe," she said in a warm, throaty voice, "you are too kind. May I introduce you to my cousin?"

Whereupon, Caroline Kemble led the city's most distinguished visitor of the year 1827 over to Jeremy and with a coolly triumphant smile said, "This is Jeremy Biddle. President Monroe and I met on the steamer. Who are these gentlemen, Jeremy dear?"

Jeremy managed to stutter out the identities of Stapleton and Sladen. The ex-president shook their hands and said, "You have the most interesting cousin, Mr. Biddle. She told me stories of her grandmother's adventures in New Jersey during the Revolution that deserve to be put into a book. I have a particular fondness for that state. I was with Washington at Trenton in '76. I saw how our little victory ignited patriotism in her people."

"You're too modest, Mr. President," George Stapleton said. "As I recall from my history books, you received a wound at Trenton, leading a charge on a Hessian gun."

"Who'd believe young fellows remember things that happened so long ago," Monroe said, immensely pleased at George's compliment.

Hurrying to Monroe's side were his daughter, Mrs. Maria Gouveneur, and her numerous family as well as the pompous mayor of New York, the Honorable Philip Hone, and a half dozen other distinguished welcomers. The ex-president beamed at Caroline Kemble for another moment. "She reminds me so much of my wife the day I married her. She's the same age," he said.

This was no small tribute. Mrs. Monroe had been one of the great beauties of her era. The ex-president went off with his relatives and the welcoming committee while the *frères trois* gazed in astonishment at Caroline Rawdon

Kemble. No one was more amazed than Jeremy Biddle. He had never seen his Ohio cousins. Like many other New Jerseyans, they had migrated west around the turn of the century.

"How did you know me?" Jeremy asked.

"Mother told me to look for the homeliest boy on the dock," she said.

George Stapleton and John Sladen chuckled. Jeremy was somewhat less amused, but he managed to produce a rueful smile. It was their first glimpse of Caroline's Western directness.

"How did you meet the president?" John Sladen asked.

"He was standing alone on the upper deck, with everyone else too tongue-tied to speak to him. I introduced myself and we chatted agreeably until we docked."

"I'm glad to see Western women have mastered the manners of democracy," John Sladen said.

This was a loaded word—even a loaded sentence—in 1827. The Democrats were a controversial movement, full of rancor against the "ruling clique" as they called Monroe and his successor, President John Quincy Adams. Their hero was General Andrew Jackson, the Tennessean who had lost the 1824 presidential election although he won a plurality of the popular vote.

"I predict women will master a great many things before our generation totters off to oblivion, Mr. Sladen," Caroline said in her oddly authoritative voice.

"Does that include the men in their lives?" Sladen asked in his wryest style.

"That depends a great deal on whether the men choose to join us—or oppose us."

"Oppose, join, you sound like a veritable revolutionary, Miss Kemble," George Stapleton said in his hearty way. George's size and stature—he had a magnificent physique—combined to give a slightly condescending tone to his words.

Caroline's blue eyes became opaque. She gazed at George with a condescension of her own that reduced him to the consistency of rice pudding. "We simply wish to be treated as intelligent beings, Mr. Stapleton. Is that asking too much?"

"Of course not," George gasped, writhing like a soldier who had just received a fatal wound. Which in fact he had. He was in love with Caroline Kemble before they left the dock. Jeremy Biddle saw a similar ardor igniting John Sladen's saturnine eyes.

Alarmed at the way things were unfolding, Jeremy asked, "Do you have the address of your school?"

"Of course. Mother was her usual methodical self." From her purse Caroline produced a letter in which Martha Kemble instructed her "dear nephew" to escort Caroline to Miss Lucretia Carter's Female Seminary on Richmond Hill. This was a good mile beyond Columbia on the west side of New York. They located Caroline's trunk among the luggage on the dock and carried it to a nearby hackney coach for the trip uptown.

Caroline gazed around her with near ecstatic delight. "Mother wanted me to go to a school in Philadelphia. But I insisted on New York."

Her escorts pointed out the principal sights—majestic Trinity Church, in whose graveyard Alexander Hamilton and other revolutionary-era giants lay, the elegant new City Hall in its green park, their alma mater's ivy-covered walls.

"That's where I really wanted to go," Caroline said, gazing up at Columbia's tiers of windows. "At my grandmother's suggestion, I wrote to them. They replied that no female could possibly survive their *rigorous* course of study without destroying her constitution. Tell me, gentlemen—did you find the study of Greek and Latin verbs threatened your nervous systems?"

"Not nearly as much as you're threatening them, Miss Kemble," George Stapleton said.

Jeremy had heard family tales of Caroline's grandmother, the formidably named Katherine Stapleton Rawdon. She too was a relic of America's revolutionary days—approaching her eighties now. Jeremy gathered Mrs. Rawdon had some strong ideas about women's rights and the equality of the sexes. These were not uncommon among the women of her time. The Revolution had stirred up a great deal of intellectual dust among all sorts of people. But fifty years had passed—and for most of America the dust had long since settled into the comfortable ideas that had guided the world since Adam's day. Men were husbands, fathers, and masters; women were wives, mothers, and helpmates.

"You're no better than your antiquated professors," Caroline said. "You refuse to take me seriously."

"Miss Kemble, it's impossible for any man with eyes in his head *not* to take you seriously," George Stapleton said.

"Oh? I must scar my face with acid, cross my eyes, knock out a tooth or two—and then you might actually listen to my opinions? I despise your attitude, Mr. Stapleton. Until you reform it, I haven't the slightest desire to speak to you again."

Jeremy Biddle could scarcely believe his ears. Neither could John Sladen. Here was a woman who coolly—or better, heatedly—flung defiance in the face of a young man who stood to inherit a minimum of a million dollars. Caroline was undoubtedly aware of George's future fortune. She was his distant cousin, thanks to a long-ago marriage between George's great-granduncle and her great-grandmother.

While George floundered, the hackman cracked his whip over his team of bays and they rolled briskly uptown to Miss Carter's Female Seminary. Caroline spent the rest of the journey telling them she was sure she would hate the place. The course of study consisted of French, piano playing, and sewing. These were the three arts society believed an educated young woman required to be an adequate wife and mother.

"Not a word about history or literature!" Caroline said.

"What are some of your favorite books, Miss Kemble?" John Sladen asked.

"Gibbon's *Decline and Fall of the Roman Empire* is my supreme favorite," Caroline said. "I also enjoyed Chief Justice Marshall's life of George Washington, David Hume's *History of England,* and Mercy Otis Warren's history of our revolution. The latter I'm sure none of you have read, it being by a mere *woman.*"

George Stapleton, not the most industrious of students, had trouble keeping his jaw from succumbing to the law of gravity. Even Jeremy Biddle, who prided himself on some attention to their courses, was amazed. John Sladen's eyes glittered with dark delight.

"I'll be happy to loan you some of my books, Miss Kemble," Sladen said. "May I also say I read Mrs. Warren's history. I found it a most interesting production."

"I think it deserves a far more substantial adjective," Caroline said.

"On that point, I regret to say we must disagree. I don't feel she dealt adequately with the military side of the struggle. I also detected a certain hostility to George Washington, born no doubt of her Massachusetts prejudices."

"You may be right," Caroline said grudgingly. "What books do you have at your disposal?"

Sladen reeled off a half dozen histories of European countries and biographies of great men, including his hero, Napoleon.

"If you would dispatch them to me, I would be most grateful," Caroline said.

"There's also an excellent circulating medium, the New York Society Library, which you can join for a trifling sum," Jeremy said.

"I fear I haven't even trifling sums available to me," Caroline said. "I'm here as a sort of scholarship student, thanks to the generosity of Mr. Stapleton's grandfather."

"The Congressman?" George said.

Caroline's voice descended an octave; she spoke in a timbre charged with sorrow. "My mother wrote to him, pleading for a loan to send me to school somewhere and appease my determination to escape the environs of Twin Forks, Ohio. He generously donated the full amount of my tuition and suggested I come East to widen my education beyond the realm of books."

At this point, the coachman opened the door and announced they had arrived at Miss Carter's Seminary five minutes ago. None of the *frères trois* had noticed that their forward motion had ceased. It was a tribute to how totally Caroline Kemble had mesmerized them. They sprang from the coach and Stapleton and Sladen carried her trunk up the steps of the modest town house. Miss Carter's Seminary was three stories high and its whitewashed brick front was badly in need of painting. It seemed to confirm the melancholy portrait of poverty and rejection Caroline had drawn for them.

A maid directed them to the front parlor, which also showed signs of genteel desuetude. The *frères trois* shifted about uneasily, none of them quite certain they were entitled to stay, yet all reluctant to leave.

"May we call upon you here, Miss Kemble?" John Sladen said. "It would give us the greatest pleasure to show you more than passing glimpses of the sights of New York."

George Stapleton violently confirmed this entertaining proposal. "*Nothing* could give us more pleasure," he said.

"I have no idea what the rules of this establishment will be. I'm only certain there will be rules," Caroline said.

"There certainly are rules!" thundered a female voice. In the doorway loomed Miss Lucretia Carter. She was at least six feet tall. She wore a black

muslin gown with round, blue buttons down the front and some sort of epaulets on her shoulders. She glowered suspiciously at the *frères trois,* as if she
was certain they were clandestine white slavers, ready to lure all her students
into some Algerian bashaw's harem.

Jeremy introduced himself as Caroline's cousin and displayed her
mother's letter to assure Miss Carter their presence was entirely proper. But
no amount of pleading could mitigate Caroline's crime of arriving with three
male escorts.

"Our young ladies may receive visitors between the hours of noon and five
P.M. on Sunday. At no other time are visitors welcome," Miss Carter said.
"Young ladies are expected at all other times to apply themselves to their
studies."

"I'm sure Miss Kemble will demonstrate her eagerness to do that," Jeremy
said.

The *frères trois* turned to make brief bows to Caroline. "I hope you'll send
me some of those books, Mr. Sladen. I'm sure I would enjoy them," she said.

"Books?" Lucretia Carter said. "You will have no need of books other
than those assigned to you, miss."

"These were books on politics and history," Caroline said. "Subjects that
interest me extremely."

"No self-respecting lady *ever* displays an interest in such mundane matters," Miss Carter said. "Come with me, miss. I'll show you to your room."

The *frères trois* trooped glumly into the street. Sladen stared up at Miss
Carter's Female Seminary with more than usual spleen on his sardonic face.
"My God, Stapleton," he said. "Didn't your grandfather investigate this miserable school before sending a young woman so fine—so intelligent—to be
incarcerated in it?"

"Grandfather considers himself enlightened to believe in women's education," George said. "And he is. He was born in 1742, for God's sake! I'm
sure this place is no worse than other schools."

"I begin to think this will cure me of that tendency to self-pity that you
see as the chief defect of my character," Sladen said.

"I don't think there's any need for this storm of sympathy," Jeremy said.
"Cousin Caroline seems to me perfectly capable of taking care of herself. I'm
inclined to feel sorry for Miss Carter."

"What would Napoleon do in a situation like this?" Sladen asked rhetorically. "We should launch a military campaign to rescue Cousin Caroline from
intellectual and spiritual debasement."

"I think it might be simpler to persuade my mother to let her live with her
and my cousin Sally in our town house," George said. "She could become a
day student at Miss Carter's and we could visit her to our hearts' content."

George was lazy but he was not stupid. He smiled mockingly at Sladen,
who could only gaze glumly back at him. Jeremy knew what Sladen was
thinking: *The million-heir has done it again. He has reminded us of how
insignificant the rest of us are.* Jeremy occasionally worried about Sladen's
bouts of envy when he contemplated George Stapleton's wealth. The Sladens
had fought in the Revolution and traced their lineage back to the seventeenth
century. But various kinds of bad luck had pursued them for generations.

"Your mother doesn't approve of me. It probably has something to do with the cut of my clothes," Sladen said to George. "Or my failure to elevate my pinkie when I drink my coffee."

George's mother, Angelica Stapleton, was a tremendous snob. Hauteur came as naturally to her as breathing. It had a lot to do with being born a Van Rensselaer, heiress to half the Hudson River valley.

"I'll make sure she lets you call now and then," George said with a grin. "I see no need to take unfair advantage."

There it was, out in the open already. Jeremy's two best friends were about to become rivals for Caroline Kemble's affections. If he could have foreseen the impact this contest would have on all their lives—not to mention the history of the country—he would have concocted some scheme that would have sent Caroline back to Ohio to commune with tree stumps, no matter how melancholy it made her—or how guilty it made him.

But Jeremy had no more ability to read the future than any other man in the year 1827. He even entertained the foolish optimism that as an already experienced third, he could cushion the hard feelings that would inevitably emerge in this interesting drama. He was like a novice seaman, sailing into his first hurricane.

T W O

BACK IN THEIR ROOMS AT COLUMBIA, Jeremy made his first attempt to pour oil on their already troubled waters. "I want a solemn promise that you'll both conduct yourselves as gentlemen," he said. "No matter what this willful creature does or says, you won't allow it to destroy our friendship. Agreed?"

"Agreed," declared Messrs. Sladen and Stapleton with perfect equanimity.

"You're both gambling on the unknown, the unforeseeable. You're about to explore life's ultimate mystery—the female mind."

"I prefer the word *soul,*" George said. "*Mind* is utterly inadequate to describe the sensations her eyes stir in me. They can only emanate from some supernatural realm."

At times the George Stapleton of 1827 sounded like a fool. This can happen if a fellow reads too much poetry in college. Jeremy was confident that his best friend would grow into a man once he escaped his mother and the unreal groves of academe.

Jeremy was baffled by the nasty confidence in John Sladen's eyes. How could he hope to win this woman in competition with George Stapleton? While Jeremy did not presume his cousin Caroline was mercenary, he found it hard to believe any woman, raised in comparative poverty, could ignore the attraction of a million dollars, especially when it came in the person of a man as good-natured, as companionable, as muscular, as George.

Jeremy puzzled over why John Sladen was even entering the contest. His best hope for a strong start in life was marriage to a wealthy young New York woman whose parents would support his early years as a lawyer and push clients his way. Sally Stapleton, George's cousin, had been a perfect choice—and she seemed more than amenable to John's attentions. But he had abruptly abandoned his pursuit just when his prospects seemed promising.

Jeremy was too young to understand how deeply resentment can alter a man's soul, how anger can become a kind of barely controlled force that drags him headlong into desires and acts that he cannot explain to anyone, including himself. In the matter of politics, Sladen was already displaying this tendency. He was a frequent visitor to Tammany Hall, headquarters of the city's Democrats, who worshiped before portraits of Andrew Jackson and cavorted around the General's symbol, a hickory pole, at election time. Almost every successful merchant in New York would have severe doubts about his daughter marrying a Democrat. But John persisted in his politics, ignoring Jeremy's advice.

In his melancholy way, John Sladen was as romantic as George Stapleton. But John's hero was Byron, the dark angel of the new breed of poets, while George admired gentler spirits, such as Wordsworth and Keats. Jeremy should have realized that spleen made a mockery of the calculation that John claimed to admire. The scorn that dominated his feelings was at war with the very idea.

George soon made good on his promise to persuade his formidable mother to take Caroline Kemble into her Beekman Street town house. As her only son, he could cajole her into almost anything he really wanted. He allowed her the illusion of ruling his life in matters romantic because it suited his indolent easygoing nature.

Caroline was immensely grateful to George for this emancipation—and to Jeremy, for obtaining her mother's approval of it with a letter assuring Aunt Martha that her daughter's studies would proceed uninterrupted. Even schoolmistress Lucretia Carter had to grudgingly agree that Caroline would obtain a far more ladylike polish in the gleaming interior of the Stapleton town house.

Angelica Van Rensselaer Stapleton put great stress on appearances. Her house was a treasure trove of fine furniture and Turkey carpets, weighty silver and Sevres dinner services. To Caroline, raised in an Ohio farmhouse, the place looked like a palace. But she retained her implausible hauteur that men found irresistible.

George persuaded his mother to invite the *frères trois* to a triumphant dinner a few weeks after Caroline's arrival. To the table Angelica added his cousin Sally, a year older than Caroline, and her latest beau, an up-and-coming lawyer named Fenimore Gardiner; the writer Washington Irving, who was an old girlhood friend; and several others of his vintage. It was a merry gathering, with frequent quotations and praise for Mr. Irving's books on New York and his much acclaimed sketches of English life. Short, plump, and genial, Mr. Irving was elegantly dressed like the aristocrat he had been from birth. He looked as if he had been born to sit at well-appointed dinner tables.

Good cheer and light conversation predominated until John Sladen asked Mr. Irving what he thought of the administration of President John Quincy Adams.

"I think he's set the country on a good course. Whether he can keep her on it is the question," Irving replied.

"You're not troubled by the corrupt bargain on which his presidency is based?" Sladen asked.

Sladen was referring to an arrangement Adams had apparently made with Senator Henry Clay of Kentucky, whereby Clay threw his support to Adams in return for a promise that the Kentuckian would become secretary of state. The deal had been crucial to Adams's success in the balloting in the House of Representatives. The presidential election had landed there when none of the four candidates received a majority of electoral votes.

Irving was markedly cool to the indignation Sladen seemed to be professing. "Politicians are always making bargains," Irving said. "Not all of them are corrupt."

"But this one, sir, which involved the selling of the presidency and the deprivation of the man who led the vote, General Jackson—"

"That was the best thing that could have happened to the country," Fenimore Gardiner said. "Andrew Jackson isn't fit to be president of a barnyard!"

"I'm inclined to agree with Mr. Gardiner, without the animadversion of the barnyard," Irving said with a placid smile. "I suggest you read my first book, *The History of New York* by Diedrich Knickerbocker. Amongst the jokes you'll find some interesting comments on the dangers of too much democracy."

"I've read it, sir. But I found its politics impossible to praise," Sladen said.

A gasp ran down the table. Sladen was virtually insulting the most famous American writer of his time. "May I say that I too read it," Caroline Kemble said. "It's one of my very favorite books, even though I too am a devotee of this movement Mr. Sladen so recklessly worships—democracy. But for a very different reason. I hope it will give more scope to women's rights and abilities."

"I fear no lady can come in contact with the brawling shouters and shovers for democracy without becoming tragically coarsened, Miss Kemble," Irving said.

"I agree—absolutely!" said Fenimore Gardiner.

"So do I," said Angelica Van Rensselaer Stapleton, who was beginning to regard the entire conversation with distinct disapproval. Slim and erect, with angular, fine-boned features, she had a royal manner, which her exquisitely curled blond hair and fondness for diamond jewelry did nothing to diminish.

It was a classic confrontation between youth and age—with Fenimore Gardiner deserting his generation to join the previous one. Irving was clearly uncomfortable, but Sladen would not drop the subject. "Your attitude puzzles me, Mr. Irving. Once, as I understand it from my late father, you were a staunch supporter of Colonel Aaron Burr, a sentiment my father shared so extravagantly it led to his ruin. Without Colonel Burr there would be no Tammany Hall, the very engine of democracy here in New York."

"It's been twenty years since I supported Mr. Burr. Neither he nor I could foresee the consequences of all our youthful indiscretions," Irving said. "I saw the Colonel on the street only the other day. He was looking a bit shabby, I'm sorry to say."

"Mr. Irving," George Stapleton said, "while you were in Europe, you met many of the English poets. Would you share your impressions of them?"

"Shelley was my favorite," Irving said. "Partly because he had the most extraordinary wife. Any man who could write good poetry and keep Mary Wollstonecraft happy had to be a genius. After his death my playwright friend John Payne made the mistake of proposing to her. But she said Americans lacked moral grandeur—which eliminated me from the line of suitors as well."

"I'm a shameless worshiper of her mother," Caroline Kemble said. "One of the first books I read as a girl was her *Vindication of the Rights of Women.* My grandmother considers it the greatest book ever written."

"An utterly seditious, atheistic document!" cried Angelica's large, forbidding sister, Henrietta Van Rensselaer.

"Was Shelley's Mary an atheist?" Caroline asked Mr. Irving, ignoring Aunt Henrietta. Caroline seemed almost too eager to anticipate the answer to this question.

"I'm quite certain she was. She and her mother both saw atheism as a prerequisite for revolution," Irving said. "But my friend Payne was confident he could lead her to a commonsensical faith."

George began a labored defense of Shelley's atheism, which he maintained was not intellectual but emotional, born of his sympathy for the poor and the oppressed. George was plainly trying to defend Caroline's apparent approval of this stark theological stance.

"You may be right," Irving said. "But I fear the political timing of their poetic call for a new revolution was atrocious. After two decades of war and carnage in the wake of France's upheaval, the world yearns for peace and stability. We've turned to the church, the school, the home, the government of men of proven talents and virtue, with a sigh of relief."

"Amen," said Fenimore Gardiner.

It was the triumphant voice of conservatism. Mr. Irving's sunny optimism and aristocratic view of life made it sound inevitable to those of his age at the table. But the younger generation, minus Fenimore Gardiner, resisted this paean to the status quo.

Even George Stapleton found himself among the doubters. "I would almost suffer a revolution if it produced something as beautiful as Shelley's 'Ode to the West Wind,' " George said.

"I'd suffer one without it," John Sladen said, gazing down the table at Caroline Kemble. She was wearing a lingerie gown of faded red, obviously something she had inherited from her mother. The short sleeves and high neckline were distinctly unstylish. But her bare, sinuous arms, her marvelous face, caught every male eye. She was unquestionably the most beautiful woman at the table. John was ready to upend the entire social order to possess this tantalizing creature.

"I fear neither of you young gentlemen have actually seen a revolution. It would change your minds, with or without an ode to the west wind," Washington Irving said.

"How true!" said the older generation virtually in unison. The excesses of the French Revolution had left deep scars in the human psyche everywhere—including distant America. Jeremy Biddle found himself inclined to agree with the seniors. His father had told him of mobs storming through the streets of his native Philadelphia, threatening to drag President George Washington out of his house and hang him.

"We've survived one revolution," John Sladen said. "Why not another?"

"Our revolution, my dear young sir, was actually a rebellion," Washington Irving said. "There was no revolt against the social order—excepting those supernumeraries from England who pretended to be at the top of it."

"Exactly," declared the older generation in another burst of choral agreement.

The dinner party ended in a rather strained atmosphere. After George's mother bid Fenimore Gardiner and the older guests good-bye, she returned to the front parlor with a forbidding frown. "George," she said, "would you mind staying for a half hour or so? There's something I want to discuss with you."

That was the signal for John Sladen and Jeremy Biddle to depart—and for Caroline and Sally Stapleton to retreat to their rooms. Alone, mother and son faced each other warily. "What extraordinary taste in friends you have, George," Angelica said. "I think I've remarked more than once on the peculiarity of your association with Mr. Sladen."

"He's the cleverest man in my class, Mother," George said. "Jeremy and I understand him very well, I assure you. He's in no danger of seducing us into his wild political ideas. We see it as our task to moderate his opinions and make a useful citizen out of him."

"I have grave doubts about such pretensions to benevolence. But they're mild compared to my thoughts of the extraordinary creature you've foisted on me as a houseguest. Does Caroline Kemble truly believe those opinions she declaimed at our table tonight? Mary Wollstonecraft! A woman whose private life—not to mention her public opinions—would bar her from every respectable home in England or America! Even France!"

"She's grown up under the influence of a grandmother who married a freethinking Englishman. I have no doubt you can easily persuade her to change her ways with a little kindness, Mother. Remember how often Father used to talk of the power of kindness?"

"He had a Quaker mother," Angelica Stapleton said. "Mine was Dutch—more inclined to a switch than a swatch of piety."

Thirteen years of widowhood, of managing her own affairs in a man's world, had made Angelica Stapleton a rather hard woman on the surface. George knew her well enough to stand his ground. "Kindness is more than piety, Mother. Make her a daughter for a little while, as you've done with Sally. The girl's starved for affection, I assure you."

This conversation must strike some readers as unusual—a young man lecturing his mother on maternal affection. But George Stapleton's predominating characteristic was his remarkable sympathy for the emotions of others. In some respects he was a new kind of American, softened (too much, some would say) by the decades of prosperity in which he had been born and raised, gentled by the revolution in psychology that poets such as Keats and Shelley signaled, in which the intellect that ruled the eighteenth century had given way to the preeminence of feeling.

"Be generous to her, Mother. Buy her some decent dresses. Persuade Sally to introduce her to some of her friends. Make her feel truly at home in this house and I guarantee you her extreme feelings will vanish like hoarfrost before a spring sun."

"You're really the most extraordinary creature, George. No young man of my youth would ever have said such wise things to his headstrong mother."

"None of them had a mother he trusted absolutely. I know how generous your heart is, Mother, though you struggle to conceal it."

"That's sheer flattery, George!" Angelica Stapleton said, although she was pleased by the compliment. What woman could resist it? "Now I must ask you an important question. What do you hope to gain from my reformation of this wild Ohio creature into a sensible woman?"

"A loving wife," George said.

THREE

JOHN SLADEN BEGAN THE CONTEST BY borrowing ten dollars from George Stapleton to take Caroline to the Bowery Theater. This splendid new building was a testament to New York's growing opulence. Illuminated by hundreds of glass-shaded gas jets, it boasted no fewer than three thousand plush seats. The play was *Pocahontas* by George Washington Parke Custis, the step-grandson of George Washington.

It was not a very good play but the actors brought the old story alive. After rescuing John Smith from being burned at the stake, Pocahontas married John Rolfe with the approval of her father, Chief Powhatan. The most striking character was imaginary—Pocahontas's former Indian lover, Matacoran, whom John Smith defeats in battle. In the final scene, as a show of amity, Smith frees him. Matacoran spurns the gesture and refuses to surrender to the white men. He will go west to "the utmost verge of the land the Manitou gave his fathers" and live there "wild and free."

Somewhat improbably, John Smith hails this defiance and declares "the esteem of the English" will go with him.

Strolling back to the Stapleton town house on Beekman Street through the usual evening throng, John Sladen asked Caroline if she agreed with Matacoran. Would she prefer to live wild and free rather than submit to society's often idiotic customs and laws?

"I would never *submit* to being a slave to such things," Caroline said. "But if I chose to accept them, with the approval of my heart and head, that would be a different matter. Having grown up in Ohio when it was a wilderness infested by bears and Indians, I'm not averse to a little civilization."

"Do you really have such freedom of choice? Aren't women in somewhat the same condition as Indians and Africans? Creatures who must make the best terms they can manage with the ruling power?"

"We have our ways of ruling them in return."

"Excuse me," John said. "I shouldn't be inflicting my prejudices on you. When you spend most of your time with the rich, you grow weary with their smug conviction that they're always right."

"Are you talking about George Stapleton?"

"George is my friend. I don't cast aspersions on my friends. He struggles to overcome the inevitable deficiencies of being born rich. I'm thinking more of that insufferable prig Fenimore Gardiner. Or his suave mentor, Washington Irving. Do you know why Irving is so ready to defend the administration of President John Quincy Adams?"

Caroline could only shake her head. In her rural Ohio isolation, she knew little about the details of contemporary politics, beyond the broad clash between Democrats and conservatives, who were called Federalists in those days.

"Mr. Irving's just been appointed ambassador to Spain. A nice comfortable sinecure that will leave him with no need to fret about making money from his half-baked books."

"You feel his opinion of the president is for sale?"

"I feel it's been bought."

"I must confess I thought he was rather callous, the way he brushed aside your mention of your father's devotion to Aaron Burr."

"Thank you."

"My father too had an attachment to Mr. Burr. He was one of the young bravos who joined his expedition to conquer Texas and possibly Mexico in 1806. My father never forgot the eloquence with which Mr. Burr described his dream of an American empire on the Rio Grande. It haunted him to the day of his death."

Sladen was too stunned to speak. Discovering this link between his lost father and Caroline's father had transcendent meaning for him. He was instantly convinced that destiny had brought them together.

"I don't understand why an attachment to Mr. Burr would ruin your father in New York," Caroline said. "It did my father no harm in Ohio."

"It's a nice illustration of the way New Yorkers play dirty politics," John said, making no attempt to disguise his bitterness.

He described how ardently his father had admired Colonel Aaron Burr as he rose to power, first as U.S. senator, then, with the backing of Tammany Hall, as vice president on the triumphant ticket with President Thomas Jefferson in 1800. But Jefferson wanted his friend James Madison to succeed him and quietly undercut Burr, with the eager assistance of the Colonel's numerous enemies in New York. Thomas Sladen had remained loyal even after Burr killed Alexander Hamilton in their famous 1804 duel, making himself a political pariah in New York. Burr compounded this blunder with his 1806 expedition down the Mississippi to conquer Texas, then a Spanish possession. President Jefferson indicted him for treason, accusing him of planning to detach the Western states from the Union and form a new nation. Burr was acquitted but his political reputation was ruined, this time on a national scale.

All but a handful of Burrites made their peace with Jefferson and his New York satellite, Governor George Clinton. Stubbornly clinging to his fallen idol, Thomas Sladen saw his law practice dwindle to nothing, and old friends cut him in the street. Eventually, his morale collapsed and he fled west, a fugitive from numerous creditors.

"Unfortunately, he didn't live wild and free," Sladen said. "He fell off a steamboat and drowned in the Ohio River."

"Oysters, fresh oysters!" bawled a fat, red-faced Irishwoman on the corner of Barclay Street and Broadway. She had her fare spread on a bed of ice in her rolling cart.

"Let's eat some of New York's favorite food," John said. "Maybe it will cool the fever in my brain that Aaron Burr tends to ignite."

Pity flooded Caroline's heart. She saw how vulnerable he was beneath his truculent manner. She was discovering—or displaying—one of the more intriguing sides of the feminine mind. The prouder the woman, the more susceptible she is to that strange emotion that lives on the border of love—but in the end is love's enemy.

Caroline let John lecture her on the shapes and sizes of New York's oysters. He called them the *pâté de foie gras* of the poor. They each devoured a half dozen of the crusty creatures sprinkled with a peppery tomato sauce, which the Irishwoman claimed was her own invention. It was a happy end to a pleasant evening. Caroline told him how grateful she was and they parted with her assurance that she would be happy to see him again soon.

At 19 Beekman Street, Caroline found Angelica Stapleton and her sister Henrietta playing whist in the second parlor. Caroline described the play and rhapsodized over the beauty of the Bowery Theater. Angelica Stapleton was unimpressed by Caroline's rural enthusiasm. She had hesitated to let Caroline go near the place. Although some of her friends went regularly, others felt theatergoing exposed them to taunts and catcalls—and occasional saliva—from the proponents of democracy in the balconies. She was shocked to discover that John Sladen had bought tickets in the very headquarters of that part of the audience, the second balcony.

"How could you stand the smell?" Angelica asked.

"I grew up on a farm," Caroline said.

"I'd be more concerned by their language and behavior," Henrietta Van Rensselaer said. She was inclined to give no quarter to the lower orders.

"They were as well behaved as the congregation at the Twin Forks Presbyterian Church," Caroline said, summoning the only comparison she could make.

"Humph," Henrietta said, still skeptical. "I prefer the opera. It attracts less riffraff."

Angelica Stapleton gave Caroline one of her frosty smiles. "If you propose to go out this way, you should dress the part. Perhaps we ought to do some shopping tomorrow."

The next day being Saturday, at ten o'clock Caroline and Angelica and Henrietta set forth on a round of the great stores and small shops. By the time they returned at three o'clock, Caroline had acquired a half dozen dresses in the latest London and Paris styles, with their full sleeves, low necklines, and richly embroidered hems. The skirts danced tantalizingly just above the ankle—which had not a little to do with their winning universal male approval. To this basic wardrobe they added for nightwear a blue turban decorated by white peacock feathers, several daytime feathered bonnets, a handsome muff, a half dozen pair of stylish shoes, and—the pièce de résistance—a sky-blue redingote with bands of white corded silk down the front. It looked made-to-order for Caroline's tall, slender figure.

"How can I ever repay such generosity?" Caroline said as she tried on the dresses to the reiterated approval of the two older women.

"We enjoyed every minute of it," Angelica Stapleton said. "It made us feel young again."

"Believe it or not," Henrietta said wistfully, "I had a figure like yours once. But then I fell in love with oysters and game hens and the like." She now weighed enough to squash a small boy if she ever fell on him.

The following Saturday, George Stapleton invited Caroline on a trip to the Elysian Fields. This was a pleasure park in Hoboken, created by steamboat builder John Stevens. At its center was a small circular railway, with a miniature steam engine and cars, similar to the larger ones Stevens hoped to build across New Jersey. Other men were laying tracks for the iron horses in Massachusetts and Maryland.

They crossed the Hudson in a private pinnace George had hired for the occasion, with a crew of four. The sailors served champagne and lobster en route—a somewhat stark contrast to the humble oysters on a dirty plate that John Sladen had bought Caroline.

George boyishly suggested a ride on the little train. As it chugged along, he remarked that his grandfather, Hugh Stapleton, thought they should invest in railroads. His Uncle Malcolm, who oversaw the family textile factories in New Jersey, was opposed. "What do you think?" George asked. "Can women's nerves handle the speed of these things? They'll go thirty, even thirty-five miles an hour."

"I wish you men would stop worrying about our nervous systems," Caroline said. "Where did you get that silly idea? Who has the babies of this world? Just because you fight an occasional war and have more muscles doesn't mean you have a monopoly on steady nerves."

"You're probably right," George said. "Come to think of it, I've never seen my mother nervous about anything. I think I'll vote in favor of the iron horse."

"I didn't realize you were already involved in the family business."

"Only on large matters—and my vote doesn't carry a great deal of weight. But my grandfather and uncle feel I should get involved—since I'll eventually be responsible for the whole works."

"In the meantime, are you going to study law like your friend Sladen?"

George shook his head. "My brain doesn't work that way. I hate arguments. I've been thinking of becoming a poet."

"Can a man make a living at that?"

"I don't have to make a living. I can exist quite comfortably for the rest of my life without doing any serious work. Our mills and ironworks are run by competent managers. But it seems reprehensible not to try to contribute something to Young America's achievements."

Young America was the slogan of the hour. Everyone saw the country as a huge, energetic twenty-year-old. "Have you written any poetry?" Caroline asked.

"Reams of it. But Sladen's convinced me it's wretched stuff. I think your cousin Jeremy agrees with him but he's too kindhearted to tell me."

"I'd love to see it."

"Would you really? I think of you poetically all the time. In fact, the moment I saw you on the steamboat dock, some lines from Wordsworth's 'Phantom of Delight' leaped into my mind."

Softly, with the shining Hudson River for a background, George recited:

A lovely Apparition, sent
To be a moment's ornament;
Her eyes as stars of Twilight fair;
Like Twilight's, too, her dusky hair.

The chugging engine reached the end of its circular line. George helped Caroline off the car. "I prefer the later lines in the same poem," she said. "Where the poet recovers his common sense and sees:

A Being breathing thoughtful breath
A Traveler between life and death;
The reason firm, the temperate will,
Endurance, foresight, strength, and skill.

George smiled and trumped this subtle rebuke:

A perfect Woman, nobly planned,
To warn, to comfort, and command.

"I'm not at all sure I need to be warned—or commanded," Caroline said.

George avoided an argument. In the distance a band had begun playing Viennese waltzes. He led Caroline to a dance floor laid out beneath chestnut trees glowing with the reddish gold of autumn. They glided out on the floor, in step to the sinuous music.

"I have a confession to make—which may annoy you even more than my Wordsworth eruption," George said. "That night, as I lay in bed hoping to dream of you, a stanza from another poem leaped into my mind. I make no attempt to explain it."

With a half smile, George recited:

I saw pale kings and princes too
Pale warriors, death-pale were they all;
They cried—"La Belle Dame sans Merci
Hath thee in thrall!

Caroline abruptly stopped dancing and said, "I have a confession to make in return. I've often imagined myself as the heroine of that poem. Without an iota of remorse."

"I don't understand where, or how, you've acquired this wonderful pride. I admire it but I don't understand it."

"From loneliness, Mr. Stapleton. You can't imagine the things a person can acquire from loneliness."

"But you have brothers—"

"A person can be lonely in the most crowded house."

They spent the rest of the afternoon discussing the poems that Caroline had found especially consoling in her years of loneliness. George Stapleton returned to Columbia babbling apostrophes to her beauty, her intelligence, her sweet sad pride. He put John Sladen in such an atrocious mood, Jeremy Biddle feared an outbreak of violence. He hastily decreed a new rule in the contest. Henceforth they would escort Caroline in a group. That way, the two rivals could watch each other in action and make sure no sinister advantages were being taken—while he, the complaisant third, acted as umpire.

Caroline was consulted and she readily agreed to the proposition, which was put to her as an economy measure. In the meantime, Sally Stapleton had been introducing her to a number of her friends, and they soon collected a half dozen couples who were usually ready to join them for a party. This agreeable group, which John Sladen dubbed the Golden Horde because they were all rich, became the nucleus of their social lives for the winter.

Like all wealthy New Yorkers, as soon as the snow fell, the Golden Horde hauled their family sleighs out of their barns. Soon scarcely a weekend passed without an expedition up Manhattan Island into the country behind teams of fast horses, followed by skating on Van Cortlandt's pond in the Bronx or some other body of frozen water. The *frères trois* insisted on Caroline's joining them in the Stapleton sleigh, sitting with George on the way out and John on the way back.

John Sladen and Jeremy Biddle were not good skaters. The latter had a bad leg, broken in a fall from a horse when he was fourteen. Growing up a poor boy in New York's lower wards, John had found little time to skate. He had gone to work at the age of eight or nine, running errands for tenants in his mother's boardinghouse. As he grew, the cost of new skates was usually beyond his mother's pinched exchequer.

George Stapleton skated with such effortless ease, he seemed to have been born on the tricky blades. Caroline, growing up in the country with a pond on her parents' farm, was almost as good. As a result, John and Jeremy, after wobbling around the ice for a half hour, often retreated to the fire to watch George and Caroline, Fenimore Gardiner and Sally Stapleton, and the rest of the Golden Horde zoom around the ice with the abandon of a lifetime on skates.

"I'm beginning to dislike this en masse idea of yours, Jeremy," John said one day in mid-December as they watched George and Caroline doing beautiful figure eights on Van Cortlandt's pond. "It makes me doubt your neutrality in this contest. I keep coming off as second best—on skates and in conversation. Half of these simpering scions won't even speak to me."

"They fear your sharp tongue and dislike your democratic politics, my friend," Jeremy said. "If you lower your voice and moderate your opinions, you'll be as popular as anyone."

"What if that offends some essential part of my soul?"

"If you hope to practice law in New York, you're looking at a slew of prospective clients out there."

"You're beginning to disgust me, Jeremy."

Jeremy was more than a little upset by this remark. He tried to tell myself it was part of the difficult task of being a third. But he was still brooding a half hour later when George Stapleton led the Golden Horde in another winter ritual—a retreat to a warm tavern, where they consumed quantities of hot flip before a roaring fire.

Someone produced a mandolin and called on George for a song. "Do you know 'The Minstrel's Lament'?" George asked.

The musician struck a few chords of this familiar song and George began singing some new verses he had written for it. He gazed boldly at Caroline, who lay on one elbow before the fire, smiling at him.

Who can resist the beauty of those eyes
That whisper of springtime's silken skies?
Not I. Not I.

Who can resist those lovely arms—
That promise happiness beyond the world's alarms?
Not I. Not I.

It was mediocre poetry but George had a fine tenor voice. He went on to annotate the beauty of Caroline's hair, lips, skin and soul. Soon the rest of the party was joining him in his chorus, murmuring, "Not I. Not I," to their women. John Sladen stood with his arm on the mantelpiece, gazing gloomily down at Caroline. For a moment Jeremy felt sorry for him. But he soon discovered almost as much pity for himself—as he watched Fenimore Gardiner sighing "Not I" to Sally Stapleton. For the first time Jeremy began to doubt the value of being a third.

FOUR

A WEEK LATER, THE *FRÈRES TROIS* invited Caroline to a college Christmas party at the North American Hotel and discovered she had accepted a dinner invitation for that night—from Fenimore Gardiner! At first they imagined that nothing less than civil war had broken out in the Stapleton household on Beekman Street. George was dispatched to make a reconnaissance and returned with semigood news. His cousin Sally claimed to be "not in the least angry" about Fenimore's sudden shift in ardor. Angelica Stapleton said she was relieved, because she thought *Fenimore* rhymed all too well with *bore*.

Jeremy promptly invited Sally to the Christmas party and found her as agreeable as her cousin George, with the added attractions of a pert nose, winsome eyes, and an excellent figure. John Sladen paid no attention to her whatsoever, leaving Jeremy in possession of the field. He thought he was progressing nicely until Sally consumed a glass of wine. Then she confided to him her secret opinion of Caroline and John Sladen.

"They're made for each other," she said. "Two of the most unscrupulous egotistic individuals I've ever encountered. I don't believe they have an iota of honest sensibility in their souls."

"I thought you'd be denouncing Fenimore Gardiner," Jeremy said.

"He was simply marking time with me, waiting for something more spectacular to appear over the horizon."

Jeremy found it hard to fathom Sally's wrath at John Sladen and Caroline Kemble. He decided the first half could be attributed to John's cold-blooded decision to ignore Sally. Caroline was more of a puzzle. Having no sisters, he did not have a clue about the way women related to each other. He launched a cautious question about Caroline's conduct.

"She hasn't made a single friend among the girls I've introduced her to," Sally said. "Every one of them has found her the most insensitive creature they've ever seen. She treats me as an object of pity."

"Pity?" Jeremy could not believe it. Sally was hardly Caroline's equal in beauty. But she was far from unappealing to his eyes. "Has she said anything to lead you to this opinion?"

"She doesn't have to. It oozes from every look, every word she speaks. She advised me on what to wear to this party! Imagine? Three months ago she didn't have a decent dress to her name until Aunt Stapleton bought her a wardrobe. Then she returned some dresses she borrowed from me with a remark about finally having something nice to wear."

Jeremy was getting a first glimpse of the impact Caroline had on other women. It would take him somewhat longer to realize how deeply John Sladen had wounded Sally with his on-again off-again attentions a year ago.

Sladen was by far the more rattled by Fenimore Gardiner's sudden pursuit of Caroline. "I begin to think your beautiful cousin is a fortune hunter at heart," he growled at Jeremy.

Jeremy defended Caroline's right to accept an invitation to dinner from any eligible bachelor. "It seems to me this freedom is a natural right under the tenets of *democracy*," he said. He got nothing for his sarcasm but unintelligible growls and curses.

On New Year's Day, 1828, Caroline joined the *frères trois* and Sally made a fifth for a round of visiting at the homes of the Stapletons' numerous friends. This old New York tradition, inherited from the Dutch, made the first day of the year into a saturnalia for some. But sensible people did not drink everything that was poured into their glasses at every house. Jeremy noticed John Sladen was not following this judicious policy. Jeremy had seen John drunk in the past and knew the symptoms. He became more and more morose—and argumentative.

At the Gardiners' home on St. Paul's Park, a lovely green enclave surrounded by the houses of Schuylers, Hamiltons, Stuyvesants, and other old New York families, Fenimore Gardiner almost broke arms and legs shouldering through the crowd to greet Caroline the moment they came in the door.

"And Sally darling," he added, kissing her hand as well.

"Tell me, Fenimore, are you related to that new novelist Jim Fenimore Cooper?" John Sladen asked.

"His full name is *James* Fenimore Cooper," Gardiner replied in his patronizing way. "I believe we're distantly related. I happen to be a member of his Bread and Cheese Club."

"I've heard you were the model for his woodland hero, Natty Bumppo," John said.

"I'm flattered—but I fear I have none of the forest skills Mr. Bumppo has in such abundance," Gardiner said. "Miss Kemble, my mother said she would like—"

"The name Bumppo is a code, Gardiner," John continued, his face expressionless. "Mr. Cooper is a student of phrenology, the science of head shapes. Natty Bumppo stands for a particular kind of man, with a head that leaves the brain peculiarly compressed. He's incapable of thought."

"My dear sir," Gardiner said. "You seem to be insulting me in my own parlor."

"I believe this house belongs to your parents, Gardiner. That's typical of the Bumppo personality. He's fitted only for the rude communism of the forest. I've investigated your law practice. It consists almost entirely of notes to pretty women."

"I admit a predilection in that direction," Gardiner said. "Now, Miss Kemble, may I—"

"Gardiner," John said in the same cutting voice. "Isn't it clear by now I want to fight you? You've trifled with the affections of Miss Stapleton, a woman I greatly admire—and you're doing the same thing with Miss Kemble, a woman I happen to love."

"I must ask you to leave my house, sir!" Gardiner said. "Mr. Stapleton, Mr. Biddle, please escort your friend Sladen from these premises before I summon a constable. We have one on call on days such as these, for the very reason Mr. Sladen represents. Some with pretensions to being gentlemen cannot hold their liquor."

"I'm sorry to admit that Mr. Sladen has had too much to drink," George Stapleton said. "But I fear he's expressed sentiments that Mr. Biddle and I thoroughly share. Happy New Year to you and your estimable parents, sir."

George was almost as drunk as John. He turned to Caroline, who was looking somewhat dazed, and Sally, who could scarcely conceal her delight. "Ladies, I hope you'll continue to accompany us on our holiday round?"

"Of course," Sally said.

Caroline accepted Jeremy's arm and they followed the others out the door without saying a word. But in the Stapleton coach she said several dozen.

"Was that diatribe part of a carefully conceived plan?" she asked. "Am I to despise all three of you, or only one?"

"There was nothing planned about it," John said. "I'll write him a letter of apology tomorrow."

Caroline's anger mounted as the carriage lumbered through the crowded streets. "You think you own me? Is that it?" she cried, turning on George Stapleton. "Because your mother bought me a wardrobe?"

"The voice of truth—and friendship—forced me to speak," George said.

"Take me back to Beekman Street. I've had enough of your wonderful New Year," Caroline said.

They obeyed her, leaving Sally Stapleton marooned until Jeremy volunteered to escort her to calls on several friends on her personal list. They had a good time together until she brought up the subject of Caroline on the way home.

"They're both in love with her, aren't they," Sally said. "George and John."

"I'm afraid so."

"How awful. I don't think she's capable of loving a man—or even a child. She loves no one but herself."

"I hope you're wrong." Jeremy simply could not believe Caroline was the supremely egotistic being that Sally saw.

Back at Columbia, Jeremy found John Sladen and George Stapleton both drunk, facing each other with pistols in hand on opposite sides of George's bedroom. "Stop!" Jeremy shouted.

They ignored him and pulled the triggers. The hammers clicked on empty chambers. "We're rehearsing the inevitable denouement of our tragicomedy," John said. "I've made it clear to Stapleton here that if he persuades Caroline Kemble to marry him, I intend to challenge him. I consider it an act of friendship—giving him a fighting chance to kill me. If she becomes engaged to Fenimore Gardiner, I intend to shoot him in the street like the swine he is."

"I've made it equally clear that I'll welcome the challenge," George said thickly. "He's embarrassed Caroline before half of New York. The best and only thing to do with such a piece of social vermin is remove him from the scene."

"You're both talking total idiocy!" Jeremy shouted. He snatched the pistols out of their hands and locked them in a cupboard in his room. He told John to go to bed and gave similar orders to George. While they enjoyed the slumber of the ossified, Jeremy lay awake staring into the future. It looked as dark as the New Year's night.

In the morning he persuaded his two friends to shake hands. But he could see that the precarious truce he had arranged with his en masse socializing was shattered. John and George began pursuing Caroline with a grim persistence that left no room for third-party benevolence. Jeremy decided they could both go to hell and began pursuing Sally Stapleton.

Two or three days a week, John conspired to meet Caroline as she walked back to Beekman Street from Miss Carter's Female Seminary. Frequently he brought her a book he had just finished reading—such as Virginian John Taylor's weighty tome, *Inquiry into the Principles and Policy of the Government of the United States*. This was the literary eruption that had begun the revolt against conservative supremacy in America. John urged Caroline to pay particular attention to Taylor's dissection of the nature, origin and consequences of aristocracy. "He's the supreme champion of free institutions in America," he said. "He proves that aristocracy leads inevitably to stifled souls, to wretched oppression, to the destruction of spiritual and finally political liberty."

Caroline found Taylor's labyrinthine prose almost impenetrable. But she had no difficulty getting the message John Sladen wanted her to receive. No woman who claimed to be a champion of more freedom for her sex—and for people in general—should consider marrying that quintessential aristocrat George Stapleton.

John descanted to her on what he considered the most important turning point in American history—when the Republicans, the disciples of Thomas Jefferson, fought the Federalists, the followers of Alexander Hamilton, and apparently won a great victory in the year 1800, thanks to Aaron Burr's political wizardry in New York. Only to have President Jefferson announce in his inaugural address, "We are all Republicans, we are all Federalists."

This fatal Jeffersonian compromise left America adrift between aristocracy and democracy, John told her. "It's up to our generation to rescue democracy."

Sladen was by no means the only man who harbored such violent thoughts in 1828. People were bewildered by the rapid rise of factories and financial markets. Down on Wall Street men were making and losing fortunes speculating on stocks in textile and steamboat and turnpike companies, while the cities filled up with immigrant laborers and ex-farmers who could no longer make a living on the land.

On their walks, John Sladen showed Caroline the other New York that existed beside the glittering houses of the rich—people living in cellars and attics, often without heat during the bitter winters. He pointed out the prostitutes prowling even respectable streets such as Broadway, desperate women who had been reduced to selling their bodies for a few dollars a night. He took her to his mother's boardinghouse on Maiden Lane, where two dozen workingmen lived, some trying to save enough money to marry, others with a wife and a child crammed in one room, hoping for promotion or a windfall that would enable them to buy a house. He introduced her to his sad-faced, harassed mother, her hair gray, her back stooped from making too many beds. She was a stunning contrast to Angelica Stapleton's sleek haughty resplendence.

One day John took Caroline to a rally organized by the Democrats of Tammany Hall. She heard orators call for a ten-hour day for every laborer instead of the current sunup to sundown. She heard other speakers denounce the smug superiority of the rich. "Did Thomas Jefferson write all men were created equal or didn't he? How is it that some people eat prime beef off fine china while others live on stale bread and soup?" roared a red-faced man named Samuel Swartout.

After the rally John introduced Swartout as his "second father." A barrel of a man with a booming voice and a nose that seemed to have spent too much time in a liquor glass, Swartout told her "Johnny" was the cleverest young man in all New York. That was why he and Colonel Burr had taken up a collection among the Tammany faithful to create a scholarship fund to send him to Columbia.

"He's the last of the Burrites," John said as Swartout turned to greet other listeners.

"How does he live?" Caroline asked. Swartout's clothes were threadbare.

"He was a customs inspector until recently. The aristos have turned him out. I fear he's now depending on the generosity of friends."

Sometimes they sat in St. John's Park and read the newspapers. John knew the story behind all the political headlines. Each paper had its own bias, which he expertly explained. He was equally well informed about personal stories. He pointed to a description of an elaborate funeral for a businessman at Brick Presbyterian Church.

"They say he died of overwork, but the real killer was laudanum," John said. "He'd gone bankrupt last month."

This painkiller, mixed with liquor, was often used by suicides. One of the oddities of Young America, with its furious pursuit of profits and prosperity, was the sharp rise in suicides as a side effect of the numerous bankruptcies.

Caroline said she could not imagine taking her own life. How could any person do it?

Sladen glowered at her. "It can be an honorable choice for a defeated man. I don't believe my father fell off that Ohio steamboat."

Once more John Sladen stirred that dangerous emotion, pity, in Caroline's heart. Pity not only for the fallen and forlorn and struggling in New York but for him, who could so easily topple back into that squalid world. It was essentially the same emotion that had stirred George Stapleton and Jeremy Biddle to offer John their friendship. But with Caroline, the emotion had a different, far more ominous timbre. She saw Sladen's essential loneliness and it stirred a response in her own lonely heart. She too had tasted the darkness of poverty and a dismal future. Finally there was the physical man, the slim angular body, so different from George Stapleton's huge muscular frame, the harsh bony face with its perpetual semiscowl, on which an occasional smile was like a burst of light.

Suddenly Caroline wanted to share her most painful secret with him: "My father died a terrible death too. He was captured by Indians during the War of 1812 in Ohio. They dug a deep pit and made him stand up in it while they packed dirt all around him. Then they scalped him. He lived for another three hours, begging them to kill him. Finally they built a fire behind his head and kept it going until there was nothing left but a whitened skull."

John lifted her hands to his heart and held them there in a wordless gesture of sympathy. Tears streamed down Caroline's cheeks. "That's why I don't believe in God," Caroline said. "Why I'll never believe in Him."

"I know exactly what you mean," John said.

George Stapleton waged a totally different campaign for Caroline's love. On weekends he took her to dinner in the dining rooms of the best hotels. He invited her to balls at these glittering emporiums, or at private houses. One afternoon they went to John Vanderlyn's art gallery, where the popular painter displayed immense panoramas of London and Paris. George talked casually of visiting these great cities as a boy with his mother. He pointed out the palaces, the museums, the famous restaurants.

"How I yearn to show these things to you," he said.

"How I yearn to see them," Caroline said. Silently she added, *But must I marry you to get there?* More and more, she disliked the way George seemed to think he could bribe her into capitulation. George did not think of it that way, of course. He was doing what came naturally to a rich young man. But he badly misjudged the depth and intensity of Caroline's pride.

A month or so after taking Caroline to the Tammany meeting, John Sladen played his trump card. He arranged a meeting with Aaron Burr. He led her down Frankfort Street to a narrow, rather ramshackle three-story building. Beside its door was a faded sign: A. BURR, ATTORNEY AT LAW. Mounting dusty wooden stairs, they knocked on the door and found a clerk toiling over a piece of foolscap. "Is Colonel Burr free?" John asked.

In a moment Caroline was being greeted by an affable, gray-haired man whose coat sleeves were frayed and his shirt faded from too much washing. "This is Caroline Kemble from Ohio, Colonel," John said. "The young woman I mentioned to you. Her father signed up with you in 1806."

"Sit down, Miss Kemble," Aaron Burr said. "I remember your father as one of the most enthusiastic members of my little band. John has told me about your extraordinary interest in history and politics. Some of the books he's loaned you came from my shelves. But he utterly failed to convey a true estimate of your beauty."

It was hard to believe this sad-eyed shabby old man had once been vice president of the United States and hobnobbed with Thomas Jefferson and James Madison. His voice was remarkably youthful, and the sadness diminished in his eyes as he talked about his passionate belief in the education of women. He told Caroline how he had taught his daughter, Theodosia, to speak French at age four. He described the course of studies he had given her—Latin, Greek, mathematics—which equaled anything taught at Princeton or Columbia. Caroline found herself charmed, even fascinated, by the strange authority Burr emanated. She could see why her father and John Sladen's father had believed in him.

"Read the best books, my dear Miss Kemble, the old ones and the new ones," Burr said. "Only by acquaintance with our greatest minds can you live without illusions."

"Do you equate that with happiness?" Caroline asked.

"Of course not. Happiness is a gift of fate. But the best writers—above all the historians—will enable you to accept what fate disposes."

Caroline was touched by the elegiac tone. She knew from John Sladen that she was seeing a man in the wreckage of his life—his daughter, Theodosia, drowned at sea, his name synonymous with treason in most circles. She found herself admiring Aaron Burr's mournful dignity.

"Mr. Burr, what were you doing on the Mississippi in 1806? Were you simply hoping to get rich? My father always defended you against that charge."

Aaron Burr sat back in his chair for a moment, gazing at Caroline with new admiration. "She is extraordinary," he said to John Sladen.

Burr paused for another long moment and began, "I was pursuing fame, Miss Kemble. The same prize I was pursuing when I looked down the wrong end of Alexander Hamilton's pistol. It's a prize that your generation no longer understands. You tend to confuse fame with notoriety, thanks to our ubiquitous newspapers. But for the men of my era, fame was the greatest honor a man could wrest from history. Ultimate fame belonged to those who were *conditores imperiorum,* founders of states and empires. Men like Cyrus of Persia, Julius Caesar, Napoleon."

"You were going to found a new country in Texas?"

"In Texas—and Mexico. That was our ultimate goal. Texas was the vast emptiness it remains today. But Mexico was a nation waiting to be born, a seething mass of Indians and mixed bloods and criollos oppressed by a thin veneer of rulers from Spain. Its gold and silver mines alone had the wealth to make it a major power. Texas would have been our American province, from which we ruled the entire region to the Isthmus of Panama."

"This is what you told my father?"

Burr nodded.

"He died when I was barely three years old. I've only overheard scraps of his dreams—from my mother."

"Texas still awaits its Americans," Burr said. "They may yet become the rulers of Mexico. That country will be nothing but a barely organized chaos without American leadership. I was too early, too impatient to seize fame—too desperate for money to pay the debts I'd accumulated playing American politics—"

He caught himself before anguish completely dominated his tone. After a brief inner struggle he regained his air of cool detachment. "We're not here to catalog my misfortunes—but to salute the future that you and John represent. May you both devote yourselves to fame! Why shouldn't women share it with men? They can do as much, perhaps more, to create it!"

He leaned forward, talking almost exclusively to Caroline now. "Women by their very natures understand more of life's paradoxes and contradictions. Perhaps they can help unravel the knottiest problem in an American search for fame. We want to be powerful—and good. Only a few of us understand we can't be both things. At some point we must choose—and let fate decide the rest."

Caroline did not speak until John Sladen had returned her to the Stapleton town house on Beekman Street. "Thank you," she said. "I'll never forget this day."

By this time spring was thawing the landscape—and George Stapleton played *his* trump card. He invited Caroline to spend the weekend with him in Bowood, the mansion that his grandfather had built on the banks of the Passaic River, not far from the family's textile factory, Principia Mills. The bustling city of Hamilton had grown up around this industry, but Bowood remained an island of green peace in its hundred-acre park. The mansion was in the classical mode, somewhat resembling the White House in Washington, with a white-pillared portico over the entrance and two substantial wings of whitewashed brick. From Bowood, for the first two decades of the republic, the Congressman, as everyone called Hugh Stapleton in memory of his years spent in the Continental Congress of the Revolution, had ruled the political landscape of New Jersey.

The death of his older son, George's father, in the War of 1812 had deprived public life of much of its savor. In most of the country, because they failed to support the war, his Federalist party had been obliterated by Thomas Jefferson and James Madison's Republicans. Hugh Stapleton had retired from the U.S. Senate in 1818. But his wealth and political connections still made him a kind of paterfamilias to the state's politicians. He was growing somewhat feeble as he approached his eighty-sixth birthday, but his mind remained clear and his judgment keen.

He also quickly demonstrated he had not lost his eye for beautiful women. "My God!" he said as George escorted Caroline into Bowood's main parlor. "It's the goddess Athena in the flesh, come down to hector us petty mortals."

The comparison was apt. There was something goddesslike in the way Caroline moved and spoke. That day her regal beauty was enhanced by a new outfit, with an embroidered, colored-silk bodice and a white muslin skirt finished by more yards of brilliant embroidery. A straw hat with a half dozen soaring ostrich plumes added to her majesty.

"I'm not wise enough to be a goddess," Caroline said. "If I have to choose a woman out of old mythology, I prefer Helen of Troy. How glorious it must have been to have tens of thousands of Greeks and Trojans fighting to decide your destiny."

"I like a woman with large ambitions," the Congressman said. "My daughter-in-law tells me this big lummox is madly in love with you."

"He hasn't so much as mentioned it to me," Caroline said, giving George a sly look.

"How can I be more explicit?" George said.

"How many times have I told you, George, poetry doesn't get you anywhere," the Congressman said. "American women want the offer stated in prose. They're simultaneously the most romantic and the most realistic women in the civilized world. Would you agree with that, Miss Kemble?"

"Absolutely," Caroline said, liking the old man more and more. He still wore the knee breeches and tight waistcoats of the revolutionary era. But his eyes sparkled with shrewdness and gaiety. Here was a man who had won the crucial battles of his life and seemed unburdened by regrets.

"I'm embarrassing you both with my salacious curiosity," the Congressman said. "I'm afraid I'm anxious to see George get a running start in life. He has a certain tendency to indolence."

"Grandfather, I haven't failed a single course at Columbia."

"I mean moral indolence, George. You seem to enjoy not being able to make up your mind about a career. Regrettable at a time when the country is crying out for leadership. What do you think, Miss Kemble?"

"We seem to be adrift between aristocracy and democracy. I didn't realize how adrift until I came to New York."

"A perfect analysis!" the Congressman said.

For a moment Caroline felt guilty, remembering she had acquired this political wisdom from John Sladen. But why couldn't women put a new twist on the adage that all was fair in love and war?

"I want this young man to go into politics," Hugh Stapleton said. "But he seems to flinch from the toil and trouble."

"Grandfather, it no longer seems to be a profession where a gentleman is welcomed—much less respected."

"Then stop being a gentleman!" the Congressman said. "Gentleman! That's your mother's starchy old New York nonsense. The Van Rensselaers have never gotten over owning half the Hudson River valley. The Stapletons were in business, politics, trade, from the start. Gentleman! My God, I wish you'd known my father. He was as big as you but he didn't have a genteel bone in his body. He drank like a shipful of sailors and was happiest in the North woods with a bunch of Senecas, painted for the warpath. He was a bona fide member of their tribe. As for my mother, she sent gentlemen to bankruptcy court year in, year out because they didn't read the fine print in the contracts they signed with her. When it came to 'improving some moneys,' as she liked to put it, Catalyntie Van Vorst Stapleton was the most dangerous businesswoman in America."

Caroline listened to this marvelous monologue with amazement—and elation. This old man touched something important in her soul. She did not understand what it was, but she liked it. Did he know exactly what he was doing—imparting a vision of what she could achieve as George Stapleton's wife? If George's mother could fill his head with nonsense about being a gentleman, why couldn't she fill it with this fascinating alternative? Why couldn't she manage Congressman—Senator—yes, even President George Stapleton's ascent to fame?

FIVE

THE CONGRESSMAN SEEMED TO SENSE THE electric communion he
had created with Caroline. He talked more to her than to George for the next
hour as they sipped Château Y'Quem, Hugh Stapleton's favorite wine. First
he wanted to know what she thought of New York.

"I adore it," Caroline said.

"I thought you might—from that letter your grandmother wrote me, describing you as a 'woman of spirit.' My dear wife had the same reaction,
though with her it was complicated by her Quaker background. She was very
beautiful and I bought her dresses by the dozen. When her mother came for
a visit, she took one look at Hannah's wardrobe and said, 'Oh, my dear girl,
I fear for thy salvation.' "

They all laughed heartily at this quaint memory of a vanished America.
The Congressman asked Caroline's opinion of Miss Carter's Female Seminary.

"Abominable," she said.

"I'm not surprised," Hugh Stapleton said. "The education of women in
this supposedly progressive country is one of our chief disgraces. My wife
never ceased drumming that idea into my head. We often regretted never
having a daughter. We would have made sure she had first-class schooling,
even if she turned into Mary Wollstonecraft."

"What did your wife think of her?"

"She was put off by Mary's atheism. Otherwise she agreed with every
word."

The Congressman's smile was almost gleeful. He could see George was
scarcely able to conceal his amazement that his grandmother, often described
in saintly terms for her numerous charities and her passionate detestation of
slavery, had been an admirer of the great female radical.

"Mary is one of Caroline's patron saints," George said.

"Why not? She should be the heroine of every thinking woman—up to a
point."

"Where would you designate that point?" Caroline said.

"Her private life. She ruined herself politically by going too far, scorning
marriage, having children out of wedlock. The mass of people see such disorder as ruinous to their individual happiness. They don't have the luxury of
private fortunes. The woman who wants to make progress for her sex in
America should observe the conventions, the customs, the morality, of the
majority."

"Won't she simply fade into the mass and become invisible?" Caroline
asked. "How can she have any impact?"

"By accepting the hard truth that all great changes come gradually, and watching for the opportunity to push a little harder here, and there, with her husband's help. Women will never manage this change alone. They must have loving men at their sides, men who share their convictions—and have the power to change things."

The Congressman saw that Caroline was unconvinced. He struggled to his feet. "Pontificating is an old politician's worst fault. Come into the library. There's something I want to show you."

They followed him as he stumped on his cane through the high-ceilinged rooms, full of elegant furniture by the best cabinetmakers in New York and Philadelphia. In the east wing, they entered a lofty library, rising two stories to a skylight. On the walls were numerous portraits of Stapletons. The Congressman identified the most important ones for Caroline: Malcolm, his hulking frontiersman father, his hard-eyed, sharp-featured Dutch mother, Catalyntie Van Vorst, and the Congressman's wife, Hannah Cosway Stapleton. He paused to gaze fondly at her. She was sitting in the sunlit alcove of a farmhouse kitchen. The light spilling on her lovely face created an aura of saintliness. But the painter, whoever he was, had added a realistic touch to her eyes—they were a mixture of sadness and pain.

"A day seldom passes without my wishing she were still here," the Congressman said. "Her moral sense was deeper than mine. I was my mother's son. Nothing was more important to me than a whacking profit at the end of every year. But I eventually managed to rise to Hannah's standards. I learned it the hard way, as one learns many of life's major lessons."

He caught himself, embarrassed by the way both George and Caroline were looking at him with more than ordinary interest. "Ye gods, how we codgers ramble on. I didn't bring you here to recite my ancient and well-forgotten travails. Here's what I wanted you to see."

The Congressman led them to a painting against the rear wall. On one side was the battle of Lundy's Lane, showing gray-clad Americans holding their ground against redcoated British, with Niagara Falls in the background. On the other side was the battle of the Thames, with mounted riflemen and frontiersmen in fringed leather hunting shirts fighting Tecumseh and his Indians. In the right-hand corner of the frame was a portrait of George's father in his lieutenant's kepi. On the left was a portrait of Caroline's father, Jonathan Gifford Kemble, in his hunting shirt.

For a moment Caroline found it difficult to breathe. "Did you know my father? Did he ever come here before he went to Ohio?"

"No. He didn't approve of me, I'm afraid. We were in opposing political parties. He was with Jefferson, I was with Hamilton."

"I suppose he'd be a violent Democrat if he were alive today," Caroline said.

"Undoubtedly," the Congressman said. "I gather he never forgave Jefferson for compromising with us Hamiltonians and permitting us to go on making ourselves and the country rich."

Caroline had only a vague idea of her father's politics from comments by her older brothers. How harmless the Congressman made it all seem—in contrast to John Sladen's dark denunciations of Jefferson's compromise.

Hugh Stapleton was one of the aristocrats who had multiplied his wealth and power against the democratic tide. But he was not the disdainer of democracy that Fenimore Gardiner declared himself. On the contrary, he seemed ready to accept the tide as a fact of life and cope with it.

Politics suddenly became irrelevant as she gazed at her lost father's portrait in the shadow of the battle that had cost him his life. This old man was telling her she was already part of his family. If she wanted to become a more important part—even his partner in persuading this big uncertain grandson to plunge into the turbulent politics of contemporary America—he was ready to accept her. He had brought her into this library to tell her she had the bloodline and the brains to win a place among the portraits on these walls.

The portrait, the entire painting, vanished in a blur of tears. Suddenly Caroline wanted nothing more than the privilege of resting her head on Hugh Stapleton's shoulder. "I can't believe how dear you've become to me," she said.

"If this goes any further, Grandfather, I'm going to sue you for alienation of affections," George said.

The Congressman's smile was rakish. "If I were twenty years younger, George, you might have to."

"I'll write to my mother tonight and tell her about this painting," Caroline said.

"I've already sent her a copy," Hugh Stapleton said.

The smile had grown sly, suggesting that he had known exactly what he was doing when he ordered the painting. Had he been in touch with George's mother, or her own mother? Caroline wondered. Was there a clever conspiracy among the older generation to lure her into wedlock with George Stapleton?

She brushed away her tears and studied George for a long moment. What did her *heart* say? In a flash, John Sladen was standing beside George, his lean swarthy face and hungry eyes challenging her judgment. Who lured her into his arms? Was it big muscular George? His physique made two of John Sladen. But there was some sort of strange compulsion, a wild mixture of want and need, that made her turn to John instead. In another flash, she was opening her arms to him, his angry lips were on her yielding mouth.

Caroline Kemble never forgot those flashes in Bowood's library. They were visitations from a subterranean world of darkness and blind desire. As if she had plunged into the underground river Samuel Taylor Coleridge had described in his mysterious poem "Kubla Khan" and discovered:

A savage place! as holy and enchanted
As e'er beneath a waning moon was haunted
By woman wailing for her demon-lover!

Poetry. She heard the Congressman saying, *Poetry doesn't get you anywhere. American women want the offer stated in prose.* Caroline struggled for the self-control that prose implied. For a fierce moment she resented the restraint that was expected of her. She bridled at the Congressman's casual confidence that George could capture her. She wanted the wild freedom of John Sladen's lips.

Resentment dwindled as the dinner guests arrived. First came George's lean, gray-haired uncle, Malcolm, the Congressman's younger son. His canny eyes, his hard mouth, made him an unmistakable descendant of Catalyntie Van Vorst. George had remarked that Uncle Malcolm was "born to do business." He was Sally Stapleton's father. His wife had died giving birth to Sally, and Malcolm had never remarried. With a dedication that approached asceticism, he had sent Sally to New York to live with Angelica Stapleton and devoted himself to expanding the Stapleton commercial empire.

With Malcolm was Andrew Freylingheusen, the senior U.S. senator from New Jersey, a red-cheeked Dutchman who looked almost as old as Hugh Stapleton, and Philip Tilghman, a congressman who was equally ancient. They sat down to a dinner of roast pork and vegetables in Bowood's wainscoted dining room, served by black maids, presided over by a stern, gray-haired black butler named Peter in tasteful maroon livery. All Bowood's servants were black, descendants of Stapleton slaves freed after the Revolution, reportedly at Hannah Cosway Stapleton's insistence.

George and Caroline remained silent as the older men analyzed the political situation in Washington, D.C., and New Jersey. Everyone seemed to agree that in the upcoming election the supporters of President John Quincy Adams and his secretary of state, Kentuckian Henry Clay, who called themselves National Republicans, were in trouble. In Pennsylvania and New York, the Democrats were growing stronger by the day with their raging attacks against the aristocratic Adams and Henry Clay's so-called American System, which envisioned business and government as partners in building the country. New Jersey, thanks largely to the influence of the Stapletons and a few other prominent families, remained loyal to the president, but the Democrats were contesting every office.

"This is your opportunity, George," the Congressman said. "Come out here and stand as a National Republican. A young American ready and eager to speak for the American System as well as your native state. Tilghman here is ready to step aside in your favor."

"What can one congressman do if the Democrats sweep the country?" George said.

"They won't sweep New England. Henry Clay will hold Kentucky in line. Delaware and Maryland are still with us," Hugh Stapleton said. "Upstate New York and Ohio are fairly firm. There'll be a decent block of votes against these fellows."

"Young vigorous voices will be especially needed in the House of Representatives," Congressman Tilghman said. "There's a tendency to mob rule in that chamber."

"It's vital to have people from the Middle States who can talk sense about tariffs and banking," Malcolm Stapleton said. "Some of these dimwit Democrats are for free trade. That would be tantamount to shutting down Principia Mills and every other textile mill in the country and handing the whole game to the British. A hundred thousand people would be thrown out of work."

"Why are the Middle States so important?" Caroline asked.

"The Yankees are obnoxious and disliked by everyone in the West as well as the South," Hugh Stapleton said. "Their ideas are sound but their personalities are a disaster."

The elders unanimously predicted Jackson would make a terrible president. He was an ignoramus, a hothead and a bully. Glumly, they weighed and found wanting the National Republicans' attempt to paint the General as an adulterer and a blackguard because he had married his wife before her divorce from her first husband was legal. Some accounts tried to make it sound as if Jackson had kidnapped her from her first husband's house.

George remarked that these gutter tactics were proof that decency had vanished from politics. Why was the supposed party of the best people stooping so low?

"Desperation," Hugh Stapleton said.

After dinner, Freylingheusen and Tilghman departed and the talk shifted from politics to business. The Stapletons had invested thousands of dollars in toll roads and bridges all over New Jersey. They had put even more money into a canal that would connect the Delaware River to the Raritan River. They also had money in John Stevens's steamboat company. Should they finance Stevens's railroad or block it in the state legislature? Caroline realized the family more or less controlled this body, and the state's governor.

"George was telling me only a few weeks ago that he's *strongly* in favor of investing in railroads," Caroline said. "Isn't that right, George?"

"Yes, I think I did say that." George seemed to barely remember their conversation in Hoboken.

Delight gleamed in the Congressman's old eyes. "That's the first sensible thing I've heard from George in an age," he said.

Malcolm Stapleton grumbled that a successful railroad would wipe out their money in toll roads and bridges and endanger their canal. "Better to cut losses early for bigger profits later," Hugh Stapleton said.

He gave Caroline an owlish smile. "We decided a long time ago that whoever controls transportation across New Jersey stands to make a fortune. We're sitting between the two most prosperous states in the Union, New York and Pennsylvania."

"All right. I'll talk to Stevens about the railroad," Malcolm said. "How much of a share do you think we should give him?"

The Congressman shook his head. "He'll drive too hard a bargain if we deal only in railroad stock. Suggest a merger between the canal and the railroad. The Joint Companies. Form a new corporation by that name and issue stock in it. That way we're the logical majority shareholders."

For a moment Caroline felt transported into a trance state. Could this be happening? She was sitting at this splendid mahogany table, surrounded by gleaming sideboards and bombé chests, listening to these calm canny men making fortunes, plotting how to influence the future of the country. She had already cast George's vote in a crucial family decision. The thrill—there was no other word for the emotion Caroline felt—vibrated in her flesh. She was discovering that power had its unique pleasure. And this was merely business.

What would she feel if she persuaded George Stapleton to join her in the pursuit of fame?

Could it compare to that flash of subterranean desire she had felt in Bowood's library? As a woman, she was supposed to be less vulnerable to such dark impulses. Invulnerable, in the opinion of some philosophers. Men were dragged down by their animal hungers. A woman's soul was composed of finer materials. Did she believe that?

Yes.

That answer sealed the bargain Caroline made with herself and with fate, with the ambiguous memory of her lost father, with the loneliness and anger of her girlhood. Sitting at Bowood's gleaming mahogany dining table, she chose George Stapleton over John Sladen and assured herself she was content. No, more than content—she was *happy*. She was catapulting herself into a world she had scarcely imagined a year ago. A world charged with energy and hope as well as power—infinitely more exciting than the defeated sadness of Aaron Burr.

George had trumped—and won.

On the steam ferry returning from Hoboken the next day, George led Caroline out on the deck. It was an afternoon of magnificent spring sunshine. The Hudson flowed swiftly past the ferry's cleaving prow in its final rush to the sea. New York's great harbor spread below them, dotted with ships of all nations. Ahead, the city with its church spires and slate roofs sparkled in the brilliant white glow.

"If I'm not mistaken, I think you love Grandfather as much as I do," George said.

"It was adoration at first sight," Caroline said.

"You know you're already the mistress of my heart. Can I make you mistress of Bowood as well?"

"I want more than Bowood, George. I want you to run for Congress. I want a husband who'll play a part in the history of this country. I want to be his partner in business, in politics, as well as in love."

"But I don't care about those things—compared to what I feel for you. For me happiness is you and me—and our children—in Bowood."

George's broad handsome face was contorted with confusion and dismay. He saw himself ensconced in Bowood, writing poetry and history, comforted by his beautiful wife and children. Caroline was unmoved.

"George, I want more than happiness from my life. I want adventure, accomplishment, fame!"

"Won't having our children be an accomplishment?"

"That doesn't take any brains, George. I want to use my head, as well as my heart."

"All right," George said with a sigh. "I'll run for Congress."

"You'll like it, George. You'll learn to like what makes me happy. Because that will help me make you happy."

Hoooonk! The ferry's smokestack emitted a derisive hoot as they approached the dock. Was the god of the nineteenth century, the genius who had inspired the machinery that was transforming the world, commenting on this overconfident prediction? If so, neither George nor Caroline noticed it. The young are seldom prey to doubts.

George Stapleton took a small jewelry box from his pocket and revealed a ring with a huge diamond set in the center. "This was my grandmother's wedding ring," George said. "The Congressman gave it to me last night after you went to bed. He wants you to have it."

Caroline felt instantly wary, reluctant, almost angry. Should she accept a marriage ring from that woman with the sunny aureole around her saintly face? Were there powers here that she did not understand? She was infinitely different from that woman. Although she knew almost nothing about Hannah Cosway Stapleton, for some reason she feared her. Never would Hannah have had those flashes of dark desire. Never would she have exulted in power for its own sake. This woman represented a spiritual side of the Stapletons' heritage that Caroline Kemble in her bitter loneliness, her defiant admiration of Mary Wollstonecraft's atheism, disdained. Had George Stapleton, with his devotion to poetic beauty and the idealism of the gentleman, inherited this tradition?

If he had, she would drive it out of him, Caroline told herself with a grim intensity that was out of all proportion to the romantic moment they were acting out. Gently, George slid the ring on her finger and kissed her on the lips for the first time.

"I love you," he said. "I love you, love you, love you."

"I love you too, George." Caroline let him crush her to his broad chest.

Caroline was not lying. More precisely, she loved the George Rensselaer Stapleton she planned to manufacture out of the present undefined gentleman poet. That future George, the man who strode the corridors of power, who won the cheers of the American people, she would love extravagantly.

And John Sladen? She would love him too, in memory. He would inhabit those measureless caverns through which Alph, the sacred river, ran down to a sunless sea. The ghost of another Caroline Kemble would linger with him in that "miracle of rare device, a sunny pleasure dome with caves of ice."

Caroline carefully blotted from her memory two other lines from that eerie poem.

And all who heard should see them there.
And all should cry, Beware! Beware!

SIX

"HOW COULD YOU DO IT?" JOHN Sladen raged. "How could you let him capture you with the clanking clatter of a million dollars' worth of cheap cotton cloth? Did you ask that old bastard how much he paid his workers? Most of them are women, you know. Poor farm girls like yourself, herded into those airless sheds from sunup to sundown. That's where your million dollars came from. That's what paid for Bowood's silver salvers and marble mantelpieces and Turkey carpets!"

Caroline was descending Broadway on her way home from Miss Carter's school. In a month she would graduate. A month later she would marry George Stapleton at Bowood. John Sladen seemed oblivious to these realities. He stalked beside her, ranting, almost shouting at her, his eyes raw with pain. Day after day he met her on upper Broadway and berated her all the way down to Beekman Street.

Caroline told no one about it. She let Sladen lash her verbally for an hour each day. In her room at 19 Beekman Street, she lay on her bed and wept for another hour. Why was she letting him do this to her? She asked herself the question a hundred times. She had no answer.

George Stapleton would have pounded John Sladen to jelly if he knew about it. Jeremy Biddle would have dragged him to the nearest tavern for a long not very friendly lecture. But all they knew was Sladen's extreme dismay when he heard the news of Caroline's engagement. He lost all the laboriously learned manners of a gentleman and called George a scheming son of a bitch and a dozen other names he had learned growing up in New York's back streets. He had moved out of their Columbia rooms to a nearby boarding-house, where he spent most of the day drunk. Various professors warned him that he was endangering his prospects of graduation. He ignored them.

Jeremy went to see John several times to try to talk some sense into his head. Sladen called him a toady, a buttsuck and other picturesque names and mocked his plans to marry Sally Stapleton as more of the same worship of the rich that had seduced Caroline. Jeremy was so offended he ceased all communication with him.

At times, as Caroline lay in her room after enduring a Sladen tirade, she pondered Hannah Stapleton's ring on her left hand. Was this the reason for her submission? Was she accepting this abuse like a Quaker saint, trying by her refusal to defend herself to tell John that she loved him in a part of her soul, even though she did not choose to marry him?

On weekends she journeyed to Bowood to see the Congressman, who was overjoyed by the news that she had accepted George. He was even more pleased by George's announcement that he was going to run for Congress. George's mother, Angelica, on the other hand, was anything but pleased. She tried to persuade Caroline to change George's mind and was not a little dismayed to learn her future daughter-in-law thoroughly approved of it. Caroline soon realized there was considerable tension between Angelica and the Congressman.

"My dear," Angelica said, "do you realize you'll have to live in *New Jersey?*"

"I've lived in Ohio and survived it," Caroline said.

"But you'll have to live with that domineering old man!" Angelica cried.

"I happen to love him."

None of these triumphs large and small seemed to give Caroline the slightest power to resist John Sladen's abuse. She had almost begun to tolerate it—even to like it in some strange way—when it suddenly ceased. For two days there was no trace of that lean, disheveled figure, that ragged voice, those tormented eyes, on Broadway. On the third day a boy of about ten, with the dirtiest face she had ever seen, approached her.

"Is youse Caroline Kemble?" he asked.

"Yes."

"There's a man named Johnny in me mudder's house that wants to see youse."

She followed the boy down side streets to a narrow cul-de-sac off Chambers Street. The three-story house sagged so seriously, it looked ready to collapse at any moment. This was a not unrealistic possibility in New York, where buildings were built quickly on the cheap and frequently came crashing down on their unlucky inhabitants. Caroline found John Sladen in a smelly basement room that reeked of rum. He looked more like a specter than a living man.

"John!" she said. "Are you ill?"

"It's terminal, I assure you. I won't be around to disrupt your wedding. I entertained a fantasy of going to the church and rising to the occasion when the parson asked if anyone had an objection. But it was never more than a pathetic dream."

"What's wrong with you? I'll tell George or Jeremy. They'll get a doctor."

"They'd like nothing more than to prop me up for a month or two so they can gloat over the walking corpse. I'm not going to give them the pleasure. I have the only physician I need. Dr. Laudanum." He gestured to a bottle full of greenish fluid on his night table.

"No!"

"I wanted to see you one more time—to tell you I forgive you. You had no idea you were dealing with such a frail creature. A man playacting at being a hero out of Byron—with nothing inside him but vapor and the stink of the gutter. You made me imagine I could attempt something magnificent with you beside me. When you turned away, you forced me to face what a joke, a fake, I am."

"You will do something magnificent, John. You don't need me. You have the mind, the spirit, the knowledge. You have a voice that must be heard."

He shook his head. "The only person I wanted to hear it is no longer interested."

"Not true, John. Not true. I'll always be interested. I'll always respect—honor—what we felt for each other, what you shared with me about your hopes for this country."

"That must be Falstaff's honor you're talking about. The honor I imagined was stronger than the iron bars the Stapletons make at Principia Forge. Stronger than the strongboxes full of banknotes in their vaults—"

"John, please!"

Pity was mingling with subterranean desire in her soul. She wanted to soothe this man's pain, the pain she had caused—she wanted to resurrect the democratic warrior she had broken. She wanted to save him from the oblivion he seemed to be courting in her name. The new century's shift from thought to feeling, from reason to passion, had exposed millions of souls to spiritual earthquakes. One was heaving in Caroline's heart now.

She sank down beside him on the bed. "How can I prove to you that I care?"

There was no need for an answer. His lips were on her mouth. The bed was closer than close. She was a child of Mary Wollstonecraft. Sin was no barrier to the desire those visionary flashes had revealed at Bowood. There was only the faint voice of calculation, dismissed in the maelstrom that was engulfing her. The imagery of the underground river in "Kubla Khan" leaped in her soul:

And from this chasm, with ceaseless turmoil seething,
As if this earth in fast thick pants were breathing

Underground, it was all happening underground. Above on the civilized earth paraded naive George and jealous Jeremy and haughty Angelica and her pious little niece Sally. Yes, and strutting Fenimore Gardiner and a hundred other gentlemen just like him, pumped full of gaseous pride by their money and bloodlines. On they paraded in the indulgent spring sunlight, convinced of their knowledge of the higher truths while down here in the cellar of the soul another truth was being discovered. A truth that lay voiceless until the agile tongue awoke it, that was as insubstantial as air until caresses gave it flesh and pulse and heartbeat. Would it become another monster, like the one Mary Wollstonecraft Shelley concocted for Dr. Frankenstein?

Caroline Kemble did not care. She did not care. She did not *care*. She was beyond any and all calculation, judgment, prediction. She was a woman in love with grief, with pity, with despair. John Sladen was above her now in the stillness, thrusting, there was a sweet, tearing pain—she welcomed it, treasured it, wanted pain as much as she wanted John Sladen, as much as she wanted love, as much as she wanted proof of her honor, as strong as any man's, as any woman's, this love that consumed and subsumed, that joined her to the women of history and myth, from Helen of Troy to Virgil's Dido to Dante's Beatrice to Abelard's Héloïse, love and the world well lost, she did not care care *care*.

It was over. The pale blood of her maidenhead speckled the grimy sheets. They lay silent for a long time, their lips, their naked bodies, touching. "I want to marry you," John Sladen said.

"Impossible," Caroline said. "The engagement has been published in the newspapers. George will kill you."

"More likely I'll kill him. I can use a gun. He's a bigger target."

"Insane! Don't you remember what happened to your hero, Colonel Burr? To your father? What do you think your future would be if you killed Angelica Van Rensselaer Stapleton's only son? You'd be a pariah. I'd be something even worse."

"There are other cities. It's a big country."

"I wanted to show you how much I loved you."

"And you discovered the real meaning of the word. Caroline, we can't turn our faces away from this truth without becoming hypocrites forever. An American Dante would consign us to the deepest pit of hell, infinitely below Paolo and Francesca. Can't you hear Virgil telling the tale of Caroline and John, the lovers who denied their love, the morbid details of their hollow lives?"

Frantically, Caroline struggled against the current that was sweeping her headlong into a sunless sea. "I must *think*," she said. "Think and think. In the meantime, you must pour that laudanum into the gutter and return to college. We'll meet here in two days to discuss this—this . . ."

"Truth."

"Yes." Her voice tolled like a funeral bell in her ears. "Truth."

Caroline spent the next two days in torment. Thought seemed impossible. Her broken sleep was full of images of desire. A letter from the Congressman, inviting her and George to join him for an eighty-sixth birthday celebration at Bowood, only multiplied her anguish. She sat through her classes at Miss Carter's school in a daze. She lost track of conversations at the Stapleton dinner table. Sally Stapleton joked about letting love befuddle her.

On the second afternoon, Caroline wound her way back to John Sladen's basement room. She found the place cleaned and almost fragrant. John had shaved and found some decent clothes. Somehow that only made him more irresistible. The bed loomed in the corner, a deceptive expanse of snowy purity.

"Have you thought?" he asked.

"Have you?"

"Only of you. Nothing but you."

"You haven't gone back to college?"

He shook his head. She felt a lurch toward despair. Had she hoped that confronting his friend George Stapleton might change his mind? Or the stern voice of reason that prevailed in Columbia's halls might dissipate his madness?

"You promised me!"

"I only promised to throw away the laudanum."

He drew her to him for a violent, authoritative kiss. "I begin to think we must revise our ideas about happiness," he said. "Our intellects are puny pygmy creatures compared to our passions. They're the true gods. They have to be propitiated or they'll destroy us."

He began to undress her. She could stop him with a word, a look. But she let him do it. "I thought there were no gods or goddesses," she said.

"Except the ones we create," John said. "We're creating one here. A god of love that will guarantee us happiness for the rest of our lives."

It made no sense. He had no money—and no prospects of making money if he became involved in an ugly breach-of-promise lawsuit or a duel or both. She would be stigmatized as a slut—even if there were no eyewitnesses to her visits to this basement room. Caroline saw these realities with incandescent clarity. But they did not matter compared to her desire for this man, to the wish to be held and to hold, to possess his dark presence and simultaneously surrender to it. Why why why?

The question clanged in her mind like a runaway fire bell, but it was much too late. They were in bed again, naked, kissing, entwined. The alarm bell dwindled to a distant tinkle as the waters of Alph rolled over them and they sank into its sunless depths.

For the rest of the week, Caroline came to John Sladen's room every day. She thought of nothing but what would happen and what had happened there, in the underground world of their love. Each day she felt doom swirling around the sagging house. It oozed down the stairs like the fog that sometimes prowled New York's streets. They were both doomed, but it did not matter. Their god of love was an underground deity, as blind as a mole to the disaster creeping toward them on the earth's malign surface.

Had she become two persons? The underground Caroline who loved John Sladen in those forbidden afternoons and the surface Caroline who dutifully accompanied her future mother-in-law to shop for her bridal trousseau, who discussed her honeymoon in Europe with George Stapleton on weekend visits to Bowood, who listened to the Congressman's advice on cities to see and others to avoid in Italy and France? It was madness of a sort she had never imagined she could perpetrate—and she did not know how to stop it. Only doom could rescue her—and simultaneously destroy her.

Doom finally arrived, late the following week. As the lovers lay in their subterranean bed toward the end of another passionate afternoon, a hand knocked on the door. Jeremy Biddle called, "Are you in there, Sladen? I've got some bad news from college."

A more unlikely choice to impersonate doom could hardly be imagined. Awkward, limping Jeremy wore the face of an American everyman. Sheer accident—and the habits of a third—had thrust him into the role. John Sladen's reckless nature made another large contribution.

Jeremy had tracked Sladen to this tenement basement out of a stubborn sense of responsibility for John's endangered future. Several professors had announced that unless he returned to class and took the final examinations that were to begin the next week, he would not graduate. The tenement was not the boardinghouse to which he had originally retreated. But the building was well known to Columbia students. It was their favorite brothel.

Since John had resolved not to return to college, he might have remained silent behind his closed door and Jeremy would have gone away after a few more knocks. John's choice of residence had already discouraged Jeremy. But

John decided it was time to reveal his triumph to a man who would report it to George Stapleton.

With nothing more than a dressing gown around him, John flung open the door and invited Jeremy into the room. Caroline shrank under the covers of the bed. "What's your news, Biddle?" John said.

"I begin to think it's irrelevant," Jeremy said. "It has to do with your graduation. From what I see here, I doubt if it will ever take place."

"What you see here is the triumph of love over money," Sladen said. "The victory of the truth over gilded lies."

"I'm afraid I see something very different," Jeremy said. "We might start with the betrayal of a friend and the ruin of a beautiful young woman. We might add the morals of a scoundrel and the seduction of a virgin. Plus the baseness of a swine and the sad folly of the uncontrolled heart. I could add to the list almost indefinitely. But I prefer to take action."

With a decision that amazed Caroline, Jeremy strode across the room and contemplated his beautiful cousin in her bed of shame. She did not look very beautiful, her hair streeling and matted on her sweaty cheeks, the cheap bedclothes clutched to her pulsing throat. "Get out of that bed and dress yourself with all possible dispatch," he said. "You're returning to Beekman Street immediately."

Jeremy was speaking out of his years of affection for George Stapleton. In some ways he was closer than a brother to him. He had spent his schooldays and almost all his summers at Bowood with George since Jeremy was fifteen and his father's death and his mother's remarriage had made him feel less than welcome at home in Philadelphia.

Never before had John Sladen seen this ferocious Jeremy. John had grown accustomed to thinking of him as the complaisant third. John's first impulse was to bluster. "Caroline, you're not required to obey any orders from him."

"Sladen," Jeremy said, "this woman was placed under my protection by her mother. She's legally still a minor. If you try to interfere in any way, I'll put you in jail. Scum like you may be indifferent to the law, but they're not above it."

"This woman is my wife! In all but name."

"Don't say another disgusting word! If you try to stop her from leaving this room, I'll beat you senseless."

"How do you plan to do that?" John sneered. He was a head taller than Jeremy. He had done his share of fighting on the mean streets of his youth.

"Like this." Jeremy sank his fist into John's stomach. As he doubled over in agony, Jeremy hit him with an uppercut that sent him crashing into the wall. Among the many sports George Stapleton and Jeremy had enjoyed during their summers at Bowood was boxing.

Jeremy turned to a wide-eyed Caroline. "Get dressed!"

Wrapped in a sheet, she clutched her clothes and retreated to a corner. Jeremy kept his eyes on the groaning John Sladen as he dragged himself to a chair, clutching his bleeding mouth and bruised stomach. In 120 seconds by Jeremy's watch, Caroline was dressed. He led her upstairs to the street.

"I won't ask you why this happened," he said as they walked downtown. "I don't believe any explanation is possible—or needed. Here's what you're going to do when you get to Nineteen Beekman Street. You'll go up to your room and write a letter to John Sladen informing him that his conduct has convinced you that he must leave New York immediately. State in the plainest terms that you do not love him. Instead, you love George Stapleton and intend to marry him on the third of June, 1828, as published in your engagement notice in the newspapers."

"But I do love him," Caroline sobbed.

"You don't anymore. Your infatuation is over. You were seduced, you succumbed—but it is *over*."

Jeremy seized Caroline's arm as they walked past Parton's Hotel. In front of it in the gathering dusk was a pretty redhead in a sky-blue gown. "Do you see that woman? She's a prostitute named Edna Kane. A favorite among Columbia students. That's what you could become if you persist in thinking John Sladen loves you."

At 19 Beekman Street, they were greeted in the hall by Sally Stapleton. Her shrewd eyes took in Caroline's tearstained face, her roiled hair, her disheveled dress. Jeremy decided the only policy was a bold-faced lie.

"Caroline felt ill and stopped at Columbia to ask me to escort her home."

"What's wrong?" Sally said, all concern.

"I felt . . . dizzy—feverish," Caroline said.

"Let me help you upstairs," Sally said.

In five minutes Sally returned to report Caroline was lying down. Jeremy chatted agreeably with Sally for another ten minutes. Caroline descended the stairs in a green nightrobe. She had washed her face and combed her hair.

"I'm getting more absentminded by the hour. I found this letter to my mother I wrote yesterday and forgot to mail. Could you take care of it for me, Jeremy dear?"

"I'll be delighted."

Jeremy took the letter and Caroline retreated to her room. In five minutes he was on his way back to John Sladen's basement. Sladen was sitting by the half window drinking rum. Music and laughter drifted down from the upper floors. The ladies of the evening were already in business.

Jeremy gave Sladen the letter. He read it and crumpled it in his fist. "What did you do, dictate this to her? It reeks of your insufferable so-called morality."

Jeremy smoothed the letter on his thigh and read it.

Dear John,

Jeremy is right. For our mutual salvation, we must part forever. I have pledged my love to George Stapleton. It is an obligation I must fulfill if I am ever to regard myself as a woman of honor. Your conduct has convinced me we could never be truly happy together. I think it would be better for both of us if you left New York as soon as possible.

Sincerely,
Caroline Kemble

Except for the word *salvation,* which gave too much away, Jeremy could have dictated it himself. He put the letter in his pocket. At this point, he believed John Sladen was not above blackmail.

"I hope you'll take that advice about leaving New York," Jeremy said. "I'm prepared to speed you on your way."

"What do you mean?"

"I mean money. I'll give you a hundred dollars* to leave tomorrow."

"That's a lot of money, Jeremy. Where will you get it?"

"From George. I'll tell him it's a gambling debt."

"You must still be worried about me."

"I am," Jeremy freely admitted. "I believe you're capable of trying to lure Caroline back here or to some worse den."

"Did it ever occur to you that I intended to marry her?"

"No, it never occurred to me. In my acquaintance, men who want to marry women don't ruin them first."

"Ruin," Sladen sneered. "She's never been happier. She never will be happier. Whenever she goes to bed with that chunk of million-heir beef, she'll think of me."

"You may be right. I consider that a kind of ruin. Do you want the money?"

"Yes. I want to get as far away from New York as possible. Do you have any suggestions?"

"New Orleans. I understand the mortality from yellow fever is high."

"New Orleans," Sladen mused. "Get me the money and I'll be on my way."

"A bank messenger will hand it to you at the Bowling Green steamboat dock tomorrow morning. If you attempt to communicate with Caroline in any way before you leave, the offer is void."

"Don't worry, Jeremy. I won't communicate with Sally either."

"You're scum, Sladen."

"You're more of the same, Jeremy. Except you're going to be rich scum."

Jeremy looked around the ugly basement room, thinking how it recapitulated his friendship with John Sladen. He had persuaded George Stapleton to join him in welcoming the raw angry fugitive from the lower depths of New York to Columbia, to a future that promised him a life of gentility and some degree of wealth. It was ending here in this malodorous hole, a paradigm of the degradation he had tried to escape. Never again would Jeremy be an optimist about the United States of America.

---

*This was almost a half year's salary for a workingman.

BOOK

TWO

O N E

ON JUNE 3, 1828, THE WEDDING of Caroline Kemble and George Stapleton took place in a tent on Bowood's green lawn. Caroline's family— her mother and four brothers—arrived from rural Ohio wearing clothes that were largely homemade. The colors were occasionally brilliant, but the dyes used to create them were erratic, so that coats shaded from cerulean in the front to dark blue in the back, or from magenta to pink. Her mother's dress was a relic of the 1790s, spotted here and there with mildew stains. Caroline's grandmother Kate Stapleton Rawdon was unfortunately too ill to come.

Angelica Stapleton and her sister, Henrietta Van Rensselaer, arrived in an elegant coach drawn by four white Arabian horses. Their Paris gowns, their diamond and pearl necklaces, their carefully coiffed hair, made one of Caroline's brothers exclaim, "You look like actresses!" Since actresses were considered only a step above prostitutes in 1828, the New York ladies did not take this honest farmer's opinion as a compliment.

The governor of New Jersey, the chief justice of the state supreme court, and most of the state legislature were also in attendance, as well as the state's two U.S. senators and five congressmen. Colonel John Stevens sailed up the Hackensack River in one of his steamboats and finished the journey to Bowood in a Stapleton coach. The Honorable John Quincy Adams, the president of the United States, with whom Hugh Stapleton had served in the U.S. Senate, sent his compliments and best wishes.

The bride was more than worthy of this distinguished company. She wore a gown of the purest white damask, with bands of inlaid mother-of-pearl and lace. In her jet-black hair she wore a single white rose. In her arms she carried a bouquet of lilies. The Congressman escorted her up the aisle, a gesture that advertised his approval of the match—something that was probably not far from his canny brain.

George's cousin Sally was Caroline's only attendant. It was a proof, if any were needed, that the new Mrs. Stapleton had little interest in or capacity for friendship with other women. Not a single fellow student at Miss Carter's school nor a young woman from the circle of couples with whom she had partied in Manhattan had become close enough to win inclusion in the ceremony.

Jeremy Biddle had to listen patiently to Sally Stapleton's biting observations on this point. He would have been glad to see Caroline at the altar, without Sally, without the Congressman, in a dress of tatterdemalion. Caroline's attendance was the only thing he cared about. Until the last moment, he was unsure if the subterranean powers that had seized her soul might not hurl her onto a steamboat to New Orleans.

John Sladen had departed for that distant port on schedule, Jeremy's hundred dollars in his pocket. But Caroline displayed no gratitude toward Jeremy for her peremptory rescue. On the contrary, whenever she saw him, loathing flashed across her face. She seemed barely capable of controlling her detestation. But she went steadfastly ahead with plans for the wedding, and Jeremy began to think the source of her emotion was simply his knowledge of her infidelity. If that was the case, Jeremy told himself, he would gladly bear her dislike lifelong for George Stapleton's sake.

At the wedding banquet in Bowood's ballroom, George whirled Caroline around the floor to the music of a Viennese waltz and stopped at the family table. "Jeremy," he said, "I give you the honor of the second dance with the queen."

"Careful George," Jeremy said, "you're not sounding like an American politician."

"An American can have a queen—of his heart," George said.

"I think the Congressman deserves the next dance far more than Jeremy," Caroline said. "He's the king of my heart."

"I told you I was going to sue for alienation of affection, Grandfather!" George said.

"By tomorrow morning she'll have changed her tune, George," the Congressman said, bringing shocked expressions to the faces of Angelica Stapleton and her sister, Henrietta Van Rensselaer. Their straitlaced generation had banished eighteenth-century ribaldry from New York's drawing rooms.

Hugh Stapleton circled the floor with Caroline and returned to the table declaring his ancient legs had better be replaced by younger ones. This time Caroline could find no plausible excuse to avoid Jeremy. She kept him at a rigid distance as they moved out on the dance floor.

"I wish we could become friends again," Jeremy said. "You have nothing to fear from me."

"I'm glad to hear that." Caroline's face remained frozen.

"I hope you've heard nothing from a certain pseudo-gentleman."

"If I had, you'd be the last person I'd tell."

"Who'd be the first?"

"No one. I've put him out of my mind—and heart. I hope you'll allow me to do the same thing with you."

"What do you mean?"

"You won't be welcome in my house. I may be forced to invite you occasionally, if you marry Sally. But you'll never be welcome. If you persist in coming, I'll ruin your friendship with George."

"I don't understand you. Why do you despise me?"

"Because of way you've wormed and wound your way into George's confidence. That pseudo-gentleman of our mutual acquaintance was right when he called you the ultimate toady."

Jeremy writhed on the shaft of that brutal thrust. He was among the first victims of the dilemma of riches in democratic America. He liked—yes, even loved—George Stapleton as the friend of his boyhood and young manhood.

It was years before he thought of George as rich. But others found it hard, if not impossible, to imagine the friend of a rich man as anything but a sycophant in pursuit of a share of his wealth.

"George is going to become a very powerful man. Possibly the president of the United States. I don't intend to let anyone influence him but me," Caroline Kemble Stapleton said.

There it was—the gauntlet that Caroline had flung down and dared Jeremy to pick up. He was tempted to tell her he had no desire to influence George Stapleton. But he realized that would have been a lie. His years as a third had made him all too aware that George needed hardheaded advice.

Jeremy spoke more out of the pain of that word *toady* than any vision of the future: "Let me reassure you that there's no need to worry about me intruding on your household. Whether Sally accepts my hand or not, I intend to return to Philadelphia and make my own way there, with no help from anyone."

"Good," Caroline replied. "That will remove both of you from contention."

Jeremy returned Caroline to George, feeling dazed by the raw intensity of that exchange. He invited Sally Stapleton to dance, and before they had circled the floor, he heard himself asking her to marry him. She gave him a wary look. "Is this Caroline's idea?"

"Good God, no," he said. "I'm sure she'd rather see me marry almost anyone but you."

"You seemed to be having a rather tense conversation just now."

"It was a bit unpleasant. She told me I wouldn't be welcome in her house. She considers me the ultimate toady. Whereas I consider myself George's ultimate friend."

There were tears on Jeremy's cheeks. "Sally, I wish—I need—your love more than ever now," he babbled.

"You have it, Jeremy. You've had it for six months," Sally said in her calm, direct way. "Why do you doubt it?"

"That conversation with Caroline makes me doubt almost everything about myself."

"I despise that woman. Now you've given me a reason to hate her."

Jeremy was too overwrought to consider the possibility that he had laid the groundwork for a ruinous family feud. "I want to live in Philadelphia. Far away from Caroline, Aunt Angelica, and Aunt Henrietta, among others. Will that trouble you?"

"Not in the least."

"I love you more and more and *more,*" Jeremy said, pressing her against him until he glimpsed Aunt Henrietta watching them, disapproval all over her fat frowning face.

The wedding breakfast ended around 2 P.M. But that by no means closed the festivities for the day. Caroline, George, his uncle Malcolm Stapleton, and the Congressman rode into the city of Hamilton in the family coach to join a huge party at Principia Mills. The looms and shuttles had been shut down and everyone had the afternoon off. The mostly women employees had been urged to invite boyfriends and brothers from the city and countryside to enjoy the fun.

There was dancing on the open plaza before the main buildings to music from a band of local fiddlers. Dozens of pounds of cracked crabs and oysters and lobsters were spread out for all to enjoy. A well-spiked punch flowed freely.

At the end of the afternoon, the Congressman mounted a table and introduced George and Caroline to the merry crowd. "Someday he'll be your boss," he said. "I thought you'd want to meet him—and *his* boss."

That drew a laugh, and the Congressman, perhaps realizing the jest might be almost too close to the truth, added he was only joking. "There's something else George wants to tell you."

He turned to George, who stepped forward on cue. "I'm no speechmaker," he said, "but I've come back here to New Jersey with a desire to do something for the people of my native state. I want to represent you in Congress at this difficult moment in our history. It's time to give people my age a voice in Washington—to bring Young America's ideas to the fore. I want to keep the country growing and producing for all Americans, and I'll make sure New Jersey gets its rightful share of the federal government's attention. Our industries will be protected and our canals and toll roads well funded—I guarantee it!"

The crowd's applause was polite—no more. Although George did not mention the National Republicans, no one had any doubt that he would vote with them if he was elected.

Caroline kissed George on the cheek and whispered, "That was wonderful." The Congressman had written the speech. Caroline had made George rehearse it a dozen times in the last two days. She had left no doubt that a good performance was as important to her as the vows they would exchange at the altar.

George barely managed to muster a smile in return for her kiss. He was less than happy with kicking off his election campaign at his wedding. It had been his uncle Malcolm's idea. George had wanted to take Caroline directly from Bowood to a ship for a three-month grand tour of Europe. Uncle Malcolm and the Congressman, assessing reports from their political operatives around the state, had decided George had better stay home and campaign hard. The Democrats were looking more and more formidable.

Almost as if someone wanted to prove the wisdom of this advice, as George was helping Caroline down from the table, a voice in the crowd yelled, "Three cheers for Andrew Jackson."

"Hip hip hooray!" roared the crowd. "Hip hip hooray. Hip hip *hooray*!"

The Congressman, still up on the table, forced a smile at this outburst of Democratic defiance. "We all admire General Jackson," he said. "It's *President* Jackson that worries me."

The bride and groom spent their first night together at Bowood. If George noticed Caroline was not a prima facie virgin, he said nothing about it. He was sophisticated enough to know that lack of the most obvious proof meant nothing. She made sure her demeanor was virginal—not a difficult task. A half dozen visits to John Sladen's bed hardly made her a courtesan.

Caroline found George's ardor more than matched his huge physique. She wanted to make him happy and she vowed in her willful way that she would make herself happy too. She put all comparisons with John Sladen out of her mind. He was gone into the darkness of distance. The underground river was mere poetry. Never again would she let her imagination distract her. She wrapped her arms around George Stapleton and kissed him with wild fervor.

After the consummation, Caroline lay in George's arms and confided to him her plan for the future. He would go to Congress and make a name for himself, with her help. Even if Andrew Jackson was elected, he was already an old man. What lay beyond his presidential term was an unknown world that they would explore—and master—together.

"You're the only world I want to explore," George said, kissing her white throat.

"You can do both, George."

"What if I'm no good at politics? Will you still love me?"

"You *will* be good at politics, George. I'm absolutely sure of it."

The next morning at breakfast the Congressman's eyes were full of more good-natured ribaldry. Before he could say a word, Caroline greeted him with a kiss and a sigh. "Your reign as king of my heart is over," she said.

"So soon? I thought I might linger for a week or two . . ."

She shook her head and kissed George coquettishly on the cheek. "It only took a single night."

George looked uncomfortable. Jeremy Biddle detected a certain theatricality in Caroline's performance. But he was a realist. He did not expect her to abandon her feelings for John Sladen overnight. He still believed that George's love would eventually prevail.

For their honeymoon, Caroline chose a trip to Washington, D.C. The newlyweds rode to Hackensack with bluff, hearty Colonel John Stevens, whose steamboat carried them down the Hackensack River to the Hudson, where they boarded a larger steamboat for Baltimore. From there it was only five hours by carriage over a good road to the national capital. In two days they were ensconced at the Franklin House, a large, comfortable establishment on I Street, run by an Irishman named O'Neale and his vivacious, dark-haired daughter, Peggy, who seemed on bantering terms with every patron.

Compared to New York, the Washington, D.C., of 1828 was little more than an extended village. The population barely exceeded twenty-five thousand. As much as a mile separated houses on many of the main avenues. The marble Capitol, rebuilt from the fiery ruin inflicted on it by the British in 1814, had a low, ugly wooden dome; it squatted on its hill like a disheveled general without an army, surrounded by the equivalent of a parcel of ragged little boys—such was the appearance of the straggling, sagging houses at the foot of the hill.

George expressed some dismay at this evidence of a social desert. But Caroline was unbothered. She had come to Washington to meet the politicians. The Congressman had given the newlyweds introductions to a half dozen prominent figures, including Secretary of State Henry Clay and Vice President John C. Calhoun. They swiftly discovered these gentlemen were much too embroiled in the politics of the hour to give them more than a polite hello.

Both houses of Congress were locked in a furious argument over a new tariff bill. Vice President Calhoun arranged for the Stapletons to get passes that admitted them to the debates in both the Senate and the House. As far as George Stapleton was concerned, the word *tariff* had dullness and pettifogging details embedded in its two syllables. Caroline was almost ready to agree with him. She was far more fascinated by the contrast in the two chambers of the legislature.

The congressmen met in a large columned hall hung with tasseled crimson curtains that matched the crimson canopy over the Speaker's desk. Beside each representative's desk was a brass spittoon; these were much used by a majority of the Southern and Western representatives. Disorder reigned in the House. Members bellowed speeches into the echoing air, but ten feet away, no one could hear them; the acoustics were atrocious. Other members read newspapers, chatted with visitors, or shouted insulting remarks at the speechmaker. With over two hundred members confronting him, the Speaker seemed incapable of maintaining order. Beside his rostrum stood a fat man in a homespun shirt, eating a large sausage. The Speaker occasionally glanced at him with dismay, but he did not seem to have any power to discipline him.

The nation's forty-eight senators met in a small, handsomely paneled, domed room. They sat at large mahogany desks on raised platforms listening to the debates or writing letters to constituents. Vice President Calhoun presided over their proceedings with stern dignity. The senators treated him and each other with elaborate courtesy. Caroline decided that George Stapleton should become a senator as soon as possible.

In both houses, the Stapletons were astonished by the passion with which the politicians debated the tariff. Members from the West and the South seemed to regard it as an attack on their lives, their fortunes, and their sacred honor; while members from the Middle States and New England ferociously defended the bill as a test of true patriotism.

In the Senate, Caroline noticed a woman around her age who was following the debates with intense interest. Using a small lap desk equipped with an inkwell and pen, she took extensive notes on each speaker's remarks. In the gallery of the House, Caroline noticed the same woman, doing the same thing. She was as tall as Caroline and carried herself in a similarly regal way, but her features had a somewhat severe, almost mannish cast—the kind of looks men called handsome rather than beautiful. Hers were redeemed from severity by her thickly curled, intensely black hair.

That night, at supper at the Franklin House, Caroline found herself sitting beside the woman. In those early Washington days, guests mingled indiscriminately in hotel dining rooms. Caroline nodded and won a smile of recognition.

"Did you enjoy the fireworks today?" the woman asked.

"I would have enjoyed them more if I understood them," Caroline said. "We're newcomers from New York—I mean, New Jersey."

"I'm Sarah Childress Polk from Tennessee. This is my husband, Congressman James Polk."

She gestured across the table to a short, extremely handsome young man with a high broad forehead, penetrating dark eyes, and a slender frame. Polk was talking intently to a short rotund man with a bald head and a knowing mouth. Caroline introduced George; Polk and his friend, whose name was Churchill C. Cambreleng, joined the conversation. Cambreleng was a Democratic congressman from New York. Caroline had heard John Sladen speak of him with approval.

"George is running for Congress," Caroline said. "We're on our honeymoon. We thought we'd see what life in Washington is like."

"I hope you're supporting General Jackson," Sarah Polk said.

"I'm afraid George is a National Republican by inheritance," Caroline said. "His grandfather represented New Jersey in the Senate for over twenty years."

"We'll do our utmost to convert you to the true faith," Sarah Polk said.

"So she let you marry her before you won, eh?" Congressman Polk said. "Sarah insisted I had to prevail at the polls first. It's quite a tribute to your charms, George."

Sarah Polk gave Caroline a smile that communicated far more than tolerance of her husband's humor. *We understand each other,* it said. Caroline felt a flash of kinship, of sympathy in its root meaning, which she had never felt before for any woman.

"All this only proves my contention that a strong-willed woman can persuade a man to do anything—even jump from the roof of the Capitol—if she puts her mind to it," said Congressman Cambreleng. "You ladies are living proof of why I'm a bachelor and intend to remain one."

"Allow me to defend myself against my husband's accusations," Sarah Polk said good-humoredly. "When he came to me with a marriage proposal, he was known for a certain instability in his affections—and in the general conduct of his affairs. I thought I was entitled to a demonstration that his vows of reform were in earnest."

"If they weren't, they are now," Cambreleng said. "Never have I seen a more complete love slave."

"You, sir," said Sarah with the same good humor, "are an enemy of society. That a scoundrel like you should be sent here to pass laws is a commentary on how little appreciation New Yorkers have for national politics."

Cambreleng seemed to consider this a compliment. "No doubt about it. We New Yorkers live only for local pleasure. Pure—and impure—local pleasure."

"As long as you support General Jackson, I forgive you," Sarah Polk said. "I only hope God will do likewise."

Here was a woman who talked to men as an equal. Caroline was dazzled. "I'm eager to become your political pupil," she said. "I've just spent a year in a school where I learned nothing."

"Careful," Cambreleng said. "Sarah allows no dissent in her classroom. Witness this recent graduate. If Polk ever disagreed with her, the shock would be so great it would knock down every building in this excuse for a city."

"That may be a testament to affection, and admiration, Mr. Cambreleng," Caroline said. "Something every wife hopes to win from her husband."

"Well said," drawled Polk, cheerfully lighting a cigar. If Sarah was the tyrant Cambreleng claimed, the Tennessee congressman did not seem troubled by it.

"I can see you have a mind which can easily master politics on your own, Mrs. Stapleton," Sarah Polk said. "But you may appreciate what will transpire here tomorrow if I explain a few things. These gentlemen and the rest of the Jacksonians are in for a rude shock."

She gestured to her husband and Cambreleng and swiftly explained the passionate quarrel that was dividing House and Senate. The tariff was the brainchild of Secretary of State Henry Clay, and President Adams, who were exponents of the much touted American System. The National Republicans said America needed high tariffs to protect fledgling industries and to produce the money needed to build canals and roads and bridges to improve the country's transportation system. The South and the West saw the tariff as a tax on them. They had to pay higher prices for American-made goods. Meanwhile, many nations were slapping retaliatory tariffs on American cotton and wheat, hurting Southern and Western farmers.

"Some Democrats, such as Senator Martin Van Buren of New York, have joined the supporters of President Adams and proposed a tariff so high, it's certain to outrage the South and West," Sarah Polk said. "The Jacksonians thought it would be voted down by both houses. But I've been listening to the debates. Tomorrow, I predict it will pass—and woe to the politicians from the South and the West who go on the record as voting for it."

"If it passes, does it mean General Jackson will be defeated?" Caroline asked.

"No, General Jackson is an irresistible force. He'll denounce the tariff and run against it. Though I think he could run for it and win. He's become the people's hero. Whatever is wrong in Washington, they think he can fix it."

"Can he?" Caroline asked.

Sarah Polk's smile was enigmatic enough to be worthy of the Mona Lisa. "He'll try. Of that much you can be certain. General Jackson always tries to fix things. He's a man of action."

Caroline remembered what she had told George about General Jackson being an old man whose influence would soon vanish. Had this clever woman also drawn that conclusion? Was she also saying that some things were wrong in Washington that not even General Jackson could fix?

Caroline was sure of only one thing. She wanted to be Sarah Polk's friend. The way Mrs. Polk pronounced that phrase *national politics* stirred Caroline almost as much as her dinner-table conversation with Hugh and Malcolm Stapleton. Here was another woman who relished the intricate sensations of power.

T W O

By the time they parted at the end of dinner, Sarah Polk had invited Caroline to breakfast with her and to spend the morning in the Senate gallery. Congressman Polk and Cambreleng invited George to be their guest on the floor of the House.

Upstairs in their rooms, George remarked that he found Mrs. Polk to be a rather cold woman, but he liked her husband. "It's possible that Mrs. Polk may only be capable of political warmth," Caroline said. "Since you said almost nothing to indicate any sympathy for General Jackson, she naturally put you at a distance."

"You call that natural?" George said. "I don't think it's healthy for a woman to become absorbed in politics that way. It cuts off the ordinary emotions that make women so important in our lives."

"Perhaps extraordinary women don't have ordinary emotions, George."

"I hope you aren't speaking for yourself."

"I want to be both women, George. I want both kinds of emotion. I want to be your ordinary wife, and your extraordinary political partner."

George caught her in his arms and gave her a passionate kiss. "You'll never be my ordinary wife."

Their lovemaking that night was by far the most fervent of their marriage thus far. Even at this early stage, Caroline needed an extra dimension to bring her feelings to bed with her. She sensed it had something to do with the effort she had made to seal off those subterranean desires that had flung her into John Sladen's arms. But she chose not to worry about it.

The next morning she began exploring that extra dimension with Sarah Polk. They breakfasted late, after the men had departed for the Capitol. Caroline asked Sarah the name of the strange man who was eating a sausage in the House of Representatives. "That's Sausage Smith, the new Democratic congressman from Ohio," Sarah said. "A man of the people if there ever was one. If you think he's bad, wait until you meet Davy Crockett from Tennessee. He parades around in a coonskin hat and hunting jacket."

Caroline realized Sarah saw her as an Easterner who would be shocked by crude Westerners. "I grew up on a farm in Ohio," she said. "We had similar types in our neighborhood."

Sarah was pleased to discover Caroline was a fellow Westerner. "I never would have gathered it from your accent."

"One of the few worthwhile courses at the finishing school I attended in New York was speech. They insisted we had to talk as Eastern ladies."

"Why did you and your husband decide to go into politics? I happened to meet a New Jersey congressman after dinner last night. He told me George Stapleton is one of the richest men in America—or soon will be, when his grandfather and uncle die."

"I told George he would have to do it if he expected to marry me."

"Do you have a private fortune?"

"On the contrary."

"Remarkable. What would you have done if he said no?"

"Gone to New Orleans with another man—who's been a Jacksonian virtually from birth."

"Does he have a private fortune?"

"No."

"My interest grows by leaps and bounds. You make my ambush of Mr. Polk seem timid, Mrs. Stapleton."

"Aside from being from Tennessee, why do you support General Jackson?"

Sarah Polk hesitated for a moment over her coffee. "I'll be as frank as you. Five years ago, Mr. Polk went to Mr. Jackson and asked him what he could do to further his career. Mr. Jackson replied in his blunt way, 'Stop your philandering! Settle down with a wife and devote yourself to her—and serious politics.' "

Mrs. Polk stirred more sugar into her coffee. "Mr. Polk, no doubt hoping to divert the General, asked him whom he should marry. 'Sarah Childress,' the General replied. 'Her wealth, family, education, and health are all superior. You know her well.'

" 'I shall go at once and ask her,' Mr. Polk said."

Sarah Polk's smile suggested she was not at all distressed to be singled out by General Jackson this way. "The General was an old friend of my father's. I'd known Mr. Polk since he was a schoolboy. I'd long since concluded he was the handsomest man in Tennessee. But I controlled myself and suggested he run for the state legislature and win before we announced the banns. Wouldn't you agree that was a prudent thing to do?"

"Unquestionably. I see why you support General Jackson. You've almost made a convert of me."

"Is General Jackson popular in your part of New Jersey?"

"Popular enough to get three cheers at our wedding when George announced his candidacy."

"I must convince you of Jackson's national importance. He represents a reaction against the aristocrats of the East, the Adamses and their toadies like Henry Clay. They've been in power too long. Their so-called American System is as corrupt as Alexander Hamilton's Federalism."

"Here's where I need some education," Caroline said. Praise of Alexander Hamilton was often on Hugh Stapleton's lips. If her father-in-law was corrupt, she failed to detect any evidence of it.

"The system is nothing but Hamilton's consolidated government, run for the Eastern rich and powerful, with some soothing Kentucky syrup à la Clay poured over it," Sarah Polk said with a fervor that almost matched some of the oratory Caroline had heard the day before in the Senate.

"And you, the Jacksonians, plan to abolish the tariff—change the whole system?" Caroline said, almost shuddering at what Hugh Stapleton would say if George became a Democrat.

"Of course not," Sarah Polk said with her Mona Lisa smile. "On the stump we talk about abolishing it. But nothing is ever done *totally* in American politics—if the other side has some power. In the end there's always a compromise. That's the genius of our politics, the fine art of compromise."

They set off to the Capitol, a half mile down Pennsylvania Avenue's uneven brick sidewalks. "When it rains, these bricks vanish into the mud," Sarah Polk said. "New Yorkers like Cambreleng are fond of deploring our primitive capital. But it doesn't look much worse than Nashville to my eyes."

An odd sound struck Caroline's ears. The clink and jangle of metal. Toward them down the middle of Pennsylvania Avenue trudged a long coffle of black slaves, chained ankle to ankle. Their clothes were in tatters. Many of them looked emaciated. At the head and rear of the column strode two white men armed with rifles. Big black whips jutted above their belts.

Sarah Polk did not even notice the procession. She continued to talk humorously about the limitations of Washington, D.C., as a city until she realized Caroline was staring at the blacks. "I've never seen slaves before. We have blacks in New Jersey, but they're all free," Caroline said apologetically.

"You'll soon get used to them if you spend much time in Washington," Sarah Polk said. "This is a Southern city. They buy and sell them on the street outside the White House."

"What inspired your interest in politics?" Caroline asked as the coffle passed.

"Joseph Addison's play, *Cato.*"

"I loved that play too. Especially that line ' 'Tis not in mortals to command success, but we'll do more, Sempronius; we'll deserve it.' Those words made me understand the sublime."

Sarah Polk nodded. "The night I finished *Cato,* I dreamt I was in a domed Roman temple. There were statues of heroes on all sides of the rotunda. Before them, women wearing long robes were chanting prayers, performing dances, singing hymns. I asked an old man in a toga where I was. 'You're in the Temple of Fame,' he said.

"I asked him what these women were doing. He frowned at my ignorance and said, 'Without their powers, none of these great men would be on their pedestals.' "

By this time they were at the foot of the hill on which the Capitol stood. Sarah Polk gazed up at its massive classical bulk. Except for its ugly wooden dome, it might have been transported intact from a hill overlooking the forum of ancient Rome.

"That dream made me think women can play a part in American history," Sarah said in her low intense voice. "We too have powers that men neither possess nor understand. The power to persuade, the power to disarm enemies, the power to sustain our heroes."

Caroline told Sarah about her visit to Aaron Burr and his discourse on the true meaning of fame. Sarah nodded. "He, Hamilton, Jefferson—they all understood it. General Jackson is the last of their breed."

For the rest of her life, Caroline remembered that moment on Pennsylvania Avenue. She sensed she and Sarah Childress Polk were joining a secret religion, a worship of fame. In a corner of Caroline's soul, there was a momentary pocket of resistance. She wanted to see herself—or Sarah—on one of those pedestals.

"The wages of fame," Caroline said. "Is that our only reward?"

"In the White House, the wages of fame can be shared equally," Sarah said. "I've talked to old men who remember the administrations of John Adams and James Madison. They left no doubt that Abigail Adams and Dolley Madison wielded as much power as their husbands, behind the scenes."

With long, determined strides, Sarah led Caroline up the hill to the Capitol and turned to look down Pennsylvania Avenue at the executive mansion. In the bright summer sunlight, it shimmered and glowed like a mystic vision. "It's the summit of American fame. Why not try for it?" Sarah said.

Inside, they were escorted to one of the couches on the Senate floor reserved for important visitors. Sarah unlocked her lap desk to resume her notetaking. "I had this designed from a larger model made for Mr. Jefferson," she said.

That day the Senate debate on the tariff thundered to a climax. Southern orators, particularly from South Carolina, denounced it as "the tariff of abominations." Sarah Polk coolly added her commentary to their rhetoric. "Charleston is a city in decline. They thought they could live on their plantations and let their Negroes breed them into wealth. Instead it's turned out to be bankruptcy. This has stirred resentment—which they naturally blame on everyone besides themselves."

When Daniel Webster, the swarthy, dark-browed senator from Massachusetts, rose to thunder an equally violent defense of the tariff, Sarah whispered, "There you see a politician who never speaks without someone putting money in his pocket. Greed is the foremost weakness of the Yankees. The second is self-righteousness."

New Jersey's two senators defended the bill, using phrases that might have come straight from Hugh Stapleton's lips. Caroline was surprised that not a sound came from New York, where cotton mills were few and radical rich-hating Democrats like John Sladen were numerous. Surely they would join the Southerners in denunciations?

A query to her political guide produced a political answer. "The Democrats had an emergency meeting last night and made some last-minute changes in the bill. The tariff on raw wool has been jacked up to favor New York's upstate sheep raisers. They far outnumber New York City's radicals. The same policy will please Ohio, Missouri, and Kentucky—wool-growing states General Jackson has to carry to win. Pennsylvania is happy, and silent, because we've upped the rate on imported iron."

Caroline began to perceive that national politics was the fine art of keeping a majority of the people happy. But she could not help noticing the tendency among Southerners to be extremely unhappy. One senator roared that if South Carolina was continually ignored this way, there would come a time when she would assert her rights at the point of a gun.

"Virginia," declared an agitated senator from the Old Dominion, "created this Union through the genius of her soldiers such as Washington and her statesmen such as Jefferson and Madison. She can unmake it the same way."

Sarah Polk leaned over and whispered, "Pay no attention. They have no place to go but General Jackson. They'd all fall on their swords before voting for John Querulous Adams."

On the dais, Vice President John C. Calhoun's wrathful face suggested Sarah Polk might be dismissing the South's anger too casually. Caroline was still a pupil and she banished the intuition for the time being. But she never forgot Calhoun's forbidding glare as the Senate voted the Tariff of Abominations into law.

There was another reason for the persistence of this memory. Moments before the vice president gaveled the Senate into recess, Caroline was assailed by an overwhelming nausea. She fled to the indoor toilets that were among the distinctions of the new Capitol and lost her breakfast.

Alone in the water closet, Caroline wondered what was wrong. Was she coming down with cholera or some other dreaded disease? Or was there another, more probable explanation? It was now almost two months since her first tryst with John Sladen. She realized she had not menstruated since that disastrous day. She was so irregular, and her mingled grief, rage, and relief over the abrupt end of her affair with Sladen, followed immediately by the preparations for the wedding to George, had so distracted her, she had paid no attention to the lapse.

Caroline did some rapid arithmetic in her head. She was liable to give birth only seven months after her wedding. What should she do?

On the way back to the hotel, Sarah Polk talked politics. She was more than satisfied with the final disposition of the tariff bill. Her fears of negative reactions in key states had been laid to rest. The Democrats' last-minute changes virtually guaranteed General Jackson's election.

"What about the story that General Jackson abducted or seduced his wife away from her first husband?" Caroline asked. "It's made a great stir against him in some parts of the East."

Sarah Polk began a tense, surprisingly defensive explanation. Rachel Donelson had left her brutal, unfaithful first husband before Andrew Jackson met her. They had married in Natchez, assuming the husband had obtained a divorce in Virginia. When they discovered he had waited a full year to do this and then obtained it on the grounds of adultery, they were remarried in Tennessee. No one in Nashville considered Rachel an unfaithful wife. She was received everywhere with respect and courtesy.

"I suppose it proves one thing. A woman can love more than one man," Caroline said.

"If she has command of her soul, she can deal with that misfortune." Sarah Polk studied her so intently, Caroline thought for a moment she had penetrated her secret. "Are you ready to become a convert to General Jackson?"

"I'm not sure it can be done, or what we'd gain from it."

"My congressman friend from New Jersey says he could persuade one of the candidates on the Democratic ticket to drop out of the campaign. That would give George a place to fill."

"What would you gain from that?"

"George's name would bolster our whole New Jersey ticket."

"What would that Democratic dropout gain?"

"A nice job in the New York Customs House or something comparable in Europe. We intend to show no mercy to Republican officeholders. General Jackson says they're all corrupt. He's going to reform them out of business."

"You do make politics interesting," Caroline said.

"From a personal point of view, I'd gain a friend to whom I could speak freely. I assume you're coming to Washington with your husband?"

"You don't think George can win as a Republican?"

"I think his chances of winning as a Democrat are far better. A change of parties by someone with his lineage will do a great deal to make him a national name."

When George returned from his session at the House of Representatives, he unnerved Caroline by complaining about the tiresome day he had spent in that chamber. "Talk about blowhards. They've got them by the dozen. And fanatics. The Southerners talk about the tariff as if it were boiling oil about to be poured on the heads of their wives and children. That fellow Cambreleng is with them, heart and soul, denouncing rich Northern businessmen as if they ate babies for breakfast."

"It's just rhetoric, George," Caroline said. "They have no place to go but General Jackson."

"I don't understand it. How can intelligent men be against a tariff? What other crazy ideas does Jackson stand for?"

"Reform."

"Reform of what? The system seems to be working pretty well, as far as I can see. The country's prosperous."

"The people are tired of the old faces. They want a new leader."

"Whoever said the people were always right? Don't you remember Grandfather saying without the tariff the mills would be out of business?"

"Calm down. In American politics, in all politics, I suspect—English, French, Spanish—there's a world of difference between what you say and what you do. General Jackson has no intention of abolishing the tariff. As a Jacksonian Democrat from New Jersey you can probably get a higher tariff on cotton cloth—if you go along with a lower tariff on woolens, which will only hurt New England."

"That's dishonest."

"No it isn't, George. It's politics."

George sat down on the bed. "Where did you get these ideas?"

"From Sarah Polk."

"It's crazy. What would Grandfather say if I ran as a Democrat?"

"We'll talk him into it. He's a reasonable man. Mrs. Polk says she can arrange to remove one of the Democrats who's running against you. I think the Congressman would like that idea."

"I couldn't agree to such a thing unless I was truly convinced that Jackson was the best candidate."

"Then there's only one thing to do. We'll go see the man himself."

"Go to Nashville? That's almost a thousand miles away."

"Sarah Polk will arrange it. In ten or fifteen years, she's going to put James Polk in the White House, George. I want you to succeed him. You can't do it as a National Republican. That party's dead. The Democratic Party is about to be born. It's the party of Young America. Where we belong."

George sank onto the bed. "You're amazing."

He was still far from convinced. Caroline decided it was necessary to risk the ultimate revelation. "I've got some more good news, George. I'm pregnant."

"You're sure?"

"A woman knows when it happens, George."

"Caroline! My God—"

George knelt beside her, kissing her hands, her arms, her neck—an ecstatic almost-Democrat, virtually on his way to Nashville to meet Andrew Jackson.

THREE

CONGRESS, HAVING APPROVED THE TARIFF OF Abominations, adjourned so its members could go home and hurl themselves into the 1828 campaign. This enabled Sarah and James Polk to offer themselves as traveling companions to Tennessee. As they boarded a stagecoach in front of the Franklin House, the pretty daughter of the owner, Peggy O'Neale, dashed up to them. "Oh, Mrs. Polk," she said. "I'm glad I caught you. I have a letter for Senator Eaton. Would you mind taking it to him?"

"Not at all," Sarah Polk said.

"I'm much obliged," Peggy said. "Give General Jackson my love."

As they rode into Maryland, Sarah gazed at the letter and said, "If I were a different sort of woman, I'd steam this open and read it. But my Presbyterian conscience won't allow it."

"Well, I'm not a Presbyterian," James Polk said, reaching for the letter.

Sarah shoved it firmly into the bottom of her purse. "I'd still be guilty. We'll have to allow time and circumstances to tell us the truth."

Sarah explained to the Stapletons that pretty Peggy was a widow; her first husband had been a naval officer who had recently died at sea. Well before his death, while he was on the bounding main, she had become almost too friendly with John Henry Eaton, the senator from Tennessee. There was talk of a marriage, but Sarah opined it was too late to save her reputation.

A day later, they rumbled west along the Great National Turnpike, one of the first "improvements" of Henry Clay's American System—a sixty-foot-wide macadam highway that ran from Fort Cumberland in western Maryland to Columbus, Ohio. They rode in a Blue Safety Line stagecoach pulled by four strong horses, who were changed every ten miles. Rolling at a brisk pace, they passed dozens of lumbering freight wagons and hundreds of plodding Conestoga wagons crammed with Eastern Americans and recent immigrants moving west.

Congressman Polk said over a quarter of a million people were using the road each year. If the influx continued, the West would soon equal the East and South at the polls.

George could not restrain himself from noting it was rather ironic that the Democrats opposed the American System—when it was responsible for doubling the population of the West, where they were strongest.

"Followers of General Jackson would oppose anything Henry Clay sponsored, even if God himself endorsed it," Polk said.

Sarah Polk explained why. Ten years ago, Andrew Jackson had been ordered to lead an army into Spanish-owned Florida to punish Seminole Indians and runaway slaves who had been raiding into Georgia and Alabama. He had conquered the entire colony and hanged two Englishmen who had been supplying the Indians with guns and ammunition. Both Spain and England threatened war. Henry Clay, the Speaker of the House at the time, denounced the General as a military adventurer and called for a vote of censure. But supporters of General Jackson defeated the Kentuckian's attempt to destroy him.

"Very early, Mr. Clay saw the General as his chief rival for the votes of the West," Sarah said. "Men talk about issues, but a great deal of their politics is personal."

"Would women be any different if they had the vote?" Polk asked her.

"Probably not," Sarah said.

George Stapleton entertained them with the early history of the national road, which George Washington helped British general Edward Braddock begin in 1754, en route to the bloody Indian ambush that killed the general on the site of contemporary Pittsburgh. George planned to start his verse history of the American Revolution with Washington's exploits in that long-forgotten war. Polk playfully offered him ten dollars to become the first subscriber to his opus.

"I think you'd be better advised to write a verse biography of General Jackson's military career," Sarah Polk said. "The senator we mentioned to you, John Henry Eaton, has risen to fame on a prose version of his life. It's no great shakes in my opinion. General Jackson deserves the kind of heroic rhythms Homer produced in praise of Achilles."

"You make me more and more eager to meet this man," George said. Together he and Caroline had drafted a letter to his grandfather, making their trip west seem a part of their honeymoon. Only casually, in the last line, did they mention the possibility of meeting General Jackson in Nashville.

In two days they were in Pittsburgh, where two great rivers, the Monongahela and the Allegheny, met to form the mighty Ohio. The town was already redolent with the smoke of burning coal that in ten years would blacken the very air. They spent the night at Hart's Tavern, where a huge painting of General Jackson hung in the taproom. The place was jammed with stevedores and riverboat men, many of whom asked the Polks to give the General their warmest regards. He had usually stopped at Hart's on his trips to and from Washington when he was a senator from Tennessee.

Several other Democratic congressmen were holding court in various corners of the taproom while the Stapletons and Polks ate dinner. The tavern rang with toasts in praise of General Jackson. A number of drinkers glanced suspiciously at George, whose stylish clothes differed markedly from the rough outfits favored by the men of the West—at least in this river town.

"Who's this, Polk?" asked one hulking keelboat man in knee-high rubber boots. "Some Philadelphia reporter on his way west to slander the General?"

"Mr. Stapleton is running for Congress from New Jersey—on the Democratic ticket, we hope," Polk said.

"Doesn't look like a Democrat to me," the keelboater growled.

"He's a rich Democrat," Polk said. "Nothing wrong with that."

"The hell you say!" roared the keelboat man. "He's a Nancy if I ever saw one. Five bucks I can take him in an arm wrestle."

Polk glanced across the table at George, who nodded. "I'll take the bet," the congressman said.

He laid five dollars on the table. The keelboat bruiser laid five dollars on top of it, pulled up a chair, and slammed his elbow on the table, his arm erect. George calmly removed his green frock coat and embroidered white vest and placed his palm in the keelboater's hand.

"Give the signal, Congressman," he said.

"Three two one—begin!" Polk said.

A crowd had gathered around the table, nasty grins on their faces. They were looking forward to the humiliation of this Eastern swell. Caroline was dismayed. She was sure George was going to lose. She did not want that to happen. He might change his mind about associating with these crude nasty-tongued Democrats.

The keelboater pushed first. The muscles in his neck bulged. He grunted like a sow in heat. George's arm vibrated but did not move backward an inch. Then George pushed. Without making a sound, he slowly bent the keelboater's arm back, back, back, until his knuckles touched the table. With a groan, the bruiser rolled out of his chair and crashed to the floor. The crowd roared their approval and pounded George on the back. Caroline felt a rush of delighted pride.

Congressman Polk seized the money and hailed a passing waiter. "Rumfustians all around," he said, gesturing to the circle of onlookers.

In moments a dozen flagons of rumfustian were on the table. Sarah Polk ignored them. Caroline was relieved to discover women were not expected to drink this lethal mix of brandy and ale and bourbon.

"To the democratic equality of all Americans, East and West, North and South, under the leadership of Andrew Jackson," Polk said, raising his flagon.

"I'll drink to that," said the keelboat man ruefully. "Maybe I just learned a democratic lesson."

Everyone downed their rumfustian. Caroline noticed James Polk took only a small sip. The keelboater and George shook hands and everyone gave them three cheers.

Up in their room, Caroline kissed George and said, "I never dreamt I was marrying a Hercules."

"We played that little game all the time in the taverns around Columbia," George said. "Johnny Sladen and Jeremy Biddle won a lot of money betting on me."

Caroline heard John Sladen's name without a tremor. Had he vanished from her soul as totally as he had disappeared from her life? She hoped so. "I'm the only one who's betting on you now," she said, kissing George. Pittsburgh became another memorable midnight in their honeymoon's progress.

The next morning the Stapletons and the Polks boarded the *Star of the West* steamboat and headed down the Ohio to the mouth of the Cumberland River, near Paducah, Kentucky. At their numerous stops along the way, many Kentuckians boarded the boat. Not a few of them were partisans of Henry Clay. That night in the dining room, one of them, a red-faced fellow as burly as the Pittsburgh keelboat man, overheard Caroline say something to Sarah about "Mr. Polk."

"Which is Congressman Polk, the great champion of General Jackson?" the Kentuckian asked.

"I'm proud to accept that title, sir," Polk said.

"Which of these is your wife?" the fellow said, looking insolently at Caroline and Sarah. "Or are you like General Jackson when it comes to the fair sex—and never bother to ask who's married to who?"

For Caroline and George, it was a stunning glimpse of the way the opposition was using the story of Jackson's marriage to smear him. "Sir," Polk said, "you've just insulted two ladies in one breath. On their behalf, I hope you'll immediately apologize—or I'll be forced to ask you for satisfaction."

Now Sarah Polk was looking horrified. Her husband had just challenged this man to a duel. "I wouldn't waste a bullet on a pismire like you," the Kentuckian said.

George Stapleton stood up and tapped him on the shoulder. "This lady happens to be my wife," he said, pointing to Caroline. "I'm afraid I must ask you for satisfaction too."

The Kentuckian rose to his feet. He was as tall as George and a good deal heavier. "You're a bigger pismire. But you get the same answer. Anyone who votes for Andrew Jackson is a de facto convicted whoremaster! If you want satisfaction, swallow this."

He balled his big hand into a fist in George's face.

"That suits me just fine," George said.

He sank his right fist into the Kentuckian's bulging belly, then clouted him in the jaw with a left hook. The man flew half the length of the dining room. All the women except Caroline and Sarah fled screaming to the outer decks.

Scrambling to his feet, the Kentuckian came at George in a roaring rush, eager to fight in the kicking, gouging Western style. George caught him in a wrestler's grip and threw him over his shoulder. The Kentuckian came down with a crash that shook the steamboat.

"Had enough?" George said.

The Kentuckian's answer was a kick in the groin. As George staggered back in pain, the man came after him, his thumb thrust like a knife blade at George's eyes. George caught the fellow's wrist and again threw him over his shoulder. This time George seized him by the shirtfront and slugged him until the man lay groaning at his feet.

"I still haven't heard you apologize to these ladies," George said, his fist raised for another punch.

" 'Pologize," the fellow said through loosened teeth.

James Polk led the way to the steamboat bar, where he bought drinks for all the male passengers. He explained that George was traveling to Nashville to meet General Jackson and decide whether to support him.

"If this fellow isn't a Jackson Democrat already, I'll eat my shoes," Polk said.

Four days later, the Polks and Stapletons debarked at a Cumberland River dock about eight miles above Nashville. A half dozen small black boys were lounging against the pilings. "Which one of you fellows can run fastest?" Polk asked.

They pointed to a lanky boy of about ten. Polk gave him a nickel. "Get up to the Hermitage and ask them to send down the coach."

In ten minutes a yellow coach with glassed windows and lace curtains, as fine as any vehicle in the Stapleton carriage house, came rumbling down the hill, drawn by four white horses. The coachman was a big black man in overalls and bare feet—not exactly a match for the spiffily uniformed blacks who drove the Stapleton coaches. George and Caroline were getting their first glimpse of luxury, Western style.

The Polks greeted "Hannibal" as an old friend. When they introduced the Stapletons to him as friends from New Jersey, the big fellow's eyes glowed. "That's where my daddy come from. Always talked about gettin' back there someday."

In another ten minutes they were debarking in front of the Hermitage, Andrew Jackson's white-pillared brick mansion. It was an imitation of George Washington's Mount Vernon, with a central hall dividing the house into east and west wings. The broad front lawn was shaded by a dozen gigantic trees. On the east side was an acre of lovely flowers, interspersed by brick walks. George was amazed. Like most Easterners, he imagined Westerners living in crude log dwellings, only a step above Indian longhouses.

General Jackson emerged from a small brick building on the west side that he used for an office. Although he was wearing a plain blue coat and faded tan pantaloons folded into riding boots, never had Caroline seen a man who looked more like a soldier. His white hair bristled straight up like the crest of a hussar's helmet. He approached them with a long swinging stride, his back straight as a gun barrel, a pleased smile on his lined, angular face. With him was a shorter, more mundane-looking, red-haired man, whom Sarah Polk identified in a quick whisper as Senator John Henry Eaton.

Jackson shook Polk's hand and embraced Sarah. "And these are the Stapletons from New Jersey?" he said to her. "Your letter came to hand yesterday. I'm impressed by anyone who'd travel a thousand miles to meet a broken-down old soldier."

"They're on their honeymoon, General," James Polk said as Jackson shook George's hand. "They're looking for any excuse to prolong their pleasure."

The General laughed heartily. "That's exactly the sort of medicine a Democratic candidate needs to keep his head on his shoulders.

"Mrs. Stapleton," Jackson said, kissing Caroline's hand with a courtly bow. "As an old codger who remembers every moment of his own honeymoon, may I say that a single glance at your loveliness should have been enough to make Congressman Polk's explanation unnecessary?"

"That's a compliment I'll always remember, General," Caroline said.

Jackson introduced the Stapletons to Senator Eaton, and Sarah Polk produced Peggy O'Neale's letter. The senator seemed momentarily flustered. "How is beautiful Peggy?" Jackson asked.

Sarah Polk said she was fine. Jackson pronounced her one of the most charming young women in Washington and led them into the Hermitage. In the west parlor he introduced them to Mrs. Jackson, a fat sweet-faced woman who spoke in a sad wheezing voice, but could not have been more hospitable. With her was her handsome nephew, Andrew Jackson Donelson, and his pretty blond wife, Emily, and two other young women, who were as well-gowned as Caroline and Sarah Polk. Only Mrs. Jackson wore frontier calico—and puffed cheerfully on a pipe.

"The rules of this house are very simple," she said. "The General and I undertake to look after none but our lady guests. The gentlemen make do as they can. If they want anything from a gun to a cigar, they need only ring for a servant. The sideboard is always ready to provide them with refreshments."

At dinner two hours later, Caroline was surprised to discover General Jackson did not sit at the head of the table. He left the place of honor to his biographer, Senator Eaton. The General sat between Sarah Polk and Caroline and demanded a detailed accounting of Washington's latest romances. Sarah had a veritable roster of names at her command, and the General had a shrewd or witty comment for almost every match.

While he seemed to be giving them his full attention, he suddenly turned away to hurl a delighted growl toward James Polk. The congressman was entertaining the rest of the table with an account of George Stapleton's thrashing of the insulting Kentuckian. "I wish I'd been there," Jackson said. "What was the nature of his insult?"

Glancing nervously toward Mrs. Jackson, who was absorbed in conversation with Emily Donelson, Polk gave the General a hurried version of what had been said.

Jackson's blue eyes blazed white fire. His whole countenance became almost incandescent. "Mr. Stapleton," he said, "you have put me and mine in your debt. You may call upon me for any favor at any time and it shall be yours—including the deed to this property!"

The General gulped some claret with a trembling hand. Alarm spread over every face. He looked as if he might be on the brink of apoplexy. "That men could sink as low as Adams and Clay and their detestable gang almost destroys my faith in this country," he said. "To wage war against an innocent woman—and to involve younger innocent women in their slanders! If I win this election, by God I'm tempted to celebrate my inauguration with a hanging!"

"Pappy, Pappy," Mrs. Jackson said. She understood the reason for his rage without hearing the grisly details. "Calm yourself. As long as I have my Bible and my pipe, no arrows can harm me, no matter how dipped they are in gall and wormwood."

She turned her plaintive eyes to the other guests. "But I will say this here and now. I would rather be a doorkeeper in the house of the Lord than live in that palace in Washington."

"If I didn't believe our country was teetering on the brink of destruction from internal enemies, I'd never ask you to endure it, my dearest," Jackson said.

Both Caroline and George were amazed and touched by the passionate sincerity of the old warrior. He truly believed that Henry Clay and John Quincy Adams were destroying the country. Their campaign of slander against him and Rachel was de facto proof that they were criminals with gross misdeeds to hide. Their policies became not merely mistaken but corrupt and evil. In Jackson's presence it was hard if not impossible to resist sharing this conviction.

The contrast between the General's hot-blooded passion and Hugh Stapleton's cool intellect was, Caroline suspected, more than a difference in personalities. It was an index of a profound change in American politics from the era of Washington and Jefferson to the age of Jackson. She and George were face-to-face with more than a man in the dining room of the Hermitage. History spilled from Andrew Jackson's hard lips and leaped in his electrifying eyes.

FOUR

AFTER DINNER, THE PARTY DIVIDED BY sexes. The ladies gathered in the east parlor around Mrs. Jackson while the men followed the General into the west parlor. Mrs. Jackson talked at length about her life with the General. In thirty-seven years they had never exchanged a difficult word. Their only disagreement was about his acceptance of numerous public assignments that took him away from home. She viewed the presidential contest as the ultimate disruption of their private lives.

Caroline listened to this plaintive recital with a mixture of sympathy and impatience. She yearned to be in the west parlor with the men, discussing politics. She was sure Sarah Polk felt the same way.

Later that night, in their bedroom, Caroline asked George what the men had talked about. George scratched his head and admitted to being confused. "The Polks, who seem to be quintessential Jacksonians, are against the tariff and internal improvements. The General says he's for them."

"What else did he say?"

"At first he seemed to lump Grandfather in with John Quincy Adams and President Monroe. The old aristocrats, he called them. His friend Eaton must have given him an earful about the family, painting us as power hungry as well as rich. But the General changed his mind when I told him about Great-Grandfather Malcolm hobnobbing with the Senecas and shooting up the French and their Indians. When he heard my father'd gone to West Point and died at Lundy's Lane, his eyes filled with tears and he said, 'Now I know why I liked you on sight. You're one of the Roman breed. We need men like you in Congress.' "

"Wonderful!" Caroline said. "Did Mr. Polk speak up on your behalf?"

"Most definitely. I get the feeling that Polk's not thrilled by Eaton, who more or less keeps everyone else a good distance from the General. He's managing the campaign."

"So it all went swimmingly?"

"Not completely. The General got onto banks and paper money. He talked as if they were creations of the devil. I was afraid to tell him we're majority stockholders in the biggest bank in New Jersey."

"That was wise," Caroline said. "I think we should be careful what we say to him."

"I've never met anyone like him. He's overpowering. When he looks at you, those eyes seem to bore into your soul. He's a piece of walking, talking history. He fought in the Revolution—at the age of thirteen! He truly loves this country. He's risked his life for it a hundred times. He wants everybody to feel—not just think—as he does. Maybe that's a good thing. The tactics of the other side—defaming a sweet old woman like Mrs. Jackson—are truly despicable."

While they were talking, they were preparing for bed. George said those last words as he lay down beside Caroline. "I'm so proud of you," she said, wrapping her arms around him. "You've *captured* him as much as he's captured you. No one but a *man* can do that with Andrew Jackson."

Caroline kissed George passionately. Power emanated from Andrew Jackson. It aroused her more than any imaginable caress or poem or song. She wanted George to emanate some of that power as soon as possible. "Now do you think I can be your political partner as well as your wife?"

"I never really doubted it," George said, returning her kiss.

Was Caroline aware that they were creating a pattern of rewards in the bedroom for George's performance outside it? Probably not. She was as mesmerized by Andrew Jackson as George. Both fatherless from an early age, they were easy quarry for a man who took charge of virtually every young person he met.

To understand Jackson, one must study the habits of Irish and Scottish leaders such as William Wallace and Red Hugh O'Neil. It was their hot Celtic blood that boiled in Old Hickory's veins, their warrior sense of honor and pride that drove his impulsive judgments, the code of the chieftain that made him play father to the whole world.

The next day, General Jackson announced the morning would be spent in the woods, gunning for quail and wild turkey. The men quickly changed to buckskin and boots, except George, who had packed little except dress clothes, thinking he would spend his honeymoon in Washington, D.C. General Jackson sent one of his house servants down to the slave quarters. He came back with the enormous black coachman, Hannibal. He wore a pair of dirty overalls.

"Stand next to Mr. Stapleton," the General said.

Hannibal obeyed. He and George were roughly the same size. The General asked Hannibal if he had a pair of clean overalls. He nodded. "My mammy done the wash yesterday, massa. But she won't let me change till Sunday 'cause she say I dirty everything so fast in that stable."

"Get the clean overalls up here for Mr. Stapleton."

While they waited for Hannibal to return, George asked Jackson how many slaves he owned. "A hundred here and another fifty on a cotton plantation in Mississippi," he said. "I wish I could afford free labor. But with the price of cotton so low, I don't expect to see the day when we can manage without bondmen."

"We consider ourselves fortunate to have escaped the problem in New Jersey by passing a gradual emancipation law," George said. He did not mention that Hugh Stapleton was the driving force behind that law, in obedience to the repeated demands of his Quaker wife.

"There's talk of one here in Tennessee," Jackson said. "But where will these poor people go? I freed one of my men in 1816 for his service with me at New Orleans. He's still living here. Only a few months ago, my nephew inherited a plantation from a relative who had freed his blacks if they would agree to go to Liberia with the Colonization Society. They refused to go."

Hannibal returned with the overalls and George soon appeared wearing them. John Henry Eaton joked about George being sentenced to pick cotton if he did not handle his gun up to the General's expectations. The men departed in an open carriage with Hannibal and two other blacks following in a buckboard. Caroline settled on the veranda with Sarah Polk, who was visibly nervous and grew more so as guns began booming in the distance. She confessed that James Polk was not adept with a gun. He had been sickly for most of his youth and never had a chance to master the sports that most male Tennesseans enjoyed.

Caroline wondered if George knew how to handle a gun. She got her answer two hours later, when the shooters returned. The smiling blacks in the buckboard held up a dozen birds. "It's a good thing we didn't make any bets with this fellow," Polk said as they got out of the carriage. "We all would have wound up picking cotton."

He was talking about George, who had made six of the twelve kills. "It's no different from shooting ducks in south Jersey," George said modestly. "My grandfather and uncle took me down to Barnegat Bay every September until I went to college."

General Jackson beamed at George like a proud father. "No duck ever flittered and skittered like a Tennessee turkey," he said. "If we have the misfortune to fight another war, I'm going to put you in charge of training sharpshooters."

"Hannibal deserves at least half the credit," George said. "He has a sixth sense for which way a bird will go. I had my gun ready for every shot."

The blacks took the birds around to the kitchen at the back of the house. "By the way," George said, "Hannibal asked me to buy him and take him back to New Jersey."

"You can have him at half price," the General said. "He's a troublemaker. He's run away twice. I've never whipped a slave, but I told him the next runoff would get him forty lashes."

"How much would he cost, General? Our family could use a good coachman. The man we have is getting old."

"A prime young fellow like him? About a thousand dollars. You can have him for five hundred."

"Agreed," George said.

In their bedroom, George explained the transaction to Caroline. In the woods Hannibal had told him that his New Jersey owners had sold his father and mother south to escape the state's emancipation law. The black was bitter because he felt he had lost his chance for freedom. Under the law he would have become free at age twenty-one.

"I didn't know you were such an emancipationist," Caroline said. Growing up in Ohio, she had little or no contact with blacks. Slavery was an abstraction to her.

"I'm not. But when I see a chance to right a wrong—the fellow really helped me win that shooting contest and shut up Eaton—and we do need a coachman."

In 1828, people could have this sort of conversation with no sense of attempting to deal with slavery as an institution. It was still merely a fact of Southern and Western life, as ordinary and as apparently permanent as birth, death, and taxes. If George and Caroline could have foreseen the role Hannibal and his family would play in their lives, they would have discussed his purchase in far more somber tones.

That night at dinner, Mrs. Jackson did not come to the table. She was feeling "poorly." Her niece Emily also skipped the meal to keep her company. That left Caroline and Sarah Polk as the only two women at the table. Once more the General sat between them, entertaining them with reminiscences of his sojourn as governor of Florida in 1819. The men talked about the political campaign, John Henry Eaton examining the Jacksonians' chances in each state. Caroline strained to hear both conversations.

As they finished their coffee, James Polk said, "Perhaps it's time for us to discuss New Jersey politics with Mr. Stapleton."

"Maybe," said Eaton.

"No maybes about it," General Jackson said. "I want this fellow in our party—if he's willing to come. Are you, Stapleton?"

"I begin to think I am," George said.

The men were on their feet, about to depart for the west parlor. "Why can't we talk right here?" Caroline said.

"Yes, why not?" Sarah Polk said.

"There's nothing that interests me more," Caroline said.

"James is well aware of my tendency in the same direction," Sarah drawled.

"General?" John Henry Eaton said.

"I have never in my life hesitated to surrender to a beautiful woman. When two of them join forces, there can't be even a shadow of a contest," Jackson said.

The men sat down again and Eaton produced a list of the Democratic candidates for Congress in New Jersey. They were running "at large" on a statewide ticket, instead of for individual districts. Eaton knew them all and thought there would be no difficulty about persuading one of them, a Dutchman named Van Brunt, to step aside so George could be added to the ticket.

"But I must ask a blunt question here," Eaton said. "Will Stapleton strengthen our slate? I fear he doesn't know how to run a Democratic-style campaign. He's likely to sit home on his porch until November, the way his grandfather campaigned, waiting for the voters to pay tribute to his bloodline."

"What do you say to that, young fellow?" Jackson asked.

Caroline fixed her eyes on George's face, silently exhorting him to stun Eaton with a ferocious reply. Instead, he was humble. "I'm afraid you'll have to explain what a Democratic-style campaign is, exactly."

"It's a Tennessee campaign," General Jackson said. "You get out in the country and shake the hand of every living soul you can find. You go into the fields to talk to the plowmen, into the church halls and Masonic halls to speak to every club and association and committee in existence. You kiss the babies and dance with the wives. You hire a newspaper to back you and print all your speeches. If you can't find a paper, you start one. You leave nothing to chance."

"It's the art of war applied to politics," James Polk said cheerfully.

"It's the art of making every voter in the state believe you consider him your *equal*," Eaton said. "Can you do that, Stapleton?" He clearly did not think so.

"Of course he can do it!" Caroline said. "He will do it."

"I'm an American," George said. "That means I already believe all men are created equal."

"A lot of Americans have lost sight of that great proposition," Andrew Jackson said. "It's my purpose to help the country regain it. Are you with me, heart and soul?"

The old man leaned toward George, the personification of an irresistible force. Instead of a flaccid yes, an echo of his wife's declaration, George reached across the table and shook Andrew Jackson's hand. In that moment, George Rensseler Stapleton became a Democratic politician.

FIVE

IN BOWOOD'S MAJESTIC LIBRARY, WITH THE portraits of his ancestors staring down at him and Caroline, George Stapleton cleared his throat and said, "I hope this won't upset you, Grandfather. But Caroline and I have decided I should run for Congress as a Democrat."

Hugh Stapleton sat up in his wing chair, his eyes almost as fiery as Andrew Jackson's. "What did they do to you in Tennessee, operate on your brains and replace them with cabbages?" he roared.

He directed not a little of his wrath at Caroline. She saw what she already half knew—he had looked on her as a confederate and companion spirit. Avoiding the accusation in his eyes, she let George do most of the talking. He swore that he went west ready to argue for the National Republicans, to defend Adams and Clay. But his encounter with the slander against Mrs. Jackson had changed his mind.

"How would you feel, Grandfather, if someone had attacked Grandmother that way?"

"Precisely as General Jackson feels, no doubt. But does that entitle me to become president and wreck the country?"

"I had several long talks with Sarah Polk, Congressman Polk's wife," Caroline said. "She assures me that no one has any reason to fear the radical theories being spouted by some Democrats."

"In fact," George said, "the General told me he was in favor of a strong tariff and internal improvements."

"That's not what his followers are saying in New York and New Jersey," the Congressman growled.

"I think they're running a different General Jackson in each section of the country," Caroline said. "But the best argument of all, Grandfather, is this: George can win as a Democrat. It automatically defuses any attempt to slander him because he's rich."

"What makes you think the voters will believe his transformation?"

"This." George handed Hugh Stapleton a letter, which he opened and read:

To the citizens of New Jersey:

I recommend without reservation the election of George Stapleton on the Democratic ticket. He is exactly the sort of young American we need in Congress to support my program.

Andrew Jackson

"That's hard to quarrel with," Hugh Stapleton admitted.

Caroline saw he was still disappointed. The old man had envisioned George campaigning for the right to represent New Jersey on the merits of his grandfather's fame—Hugh Stapleton's service in the Continental Congress, his friendship with George Washington and John Adams and Alexander Hamilton, his creation of Principia Mills and Principia Forge, which had given employment to hundreds of people. It was hard for him to realize these historic names meant little to the new generation that was rising up to take charge of America. Even harder to accept was the realization that his mills, his iron factory, his bank, were ready targets for those who saw him as an exploiter of the poor and dispossessed. In America, the wages of fame were constantly depreciated by time and envy.

Not even the news of Caroline's pregnancy cheered the old man. He slipped into a slow decline. With George out campaigning every day, it was Caroline who witnessed Hugh Stapleton's quiet withdrawal from the field of fame. He spent more and more time in Bowood's library, putting his voluminous papers in order. He lost interest in the newspapers, which he had previously devoured with the seasoned eye of the veteran politician. Although he was unfailingly polite to Caroline, there was a subtle reproach in his patent lack of interest in George's campaign.

Not nearly as polite was George's uncle Malcolm. He visited his father at least once a week and saw what was happening with the cold eyes of a businessman who had little respect for politics. One day in late September, when Malcolm was leaving Bowood, Caroline hurried to say good-bye to him. "I wish you could come more often," she said. "You always cheer Grandfather so."

"Does his melancholy trouble you?" Malcolm said. "Is it possible you have a bad conscience?"

"What do you mean?"

"You know exactly what I mean. How could you repay his affection for you by pushing your husband into the Democratic Party? He could have stopped George's infatuation with you anytime he chose. Angelica and Sally both begged him to do it. Instead he gave you his blessing. This is his reward."

"I didn't push my husband anywhere. He went of his own free will."

Malcolm contemptuously dismissed this half-truth with a shake of his le-
onine head. "I can't believe anyone raised as a gentleman can willingly support
that Tennessee brawler, adulterer, and murderer."

"I've met General Jackson. He's as much a gentleman, a man of honor
and integrity, as any person I've ever seen or hope to see."

"Then why is he being supported by the scum of the earth? George Stapleton is out there campaigning with would-be Robespierres and Dantons,
men like Samuel Swartout who talk about the day of reckoning for the rich—"

"If George wins he'll have a voice in the councils of the party. He can
oppose these extremists."

"Even if he manages such a miracle, that won't be much consolation for
Father. He'll be dead—of a broken heart. I may soon follow him. Disgust,
I've been told, is a strong inducer of apoplexy."

Good riddance to both of you. The blazing words shocked Caroline. She
groped for a more genteel reply and could find none. She whirled and fled
upstairs. Malcolm Stapleton was a formidable enemy. It was almost as unnerving to discover his daughter, Sally, and George's mother had equally low
opinions of her.

This upheaval had a major impact on Jeremy Biddle. He had asked Malcolm's permission to marry Sally and had won his consent. The wedding was
set for early October. Jeremy had already informed everyone of his plans to
move to Philadelphia. He had even signed a lease on a house. A week before
the ceremony, a letter from Malcolm summoned him to Bowood.

Jeremy was not surprised to discover a gigantic hickory pole on the man-
icured lawn in front of Bowood. George had written him a long letter, telling
him about his conversion in Nashville. Neither George nor Caroline were at
home to greet the visitor. George was campaigning in Newark, close enough
to make a trip for Caroline feasible in spite of her advancing pregnancy.

The Congressman and Malcolm greeted Jeremy in the library. He was
distressed by how feeble Hugh Stapleton had become. He did not rise from
the chair when they shook hands. Before Jeremy could inquire into his health,
Malcolm launched into the reason for his visit.

"Father and I have been discussing the future. While we think it's com-
mendable of you to move to Philadelphia and make your own way, we've
begun to think it's neither wise nor convenient. As my daughter, Sally will
inherit a fifty percent interest in the Stapleton properties. George's plunge into
Democratic politics makes it less likely that he'll have the time or inclination
to do much in a business way. It's been our experience that there's no substitute for ownership when it comes to managing a business."

On he talked in his hard cold voice, that word *business* clanging against
Jeremy's brain like the tongue of a large bell. "In short," the Congressman
said, "we feel it would make Malcolm and me rest easier if you settled here
after your marriage and began working with Malcolm with an eye to becoming his successor."

The calm faintly elegiac way he said "rest easier" dissolved whatever feeble
resistance Jeremy had to this generous offer. It sentenced him to a lifetime of
toil in a field that did not truly inspire him, compared to the law. But it
guaranteed ample comfort and wealth. Only one thing made him hesitate.

"What does George think of this?" he asked.

"He hasn't been consulted. Nor has Caroline," Malcolm said stonily.

The Congressman said nothing. He looked vaguely embarrassed. But his silence left little doubt that he endorsed his son's harsh tone. "George is my closest friend. I couldn't do it without his consent," Jeremy said.

"Then talk to him," Malcolm said.

"If all goes well," Hugh Stapleton said, "we'll arrange for you to be the majority stockholder in the parent company."

"In business there's no place for compromises. One man has to be in charge and make the final decisions," Malcolm said.

"I wouldn't tell that to George for the time being," Hugh Stapleton said.

Jeremy felt dazed—and not a little apprehensive. He was tempted to tell them of Caroline's hatred. But that would have led to explanations he was not prepared to make. He had resolved to tell no one about John Sladen.

Jeremy borrowed a horse and gig from the Bowood stables and headed for Newark. On the road, he saw the Stapleton coach approaching—its royal crimson sides, with the gold crest of the corporate seal of Principia Mills on the doors, was much too vivid to miss. He waved to the coachman and he slowed the horses.

Caroline leaned from the window, a chilly smile on her lips. "What brings you to New Jersey?" she asked.

"Oh, I just thought I'd drop over to see George."

"Why? Your wedding is next week. Have you forgotten he's your best man?" Caroline said, her eyebrows arching.

A poor liar, Jeremy floundered through a dubious story about visiting Malcolm Stapleton to discuss some details of Sally's dowry before they left for Philadelphia—and deciding to see George campaign as a Democrat. Caroline did not believe a word of it.

"Is George still in Newark?" he asked.

"He's on his way to Bloomfield to speak to the leather workers there."

"Can I catch up to him this evening?"

"He's spending the night at Mason's Tavern." Caroline slammed down the coach window, making it into a statement of her opinion of Jeremy and his evasions.

Jeremy rode on to Bloomfield. Along with Newark and Rahway, it was one of the "leather towns" where burgeoning factories were turning out shoes, gloves, and other products. They all used the invention of a clever Yankee who had figured out how to slit a cow's hide into several layers, marvelously multiplying its value.

At John Mason's commodious brick and timber tavern, Jeremy asked a knot of men outside for George Stapleton's whereabouts. Out of the crowd stepped a black man at least as big as George. "Master—I mean, Mr. Stapleton's in the taproom, buyin' drinks all around," he said with a cheerful grin. "Sure takes a lot of liquor to win an election in New Jersey. Almost as much as Tennessee."

Jeremy would soon learn that this was Hannibal, the big black George had purchased from General Jackson and brought back to New Jersey. George had freed him and put him to work as his coachman. Driving George around the state in a gig, he had proven himself a political asset by mingling in the crowd and telling stories about General Jackson as the kindly master of the Hermitage—and about the General's praise of George's marksmanship.

In the taproom, Jeremy found George at the bar, a flagon of ale in his hand, telling a room of rapt listeners about his fight with the Kentuckian who had insulted General Jackson's wife—and the General's gratitude. George looked tired and his normal baritone had a ragged edge to it. But he went on to eulogize Jackson with passionate sincerity. "The man is the leader we want and need in this country! I'm proud to have his endorsement."

Like Hugh Stapleton, Jeremy was inclined to ask why outrage over a slandered wife was a good reason for electing Andrew Jackson president of the United States. But there was no doubt from the fervor with which the drinkers responded to George's toast that they thought it was an unbeatable argument.

"Tell us again how he *looked*," said a stumpy man whose hands were stained dark brown from the chemicals used in the leather factories.

"We hear his health is so bad, he may die in office," said another man, who had splotches of the dye on his face.

"He looks his age," George said. "But I spent a day gunning in the woods with him. He climbed hills without a puff and got his share of birds."

A collective sigh escaped from every breast. George went on to describe Mrs. Jackson as a saint. He said she was a woman out of the Bible, as pure and devoted as Abraham's mate.

"Now Congressman," said a fat little man in a cheap frock coat, "let me introduce each of these good Democrats to you. There's more waiting outside to meet you."

He solemnly introduced every man in the room. George shook each extended hand. Not a few were grimy, but he did not seem bothered in the least. He listened patiently as one man told him how his brother had fallen into a priming vat in the local factory and had been scarred for life. George asked if he was a veteran of the War of 1812. If so, he would do everything in his power to get him a government pension. Alas, the man was not a veteran. George said he would try to get him work at Principia Mills. So it went, tales of woe mingling with hurried words about old links to the Stapleton family and murmured thanks for supporting Andrew Jackson. There was little doubt that George's switch to the Democrats was a political coup of the first order.

The men streamed out the door, contentment—in part a tribute to the drinks they had downed—on every face. In marched another contingent for more drinks and another recital of General Jackson's virtues and glowing health. It took almost two hours before the little man in the frock coat announced George could rest from his labors. Jeremy went up to the bar and said, "He's got to stand one more round for a National Republican."

"Jeremy!" George said, swatting him on the back. George introduced him to the fat little man. He was Adam Hosmer, chairman of the Bloomfield Democratic Committee. George explained that the Democrats had county and city and town committees throughout the state. It was a new idea in American politics—it gave voters a sense of participation in elections. Hosmer treated Jeremy to a panegyric of George as a politician. He was born to help the people regain control of the federal government, which Hosmer seemed to think had been stolen by the nefarious followers of President Adams and his corrupt friend Henry Clay. This struck Jeremy as egregious nonsense but he smiled and nodded in apparent agreement.

Eventually Hosmer went home for his supper, and George gazed at Jeremy across the top of a renewed pint of ale. "To President Jackson," he said with a grin.

"To Congressman Stapleton," Jeremy retorted.

"I could see you didn't agree with him," George said, nodding after Hosmer. "But he's a good fellow. They're all good fellows. This whole thing has been an education for me, Jeremy. I've met the ordinary American for the first time. I've learned to share his hopes and fears. I've been saddened by his hardships and touched by his faith in this country. Win or lose, I'll be a different man thanks to this experience."

Jeremy told himself not to be surprised. George's large heart, his quick sympathies, made him a natural Democrat. Jeremy thought George was talking sentimental twaddle, but he realized this was hardly the time or place to get into a political debate.

"I wish I could vote for you," Jeremy said. "Maybe I will the next time you run. It looks as if I'm not going to Philadelphia after all."

"You're going to settle in New Jersey? Jeremy, that's great news!"

"Hear me out before you say that."

Jeremy told him about his meeting with Hugh and Malcolm Stapleton—and their offer. "That's even better news," George said. "I can't think of anyone I'd rather have running the business side of things."

Jeremy had George's consent. That was as far as Hugh and Malcolm Stapleton had advised him to go. But George Stapleton was Jeremy's best friend, closer in his mind and heart than a brother. He could not practice even the smallest deception on him. He told George the rest of the proposition. "They want me to have a controlling percentage of the family stock," Jeremy said. "To guarantee my independence in business decisions. Of course we'll share the profits equally."

"Why did they recommend that?" George said. "I can't imagine a situation in which you and I would disagree about anything important."

"Apparently, they feel it could happen. People change as they grow older. Their children—their wives—influence them."

George was too intelligent to deceive with such banal generalities. "Caroline. Uncle Malcolm has never liked her. But I don't see why Grandfather has gone along. I thought he adored her."

"He did, until you decided to become a Democrat."

This was hard for George to accept. But he realized it was probably true. He was far more troubled to think he and Caroline had hurt the old man than he was concerned about who would control Principia Mills. This regret reinforced his readiness to accept the arrangement that the older generation had decreed for the companies. It was a kind of expiation, a gesture of reconciliation with Hugh Stapleton.

"I'm sure it's for the best all around," he said. "I agree wholeheartedly with Grandfather's estimate of my business abilities, and I'm delighted someone as hardheaded as Uncle Malcolm puts such a high value on yours."

As they drank to harmony and happiness, Jeremy realized how much he could not tell George. He could not reveal that his uncle and his grandfather had advised Jeremy to deceive him. He could not admit that he would probably have refused the offer if a strictly equal division had exposed him to Caroline's hostility. Jeremy sipped his ale and listened to George puzzle over why his grandfather thought he might be unduly influenced by Caroline. Of course he listened to her advice, especially on politics, where she was surprisingly shrewd. "But I make up my own mind. That would be especially the case in a business decision."

Naturally Jeremy agreed with him. It was the beginning of years of guilt for his inability to tell his friend the whole truth. The beginning of the long, slow spiral into multiplying evasions until that terrible moment when Jeremy discovered the truth's slow, relentless urgency, like a bullet lodged in the body, working its way to the surface by a process too obscure for the mind to comprehend.

S I X

A WEEK LATER, GEORGE RETURNED TO Bowood to be Jeremy's best man at the weeding. In their bedroom the candidate and Caroline talked first about the campaign. There were growing signs that he might lead the Democratic ticket in the state. Many National Republicans had endorsed him, particularly in North Jersey, where the Stapleton name was potent. But George had doubts about General Jackson's ability to carry the state. The slanders against him—for adultery, for killing several men in duels, for hanging six deserters during his military years—were troubling many voters.

Then George mentioned, almost casually, that Sally and Jeremy were not going to Philadelphia. They would be neighbors—and partners in the Principia companies. Even more casually, he described the decision to give Jeremy eventual control of the businesses.

"How could you agree to this without consulting me?" Caroline said. "Don't you see how ruinous this could be to me—to both of us?"

"What are you talking about?"

"Your cousin Sally hates me. And so does your friend Jeremy Biddle."

George was openmouthed. "Caroline, you're talking nonsense. Jeremy's never even hinted such a thing. Sally is another matter. I don't pretend to understand why or how women take dislikes to each other. But it will surely pass as you grow older and more mature."

"My dislike for her—and her hatred of me—has nothing to do with immaturity. It has to do with snobbery—her inborn inability to admit a mere farm girl from Ohio could possibly be her equal in taste and intelligence. I'm telling you here and now you've made a terrible mistake, George. You should have objected violently to the whole idea. You should still object—for my sake!"

"How can I do that when I don't think it's a mistake? I don't have much head for business. Politics—Democratic style—is all-absorbing. I won't have time to run the business and win elections."

"You'll soon be a senator. That only requires you to campaign once every six years."

"Your optimism exceeds mine. Most people don't reach the Senate before the age of forty. Anyway, the basic fact remains—I agree with the idea. I welcome Jeremy as a friend and business partner."

"I thought I was your partner."

"You are too. A man can have more than one partner." George tried to give her a reassuring kiss. "Darling, calm down. I've never seen you so upset. I'm beginning to fear for the baby."

"You don't understand—or care," Caroline said, avoiding his lips.

Jeremy was forever linked in her mind with John Sladen. Jeremy's presence lured John back into her soul. But she could not explain that to George. She left him to puzzle over her seemingly irrational hostility to his best friend—and to worry about the way she seemed to transfer some of it to him.

For the moment, things remained relatively calm on the surface. The wedding went off without any complications. Sally and Jeremy sailed off on a two-month grand tour of Europe. While they were gliding down the Grand Canal in Venice and prowling the ruins of the Roman forum, George was trekking through South Jersey in search of votes. His Quaker grandmother won him wide approval among the numerous Plain People in that part of the state, in spite of his support for that "man of war" Andrew Jackson.

In mid-October, George was in Trenton, just across the Delaware from Pennsylvania, when the first election results reached him. (In 1828, there was no single election day; the states set a variety of dates.) General Jackson had swept the Keystone State by a margin of two-to-one and had done almost as well in Ohio. Next came word that he had carried Kentucky, Henry Clay's home state. Over the following two weeks, evidence of a landslide mounted. The South gave the General massive majorities in every state.

By the time New Jersey voted, it was almost an anticlimax. As George had feared, many Quakers disliked Jackson's violent reputation, and even more of the state's mostly rural voters were suspicious of a man who was backed by the city slickers of Philadelphia and New York. The Garden State went for Adams, but all five Democratic candidates were elected to Congress, with George Stapleton running ahead of the nearest contender by ten thousand votes.

Adam Hosmer and two dozen other Democratic committee chairmen from nearby towns rushed to Bowood to congratulate George. Hundreds of citizens from their towns and the city of Hamilton joined them. George was obviously the coming man in the New Jersey branch of the Democratic Party. A celebration was soon under way on the lawn. The servants lugged out gallons of champagne punch to fuel the merriment.

Caroline sent Malcolm Stapleton a note, suggesting he let the mills out early to join the party. She got a chilling reply.

With an ignoramus from Tennessee in the White House, I do not think we can afford to lose a single penny of profit. We will need to husband every dollar to survive the difficult years ahead. Congratulate George on his congressional victory, nonetheless.

Hugh Stapleton also declined to mingle with the Jacksonians who cavorted around the hickory pole on Bowood's lawn. He pleaded indisposition and stayed in his bedroom. Behind his smiles and handshakes, George Stapleton concealed a growing uneasiness about his decision to become a Democrat. He was finding out that life is full of conflicting choices.

At supper later that night, Hugh Stapleton was resolutely cheerful. He joked about surrendering his nickname, "the Congressman," to George and toasted him and President Jackson. He gamely admitted that no one could foresee the future. He could remember more than one friend predicting that George Washington would make a terrible president. But the new congressman detected the vein of sadness in his grandfather's manner.

So did Caroline, but she was far more prepared for it, having spent most of her time at Bowood during the previous months. She had given up trying to soothe the old man. Unfortunately, George judged her silence as coldness.

That night in the library, she urged George to write a letter of congratulations to Andrew Jackson. George agreed, then asked if she too was troubled by Hugh Stapleton's melancholy. She responded by showing him Malcolm Stapleton's note.

"You're the family leader now, George," Caroline said. "You can't let these old men—or your friend Jeremy Biddle, who agrees with them—get in your way. That's why I fear the worst over the agreement you've allowed Jeremy to make."

"I know Jeremy's not a Democrat, but he's a decent honest man," George insisted. He fingered Malcolm's note. "I also don't think Grandfather shares Uncle Mal's harsh attitude."

"Perhaps not." Her cold tone indicated she considered George's sentimental regret was irrelevant.

"I wonder if we should try to make the old gentleman feel better about it all."

"There's nothing you, or I, can do."

"Nothing? Caroline, a woman can do so many small, tender things."

"But I don't choose to. Having been excluded from the family's councils, why should I humble myself, play the apologist?"

"Not even for my sake?"

"Not even for your sake."

For the first but not the last time, George was learning the danger of offending Caroline Kemble Stapleton. In the weeks that followed, George repeatedly tried to communicate his regret, and his deep, unshaken affection, to his grandfather. But it was difficult to do. His time was devoured by delegations of Democrats from distant parts of the state and congratulatory letters from New York and Pennsylvania Democratic politicians, who had to be answered promptly. Swarms of government-job seekers implored him for help. Anyway, a man lacks the gift of subtle emotional communication. In spite of all George's efforts, Hugh Stapleton remained out of reach behind his politeness, his memories.

In December, Sally and Jeremy returned from their honeymoon and began living at Bowood while their own house was being built. Malcolm Stapleton felt they would be more comfortable there than in his widower's cottage. Caroline did as little as possible to make them welcome, using her pregnancy as an excuse to dine in her room and otherwise avoid them.

One morning the gray-haired local postmaster personally brought to Bowood a letter addressed to George. The old man excitedly pointed to the return address: *A. Jackson, Nashville, Tennessee*. It was written by Andrew Jackson himself, in his highly original scrawl.

Dear Congressman Stapleton:

> *Your letter came safely to hand yesterday. I thank you for your congratulations, which really should be extended to the people of this great nation. I am only their humble instrument. I congratulate you in turn on your election. I look forward to working with you on the great task of reforming our national government.*
>
> *I wish I could say I was elated by my election, but truth compels me to admit my mind is depressed. You and your wife know better than most the reason. Mrs. Jackson is less than happy at the prospect of going to Washington and facing many of the foul wretches who slandered her so cruelly over the past six months. But we will both do our duty in response to the people's summons.*
>
> *I hope you and your beautiful wife are continuing to enjoy honeymoon transports and will do so for years to come.*

Again, George felt the grasp of Jackson's paternity. He was glad, fiercely glad, he had embraced this old warrior's cause. Thanks to Jackson's candor, he also realized his own tincture of regret for his Democratic triumph was not so unusual. There are often gaps between public triumphs and private emotions. George was encountering one of history's dominant motifs: irony.

George showed Jackson's letter to Jeremy Biddle as he departed for Principia Mills. He agreed it was a moving document. "I'm going to show this to Grandfather," George said. He thought it might win the old man's sympathy and bolster the case for his grandson's Democratic status.

Jeremy paused in the hall to see if the mail had brought a letter for him or Sally. His examination of the dozen or so letters was broken by a cry of anguish in the upper hall. "Grandfather!"

Jeremy rushed upstairs to find George embracing a tearful Sally outside Hugh Stapleton's bedroom. Caroline, extremely pregnant, was standing in the doorway of her room in a negligee and robe. In Hugh Stapleton's bedroom, Jeremy found the Congressman stretched on the canopied bed, clothed in the old-fashioned breeches and waistcoat he favored. He had apparently finished dressing when the stroke or heart spasm seized him. He had lain down and calmly greeted death with the same composure with which he had confronted life.

The funeral was an ordeal for everyone in the family. Newspapers in New

York, New Jersey, and Philadelphia published long résumés of Hugh Stapleton's career. Not a few Democratic papers underscored his grandson George's conversion to the party of the people. This did nothing to raise Malcolm Stapleton's spirits. But the whole family was consoled by the dozens of eulogies that praised the patriarch's disinterested patriotism. They applauded his loans to the Continental Congress from his private fortune in the closing years of the Revolution. They commended his support of the War of 1812 even after it had taken the life of his older son and many of his New England Federalist colleagues in Congress were urging a peace of surrender and even secession from the Union.

Caroline insisted on participating in all the ceremonies, including the graveside prayers that laid the old man to rest beside his wife in the cemetery at Great Rock Farm, the family's original New Jersey property, about twenty miles from Bowood. It was still a producing farm, run by the descendants of some of the black slaves who had originally worked it.

As they jolted back to Bowood over wretched country roads, Caroline became more and more agitated. She twisted the engagement ring on her finger as if she yearned to tear it off. She was barely aware of what she was doing. Hugh Stapleton's death had forced her to confront her guilt for taking his grandson away from him and from the family's traditions. It was a far keener emotion than George's sentimental regret. For a little while she had treasured the sense of fatherhood the old man had offered her. Now she was assailed by a new kind of loneliness. Jeremy's reappearance in such a powerful role made her feel beleaguered, incapable of explaining her deepest feelings to anyone—even herself.

As Caroline stepped out of the carriage in front of Bowood, she clutched her side and cried out. The first of many labor pains had just jolted through her body. Jeremy leaped in a gig and raced off to summon the family doctor. George carried Caroline upstairs, where Sally and several of the women servants undressed her. By the time the doctor arrived, the pains were multiplying. Caroline's cries echoed through Bowood all afternoon and into the night.

George paced the library fearing the worst, hoping for the best, like fathers since civilization began. He and Jeremy talked about enrolling the boy in Columbia immediately, of buying him a pony and other toys—the sort of nonsense men blabber to conceal how utterly superfluous they are in this fundamental process.

At midnight Sally came downstairs with a smile on her weary face. "Congratulations, George, you're the father of a healthy baby boy."

The men rushed upstairs to find Caroline propped up in the bed, holding the infant, who had apparently taken a quick look at his surroundings, decided they met with his approval, and gone to sleep. His finely sculpted features had an unmistakable resemblance to John Sladen's. Jeremy held his breath. Would Caroline's luck hold?

His worry was superfluous. As any lawyer can testify, evidence, like beauty, is often in the eye of the beholder. George picked up the child and held him against his broad chest. "He's beautiful, Caroline," he said. "What shall we name him?"

"He looks like my father," Caroline said. "The dark hair, the mouth . . ."

George hesitated. He wanted to name him after Hugh Stapleton. "I see Grandfather too."

"I don't."

"It's Jonathan then. You've earned the right to the first pick. How about Hugh for a middle name?"

"All right," Caroline said without enthusiasm.

"I'm glad he came early. He'll be old enough to take to Andrew Jackson's inauguration, won't he?"

"Of course," Caroline said.

As Sally and Jeremy undressed for bed, he found himself facing an inquisitive wife. "George and Caroline have been married seven months," she said. "That baby is no seven months child."

"So?"

"I can't believe George, the man of honor, took advantage of dear Caroline. Or am I to conclude that this was how she landed him?"

"Perhaps it would be best to draw no conclusions."

"Are you defending her—after the way she's treated you?"

"I'm defending her—and George. Whatever's happened is something we're dutybound not to discuss—out of family loyalty, elementary decency, and good manners."

"You mean to say I can't speak my mind to you here, in our bedroom?"

"Of course you can. But . . ."

"But what?"

Abandoning his vow of perpetual silence, Jeremy told Sally about Caroline and John Sladen. He immediately realized he had made the worst mistake of his life. Sally was stunned and horrified beyond all his expectations. He should have known she might feel that way. She had spent her girlhood and youth in the company of Angelica Stapleton and her sister, Henrietta, two of the most proper women in New York.

Worse, Sally disapproved of Jeremy's concealing the affair from George and allowing Caroline into the family. "How could you have done such a thing?" she cried. "You should have given each of them a hundred dollars and sent them both to New Orleans."

"George loved her!" Jeremy said.

"He would have gotten over it," Sally said with the merciless realism that comes so easily to some of her sex.

"I did what I thought was best."

Sally turned away, trying, and failing, to conceal the contempt on her face. Jeremy realized that she would never have confidence in him again. He lay awake most of the night, wondering if he was on his way to the overheated place that is paved with good intentions.

BOOK

THREE

ONE

ON JANUARY 2, 1829, THE LOCAL newspaper, the *Hamilton Beacon*, reached Bowood with a stunning report from the West in its right-hand column: "Mrs. Jackson Dead!" The editor went on to tell his wide-eyed readers that Rachel Jackson had died at the Hermitage on December 23 and had been buried the following day. It described Andrew Jackson as "grief-stricken to the point where there is serious concern for his survival."

Caroline immediately wrote to Sarah Polk, begging her for a complete account of the tragedy. In a postscript she mentioned she had given birth to a son. Two weeks later, as the new congressman and his wife were preparing to depart for Washington, D.C., Sarah's reply reached them. She and her husband had not been in Nashville at the time of Rachel Jackson's death (the Polks lived in Columbia, Tennessee), but she had obtained her information from friends and family when they rushed to the Hermitage to extend their sympathy to the General.

> *As you know, Mrs. Jackson had little enthusiasm for going to Washington, and her anxiety about the impending journey weakened her already faltering health a good deal. In mid-December she permitted the ladies of Nashville to take her to the city to outfit her with a trousseau that would enable her to grace her role as the President's wife. While waiting in a newspaper editor's office for a carriage to take her home, she picked up one of the scurrilous pamphlets the Adams-Clay clique had circulated about her marriage. When the coachman arrived, he found her sobbing hysterically. At the Hermitage, she swooned and physicians had to be summoned. They bled her and she seemed to recover. But three days later, while preparing for bed, she collapsed and died moments after the General, summoned by a servant's cries, reached her. The General could not believe she was gone. He begged the doctors to try to resuscitate her. For the next twenty-four hours, he sat by her bed holding her cold hand. It was a scene so affecting, no one, man or woman, could describe it to me without tears. The next day Rachel was buried in a dress of pure white, a fitting symbol of her stainless soul. At the graveside, tears coursed down the General's cheeks for the first time since his beloved's death. "I know 'tis unmanly," he said, "but these tears are due her virtues. She shed many for me." Then he mastered himself and spoke in a voice that seemed to come from another*

world. "In the presence of this dear saint I can and do forgive all my enemies. But those vile wretches who have slandered her must look to God for mercy."

I fear we are facing some stormy political weather. The newspaper stories of General Jackson's imminent demise are exaggerated. Though he is heartbroken, the flame of life still burns furiously in his soul. I congratulate and envy you on your elevation to motherhood and look forward to seeing you and George and little Jonathan in Washington.

Your friend,
Sarah Polk

To Washington, D.C., George and Caroline and little Jonathan went, taking with them several of Bowood's servants—Hannibal, the big black whom George had brought from Tennessee; Tabitha Flowers, a pert young woman of his race whom Hannibal had married since he came to Bowood; and Harriet, the mansion's rotund cook. Caroline and Sally Biddle almost came to blows over Harriet. Sally and Jeremy were about to move into their new house, and Sally tried to pirate Harriet for their kitchen. Jeremy suggested they draw lots and Caroline won.

In Washington, Caroline and George found the new house they had rented at 3600 Pennsylvania Avenue chaotically incomplete. Plaster was still oozing from the walls, the coal stove in the kitchen had no connection to the chimney, the indoor toilet threatened to flood the first floor every time it was used. They sought shelter at nearby Gadsby's Hotel, only to learn not a room was to be had there or anywhere else in Washington. At least ten thousand people had poured into the city to attend Andrew Jackson's inauguration.

They settled for dinner at Gadsby's where they enjoyed a cordial reunion with the Polks—and discovered the topic that was standing official and unofficial Washington on its ear.

"John Henry Eaton has resigned from the Senate and become General Jackson's secretary of war. He's also married Peggy O'Neale," Sarah Polk said, her eyes alight with unladylike glee. "A great many people think the two things will mix like oil and water—or honey and vinegar."

The Polks' dislike—or to put it more exactly, jealousy—of Eaton was no longer concealed behind politeness. Several other Jackson Democrats at the table chimed in with similar sarcasm. "If Peggy is a lady," chortled Congressman Churchill C. Cambreleng, "then I'm a candidate for presiding bishop of the Methodist Episcopal Church."

"Unfortunately," Sarah Polk continued in a more sober tone, "General Jackson insists Peggy is a lady."

"Does that mean we can look forward to Mr. Cambreleng's nomination to the episcopacy?" George asked.

"More likely his appointment as third secretary in the American consulate in Tierra del Fuego—if he persists in his opinion," James Polk said.

"You gentlemen misjudge me," Cambreleng said. "Simply because I personally have no moral character worth mentioning doesn't mean I don't insist on it in others. My aim in life is complete hypocrisy. That's what American politics is all about."

After dinner, while Polk and Cambreleng discussed with George what House committees interested him, Sarah Polk told Caroline she was seriously alarmed about the Eaton problem. "On January first of this year, Major Eaton married Peggy at the General's direct *order,*" she said. "That has only inflamed the gossip."

The gossip, summarized by Mrs. Polk in her incisive way, was juicy. Peggy's previous husband had been a U.S. Navy purser who had trouble keeping good accounts. A Southern Adonis with a small brain and a fondness for alcohol, John Timberlake had wooed and won Peggy when she was sixteen. While the purser was at sea, John Henry Eaton moved into the hotel that Peggy's father owned, the Franklin House. Peggy's conduct with him was flagrant enough to attract the notice of Mrs. James Monroe, who had banned her from receptions at the White House.

Early in 1828, Timberlake's accounts were such a mess that the Navy threatened to dismiss him. Senator Eaton had posted a bond of ten thousand dollars to enable the impugned purser to sail for the Mediterranean aboard the USS *Constitution,* where he died, according to the Navy, from acute drunkenness. Others claimed he had cut his throat because his wife was living in sin with Senator Eaton.

Caroline immediately pointed out the striking similarity between Peggy's story and General Jackson's rescue of his beloved Rachel from the arms of another rascal. "That's exactly what worries me," Sarah Polk said.

For the rest of the week, the Stapletons struggled to make their house livable. In their forays onto the streets, they noticed incredible numbers of people wandering in search of amusement. Many of them seemed to have recently arrived from places like Pittsburgh and Nashville. They wore the rough clothes of the West and seemed to regard anyone well dressed as an enemy. If a gentleman stared at them in a way they considered too curious, he was liable to end up on his back with a broken jaw. A startling number of them were drunk, even at nine o'clock in the morning.

At the Stapleton's dinners at Gadsby's Hotel—the stove in the Pennsylvania Avenue house was still unattached—amazed politicians such as Cambreleng reported the visitors were sleeping five to a bed in nearby Alexandria. Others slept on billiard tables or on floors. "I'm beginning to understand how the Romans felt when the barbarians breached the walls," said Cambreleng. In spite of his radical politics, he was a New York snob.

"They all seem to think the country has to be rescued from some dreadful danger," George Stapleton said. "I'm beginning to think General Jackson went a little too far in his denunciations of Mr. Adams and Mr. Clay."

"They're good people," James Polk said. "A little rough maybe. But their hearts are pure." As a Tennessean, his faith in democracy was not easily shaken.

"You've put up with Sausage Smith," Sarah Polk told Cambreleng. "This is more of the same, multiplied by a thousand."

"Ten thousand," Cambreleng said.

To escape these excited followers, General Jackson had entered the city under cover of darkness on February 12 and taken shelter at Gadsby's. As soon as his devotees discovered his whereabouts, they had besieged him day and night as he struggled to form a cabinet. The Polks said great numbers of these fellows were hoping for federal jobs. They had translated Jackson's call for reform into "Turn the rascals out." With this sentiment the Polks were in hearty agreement. The congressman had a list of job candidates from his district that he hoped to submit to Old Hickory the day after he settled into the White House.

On the morning of March 4, 1829, George and Caroline arose early. She nursed little Jonathan and left two bottles of milk with Tabitha Flowers, who was serving as the baby's nurse. The Stapletons expected to be gone most of the day. There was to be a reception at the White House after the inaugural ceremony.

Joining the Polks, at ten o'clock they set out down crowded Pennsylvania Avenue as cannons boomed. The ground was soft underfoot. Patches of snow lay in the fields. They knew that the General had vetoed an elaborate military parade. He had also declined to make a courtesy call on President Adams, whom he now regarded as Rachel Jackson's murderer. He was going straight from Gadsby's to the Capitol.

Around them the crowd suddenly erupted with cries of admiration and excitement. "There he is. Old Jack! He's walking! Ain't that just like him?"

Preceded by a tottering company of elderly soldiers of the American Revolution and a half dozen younger officers who had served at the Battle of New Orleans, Jackson strode past them in a long black coat, black suit, and black tie. He would not allow even this triumphant day to interrupt his mourning for Rachel. But his smile was wide and genuine as he responded to the cheers of the crowd. Occasionally he raised his hand in a friendly wave.

"Sublime!" Sarah Polk said. "The servant saluting his sovereign, the people."

Before the Capitol swarmed an amazing mass of humanity. The next day, newspapers estimated the crowd at thirty thousand. The Polks and the Stapletons followed the presidential line of march around the multitude and made their way into the Capitol by the basement. They followed Jackson to the Senate chamber for the swearing in of his vice president, John C. Calhoun. The South Carolinian had been Adams's vice president too but had switched sides and backed Jackson in the election campaign.

"We must all be polite to Mr. Calhoun," Sarah Polk whispered to Caroline as they settled into gallery seats reserved for congressmen. "Since General Jackson has declared he'll only serve one term, Mr. Calhoun is his logical successor."

The most noteworthy sight of the brief ceremony was an empty chair in front of the dais, reserved for ex-president Adams. He had repaid Jackson's enmity by boycotting the inauguration.

Precisely at twelve o'clock, the congressmen and senators followed Andrew Jackson onto the East Portico, where he was to be sworn in. A marine band burst into "The President's March" as he appeared, flanked by U.S. marshals, followed by the justices of the Supreme Court. Artillery boomed a twenty-four gun salute. The cannon were almost drowned out by the roar when the people saw Jackson.

For a moment, Jackson stood silently on the portico staring down at the crowd. His sunken, deeply grooved cheeks, his formidable nose, his stern mouth, seemed as stony as the marble building behind him. Then, in a gesture that no one who saw it ever forgot, he bowed low to the people assembled in their majesty. Instantly the color of the crowd changed from the mixture of dark brown and black that had prevailed while they waited for their hero. Every hat was doffed and faces radiant with adoration and joy were visible around the huge semicircle.

The president read his brief inaugural address, barely ten minutes in length, in which he promised to reform the government and restore liberty to the people. Few beyond the first rows of spectators on the sloping hill below the Capitol could hear it. But no one seemed to care. When he finished, aged Chief Justice John Marshall, looking almost as discouraged as he felt—he had made no secret of his loathing for Democrats—administered the oath of office. Caroline noted how fiercely Jackson pronounced the most important words of the oath: "preserve, protect, and defend the Constitution of the United States."

Jackson shook hands with Chief Justice Marshall and Vice President Calhoun and turned once more to the people. Again he saluted them with a deep bow. The crowd went berserk. They burst through the ship's cable that had been stretched across the lower part of Capitol Hill and swarmed onto the portico. Congressmen and senators and their ladies were jostled aside in the furious attempt to shake Old Hickory's hand.

Federal marshals formed a cordon around the new president and got him off the portico before he was trampled to death. At the west entrance to the Capitol, the marshals had a white horse waiting for Jackson. He mounted it and rode down Pennsylvania Avenue, escorted by the chief U.S. marshal, surrounded by the ecstatic, cheering crowd. It was a veritable river of humanity, most on foot, others in gigs and on horseback. Gazing down at the immense procession, James Polk took out his tickets for the inaugural reception at the White House and tore them up.

"James!" Sarah said. "What in the world did you do that for? Shouldn't we go to the reception to congratulate President Jackson?"

"Calm down, darling," Polk said. "Of course we're going. But we won't need tickets." He pointed down at the crowd. "They're all going. They're inviting themselves!"

When the Polks and the Stapletons reached the White House, the building was surrounded by at least two thousand people in a wild mixture of Eastern broadcloth and Western homespun. From inside came a dull roar that seemed to make the mansion vibrate. People were leaping into the house through the French windows; others were leaping out. From the front door staggered a dignified man whose tie was askew, his black top hat dented. Blood dribbled from his nose. Beside him, his weeping dark-haired wife clutched a green dress with a huge rip in the skirt.

"It's the reign of King Mob!" the man said.

As the couple fled across the lawn, an alarmed Sarah Polk identified the man as Associate Justice Joseph Story of the Supreme Court.

"Definitely not a Democrat," said James Polk. "Let's join the party!"

Into the front hall they plunged, to discover they barely had room to breathe. Blacks, whites, men, women, were packed into the place, staring wildly around them like immigrants in the hold of a sinking ship. None of them seemed to have any idea where to go. There was not a sign of anyone in authority to tell them.

"Where's the eats?" bellowed a huge fat man in a rough wool shirt.

"Forget the eats," whooped another man around the same size. "Where's the whiskey?"

After a severe struggle, the Polks and Stapletons worked their way into the spacious East Room. The crowd was just as dense and even more unruly. At the far end of the room, doors opened and waiters began carrying in tubs of orange punch. Other servants had trays of wineglasses. The crowd surged toward them and the servants flew in all directions. The punch cascaded across the rug, the glasses were crunched beneath a hundred boots.

"Shee-it!" shouted a tall, thin man sporting a dirty white cravat. He spewed a stream of tobacco juice at the floor, narrowly missing Caroline's skirt. She realized the rug was streaked with this yellow slime, along with clumps of mud from everyone's boots.

"Where's Old Hickory?" cried one man. A dozen other voices took up the shout. Several Westerners climbed up on the sofas to try to find the president. Caroline winced at the sight of clods of mud from their boots oozing across the expensive blue and red upholstery.

Andrew Jackson Donelson, the General's nephew, whom they had met in the Hermitage, rushed up to them. "Just what I'm looking for," he said. "The General needs reinforcements. He's in danger of being crushed to death."

"I think Stapleton here is the sort of behemoth you can use," Polk said. "I'll stay here and guard the ladies."

Struggling through the mob in Donelson's wake, George found Jackson pressed against the windows in the room known as the elliptical salon. He looked more than a little worn and dismayed by the pandemonium around him. The deep lines of grief added another dimension of old age to his pallid face. George was struck by the thought that if they did not get the man out of this chaos, he might collapse.

John Henry Eaton and two other men were Jackson's only guards. They rallied at the sight of George's bulk. "Here's what we need," Eaton said. "A battering ram."

"You lead the way, Congressman. Head for the south door. We've got a carriage waiting," Donelson said.

The other four men formed a cordon around Old Hickory. George plowed into the crowd, knocking people in all directions, calling, "Make way for the president!" In ten minutes of wrestling and shoving, they reached the south entrance, where a black man sat on the box of a waiting carriage.

"You and your beautiful wife will be my guests here as soon as possible, Congressman," Old Hickory said as the others helped him into the vehicle.

In the East Room, Sarah Polk was finding it hard to conceal her growing dismay at the conduct of the crowd. "If something isn't done, the majesty of the people may vanish from American politics," she told her husband. "Justice Story is right. This is a mob in action."

"What do you think we should do? Call out the army?" Polk said with more than a little impatience.

Caroline was barely listening to this political quarrel. Over by the windows, her eyes had found a face in the crowd that caused a violent upheaval in her soul. John Sladen was leaning over a dark-haired woman in an armchair, smiling possessively down at her. The woman's features—a delicate nose, a small, tremulous mouth—were unimpressive. Her skin was exquisitely white, almost marblelike in its perfection. She was eating jelly from a glass, using a gold White House spoon.

A moment later, George rejoined Caroline and the Polks, his brow sweaty, his tie crooked, a rip in his coat, to report that the president had departed. "Let's imitate his example," James Polk said.

As they left, White House servants lugged tubs of punch out on the lawn. Many of the celebrants followed them, whooping and howling around the refreshments like Indians on the warpath. Fights broke out as they jostled each other for a drink. Soon a half dozen Western bruisers were gouging and kicking each other on the green lawn.

"The people can occasionally get out of hand," James Polk said as they strolled back to Gadsby's Hotel.

"Maybe they're entitled to an upheaval now and then," George said. "Jefferson said we needed a revolution every twenty years."

"It looked as if we were getting one today," Sarah Polk said, still struggling to preserve her democratic faith in spite of what she had just seen at the first people's inaugural.

Caroline said nothing. She was far more concerned with the reappearance of John Sladen in the middle of that rowdy tumult. Did it threaten her with another inner revolt, a loss of control to the blind desire to possess and be possessed by that defiant yet somehow pathetic spirit?

Not likely, she told herself, recalling her former lover's elaborate attention to the dark-haired woman. Caroline was almost glad she had seen John surrounded by the people at their clownish worst. The memory would armor her against sentimentality as she maneuvered George through the contradictions of democracy to fame.

T W O

THAT NIGHT, GEORGE AND CAROLINE DRESSED for the inaugural ball. Her toilette was much more intricate—and her task of improving nature's gifts was complicated by an intense desire to look her best. George occupied himself with writing a letter while he waited. When she anxiously asked, "How do I look?" he pondered her high-waisted, maroon silk gown topped by a headdress of jeweled, buckle-embroidered sheer white lawn and told her the question was superfluous.

"Who are you writing to?" she asked.

"Jeremy Biddle. I thought he'd enjoy a firsthand account of the inauguration."

"Why?"

"Darling, he's my best friend."

"He'll use it against you. He'll show it to your uncle Malcolm, who'll go around the city claiming it proves that the people are a great beast, exactly as your grandfather's idol Alexander Hamilton said they were—and George Stapleton is an idiot for encouraging them."

"Darling, I can't imagine Jeremy or Uncle Malcolm doing such a thing."

"I can. You're much too trusting, George. It's going to be your major problem as a politician."

George left the letter unfinished and they departed for the Washington Assembly Rooms at C and Eleventh Street. What passed for District of Columbia society in 1829 held balls in this building throughout the year and sent their sons and daughters to learn the art of the social dance from the proprietor, a courtly Italian named Carusi. The white-walled, barnlike ballroom was decorated with evergreens and flowers; a huge American flag dangled from the ceiling.

King Mob was nowhere to be seen. Tickets cost $20—a month's wages for a workingman. Only ladies and gentlemen in evening dress were admitted. The Democratic Party's elite and their wives numbered at least twelve hundred, and the ladies' elaborate gowns of brocade piped with coral satin, of blue silk or India muslin trimmed with roses and delicate hand embroidery, must have enabled a small army of dressmakers to live in comfort for the rest of the year. The Polks had arranged a table that included Andrew Jackson Donelson and his blond wife, Emily, and James Hamilton, a son of the founding father. Hamilton was a devoted Jacksonian and responded agreeably to George's story of his grandfather's reaction to his becoming a Democrat. Hamilton said half his family had denounced him and his mother had stopped speaking to him.

As the man who had led the Democratic ticket in New Jersey, a state the Democrats had previously contested in vain, George was something of a celebrity. On the dance floor, Hamilton introduced him to Vice President John C. Calhoun and his wife, Floride, as "the conqueror of New Jersey." Calhoun expressed warm memories of George's grandfather in Congress.

"Mr. Vice President!"

A familiar voice. Caroline turned to discover red-haired Secretary of War John Henry Eaton and his new wife, Peggy. She was wearing a white silk gown that glittered with mother-of-pearl inlays on the skirt. At her throat she wore a diamond brooch that would easily have purchased any house in Washington. A turban of peacock blue velvet set off her thickly curled, dark hair and vivid oval face, with its curving, full-lipped mouth and bold blue eyes. An extraordinary odor of toilet water enveloped her. Caroline wondered if she had bathed in the stuff.

"I don't think you and Mrs. Calhoun have met my wife, Peggy," Eaton said.

Calhoun kissed Peggy's hand. "I haven't met her as your wife," he said. "But I've known her for many years as one of our city's most charming women. This is my wife, Floride."

"How do you do," Floride Calhoun said. Her heart-shaped face, framed by two loops of smooth, inky black hair, was devoid of expression. Her dark eyes were half-hidden under drooping imperious lids. Her prim cupid's-bow mouth, her chiseled nose, exuded pride—and relentless disapproval. She did not say a word about Peggy's spectacular gown or attempt so much as a breath of the kind of pleasantries women exchange on such an occasion.

"I wore a dress just like this to my wedding," Peggy said. "John liked it so much he insisted on ordering one as a ball gown. Mother of pearl is not easy to get here in Washington. We had to send all the way to New Orleans for it."

Peggy was babbling. Caroline could see anger glinting in her blue eyes. She knew a snub when she met one. Secretary Eaton introduced her to the Stapletons. "The gown is lovely," Caroline said. "I wouldn't dare ask George to let me spend that much money on a dress."

"A sign of wedded bliss," said James Hamilton to his tall, elegant wife. Secretary Eaton introduced Peggy to them, and Mrs. Hamilton gave her the Floride Calhoun treatment: "How do you do." Whereupon she danced Hamilton out of the conversation.

Eaton expressed renewed gratitude to George for helping to rescue President Jackson from the popular frenzy at the White House. "We'll see you at dinner there shortly, I assure you," he said.

The Eatons glided into the crowd of dancers, and Caroline immediately wanted to know what he meant by his remark about dinner. George told her what President Jackson had said at the White House.

"You should tell me things like that as soon as possible," Caroline said.

"Why?" George said.

"It means we don't need Secretary Eaton to wangle an invitation. Which means I may not feel obliged to be polite to his wife."

Back at their table, Emily Donelson sat down next to Caroline. "I saw you talking to *her*. Do you intend to accept her socially?"

"I don't know," Caroline said. "I felt I had no choice but to be polite for Secretary Eaton's sake."

"I looked right through her. And through him," Emily said. "I will never sit at a table in the White House with that woman."

A moment later, the orchestra stopped playing and Mr. Carusi announced dinner was served in a room on the floor below them. Going downstairs, Caroline turned to Sarah Polk for guidance. "It begins to look as if open warfare over Peggy Eaton has already begun. What do you plan to do?"

"I don't know," Sarah said in her honest way. "Impulse bids me to be kind but conscience bids me to be cruel. I'll have to pray over it. There may be a good deal more at stake here than Peggy's reputation."

"You mean Mr. Eaton's influence with the president?"

Sarah summoned her Mona Lisa smile. "I *am* going to enjoy having you in Washington."

"Who are Secretary Eaton's allies?"

"Vice President Calhoun should be one. Mr. Eaton conducted all the negotiations that teamed him with General Jackson for the election. As a result, there are three Calhoun men in the cabinet, besides Eaton."

"Are there other contestants?"

"There are always other contestants," Sarah said. "One of them hasn't arrived in Washington yet. Martin Van Buren, the former senator from New York, now our secretary of state. He's a sly fox. Very charming. But always looking out for Martin Van Buren."

"You don't seem to like him."

"He's slippery. You're never sure what he really thinks about anything. You'll have to make up your own mind about him. I assure you he'll be *very* nice to you and George."

Dinner, as the newspapers described it not inaccurately the next day, was "composed of all the delicacies of the season"—a twenty-five-dish feast of fish and crab and lobster and game and beefsteak from a gigantic ox brought to Washington by General Jackson's Kentucky followers—all devoured with a bountiful supply of good champagne. Not far from the Stapleton-Polk table sat the members of the cabinet. Caroline noticed not one wife spoke to Peggy Eaton. But she seemed undaunted by the chill, talking vivaciously to the men who sat near her.

Upstairs, the dancing resumed and George led Caroline out on the floor. As he opened his arms to begin the waltz, he froze, his face registering disbelief. "My God! There's Johnny Sladen!"

Caroline turned and saw him too, about twenty feet away, dancing with the same dark-haired woman. George hesitated, wondering what to do. "The last time I saw him, he threatened to shoot me for taking you away from him. He seems to have found some consolation in New Orleans."

"Let's say hello," Caroline said. Instinct told her it would be better to meet John on her terms, arm in arm with George. "It's time to let bygones be bygones."

George seized her hand and strolled across the not yet crowded dance floor. "Johnny!" he said. "I should have known you'd find your way to this inauguration."

"George," John said. "I saw you at the White House, leading the president to safety. But I wasn't sure what sort of reception I'd get if I offered you my hand."

"The same one you're getting now," George said, holding out his hand. "Here's Caroline, with the same sentiment. Congratulate her. She's the mother of a beautiful baby boy."

"How wonderful." For a moment a flicker of bitterness played across John's mouth, belying his polite cheer. But he quickly composed himself and introduced his dancing partner. "This is Clothilde Legrand. Her father is the senior senator from Louisiana. He invited me to the inauguration as her escort."

"John has told me much about his New York friends," Clothilde said in a liquid Southern accent that was further complicated by a touch of France. Behind her seeming self-assurance, Caroline sensed fragility.

"But I never told her George Stapleton had become a Democrat," John said. "I only discovered it when I read the election reports in the *New Orleans Picayune*. We must meet as soon as possible to explain this transformation."

"It was accomplished by one man—and one woman," George said with a good-natured grin. "The man was Andrew Jackson. The woman I think you know."

"Has she insisted you introduce an equal rights for women bill as your first public act?" John said.

"Not yet. I wish you hadn't reminded her," George said.

"I plan to wait four or five years, until George becomes a senator," Caroline said. "It will have more impact there. We'll bribe Daniel Webster to support it."

"I see you've already learned a few things about Washington," John said.

Caroline stood there, close enough to touch him. She felt nothing, neither revulsion nor desire. She chose to see this as proof of her freedom from this man. What John thought or felt was hard if not impossible to discern, after that flash of bitterness. He seemed to be a new man, almost a stranger from another world. The forlorn fugitive from New York's lower depths had been transformed by his year in New Orleans.

George asked him how long he was going to stay in Washington. "Only long enough to make a case with President Jackson for a drastic reduction of the tariff. I'm here to help forge a union between New York's free-trade Democrats and Southerners like Senator Legrand."

"You must come to dinner, assuming we finally get a stove to cook food on," George said. "I hope you can join us too, Miss Legrand."

Clothilde Legrand said she would be delighted. Caroline was not at all sure she would be pleased to entertain John Sladen in her house. Somehow that suggested an intimacy she wanted to avoid. But she smiled politely and said she looked forward to the dinner party.

At this point they were interrupted by a florid-faced man who looked vaguely familiar. On his arm was a lady who looked more like a barmaid than a member of any elite. She had arms like a stevedore, which she left blithely uncovered, only one among several mistakes in her garishly colored evening gown.

"Caroline, you remember Colonel Swartout? My father's old friend?" John said. "Miss Kemble is now married to Congressman Stapleton here, the conqueror of New Jersey."

"I've heard of that famous victory," Swartout said, shaking George's hand and smiling jovially at Caroline. "While it's not exactly comparable to the Waterloo we inflicted on our enemies in New York, even a winning skirmish is worthy of praise."

"We New Jerseyans would never dream of comparing ourselves to New York, Colonel," George said. "We're simple farmers and honest manufacturers. We have no pretensions to being the Gomorrah of America."

"Ouch!" Swartout said. "I see we'll have to watch this fellow, Sladen."

"Obviously, marrying a clever woman has done wonders for him," John said.

"Seriously, young fellow, we must have some political conversations before long," Swartout said. "We Middle Staters must watch our flanks, lest we be overrun by the South and West. I'm happy to report General Jackson has promised me a bastion from which we can meet all comers."

"Colonel Swartout is to be the next collector of the port of New York," Sladen said.

"And this fellow will be the assistant collector at New Orleans if he wants it. I have Secretary of War Eaton's word for it," Swartout said.

John Sladen's transformation in New Orleans suddenly became explicable to Caroline. He had gone there with a letter of introduction from Samuel Swartout. That gentleman had apparently risen from political oblivion on the wings of Andrew Jackson's victory and carried Sladen with him.

She sought confirmation of this intuition from Sarah Polk, who assured her she was probably right. "The General has a sentimental fondness for the friends of Aaron Burr," Sarah said. "He was very deep in Mr. Burr's plans to seize Texas twenty years ago. He offered to testify in his defense at Burr's trial for treason in 1806."

"Is Mr. Swartout an ally of Mr. Van Buren?"

"Not at all," Sarah said with the glimmer of a smile. "He hates him. He claims that Mr. Van Buren betrayed Colonel Burr when he ran for governor of New York in 1804. Swartout leads the Jackson party in New York City. Mr. Van Buren more or less controls the rest of the state. We rather like the idea of a Democratic quarrel in New York. It weakens Mr. Van Buren's influence."

Sarah was amazed when she heard that President Jackson had made Swartout the collector of customs in New York. "That's a tremendous blow to Mr. Van Buren," she said. "It's the single most important federal appointment in the nation. The collector controls hundreds of jobs."

The orchestra was playing "The President's March." It was a way of announcing the ball was over—and reminding everyone that they were there to salute Andrew Jackson. Waiters rushed around the room serving a final round of champagne. Mounting the dais was a short, spare man with a bald head, a hooked nose, and a menacing slit of a mouth. Sarah Polk identified him as Amos Kendall, the leader of the Jackson party in Kentucky. He had been appointed to the Treasury Department with orders to clean out the Adamsites.

"To the people's president!" he shouted

"The people's president!" returned the twelve hundred members of the elite, relieved of the necessity of associating with a single one of the people in their sweaty, tobacco-spitting reality. On that note of Democratic solidarity ended Andrew Jackson's inauguration day.

Back in their house on Pennsylvania Avenue, Caroline told George what Sarah Polk had shared with her about Samuel Swartout. "I'd keep him at arm's length for a while," she said. "Let's see what Mr. Van Buren offers you before you sign any pacts with one of his enemies."

"You're a wonder," George said, cradling little Jonathan in his arms. He was far more affectionate with the child than Caroline was. She told herself it was Tabitha's job to pick him up and console him when he cried. She was already counting the days when she could stop breast-feeding him. Most doctors agreed a baby could be shifted to whole milk at the age of five or six months, depending on size and appetite.

She left George in the nursery with the baby and undressed with Tabitha's help. Tabitha was full of praise for Andrew Jackson. "Hannibal told me about him. Never lets a black man or woman be whipped on his farm. Gives them six or seven holidays a year and every Sunday off. Feeds them strong meat and fresh vegetables every day. He'll be a good president, don't you think?"

"Undoubtedly."

"Maybe he'll use his power to free black people everywhere."

"Maybe." Caroline was too sleepy to take what Tabitha was saying seriously.

"I hates it when I see them slave coffles in front of the president's house. They don't belong there. Ought to be hidden someplace in a piece of woods."

"You're right."

"Why don't you tell President Jackson that when you see him?"

"I'll try to remember."

The girl's ideas were so fantastic, Caroline stopped listening. Her mind drifted to the events of the day. John Sladen leaning over Clothilde Legrand in the White House. Dancing with her at Carusi's in such a close embrace. Suddenly Caroline was sitting on the bed beside John in that New York basement. The image of the underground river wound through her mind.

"George?" she called. "George?"

A faint response from the nursery.

"Are you ever coming to bed? It's three o'clock in the morning."

"Jonathan's still fussing."

"Tabitha will take care of him."

"Maybe you should feed him, ma'am," Tabitha said. "He don't take the milk well. Spit up a lot of it."

"Give him another bottle. Warm it this time."

"I warmed it the last time."

Caroline sighed. She would have to hire a wet nurse. She could not rush home from balls and teas and receptions to breast-feed the child every four hours.

For the moment, there was a more immediate concern. "George! I'm turning out the light."

He ambled in, shedding his evening clothes. When he lay down beside her, she turned on her side and whispered, "I thought New Jersey's conqueror would be in a mood to celebrate."

"I'm always in a mood to do that with you."

"There are times when I need you—as much or more than you imagine you need me."

"I don't imagine that. I know it."

His big hands roved her body. Gradually, the memory of John Sladen's spectral face on the bed in the New York basement began to dissolve in a rush of desire for the man beside her. He did not threaten her with shame or disgrace; he believed that he alone possessed her heart as totally as he began to possess her body.

For this celebratory moment, Caroline wanted that to be true. No, she wanted it to be true forever. She welcomed the long, slow thrusts that swept her toward a surrender that was also a kind of possession, fulfillment, promise, hope, forgiveness. The white words cascaded through Caroline's troubled soul as she drew George down the sacred river's dark current into the haunted caverns of tomorrow and yesterday, where time no longer mattered and love was a word that winged through the gloom like a creature of the night.

THREE

"ISN'T IT AS CLEAR AS HIGH noon to anyone with an unprejudiced mind?" President Andrew Jackson said. "Clay and Adams and their minions are doing the same thing to Peggy Eaton that they did to my darling Rachel. Despicable scum that they are, they don't have the courage to meet me man to man. They prefer to war on defenseless women!"

The Stapletons were in the White House dining room with a half dozen other couples, enjoying President Jackson's hospitality. The Polks sat on the opposite side of the oval table. Emily Donelson and her husband flanked Caroline and George. On either side of the Polks sat John Sladen and Clothilde Legrand, her father, portly Senator Simon Legrand, and his stocky, handsome son, Victor, who was about George's age. At the bottom of the table, opposite the widower president, sat another widower, Secretary of State Martin Van Buren.

The leader of the New York Democrats was a plump, avuncular man with shrewd, shining eyes and an amiable mouth. His fair skin and blond hair inclined him to favor creamy white vests and tan suits. He looked, someone said, as if he were always about to depart on a summer holiday. This touch of the theatrical in his tailoring made more plausible his political nickname, the Little Magician.

"What I don't understand," Van Buren said with apparently honest puzzlement, "is Mrs. Calhoun's refusal to return Mrs. Eaton's call."

"I asked Calhoun for an explanation," Jackson said. "He said there was nothing he could do. She had made up her own mind without consulting him. The next day I called on Mrs. Calhoun personally. I explained my wishes in this matter and gave her a positive order to return Mrs. Eaton's call. She rang for her butler and said, 'Show this gentleman to the door.' "

Eyes widened, brains reeled. The warfare over Mrs. Eaton had come to this: the wife of the vice president had thrown the president of the United States out of her house!

A South Carolinian by birth, Old Hickory claimed to be unsurprised by his ejection. "She's a Bonneau from Charleston," he said. "They don't come much prouder than that tribe of aristocrats. She doesn't give ten pins for my current office. As far as she's concerned, I'm still Andrew Jackson from the Waxhaws—the wrong end of the state."

Mrs. Eaton's respectability, or lack of it, was convulsing official Washington. Senator Henry Clay had been inspired to one of his naughtier witticisms: "Time cannot stale nor custom wither her infinite virginity." The wives of the three cabinet ministers allied with Mr. Calhoun had also refused to receive Mrs. Eaton in their homes or return her calls. The president had lectured the husbands furiously with no visible result. He had sent investigators to New York to refute a rumor that Peggy and her new husband had registered as man and wife in a hotel there several years ago.

Old Hickory had engaged in a shouting match with a clergyman who came to the White House with a story that Peggy had suffered a miscarriage at a time when her husband had been at sea for the previous twelve months. The Navy Department was ordered to scour its records to prove that the late purser Timberlake had been at home at least once in that previous year.

By this time the imbroglio had gotten into the newspapers. There were sly references to "Bellona"—the Roman goddess of war—who was determined to triumph over her enemies, even if she wrecked the administration. In Italian, la bellona had an even less complimentary meaning—a vulgar, well-endowed women with no morals worth mentioning. Sarah Polk whispered to Caroline that one of Peggy's severest critics, Mrs. Samuel Ingham, the wife of the secretary of the treasury, had a few secrets to hide in her past. But she was born a lady. Caroline wondered if the ostracism was aimed at excluding the daughter of a tavern keeper, whether or not she was, as President Jackson claimed, "as chaste as a virgin."

In spite of repeated lectures from the president, Emily Donelson remained adamantly determined not to call on Mrs. Eaton. Emily stayed in her room at the White House when Jackson and her husband called on the Eatons in the mansion they had rented on Pennsylvania Avenue. From the icy expression on Emily's face, the current discussion was not likely to change her mind.

Caroline remained uncommitted in this swirling political brawl. She was following Sarah Polk's lead. As congressmen's wives, they were not immediate targets of Mrs. Eaton's aggressive style. Thus far, Peggy seemed to be leaving her calling cards at the doors of the vice president, cabinet members, Supreme Court justices, and similar potentates. But so few women accompanied their husbands to Congress in 1829, she would soon descend to congressional wives. For the time being, Caroline was grateful that the Stapletons' Pennsylvania Avenue house was a good half mile from the Eatons' mansion.

For obvious reasons, Peggy Eaton was a subject that inevitably tensed Caroline's nerves. Gazing across the table, she wondered if she saw sarcasm, mockery, in John Sladen's eyes—and in the eyes of his friends the Legrands. Had he revealed to them his conquest of the wife of the conqueror of New Jersey? She could not believe it, but there was no way to reassure herself without revealing her vulnerability.

To Caroline's immense relief, James Polk managed to get the president to change the subject by mentioning a magic word, Texas. More and more Americans were settling in this huge northern province of Mexico. Did he think it was possible or probable that they could purchase it from the Mexicans the way they had bought Florida from Spain?

"An American Texas is more than either of those iffy words, Mr. Polk," Jackson said. "It's a necessity. Take a look at the map of North America. You'll see whoever owns Texas outflanks New Orleans. The nation that conquers New Orleans and holds it will destroy the United States, as surely as a murderer kills a man by strangulating his windpipe. All the commerce of the West goes down the Mississippi to that port. Without it, the West would be roiled in bankruptcy and anarchy in six months."

"I agree, Mr. President. Totally!" Senator Simon Legrand said. "You saved us from such a fate in 1815. Your wise policy will save us again. I can assure you of Louisiana's loyalty in such an enterprise. We'll put thirty thousand men in the field in a fortnight of your call to arms!"

Old Hickory beamed. Legrand had served under him against the British in the 1815 triumph at New Orleans. "I hope you'll write the secretary of state a letter to that effect, Senator Legrand."

"Consider it done."

Secretary of State Martin Van Buren said he was inclined to agree with the General about Texas. He hoped to begin exploring the subject of a sale with the Mexican ambassador soon.

"Explore?" Jackson said. "I hope you'll begin by pointing out that if they decline to sell it, we're perfectly capable of taking it from them. Negotiation with a Spaniard has never gotten us anywhere unless we laid a gun and sword on the table first, along with a pen. That's how we won Florida."

"With you as the resident of this house, General," Van Buren said, "a show of weapons by someone as unwarlike as I would be superfluous—and possibly ludicrous."

Well said, Caroline thought. She was learning so much from almost every moment in Washington. The art of flattering without seeming to flatter, the art of dissembling while seeming to speak the truth, the art of agreeing while reserving one's judgment.

Old Hickory did not conceal his pleasure at the secretary of state's compliment. "We all can't be fools who spend their lives accumulating lead in their carcasses," he said. "Let's drink a toast to Texas! May she soon be a state of this glorious Union!"

They drank the excellent claret that the president dispensed at his table. All of Washington was awed by the way this supposedly uncouth frontiersman was serving wine and food that compared favorably with the menus of Thomas Jefferson. Old Hickory had also demanded and gotten from Congress forty-five thousand dollars to finish the interior and exterior of the White House—something Jefferson and his successors had never gotten around to doing. A portico was rising on the north side of the mansion and the East Room was a wilderness of ladders as artisans created splendor where barren space had heretofore reigned.

As the dinner broke up, the president escorted Caroline from the dining room to the south entrance. "I hope you'll see it in your heart to be kind to

Mrs. Eaton," he said. "These people think they can drive me to a shameful capitulation that will leave me looking like a weak old fool before Congress and the nation. We mustn't let that happen—not for my sake, but for the people's sake."

"I'll do what I can, Mr. President," Caroline said.

She was trapped in a web of conflicting emotions about Peggy Eaton. Should she openly sympathize with her—risking the possibility that she too would end among the ostracized? What if Jeremy Biddle had been indiscreet and a coterie of people in New York and New Jersey knew the truth about her and John Sladen?

Beneath the politics, there was a deeper and more dangerous current tugging at Caroline's emotions: her sympathy for Peggy as a woman who was trying to move boldly from hotel keeper's daughter to the world of the rich and powerful. Eaton was one of the wealthiest men in Tennessee. He was as logical a successor to Old Hickory as John C. Calhoun or Martin Van Buren. Yet everything Caroline saw and heard about Peggy stirred wary doubts in her mind.

At the south portico, Caroline found Secretary of State Van Buren offering George transportation back to their house in his carriage. They said good-night to the president and rumbled into the darkness. "I don't know about you, Congressman," Van Buren said to George, "but I feel compelled to do all I can to rescue the General from this social quagmire. I plan to give a dinner party for Mrs. Eaton as soon as possible. I hope you and Mrs. Stapleton will come."

"Of course we will," George said. "Don't you agree, dear?"

"After the personal appeal the General just made to me, how can I say no?" Caroline said.

"Good. Now to another even stickier problem, in some ways. I hear you've been talking to Sam Swartout, the new collector of the port of New York."

"We've had drinks at Gadsby's," George said.

"I think you'll regret any arrangements you make with him," Van Buren said. "He has delusions of taking over the Democratic Party in New York. It simply won't happen. Instead, I predict he'll be an ex-collector within the next two years."

"Why?" George said.

"He's got the morals of a pirate," Van Buren said. "He thinks he's gotten a license to plunder. I intend to revoke that license as soon as possible."

"How will you do that?"

"I have men watching him very closely."

Caroline sensed disapproval in George's silence. The use of spies and informants would never sit well with him. If the secretary of state noticed this, he remained unruffled.

"New York and New Jersey are natural political allies," Van Buren said. "We share the Hudson River, the wealth of New York City."

"To be blunt, Mr. Secretary, New Jersey often feels in danger of being overwhelmed by New York's size and self-importance," George said.

"No doubt, no doubt. But you'll find New York's Democrats easy to get along with. The party's center of gravity is upstate, among the small farmers and businessmen, not among the capitalists of Wall Street—or the dregs of society lurking in the city's slums. Our roots are still in Jefferson's ideals of simplicity in manners, appetites, and ambitions."

"That's good to hear," George said.

"We can't offer you any patronage from the port of New York for the moment. But we can certainly do business on jobs in other ports—Perth Amboy, Camden, Cape May. Judgeships, of course, as vacancies occur. Federal attorneys, marshals . . ."

"Of course," George murmured, again barely concealing his distaste.

"You're young. Let an aging politician give you some advice. Politics is always an exchange of favors, a meeting of minds—and interests."

Caroline found herself liking this man's candor. She was also inclined to agree with his estimate of Samuel Swartout. Where did that leave John Sladen and his friends the Legrands? They were still trying to round up Southern backing for Swartout as the spokesman of the New York Democratic Party. Vice President Calhoun had shown more than a little interest in the idea. He saw that Martin Van Buren was likely to be his chief opponent for the presidential nomination in 1832, and a crippling quarrel in his home state would do a lot to ruin his chances. But Democrats from other states, notably Virginia, remained cool to the idea, preferring Van Buren and his well-oiled Albany machine to Swartout's personal politics.

"At the risk of sounding like a sententious old bore, let me suggest another adage for the young politician," Van Buren said. "Don't try to rush things. An ability to wait for the right moment is crucial. I fear Swartout is like his old master, Aaron Burr—he's not the waiting sort—one reason being a swarm of creditors hot on his trail."

The Stapletons and the secretary of state parted with protestations of warm friendship. The next morning, before they finished breakfast, John Sladen was at their door with a worried expression on his face. George invited him to have coffee with them.

"What did the Little Magician have to say to you last night?" Sladen asked before Harriet could fill his cup.

"He told us to keep your friend Swartout at arm's length," George said.

"Are you going to take his advice?"

"I'm going to think about it."

"It's time to take sides, George. Sam Swartout is a man you can trust."

"Why?"

"He's got Andrew Jackson's confidence. The Little Magician tried every trick in his repertoire to talk Jackson out of appointing him collector of the port of New York. But Jackson believes in loyalty. Sam Swartout was supporting him back in 1824, when Martin Van Buren was in bed with John Quincy Adams."

"I'm still going to think about it, Johnny."

Caroline said nothing. She was again trying to estimate her feelings face-to-face with John Sladen, this time at her own dining-room table. She found no disorder. She was as calm and distant as George.

"Are you going to join forces with Van Buren in his plan to use this Eaton mess to wound the vice president? I assure you, if that shyster succeeds in ruining Calhoun, the country will live to regret it."

"He simply seems to be trying to help the president out of a very difficult situation, Johnny," George said.

"What do you think, Mrs. Stapleton?"

John's voice had a cutting edge. The use of her married name carried an unspoken irony that only they understood. Suddenly Caroline's nerves were no longer inert. "I'm inclined to sympathize with Mrs. Eaton. I'm surprised you don't," she said.

"I sympathize with her personally. But politically, I think every intelligent man and woman should suppress the emotion. John C. Calhoun deserves to be our next president. I would go so far as to say he must be our next president if this country is to survive. We can't let a ridiculous quarrel like this ruin his chances."

"Oh, come now, Johnny," George said. "That's a bit much."

"I know it sounds far-fetched. But we're dealing with ambitious men. As president, Calhoun will conciliate the South. We'll get a lower tariff or no tariff at all. There's a danger, a very real danger, of letting the South nurse its grievances, to go on year after year feeling they're ignored and despised by the North. I've heard it a thousand times in New Orleans. My answer has always been, the Democrats of New York will stand by you, as they did when we elected Jefferson in 1800, and in every election since that date, until divisions destroyed the party in 1824 and let Adams into the White House."

"So Swartout is a Calhoun man?" George asked.

"A better way to put it is, he's not a Van Buren man. He sees that ambitious schemer destroying the Democratic Party. So do I. As president he'll do nothing for the South. He'll concentrate on doing things for Martin Van Buren and his friends."

John Sladen spoke prophetic words in the Stapleton dining room on that spring morning in 1829. But the century's catastrophe was gathering beyond their sight, over the distant horizon. He was unable to ignite a sense of danger, a fear of upheaval. The Stapletons' reactions remained more personal than political.

George had never really liked John Sladen. His violent reaction to losing Caroline had hardly buttressed George's opinion of his character. "I'm afraid you have a tendency go off half-cocked, Johnny. I speak as a friend. Don't take it personally."

"How else am I supposed to take a remark like that?"

"As a piece of advice. I don't owe any of these gentlemen my allegiance. That belongs to only one man—Andrew Jackson. Whatever Caroline and I can do to help him be a better president, we'll do, no matter who or what we disappoint. Don't you agree, dear?"

Caroline Kemble Stapleton gazed steadily at John Sladen. "Yes. I agree, *totally.*"

Again, a single word carried with it a private message that said more than a six-hour speech by Daniel Webster or Henry Clay. For a bitter moment, Caroline rejoiced at the pain on John Sladen's face. She was telling him that she and George Stapleton were married, not merely spiritually and physically, but politically. They were an enterprise over which Sladen could never hope to acquire control.

Across John Sladen's face flashed grief, remorse, and a hint of the bitter despair that had stirred ruinous pity in Caroline Kemble's heart in that Manhattan basement. "George, I know I behaved badly in New York," he said. "I'm prepared to apologize for it, to make any amends in my power. I don't want personal antagonism to intrude here. What I'm saying is too important for the future of the country."

What was he really saying? Not for the last time, Caroline began translating John Sladen's conversations with George into a personal communication intended for her. John did not consider George Stapleton capable of thinking about the future of the country. Only Caroline Kemble had that capacity. He was here, accepting the humiliation of his rout as her suitor, swallowing George's condescension, because he truly believed what he was saying—and her capacity to understand it.

"Johnny, I hold no grudge for words spoken in anger," George said. "It's not my way. I assure you there's no personal animosity at work here. Not on my part—and certainly not on Caroline's part. We're feeling our way through a new part of the forest. If we disagree, it's of no great moment. We're all beginners in this political game."

"That's true enough. But the game is not just beginning. It's closer to the halfway mark. We can't afford too many mistakes."

"When and if you see us making one, by all means feel free to come here and lecture us to your heart's content. If we disagree, let's vow here and now to stay friends. Don't you agree, Caroline?"

Friends? In a corner of her soul, the Caroline who had succumbed to pity shook her head. No, never. This man could never be a mere friend. In the center of her soul, the Caroline who had become Mrs. George Stapleton nodded and smiled serenely. "Of course," she said.

FOUR

"FORTY POUNDS OF COTTON OUT OF every hundred we grow—that's what the tariff costs us, Mr. Stapleton. Can you ask us to make such a sacrifice to keep the profits of your mills at twenty-five percent?"

The speaker was Senator Robert Young Hayne of South Carolina, a slender, fair-haired man with a petulant mouth and a deep mellifluous voice that frequently throbbed with emotion. The Stapletons were dining at the comfortable Washington house of Vice President John C. Calhoun. Senator Simon Legrand, his son, Victor, his sister, Clothilde, and John Sladen were among the twenty guests. Black servants glided around the impeccably set table, depositing an array of fish, game, and fowl that more than matched the hospitality of President Jackson in the White House.

Mrs. Calhoun, pretending utter disinterest in the tense conversation between the men, asked Caroline if she was still nursing her baby. Caroline replied that she had found a wet nurse, the wife of one of the Irish laborers who were flooding into the District to work on the many new houses and government buildings under construction. Mrs. Calhoun sighed and said she did not want to upset her, but there was always a danger of infection from a wet nurse.

"I lost my first child, the sweetest baby girl, at six months. I blamed it on the wet nurse. Ever since, I've nursed all my babies for a full year, trial though it is."

Caroline struggled to control her anxiety. She assured Mrs. Calhoun that she had tried to select a nurse whose habits were sober and family life sound. Simultaneously she tried to hear what George Stapleton was saying to Senator Hayne.

"We must and can adjust matters to our mutual satisfaction, Senator. We're not spending our profits from Principia Mills on luxurious living. We're reinvesting them in a railroad across New Jersey," George said. "Why can't Northern banks loan the South money to build railroads and steamboats to lower the cost of shipping your cotton? Eventually help you build factories to turn it into cloth."

"Shipyards, factories, are contrary to the genius of our people," Hayne said. "We're agriculturists. The sort of men and women Thomas Jefferson saw as the best guardians of American liberty."

Presiding at the head of the table, a small smile on his lined, angular face, was the vice president. His jet-black hair was brushed back in thick strands that seemed to lie uneasily on his large head. "You occupy a singularly important position in the North, Mr. Stapleton," he said in his husky voice, which did not have a trace of a Southern accent. "You can help us talk to your brethren in a spirit of moderation that sometimes escapes our high-toned temperaments."

"Calomel," Mrs. Calhoun said to Caroline. "Calomel is a great restorative to an infant if he grows feverish. Do you plan to live here in Washington, Mrs. Stapleton?"

"Yes. I'm quite fascinated by—by politics."

"Aren't we all," Mrs. Calhoun said with a smile that managed to convey a hint of menace. "Have you heard the latest outrage perpetrated by Mrs. Eaton?"

The dinner was one of several John Sladen and his mentor, Senator Legrand, had arranged for the Stapletons' education on the South's political attitudes. Legrand apparently ruled Louisiana almost as thoroughly as Hugh Stapleton had dominated New Jersey. A word from him put the new congressman and his wife on numerous guest lists. This dinner at the Calhouns was the most important so far, and the most puzzling. The vice president seemed content to preside and let more belligerent Southerners do the talking. His few remarks abhorred conflict and seemed to praise compromise.

This word seemed foreign to his wife's temperament. Floride Calhoun began telling the ladies and gentlemen within reach of her conversation about a dispute that had broken out between Peggy Eaton and the wife of the Dutch envoy, Madame Huygens. This lady, known for her temper and her generous embonpoint, had announced she was going to give a dinner party for the presidents' cabinet that would exclude Mrs. Eaton. The president was threatening to revoke the ambassador's passport and expel them from the country.

"It's bad enough that this matter has gotten into our newspapers. Now it will travel abroad," Mrs. Calhoun said. "Our friends in the White House tell us the president is so overwrought about Mrs. Eaton, he sleeps not at all. He may soon be unfit to carry on the duties of his office."

"Now, now, Floride dear," Vice President Calhoun said. "I'm sure that's an exaggeration."

"I sincerely *hope* so," Floride said.

Was there a carefully orchestrated plan at work here? Caroline wondered. What better way to ruin the health of an already grief-stricken old man than to harass him with a repetition of the slanders that had killed his wife? But there was no way to penetrate the mask of civility and good breeding on the faces around the table.

At times Caroline found herself not quite able to believe that the Eaton affair was actually happening. Peggy O'Neale Eaton was threatening the stability of the American government. Washington, D.C., made Caroline's Wollstonecraftish complaints about women's lot seem so much adolescent prattle. Women wielded amazing amounts of power in this capital city.

Caroline filled the mails with letters to Sarah Polk. Since Congress was not yet in session, Sarah and her husband had retreated to Tennessee to escape choosing sides in the Eaton imbroglio. Sarah's strict Presbyterian upbringing inclined her to support those who deplored Peggy's elevation to respectability. But she decided it would be hazardous for someone from Tennessee to express such an opinion with Andrew Jackson in the White House.

"Have you visited the South, Mr. Stapleton?" the vice president asked.

"No," George said. "A great omission, I begin to think."

"You must spend some time with us at Fort Hill. There we can stretch our minds while we relax our souls."

"I'd be honored," George said. On the dining-room wall was a fine watercolor of the Calhoun plantation in the Carolina hill country—a white-pillared mansion, its drive lined with tall cedars.

"You must also visit Charleston. You can't omit Charleston," Floride Calhoun said.

"I worry about the impression Charleston will make," Senator Hayne said. "There's grass growing in many streets. The harbor is empty. I fear a man who's lived in New York will dismiss us as poverty-stricken failures."

"Have no fear about that, Senator," George said. "New York's condescension doesn't sit well with Jerseymen."

The pleased expressions on the faces of the Southerners around the table made Caroline realize they interpreted this commonplace New Jersey sentiment as a rebuke to Martin Van Buren's ambitions. Sitting on her night table was an invitation to a dinner party that the secretary of state was giving in Mrs. Eaton's honor. It would be a severe test for all the Jacksonians in Washington, D.C. In her latest letter, Sarah Polk had advised Caroline to accept—or to retreat to her home state.

> *Let us be realistic. To offend Andrew Jackson is no small matter. You and George have won his affection. Since Mrs. Eaton's reputation is not a matter of conscience with you, it seems to me your course is clear.*

By this time, Caroline had explained to her friend that she was without religious belief. Sarah Polk had accepted this profession of atheism without a hint of rebuke. A godless life was almost unimaginable to her, she said. But it was a free country.

Vice President Calhoun was talking about the future of the United States as he saw it. The table fell silent. "The South's voice must be heard in the highest councils of the nation," he said. "Not merely heard, but heeded. We stand for liberty against the encroachments of the federal government. History already tells us this is no small concern. In 1798, when President John Adams and his Congress passed the Sedition Acts, making it a crime for a newspaper, or a congressman, to criticize the government, Virginia and Kentucky passed resolutions, written by none other than Thomas Jefferson, warning that a state may find it necessary to interpose its power to prevent the execution of an unjust law—in a word to declare it nullified."

"With all due respect to Mr. Jefferson's memory, where does that leave the Union?" George asked. "My inheritance comes down from Washington, not Jefferson. My grandfather often told me there was only one historical document worth reading—Washington's farewell address. In it, he tells us that the Union is our most precious legacy."

"No one reveres the Union more than the men of the South," Calhoun said. "We only ask that it be *administered* for the equal welfare of all the states."

The emphasis on *administered* needed no translation for Caroline. Presidents administered the government. Congress merely legislated. Across the table, John Sladen's eyes sought hers. *Now do you believe me?* he asked. Here was a man who wanted to be president—and deserved to be president. He had been a senator, a cabinet member, and had twice been elected vice president by the American people.

"Are you planning to attend Secretary of State Van Buren's dinner in honor of Mrs. Eaton?" Floride Calhoun asked Caroline.

Suddenly the room was charged with new tension. Caroline realized more was at work here than a mere exposition of the South's political views. She and George were being asked to choose sides, to shun sly, slippery Martin Van Buren and join the camp of honorable, straightforward John C. Calhoun. The decision would be irrevocable. You could not snub Peggy Eaton on Monday and dance with her on Tuesday.

Across the table, John Sladen made a final, silent plea. Caroline rejected it, for exactly the same reason that she was about to reject Floride Calhoun's ultimatum. She disliked being coerced, maneuvered, on the assumption that she and George were political children and could not think for themselves. In the momentary silence, she had also found an answer that would, she hoped, meet the exquisite standards of Washington politics.

"I fear we *must* go," Caroline said. "Not for Mrs. Eaton's sake, or Mr. Van Buren's sake. But for President Jackson's sake. We traveled to Tennessee to meet him, as you may know. We heard from Mrs. Jackson's own lips the torment the slanders against her reputation caused them. What you just told me about his sleeplessness, his agitation, made up my mind."

"But the cases are entirely different!" Floride Calhoun said.

"In the president's mind, I fear they're identical. He made that all too clear to us when we dined at the White House a month ago."

"I share my wife's opinion," George Stapleton said. "I have no illusions about our importance. But I wouldn't want to add even a speck to the president's distress."

"The man is an uncouth dotard!" Floride Calhoun said.

"Floride, calm yourself," Vice President Calhoun said.

"I'm tired of playing that humble part! I say let the storm begin! Let's put the old fool to the test!"

Caroline remembered Sarah Polk's analysis of Charleston's growing poverty and mounting resentment and marveled at her friend's perspicacity. Even more startling was this glimpse inside the Calhoun marriage, the tension between the angry Charlestonian and the levelheaded upcountry planter, between the partisan and the statesman, between the heart and the head of the South. Floride Calhoun obviously felt her husband should be president, now. She wanted him to begin asserting his right to be the master of Washington, D.C.

Riding home in their carriage, the Stapletons were silent until George spoke. "I congratulate you on your reply to Mrs. Calhoun."

"Thank you," Caroline said.

"Those are deeply troubled people. For the first time I'm beginning to worry about the future of our country."

"Let's concentrate on your future for the time being. I'm glad we agree that we have to go to Mr. Van Buren's party. But I see no reason for you to join his political party."

"I agree on that too."

The secretary of state had rented the Pennsylvania Avenue mansion in which Henry Clay, his predecessor, had resided. To the party flocked all the diplomats and their wives, including the controversial Madame Huygens, who was loud in her denials that she ever planned to insult Mrs. Eaton. The president's threat to send her husband packing had cooled her moral fervor. Numerous members of the old Washington and Virginia aristocracy also appeared. The most startling of these was Thomas Jefferson's widowed daughter, tall, austere Martha Jefferson Randolph. It was an unquestioned coup to have the daughter of the founder of the Democratic Party apparently giving her blessing to Mrs. Eaton. But the Calhouns, and the wives of the three Calhoun cabinet members, were conspicuously absent, as were Emily Donelson and her husband.

Moreover, when Mr. Van Buren led Peggy Eaton to the floor to begin the contredanse, the number of women who declined to join her was conspicuous. Only Mrs. Barry, the pretty wife of the postmaster general, displayed any enthusiasm for the performance. Caroline coolly led George into the lineup, and the musicians struck up a country tune. Never had she felt more tension in the air as they bowed and whirled and exchanged partners in the usual way.

When it ended, and the ladies fluttered their fans and the men mopped their brows, Peggy Eaton drifted across the floor to the Stapletons. "I heard what you said to that bitch Floride Calhoun the other night," she said. "I'm glad you know which side your bread is buttered on."

"I beg your pardon?" Caroline said.

"Before this is over, everyone's going to find out they can't insult Peggy O'Neale."

Peggy's extravagant use of toilet water again assailed Caroline's nostrils. There was something vulgar about this woman; it was an undemocratic thought—but an unavoidable one.

A half hour later, back on the dance floor, Peggy collided with Mrs. Alexander McComb, an admiral's wife. Older and heftier, Mrs. McComb almost knocked Peggy down—and did not apologize. Instead she muttered something to her husband about inviting the wrong people into society.

"What did you say?" Peggy cried. "Another crack like that and your husband will be commanding a sloop in Pago Pago."

"Obviously, your manners are as atrocious as your morals," Mrs. McComb said.

For a moment it looked as if the two ladies were going to start scratching and biting. An appalled Caroline looked around for their host, the secretary of state. He seemed to have vanished. She urged George to find him. George located Van Buren in the library, sipping port, while the name-calling on the dance floor reached ever higher decibels. The story would be all over Washington the next day, further embarrassing Andrew Jackson. Surely Van Buren would want to stop it. But when George urged the secretary to do something, he coolly replied it would be better to "let the heavyweights fight it out."

Obviously, Martin Van Buren did not give a damn how much Peggy Eaton embarrassed the president. His only interest in the affair was how much political capital he could coin from it. From that moment, George Stapleton ceased to like or trust this clever Democrat from New York.

A week later, the Stapletons were invited to join the president and about forty guests for an excursion down the Potomac aboard a new steam-powered navy warship. Vice President and Mrs. Calhoun were among the guests, as well as the Legrands and John Sladen. As they trooped aboard, the president stood on the quarterdeck, shaking hands with the men and greeting the ladies.

As the ship headed down the Potomac, John Sladen joined Caroline and George at the starboard railing. Toward them strolled Floride Calhoun in a saffron yellow spring dress and a small straw hat trimmed with white roses. "Good afternoon, Mrs. Calhoun," Caroline said.

"Good afternoon, Mrs. Stapleton," Floride said. "How did you enjoy Mr. Van Buren's ball?"

"It was a very festive affair."

"I heard people placed bets on whether Mrs. McComb or Mrs. Eaton would win their prizefight. Did you make any money?"

"No, but I almost wished I'd taken your advice and stayed home."

Her glance caught John Sladen's eyes. *Is that better?* she silently asked.

Down the deck toward them strolled Amos Kendall, the man whose toast had closed the inaugural ball. His hawk nose and bold gray eyes gave him a menacing air. Beside him was a shorter man with an odd-shaped, balding head and oversized eyes that made him look like a circus clown out of costume. With them was the dapper secretary of state in one of his creamy vests and tan suits.

"Here comes President Jackson's new cabinet," Mrs. Calhoun said. "I hear they meet nightly in the White House kitchen."

It was the beginning of the phrase *kitchen cabinet*, which soon became a byword for Jackson's style of government. Alienated from his regular cabinet by the Eaton imbroglio, he turned to informal advisers.

"How do you do, Mr. Kendall," Floride Calhoun said. "And Mr. Van Buren—whom I should have saluted first."

"By no means, Mrs. Calhoun. In the Democratic Party, we're all equals," Van Buren said.

Martin Van Buren introduced Caroline and George and John Sladen to Kendall. He also introduced the balding man—Frank Blair, whom he described as the best newspaperman in the West.

"Ah yes. Mr. Swartout's friends," Kendall said, his hard eyes sweeping over the Stapletons and John Sladen.

"And proud of it!" John said.

"I was discussing with these young people the Machiavellian element in politics," Floride Calhoun said. "You must be familiar with his writings, Mr. Secretary."

"If you read his books, you'll find him a much slandered man," Van Buren said. "He favors honesty and plain dealing among those in power."

"Mr. Kendall and his fellow Kentuckian, Mr. Blair, are going to establish a new newspaper in Washington," Floride Calhoun said, ignoring Van Buren's defense of Machiavelli. "It will speak for the administration. Everyone on the federal payroll recently received a subscription to it. The implication, it seemed to me, was—either you paid for your subscription or you should begin looking for another job."

"You reason too closely, Mrs. Calhoun. Like your husband. In politics, appearances are deceptive," Kendall said.

"How well we Southerners know that," Floride said. "We thought we belonged to a united Democratic Party, for instance."

"United under Andrew Jackson, madam," Van Buren said.

"How stupid of me not to realize that," Mrs. Calhoun said.

With a twirl of her parasol, she left the Stapletons and John Sladen to digest what they had just heard. Kendall, Blair, and the secretary of state also departed. Again, Caroline sensed John was asking, *Now do you believe me— trust me?* She resisted the question violently for reasons both personal and political.

"There's Jack Donelson and Emily," she said. "Let's say hello." She pointed across the deck, where the White House hostess and her husband, the president's secretary, were looking at the scenery off the port side of the ship.

"Beware," John Sladen said. "The uncrowned queen approaches."

Peggy O'Neale Eaton strolled toward the Donelsons. She was wearing a crimson red silk dress trimmed with Turkish embroidery. Its tight high waist more than emphasized her superb figure. On her dark hair was a chaplet of red roses. A brisk wind had risen, fluttering their leaves. Clutching the flowers, Peggy said, "Oh, Mrs. Donelson. Would you like to use my toilet water? It will protect your skin against this wind."

"No thank you," Emily Donelson said in a voice that could not have been more icy.

Peggy's lovely face convulsed with fury. "If you continue to insult me, you'll find your husband and you and your brats on the way back to Tennessee."

From that moment, Caroline wrote off Peggy Eaton as a hopeless case. The woman had no political judgment. It was only a question of time before she would destroy herself and her husband. In the meantime, where should the Stapletons pledge their allegiance? Beside her stood John Sladen, telling her it should go to John C. Calhoun and the wronged abused South. But where did that leave her loyalty to the unhappy old man in the White House? Was he irrelevant, a kind of king without real power, manipulated by the men around him? If that was true, her political instincts told her that the man who was going to emerge victorious from this amoral struggle was the admirer of Machiavelli, Martin Van Buren. Did that make John Sladen, with his forlorn, father-driven loyalty to Samuel Swartout, somehow pitiable?

No, no, no, Caroline told herself. She had traveled down that river once. Never, never, never again. Why was she attracted to men who backed losing causes? Suddenly she was in the Bowood library again, looking at her father's memorial. Was he the reason? Was that proud, poverty-haunted man the secret ruler of her soul? Did she feel she had betrayed him by marrying George Stapleton?

"Look," George said. "Mount Vernon."

Off the starboard bow was the white mansion of the ultimate founding father, George Washington. For almost five minutes, conversation on the deck dwindled as everyone contemplated the memory and meaning of a man who had won authentic imperishable fame.

"He's the one man we must never forget," George said. "He embodied America."

Caroline found this idolatry annoying. Her experience with Hugh Stapleton inclined her to think the past was a foreign country that no one should try to visit. Better to free themselves from its grip, to banish all the ghosts, personal and national.

"Someday, George, maybe they'll say that about you."

For a moment George's glance was unfriendly. He thought she was ridiculing him. "I mean it," she said. "Don't you think it's possible, John?"

"In American politics, anything is possible," John Sladen said.

Was that mockery in his saturnine eyes? If so, Caroline dismissed it. For a fantastic moment she had a glimpse of a future in which she and John would conspire to convince George Stapleton that he could achieve this goal—for a purpose which he did not comprehend. She did not know what that purpose would be. But she felt destiny gathering around her in this capital city, where personalities and power were in violent collision.

FIVE

"YES, HE'S DADDY'S BIG BOY. ISN'T he Daddy's big boy?" George said, bouncing Jonathan Stapleton on his large knee.

Six-month-old Jonathan giggled and gurgled with glee. "I think he looks more and more like Grandfather, don't you?" George said.

His frequent attempts to detect the family bloodline in Jonathan's looks always made Caroline uncomfortable. Every time she saw the child, she encountered John Sladen's gray eyes and thin-lipped mouth. "Yes," she said.

"Here's some iced tea, mistress," Tabitha said.

"Oh, thank you," Caroline said. Tabitha was always doing thoughtful little things for her.

It was June at its worst in Washington, D.C. Waves of soggy heat seemed to drift on the desultory Southern breeze. George had added a broad porch on the second floor of their house. It gave them a blessed escape from the heat—and a nice view of the empty fields and vacant streets of the capital. As the sun sank, the birds twittered sleepily in the trees along Pennsylvania Avenue, crickets began to chirp, the traffic dwindled.

The clop of horses' hooves reached their ears. Looking down, they saw the president of the United States, Andrew Jackson, and his secretary of state, Martin Van Buren, out for another evening ride. Over the last month, their appearance around this time had become almost a fixture of the capital scene. George and Caroline watched in silence as they passed. The significance of this deepening companionship was too obvious to mention.

"I'm glad we're going back to New Jersey," Caroline said.

"I am too," George said.

They were closing their Washington house for the summer. Few Washingtonians endured the broiling heat and stifling humidity of the place if they could avoid it. Bowood would be a haven of comfort in comparison. But Caroline was not talking about the weather. She was referring to Martin Van Buren's growing ascendancy and John C. Calhoun's steady decline as a result of the ongoing social war over Peggy Eaton.

Peggy's mastery of the president made her truculent public behavior almost irrelevant. She took all her insults and rebuffs to him and blamed them on the vice president. Sarah Polk sent Caroline a quotation from a letter that the president had written to James Polk: "That base man Calhoun is secretly saying that Mrs. Eaton is the president."

Other spies had reported to Sarah a particularly flagrant Van Buren ploy. He had confided to Peggy that he considered Andrew Jackson the greatest man who ever lived—but sternly forbade her to tell the president. Of course, Peggy passed on the remark the next time she went to the White House. Old Hickory's eyes filled with tears. "That man loves me," he said.

"Sickening" was among the milder terms George Stapleton used to describe Van Buren's oily flattery and his manipulation of Peggy Eaton to destroy John C. Calhoun. Caroline was equally repelled, but she continued to marvel at the power Peggy was wielding on one side—and Floride Calhoun was displaying on the supposedly moral side of the question. In her secret heart Caroline rejoiced at the sight of women forcing flabbergasted males to deal with them.

Caroline was also discovering how totally unpredictable history can be— how seemingly trivial quarrels and animosities can tilt events in ways that loom far longer than their petty origins. On his side, George was discovering what it meant to resist a powerful politician. For his John Sladen–inspired flirtation with Samuel Swartout, now installed as collector of the port of New York, George suddenly found it impossible to name a single postmaster to the many vacancies that occurred in New Jersey. The postmaster general and his wife were on the Eaton–Van Buren side of the quarrel over Peggy.

Worse, the editor of the *Newark Plebian,* the leading Democratic newspaper in New Jersey, suddenly began to wonder in his editorials if George was a "true Democrat." He was, after all, still rich, his uncle was still the president of Principia Mills and chairman of the largest bank in the state, and according to rumor George was paying a man five dollars a month to put flowers on his grandfather's grave—proof that he secretly yearned for a return to rule by aristocrats. Congressman Stapleton may have charmed Old Hickory at the Hermitage, but the editor decided only "deeds" would convince him. The editor's brother-in-law had become assistant collector of the port of Perth Amboy thanks to Van Buren's friend Amos Kendall, who was virtually running the Treasury Department.

Caroline told these troubles to Sarah Polk, who coolly assured her they were annoying but not particularly surprising. Similar feuds and rivalries existed in every state. Sarah advised an early return to New Jersey to assert George's leadership of the local Democratic Party. She also urged George to do unto his enemies what they were doing to him and start a newspaper of his own. Van Buren had a newspaper, the *Albany Argus,* that chastised foes and praised friends in New York. In Nashville, the *Republican* was edited by one of President Jackson's close personal friends. Every major politician had a paper manned by an aggressive editor who spoke in his behalf.

Not long after Martin Van Buren and Andrew Jackson disappeared down Pennsylvania Avenue, Tabitha returned to the porch. "Mr. Sladen is downstairs," she said.

"Send him up, by all means," George said.

The twilight was deepening on the porch. John Sladen was a figure of darkness in the doorway. "I've come to say good-bye."

"You're leaving for New Orleans tomorrow?"

"Yes."

"I hope you'll come back a congressman, Johnny," George said.

"That will take some doing. I'm still pretty much an outsider. But it's not an impossibility, if Senator Legrand's health remains good. I think I've convinced him I can be of some service."

"Undoubtedly."

"In some ways this has been the most momentous three months of my life. I've met a truly great man. Greater than Aaron Burr—or Andrew Jackson."

"Calhoun? I admire him too," George said. "But his stock is slipping steadily downhill. He's barely selling at par these days."

"That's another reason why I want to come back here. I assure you he's not going to sit passively and let the leadership of this country go by default to a scheming swine like Martin Van Buren."

"Sit down. Would you like some iced tea?" George said.

"No, no thank you. I've still got packing to do." John cleared his throat and fumbled with his hat. "I've got some news of my own. I've asked the senator for Clothilde's hand."

"Wonderful!" George's hearty tone gouged Caroline's nerves. "I presume he said yes?"

"He's delighted. He's giving us a very generous dowry. I think she'll be a good wife, don't you? She has beautiful manners. She's a sweet, lovely girl. I'm very fond of her."

"It's a wonderful choice," George said. "My only complaint is she sometimes seems too quiet. But I suppose I've seen her with Caroline and Sarah Polk. They're never at a loss for words."

"How true," John said. "I'm afraid I'm that way myself. Maybe that's why I like the idea of a quiet wife. At least one person will listen to me."

"Johnny, you're rating your powers much too low."

"Well, you're among my oldest friends. I thought I'd share my . . . my good news with you."

"I'm glad you did. I wish I could persuade you to stay for a drink. Did I scare you off with iced tea? We can have a rumfustian or some cold white wine in your hand in two minutes."

"No thank you, George. One other thing—I hope you or Caroline can find time to write me a letter now and then about what's happening here in Washington. I'm sure it would tell me more than any newspaper."

"I hereby appoint Caroline your official correspondent."

"Wonderful. Good-bye to you both. Good-bye, Caroline."

"Good-bye," she said.

She listened to John's footsteps descending the stairs. She knew why he did not stay. He had been hoping to find her alone. She knew exactly what he had wanted to say—by what he had failed to say about Clothilde. The word *love* was singularly absent from his good news. Caroline knew in John Sladen's heart that word would always be reserved for her. Had he come hoping to extract the same confession from her? What would she have said if he had asked her, challenged her, to tell him?

The birds had ceased their drowsy twitters. Darkness was almost total in the street, on the porch. "That's the best news I've heard in a while," George said. "Don't you agree?"

"Yes," Caroline said.

"I guess he's gotten over you, my dear. Do you wish it were otherwise? Do you still sometimes imagine yourself as La Belle Dame sans Merci with poor Sladen—and me—in your thrall?"

"Of course not."

"I'm glad to hear it, because you still have it in your power."

They went home to New Jersey with those words throbbing in Caroline's head. She found Bowood tomblike. The Congressman's ghost seemed everywhere: gazing from the library wall in a new painting that his son Malcolm had commissioned, watching in the shadows from the silent parlor, presiding over the exquisite Palladian dining room. George left her there for days at a time while he toured the state, hobnobbing with local Democrats and their innumerable committees.

Another strain on her nerves was Jeremy Biddle and his wife, Sally. Caroline was not thrilled to return to their proximity—especially when she discovered that Sally had more or less established herself as the first lady of the little industrial city of Hamilton. She and Jeremy had built a substantial house on the other side of the city, close to Principia Mills, so Jeremy could walk to work in good weather. Although Sally was six months pregnant, she decided to give a dinner party for Caroline and George.

How could Caroline say no? As a politician's wife, she could not risk offending anyone. Of course George was delighted to come. He and Jeremy had been corresponding about the politics of Washington and the nation, and during dinner Jeremy drew him out about his impressions of Andrew Jackson, John C. Calhoun, and Martin Van Buren to fine effect. The other guests, a mixture of local businessmen and politicians, were enthralled.

At coffee, the gentlemen stayed behind for their inevitable cigars, and the ladies withdrew to the east parlor, decorated in the cosy style people had not yet learned to call Victorian. During dinner Sally had confined herself to female topics, such as the wonderful new Lucifer matches everyone was using in their kitchens. She now gave everyone a demonstration. The matches were tipped with brimstone. All you had to do was insert the tip in the fluid at the bottom of the matchstick and you had a flame. Everyone agreed it was infinitely better than the old-fashioned flint lighters.

With no warning, Sally put away the matches and turned the conversation to the aspect of the Washington scene Jeremy had avoided at dinner—the Peggy Eaton scandal. "All of us can scarcely wait to hear your opinion of Mrs. Eaton," Sally said. "Have you returned her calls? Do you appear with her in public?"

"I have a private opinion of Mrs. Eaton, and a public one," Caroline said. "In private, I think she's a fool. In public, I tolerate her for President Jackson's sake."

"Such a dilemma," Sally said. "You must find it especially fascinating."

"What do you mean?" Caroline asked.

Sally floundered. "With your strong opinions . . . about women's role."

Caroline's self-control remained intact. But as she met Sally's eyes across the parlor, she read condescension and even contempt in her cool stare—while her polite smile became more and more mocking. No one else in the room noticed anything out of the ordinary. Everyone presumed there was nothing but the warmest friendship between Caroline and her cousin-in-law. But in that scarifying moment, Caroline realized that Sally knew about John Sladen and was implicitly comparing her to Peggy Eaton.

An incalculable rage gripped Caroline's soul. Was Sally hinting that she could wreak similar havoc on Mrs. Stapleton whenever she chose? Probably not. She was a Stapleton, after all, and Caroline now shared the name. But the mere suggestion that Sally had such power over her made Caroline seethe. She silently vowed never to set foot in Sally's house again. From that moment she found the whole city, including Bowood, intolerable.

Within a week, she had George hunting for a vacation home. Hamilton was as impossibly hot as Washington, Caroline insisted. The heat was making her and little Jonathan ill. She soon had a specific house in mind. Her grandmother Kate Rawdon, with whom she still corresponded, told her that down in Monmouth County, Kemble Manor, the home of the wealthiest branch of the Kemble family before the Revolution, was for sale.

Caroline insisted on an immediate visit. The place was a wreck, the roof leaky, the chimneys crumbling. It would cost a fortune to restore. But the view of Raritan Bay was spectacular, and the vale of the Shrewsbury River, one of the loveliest water vistas in New Jersey, was only a few miles away. George bought Kemble Manor and by August an outpouring of cash had it ready to inhabit.

For the next two months, they enjoyed an idyll. Each day George took Caroline and Jonathan sailing in a swift sloop George picked up at a bargain price in Perth Amboy. He taught Caroline to swim in a tidal creek near the property. As a farm girl from landlocked Ohio, she had a dread of the water that was not easy to overcome.

The sight of George in a bathing costume, muscles rippling, the sun glistening on his bronzed skin, stirred desire in Caroline's flesh. By now they had acquired instinctive ways to arouse each other: a kiss on the throat, a touch of a fingertip on the nape of the neck. They made love almost every night. Caroline began to think she could annihilate John Sladen and Sally Stapleton Biddle and loose-lipped Jeremy Biddle with the sheer satisfaction of being alive, of being married to this huge, amiable, passionate man.

For George too those summer months at Kemble Manor were a profound experience. He began to call it their second honeymoon. The resentment he had felt about Caroline's failure to console Hugh Stapleton ebbed into forgiveness.

Jonathan thrived too, taking his first tottering steps across Kemble Manor's parquet parlor holding his father's hand. Caroline began to take more pleasure in the child. She promised herself she would give him even more attention when he was old enough to educate.

Tabitha and Hannibal Flowers (he had taken her last name, not having one of his own) enjoyed Kemble Manor as much as their employers. They and Harriet, the fat, gray-haired cook, were the only servants. George cheerfully offered them swimming lessons, which Harriet declined. But Tabitha and Hannibal were soon splashing in the creek. There was no need to wonder what happened back at Kemble Manor after one of these sessions. About the same age as George and Caroline, they were at least as amorous.

Caroline was not entirely surprised when Tabitha informed her that she was pregnant. George congratulated Hannibal and hoped it would be a boy. "I'm waiting for Caroline to give Jonathan a brother," George said.

As if the words were black magic, Caroline's head whirled and she was assailed by that first signal of pregnancy, morning sickness. George was ecstatic. In an amorous daze, Caroline found herself welcoming the child, even if she did not look forward to the next seven months.

The new baby prompted her first political thought in weeks. "It will be a perfect excuse to avoid going to parties for Peggy Eaton," she said.

George looked gloomy. "I won't go alone."

"You most certainly will. You can imitate that widower faker Martin Van Buren."

Caroline quickly sent Sarah Polk the news. That astute politician congratulated her for the baby—and the exemption from Mrs. Eaton. "I don't look forward to returning to our overheated capital," Sarah wrote.

As September dwindled, George left for another tour of New Jersey's political circuit, and Caroline began packing for another nine months in Washington. As Tabitha helped wrap dresses and shoes in paper before putting them into trunks, she said, "I wishes we could stay here forever, missus. I never been so happy anywhere. I hates the thought of goin' back to Washington."

"Why?"

"Them slave coffles, mistress. They upset me so. To see black folks treated that way. Sold and traded like they was so much cattle. It curdles my soul, mistress. It really do."

"I don't think Southerners like slavery any more than we do. I heard President Jackson say he wished he could free all his people. He freed Hannibal."

"For five hundred of Mr. Stapleton's dollars."

The conversation made Caroline uncomfortable. Her father had freed their slaves when the family migrated to Ohio, where slavery was forbidden in the state constitution. Like his idol, Thomas Jefferson, he disapproved of the idea of slavery in the abstract, but he did not think freed blacks could live happily with whites. He had been a founding member of the American Colonization Society, which proposed to send freed blacks to Africa. But none of Jonathan Kemble's blacks showed the slightest interest in going back to the land of their ancestors. They headed for Philadelphia and New York.

That Sunday, Tabitha and Hannibal went off in the buggy to a church in Middletown, where they had found a preacher they liked. He was a Baptist who gave rousing sermons about sin and damnation and salvation through Jesus. George and Caroline, both devoid of religious belief, stayed home—although George remarked that when Jonathan grew older, they would have to select a church.

Tabitha and Hannibal returned from church with a bundle of papers in a small cardboard box. "Our preacher, Mr. Donaldson, when he heard we was goin' to Washington, give us this to take and hand out to the slaves there. What's it say, Mr. George?" Hannibal asked.

George's eyes widened as he read the papers. The Reverend Mr. Donaldson was apparently a recent convert to the idea that slavery should be abolished in the South—and in the meantime there was nothing wrong with encouraging slaves to run away from their masters. "I wouldn't bring this anywhere near Washington," George said. "It could get you in a lot of trouble."

"That's what I told him," Tabitha said. She had been learning to read with Caroline's help. "I could make out some words. Things like 'against the law' and this—about burnin'." She pointed to a line in which slaves were exhorted to burn their masters' houses and barns in retaliation for their bondage.

"What should we do with it, Mr. George?" Hannibal said. "We promised Pastor Donaldson to bring it with us."

"I'll go see Mr. Donaldson and get you out of that promise."

That afternoon, George rode over to Middletown and spent an hour with the Reverend Mr. Donaldson. He was a small, spare man whose eyes glowed with an otherworldly light. He was unimpressed when George rebuked him for sending abolitionist literature into Washington, D.C. Did he want to burn down the capital of the country?

"In this cause, many will have to suffer. We're declaring war against the slave power, Congressman Stapleton. Since you're leagued with them in the infernal Democratic Party, we're declaring war against you too."

"I'll remember that the next time you ask me for a donation to your church school," George said.

"I've seen a new light. I wouldn't take your money now."

It was George's first encounter with abolition—a movement that would make his life hell on earth in coming years. For the time being, he dismissed Donaldson and his kind as a tiny minority of extremists who could and should be ignored. Back at Kemble Manor, he told Hannibal to put the abolitionist literature in the fireplace and burn it.

"He's a powerful preacher, Mr. George," Hannibal said, as he piled the pamphlets in the fireplace. "He say all America someday gonna believe in the light he's been sent—that all black people should be free."

"I wish they were all free right now, Hannibal. But it would take more money than I've got, or the whole country's got."

George told Hannibal there were almost two million black slaves in the South. If each one was redeemed by paying his master five hundred dollars the way George had freed Hannibal from Andrew Jackson, that meant it would cost a half billion dollars to free them all. That was a lot more money that the U.S. government had at its disposal. If the slaves were freed, how could they live? Their masters could not afford to pay them wages. It might start a war in which one or the other race would be exterminated.

Hannibal listened, his brow furrowed. He adored George Stapleton, the man who had given him his freedom. But he visibly resisted the logic of George's argument. The coachman ruefully shook his big black head as he ignited one of the new Lucifer matches and set the papers ablaze. "Maybe only God can do it," he said.

BOOK

FOUR

ONE

A WEEK LATER, THE STAPLETONS LEFT for Washington, D.C., by steamboat from Perth Amboy. Pregnancy made Caroline and Tabitha both feel queasy on the water; they had a difficult trip. But their spirits improved when they reached the house on Pennsylvania Avenue and found everything spotless and shining. Sarah Polk had hired two free black women; Josephine and Nancy Parks, to give the place a thorough cleaning. Caroline promptly hired the sisters as maids.

A reunion with the Polks at Gadsby's Hotel that night provided a feast of gossip. Mrs. Eaton still reigned at the White House, but Sarah Polk thought her loose tongue and headstrong style were undercutting her support elsewhere. Far more important, President Jackson had turned totally against Vice President John C. Calhoun. He now regarded him as an enemy.

Mrs. Eaton was not the only reason. While everyone else was vacationing, Secretary of State Van Buren had sent James Hamilton on a Machiavellian summer journey to Georgia, where he met with William B. Crawford, who had once rivaled Calhoun as the leader of the South. Now laid low by bad health and political misfortune, Crawford had given Hamilton a letter that the secretary of state had arranged to reach the president by another hand.

Since 1818, Andrew Jackson had believed that John C. Calhoun was the only man who had defended his invasion and conquest of Florida that year— the military adventure that Henry Clay had tried to use to destroy Jackson as a political rival. Now Crawford, who had been in President Monroe's cabinet with Calhoun, swore in writing that the South Carolinian had wanted to have Jackson court-martialed and disgraced.

"The president showed me the letter," James Polk said. "I urged him to forget it. The whole thing is the product of hate and intrigue. But this Eaton affair has poisoned his mind against Calhoun. He's written to the vice president, asking for an explanation."

"Mr. Calhoun is said to be close to sending Mr. Van Buren a challenge," Sarah Polk said. "Meanwhile, the Southerners are in a rage. They're threatening to do unto Jackson what the party did to Adams. They're setting up newspapers in every state. At a signal from Mr. Calhoun, they'll open fire and undermine the administration."

"For the moment, Calhoun insists he's still loyal to the president," James Polk said.

"Can anyone stop Van Buren?" George asked. He described the petty humiliations the New Yorker had inflicted on him.

Polk glumly shook his head. "He's mesmerized the President. I begin to see why they call him the Little Magician."

"Some people think it's vital for the South, for the Union, for Mr. Calhoun to become president." Caroline was echoing John Sladen, but George did not seem to mind. Wasn't it true?

Sarah Polk did not seem to think so: "The South's self-pity begins to trouble me."

"I'm more concerned about the president's health," James Polk said. "Andrew Jackson Donelson told me this Eaton mess is taking more out of the old man than four years of running the country. He isn't sleeping, he's spitting blood, he gets violent headaches."

Back in their own house, George wondered what they could do to rescue Andrew Jackson from this nightmare. "Nothing," Caroline said in her hard way. "It would be better to think of what we can do to help Vice President Calhoun."

"I like him, but I think some of his ideas are dangerous."

"A good reason to become his friend and try to change some of those ideas."

Caroline told herself that she was not following John Sladen's lead here. She was reacting against her growing detestation of Mrs. Eaton. Here was a woman who found herself with immense power in her hands, and she was throwing it away with petty resentments and boorish behavior. It was not a reassuring spectacle to someone who believed in women's equality. In fact, almost all the female actors in this drama were performing far below Caroline's expectations—or better, her hopes. Floride Calhoun seemed to delight in plunging her husband into this maelstrom of animosity.

"I think you're expecting too much—to imagine that a man of Calhoun's age and stature is going to listen seriously to a first-term congressman," George said.

"You're a first-term congressman from a crucial state. The stands you take can influence people in New York and Pennsylvania. Don't rate yourself so low, George. Humility gets you nowhere in Washington, D.C."

The next day, Caroline received an invitation to tea from Floride Calhoun. She found Sarah Polk and the wives of a half dozen other senators and congressmen in Mrs. Calhoun's parlor. Floride announced her determination to continue her opposition to Mrs. Eaton. She descanted on her fixed opinion that Andrew Jackson was in his dotage. That meant someone had to take charge of the Democratic Party.

"I've urged my husband not to sit passively and let that someone be Martin Van Buren," Floride said.

She urged her guests to be on the alert for a major speech by Senator Robert Young Hayne in the Senate. It would settle, once and for all, the question of the South's place in the nation. He had been preparing it for months, with Mr. Calhoun's help. "The more ladies we have in the gallery to applaud him, the better," she said.

Everyone promised to join Mrs. Calhoun's petticoat army. Caroline almost forgot about it in the excitement of watching Congress convene and George take his oath to faithfully support the Constitution. The House was bedecked with flags for the occasion. Not a few members brought champagne and other liquors to their seats to share with friends. Several Southern members brought their hunting dogs to enjoy the excitement and slaves to serve their refreshments. For a while a carnival atmosphere engulfed the stately chamber.

"What happens now?" Caroline asked Sarah Polk, who had joined her in the gallery of the House.

"The jockeying begins."

Sarah meant the competition for seats on the more important committees. George had help from his friend Polk but opposition from Churchill C. Cambreleng, who had gone over to the Martin Van Buren faction. George asked for a seat on the Military Affairs Committee; Cambreleng, the chairman, ignored him. Polk got him aboard the Commerce Committee, another natural place for him, and the influential Ways and Means Committee. Against his will, George was shoved onto the committee that governed the District of Columbia, a job all congressmen tried to avoid.

Caroline tried to keep up with what was happening in the other parts of the government by reading the new administration paper, the *Washington Globe,* with its bold motto at the top of the front page: "The World Is Governed Too Much." George grumbled that it was a strange saying for a semi-official government paper. Editor Frank Blair had a slashing style that made everyone fear him. Quite a few of his slashes recently had been aimed at Vice President Calhoun.

On January 26, 1830, Caroline received a note from Sarah Polk, asking her if she was ready to join her in the Senate gallery tomorrow. Senator Robert Young Hayne was scheduled to give the "interesting" speech that Mrs. Calhoun had urged them to support.

Although her morning sickness left her feeling miserable for most of the day, Caroline resolutely donned a good dress and a cloak lined with white marten fur that George had given her for Christmas and rode to the Capitol with Sarah in a cab. It was 7 A.M. and bitterly cold, with a cruel wind howling from the north. The sky remained a monotonous gray as the coach jolted over the frozen ruts on Pennsylvania Avenue.

Along the way they passed two lines of slaves being marched in coffles to the auction blocks in front of the White House. They were all dressed in cheap, undyed-wool shirts and pants, without shoes. Not one wore a cloak or a coat. Caroline hardly noticed them. As Sarah Polk had predicted, she had become used to slaves and slavery in Washington, D.C. Many Southern politicians brought their slaves with them to staff their houses. Many of the government bureaucrats were Southerners with similar households.

In the Senate chamber, the gallery was already crowded with dozens of women. Floride Calhoun was in the front row, surrounded by the wives of three cabinet members and several senators. She was wearing an embroidered lingerie gown and a green velvet spencer*—an outfit no one in New York

---

*A kind of vest with long sleeves.

had worn for a decade. On the Senate floor, Caroline noticed Senator Hayne was wearing an equally odd costume—a suit of coarse homespun, not much better in quality than the cloth worn by the slaves she had seen on Pennsylvania Avenue, though his tailoring was better.

"Why is the senator wearing that dreadful suit?" she asked Sarah Polk.

"I think he's trying to advertise his defiance of Northern textiles," Sarah said. "Maybe Mrs. Calhoun is doing the same thing for Northern fashions."

Before a hushed Senate and breathless galleries, Senator Hayne began his speech with a stunning declaration. It was time, he said, to alter the arrangement of power in the Union. Hitherto, the West and New England had voted against the South on the tariff, apparently indifferent to its crushing burden on his section of the country. But in this Congress, the New England states had called for an end to the sale of public lands in the West. New England was showing its contempt for both sections in its determination to pile up wealth. They were determined to keep their workers in thrall to their factories, no matter what it cost those poor toilers in health and happiness.

It was time for the West and the South, two sections that had so much in common—a love of, a dependence on agriculture, a devotion to individual liberty—it was time and past time for them to unite and with their votes in Congress take charge of America's destiny. Let the West support the South's contention that a state had the right to nullify by a vote of its legislature any unjust law that Congress passed, and they would have a new Union.

All this was delivered with a passionate flow of language that left everyone in the chamber mesmerized. On the dais, Vice President Calhoun listened in a near rapture of approval. Several times a smile broke across his tight lips. More often, he bent over his rostrum to scrawl notes of advice to the speaker, which were handed to Hayne by scampering pages. By the time Hayne closed with a soaring peroration to "true patriotism," there was no doubt in anyone's mind that he was speaking for John C. Calhoun.

"Mr. President!"

From the door of the chamber a deep baritone voice rang out. Daniel Webster stood there, in a buff coat with large brass buttons, his dark eyes glowing, his swarthy countenance charged with emotion.

"The chair recognizes the senator from Massachusetts," Vice President Calhoun said.

"As a New England man, I cannot allow Senator Hayne's aspersions to go unanswered. Nor do I think any American would want to let them go unanswered. Aside from his slanders of the people whose love of liberty stirred the first resistance to British oppression, there is the great question he has raised in his remarks. Whether a single state can defy laws passed by Congress. In fact, if I did not mishear him, he went further—he said if the defiance he calls nullification fails to gain redress, a state has the right to secede from the Union."

Webster was right. In expanding on his remarks on nullification, Hayne had in fact mentioned secession as a final solution to a quarrel between a state and the Union. He had insisted it was a step that would require the most extreme circumstances to justify it. Still, he should never have said it. Webster, one of the nation's most brilliant lawyers, seized on this admission and made a stupendous speech, denouncing nullification and secession and extolling the Union as the bastion of American liberty.

"I go for the Constitution as it is, and for the Union as it is," he thundered. "It is the people's Constitution, the people's government, made for the people, made by the people, and answering to the people. Liberty and Union, now and forever, one and inseparable!"

Cheers burst from numerous male throats. Around her, Caroline saw tears streaming down many women's faces. Below, she saw congressmen crowding the doors of the Senate chamber. Among them towered George Stapleton. His face wore an exalted, almost hypnotized expression. There was no doubt whatsoever that Daniel Webster's words had touched the core of George's being.

On the dais, John C. Calhoun was a shaken man. His face ashen, he rapped his gavel and called, "Order! Order!" But the galleries, the floor of the Senate itself, ignored him. More cheers cascaded down. Many senators rushed to shake Webster's hand. Around Robert Young Hayne clustered a far smaller band of glowering Southerners. Floride Calhoun departed with her circle of friends, their faces equally dour.

In this first great battle of America's thirty years' war, the South had suffered a shattering defeat. Caroline made no attempt to disguise it in her letter to John Sladen the next day. She told him Hayne, and possibly Calhoun, had grievously miscalculated by even bringing up the word *secession.*

I believe there is a term in military lore, "the high ground," which wise soldiers seize and hold in a battle. Senator Hayne let Senator Webster seize the high moral ground in their dispute—and I wonder if he or Vice President Calhoun can ever regain it.

But there may be a method in their seeming madness, according to my friend Sarah Polk. What they hope to do is divide President Jackson from Mr. Van Buren by asserting the doctrine of nullification. They are absolutely confident that the President will support them—and come over to Calhoun's side.

I have my doubts. Although I sympathize with Mr. Calhoun as a wronged man, I wonder if his temper is too severe, his pride too ascendant. He and his wife seem to think they can make President Jackson become their follower by the sheer force of their political philosophy. I fear President Jackson is not the sort of man who submits to force of any kind.

This assumes, of course, that the President is in full control of his faculties. Only time will tell who is right.

I hope by now you and Clothilde are man and wife and have set up housekeeping. Let us hear from you so we can send you a wedding present.

Affectionately,
Caroline Stapleton

"Mistress, Tabitha's disappeared. She didn't come home from the market this mornin'."

"What?"

"Tabitha's gone," Harriet said. Behind the cook towered Hannibal, his wide black face contorted with dread. He was twisting his cap in his big hands until it was a shapeless rag.

Caroline was sealing and stamping her letter to John Sladen when this stunning news was communicated to her.

"What could have happened to her?" Caroline said. Nancy and Josephine Parks, the sisters she had hired the last fall, hovered in the doorway. They looked frightened.

"I don't know, mistress," Harriet said.

"Maybe she took sick and went into some friend's house to lie down. Women often get spells when they're pregnant."

"Mistress, I fears the slavers got her!" Hannibal said.

"How could they? In broad daylight?"

"Mistress, it happen all the time," Hannibal said. "Ask Nancy and Josephine here. They born in this place."

Caroline turned to the two young women. They were small, slight, rather timid creatures. They nodded simultaneously. "It happen all right," Nancy said. "They drag people into houses. Say they're runaways. Then sell them South. They got federal marshals helpin' 'em sometimes. Give them a piece of the money they make."

"I can't believe it," Caroline said. "I'll speak to Mr. Stapleton the moment he comes in."

"Oh, please, missus. You got to act fast. Can't you send me to him? No matter where he is, I'll run all the way," Hannibal said. "By nighttime, she'll be gone from this place. Put on a boat and gone."

"He's at the Capitol."

Hannibal raced out the door. Caroline repeated her disbelief that someone would kidnap a human being in broad daylight. Harriet grimly informed her that pregnant black women were considered prime targets for this sort of crime. "They gettin' two for the price of one. Makes a woman more valuable," Harriet said.

A half hour later, a gasping Hannibal returned in a near frenzy. "They say Mr. George can't be bothered. They meetin' with all the Democratic chiefs in a cork-us. Won't be free until dark."

Cork-us? Caroline realized Hannibal meant *caucus.* The Democratic Party regularly met in these semiprivate sessions to thrash out policy. "Get the carriage," she said.

Flinging on a dress, Caroline rode to the Capitol. Along Pennsylvania Avenue, they passed another long coffle of blacks being marched to the slave market in Lafayette Square opposite the White House. Caroline remembered Tabitha's frequent comments that slave trading should be banned from Washington.

At the Capitol Caroline found a page who extracted George from the Democratic caucus. Like Caroline, his first reaction was disbelief at the news she brought. But the frantic expression on Hannibal's face swiftly convinced him the crisis was real. He rushed back to the caucus and returned with James Polk, whose face acquired a gloomy cast as he heard the story.

"The obvious man to see is the chief of the federal marshals. But I fear you'll get the runaround."

"Why?"

"His brother is one of the principal traders. You should seek help from the highest possible power."

"The president?" George said.

"As a newcomer to Washington he'll also get the runaround. I recommend the vice president. He's been here for twenty years. He knows everybody."

They rushed to the Senate chamber. The vice president was on the dais, listening to a senator from Ohio arguing that the federal government should pay for roads and canals to improve the national economy. A page brought him a note from George explaining their problem. Calhoun immediately joined them in the corridor and led them to an office behind the dais.

"Let me first ask this fellow some questions," he said, turning to Hannibal. "Have you beaten your wife? Struck her when you were drunk?"

"No, sir. I'se a Baptist. Liquor don't touch my lips."

"Have you been seeing another woman? Has your wife been seeing another man?"

"No, sir! We be Christians, sir. We obey the Lord's commandments," Hannibal said, growing more and more agitated.

"Have you had any dealings with abolitionists?"

Hannibal was thunderstruck. He looked guiltily at George. "He's got a pastor in New Jersey of that persuasion," George said. "But I don't believe he's had anything to do with them here in Washington."

"These questions seem insensitive but they're necessary," Calhoun said. "These people's habits often lead them astray. Investigations have inclined us to conclude most of the so-called free-Negro kidnappings in Washington are really domestic disputes, solved by running away. One or two have been staged by abolitionists to slander slave owners."

"Mr. Vice President. Please save my wife," Hannibal cried. "I ain't never spoke a cross word to Tabitha. We ain't done nothin' in the abolition line. Tabitha's gonna be on a boat to South Carolina or Georgia this night!"

"I'll speak to the chief of the federal marshals immediately," Calhoun said. "He'll do everything in his power to find her, Hannibal. Can you describe her?"

"She's not very black. More tannish. About as tall as Mistress Stapleton here. Got a mark on her leg where some hot water burned her when she first worked in a kitchen years ago."

Hannibal could not control himself, thinking of Tabitha in that long-ago pain. He started to weep.

"Which leg?" Calhoun said, taking notes.

"The left."

"All right. The marshals will do their best. I'll see to it. Let me advise you on how to conduct yourself. Go home and be quiet. Don't gather some friends and start a riot. That will only make it impossible to find Tabitha."

Again, Calhoun explained to the Stapletons. "We've had to call out the militia several times in these cases. Two years ago the blacks burned down a suspected hiding place."

George and Caroline were bewildered as they followed James Polk into the corridor. Why hadn't the vice president expressed more sympathy to Hannibal? He displayed virtually no indignation at the commission of such a crime in the capital of the United States. They were discovering that slavery was already a kind of war zone in which John C. Calhoun had been living all his life. Like war, it tended to blunt ordinary emotion in otherwise decent men and women.

"Let's hope for the best, Hannibal," George said. "You heard the vice president say they'll search hard for Tabitha."

"Mr. George, them federal marshals ain't worth a damn!" Hannibal said. "Ain't there anything else we can do?"

"I don't know. Can you think of anything, Polk?"

James Polk glumly shook his head. It was obvious that he agreed with Hannibal's estimate of the federal marshals. The two congressmen returned to the Democratic caucus. Caroline rode home with Hannibal. He immediately rushed to the slave auction in Lafayette Square on the chance that Tabitha might appear for sale there. But the Parks sisters told Caroline this was unlikely. Kidnapped free blacks were usually held in houses and smuggled out of the city at night to be sold in the South.

George returned home with grim news. The federal marshals had searched several houses previously used to conceal free blacks and found nothing. In their bedroom, he told Caroline the chief marshal, David Wyden, struck him as a first-class scoundrel. They were interrupted by excited voices downstairs.

It was Hannibal. He gazed up the stairs, his face shiny with sweat and excitement. "Mr. George. I knows I shouldna done it, but I been to the president's house. He wants to see you. He's goin' to help us find Tabitha."

They rushed to the White House in the carriage, with Hannibal urging the horses to a gallop. Andrew Jackson was in the dining room having supper with the Donelsons and James Hamilton. The president looked gaunt and weary. But there was white fire in his eyes.

"I've heard what's happened to Hannibal's wife," he said. "Why didn't you come to me immediately?"

"Mr. President, you have so many burdens pressing on you," George said.

"I've ordered a naval blockade of the port of Alexandria. No ship containing slaves will sail without a complete inspection of its contents. I've ordered Chief Marshal Wyden to place twenty-four-hour guards on the road to Alexandria. I told him unless he finds Tabitha, he'll be looking for another job."

"Let me tell this to Hannibal," George said. He went out to the carriage and brought Hannibal into the dining room.

The big black fell on his knees in front of Jackson. "Old master, I knew you was a good man. Now I thinks you is one of God's saints!"

"I wish that were true," Jackson said. "But if there's a God in heaven, we'll find your wife, Hannibal!"

They went home feeling almost hopeful. But another day passed with no word about Tabitha. Hannibal was in agony, unable to sleep or eat. The next day was Sunday. At about eleven o'clock a heavy hand knocked on their door.

It was Chief Marshal Wyden. He was a round-faced, big-bellied Virginian, with a heavy drawl. "Well, we've tracked down your missin' African," he said, ignoring Hannibal, who stood behind George and Caroline in the hall.

"Where is she?"

"She's on the high seas. 'Fore the president started his blockade, a brig named *Fortunate Pilgrim* left for Charleston with a cargo of blacks. Some people say this wench Tabitha was among'm."

"My God, what can we do?" George asked.

"Nothin'," Wyden said. "She's out of federal jurisdiction now. She'll be sold in South Carolina. No way to stop it."

"The hell you say!" George said.

He put on a suit and rushed to the White House, taking a reluctant Wyden with him. Andrew Jackson was just returning from church. When he heard Wyden's news, Old Hickory decorated the walls of his study with picturesque oaths.

"Can you be ready to leave in an hour aboard the steam frigate *Somers*?" the president asked George.

"Of course."

"I'll have a federal subpoena in your hands, ordering the surrender of Tabitha and the arrest of the traders holding her. The *Somers* should reach Charleston well ahead of this *Pilgrim* vessel. You can meet her at the dock."

"Thank you, Mr. President."

"Don't thank me. We haven't accomplished a damn thing yet. If you run into trouble in South Carolina, contact a man named Joel Poinsett. He's just gotten himself kicked out of Mexico for trying to buy Texas at my orders. He's been writing me about the damnable politics of South Carolina."

In two hours George and Hannibal were steaming down the Potomac aboard the *Somers*, armed with a federal subpoena signed by an associate justice of the Supreme Court. Caroline had no doubt that Chief Marshal Wyden had reported what was happening to John C. Calhoun—which filled her with foreboding. She feared George was about to become part of the growing animosity between the president and the vice president. Her Washington life seemed to be whirling out of control. She rushed to the Polks' rooms at Gadsby's Hotel and told them the latest developments.

"I wish George had gotten a letter from Vice President Calhoun," Sarah said.

"Why?"

"From what we've been hearing, it would have more weight in South Carolina than a federal subpoena," James Polk said.

TWO

THE STEAM FRIGATE *SOMERS*, STRUGGLING THROUGH mountainous winter seas, passed Fort Sumter, the squat, casemated guardian of Charleston Harbor, at 2 P.M. on its third day out from Alexandria. George and Hannibal had been violently seasick for the entire voyage. George gazed at the faded pinks of the old houses fronting the broad harbor and thought Charleston was one of the most civilized-looking cities he had ever seen. But the harbor was devoid of ships, and grass was in fact growing in several streets, between rows of bristling yucca and palmetto trees. Senator Hayne's doleful description at Vice President Calhoun's dinner party had not been an exaggeration.

They tied up at a wharf in the U.S. Navy Yard and stumbled ashore. At the imposing Customs House, the collector of customs, a tall, cadaverous man named Richard Laurens, presided over an office full of dust-covered books and records. He said the ship *Fortunate Pilgrim* had not yet arrived.

When George explained why he was interested, Laurens looked grave. "I would keep your purpose here quiet, if I were you."

"Why?"

"Federal subpoenas aren't popular in South Carolina."

At the city's chief hotel, the wide-porched Palmetto House, George was told Hannibal would have to sleep in the cellar with the slaves of other guests. He would also have to eat with them. Hannibal assured George he did not mind. George gave him a note to Joel Poinsett and headed for the dining room, hoping to eat some food that would remain in his stomach. For want of company, he bought a newspaper. He was astonished by its account of the debate between Senators Hayne and Webster. Hayne was described as the clear winner. Webster's apostrophes to the Union were dismissed as "sputterings of a defective July 4th rocket."

"Congressman Stapleton?"

George gazed at a short, swarthy, slender man whose gaunt face might have peered from a sepulchre. Did everyone in Charleston have one foot in the grave? "I'm Joel Poinsett. Anyone who summons me in Andrew Jackson's name gets my immediate attention. What can I do for you?"

George told him of his errand. Poinsett looked even graver than Collector of the Port Laurens. "This is delicate. It could lead to a public disturbance of rather large proportions."

"Why in the world?"

"Nullification fever is running wild here in Charleston. The complication of secession is only a step behind it. Add slavery to the mixture and you have an almost guaranteed explosion."

"We're talking about a crime. A simple, brutal crime."

"A crime purportedly committed in Washington, D.C. Do you really expect this trader to confess? He'll deny everything. My advice is to press no charges. Simply take the poor kidnapped creature if she's on the ship and clear out of here."

George shook his head. "I intend to see justice done."

"You may end up endangering her safety as well as your own and her husband's."

"Do you have a federal attorney here?"

"Of course. I'll be glad to take you to him."

George bolted down a hasty meal of southern-fried chicken and hominy grits and followed Poinsett to the federal attorney's office. His name was Graves and he lived up to it. A short, heavyset man, he looked harassed and weary. He almost groaned when he saw George's subpoena. "I'm to serve this?"

"Isn't that your job?" George said.

"I've been thinking of resigning this office. I'm tired of being insulted on the street whenever I go out in public. This thing could get my house burned down—or me thrown into the harbor."

"I'll serve it," George said. "You won't have to say a word."

George paced the porch of the Palmetto House for the next three days, waiting for the *Fortunate Pilgrim*. Evenings he spent in Joel Poinsett's elegant house or in the houses of his friends. The Georgian doorways with fluted columns opening into long, shaded galleries, the mock-India wallpaper, and the Doric pilasters reminded him of Bowood. Charleston reeked of history. The talk he heard over the dinner tables and afterward in the drawing rooms was equally historic—about the clash of the glorious American past with the ominous present. Joel Poinsett and his friends were a beleaguered dwindling minority—the supporters of the Union.

George liked many of them and they liked him, especially when they learned he too had a lineage, a grandfather who had sat with their grandfathers in the Continental Congress, a great-grandfather who had done war dances with the Seneca. But George saw them with the eyes of a man who had met Andrew Jackson and joined the political party he had created.

There was James Louis Petigru, a dumpy little man with a long head and squinting eyes, who was considered by some the greatest lawyer in America. He loved the Union, and he loved liberty, and had no confidence in the ability of the people to preserve either. There were the Huger cousins, Alfred and Daniel, each slender, tall, chiseled of feature, Grecian of mind. There was Thomas Grimke, "the walking dictionary," whose heavy gait and ponderous frame seemed mirror images of the weighty articles he wrote in the *Southern Review*. When it came to practical politics, he was a blank page. The more they talked in their charming, acerbic, witty way, the more George began to regard these people as Southern versions of Washington Irving and Fenimore Gardiner and his mother's New York friends, bewildered witnesses to the onward rush of democracy, as appalled—and frightened—as the French aristocracy of 1789.

For these Charlestonians, George Stapleton was a double specter—a Democrat and a spokesman for the burgeoning factory system that was enabling the North to grow immeasurably richer while the South grew remorselessly poorer. It was, one told him, a clash of civilizations, Rome versus Greece, Greece versus Persia, the Sung dynasty versus the Mongol barbarians. "We're defending the past against the future here in Charleston," one declared. "We intend to do it as long as possible."

Joel Poinsett had another vision. He had spent the previous four years in Mexico as American ambassador. At President Andrew Jackson's order, he had attempted to buy Texas. When the Mexicans refused to sell, he began bribing individual Mexican politicians and surreptitiously urging them to seize power. The Mexicans had thrown him out of the country. He had come home with a low opinion of Mexico as a nation. It was "all sail and no ship." They were incapable of governing themselves. Americans should take Texas by force—and march on to Mexico City. Geography would guarantee that most of these conquering Americans would be Southerners. An empire was waiting there to restore the South to splendor and power.

Talk, George heard it all as nothing but talk by men caught in one of history's ebb tides. Again and again, he silently thanked Caroline and Andrew Jackson for making him a man who faced toward the future, not the past. Even more often, he thought of Hannibal in the cellar of the Palmetto House, Tabitha in the hold of the *Fortunate Pilgrim*. When he asked these brilliant Charleston thinkers for advice, they retreated into epigrams and musings. They came close to disliking him for trying to lure them into the gritty details of the looming present.

At midday in private rooms at the Palmetto House, Joel Poinsett arranged for George to meet the other side, tense, angry, young George McDuffie, aging Langdon Cleves, with a huge head and forehead on which a frown seemed permanently engraved—men who told him South Carolina was serious about nullification and, yes, secession. Next came Robert Barnwell Rhett, almost a caricature of a Southern gentleman, with flaring nostrils and squarish forehead, a battering ram of a man. He strode up to George on the porch of the Palmetto House at high noon on the third day, stabbed his cane into the floorboards, and said, "Why did that Tennessee barbarian send you here? To embarrass us? To make a legal case for settling an army on us? To frighten us? Tell him none of these will work. We're past being embarrassed by your ilk. We'll fight his army. We refuse to be frightened by him or anyone else."

"In the name of God, sir," George said, "I'm here as an individual."

"Aboard a U.S. Navy ship."

"That was the president's decision. I would have hired a ship if necessary. I'm here to rescue a free woman—and punish a crime."

"You're here to challenge the doctrine of nullification, to abrogate before our eyes the right of a state to act as a free and independent republic! If not, why haven't you taken your case to a Carolina court? Why, sir? Don't you believe we too have a system of justice?"

"I have a subpoena from the U.S. Supreme Court. Obtained by the president of the United States. That's all I need."

"Mr. George!"

It was Hannibal, in the street. "They say it's here. The *Pilgrim* ship."

He pointed to the harbor. There, working her way past Fort Sumter, was a square-rigged brigantine. Sails taut, she made good headway toward the city's empty wharves.

"Go to Mr. Poinsett. Tell him to bring the federal attorney," George said. "Then go to the *Somers*. Tell them to get the ship ready to sail. Ask the captain and ten armed men to join me on the wharf."

When he turned to continue his argument with Rhett, that gentleman was gone. George hurried down the broad, curving esplanade to the wharves. He was soon joined by an anxious Joel Poinsett, who told him that the federal attorney, Graves, had resigned as of last night. Commander Harrison Duane, the captain of the *Somers,* arrived with ten marines in blue-and-red uniforms. The commander was from Georgia. He had been polite and noncommittal on the voyage from Washington. George could only hope he was on his side.

Beyond the wharf, a huge crowd was beginning to gather. Off to one side, Robert Barnwell Rhett began haranguing them. George could only hear snatches of his rhetoric: "federal tyranny . . . Southern liberty . . . presidential plot."

The *Fortunate Pilgrim* was soon warping against the sagging wharf, her sailors whipping hawsers around bollards, her sails being furled by the topmen. Down a crude gangplank came the captain and his chief passenger. George had the latter's name on the subpoena. The federal marshals had acquired it from the port records of Alexandria.

"Are you Thomas Jefferson Glover?" George asked the man. He was a big, heavy-shouldered fellow, almost as tall as George. He had a black whip struck in the waistband of his pants.

"That's me."

"You're under arrest for the kidnapping of Tabitha Flowers."

"I don't know what the hell you're talking about."

"Under the authority stated here by the president of the United States, we have the right to search this ship for this woman. She's a free woman of color who was kidnapped by you or your confederates in Washington, D.C."

George said this in a voice loud enough to carry far into the crowd on the street around the dock. "I repeat, I don't know what the hell you're talking about," Glover said. "I'm a citizen of South Carolina. I don't pay no attention to federal subpoenas once I'm in my native state. You try to search this ship and you'll get this whip around your neck and this knife in your belly."

He pulled the whip from his waistband and drew a knife with his other hand.

"You'd be well advised to do nothing of the sort," said Commander Duane of the *Somers*. "If we overtook you on the high seas, as we had hoped to do, we would have searched you there. As long as your ship is in the water, I have orders from the president of the United States to search it and I intend to carry them out."

"The hell with the president of the United States!" Glover shouted.

A cheer rose from the crowd on the esplanade.

"I'm going up that gangplank. If you try to strike me with that whip or cut me with that knife, you'll wind up in the water with a broken neck," George said.

He seized Glover by the shoulder and flung him aside. Commander Duane drew his sword and put the hilt against Glover's chest. "Don't move," he said.

On the deck of the *Fortunate Pilgrim*, George seized the first sailor he met. He turned out to be the second mate. "Where's Tabitha Flowers?"

"What's she look like?"

"Light tan. About seven months pregnant."

"Oh, her. You'll find her in the stern section."

George turned. "Hannibal. She's here."

Hannibal sprinted up the gangplank. The second mate led the way to the stern section. They descended into gloom filled with an incredible stench. In the half-light they saw about two dozen black men and women in manacles, behind a set of iron bars that stretched from port to starboard, creating a cage. The deck, really the ship's bottom, was covered by about a foot of straw. Apparently they used this for a bed—and a toilet.

"Tabitha?" Hannibal called.

There was no response from anyone inside the cage.

"Tabitha!" Hannibal screamed.

"Open this lock," George said to the second mate.

He began fumbling through a set of keys. "Tabitha!" Hannibal cried again, clutching the bars.

"She's dead," said a voice in the dark rear of the cage.

The second mate had the door open. Hannibal burst in ahead of George. They floundered over the manacled bodies in the straw. The stench made George want to vomit. Hannibal sank to his knees. "Tabitha," he said. This time it was a groan. He picked up the inert form and clutched it to his chest. "Tabitha," he said, sobs wracking his huge frame.

"I got the baby," said the same voice from the darkness.

His eyes adjusted to the dark by now, George managed to make out a young black woman crouched in the corner. She had something wrapped in a cloth against her breasts.

"What's your name?" George said.

"Mercy."

He turned to the mate. "Get her shackles off. She's coming with us." The mate obeyed without any argument.

George floundered back to Hannibal. "Bring Tabitha with us. We'll take her home."

Hannibal picked up Tabitha and followed George and the mate up the ladder to the open deck. A gasp swept through the crowd when they saw Hannibal carrying Tabitha's body. When Mercy and the baby appeared, even the most slow-witted in the crowd, which now numbered well over a thousand, realized what had happened. Robert Barnwell Rhett fell silent.

George descended the gangplank and pointed at Thomas Jefferson Glover. "I want this man arrested for murder!" he shouted. He turned to an aghast Commander Duane. "Take him in custody."

Joel Poinsett seized George's arm. "You'll never get him through that crowd to the *Somers*. Let the state authorities arrest him and try him here."

"He's going to be tried in Washington, D.C., where he committed this crime," George said.

"Congressman," Commander Duane said. "I'll try to obey your order. But I think Mr. Poinsett is giving you good advice. I've only got ten men. A lot of people in that crowd have guns."

Thomas Jefferson Glover wore a confident sneer on his fleshy face. He was daring George to try to arrest him.

"Mr. George," Hannibal said. "Let the man go. Let God punish him for what he done to my beautiful Tabitha. God will do it in his good time. We don't need to depend on men."

Beside Hannibal, Mercy was visibly terrified. She clutched the baby convulsively. The child emitted a feeble wail. "The poor chile ain't had nothin' to eat since she been born," she said.

George climbed up on a barrel and faced the crowd on the esplanade. "Mr. Poinsett has convinced me that this crime of murder will be prosecuted and, I hope, punished by the courts of South Carolina. In the meantime, I'm taking Tabitha Flowers's dead body and her child back to Washington."

"That kid belongs to me!" Thomas Jefferson Glover said. "I paid two hundred dollars for this wench. It ain't my fault she died on board ship. This other wench is my property too. She's worth five hundred dollars minimum."

Joel Poinsett's swarthy complexion grew almost pale. "Shut your stupid mouth," he said.

"If there are any charges connected to this matter, send them to me, care of the U.S. Congress in Washington, D.C.," George said. "When this murderer is brought to trial, I want to hire the best lawyer in Charleston to assist the state's attorney."

Commander Duane ordered five marines with fixed bayonets to precede them up the wharf to the street. Duane, Poinsett, George, Hannibal, carrying Tabitha's body, and Mercy, carrying the baby, followed them. The other five marines brought up the rear. The crowd parted to let them pass through. No one spoke a hostile word. But there was no friendship on a single face.

In five minutes they were on board the *Somers* in the Navy Yard. Hannibal carried Tabitha into Duane's cabin and the ship's doctor examined her. He reported her body was covered with bruises and welts. She had been savagely beaten. As far as he could tell, she had died of a hemorrhage during childbirth. He also examined the baby and found it to be a healthy girl. But she was badly in need of nourishment.

Poinsett said he would find a wet nurse to feed the child. "Are you still determined to take the dead wench back North with you?" he asked.

Hannibal nodded.

"We want to bury her at Great Rock Farm, where she was born—a free woman," George said.

Poinsett winced. "Slavery's a rotten business. But it's not my doing, Mr. Stapleton."

"I know that. I'm sorry," George said. "I never realized just how rotten it was."

"It's no one's doing," Poinsett said. "It started two hundred and eleven years ago in Virginia."

"I know that," George said.

"I inquired because she'll have to be embalmed. You'll need an undertaker. A casket."

"Thank you," George said. "I should thank you for everything you've tried to do. Your hospitality—"

"It was in Andrew Jackson's name." Poinsett struggled to regain a semblance of his usual urbanity. "I hope you'll tell him the situation here in South Carolina. You're more than qualified as an expert witness now."

THREE

WHILE GEORGE WAS CONFRONTING THIS NIGHTMARE in Charleston, Caroline was being bombarded with messages from John C. Calhoun and his wife in Washington, D.C. They were both extremely upset to learn that George had departed for South Carolina without conferring with them. Mrs. Calhoun seemed to consider it a personal affront. The vice president was more polite. He assured Caroline that he simply wished to be of service. George was on a delicate mission and Calhoun wanted to do everything in his power to help him succeed.

When George arrived home, ill from another stormy voyage, Caroline urged him to see the vice president immediately. "I will do no such thing!" George said. "That man is a menace to the Union. He's infected the entire state of South Carolina with nullification and secession. They're ready to start a civil war!"

He told her about the horror of the slave ship, the appalling conduct of Thomas Jefferson Glover, the slave trader. "I agree with everything you say," Caroline said. "But calm yourself and think about this as a politician. You asked the vice president for help and then ignored him. He deserves the consideration of a visit."

"Maybe," George said. "But it will be after I see the president."

The next day George reported to Andrew Jackson on what he had seen and heard in South Carolina. Old Hickory was in his second-floor White House office, enjoying an after-dinner smoke from one of his corncob pipes. The pipe was soon flung aside, the badly needed half hour of relaxation abandoned, as George told his story.

"I've heard some of this from Poinsett in muted tones," the president said. "If what you tell me is true, it may be time to bring the sword and some hemp into this argument."

"Hemp?" George said, not used to Jacksonian terminology.

"Hanging is the usual punishment for treason! We've got the chief traitor sitting day by day in the U.S. Senate, only a breath away from the presidency. A dose of hemp applied to his hypocritical neck would eliminate that threat— and send a message to his confederates in Charleston!"

"Mr. President, I hope it doesn't come to that."

"I hope not too," Jackson growled, the eruption subsiding. "But those people had better understand no one is going to nullify any bill that Andrew Jackson signs into law. As for my cowardly federal attorney in Charleston, I'm going to charge him with malfeasance in office for refusing to serve my subpoena."

"That slave trader will never spend a day in jail. No grand jury in South Carolina will indict him."

"Probably not. The case against him is weak. He's not responsible for your wench's death, strictly speaking. He may not even be responsible for kidnapping her. Only if we got him to Washington and forced him to tell us all he knows . . ."

The president let this unlikely possibility trail off. "Are you going to the dinner at the Indian Queen?"

"I haven't heard of it."

"On Jefferson's birthday, the Democrats of Washington are having a dinner, supposedly to assure everyone that perfect peace reigns in the party. Mr. Calhoun and his friends seem to be in charge of it. Now that I've heard what they're saying about me in South Carolina, I smell a rat."

"Would you have any objection to me telling the vice president what happened down there?"

"None at all. It may wake him up to the real consequences of his infernal ideas. The man lives too much in his brain. Such men are dangerous!"

Did Jackson know he was echoing Shakespeare's Julius Caesar? Probably not. But it left George more than a little uneasy as he left the White House. The next day, he met the vice president in his private office off the Senate chamber. As George told him his story, Calhoun grew more and more agitated. He broke in with violent expostulations. "These people are reducing nullification to the lowest, the worst possible denominator! I never dreamt of using it to justify the defiance of a federal subpoena."

When George got to the discovery of Tabitha's body and the newborn baby, the vice president's eyes filled with tears. "Dear God. Fate seems to have arranged for you to get the worst possible impression of South Carolina."

"I met a number of distinguished gentlemen. Many expressed moderate views. But others seem bent on total defiance of the federal government."

"I'll get to work immediately to damp this flame. I deeply appreciate your telling me this. Believe me, sir, I mean it with all my heart when I say that I have no desire to break up our Union. I love it to the depths of my soul. It was the joy of my youth and I hope it will be the consolation of my old age."

George was profoundly moved. "As I've told you, it's the linchpin of my political creed, Mr. Vice President."

"My hope is that the president will join me in a firm stand for the right of a state to defend itself against an unjust majority. That is all I mean by nullification. His assent is all we need to quiet South Carolina."

Having just heard Andrew Jackson threatening to hang this man for treason, George was so astonished, he did not know what to say. Could Calhoun
not know what the president was thinking? Were he and his followers living
in a dream world?

"As a man of the South, a native of South Carolina, I think he must submit
to us, if he venerates Thomas Jefferson a tenth as much as he claims to do,"
Calhoun continued. "We're going to put him to the test at the Jefferson Day
dinner."

There it was again, the vice president's assumption that Andrew Jackson,
the unlearned frontiersman, had to accept John C. Calhoun, the Yale graduate
and scholar of the Constitution, as the real leader of the Democratic Party.

"I hope you'll come and show us where New Jersey stands," Calhoun said.
"Don't let this painful difficulty with your servant throw you into Van Buren's
ranks."

"I . . . I hope to attend. Unless business takes me back to New Jersey."

At home, Caroline paced the floor, trying to help George decide what to
do about the Jefferson Day dinner. A conference with Sarah Polk had revealed
they too were in a quandary. Their dislike of John and Peggy Eaton had
hardened into detestation. They were equally disgusted with Peggy's oily ally
Secretary of State Martin Van Buren. But they were even more reluctant to
rally to the Calhoun side after Caroline told them what George had heard in
South Carolina—and in the White House.

"Perhaps mere congressmen need not give a toast," Caroline said.

"It's a rare opportunity to be noticed," Sarah said in her cool calculating
way.

When George left for New Jersey with Hannibal and Tabitha's body to
bury her on Great Rock Farm, Caroline sought advice from another quarter,
John Sladen in New Orleans. He replied with an analysis of the situation as
viewed from his adopted city and state. It was absolutely necessary to shift
the focus of the argument from the Union and nullification to the real source
of the quarrel: Martin Van Buren's slimy, slithering ambition and his readiness
to do anything to further it. Calhoun had to be persuaded that a personal
contest between him and Jackson would destroy him politically. *A senile Jackson, drooling baby talk, would carry Louisiana against Calhoun, even if the
vice president's intellect were expanded to equal the godhead,* John wrote.

Should George give a toast at the Jefferson Day dinner? Most emphatically,
John wrote. It should be aimed at Van Buren. Sladen had a suggestion: "To
the Union—of all honest men." It implied that hypocrisy and intrigue could
be as fatal to the Democratic Party as differences of principle.

George returned from New Jersey with a sad, subdued Hannibal. It had
been a difficult trip. Hannibal had requested the pastor of the Baptist church
in Middletown to officiate at the funeral on Great Rock Farm. The pastor
had turned the ceremony into an abolitionist rally, replete with violent denunciations of slavery and Southerners. Reporters had swarmed around the
grave, asking George's opinion. He had deplored the way the slave trade was
conducted in Washington, D.C., and said he was determined either to make
it scrupulously honest or ban it from the city—an opinion he was sure Andrew

Jackson shared. He stressed Jackson's sympathy and help in their attempt to rescue Tabitha. The statement was widely reported in New Jersey and New York papers and was picked up by the *Washington Globe,* which printed it without comment.

Hannibal's little daughter was thriving under the care of the female slave Mercy. She was no more than sixteen and came from a farm in Delaware. Hannibal decided to name the child Tabitha after her mother. He announced he wanted to learn the alphabet so he could read the Bible to his daughter and raise her as a Christian. Caroline said she would be delighted to teach him.

To Caroline's dismay and George's chagrin, the day after he returned, they were served with a lawsuit filed by a slave trader named Quinn on behalf of Thomas Jefferson Glover, demanding $400 for Mercy. Quinn had a receipt showing Glover had purchased her from him. Glover had statements from the captain of the *Fortunate Pilgrim* and other witnesses that George had abducted her by force. George was inclined to defy him and fight it out in court. He told James Polk and several other congressmen about it.

Two days later, Polk paid the Stapletons an after-supper visit. He had a message from President Jackson. Old Hickory did not think it was the right time to make a public issue of Tabitha's tragedy. It would be best if George paid a compromise price for Mercy and let the story sink into oblivion. Polk was candid about the president's reasons. "He can't afford to seem to pick a quarrel over slavery with Calhoun on the attack."

Caroline could see George was tempted to defy Polk and the president. "Let us think it over," she said. "George feels deeply about this."

Polk offered to conduct the negotiation with Quinn, who was at least as repulsive in his manners and appearance as Thomas Jefferson Glover. George thanked the Tennessean and he departed.

"I'm not going to do it," George said. "I don't care what anyone says, including the president."

"George, don't let emotion control you. You must never stop thinking, no matter how strongly you feel about something."

George did not realize he was hearing the essence of Caroline's creed, the words she lived by. Perhaps she herself did not realize it at this point. "I'm not sure I agree with that," George said.

Caroline became extremely agitated. "You have a part to play in this country. Possibly a great one. Don't throw it away over a minor matter."

"Is it minor? Does Tabitha's death mean that little to you?"

"It means a great deal to me personally. I mourn her as much as you. But in the grand scale of American politics, it *is* a minor matter. What will you gain by embarrassing the president and aligning yourself with the abolitionists? Do you want to be marked as one of them?"

"Of course not. They're as repulsive as the slave traders."

"If that's what you *think,* then you have no choice but to consent to the president's plan."

Her logic was irresistible. George slowly descended from his pillar of righteousness. "You have a point."

She sensed he might be ready to agree to something far more important.

"I've thought about the Jefferson Day dinner. I think you should offer a toast." She gave him John Sladen's suggestion, without mentioning its source.

"To the union of all honest men," George mused.

"No. To the *Union*—of all honest men. You should pause on the word *Union* just long enough to gather everyone's attention. Then add the close. If you're sitting near Mr. Van Buren—as I hope you will be—stare hard at him as you finish it. So everyone will have no doubt about what you mean."

"To the Union—of all honest men." George swept her against him. "I like it."

The next day, George told James Polk to offer Quinn two hundred dollars for Mercy. By nightfall the deal was struck and George told Mercy she would be a free woman as soon as he filed her manumission papers with the District court. Caroline hired Mercy as a nurse for little Tabitha and for thirteen-month-old Jonathan Stapleton, who was toddling around the house, threatening to destroy everything in his path. George spoiled him shamelessly, and Harriet, their cook, was no better. Only Caroline attempted to impose some discipline, often with the flat of her hand on his bottom. He never shed a tear. Instead, he confronted her with those defiant gray eyes, which often stirred anxiety—or was it guilt?—in her soul.

At last winter yielded to Washington's early spring. The streets turned to rivers of mud. Ladies lost their shoes in them and even men lost an occasional boot. The city buzzed with the anticipated excitement of the Jefferson Day dinner at the Indian Queen Hotel. Ladies were not invited, a policy that irked Caroline and Sarah Polk and several other congressional wives. Caroline and Sarah resolved to have supper in the hotel dining room and find a way to penetrate the ballroom, where the banquet was being served, when the speeches and toasts began.

The newspapers were thick with speculation over what the president would say about nullification and the Union. Columns of densely packed print pointed out he had repeatedly declared himself a states' rights man and deplored a federal government with the power to menace liberty. The pro-Calhoun papers seemed to be preaching sermons to the president, virtually telling him he had no choice but to submit to party doctrine. The *Globe,* on the other hand, denounced nullification as a gross violation of the great democratic principle of majority rule and reprinted editorials from other papers, not a few from the South, echoing this sentiment.

The great day, April 13, 1830, arrived in a burst of spring sunshine. George rehearsed his toast to Caroline's satisfaction a dozen times. Sarah Polk warmly approved it. But she had counseled James Polk to remain silent. He was launching a campaign to become Speaker of the House of Representatives. He could not afford to offend anyone in the party if he hoped to achieve this ambitious goal. Caroline asked Sarah if she would ask one of the managers of the banquet to seat George close to Martin Van Buren. With a devilish, un-Presbyterian smile, Sarah said she would try.

By now Caroline was eight months pregnant. But she did not allow that to deter her from witnessing this climactic event. Sarah Polk had done her utmost to find out what the president was going to say—and failed. Her best friend inside the White House, Emily Donelson, had gone home to Tennessee rather than serve as a hostess when Peggy Eaton came to dinner. That quarrel still bubbled and seethed beneath the surface of the political confrontation at the Indian Queen.

Sarah's diligence on another front had been rewarded. She discovered the ballroom of the Indian Queen Hotel was two stories high and had a number of boxes on the second floor that would overlook the banquet. The manager of the hotel had assured her it would be easy to arrange for them to occupy one of these vantage points when the verbal fireworks began.

At noon on the great day, Caroline was trying to decide which dress to wear when Josephine Parks knocked on her bedroom door. "Mr. Sladen is downstairs."

Caroline was stunned—and for a moment, embarrassed. Somehow she did not want him to see her carrying George's child. It was a primitive, instinctive reaction that she quickly brushed aside. She greeted him in the front parlor with a smile. "What a delightful surprise!"

"I thought it was simpler to come ahead than to write. There's been a special election to replace the congressman from the third district, who resigned and has since died of cancer. With some help from Senator Legrand, I've won the seat."

"Wonderful!"

Did she mean that? Did she want this man in Washington? Yes, the rational Caroline angrily told the side of her soul from which her primitive primary feelings rose. What better moment for John to come? Her ballooned shape virtually proclaimed her identity as Mrs. George Rensselaer Stapleton.

"Has Clothilde come with you?"

"No. She's pregnant too. Not in the best of health, I'm sorry to say. Whereas you look positively glorious. There must be some Indian blood in you. You look ready to give birth and hoe corn on the same day."

"Are you going to the great banquet tonight?"

"Senator Legrand says there's not a ticket left."

"You can come with Sarah Polk and me. We're planning to spy on these all-powerful males from a ballroom box."

So it was arranged. John joined them at the Indian Queen at 5 P.M. Did the huge painting of Pocahontas that hung over the hotel's front door remind him of their evening at the Bowery Theater? He did not mention it. Instead he entertained them with tales of Louisiana life—the opulent plantations on the rivers and bayous, New Orleans with its splendid opera house and theaters and the exotic women who lived on its back streets, the quadroons and octoroons who became the mistresses of the men who made millions on the Cotton Exchange. Sarah Polk claimed to be shocked, but she was as fascinated as Caroline.

As they finished supper in the dining room, the manager rushed to their table to report Senator Hayne of South Carolina had begun the night's first speech. They hurried upstairs to the box, which had a curtain on two sides that shielded them from the eyes of the diners on the floor below them. Caroline noticed shadowy faces in several other boxes. One of them, she was certain, was Peggy O'Neale Eaton.

Below them, the president sat at one end of the head table. Facing him at the other end was Vice President Calhoun. Between them ranged members of the cabinet, the master of ceremonies, and other notables. The rest of the diners sat at two parallel tables that met the head table, forming a large U. Over a hundred congressmen and senators were among the diners, as well as numerous high-ranking members of the army and navy and government civil servants.

George was sitting beside James Polk rather far from the head table. Caroline was pleased to see that Martin Van Buren was only a few places away from him. "They planned to seat Mr. Van Buren well below the salt anyway," Sarah whispered. Caroline was well aware that "they"—the banquet's managers—were all Calhoun men.

Senator Hayne's speech was a flowery eulogy of Jefferson and his firm belief in states' rights as the bulwark of American liberty. He closed with the first toast of the evening: "The *Union* of the states, and the *sovereignty* of the states." When he sat down to polite applause, the rest of the twenty-four formal toasts began. The first few were inarguable tributes to Jefferson, but the next speakers called on the party to abandon once and for all the high tariff that was supposedly bankrupting the South. The Pennsylvania congressional delegation rose in a body and left the room. Grim-faced, the succeeding speakers persisted in proclaiming the transcendence of states' rights. The closing toast saluted "the doctrine contended for by Senator Hayne against Senator Webster." In a word, nullification.

Tension seeped into the room as the waiters began clearing away the dessert dishes and the time for voluntary toasts arrived. Everyone knew the president would offer the first toast. Throughout the formal toasts, his face had remained expressionless. He drank to them with no visible enthusiasm, but he drank. Was Calhoun right? Caroline wondered. Was Jackson going to capitulate to this drumfire of Southern solidarity?

Finally, the master of ceremonies, a portly Virginian named John Roane, rose: "The President of the United States."

Jackson stood up. For a moment his eyes swept the room. Then they returned to the head table. Down its length he glared at John C. Calhoun. "Our federal union—*it must be preserved.*"

Jackson raised his glass, a signal that meant everyone was required to stand and drink with him. All eyes were on the vice president. Would he refuse to rise? No, he was on his feet. His hand trembled slightly and some of the amber wine spilled on it as he drank to those ominous words.

Everyone sank into their seats. John Roane stood and said, "The Vice President of the United States."

Calhoun rose. He did not glance at the audience. His gaze was fixed on Jackson. "The Union. Next to our liberties, most dear."

A low murmur circled the room. It was a superb reply to the president's stunning challenge. But Calhoun, ever the scholar/politician, could not leave it there. "May we all remember that it can only be preserved by respecting the rights of the states and distributing equally the benefits and the burdens of the Union."

Caroline heard John Sladen mutter, "No!" under his breath. Did she feel the same disappointment in her heart? Below them, the master of ceremonies called on the next personage in order of political importance: "The Secretary of State."

Martin Van Buren rose. He was wearing one of his creamy tan suits and a yellow vest. "Mutual forbearance and reciprocal concession. Through their agency the Union was established. The patriotic spirit from which they emanated will forever sustain it."

John Sladen whispered in Caroline's ear, "That means everything—and nothing. Machiavelli couldn't have said it better."

Toasts to the Union, the South, to the Founding Fathers, were lofted across the spacious room, which was decorated by two busts of Jefferson and a full portrait of Washington. Finally came the one for which Caroline and John Sladen and Sarah Polk had been impatiently waiting. "Congressman Stapleton of New Jersey," said the master of ceremonies.

George rose, his glass held high. His size made an instant impression on everyone. He paused, exactly as Caroline had rehearsed him, until all conversation ceased. His strong baritone rang out, "To the Union"—he gave Secretary of State Van Buren a stony stare—"of all honest men!"

The impact of these words on the Little Magician was nothing less than astounding. A gamut of emotions played across his usually imperturbable face: anger, shame, rage. The words had a very different effect on the rest of the company. A murmur of astonishment swept the room. Everywhere men turned to whisper to their neighbors. The banqueters rose to drink and the secretary of state remained seated, only struggling to his feet at the last moment. He glared at George Stapleton and gulped his wine as if it were a noxious poison.

In their box, John Sladen whispered to Caroline, "It worked! I knew it would work!"

"What are you talking about?"

"In this very room, twenty-eight years ago, Vice President Aaron Burr gave that same toast before he returned to New York to run for governor. Remember my telling you Martin Van Buren betrayed him in that race? We've reminded everyone with a shred of historical memory that Van Buren began his career with an act of treachery."

The room buzzed with excitement. Men dashed from one parallel table to another, telling friends the real significance of George's toast. Van Buren sat silent, glowering at George, who was beginning to look bewildered by the uproar he had stirred. Someone rushed to the head table and whispered in Vice President Calhoun's ear. A pleased smile broke across his hitherto grim face. He looked down the room in George's direction and raised his glass for a second toast to his sentiments, now that he understood their full relevance.

Caroline did not know whether to be pleased or appalled. Was it a good thing for George to associate himself with Aaron Burr, a politician who was ending his life a forlorn disgraced failure? And to arouse the violent enmity of Martin Van Buren, Andrew Jackson's favorite? It would all depend on what Old Hickory thought of it. She turned her eyes to the other end of the head table. The president's chair was empty.

F O U R

AS THE DINNER BROKE UP, MARTIN Van Buren scuttled into the night without saying a word to anyone. Southerners and Northern allies of John C. Calhoun rushed to shake George's hand. Spherical Congressman Dixon Lewis of Alabama, who reportedly weighed 420 pounds, whacked him on the back. "It was a hit, my dear young friend," Lewis chortled. "A veritable smash. He quailed, he caved. To think that old Burr, whom my father worshiped, could be resurrected to such effect."

George managed to smile through this and other effusions. He met Caroline and Sarah Polk and John Sladen in the lobby of the Indian Queen and expressed his surprise and pleasure at discovering John had returned to Washington as a congressman. Sarah Polk congratulated George on his toast. Her husband joined them and declared George had achieved instant fame in seven words.

"Julius Caesar did it in three," John said. "You've still got a ways to go, George."

"I'll get to work on it," George said, good-natured as usual.

It was a balmy night. The Polks said they would walk back to Gadsby's Hotel. John Sladen was staying at Senator Legrand's house, only a few blocks from the Indian Queen. George and Caroline rode home in their carriage alone.

George's voice came out of the darkness with a rather harsh edge. "What the hell are they all talking about? That toast—it's got something to do with Aaron Burr?"

Tell him the whole truth? No, it would be too dangerous. "Apparently the words somewhat resemble a toast Mr. Burr gave at a dinner here in Washington not long before he ran for governor of New York in 1804—a race in which Mr. Van Buren betrayed him."

"Did you know that?"

"Of course not. It was—a fortunate coincidence, don't you think?"

"I'm not so sure. I think I've made a rather formidable enemy."

"You didn't think Mr. Van Buren would be pleased by the words, even without the allusion to Burr, did you?"

"I thought they were vague enough to mean no one in particular. Wasn't that the idea?"

"George, it was the most talked about toast of the night, after the president's. You've established yourself as a man to watch."

"A man Van Buren is going to watch, that's for sure."

"Everyone is going to watch. I guarantee it."

The next day, Caroline asked Sarah Polk to make cautious inquiries into Andrew Jackson's reaction to George's toast. She implored John Sladen to persuade Senator Legrand to use his friendship with Old Hickory to protect George from the president's all too possible wrath.

Her fears proved to be groundless. A week later she received a flattering note from the president. In the absence of Emily Donelson, would she consent to be his hostess at a dinner the following Saturday at the White House? Mrs. Eaton would be among the guests.

Caroline sent her regrets, pleading her advanced pregnancy. This prompted a visit from Old Hickory the following day. He said he wanted to make sure she was well. He was reassured by her healthy complexion. "I can see you're going to present us with another Democratic voter," he said.

"What if it's a girl, General? Will you campaign for reelection on a platform of votes for women?" Caroline asked.

"If she's as beautiful as her mother, I might be foolish enough to try it. Seriously, are you and George among those who think these old bones should endure another term?"

"The country would be the better for it, I'm sure, General."

"Van Buren has been urging it on me," Jackson said in a musing way. "Which reminds me. I liked your husband's toast the other night. Did he like mine?"

"He adored it, General. The Union is his guiding star."

"So he told me. It's Van Buren's too. Assure him of that."

"I will, I promise you. But George regrets—he truly regrets—the differences between you and Mr. Calhoun."

"So do I. It's up to him to mend them. Otherwise, he'll end up like Mr. Burr. That was a very salient warning your husband sent him the other night."

Caroline smiled and nodded in agreement, managing to conceal her amazement. The president thought George had been reproaching Calhoun! It was a stunning example of how isolated a man can become in the White House. He hears only what his inner circle chooses to tell him. In Jackson's case, it was also an example of how totally Martin Van Buren had mesmerized him. Seated so far apart, Old Hickory had missed the Little Magician's visible chagrin.

Caroline rushed word of Old Hickory's visit to Sarah Polk, who came for tea and eagerly devoured the news. She was especially struck to hear that Van Buren was urging a second term on Jackson. "That will devastate Mr. Calhoun. No man can endure three terms as Vice President. They'll be making jokes about him. Always a bridesmaid, that sort of thing. The office is a nullity in the first place."

Martin Van Buren soon demonstrated he was capable of more than an intriguer's game in Washington, D.C. In successive weeks, the legislatures of New York, which he controlled, and Pennsylvania, which hated Mr. Calhoun for his opposition to the tariff, nominated Andrew Jackson for a second term. In a less conspicuous way, Van Buren went to work on George Stapleton. Editors of two more New Jersey papers began making hostile comments about the "aristocratic" congressman. One published outrageous lies about George and Caroline living in a palace in Washington. The second said he had a mistress in Charleston and had recently commandeered a navy ship to take him there for a visit.

These attacks might have become a serious matter. But George now had an ally in New Jersey who was ready to play politics as ruthlessly as Van Buren. Jeremy Biddle had become president of the newly opened Camden & Amboy Railroad. The Stapletons owned it almost entirely, having bought out the restless Colonel John Stevens, who was always looking for new fields of invention to conquer. The line was fabulously profitable from its first day of operation. Jeremy, who privately called the Democratic Party the Demagogue Party, put his loyalty to George above his political opinions.

In the matter of the two papers, Jeremy simply paid each a visit and asked the editor what he wanted to do: publish a correction of his slanders or face an opposition paper, which Jeremy, as George's spokesman, was prepared to launch the following week. The correction was in print the following day. The original Van Buren satellite paper, the *Newark Plebian,* was transformed by Jeremy's buying the enterprise from the stockholders at a price they could not refuse, firing the editor, and making it the official Stapleton organ for the state. The paper was soon telling its readers that Congressman Stapleton was the genius behind the Camden & Amboy. That proved he was a man of the people, eager to create hundreds of jobs for the citizens of New Jersey.

Meanwhile, in Washington, Caroline gave birth to another boy. He was a beautiful child, with a swatch of dark hair, dark eyes, and remarkably well-formed features. Unlike his brother, Jonathan, he was a placid baby, seldom crying, breaking into gurgles and smiles at the slightest provocation. George called him the love child, remembering their idyll at Kemble Manor.

Nevertheless, there was a wrangle over his name. George pushed for Malcolm after his uncle, but Caroline adamantly resisted until they reached a compromise. His middle name would be Charles, after her oldest brother, and Caroline reserved the right to use that name. She had no special affection for her brother. She would have called the child Lucifer before she used Malcolm. She had never forgiven him for his bitter lecture when George became a Democrat. George, satisfied that he had made a gesture of reconciliation to his uncle, agreed to the arrangement.

Beyond the nursery, the political giants continued their war. Martin Van Buren grew more and more confident of his influence over Andrew Jackson. He persuaded the president to veto a bill that provided federal funds for a road between Maysville and Lexington, Kentucky. Jackson added a message saying the administration opposed all such outlays unless they furthered interstate commerce. This doomed a dozen other roads and canals various states were attempting to build. Many noted it also enhanced the value of New York's Erie Canal, which was pouring undreamt-of riches into that state from the Midwest.

In the House, George Stapleton rose to criticize the Maysville Road veto. In phrases that came easily to his New Jerseyan lips, he said that behind it lurked New York's greed for money and power. He treated the House to a disquisition on how the city of New York had prevented the development of the New Jersey side of the Hudson by arguing for the last thirty years in a tangle of lawsuits that they owned the land servicing the river up to the low-water mark. They were aiming at a similar monopoly for the Erie Canal.

The speech played well in New Jersey and almost as well in the West and South. Caroline had helped George write it, with some clandestine assistance from John Sladen. A few days later, George received a summons from the White House. Old Hickory paced his office, puffing on one of his pipes.

"Why don't you like Mr. Van Buren?"

"I think he has the makings of a tyrant, General."

"Oh?" Jackson was amused. "That's what they're saying about me."

"He wants everyone to fall in line to make sure he's your successor."

"You think so?"

"It's my impression."

"Mr. Calhoun doesn't expect everyone to fall in line—including me?"

"Mr. Calhoun has his flaws, General. I freely admit them. But he's a man of honor. He doesn't stoop to intrigue."

"You're wrong. I thought so too, for the better part of the last twelve years. His conduct with Peggy Eaton changed my mind. Now I find him admitting—*admitting*—that he lied to me about his support of my conquest of Florida!"

From his desk Jackson snatched a letter that was almost as long as a book. In no less than thirty-two pages, John C. Calhoun angrily defended himself against "secret enemies" in the White House who were slandering him. The president had sent Calhoun the letter that his old enemy William Crawford had written, accusing him of the Florida perfidy. Calhoun had responded with this thinly veiled attack on Van Buren, and a haughty refusal to discuss the Florida accusation. That only convinced Jackson of his guilt.

George asked if he could take the letter home and read it. The president gave him his permission. George convened a meeting with Caroline, the Polks, and John Sladen to consider it. They were fascinated—and horrified. Sladen pronounced it a political disaster for Calhoun.

"Someone's got to persuade Calhoun to take a milder tone toward the president," James Polk said.

"Are you volunteering?" Caroline asked.

"I'm from Tennessee, remember? That makes me part of the conspiracy."

"It will have to be George," Sarah Polk said.

"I agree," Caroline said.

"I'm no diplomat," George protested.

"You'll become one before this is over," John Sladen said.

So George became a combination letter carrier and special pleader between these two intensely suspicious, angry men. Back and forth letters went, with George and John Sladen slowly persuading Calhoun to take a more temperate tone. Always George was conscious that they were boxing in the dark against Martin Van Buren. The Little Magician lurked behind the White House doors, skewing Old Hickory's reaction to Calhoun's wary approach to a reconciliation.

After two months of this clandestine diplomacy, John Sladen made a daring proposal to Calhoun. Why not publish the entire correspondence? Sladen pointed to numerous references to the vice president's secret enemy inside the

White House: "Everyone knows who you're talking about. It would strike Van Buren like a forty-pound shot."

The idea appealed to Calhoun. It combined a smashing blow at Van Buren with an implied criticism of Jackson, as his dupe. This aspect made George less than enthusiastic. "You couldn't publish it without the president's permission," he said. "His letters are clearly confidential."

"True. Can Andy's approval be obtained?" Calhoun said.

Again the "council of state," as George began to call the meetings with the Polks and Sladen, was convened at 3600 Pennsylvania Avenue. James Polk thought it would be dangerous to broach the topic directly to Andrew Jackson. He was likely to issue a thunderous no. "It might be better to have someone in the inner circle read it and recommend it."

"Who?"

"Eaton, perhaps. He's jealous of Van Buren's influence with Jackson. The Little Magician has all but shoved him aside. He might even suggest things that ought to be changed before Jackson sees the manuscript."

"Perfect. Will you talk to him?" George said.

"Let's both talk to him."

The next day Congressmen Stapleton and Polk visited John Henry Eaton in his opulently furnished house opposite the British legation on Pennsylvania Avenue. George thought the secretary of war was looking haggard. The conflict over his wife continued, and Peggy was not winning it. At dinner party after party, a half dozen, sometimes a dozen, empty seats testified to wives who chose to stay home rather than sit near Mrs. Eaton. George could imagine without much difficulty the tantrums Peggy was throwing in private.

George told Eaton about the exchange of letters. "I know about it," he said. "So does everyone else in Washington."

"Mr. Calhoun thinks publishing these letters would clear the air on both sides—and might expose a certain party to the sort of notice he deserves," Polk said.

"Would you read them and, if you find the manuscript meets with your approval, show them to the president?" George said.

Eaton's eyes remained opaque. He knew they were playing high-stakes poker. They were offering him a chance to undermine Van Buren and regain his role as Jackson's closest adviser. "I'll be glad to read them."

A day later, he summoned George to his house and gave him a dozen suggested changes—mostly deletions from the president's letters, and a few from Calhoun's. George noticed he did not delete any of the snide, thinly veiled references to Martin Van Buren. Calhoun readily agreed to the changes. Two days later, George returned with the corrected manuscript, set in type. Eaton glanced coolly at it and nodded in approval.

"Do you think you can show this to the president now?"

"I think so," Eaton growled. "Unless you hear from me, you can proceed."

Eaton's curt manner worried George. But he decided it was only the tension of the situation. He was risking the residue of his influence with Jackson, who might take a dim view of publishing the letters. A week passed without a word from the secretary of war. George told Calhoun he assumed they were free to proceed. Two days later, the letters appeared in a well-printed fifty-page octavo pamphlet entitled "Correspondence between Gen. Andrew Jackson and John C. Calhoun . . . on the subject of the course of the latter in the cabinet of Mr. Monroe, on the occurrences in the Seminole War." They were backed by a ferocious editorial in the *Washington Telegraph,* whose editor supported Calhoun, denouncing intrigue and backstairs throat-cutting in the Democratic Party.

The publication created a sensation throughout the country. Suddenly the rest of the United States discovered the clandestine struggle for power raging in Washington. Few people had any difficulty identifying Mr. Calhoun's unnamed enemy.

Two days after the pamphlet came out, George was summoned to the White House. He confronted an enraged president. "Now what do you think of your friend Calhoun?"

"What do you mean, General?"

"He's cut his own throat. He's published parts of my private letters without my consent!"

"But, General—"

"The man is dead. Cut yourself loose from his corpse, I urge you, my dear young friend. I know every young man tries to attach himself to a rising star. I was that way myself in my salad days. But the wise man should know when he's made a mistake!"

Never had George seen Andrew Jackson in such a passion. He reeled home to tell Caroline of the debacle. "What happened? How could he say he never saw the manuscript? Is he lying?"

"Of course not," she said. "Eaton double-crossed you. He never showed him the letters. It's his revenge against Calhoun—in Peggy's name. In fact, I would bet the price of this house, or the Eatons' house, that Peggy made him do it. Is there anyone in Washington she hates more than Vice President and Mrs. John C. Calhoun?"

There was no other answer. The Polks and John Sladen mournfully agreed with Caroline. George could only go to Calhoun and pass on the bitter news of Jackson's irreconcilable wrath. He found the vice president reading the *Washington Globe,* which thundered denunciations of him as a renegade Democrat who must be expelled from the party. George was amazed to find him smiling at this rain of abuse—and unfazed by the news of Jackson's reaction.

"Let the president rave and the *Globe* roar. The country is shouting my vindication." Calhoun pointed to a pile of letters on his desk. "They're arriving at the rate of fifty a day."

It was true. The nation as a whole and most of Washington, D.C., ignored the *Globe's* fulminations that Calhoun had committed an unforgivable sin by washing dirty political linen in public. Instead, most people were disgusted by Van Buren's role in dredging up a long-dead quarrel to push his presidential ambitions. No one rejoiced more vehemently over this eruption of disapproval than John Sladen.

In the next few months, Sladen became a virtual habitué of the Stapleton house. He constantly dropped by with the latest report on the secretary of state's accelerating political decline. He showed Caroline a letter from a Louisiana constituent who declared, "Van Buren is a gone dog. He is *done.*"

John gleefully reported that the Little Magician was no longer the man who never missed a party. He was spending more and more time alone in his big house on Pennsylvania Avenue. When he ventured out, he looked wan and spiritless.

Those months created a precarious happiness in Caroline's troubled soul. Three or four times a week, she saw love in John Sladen's somber eyes—and silently returned it. She began to believe this love could remain unspoken but real, while she struggled to sustain and express another kind of love with her husband. In that love the body acted and the tongue spoke affection. At first the double miracle seemed a possibility. But discord from a source she could not tolerate suddenly disrupted this probably impossible dream.

George began disagreeing with her and John Sladen about their passionate detestation of Martin Van Buren. George got this opinion from Jeremy Biddle, with whom he continued to correspond, in spite of Caroline's spasms of disapproval. As a distant spectator, Jeremy advised George to espouse a peacemaker's role, to give speeches in Congress deploring the lack of harmony in the party, urging everyone to compose their differences. Jeremy even wrote one speech for George (with some help from the new editor of the *Newark Plebian*), which George gave in the House to considerable effect.

John Sladen scorned this gesture and Caroline echoed him, which meant George had to endure some bedroom lectures. Buoying John's self-confidence and his prestige with Caroline was his elevation to John C. Calhoun's inner circle. Sladen dazzled the older man with the range of his reading and the vigor of his ideas, which included a wholehearted approval of nullification as a doctrine that the great Jefferson himself had sanctioned. Sladen and Calhoun were a well-matched pair: they both tended to find most of their political enthusiasms in their heads, ignoring the existence of primal emotions such as ambition, envy, and hatred.

One day, Sarah Polk was having tea with Caroline when John Sladen appeared with yet another rumor about the secretary of state. "He's told some of his friends in New York that he's going to resign. It's the only thing he can think of doing to win some public sympathy. Of course we'll do our best to make it an admission of guilt."

Caroline invited him to stay for a cup of tea. John shook his head. "Sam Swartout is in town, trying to persuade the president to consider him the new political leader of New York. He's got a hundred letters from prominent Democrats telling Old Hickory that Van Buren is beginning to stink up the party. Senator Legrand has arranged a meeting at the White House."

Sarah Polk waited until the front door slammed before speaking. "Mr. Sladen doesn't seem to have heard of an old political axiom: there's such a thing as killing a man too dead. He can come back to haunt you."

"What do you mean?"

"If Mr. Van Buren can convince the world that there's a vendetta against him, the people will switch their sympathy to his side of this business."

Caroline hesitated, unable to tell her closest friend how well she understood John Sladen. "You don't think Van Buren is a gone dog?" She had showed that picturesque Louisiana letter to Sarah.

"I don't think anyone who retains Andrew Jackson's backing is gone—until rigor mortis sets in."

That evening, Caroline and George were sitting on the second-floor porch, enjoying the cool twilight of mid-May, when Josephine Parks announced Congressman Sladen had returned. Caroline knew why he had come and sensed from his crestfallen expression that the news was not good.

"How did things go at the White House?" she asked.

"The president practically threw Sam Swartout out of the place. He told him he was loyal to the friends who were loyal to him, and at the top of that list sat Martin Van Buren."

"He's a very headstrong old man," Caroline said.

"*Pigheaded* is a better word," Sladen said.

"Johnny, I see no point in getting so involved in this quarrel," George said. "You're not from New York anymore. This means nothing in Louisiana."

"I think you're wrong, George. I've talked it over with the vice president. He agrees with me—this vile schemer Van Buren must be destroyed, one way or the other. Even if it involves teaching Andrew Jackson a lesson."

"I begin to think he's right," Caroline said.

"I think all three of you are wrong," George said. "Let Van Buren stew in his own juice. He may wind up a cooked goose and Jackson will have to get rid of him. If it doesn't go that way, we'll have to live with him."

"Live with a lying schemer? I disagree, George!" John said.

Caroline silently vowed to change her husband's wayward opinions. Little by little she was losing touch with the hard, cool intellect that had guided her choice of George Stapleton as a husband. She was drifting toward becoming John Sladen's advocate; yes, even his secret political partner. She was less and less able to see that John, forever searching for a replacement for his lost father, had found one in John C. Calhoun, a man whose intellect also ranged over the history of law and politics in search of axioms that justified his antagonisms. They would soon demonstrate the dangers of this mind-set in an act of *folie à deux*.

FIVE

CAROLINE READ THE MOST ASTONISHING NEWS of the year 1831 in the *Washington Globe:* "President Jackson's Cabinet Resigns." John Sladen's rumor had turned out to be true, up to a point. Martin Van Buren had resigned as secretary of state to escape the aura of shame and subterfuge that Vice President Calhoun's pamphlet had woven around him. But the resignation of the rest of the cabinet was a total shock.

George was at a meeting of the House committee that governed the District of Columbia. Two more kidnappings of free blacks had recently come to light, and the free Africans of the District had staged an angry demonstration in front of the federal marshals' headquarters. Hannibal had been among the leaders and had gotten himself arrested for punching a marshal.

Caroline rushed to consult Sarah Polk about the cabinet's dissolution. As usual, Sarah had an inside-the-White House version, thanks to James Polk's friendship with Andrew Jackson Donelson, Old Hickory's secretary. "Mr. Van Buren has demonstrated he's by no means out of the game," Sarah said. "He persuaded the president to see his resignation as an act of loyalty—and proved it by persuading John Henry Eaton to resign with him, removing Peggy from the battlefield. The Little Magician then advised the president to demand the resignation of the rest of the cabinet, especially the Calhoun men whose wives had snubbed dear Peggy."

"What will Mr. Van Buren do now?"

"He's about to become ambassador to the Court of St. James, the most prestigious gift in the president's power. Mr. Eaton and Peggy are going to become ambassador and ambassadress to Spain."

Sarah's wry tone made it clear that she was staying aloof from this latest contretemps. She had managed to steer James Polk through the Eaton imbroglio without losing the friendship of Martin Van Buren, John C. Calhoun, or Andrew Jackson. Caroline was forced to admire her shrewdness. But she remained enmeshed in John Sladen's passionate detestation of Van Buren and his fierce devotion to John C. Calhoun.

John was waiting for her in the parlor at 3600 Pennsylvania Avenue when she returned home. He was wrestling with little Jonathan, a sight that made her tremble. The sharply angled features, the gray eyes, the taut mouth, were so similar. She ordered herself to get used to it.

John leaped to his feet. "You've heard the news? We've driven the schemer out of the country! He's running three thousand miles for shelter."

"He's taken Eaton and Peggy with him. The president must be grateful for that."

"I wonder. I heard that the president visited Peggy to explain matters. She was extremely cold, almost insulting to him. If the old boy thought this latest Van Buren scheme was going to make her happy, he can't be too pleased by the result."

"Perhaps not."

"As a delicious bonus, Eaton will replace that pompous fraud Washington Irving as ambassador to Spain. There's a nice story making the rounds about the president's opinion of old Washy. When someone told him Irving was our most famous author, Old Hickory said he had never heard of him."

John paced the room, gesticulating as if he were making a speech to Congress. "We've got the Little Magician on the run. It's simply a matter of choosing the right moment to finish him off."

"Finish who off?" George Stapleton loomed in the doorway. Caroline flinched at the way his sheer physical presence overwhelmed John Sladen's slender frame. Behind George stood Hannibal. The big black had a livid purplish welt across his face.

"Hannibal, what happened to you?" Caroline asked.

"They whipped me bad in dat jail, missus."

"I paid his fine and got him out of there. His back is a mess," George said. "I've sent Mercy for our doctor." He told Hannibal to go upstairs and lie down until the doctor arrived.

After a suitable pause, John answered George's question. "We're talking about the dissolution of the cabinet, and the Little Magician's flight to London."

"I've heard a slightly different version," George said. "He's staying around and handpicking all the replacements."

"If the vice president plays the card I'm recommending," John said, "they'll all have to come crawling to him—the cabinet, the presumed ambassador, and the president."

"What card might that be?" George asked.

"I can't tell you yet. It will take some negotiations with several people."

John seized his hat and departed. It was not the first time Caroline noticed he was uncomfortable when George was at home.

George was irked by John's portentous secrecy. "He acts as if he's a member of Calhoun's cabinet."

"He is, in a way. The vice president's very fond of him."

For a moment, Caroline was unnerved by the antagonistic expression on George's face. She thought he was going to say, "So are you."

But George was thinking less dangerous thoughts. "I'm not at all sure that Calhoun's victory is as complete as he and his inner circle think it is. He's made an enemy of Andrew Jackson—no small matter."

"Aren't you pleased to see a schemer like Martin Van Buren driven out of the country? Have you forgotten the way he tried to bully you into joining his faction?"

George shrugged. "That was just a little political mud-wrestling. A man shouldn't take those things too personally."

"What about his use—or better, abuse—of Peggy Eaton?" Caroline said, growing more and more irritated at George's pose of superior wisdom.

"Less than admirable, I admit. But in retrospect, wouldn't it have been better for all concerned if Mrs. Calhoun had never mounted her high horse and started the whole thing—or John Calhoun had sat her down and told her to stop it the minute she started?"

"You don't think a woman has a right to her own opinion in such matters?"

"She can have an opinion. But in politics, people often have to swallow their opinions temporarily, sometimes permanently."

"That strikes me as cowardly—and demeaning."

"Not at all. A political party is like an army. If you read military history, you'd see what I mean. Before a battle, there may be a dozen different opinions about the best way to fight it, or whether to fight it at all. But once the commander in chief makes up his mind, every soldier in the army fights the battle the general's way no matter what he thinks of it."

"Cowardly—and demeaning! You leave women totally out of the equation with that comparison. I thought we'd come here as political partners!"

"Darling, calm down. We're just having a friendly discussion. I'm sharing a little of what I've concluded after three and a half years in Washington."

"It's neither friendly nor sharing. You're *informing* me that my opinions may or may not be important, depending on what you—or someone more powerful than you—thinks of them."

"They'll be important to me, but they may not be correct or timely or well informed."

"Let's end this discussion now! You've said far too much already."

George was baffled by the upheaval his candor had triggered. At dinner, Caroline barely spoke to him. In their bedroom, she flung herself under the covers and turned her back to him, making it clear that even a kiss would be unwelcome. She dimly realized she was acting irrationally. She could not see that the roots of her anger lay in George's cool disregard for John Sladen's elation—and his judgment on Floride Calhoun. In that woman's abrasive arrogance, she sensed the same discrete resentment at women's lot that so often surged in her own soul. They were spiritual sisters. She rejoiced—yes, *rejoiced*—at the turmoil Floride had caused in Washington with her decision to snub Peggy Eaton.

"I'll tell you what I begin to think," George said, his good nature deserting him as he undressed for bed. "This whole thing is a concerted plan by both Calhouns to humiliate and subjugate Andrew Jackson. It's been a grab for power on their part every bit as calculating as Martin Van Buren's. From what I've seen in the White House and South Carolina, it's going to explode in their faces."

George extinguished the oil lamp and they lay there in the darkness, two antagonistic political partners. Once more Caroline was assailed by her sense of George's physical bulk. It seemed to be a correlative of his disagreement. Whereas Sarah Polk's control of James Polk seemed not only plausible but possible—because of his modest size.

Say you're sorry. Tell him he may be right? The wisdom of ending this quarrel was all too apparent. She had entertained the same thoughts about the Calhouns as possibly devious plotters. But Caroline sensed if she turned and accepted George's good-night kiss, it would lead to another kiss and another kiss and the surge of desire, the submission and surrender that his lovemaking imposed on her. It would be an implied abandonment of her precarious claim to the leadership of their joint political venture. No, Caroline vowed. She would make him submit, no matter what it cost them in the dubious annals of marital happiness.

The quarrel continued while the principals in the drama went their separate ways, Mr. Van Buren to London to take up his duties at the Court of St. James, the Calhouns, the Polks, and John Sladen to their respective states until the next session of Congress began. The Stapletons went directly to Kemble Manor; Caroline was even more determined to avoid any contact with Jeremy and Sally Biddle.

As far as married love was concerned, a kind of truce was established. George was permitted to resume his husband's privileges, but on Caroline's terms, without any of the willed, willful surrender that had made the act so meaningful to them both. In her heart, her spirit, Caroline had withdrawn from George. She chose to live in those poetic caves of ice until George acknowledged his faults with a humble, even a humiliating, surrender.

From Louisiana and elsewhere came a stream of letters from John Sladen. He was traveling through the South and West, piecing together a coalition that would enable John C. Calhoun to play his final card against Martin Van Buren. When he revealed the nature of this card to Caroline, she was left breathless at its daring. It would, or could, be a blow that sent both Martin Van Buren and Andrew Jackson reeling. She did not so much as mention it to George. She was sure he would not approve of it. Moreover, he was a corollary to the plot: *As a Senator, George could be a major player in this drama,* Sladen wrote.

The term of New Jersey's senior senator, Henry Freylingheusen, would expire in 1832. Caroline pressed George to press Jeremy Biddle to press Uncle Malcolm to persuade Freylingheusen to retire and propose George as his replacement to the complaisant New Jersey legislature. Most of the legislators currently were Democrats, which made the proposition easier. No matter what their party affiliation, few lawmakers were inclined to differ with the powers that controlled the Camden & Amboy Railroad and the other components of the Stapletons' business empire.

Jeremy agreed with his best friend that four years in the House of Representatives was enough to qualify as a democratic obeisance to the common man. The Senate was where he belonged. He could speak for New Jersey with a far more effective voice when his vote was one of 48 senators rather than 260 congressmen. Malcolm Stapleton was invited for a weekend at Kemble Manor, where he beamed at his pseudo-namesake, Malcolm Charles, now five months old. Servants and George were instructed to call the baby Malky for forty-eight hours. Caroline could not have been more charming to her heretofore despised uncle-in-law.

All this subterfuge turned out to be superfluous. Malcolm, his fear of Andrew Jackson subsiding, had no objection to George becoming a Democratic senator. He thought the National Republicans, united behind candidate Henry Clay, had a good chance of defeating Old Hickory in the upcoming election. The Eaton scandal, the cabinet reshufflings, the feud with Calhoun, left Jackson's administration looking chaotic and mismanaged. That made it all the more important to secure George a political seat that would leave him invulnerable for the next six years. As usual among the Stapletons, blood was thicker than politics, money, and almost everything else.

Jeremy was the only sufferer from this intrigue. Sally insisted on blaming him for its success, and a frost that sometimes approached the Ice Age descended on their bedroom. Matters in that arena had never entirely recovered from the foolish confession Jeremy had made after the birth of Jonathan Hugh Stapleton.

Shortly after George's elevation to the Senate was assured, the nation's newspapers reverberated with the story of a slave rebellion in Virginia. A self-appointed black preacher named Nat Turner had organized an African army that killed fifty-seven white men, women, and children before being dispersed by hastily summoned local militia companies.

John Sladen's previous letter had left him in Virginia, en route to South

Carolina to see Vice President Calhoun. Caroline spent several restless nights wondering if he had been caught in Nat Turner's violent path. A letter from Charleston relieved her of this fear. But it added new urgency to what they now called "the plan."

> *I missed Nat Turner and his warriors by only twenty-four hours. If I had started a day earlier, I might have been one of his disemboweled, decapitated victims. I rode along his path of would-be conquest as the dead were being mourned and heard firsthand descriptions of his butcheries from the anguished survivors. If I ever had any lingering fondness for abolitionists, this has ended it forever. The event has thrown South Carolina into a special frenzy. The governor has issued a proclamation, declaring a state of emergency because of the supposed influence of abolitionists on the slaves of this state. They are accused of smuggling in revolution along with religion. The Vice President thinks the governor is a bit hysterical. But it would be foolish to underestimate the influence of this event on the minds and hearts of everyone here. Too many have found another even more visceral reason to use the Vice President's program of peaceful nullification as a step to secession. It makes all the more vital the success of our plan. Only the reassurance of seeing John C. Calhoun in the White House can preserve the Union here.*

Back in Washington for the next session of Congress, George took his seat in the Senate. The Polks and other friends applauded his ascent. No one was more enthusiastic than John Sladen. He and his father-in-law, Senator Legrand, gave a private dinner for George and Caroline at the Indian Queen Hotel. Prominent among the smiling guests were Samuel Swartout, Collector of the Port of New York, and Vice President and Mrs. Calhoun. All this acclamation did not please George nearly as much as a scrawled note from the White House that read: *My dear young senator: New Jersey has chosen wisely and well. Come see me one of these days. Andrew Jackson.*

Sarah Polk congratulated Caroline privately, after persuading her to confess that the move was mostly her doing. "My only regret is the loss of a valuable ally in James's hopes to become the Speaker of the House," Sarah said.

Caroline assured her that George's position would make his leadership of New Jersey's House delegation all the more complete. They would back James Polk to a man. For a moment Caroline was tempted to tell Sarah the real reason for her sudden decision to make George a senator at this early date. But she feared Sarah would disapprove of John Sladen's plan to drive a stake through Martin Van Buren's heart.

John had returned to Washington without Clothilde. She was pregnant again. Their first child had only lived a month. He soon learned to visit Caroline when George was in the Senate. Together they plotted to draw Senator Stapleton into the plan. Once more, Caroline felt the thrill of power that had seduced her into George Stapleton's arms. Now it was being created by John Sladen, no longer the pitiful outcast from New York's lower depths.

She confessed her quarrel with George, and they decided it would be best to let John propose the idea to him. Caroline would provide reinforcements, when and if they were necessary. A few days later, George told Caroline he would not be home for supper. "Johnny Sladen has something very important to discuss with me. What could that be?"

"I have no idea. All he ever talks about to me are his worries over Clothilde's health."

Caroline spent the evening teaching little Jonathan his numbers. At two and a half, the boy seemed to have an uncommon interest in learning. He often sat with a book in his hand, pretending to read it. George called him "the scholar."

At about nine o'clock, George appeared in the nursery doorway. "Poppa!" Jonathan cried, running to him. George patted him on the head. "John Sladen—or better, Calhoun—wants the Senate to refuse to confirm Van Buren's nomination as ambassador to London. They want me to vote with them."

"What a brilliant idea," Caroline said. "It will totally humiliate the schemer. Make him a national laughingstock. He'll never be able to run for political office again."

"Maybe," George said, lifting Jonathan high over his head. He set the boy down and stared stonily at Caroline. "But it's also a terrific affront to the president."

"So? No one made him appoint Mr. Van Buren ambassador. He consulted no one. He's treated him as a favorite too long. Maybe it's time he was told what people think of their . . . almost unnatural relationship."

George strolled over to Malcolm Charles Stapleton's crib and picked him up for a ride over his head. Charlie gurgled with glee. "I told Sladen I couldn't do it. I couldn't do that to Andrew Jackson."

"George! This is more of that style of thinking, of philosophizing, that I've found so offensive. You make a decision like that without even consulting me. Without giving me a chance to consider it. Even on this short notice, I think you're throwing away a chance to side with the man who'll decide the future of this country for the next two decades—John C. Calhoun. Don't you see that this will make him a bigger man than any other politician in sight, including Andrew Jackson?"

"Maybe, but I don't see how all the discussion in the world can alter what I promised Andrew Jackson when I shook his hand at the Hermitage. I joined the Democratic Party under his leadership. Even if I don't agree with his leadership at all points, I can't see how I can repudiate him before the whole country."

"Well, I can. I can not only see you doing it, I can't see you *not* doing it—if you want my . . . my companionship."

Little Jonathan was looking more and more bewildered. Charlie, ordinarily the most cheerful of babies, was starting to whimper. The nursery was charged with nerve-jangling negative vibrations.

"Let's go downstairs," George said. "No point in upsetting these children."

Even before they reached the front parlor, Caroline realized she had gone much too far toward revealing herself as John Sladen's secret confederate.

"Husband," she said, kissing George on the cheek, "forgive me. I shouldn't be so short-tempered. This idea is so extraordinary, so daring, it struck me—it still strikes me—as exactly the sort of thing that I've always imagined you doing. Rather like your toast at the Jefferson dinner—demonstrating your independence, your leadership qualities."

"I seem to be more led than leading. Johnny Sladen is rounding me up like he's cajoled a dozen other senators."

"Most of them are probably Southerners and Westerners. Wouldn't it be a coup to be known as John Calhoun's spokesman in the Middle States? To have all Van Buren's former toadies from New York coming to you to see how they can ingratiate themselves with the Democratic Party's new leader?"

"It might be flattering, if it ever happened. But my conscience would still bother me. That old man in the White House has never done anything to me that warrants such a flagrant desertion."

"There you go again with your military metaphors!" Caroline had never dreamt George would be so stubborn. She had virtually guaranteed John Sladen that his vote was as good as counted. They went to bed antagonists and remained in opposition for the next week, while the Calhoun forces put pressure on waverers to gather enough votes to execute their coup.

One morning, John Sladen appeared in Caroline's parlor looking weary. "We're one vote short of a deadlock," he said. "Is George still in the ranks behind General Jackson?"

"I'll try again tonight," Caroline said. "But it begins to look hopeless."

"I knew he was a bit dim, but this transcends stupidity. It's idiocy. Van Buren will never display the slightest gratitude toward him. It's foreign to his nature."

"*I* know that, but now that he's a senator, he feels rather invulnerable to Mr. Van Buren and everyone else, except General Jackson."

"Have you told him what's really at stake? The future of the Union?"

"I'm afraid he thinks that issue is safe in the hands of General Jackson."

"It's the arrogance of the aristocrat combined with the stupidity of the democrat."

"That's enough, John!"

Suddenly they were facing each other, not as clandestine political partners, but as former lovers. "I'm attempting to continue loving my husband, in spite of these differences. Don't make it more difficult for me."

"I'm sorry."

Caroline turned her back on John to stare at a painting of Kemble Manor. The red bricks glowed in August sunshine. Wild white roses ascended the north wall. George had commissioned the painting at the end of their idyllic summer, two years ago.

When Caroline turned again, the parlor was empty. As empty as her heart, she thought. She flung herself on the couch and wept bitterly for an hour.

That night at dinner, she again asked George to change his mind. "I saw Floride Calhoun today," she lied. "She told me what people in South Carolina are saying since Nat Turner's revolt. More and more of them have begun to think secession, closing their borders, is their only salvation. Only one man can reason with them—John C. Calhoun. Don't you think that's another reason to give him your support?"

"I do support him, I will support him, in any and every reasonable gesture we can make to South Carolina," George said. "I'm in favor of lowering the tariff, of banning abolitionist literature from the mails if they insist on preaching violence. But I don't feel my support should include humiliating Andrew Jackson."

Caroline's forehead began to throb. A steel ratchet seemed to be plunging back and forth in her head, cutting through flesh and bone with exquisite savagery. "Cowardly. There is no other word for it. Cowardly."

"Caroline, I must ask you, as your husband, to retract that word."

"I won't. I can't."

She flung her napkin on the table and fled upstairs. She lay on their bed, the ratchet sawing through her skull, the pain becoming more and more intense. Somehow she welcomed it. In a bizarre way, it was a satisfactory exchange for the right to call her husband a coward. She lay there, almost encouraging the pain, as George ascended the stairs and took a suit from his closet without saying a word to her. Ten minutes later he descended the stairs and went out. He did not return home until after midnight. He ascended the stairs and slept in a guest bedroom down the hall. All that time the ratchet grooved pain into Caroline's being. She was encountering her first migraine headache.

For the next five days, she and George did not speak. Caroline spent most of the time in her bedroom in silent agony. Sarah Polk visited her and recommended a gray-haired physician named Boileau, who had treated Thomas Jefferson for the complaint. He gave Caroline chloral hydrate for the pain but told her a doctor could otherwise do little except recommend the avoidance of worry and irritation. "When I told that to Mr. Jefferson, he was president. It amused him greatly," the old man said.

By now it was the third week in January, 1832. On the night of the twenty-fifth, the Senate sat late, debating the possibility of lowering the tariff to satisfy the demands of the South. Then the galleries were cleared and the solons went into executive session to consider Martin Van Buren's nomination to the Court of St. James. The followers of Henry Clay, already an announced candidate for president, denounced the Little Magician as a tool of British interests. Several Southern senators attacked him as a backstabber and marplotter, a source of party discord, making explicit the accusations Calhoun had implied in his pamphlet. George Stapleton remained silent. Finally, Senator Hayne of South Carolina made a motion to reject the nomination.

At this point, Senator Daniel Webster left the chamber. John Sladen had negotiated this arrangement. The Massachusetts orator did not want to admit publicly that he was collaborating with his foes from South Carolina. He and Henry Clay's main interest was not the destruction of Van Buren but the humiliation of President Andrew Jackson.

Without Webster, the vote to reject ended in a tie. From the start, this had been the goal of the planners. Vice President John C. Calhoun, a delighted smile on his face, cast the deciding vote—annihilating Martin Van Buren as ambassador to Great Britain. Calhoun was so pleased, he descended from the dais to shake hands with the senators who had joined him. "It will kill him dead, sir, kill him dead," he said. "He will never even kick, sir. No, he will never even kick."

Beside George sat Thomas Hart Benton, the flamboyant senator from Missouri. A slab of a man, at least as big as George, they had struck up a preliminary friendship based on Benton's remark that they "outweigh all the rest of these pantywaists put together." Benton and George had voted for Van Buren. Now the big Missourian scowled at the chortling Calhoun and turned to a diminutive senator from Alabama named Gabriel Moore. With a wink to George, Benton said, "You fellows have broken a minister—and elected a vice president."

"Good God!" gasped Moore. "Why didn't you tell me that before I voted?"

That same night, the Polks were guests at the White House. Old Hickory was in excellent health and spirits. He charmed the ladies as usual by sitting among them, exchanging witticisms. After dinner, he led the company into the Red Room, which was hung in vivid damask that more than justified its name. He sat down before the fire and insisted that Sarah take the place of honor on his right. As they began exchanging gossip about Tennessee births and marriages, into the room strolled Senators Benton and Stapleton.

The president welcomed them with a hearty hello. Benton acknowledged the salute and stooped to whisper the news of Van Buren's rejection in Jackson's ear. The old warrior sprang from his chair, his whole frame, from his legs to his erect white hair, quivering with wrath. "By the eternal!" he roared. "I'll smash them!"

S I X

T HE NEXT DAY, WHEN S ARAH P OLK reported this scene to Caroline Stapleton, she burst into tears. Sarah was more than a little puzzled. "My dear friend, what's wrong? George voted for Mr. Van Buren. The president showered him with compliments for his loyalty. He told everyone Senator Stapleton had good and sufficient reasons to vote nay—Mr. Van Buren's conduct toward him had been less than friendly—but his devotion to the Democratic Party had lifted him above revenge. Didn't George tell you all this?"

"George and I disagreed, disagreed strongly about this matter."

"You wanted him to vote the other way, with the vice president?"

Caroline nodded.

Sarah studied Caroline's melancholy face. "My dear friend, my dearest friend, may I speak frankly to you?"

"Of course."

"I've been playing this difficult game a little bit longer than you. James and I have run into similar problems. We've finally worked out a rule. I have the right to state my opinions with all the enthusiasm and logic I can muster. But the final decision rests with him. Men are peculiar beings. I think it comes from having to take orders from their mothers growing up. If a wife insists on having her way too often, she can stir up the fear that they're being reduced to boys in diapers again."

A force, a need, propelled Caroline out of her chair onto the couch beside Sarah. She flung her arms around her. "Your affection means so much to me."

"Believe me, that feeling is more than reciprocated," Sarah said.

For a moment they clung together, stunned, almost frightened by the intensity of their emotions. Caroline retreated to the other end of the couch and struggled for self-control. "Do you think General Jackson can do it?"

"Smash them? We'll soon see." Sarah held up a copy of the *Washington Globe*. "Here's the first salvo. A call for a national convention to repudiate the insult to the president by nominating Mr. Van Buren as vice president."

"A national convention," Caroline said. This was a new idea. Previously, presidents and vice presidents had been nominated by a party caucus in Congress.

"It's General Jackson's idea, I gather. A kind of marshaling of the troops."

That evening when George returned from the Senate, Caroline was awaiting him in the parlor. She had her tea table set with a half dozen sweetmeats and cheese tidbits that she knew he liked. Above the fireplace swung a flagon of hot toddy to banish the January chill. "My dreadful headache—maybe I should call it *our* headache—is gone. I want to hear all about the famous vote."

She sprang up and kissed him. George returned the embrace with more than ordinary fervor. It was pleasing to see how eager he was to accept a truce. They sipped toddy and talked politics for an hour; George gave her fascinating quotations from the scurrilous things pro-Calhoun senators had said about Martin Van Buren in their speeches—and the vice president's exultant comments at the final vote.

"Do you think Van Buren's dead beyond kicking?"

"Far from it. The president's reaction has changed the whole argument. Now Andrew Jackson's the issue. He's going to make Van Buren vice president at this convention—and obliterate John C. Calhoun."

The next day a somber John Sladen sat in Caroline's parlor, where George had sat the night before, telling her much the same thing—and adding a denouement that both thrilled and chilled Caroline's blood.

"If Jackson goes through with this and drives John C. Calhoun out of the Democratic Party, it will be the beginning of a national tragedy. South Carolina will regard it as an insult—and act accordingly."

Last night, Caroline had attempted to complete her reconciliation with George in their bedroom. But she had found herself unable to command the surrender, to summon the sweetness that his lovemaking had hitherto stirred in her flesh. Now she understood why, facing John Sladen in the parlor filled with gray January light. Snow scratched at the windows. Was a kind of winter taking root in her soul?

On John's gaunt face lay the patina of defeat that had stirred pity in the past. She had banned that vagrant emotion from her soul in the name of marital fidelity. It was barred from the icy caverns where the underground river ran down to the sunless sea. She crouched in one of these caves, a spectator watching herself perform the rituals of secret partnership with this man, silently begging him to understand that she had no other choice, this was the best she could do.

"You think they might actually secede? Start a civil war?"

"I do. Unless Jackson surrenders on the tariff. He has to give Calhoun something to show his people."

Again, Caroline saw the unrealism in those words. Andrew Jackson had never surrendered anything in his life. Yet she could not bring herself to speak as bluntly to John Sladen as she had spoken to George Stapleton.

Pity? Or a secret wish to see some sort of upheaval that would enable her to triumph over George with a livid *I told you so?* The more she thought about it, the more Caroline preferred the second answer.

Over the next three months, the nation's newspapers churned out a semi-verdict on the Van Buren rejection. The country seemed to agree that the Little Magician was no longer the issue. The president had been insulted, his leadership of the Democratic Party challenged. The defunct ambassador shrewdly said nothing. He did not even return home from England. Instead, he toured the Continent for his "health," a hint that he was suffering sympathy-winning pangs from Calhoun's attempted deathblow. Meanwhile, the president-as-general summoned his loyal Democratic troops to Baltimore for the nation's first national political convention.

Delegations were elected by state conventions or by state legislatures. In New Jersey, Senator George Stapleton had no difficulty handpicking his contingent, with some assistance from Jeremy Biddle. There were representatives from every state except Missouri; Senator Thomas Hart Benton, who embodied the Democratic Party in that state, apparently felt a convention impinged on his independence.

Caroline and Sarah Polk stayed in Washington, D.C., while their spouses mustered in Baltimore. Caroline did not receive a line from George, but James Polk sent Sarah a full report of each day's proceedings. It was apparent from the first day that Jackson's iron hand was in control, even though he never stirred from the White House. The delegates resolved that a two-thirds majority would be required to win a nomination. The president wanted to reinforce the image of massive support for him and his chosen vice president.

Two days later, before James Polk's letter arrived with the intimate details of minor backstage maneuvering, the *Washington Globe* triumphantly reported the results: on the first ballot, Martin Van Buren had received 209 out of 344 votes for vice president. A second ballot, in response to a resolution from the floor, made the choice unanimous. The convention also approved a letter to the nominee, which stated, among other things, that his election would be "a just and certain reparation" for his "wounded feelings" as well as "an ample retribution for the injury meditated against President Jackson."

Almost as an afterthought, the delegates unanimously concurred with numerous state legislatures that had already nominated Old Hickory for another four years in the White House.

George Stapleton and James Polk returned hailing the convention as a brilliant political idea. Neither had any enthusiasm for Martin Van Buren, but he was now a fact of their political lives, the man most likely to succeed Andrew Jackson. He had the votes of New York State's ever-swelling numbers behind him—and Old Hickory's certain endorsement, if he lived to deliver it.

"Not a word was spoken on behalf of our current vice president?" Caroline said.

"His name was never so much as mentioned," George said with a complacency that made Caroline wonder if John Sladen's remarks about aristocratic arrogance and democratic stupidity were not entirely misplaced.

"I fear his name may be mentioned elsewhere before long in ways that disturb our tranquillity," Caroline said.

George and James Polk airily dismissed this prophecy. "The president has told me he plans to submit a new tariff with rates that will satisfy every reasonable man in South Carolina," Polk said.

Caroline sought Sarah Polk's eyes to see if she shared her growing skepticism about reasonable men. But Sarah's Tennessee loyalty to Andrew Jackson, and her devotion to James Polk, left her unable to doubt the reasonableness of the great American electorate. More and more, Caroline found herself wishing, yes, wanting to see further proof of her growing conviction that men were no more reasonable than women in matters political.

Over the next months, John Sladen became Caroline's prophet of unreason. He had gone to Baltimore with his father-in-law, Senator Legrand, and tried to rally an alternative candidate to Martin Van Buren. For a while they had conjured some support for Virginia's governor, Francis Barbour, but it was only a brief illusion. Now John watched Vice President Calhoun stalk the streets of Washington, a man without a party. His head was defiantly erect, yet each day in the Senate he was forced to face row upon row of men who had repudiated him in Baltimore.

John Sladen was obsessed with the similarity to the fate of Aaron Burr. He too had been refused renomination as vice president by President Thomas Jefferson and had reeled from that blow to political oblivion. John believed it was imperative for Calhoun to learn from Burr's mistakes. "I've warned him he must at all events keep the loyalty and support of South Carolina," John told Caroline in one of his morning visits.

Why? Caroline silently asked. Wouldn't it be better for Calhoun to go to Andrew Jackson and make peace with him? But that would violate another great masculine principle. A man must never admit he made a mistake. Caroline pretended to agree with John's anguished analysis of the situation. But she saw his obsession with Burr was no more rational than George's devotion to Andrew Jackson. She also saw that by embracing the hotheads in his native state, Calhoun would ruin himself as a national figure and trigger a confrontation with Andrew Jackson. She convinced herself she did not care. She only wanted one thing: to hurl *I told you so* at George Stapleton.

Over the next troubled months, the politicians concocted a chaos that transcended Caroline's secret hopes. President Jackson's new secretary of the treasury sent a revised tariff up to Congress. It called for significant reductions of many items on South Carolina's complaint list. But Calhoun's chief lieutenant in the Senate, Senator Robert Young Hayne, pronounced the revision as no better than the Tariff of Abominations that Martin Van Buren had perpetrated in 1828.

Hayne's rejection implied that Van Buren, back from Europe and once more a frequent visitor to the White House, was using a reduced dosage to destroy John C. Calhoun and South Carolina on a slower schedule. They found food for further suspicion when John Quincy Adams, who had returned to Washington as a congressman from Massachusetts, backed Jackson's bill. The image of the president as a dotard manipulated by the scheming Little Magician, who would cut a deal with Satan (aka Adams) himself, took on further substance.

George fretted over the South's reaction and tried to persuade some of his fellow senators to support a further reduction in the tariff. He was buffeted with letters from Jeremy Biddle, urging him to do nothing of the sort. Caroline secretly enjoyed this exposure of Jeremy's conservative bias. In the House of Representatives, meanwhile, John Sladen led a ferocious campaign for an absolute end of the tariff and an endorsement of free trade. This put him at odds with James Polk, who was defending Jackson's bill against all comers. Presidential candidate Senator Henry Clay pushed a tariff bill of his own, which jacked the rates to astronomical heights, hoping to unite the West and the Northeast in a revival of his American System. This further convinced the Calhoun men that they were a beleaguered band, without friends anywhere.

What a marvelous mess, Caroline thought. Best of all, there was another boiling issue that distracted George, Andrew Jackson, and everyone else from finding time to become reasonable about the tariff: the Bank of the United States. This entity was in charge of guaranteeing a reliable currency for the nation. To perform this crucial task, it utilized the entire revenue of the U.S. government, which was deposited in its vaults. From its doors this river of cash flowed to branch offices in every state, which loaned the money at reasonable rates to carefully supervised state-chartered banks, who in turn loaned it to businessmen and farmers. For the previous dozen years, the BUS, as it was called, had been in the capable hands of Jeremy Biddle's uncle, Nicholas Biddle. BUS-backed loans had helped build Principia Mills, the Delaware and Raritan Canal, and the Camden & Amboy Railroad.

Andrew Jackson had a frontiersman's dislike of banks because of their habit of calling in overdue loans on the farms and crops of his friends. He reserved a special animosity for the Bank of the United States because it was a direct descendant of the institution created by Alexander Hamilton, modeled much too blatantly on the Bank of England. All this smacked of the old Federalist elite whom Thomas Jefferson had defeated in 1800 and Jackson had finally and totally routed in 1828 with his fulminations against aristocrats. The fact that numerous lawyers who were also congressmen and senators, notably Daniel Webster, were paid fat fees by the bank in its ordinary operations only intensified Old Hickory's suspicions that the BUS was an enemy of the people.

Nevertheless, thanks to the distractions of Peggy Eaton and the feud with Calhoun, the bank might have slumbered like a dormant volcano into the president's second term if Henry Clay, casting about for an issue to challenge Jackson, had not persuaded Nicholas Biddle to ask for the bank to be rechartered in 1832. Biddle was a Clay man to his bones, a fervent believer in the American System. He was arrogantly confident, thanks to the number of congressmen on his payroll, that he could have his way—and humiliate Andrew Jackson in the bargain.

Here was an argument that was made to order for fanaticism on all sides. Caroline could scarcely conceal her delight at how confused George became as he wrestled with entreaties from his uncle Malcolm Stapleton and his best friend, Jeremy Biddle, to defend the BUS and with trumpet calls from Andrew Jackson and James Polk to destroy it. In the House of Representatives, James Polk led a feverish Jackson-driven crusade against recharter, while John Sladen and other Calhoun men rallied to the side of the bank, on the principle that it was their sworn duty to oppose whatever Andrew Jackson wanted. The corrupt hand of Martin Van Buren was perceived as another reason to defend the BUS. If it was destroyed, the nation's financial control would pass to the ever more powerful banks of New York, who were all the Little Magician's clients or vice versa.

Day and night the oratory raged. At White House dinners, the president looked exhausted, his cough sounded more and more alarming, his step seemed feeble. When Caroline expressed her concern, he took her arm and said, "Don't fret your pretty head about me, child. The bank is trying to kill me. But I assure you, I will kill it instead."

A few days later, at tea with Sarah Polk, Caroline saw similar traces of exhaustion on her usually serene face. "Is something worrying you?" Caroline asked.

"James has had a terrible attack of stomach and bowel complaints. It's always a sign that he's overworking. But I can't ask him to rest. So much depends on this struggle against the BUS. The Calhoun men have a clear majority on the committee. They're going to recommend recharter. James is working day and night on a minority report. He can't bear the thought of failing General Jackson."

"What about the tariff? I haven't heard anyone mention it in a month."

"The tariff?" Sarah said dazedly. "Who cares about that, now?"

Caroline asked John Sladen the same question and got almost the same answer. George was equally hazy about the subject that had absorbed him two months ago. He was in an agony of indecision about how to vote on the bill to recharter the BUS. To vote against it seemed to be a desecration of the Stapleton manes. His grandfather had played a major role in the founding of Hamilton's BUS. When it was rechartered in 1816, Hugh Stapleton had been the floor leader in the Senate, the man who pushed it through. Letters were cascading in from business leaders in New Jersey, urging his support. He asked Caroline what she thought he should do.

"Isn't it the first principle of your existence never to disobey President Jackson?" she asked.

George looked hangdog. It was a clear hit. He went off to his study to meditate on his mail. The great bank debate churned on, with the forces of Biddle and Clay, supplemented by Calhoun volunteers, clearly in control. Both the House and the Senate reported bills with substantial majorities in favor of recharter.

George sided with the majority, after a trip to the White House to explain to the president. Old Hickory told him if he were in George's ancestral shoes, he would probably vote the same way. "Don't lose any sleep over it, my young friend," Jackson said, his mouth a grim line in his furrowed face. "I have the means to destroy the monster right here on my desk."

"What would that be, General?" asked George.

Old Hickory picked up a pen, dipped it in an inkwell, and wrote four letters on a piece of foolscap: *V E T O.* He gave George the paper as a souvenir.

George returned to Caroline in something close to consternation. He showed her his souvenir but forbade her to show it to anyone. The next morning, she displayed it to a wide-eyed Sarah Polk. "This will raise a storm," Sarah said. "Possibly a hurricane."

Later in the day, John Sladen paid Caroline one of his political visits. He told her that the House had passed the BUS recharter bill and the Senate was expected to follow suit later in the day. He was in the midst of gloating over Jackson's humiliation when Caroline silently presented him with George's souvenir.

Never had she seen John so flabbergasted. In the icy cavern beside her soul's sunless sea, Caroline rejoiced. She told herself she wanted to witness the humiliation of all these males who purported to consult her, when not one of them, not even this man, placed any real value on her advice.

"It's never been done," Sladen said. "No president has ever vetoed an act of Congress unless he thought it was unconstitutional. But the Supreme Court has already said the BUS is constitutional. The old madman is claiming he's an equal partner with Congress! King Andrew the First! I shudder to think of what they'll say about this in South Carolina."

Hurrah, Caroline silently cheered. "What's happened to the tariff bill, by the way?" she asked.

"The tariff? Oh, the president's bill has been moving toward a vote. I wouldn't be surprised if it passed tomorrow."

The next day, the distracted House and Senate, rattled by the swirling rumors that the president was going to veto the BUS recharter, passed Jackson's original tariff bill with scarcely a word of debate. A few days later, Jackson's veto of the BUS recharter crashed through Washington and the rest of the country. He did not merely reject Congress's labors on behalf of Nicholas Biddle and company. He added to it a ferocious message, which called on the American people to join him in destroying a "moneyed aristocracy" that threatened their liberties.

George Stapleton, obviously a moneyed aristocrat, found himself in the stickiest dilemma of his young political life. When the Senate and the House failed to muster the two-thirds majorities needed to override the veto, the bank became the major issue of the 1832 presidential campaign. What to do? When he consulted his political partner, Caroline gave him two startling suggestions:

"Talk about the tariff instead. That's going to become the major issue, after Jackson wins. Portray yourself as a man who pushed for lower rates, who wants peace between the North and the South. As for the BUS, tell everyone your family owns a bank and you look forward to advising the president on how to reorganize the country's banking system after he abolishes the BUS."

It was brilliant advice. Even Jeremy Biddle had to admit it, although he had no foreknowledge of a coming crisis over the tariff. Only Caroline had this information, thanks to John Sladen. He had gone back to Louisiana virtually guaranteeing an imminent explosion in South Carolina. On the hustings in New Jersey, George managed to sound like that rarest of politicians, a wise man and a patriot.

The "Nationals," as the *Washington Globe* called the National Republicans, fought back with an avalanche of anti-Jackson cartoons and hard-hitting pamphlets financed by the BUS. One cartoon portrayed Jackson receiving a crown from Van Buren and a scepter from Satan. Another sketch, which appeared in thousands of papers, had Old Hickory in royal robes, stamping on a tattered copy of the Constitution. The Democrats responded with hickory poles, which they marched around town to attract a crowd. Next came a barbecue, fueled by kegs of beer, followed by three cheers for Jackson and the party's campaign song.

Hurrah for the Hickory Tree!
Hurrah for the Hickory Tree!
Its branches will wave o'er tyranny's grave
And bloom for the brave and the free.

The Jackson–Van Buren ticket swept New Jersey and almost every other state in the Union. The count in the electoral college was 219 to 49. Old Hickory carried every state in the South except one: South Carolina. The Palmetto State cast its vote for an unknown Virginia politician named Floyd. On the state level, the Union party, led by Joel Poinsett, was routed from virtually every office.

As usual, the Stapletons returned to Washington early in the fall of 1832. The president arrived at the White House around the same time, having spent the summer at the Hermitage. He promptly invited them to dinner. The Polks were on the guest list too and so was Senator Legrand. As the president kissed Caroline's hand and complimented her on her sky-blue Paris gown, he did not seem to have a care in the world. He dismissed everyone's congratulations on his victory by insisting it was not he but the American people who had triumphed. At the table, he seemed interested in discussing nothing more weighty than the success of some of his prize racehorses at the Nashville track.

As the main course was served, George asked Senator Legrand if John Sladen would soon be arriving in town. "He's stopped off to see some friends in South Carolina," the senator said in a low voice.

"I'm glad to hear some Jackson Democrat has a friend in South Carolina," Old Hickory said, once again demonstrating his ability to conduct one conversation and listen to another one.

Caroline had the delicious sensation of being in on a political secret. She had received a letter from John Sladen explaining why he was going to South Carolina. Remembering his success at rounding up votes to reject Martin Van Buren as ambassador, Vice President Calhoun had summoned him to help rally support for South Carolina among other Southern states. With the results of the election all too clear, they saw only one course: nullification of the new tariff and defiance of Andrew Jackson and Martin Van Buren.

"What's happening in South Carolina, General?" George Stapleton said.

"From my latest reports, it can be summed up on one word: treason!" Old Hickory said. "The nullifiers have taken control of the state government and are meditating a challenge to the tariff. I told you a while ago that situation might require a liberal use of hemp—starting with a knot around the traitorous neck of John C. Calhoun!"

Everyone goggled at George, amazed to discover he and the president had already discussed such a radical solution to South Carolina's defiance. "I can only hope these reports are exaggerated, General," George said.

"I can assure you they're entirely accurate. They're reaching me daily by navy cutter. The supporters of the Union have already met the nullifiers in a bloody brawl on Charleston's King Street. One man had his face split open by a rock."

Caroline almost could not believe the way fate was cooperating with her secret wish. Across the table, she saw new respect in Sarah Polk's eyes. Perhaps Sarah would no longer always be the advice-giver now. Perhaps Caroline Kemble Stapleton had become an equal in the Temple of Fame. But Sarah's occasional condescension had never bothered her. Caroline the huntress was emerging from her cave of ice to strike down another quarry: her large, complacent, philosophizing husband, George Rensselaer Stapleton.

George was silent for the entire ride home in their carriage. Caroline made no attempt to converse. She was waiting for the right moment to speak. She decided it should not be in darkness. She wanted both her voice to be heard and her triumphant expression to be visible in the blazing light of every lamp in their house.

Into the front hall she strode ahead of George. In the parlor, she swiftly lit three additional lamps and turned up the one that the servants had left to guide them along the hall. George stood in the doorway, puzzled by her behavior. Caroline turned from lighting the final lamp and said, "I told you so!"

George knew exactly what she meant. He whirled and mounted the stairs. Caroline rushed to the parlor door. His broad receding back intimated she was risking the happiness of their marriage. She thought of John Sladen in South Carolina, helping John C. Calhoun and his compatriots to defy Andrew Jackson and the U.S. Constitution. Was that what she wanted in her secret soul? To be the partner of a man who shouted defiance to the entire world, indifferent to its rights and wrongs? She did not know, she did not care. Caroline only knew she had to say it once more, no matter what it cost her.

"I *told* you so!"

SEVEN

SHE WAS NOT BEING REASONABLE. SHE was being—what? A woman. Caroline found no fault with that conclusion as she lay beside her sullen husband in their marriage bed. The next day a letter arrived from John Sladen, describing the mood of South Carolina. *These people are determined to defend their rights or die in the ruins. I wish I could believe they meant it. Most of them seem to think that when they issue a proclamation on November 24, nullifying the tariff act, the federal government will back down. Do you think so? What do you hear in Washington?*

She told him what she had heard at the White House the night before. *From the beginning of this mess you and your hero Mr. Calhoun seem to have made a habit of underestimating Andrew Jackson. It is time for you to face the real man and not the dotard you seem to insist on seeing. He is going to meet your proclamation with all the force he can muster. He will have no compunction about letting you and your friends die in the ruins.*

On November 26, the resolutions of the South Carolina Nullification Convention reached Washington. The delegates declared the Federal Tariff Act of 1832 null and void as of February 1, 1833. After that date, unless the federal government agreed to revise the tariff, not a cent of money would be collected in the port of Charleston. Imports and exports would be duty-free. If the federal government attempted to collect the duties by force, South Carolina would secede and fight for its independence.

From South Carolina also came a frantic letter from John Sladen to Caroline. *The ultras are in control. Vice President Calhoun made a speech at the convention, stressing that nullification was intended to be a peaceful process. He was all but ignored. They are organizing an army. All the civil and military officers of the state are required to take a test oath, declaring their support of the Ordinance of Nullification.*

George came and left the house in silence for two days. Finally he lifted his eyes to her at dinner and asked through all but gritted teeth, "What do you think I should do?"

"Offer your services to General Jackson—as a peacemaker. Tell him about the speeches you made in New Jersey, urging tariff reduction. But don't for a moment disagree with him about the use of force to answer this challenge. If you do that, you'll lose his confidence forever."

George nodded. The advice coincided nicely with his own instincts. "That sounds reasonable."

"It isn't anything of the sort. You're not dealing with a reasonable man. You won't find much reasonableness in South Carolina either."

She was taking a new tone with him. She knew it was wrong. She could see it infuriated him. But she could not help it. More and more, she had began to dislike the way she was living, married to a man she did not respect and secretly in love with a man she could not acknowledge.

"You were right," George said. "What more can I say?"

"Nothing," Caroline said.

At the White House, Andrew Jackson grasped George's hand and all but wept at his offer to be a voice of peace. "You understand there may be many who will call you a trimmer, a traitor to the Union," Jackson said.

This had never occurred to George. "Not a few people want me to smash these fellows once and for all," Jackson continued. "But it's my native state. I understand how South Carolinians think. I have the same hot blood. You and I will know that you're acting for the Union—just as I will be with my trumpet blasts of blood and thunder."

Washington, and the nation, waited breathlessly for Andrew Jackson to speak. His first statement was his annual message to Congress. He did not say a word about the nullifiers. He recommended a further lowering of the tariff and called for action against the Bank of the United States.

Many people were aghast. George met John Quincy Adams in the Capitol rotunda. "Has the president surrendered to the nullifiers? His message sounded to me like the dissolution of the Union," the ex-president said. "You must speak to him in your grandfather's name, in the name of Washington!"

George calmed the agitated old man. "Wait a day or two."

On December 10, 1832, Washington, D.C., and the nation reverberated with Andrew Jackson's "Proclamation on Nullification." It branded the doctrine a "practical absurdity, contradictory to the Constitution, incompatible with the Union." The right of secession was even more categorically denied. "The Constitution forms a government, not a league. To say that any state may at pleasure secede from the Union is to say the United States is not a nation."

Finally came the ultimate trumpet blast. "Fellow citizens of my native state, let me admonish you, I have no discretionary power on this subject. Those who told you that you might peaceably prevent the execution of the laws deceived you. Their object is disunion. Disunion by armed force is treason. Are you really ready to incur its guilt? If you are, on the heads of the instigators of the act be dreadful consequences."

Seldom before in American history had a president's words achieved such total unanimity. State legislatures, North and South, rushed to congratulate Old Hickory and offer him thousands of volunteers. Daniel Webster and John Quincy Adams jointly guaranteed him New England's support. George Stapleton rose in the Senate to pledge "the men of the Middle States" to the president's call to arms—and to ask, rhetorically, why New York had yet to be heard from.

No one realized George was acting as Andrew Jackson's agent here. At another White House meeting, Old Hickory had shown George a temporizing letter from Martin Van Buren, urging Jackson to show restraint and caution, warning him Virginia might be offended by his categorical rejection of the right to secede. The president said he was showing George the letter because he would not be shocked by it. His opinion of Van Buren was already low.

"Help me get him up to the mark," the old warrior said. George could only marvel at the General's mastery of the art of politics.

In South Carolina, a forlorn John Sladen reported to Caroline that the network of Southern sympathizers he had been struggling to create had been swept away by Jackson's proclamation like a cobweb before a housekeeper's broom. South Carolina stood alone against the obloquy and denunciations of the entire country. John C. Calhoun had plunged into a pit of political infamy deeper than anything Aaron Burr had ever known. North and South, newspapers excoriated him as a traitor second only to Judas Iscariot.

In the Senate, George Stapleton rose to recommend a drastic reduction in the tariff. Simultaneously, the White House introduced a bill authorizing the president to use force to suppress a rebellion in South Carolina. Old Hickory was using the carrot and the stick. But there was no doubt about his readiness to use the stick. He showed George a letter he had just scrawled to Joel Poinsett: "If So. Carolina opposes the execution of the revenue laws with an armed force, I will in ten or fifteen days have in Charleston ten or fifteen thousand well-organized troops and twenty thousand or thirty in their interior. I can if need be, God forbid, march two hundred thousand men in forty days to quell any and every insurrection."

Jackson showed George another letter in which he ferociously rebuked Martin Van Buren. The Little Magician's creature, the New York legislature, had finally produced a resolution of support, but it was so pale, Jackson had been disgusted by it. "Your policy," he told his new vice president, "would destroy all confidence in our government both at home and abroad."

While Washington held its breath and the days marched inexorably toward the February 1 deadline set by the South Carolina Ordinance of Nullification, George's tariff bill was ambushed by an alternative bill proposed by Henry Clay, who was eager to fish in troubled waters in the hope of a prize catch that would give him a running start for the presidential campaign of 1836. As the senators squabbled, into the chamber stalked a figure who looked more like an apparition than a real man: John C. Calhoun.

Coldly, he presented his credentials to the senator who was sitting as president pro tempore of the Senate. (Martin Van Buren would not be sworn in as vice president and new Senate presiding officer until March 4, 1833.) Calhoun announced he had resigned as vice president and had been elected senator by the South Carolina legislature, replacing Senator Robert Young Hayne. In a brief, grim speech, he said he was here to defend his state's right to nullify the tariff—peacefully.

At 3600 Pennsylvania Avenue, Caroline Stapleton was talking to John Sladen. "Calhoun's courage awes me," he said. "He knows that if hostilities break out in South Carolina, the president is very likely to arrest him for treason. But this cause has become his life. Never before have I seen someone who *lives* his thoughts, who'll stake his very existence on his convictions. We must get George to support him."

"I've already taken care of that." Caroline told John how she had sent George to the president with his offer to play peacemaker.

John was ecstatic. "You anticipate my thoughts now. How wonderful."

How wonderful, and how sad, Caroline thought as she gazed at her secret lover. Never could their love be consummated in the way that other lovers, from Hero and Leander to Héloïse and Abelard to Tristan and Isolde, had made immortal. Perhaps they were living a new myth here. Were the acolytes of the Temple of Fame bound by a peculiar code of honor to the man to whose elevation they had dedicated their lives? Like the vestal virgins of ancient Rome, was their influence dependent on a bizarre chastity, which transcended the wayward wanderings of their hearts?

How she yearned to discuss this inner secret with Sarah Polk. Did she have a secret lover in Tennessee? A larger-souled more intelligent man than earnest James Polk, who seemed to have as his chief recommendation a willingness to work himself to the brink of exhaustion? His intellect was, if anything, more limited than George Stapleton's.

That day, after John Sladen departed, Caroline Kemble Stapleton began a diary. It was a significant gesture. Diarists are among humanity's stranger beings. They acknowledge by the very act that there is no one who can hope to understand their inmost selves. They become, by a strange necessity, their own best friend. Side by side with this inward confession often stands a secret desire to let the world ultimately discover how their two selves, the outer and the inner person, experienced or, if they have access to power, influenced the history of their time. History was being made here in Washington, and Caroline Stapleton's ultimate purpose was to leave the world proof that a woman could and did play a part in it.

That night George returned from the Senate with the news of Calhoun's arrival. "How incredibly heroic," Caroline said. "Even if you don't agree with him, you must admit his courage."

"I do. The man is a tragic figure."

"You should do more than merely push a tariff reduction. He sees you as an agent of Andrew Jackson, a man he now hates. He won't accept it as a true peacemaking gesture. Tell him you're prepared to do everything in your power, personally, to help South Carolina. Your bank will lend them money, help them build railroads. Become his friend, George."

"At the moment, that's politically comparable to embracing Benedict Arnold, if he were still around. I've gotten quite a few letters from people who don't think we should concede anything to South Carolina. Jeremy Biddle wants to see them invaded and totally subjugated to make sure this nullification-secession disease never gets loose again."

"That sounds typical of his simplistic mentality. There's only one way for the disease to be cured—by creating bonds of friendship and trust between the North and the South. That was why I urged you so strongly to support Mr. Calhoun from the start."

I told you so was an unspoken whisper in this sermonette. George Stapleton bowed his big head and agreed to do his utmost to persuade John C. Calhoun that he was his friend, and the South's friend. Caroline's policy produced almost magical results. Virtually alone in Washington, a pariah to whom no one spoke except fellow South Carolinians, Calhoun grasped George's proffered hand of friendship.

Soon the former vice president and John Sladen were seated at the Stapleton dining table, discussing what the Merchants Bank of Newark and additional loans from the overflowing coffers of the Camden & Amboy Railroad could accomplish in South Carolina. Excitedly, Calhoun produced a map of his state and drew a snaking line from Charleston over the uplands to the western border. "A railroad there, sir," he said, "could work the resurrection of Charleston and the whole state. It could become the chief carrier of goods and produce from the West for export, at twice the speed it takes to ship stuff a thousand miles down the Mississippi to New Orleans."

"Careful, Senator," George Stapleton said. "You have a Louisiana partisan here who may do his utmost to torpedo that idea."

"Nonsense," John Sladen said. "At the rate the West is growing, there'll be more than enough business for both routes."

Calhoun smiled at John with not a little of the fondness of a father for a son. "I'm constantly impressed by this young fellow's breadth of mind."

History, Caroline thought. They were making history here beyond the reach of the power gods such as Andrew Jackson and Daniel Webster and Henry Clay. But she wondered if John C. Calhoun would survive this crisis. Her woman's eyes found alarming signs of exhaustion on his lined face. Again and again a feverish cough tore at his throat. She saw this man was risking his life for his beliefs in more ways than his defiance of Andrew Jackson.

The conversation turned to the present crisis. Calhoun revealed that he had advised South Carolina to repeal its February 1 deadline. "I've decided we can wait until March fourth. Congress will have adjourned and we will see what nullification has accomplished in a reduction of the tariff."

"Some people will say we're bending to Jackson's proclamation, but it's nothing of the sort," John said.

After Calhoun and Sladen departed, Caroline poured George another cup of coffee and said, "How does that make you feel? I think you can claim some responsibility for the repeal of that deadline."

"I don't think postponing it will impress Old Hickory," George said. "His latest reports from South Carolina are not encouraging. They've issued a defiant answer to his proclamation and they're still organizing an army."

"All the more reason to press ahead as a peacemaker."

In Congress, George struggled to pursue this course. But Calhoun decided he preferred Henry Clay's tariff bill, which offered far less generous terms, because Clay's bill was untainted by any connection to Andrew Jackson. The tariff soon became a minor drama compared to the debate on the president's Force Bill. As long as the South Carolinians insisted on reserving the right to nullify this latest tariff if it did not suit them, Jackson insisted on Congress giving him the power to crush them and their army.

Caroline invited Sarah Polk to join her in the Senate when John C. Calhoun rose to attack the Force Bill late in February. They sat on couches only a few feet away from him. The man looked even more exhausted than he had at the Stapleton dinner table a month ago. John Sladen had confessed that he too was worried about Calhoun's possible collapse. But he spoke for most of a day, summoning examples of tyranny from history, excoriating the Force Bill as the death knell of liberty in America.

Caroline could see angry disagreement on George's face. She summoned a page. *Don't say a word,* she scribbled on a piece of paper and sent it over to him. He crumpled the paper in his big hand and slumped in his seat. As Calhoun sat down, Senator John Forsyth of Georgia rose to answer him. How could he expect any sympathy, Forsyth asked, when South Carolina had repudiated the republican form of government that the Constitution guaranteed?

Calhoun struggled to his feet once more. He scowled down at the slim, elegant Forsyth, who sat only a few feet away from him, and said these were the most ominous words he had ever heard. Couldn't Forsyth see that if Andrew Jackson could claim the power to invade a sovereign state to destroy a peaceful act of nullification, another president, elected by Northern abolitionists, could do the same thing to overturn the "domestic institution" on which the South's tranquillity depended—slavery? All in the name of his interpretation of republican government? Didn't Senator Forsyth realize that a growing number of people in the North were prepared "to drive the white population from the Southern Atlantic states?"

Senator Forsyth dismissed Calhoun's remarks with a few curt words. But Caroline suddenly saw why John Calhoun had returned to Washington to risk Andrew Jackson's murderous wrath. It was not merely to defend his finespun constitutional theory of nullification. It was to unite the South behind South Carolina to defend themselves against this primal fear of a race war.

On March 2, 1833, the day before Congress adjourned, the Force Bill was put to a vote. There was no doubt that it would win by a hefty majority. Rather than endure this humiliation, Calhoun stalked out of the chamber, followed by eight other Southern senators. Only one opponent remained, Senator John Tyler of Virginia, who cast the lone vote against it.

Caroline sat on one of the couches in the midst of the solons, watching complacently. She had spent three hours arguing with her husband last night, persuading him either to vote against the bill—or abstain. *I told you so* whispered its powerful undertone in the quarrel. Finally, George decided he would stay home. She noticed Henry Clay, at the last moment, also fled from the Senate chamber rather than vote.

Beside her sat Sarah Polk, who clearly doubted that George was as sick as he claimed. He had been hearty and healthy at a dinner party given by Senator Legrand only two nights before. Sarah did not know that John Sladen had steered Caroline out of the party to argue passionately for this policy—to be stopped in midsentence by Caroline. "I'm waiting until tomorrow night to talk to him."

"Give George my best wishes for a speedy recovery," Sarah said as the politicians and spectators streamed from the Senate chamber.

"I'm sure he'll be fine by tomorrow morning. He's something of a hypochondriac."

"Especially when swing votes are taken?"

"Then I'm subject to the hyp."

"My dear friend, I begin to worry a little about the game you're playing."

"Would you have let James vote if he were from New Jersey instead of Tennessee?"

"Probably not," Sarah admitted with a wan smile.

Outside, Sarah accepted Caroline's offer to take her back to Gadsby's Hotel in the Stapleton carriage. Winter gripped Washington with icy, wind-whipped fury. At home she found John Sladen drinking toddy with George. She told them how the final vote had gone. John had difficulty concealing his delight when she reported eight Southern senators had walked out with Calhoun and Virginia's John Tyler had voted a defiant no.

George was perturbed. "I suppose that makes all the more important what Johnny is urging me to do."

"I'm here as Senator Calhoun's emissary," Sladen said. "He's leaving for South Carolina tonight. He wants to get there before the Nullification Convention reconvenes. He has no idea whether the ultras will approve the rather piddling reduction of the tariff he accepted from Henry Clay. They may still opt for secession and defiance of Andrew Jackson. Mr. Calhoun thinks the presence of a Northern senator, who proposed a far more generous tariff reduction, who abstained from voting for Jackson's Force Bill, who comes offering money as well as friendship to the state, would have a powerful effect on the ultras."

"George, you *must* go," Caroline said.

"I'd like to discuss it with the president, first."

"George, that bloodthirsty old man wants a war. He'll talk you out of it. Be your own man, George. Stand out from the crowd. You've already done it by abstaining on the Force Bill. Lead, don't follow!"

"Amen," John Sladen said.

"All right," George said.

In two hours, Senator Calhoun was at the door in a hired coach. "Your offer to make this journey in such wretched weather has done more to give me hope for the future than anything I have seen or heard since I've returned to Washington."

George, still unhappy about not consulting Andrew Jackson, murmured something about hoping to make a contribution to peace and union. "You shall," Calhoun said. "We shall do it in our different ways. Thank you for your help, John. Mrs. Stapleton, I hope I can return your husband to you, no worse the wear, in two weeks' time."

The coach rumbled into the twilight, heading for Alexandria, where the travelers planned to take the mail packet to Charleston tomorrow at dawn. John Sladen followed Caroline back into the house and seized her hands.

"My dearest love," he whispered. "My dearest, dearest love."

"Stop!" she said, pulling her hands free and retreating into the parlor.

"I *have* to say it. I think it constantly. I have to say it at least once."

"All right. You've said it."

"Do you feel the same way?"

"Of course. Why else would I be bullying my husband into doing something he doubts to the depths of his soul?"

John struggled with a wild mixture of joy and sorrow. "I'll never mention it again. Or touch you. But I had to know."

Caroline said nothing. She was hearing her fate. Could she embrace it? She was not sure. She felt as empty as a scarecrow, as stupid as a stuffed doll.

"The struggle is just beginning. You know that."

"Yes."

"The South has learned a bitter lesson from this experience," John said. "One state can't go it alone. That's the chief reason Calhoun's returned to the Senate. To rally the South to our side."

"I know."

John's smile was as wistful as it was adoring. "Why do I bother to explain things to you? You're always ahead of me."

"Sometimes."

"One state can't secede. But if a whole region, a whole people, secedes, that's another matter. That will make the millionaires and manufacturers of the North think twice about voting for a Force Bill."

"What about the Union? Isn't Calhoun sincere about that?"

"There'll still be a Union. But it will be on our terms."

So that was where they were going. Did she agree with this bitter vision? She saw John Sladen's part in it, the visceral resentment against those who had destroyed his father, the gruesome proofs supplied by Nat Turner that the South had no alternative but the perpetual subjugation of its 2 million— soon to be 3 million—African slaves, the blend of anger and ambition that had led Calhoun to challenge Andrew Jackson. She saw it all but it did not really matter. She and this man were bound by something deeper and more compelling than politics. Something more profound and mysterious than the Temple of Fame.

Would she ever emerge from her cave of ice and bear ultimate witness by placing her lips on his longing mouth? If history gave birth to this dark consummation, would she feel free to seek the other consummation they both denied themselves? No, never, Caroline told herself. But the words did not still the wild longing in her soul.

EIGHT

HISTORY. GEORGE STAPLETON FELT IT BEATING in his blood too as he headed south with John C. Calhoun. He had grave doubts about allying himself with this bitter angry man. At Alexandria, they made a dismaying discovery. The Potomac was a sheet of solid ice. No mail packet could sail unless there was a break in the weather, which seemed unlikely.

Senator Calhoun rushed into a general store and bought a newspaper. It happened to be an edition of the *Washington Globe*, filled with its usual denunciations of him. He gave George half the pages and advised him to insert it under his shirt, next to his chest. "I've found nothing better to keep pleurisy at bay."

George shivered in his bearskin coat. Calhoun was wearing an equally thick coat of otter skins. The temperature was in the twenties. "We'll have to go by fast stagecoach," Calhoun said.

A company ran daily stages south from Alexandria. At first they said they had suspended service because of the cold. When George offered to double the driver's wages, they hitched up a team of horses and began the overland journey on the roads grooved with deep, frozen ruts that forced the driver to proceed at the pace of a creeping infant.

It took them twelve hours to reach Newport, Virginia. The driver was exhausted and the horses were near collapse. The proprietor of the Eagle Tavern, who ordinarily supplied fresh horses to the stagecoach company, was not inclined to risk his steeds as replacements. He urged them to return to Washington or wait by his warm fire until the harbor thawed.

"We'll have to use the mail carts," Calhoun said to George. "They're required by law to keep going."

"There's one outside, on its way within the hour," the tavernkeeper said. He obviously regarded Calhoun as insane.

What could George say? The senator was old enough to be his father. If he was willing to risk these open carts, George had to volunteer to join him. For the next eight days and nights, they jounced south in these springless, coverless vehicles, exposed to drizzling rain and occasional snow showers, with only mailbags and their heavy coats for warmth. In spite of the newspapers across his chest, George developed a persistent cough. Calhoun was not in much better shape, with a head cold that left him gasping for breath.

Sleep was snatched in fitful hours against the mailbags. Food was gulped down in roadside taverns, the walls greasy with smoke from burning pine logs. It was white bread and chicken fixings one meal, brown bread and common doings the next meal, and vice versa, while neighborhood folk, white and black, stared in wonderment at these strange travelers in their furry greatcoats.

Inevitably, they began talking to each other with ever greater frankness as their ordeal lengthened. George confessed his grave doubts about nullification and declared secession unthinkable. Calhoun said the Union remained a precious entity to him as well. He expounded his faith in nullifying laws as a peaceful legal protest but admitted that the people to whom he was preaching had a tendency to prefer violent solutions. "There's a great preponderance of Irish and Scottish blood in South Carolina," he said. "Particularly in the uplands, where I have my roots."

"Senator," George said after another hour or two of silent jouncing, "why didn't you stop Mrs. Calhoun when she decided to snub Mrs. Eaton?"

They rode a good mile without an answer. A thin rain began to fall from the leaden sky. "How long have you been married, Senator?" Calhoun asked.

"Four and a half years."

"Have you and your wife had any serious disagreements?"

"One—or two."

"Have you tried to change her mind once it's made up?"

"Yes."

"Did you succeed?"

"No."

"I married Floride on January eighth, 1811. That computes to twenty-two years. I took her away from the city life she loved in Charleston to the loneliness of the up-country, to managing Fort Hill when I was in Washington, to seven pregnancies. She's never said a single word of complaint to me. But there've been times when her temper made me aware of what she'd sacrificed for me—in comfort, in social pleasures, in sheer physical risk. Add to this my habit of solitary thought, of thinking out for myself, consulting with no one, my chosen course. Yet her love for me, her ambition for me, has remained inviolate. How could I say no when she chose to assert herself in this affair?"

"I see your point—all too well."

"In my heart, I shared her disgust. There was something degrading in this fellow Eaton, Jackson's favorite, embracing his whore in public. It seemed a sort of paradigm of the degradation that Jackson's followers seemed determined to impose on us all. You've seen Sausage Smith in action. Then there's Kendall and his hired libeler, Blair, at the *Globe*. And slimy, slithering Van Buren and his friends from New York. I couldn't—I still can't—deny that my heart assented to her judgment. Someone needed to erect a standard and declare, 'Thus far and no further.' I will candidly admit that I thought Jackson would beat a retreat, considering how roughly his character and his wife's character had been handled in the campaign. I'm a politician, my young friend. A proud badge, in my opinion. I knew your grandfather slightly in his last years in Congress. He considered it an honorable title. Do you?"

"Yes."

"I've heard reports that your wife operates you, rather like Polk's wife runs him. I hope the rumor's not true. A woman's judgment can be as good as a man's and even superior on some things. But there are so many intangible matters between men that they can never grasp."

"The rumor's not true, though I have great respect for Caroline's intelligence."

After another hour of silence in the drooling, icy rain, Calhoun began again. "This is no local affair. I hope you realize that. The British are in this game. They own half the stock in the Bank of the United States, which gives them tremendous leverage in Congress. They're eager to buy what they couldn't conquer in 1776 and 1812. They're behind the abolitionists. They'd love to abolitionize the South. If it doesn't bring on a race war, it will at the very least double the price of our cotton. That would leave their India cotton preeminent in the world market."

George groped for words. This man's mind roved so far beyond his horizons.

"I've heard your father was killed in the war of 1812. Is that true?" Calhoun asked.

"Yes."

"That makes this journey doubly generous. You're risking your health for one of the fools who started that war. Along with my asinine friend Henry Clay. The War Hawks, they called us. Do you remember any of it?"

"Only that I thought you were wonderful. I was eleven years old. I read your speeches in the newspapers. I thought they breathed pure patriotism."

"They did, for an eleven-year-old. Henry Clay and I thought we could conquer Canada without shedding more than a few drops of American blood—doubling the size of the country. We thought the British were too preoccupied with fighting Napoleon to the death to stop us. It was the first—and last—time I underestimated the British. They're a formidable people. We were lucky to escape that war as a whole country. New England almost seceded, you know. Daniel Webster conveniently forgets that in his apostrophes to the Union."

"My grandfather refused to attend the Hartford Convention."

"I know. I heard him denounce it in the Senate. Even though he knew it reduced him to a man without a party. I remember something he said at that time. Maybe you've heard him repeat it. 'Better a man without a party than a party without a man.' "

"I've never heard that before."

"It's worth remembering. I've never forgotten it."

George was tremendously moved. His grandfather's lost words summed up what they were doing here, talking one man to another, without anything between them but their wish to preserve the Union. The mail cart jolted on through the night, the rain replaced by a bitter northeast wind.

In another twenty-four hours of brutal jouncing, they were in Columbia, the capital of South Carolina. It was a comfortable-looking town, with tall trees lining the wide streets. The houses reminded George of Charleston; many displayed the same delicate ironwork and columns over high-arched basements. The capitol building was a handsome classical temple, with huge Doric columns. Not far away was a swarm of horses and buggies in the street outside a building of gray-painted brick, the home of South Carolina College. That was there the Nullification Convention was meeting.

George had to help the exhausted Calhoun out of the mail cart. They were both splotched with mud and grime. But Calhoun insisted there was no time to change their clothes or rest. After a minute of leaning on George's broad shoulder, he pronounced himself strong enough to proceed under his own power and walked slowly, painfully, into the building.

On the rostrum at one end of the hall stood George's Charleston acquaintance Robert Barnwell Rhett, feet spread wide, his nostrils flared in defiance. "I dare any man here to stand up and say he loves the Union," he roared. "There is only one course for South Carolina, a course which will unite the South behind her: immediate secession!"

While Rhett ranted, Calhoun moved around the hall, shaking hands with startled delegates, introducing George as a fellow senator. "This man has ridden eight days and nights in an open cart with me to let you know there are some Northern Democrats on South Carolina's side."

Many reactions were barely polite. Not a few men told Calhoun they thought he had sold them out on the tariff and he might as well have stayed in Washington. "We just passed a motion to censure you for failin' to do your duty," snapped one young hothead in an elegant blue coat and green silk vest. Others told Calhoun they were going to nullify this new tariff and secede, no matter what he said. With a patience and endurance that made George marvel, knowing his physical condition, Calhoun heard out the protesters. Quietly, insistently, Calhoun told them they were wrong; South Carolina could not win a war with the rest of the country. The South was not united behind them.

Calhoun told them what Senator Forsyth of Georgia had said about South Carolina abandoning the protection of the Constitution and asked George to bear witness. Calhoun advertised Senator Stapleton as a military historian who agreed that they would be starting a war they could not win.

On the rostrum, Robert Barnwell Rhett ended his diatribe with another challenge for anyone to testify to his support for the Union. Only one man, an aged veteran of the Revolution with a missing leg, rose. But most delegates were no longer paying attention. Around the hall there was a swelling murmur over the news that Calhoun had arrived. Robert Young Hayne, recently elected governor of South Carolina, took over the rostrum and announced Calhoun's presence.

"Senator, would you be good enough to give us your views?" he asked.

Calhoun wisely said no. He was in no condition to make a speech. But he said he was eager to converse with delegates singly or in small groups.

"Governor Hayne," George said. "Speaking as a friend as well as a fellow traveler, I think Senator Calhoun and I would make more sense if we allowed ourselves a few hours of rest in a bed. We've spent the previous eight days and nights in a mail cart. I'm young enough to stand it, but I fear for the senator's health."

"Do I hear a motion to adjourn until these gentlemen recuperate?" Hayne asked.

A thunderous assent. A carriage was soon at the door, and in fifteen minutes George was lying in a tub of steaming hot water on the upper floor of a nearby private home, his fetid clothes gathered for the wash by a smiling black servant. He fell asleep twice in the tub. Cleansed, he plunged into a feather bed and slept dreamlessly until a hand shook his shoulder. He gazed up at John C. Calhoun. He still looked exhausted. But he had changed into fresh clothes. The haunted determination that suffused his face summoned George to battle.

"The committee that deals with the nullification ordinance is meeting."

George struggled into his clothes. His head was throbbing; his breath created a sawing sensation in his chest. A wave of chills assailed him. It began to look as if the pages of the *Globe* had not protected him from pleurisy after all. But he said nothing to Calhoun as they trudged into the cold March night.

In a classroom of the South Carolina College a dozen members of the Nullification Committee hunched in student seats. The chairman was Calhoun's close friend Francis Pickens, slim, with a firm precise mouth and a proud tilt to his head. Several members handled Calhoun as roughly as some of the delegates he had encountered when they first arrived. He met them with the same patient courtesy—and unswerving opposition.

"The nullification ordinance must be repealed," he said.

"You mean we're beaten?" Robert Barnwell Rhett snarled.

"Yes. Congress has authorized the president to smash us to smithereens."

"Then it's over?" asked another man. "We have to go home and face our friends, our wives and children, looking like fools?"

"By no means. We'll proclaim a victory. In fact we have every reason to claim one. We've made them reduce the tariff. But the Force Bill is a defeat for peaceful nullification. It would be foolish to deny it."

"It's a damnable unconstitutional disgrace!" Robert Barnwell Rhett roared.

"I agree with the unconstitutional part," Calhoun said. "The framers never intended to give a president such power. But nine Southern senators voted against it. My journey to Washington was not a waste of time."

He turned to George Stapleton. "Here's another man who refused to vote for the Force Bill. Senator Stapleton is also a harbinger of hope in matters not purely political. He wishes to extend more than a hand of friendship to the South. His family owns the most successful railroad in America. He's eager to loan us the money that will help us build one in South Carolina. A railroad that will bring prosperity to our state, from the up-country to the sea—and help us bind the West in a coalition that will break the Yankee stranglehold on our throats."

The committee was gazing at George with a confusing mixture of respect and suspicion. "What does he want for all this benevolence?" Robert Barnwell Rhett said. "Mortgages on everything we own?"

"He expects a fair return on his investment, of course. But he also wants the satisfaction of knitting together our fractured Union. He's a Union man to the bottom of his soul. As I am."

The committee gazed at George as if he were some strange species of animal from the Russian tundra or the jungles of Africa. "Is this a fair exposition of your views, Senator Stapleton?" Francis Pickens asked.

"Eminently," George heard himself say.

The throbbing in his head had reached steam-engine proportions. A bayonet of pain drove through his chest with every breath. His flesh felt on fire. It was not simply the onset of pleurisy. It was also the sense of uneasiness that pervaded his being as he listened to Calhoun and Francis Pickens and Robert Barnwell Rhett. He wanted to take Rhett by the back of the neck and bang his head through the wall. He wanted to seize Calhoun and Pickens and shake them the way a parent shakes a child out of a nightmare. The Union was at risk in this room, in this city, and nothing George had heard from any of these men, including John C. Calhoun, allayed that sense of oncoming disaster.

"I for one am convinced," Francis Pickens said. "Shall we take a vote on Senator Calhoun's motion to repeal the Ordinance of Nullification?"

The vote was eleven to one. Robert Barnwell Rhett was the sole holdout. The next day George was too sick to get out of bed. Calhoun reported to him that after several hours of oratory, the convention had agreed to repeal the ordinance. Peace was now guaranteed. In a final gesture of defiance, they recommended that the legislature nullify President Jackson's Force Bill. Calhoun called that ridiculous gesture "a bit of salve" for the unreconcilables like Robert Barnwell Rhett.

"I wish you were on hand to hear how many gentlemen credit you for changing their minds," Calhoun said.

George nodded. He could no longer talk above a croak. A doctor had bled him and administered blisters to his aching chest. He was under orders to take cold baths to bring his fever down. None of these medical remedies worked very well. For the next several days, he drifted in and out of delirium. A haze of smoke or fog filled the room. Through this murk he saw Tabitha sitting beside his bed, weeping and wringing her hands. Suddenly she changed into John C. Calhoun, who changed into Hugh Stapleton, wearing a cocked hat and wielding a telescope through which he peered into the distance. The Congressman seemed to be trying to tell him something important. But a hand was over his mouth. Only muffled words emerged: "trairous." Was that *traitorous*? George's eyes traveled from the hand up its attached arm to discover it belonged to Caroline Kemble Stapleton. She had a smug smile on her face. "What the hell are you doing?" he roared.

"George, I'm here to help you," Caroline said. "Take some of this broth."

The haze that filled the room slowly cleared. Caroline was sitting beside his bed, wearing a green dress with a white lace bow at her throat. Her lovely face was the opposite of smug; it was full of loving concern. She had a bowl of steaming soup in her hand. "Where am I?" George asked.

"In Columbia. President Jackson sent me down here on a navy frigate to nurse you. It was Senator Calhoun's idea. I've been feeding you this old Indian herbal remedy that Sarah Polk gave me. It seems to work."

George swallowed some of the soup. It tasted like rusty iron filings had been boiled in it. "I'll either get better or die to stop drinking that stuff."

"Your fever is almost gone. The Calhouns have invited us to Fort Hill where you can recuperate for the rest of the summer if need be."

Senator Calhoun poked his distinguished head in the door. "How is he this morning?"

"He knows where he is, and who he is," Caroline said.

"Good. We'll leave for Fort Hill tomorrow."

By the time they reached the white-pillared house in the up-country, it was the last week in March. Spring had finally conquered winter. Trees were budding, the grass was green. Floride Calhoun and her petite pretty daughter, Anna Maria, greeted Caroline and the two senators at the portico. Calhoun had warned them that George was a hospital case, and solicitude breathed in their caressing Southern voices. He was hustled upstairs to a big double bed overlooking the front lawn.

The next day George was well enough to join Caroline for a tour of the plantation. Calhoun led them down to the slave quarters, where "master" was greeted with extravagant expressions of joy by men, women, and children. At the head of the group was Old Sawney, son of the first slave whom Calhoun's father had purchased and brought from the coastal lowlands to help him grow cotton in the high hills.

"Sawney is as close as I've come to a brother," Calhoun said. "We hunted and played together as boys. There's many a coon we caught together, right, Sawney?"

"Many a one, master, many a one." Sawney was a short, burly man, coal black, with thick white hair.

"How do you do?" George said, holding out his hand.

Sawney looked surprised. He was not used to people shaking hands with him. He finally let George take his hand, but he made no attempt to squeeze George's hand in return.

The Africans, about fifty in number, lived in a big stone house about an eighth of a mile from the main house. Children peered from a dozen windows. In front of it was a shed in which a huge pot of stew bubbled, tended by an aging black woman. Calhoun explained that each family raised its own vegetables and received a ration of salt meat and cornmeal from the storehouse each week.

A tall middle-aged black woman approached Calhoun. "Master, I don't want to go to Alabam. I don' care if you send all my chilluns. I don' want to go."

"All right, Betsy," Calhoun said. "You can stay here. Don't you want to keep your youngest boy, Peter, here too?"

"I'd like it, but you gon' to let him?"

"Of course I'll let him."

"Oh, thank you, master!" Betsy said.

Walking back to the main house, Calhoun explained that his son Andrew ran a large cotton plantation in the hot Alabama bottomlands. "It's very hard work, so we rotate our slaves. I send him twenty-five for six months, and he returns twenty-five here to recuperate in this healthy climate."

As they reached the portico, Floride rushed out. "Jimmy has cut his foot badly with a hoe. I've sent for Dr. Parks. I'll see to him in the meantime. Tell him we're in the south forty."

She vanished down the path that led to the cotton fields. Calhoun sighed. "I always feel guilty when I come home and see how much work Floride does, day in, day out. At all hours of the night she's down at the quarters giving them medicine. Or tending emergencies in the fields, like that one. Or settling quarrels about who works with whom."

"Is Sawney a foreman of sorts?" Caroline asked.

"No, he hasn't much inclination in that direction. He does as little work as possible. I fear I've spoiled him a good deal. We have a white overseer who bosses the field hands."

A tall stooped slave passed them on the path. Calhoun caught his arm. "How are you, Andrew?"

"Just fine, master."

"Andrew is a very good shoemaker. He earned so much money selling shoes he made after hours to nearby planters, he bought his freedom from me. He went to Philadelphia with his wife. He came back last year, half-starved. The white shoemakers smashed up his shop three times and finally drove him out of business. We're hoping we can set him up in business in Charleston."

Calhoun left George and Caroline on the portico with his daughter, Anna Maria. Caroline was surprised to discover the young woman was intimately aware of what was happening in Washington. "Father sends me all the newspapers. He's told me about your generous attitude toward the South. It's the first hopeful thing I've heard in months."

George murmured something about preserving the Union.

"In Boston they're holding monthly meetings calling for immediate freedom for the slaves. Are people saying similar things in New Jersey?"

"A few. Very few."

"It makes one so fearful of the future. I almost hesitate to marry and bear children. At times I feel I'd be happiest working with Father, defending the South. I've helped him prepare some of his speeches—researching quotations and precedents, that sort of thing."

Anna Maria's sadness stirred George's sympathy. "I can't believe reasonable men, with the same heritage, won't sit down in Congress and solve these problems."

"I'm sure George is right," Caroline said.

"Fire!"

The cry abolished politics. Senator Calhoun rushed out on the porch. One of the house servants dashed up to them. "The barn, master!"

Calhoun and George raced to the big wooden structure. Flames were poking livid snouts against an upper window. "Get buckets!" Calhoun shouted to several slaves.

George charged into the barn. The fire was in the loft. He climbed up and saw it crackling beneath a bale of hay that someone had set against the window. The bale reeked of some sort of pungent liquid.

"Stand back!" he shouted, and flung the bale from the loft into the center of the barn. By that time a half dozen slaves with buckets had arrived, and they hurled water on it. George stamped out sparks in the hay around the window and recommended a thorough dousing. The slaves climbed up with buckets and finished the job.

"How could a fire start up there?" Calhoun said as they returned to the house.

"It was set!" Floride was waiting for them on the portico, as angry as she was distraught. "It was set by one of Sawney's tribe!"

"Oh, tut tut, Floride," Calhoun said.

"I've told you a dozen times that fellow has never been the same since you took him to Washington ten years ago and he talked to free Negroes. He and his sons and daughters and nieces and nephews are going to kill us all."

"My dear, you're exaggerating, I'm sure of it."

"Get someone to find who started that fire. I insist on it."

"It could have been an accident."

"Get someone!"

George and Caroline discovered this meant summoning one of the older Africans and promising him fifty cents if he found out who set the fire. In an hour the fellow was back with the information. "Henry done it."

"What did I tell you?" Floride said. "He's Sawney's favorite nephew."

Calhoun summoned Henry to judgment. "Why did you set the fire?" he thundered.

Henry trembled and looked as if he was about to sink to his knees on the brick path that led to the porch. He was about eighteen, chunky, with Sawney's square jaw. "Was n'accident."

He looked past Calhoun at George and Caroline as he said this. Caroline suddenly wondered if their visit was the reason for the fire. Sawney stood in the circle of blacks watching the interrogation. His eyes too were on the Stapletons. Were the Africans trying to tell these Northern visitors something they regarded as important? Something to do with their readiness to imitate Nat Turner if they got a chance?

"I'm going to have to whip you, Henry," Calhoun said. "You know I hate to whip anyone. But this was a very bad thing to do. Is it because you don't want to go to Alabama?"

"I dunno, master. Maybe."

"You all have to work part of the year in Alabama because we need the money to buy clothes and food for everyone. Do you understand that?"

"Yes, master," murmured the crowd. Caroline noticed Sawney said nothing.

Henry was locked in the smokehouse until Fort Hill's overseer finished supper. He sauntered over from his house on the edge of the cotton fields with his whip in hand. He was a small, hard-faced man, with buck teeth. "Give Henry twenty-five strokes," Calhoun said. "He's in the smokehouse."

They sat on the portico sipping lemonade until the crack of the whip filled the warm spring night. Twenty-five times it cracked and each time Henry screamed with pain.

"Now will you believe me?" Floride said.

"He was just trying to say he didn't want to go to Alabama," Calhoun said.

"You should have given him fifty," Floride said

George and Caroline were grateful for the darkness, which concealed any wayward expressions that might be forming on their faces. *I told you so* reverberated in George's ears with a special irony. Was he here because the woman sitting beside him had used that expression with passionate savagery? Or was it because he genuinely wanted to save the Union? Or both?

"You should sell Sawney. If you truly cared about the safety of your wife and daughter, you would," Floride said.

"I'm sorry, Floride. I couldn't possibly sell him."

"Senator Stapleton, Father tells me you hope to write a history of our War for Independence," Anna Maria Calhoun said.

Anna Maria had read a dozen books on the subject, including John Marshall's *Life of George Washington*. They began a discussion that lasted through dinner, with Senator Calhoun a lively participant. He had made a close study of the politics of the Continental Congress. Even then, the Southern states tended to vote as a bloc and their chief opposition was New England. Both sides tried to build coalitions with the Middle States.

Anna Maria gazed at her father with rapt adoration. "So it was this way from the start."

"I fear so," Calhoun said.

Floride did not say a word. The American Revolution bored her. She abruptly changed the subject over coffee. "Texas, Senator Stapleton. What do you hear of it in New Jersey? All our young men talk about it day and night. A number have already gone there."

"I only hear about it when I go to the White House," George said. "It's often on the president's mind. He says we must have it, sooner or later. He prefers sooner."

"I'm sorry to hear that," Floride said. "I hate to think I might agree with anything Andrew Jackson says."

I told you so resounded in George's head long after he finished dinner and went to bed. It coiled around his brain like the crack of the overseer's whip. Beside him, Caroline whispered, "I'm almost glad you got sick and brought me down here. You have to see their situation before you realize why they think the way they do."

"What do you mean?"

"The blacks. The women are terrified of them. Mrs. Calhoun told me they outnumber the whites three to one in this county. Around Charleston it's more like five to one."

George stared into the silky spring darkness of South Carolina, wondering where love, and history, were taking him.

BOOK

FIVE

ONE

CAROLINE KEMBLE STAPLETON LOOKED AROUND THE large, opulently furnished parlor of her home at 3600 Pennsylvania Avenue. In one
corner, Margaret Bayard Smith, a gray-haired grande dame of Washington
society, was telling Congressman John Sladen of Louisiana the story of her
recent visit to Monticello, Thomas Jefferson's old home. She had found the
mansion a pathetic wreck. "Rotting terraces, the lawn plowed up and cattle
wandering among the Italian vases, the stone that marks Mr. Jefferson's resting place defaced and broken, and not even a slab or piece of wood to mark
the grave of his beloved daughter. I asked myself, 'What is human greatness!' "

In another corner, Sarah Childress Polk and her husband, Speaker of the
House of Representatives James Polk, were talking politics with austere Sen-
ator Silas Wright of New York. Tomorrow, March 4, 1837, Martin Van
Buren would be inaugurated as president of the United States, and Senator
Wright would become the most important man in the Senate, the White
House's spokesman. In the House, James Polk would bear this unenviable
burden. Listening closely to their muted council of war was beefy, red-faced
Reuben Whitney, the most important lobbyist in Washington. He represented
the state banks into which the government now deposited its rivers of cash,
since Andrew Jackson abolished the Bank of the United States.

On the other side of the room, Senator Daniel Webster of Massachusetts,
his beetling black brows adding dark majesty to his broad forehead and massive chest, was telling one of his comic stories to a group that included Senator
John C. Calhoun and his chief spokesman in the House of Representatives,
stumpy George McDuffie. "Recently one of my constituents accused me of
being no different from a Southern politician. I told him he was absolutely
right. Have I ever been known to leave a glass of brandy undrained? Have I
ever stayed in town five minutes after someone challenged me to a duel? Have
I ever paid a debt if I could avoid it?"

Calhoun and McDuffie laughed as heartily as everyone else. Good humor
was the rule in Mrs. Stapleton's salon. Her skill at mixing the prominent from
all parties and all parts of Washington society was by now an established fact.
One attraction was the cuisine, prepared by Henry Orr, a free black who had
become Washington's premier caterer. Side tables abounded with castles of
quartered oranges glazed with yellow sugar, ice cream molded into the shape
of doves, a dozen different cakes and tarts, all served with warm apple toddy

or the best French wines. But the palate took second place to politics. People said things—and heard things—in Mrs. Stapleton's parlor that made it a Washington institution, only slightly less important than the House and Senate.

Her invitations were a compliment—and a summons that few dared to ignore. As if to prove the point, through the door came Henry Clay of Kentucky. He had just suffered a horrendous blow—the death of yet another daughter, this one the senator's favorite.

"Senator," Caroline said. "I am so pleased, and so flattered, that you felt well enough to come. What can I say beyond how much the sad news has wrenched all our hearts."

"Thank you, thank you," Clay said, his angular face haggard with grief.

Senator Calhoun slipped away from the Webster group and joined them. "Mr. Clay, may I speak from the heart and tell you, having a beloved daughter that God has thus far spared me, how much I have felt for you since I heard the news yesterday."

"Thank you, Mr. Calhoun, thank you."

Webster joined them to speak similar words. He flung his arm around Clay's stooped shoulders and led him off to the corner where he had set up a kind of kingdom, as was his style. In a few minutes, he had Clay smiling and even laughing at another of his stories—and telling a few of his own in his best Kentucky style.

Caroline turned to see if any more guests were coming down the hall. On the stairs she spied her eight-year-old son, Jonathan, and his chunky six-year-old brother, Charlie, peering through the rails at the famous and important in the parlor. The two were so different looking, she felt a spasm of embarrassment that all but ruined her good humor.

"Get to bed, you two, or there'll be no dessert for a week!" she said.

John Sladen strolled to the door to wag his finger at the boys. "You heard what the wicked witch said! Get going or she'll change you into frogs who won't be able to do anything but croak, "Y-e-s, M-o-th-er.""

He croaked the last words with a skill he told them he had acquired from listening to the thousands of frogs that haunted his Louisiana bayou.

"Do you have a gumdrop?" asked Charlie with his endearing lisp.

John carried in his pocket a special brand of soft sweet candy from a New Orleans confectionery shop. It had made him the house's favorite visitor as far as Jonathan and Charlie were concerned.

"Can I?" Charlie asked Caroline.

"Oh, I suppose so!" Caroline said.

"I'll take some too," Jonathan said, elbowing Charlie aside.

They snatched the candy and fled upstairs. "A wonderful party," John said, gazing into the crowded parlor. "But you never give any other kind."

"I wondered about inviting Mr. Calhoun, after his attack on the president today."

"Everyone leaves their politics at the door here, thanks to you."

"Thanks to you as well."

The last four years had seen politics of almost insane virulence raging in the Senate and the House. John Sladen had been among the most violent participants in the seething quarrels over President Jackson's decision to destroy the Bank of the United States by removing its federal deposits, a move that threw the nation's monetary system into turmoil. One day John had pulled open his coat to show Caroline the small pistol he was carrying to the House of Representatives. A congressman from Georgia had threatened to stab him if he repeated a charge that the man was a paid toady of the BUS.

That was when Caroline sat John Sladen down and took charge of his political destiny. She told him that his style must change. From an abrasive, screaming, snarling attack dog, he must espouse the ways and wiles of the feline species. He must imitate George's good nature, even if he did not possess it—adding to it a silky, smiling dimension of subtle flattery and cheerful cajolery. Unless he made this change, Caroline vowed she would bar him from her salon and write him off as hopeless.

It had been a turning point in their relationship. From the advice-giver he had become the advice-seeker. Whatever else remained between them beneath the surface of their political lives continued to ferment. But this new balance of power became the preeminent fact of their existence.

"Mr. President!" Caroline said.

In the doorway was the evening's ultimate test of Mrs. Stapleton's salon: ex-president John Quincy Adams, now mere Congressman Adams. Caroline had learned how much he liked to be called Mr. President in private. Stumping on his cane, the short, thick-bodied old man seemed to glare at Caroline at first. But he was simply nearsighted.

"Ah, Mrs. Stapleton," he said. "I've brought two uninvited guests. I hope you don't mind."

"Of course not."

Through the front door strode the famous British actor Richard Kemble and his beautiful daughter, Fanny. Her perfect complexion, the dark hair in strategic ringlets framing her small almost childishly innocent face, made Caroline feel alarmingly old. But she was too good a hostess not to recognize a coup when she saw one.

"Mr. Kemble and Miss Kemble. What an honor! I saw you only last night in *Romeo and Juliet*. It was an unforgettable performance."

"Mrs. Stapleton, you're too kind," Fanny said in a liquid voice that seemed to echo a thousand Wordsworthian brooks. "Father and I were dining with *President* Adams here, whom we had the pleasure of meeting in Boston. He suggested you wouldn't mind if we *imposed* on you for coffee and a chance to see your *marvelous* coterie."

"Come into the parlor and meet some of our guests. This is Congressman John Sladen of Louisiana."

"Ohhhh," Fanny said with a sibilant breath that virtually melted John down to his shoes. "We'll be in New Orleans in a month's time."

"I'll be there without fail to take you to dinner," John said.

Caroline managed a smile. This was a recent development—his openly flirting with pretty women before her eyes. But how could she object?

Into the parlor Caroline led John Quincy Adams and the Kembles, thinking how glad she was that the congressman/ex-president had brought them.

Without these exotic creatures, she wondered if even her dedication to political harmony could have avoided an explosion of rancor at the sight of the old Yankee. For the past two years, he had been throwing the House of Representatives into chaos by presenting dozens of petitions a week from abolitionists demanding that slavery be banned in the District of Columbia—and in the entire South. Invariably he ignited furious shouting matches with Southerners who insisted that the petitions be either ignored or totally barred.

Now, in their rush to greet the Kembles, people barely noticed old John Querulous Adams, as Sarah Polk still called him. At the head of the pack was Henry Clay, who had been romantically linked with Fanny a year or two ago in Philadelphia. She greeted the senator from Kentucky as "my *dear* Henry," which sent not a few eyes revolving toward the ceiling. In a scene worthy of the stage, she kissed him tenderly on the cheek and extended her sympathy for the loss of his daughter.

Watching, Caroline admired the way Fanny Kemble had mastered the art of charming and tantalizing men. She seemed utterly satisfied with the exercise of this skill. Did she have any personal feelings? Caroline wondered. Was there a man or men anywhere to whom she had succumbed? Caroline suspected not; a mastery of the art of dissembling or acting (was there any real difference?) tended to diminish the capacity for personal emotion. Caroline was discovering that was one of the principal sacrifices required of the women of the Temple of Fame.

Fanny began holding a kind of court in the middle of the parlor. "Mr. Adams and I had the most fascinating conversation about Shakespeare during dinner. He maintained that the man was immoral. Glorifying courtesans like Cleopatra. He even insisted that *Romeo and Juliet* taught nothing but sympathy for fornication!"

"I did, I did," Adams said. "I will debate the matter with anyone here."

"We've learned, Mr. Adams, the folly of debating you," James Polk said. As Speaker of the House, he was the frequent target of Adams's vitriol in Congress whenever Polk tried to dispose of his endless abolitionist petitions.

Adams grinned almost fiendishly at Polk.

"What other plays of Shakespeare have fallen under your ban, Mr. Adams?" Sarah Polk said.

Sarah despised the old man. She maintained he was a hypocrite who did not care an iota about the enslaved blacks. His only interest was in embarrassing Andrew Jackson and the other Democrats who had kicked him out of the White House.

"Why, Mrs. Polk, surely you can't favor *Othello*," Adams said in his supremely self-righteous way. "As a play it just doesn't scan. Though I'll say this for old Shakespeare: he gave Desdemona exactly what she deserved for marrying a nigger."

At that moment Henry Orr offered Adams a fragrant glass of mulled wine, the ex-president's favorite drink. Adams gazed into Orr's impassive black face without a flicker of emotion. So much for abolitionism, Caroline thought.

Fanny gazed at Adams in her seemingly innocent way. "I sometimes think, Mr. President, that you're a very good man and a very wicked man all in one remarkable package."

Adams gazed defiantly from Webster to Calhoun to Clay, eventually including almost everyone in the room in his cold gaze. "Aren't we all?"

"There's one man I would exempt from that charge, sir," John Sladen said. "The husband of our hostess, Senator George Stapleton. If there's a piece of malice in his large frame, I haven't found it. I dare say no one here has, or ever will."

"To Saint George," Henry Clay said. "May he soon slay all our dragons and gorgons—with no reference to present company, of course!"

Everyone good-naturedly drank to George. "Where is the senator, Mrs. Stapleton?" John Quincy Adams asked.

"At the White House. He felt compelled to wish the president a fond farewell."

"I'd be inclined to wish him a very different good-bye," Adams said. "As would most of the people in this room. Thank goodness we're forbidden to be disagreeable in the presence of beauty."

He raised his glass, first to Caroline and then to Fanny Kemble, and offered the rest of the room a mocking bow. As usual, he was giving a superb performance.

In the White House, Senators George Stapleton and Thomas Hart Benton were among the small group that had gathered in the upstairs study to hear President Andrew Jackson read over the final version of his Farewell Address. It was to be printed in the *Washington Globe* tomorrow. The two solons were among the select few who had been asked to read previous drafts of the document and suggest changes. Roger Brooke Taney, the new chief justice of the Supreme Court, had done most of the writing.

The president thanked them again for their help with the address. "I hope I've satisfied you on the matter of the Union, Stapleton," Old Hickory said.

"You have entirely, Mr. President."

Jackson flipped the pages to the opening paragraphs and read the key sentence again: "At every hazard and at every sacrifice the Union must be preserved."

"Amen," said Benton.

"President-elect Van Buren doesn't like it," Jackson said. "But I refused to put in a single qualifier."

"I think I'll clip the whole paragraph and mail it to Senator Calhoun," Senator Benton said. "He disgraced himself and the Senate today with another attack on you."

"What did he call me this time?"

"Tyrant, dictator, the usual names. Then he accused you of a breach of the privileges of the Senate because you called him a liar in your letter last week. He claimed as a legislator he had the right to judge you but you had no right to judge him."

"I should have hanged him when I had the chance."

"History may well agree with you," Benton said.

"If I'd challenged Clay when he called me a would-be Caesar in 1819, I would have killed him. Think how much better off we'd be without those two."

"It would be a peace that surpasseth understanding," Benton agreed.

George thought Chief Justice Taney, a devout Maryland Catholic, looked uncomfortable about these murderous Western sentiments. Georgia-born Secretary of State John Forsyth's smile suggested he took a more benign view. When it came to hanging and dueling, the South and the West were in agreement most of the time.

The president's tall, diffident adopted son, Andrew Jackson Jr., who was serving as his secretary, gathered up the sheets of the Farewell Address to deliver to the *Washington Globe.* As he departed, a thunderous roar erupted in the hall. "I'm here to see the president!"

Everyone knew instantly that it was the spherical Democratic senator from Ohio, William "Earthquake" Allen. He had the loudest voice in Washington. Into the study he lumbered. "Mr. President," he shouted. "I couldn't let you go without paying you m'personal respects."

Earthquake was drunk but Jackson greeted him with his usual courtesy. They shook hands and Old Hickory said, "I think this occasion permits me to break my doctor's rules. Let's open a bottle of Madeira."

The old warrior had been seriously ill for the last six weeks. Twice he had hemorrhaged blood from his lungs. Rumors of his death had swept the city a half dozen times. That had not prevented him from dashing off scorching letters to Calhoun, Adams, and other enemies in Congress who were using the last days of his presidency to denounce him.

One of the White House's black servants swiftly produced the Madeira. Everyone soon had a glass in his hand. "To the greatest president!" bellowed Earthquake Allen.

Everyone drank without a contrary word or, as far as George could see, a negative thought. Excepting George Washington, Senator Stapleton was inclined to agree with Earthquake. Old Hickory lit one of his corncob pipes and puffed away for several silent minutes. George realized Jackson's eyes were on the face of a grandfather clock in the corner. Soon all eyes were on the same timepiece, as the minute hand approached midnight.

Twelve chimes broke the stillness. Jackson's mouth relaxed into a semismile. "Gentleman, I am no longer president of the United States, but just a citizen like any of you."

"There'll never be a citizen like you, General," roared Earthquake Allen.

George could think of nothing appropriate to say. He silently extended his hand, and Jackson grasped it with the same tough squeeze that had hauled George into the ranks of the Democratic Party at the Hermitage eight years ago. Benton, Forsyth, and Taney also felt words were superfluous and imitated George.

From a shelf to his right, Jackson took down a small book and turned its pages as they left the room. Andrew Jackson Jr., standing in the open doorway, whispered, "That's Rachel's Bible. He reads a chapter every night."

As the door closed, the ex-president's voice followed them into the hall: "Gentlemen, don't for a moment lose sight of Texas!"

The four years of Andrew Jackson's second term swarmed through George's mind as he walked down Pennsylvania Avenue in the cold March night. It had been a wild ride. The president's decision to destroy the Bank of the United States had released an orgy of inflation and speculation. Banks began issuing their own currency under loose state laws, and the price of everything began gyrating skyward. Thousands of businessmen stormed Congress begging the lawmakers to do something, anything, to get the economy under control. The followers of John C. Calhoun joined the forces of Henry Clay and Daniel Webster in ferocious attacks on the president.

From New Jersey, Jeremy Biddle and George's uncle Malcolm Stapleton sent him a stream of letters denouncing Jackson with similar vehemence. Malcolm died of a stroke while dealing with a strike at Principia Mills, caused by the wild inflation. Sally Stapleton blamed Andrew Jackson, and by association, George, for his death. Jeremy reiterated his personal friendship as often as he repeated his angry criticism of Jackson's economic policy, but George sensed his best friend was growing more and more beleaguered and unhappy.

That makes two of us, George found himself thinking. But he quickly corrected this lapse into gloom. True, his marriage with Caroline had its problems. But what marriage didn't? John Sladen had admitted to him in a moment of bitter candor that Clothilde Legrand had become more and more erratic in her moods and attitudes. In a family tradition inherited from her mother, she seemed to resent John's immersion in Washington's politics and sulked on their plantation or in their house in New Orleans. Floride Calhoun had announced a similar determination to shun Washington, for reasons Calhoun could only hint at with words like "temper."

George found himself thinking of Andrew Jackson's final order. Texas was his most explosive legacy. He had sent a series of envoys to Mexico City to negotiate a peaceful purchase. When the Mexicans declined to cut a deal, Old Hickory had encouraged his six-foot-six Tennessee protégé, Sam Houston, to go down there and organize an army from the thousands of American settlers in the territory. When the Mexicans responded with a bigger army, Houston had routed them and captured the president of Mexico, General Santa Anna.

Houston had shipped Santa Anna to Washington, where he told Andrew Jackson that he was agreeable to selling Texas for three or four million dollars if he got some of the cash. As a member of the Senate Committee on Foreign Relations, George had met this smooth, smiling political soldier two months ago and had been impressed by his apparent candor and reiterated desire for peace. Caroline predicted that the moment he got back to Mexico, he would renege on his promises—which was exactly what he did.

Meanwhile, John C. Calhoun had risen in the Senate to welcome Texas into the Union—as a vast new territory in which to expand the domain of slavery. Abolitionists in New England had screamed in rage and battered their politicians with thousands of letters opposing the idea. It had been deplorable politics on Calhoun's side if he was sincere about supporting the Union. When George asked him privately what he thought he was doing, he had claimed to be merely telling the truth. At home, Caroline had been Calhoun's advocate, arguing that it was better to bare the fundamental quarrel over Texas sooner rather than later, so that neither side had any illusions.

Jackson, cursing Calhoun, had backed away from immediate annexation and announced the United States could only acquire Texas by new negotiations with Mexico and the consent of the Texan people. Houston, obedient to the chieftain's wishes, had set up the Republic of Texas and hunkered down to wait for the moment when Jackson decided the issue had fermented in the national mind and the Mexicans were ready to accept the inevitable.

The bank and other issues had distracted and divided the Democrats. Texas, awash in debt, began making ominous noises about an alliance with England. Only in the last week of his presidency had Jackson taken the next cautious step. He had allowed both houses of Congress to pass resolutions recognizing the Texas Republic—and dispatched a diplomat to represent the United States at Sam Houston's capital. Old Hickory was leaving this gigantic thundercloud on the southern border for the administration of Martin Van Buren.

Why did that name stir noxious fumes in his brain? Senator Stapleton had supported the Little Magician's candidacy. George had been a good Democrat. He had gotten to know Van Buren better during the four years he had presided over the Senate. He was able, he was shrewd. But he never won George's respect. He still remembered the man who had flattered his way into Andrew Jackson's affections.

George realized he half agreed with Davy Crockett, the contrary Tennessean who had penned a ferocious assault on the Little Magician during the presidential campaign. *Van Buren is as opposite to General Jackson as dung is to a diamond. . . . When he enters the Senate chamber, he struts and swaggers like a crow in the gutter. . . . It would be difficult to say, from his personal appearance, whether he was man or woman, but for his large side whiskers.* In Crockett's wake was a swarm of nicknames that testified to similar opinions of Van Buren: the Red Fox, the Weasel, Sweet Little Fellow, the Flying Dutchman, the Mistletoe Politician.

A lot of voters had agreed with Davy Crockett and his friends. Henry Clay and his followers had organized themselves into a new political party, the Whigs, which imitated the Democrats with local committees and campaign rallies and rousing newspaper coverage. They had come close to putting another Western general, Ohioan William Henry Harrison, in the White House. Van Buren had carried a bare fifteen states.

New Jersey was not one of them. Jeremy Biddle, prodded by his wife, had announced he was a Whig and poured thousands of dollars into the Harrison campaign in the Garden State. Jeremy wrote George a tortured letter, desperately trying to salvage their personal friendship. George assured him he had nothing to worry about on that score.

Privately, George took a certain satisfaction in New Jersey's defection. Its congressional delegation remained Democratic. Van Buren could hardly reproach him. The Little Magician had also failed to carry Tennessee, where Crockett's biography and those savage nicknames had a cruel impact.

With a better name for their political party, Clay and company might have trounced the Democrats. The choice of *Whig* testified to the way Andrew Jackson obsessed the minds of every politician in the country. The name was drawn from English history, when Whigs opposed the tyranny of the king. Clay and his followers thought the moniker would be a good way to remind people that "King Andrew" was still running the Democratic Party.

But the uncrowned king and his courtier had prevailed. Tomorrow morning Martin Van Buren would become the eighth president of the United States. It was going to be an odd sensation, serving a president he despised. After eight years in the service of a man he loved.

George had made the mistake of saying this to Caroline yesterday. He had gotten a lecture about the unimportance of one's personal feelings in politics. Mrs. Stapleton seemed to have forgotten the way she had argued on the opposite side of that principle when she allied him with John C. Calhoun. For a moment an alien voice raged in George's mind: *Maybe this time I'll get a chance to say I told you so.* But he had not spoken these abrasive words. Instead he had listened like a good boy to mother's latest scolding.

Although he carefully excluded the thought from his mind, Senator George Stapleton was not a happy man.

TWO

"MR. CALHOUN IS SO GRATEFUL FOR the money you've loaned the South Carolina Railroad. He predicts its success could change the temper of the state," Caroline said.

"That's good to hear," George said. "Jeremy Biddle still says we're never going to see a cent of profit."

"That's typical of his narrow, penny-pinching mind."

Caroline was already in bed, wearing a pale blue nightgown. Her hair was carefully wrapped in a gauze turban to protect her curls for the inauguration tomorrow. The swirls of white cloth isolated that perfect face, making it seem like a piece of sculpture. George had felt a rush of desire when he walked into the room.

Instead of a kiss, Caroline gave him an exhaustive report on what was said and what was hinted and what was unsaid at the night's salon. He sipped a brandy and soda and barely listened until she got to Texas.

"Senators Calhoun and Webster had a fascinating discussion about Sam Houston—whether they could trust him. Senator Clay chimed in with the story of the way Houston had abandoned his wife of four weeks and gone off to live with Indians in Oklahoma! Mr. Calhoun said he was afraid the English were planning to call in all the money they were loaning Houston and set up an abolitionist state on the southern border. Mr. Webster said he hoped the English tried it. It would drive every abolitionist in New England into eternal silence. Everyone turned to Silas Wright as Martin Van Buren's spokesman and asked his opinion. He said, only half-humorously, that the president-elect wished Texas would just go away."

George told her Andrew Jackson's farewell words.

"If Mr. Calhoun were the president, he'd keep everyone's eyes on Texas. But Machiavelli's twin brother will do nothing. I'm sure of it," Caroline said.

George finished his drink and sat down beside her on the bed. "Did everyone congratulate you on your stunning appearance, as usual?"

"I was hopelessly upstaged by Fanny Kemble."

"I wouldn't have given her a passing glance. She's not my type."

"Johnny Sladen gave her more than several passing glances."

"From what I hear around town, Johnny is paying passing glances to quite a few unattached ladies. I guess they have different ideas about marriage down in Louisiana."

"He paid you the nicest compliment." She told him John's toast.

George winced. "That's laying it on a bit too thick."

"George! He meant it."

"I suppose so. But tomorrow he'll be after me to loan another half million to the Louisiana and Pensacola Railroad. Or invest another fifty thousand dollars in Sam Swartout's Galveston Bay and Texas Land Company. I don't like the way Sam piles on mass meetings at Tammany Hall in favor of annexing Texas without telling anyone that he and his friends own half the Gulf Coast and annexation will make them millionaires. If the Whigs get hold of that information, we'll all look like crooks."

"It's a perfectly legitimate enterprise. George Washington had money in land companies."

"I suppose so. But it still makes me uneasy. Jeremy Biddle says—"

"How many times do I have to tell you I don't give a damn what he says!"

George paced the room, struggling to control his temper. He still wanted to make love to his wife. They had not touched each other, beyond a polite kiss or two, for ten days. "I begin to think we should only talk politics on the first floor."

"George, I couldn't possibly. Not tonight. You'd ruin my hair."

Tomorrow night she would be too tired from the inaugural ball. Last night, by the time he came home from a late session of the Senate, she had coated her face with a half pound of beauty cream.

"I'm sorry," Caroline said. "I love you just as much—"

"I love you too."

He kissed her, undressed, turned out the oil lamp, and slipped into bed beside her. He told himself Caroline's diminished enthusiasm for sex had nothing to do with love or politics. Two years ago she had given birth to a baby girl who had only lived a week. Last year she had had a miscarriage, an incredibly messy business in which she had lost at least a gallon of blood.

On Caroline's side of the bed lay a woman who found it more and more difficult to simulate enthusiasm in her sexual encounters with George Stapleton. Her fear of another pregnancy had begun to blend with more fundamental problems, above all Senator Stapleton's increasing political independence. John C. Calhoun's warning about the limits of a woman's advice had taken deep root in George's psyche. Caroline did not realize this of course. She and John Sladen still congratulated themselves on cementing this unlikely partnership between North and South.

Meanwhile, Calhoun, Sladen, and others struggled to unite the South for a regional confrontation with the industrial North that would annihilate the tariff and demolish the abolitionists once and for all. The surprising strength of the new Whig party among the planter aristocracy had put a serious dent in these hopes, outside of ever faithful South Carolina. The new president, Martin Van Buren, also put his not inconsiderable talents for conciliation into reassuring Southern Democrats that they had nothing to fear from the abolitionists while he was president, further isolating Calhoun.

Why not accept this new status quo? Caroline asked herself as she lay awake for an hour after her husband's deep breathing signaled sleep. After Andrew Jackson, the country needed a rest. The Van Buren administration would be boring and humdrum, but peaceful. Unfortunately, she agreed with John Sladen that it would be a peace of deception, a peace built on the lies and half-truths of the schemer in the White House.

Caroline despised President-elect Martin Van Buren far more venomously than George. Lately, Caroline had begun borrowing most of her political emotions from John Sladen. Was it an attempt to compensate for the other thing she failed to give him? Over the last four years, she had watched his hopes dwindle as he began to wonder about the nature of the love she had confessed in 1833.

Was she becoming La Belle Dame sans Merci? Was that hidden wish, once confessed to George but now, she hoped, long and safely dismissed, the ultimate satisfaction she sought for being born a woman? No, no, a thousand times no, Caroline told herself. She wanted to be a loving woman. She was a loving woman, within the terrible limits of her situation. She tiptoed into her study and for another hour poured out these anguished thoughts to her only confidant now, her diary. Only in these white pages could she tell the whole truth to her secret self.

The next morning she was awakened at seven by Jonathan and Charlie romping in the hall outside their bedroom. Mercy, their nurse, was simply unable to control the two boys. But George, still troubled by Tabitha's death, would not hear of letting her go. He was equally immune to Caroline's complaints about Hannibal. The big black had become involved with other free blacks who wanted public schools in the District of Columbia. They had petitioned Congress, and George had urged Speaker of the House James Polk to put some pressure on the committee that presided over the District. Sarah Polk had begged Caroline to change George's mind. Any such gesture by the Speaker would have imperiled Southern votes for Andrew Jackson's program. George had stubbornly declined to cease and desist, and when Polk failed to act, Senator Stapleton donated fifty thousand dollars to found a private school for the blacks. Little Tabitha Flowers, Hannibal's daughter, was enrolled in it.

Caroline was convinced that Hannibal had become an abolitionist and regularly smuggled tracts from the Reverend Mr. Donaldson into Washington. But the big coachman vehemently denied it. He said Jesus had told him to forgive Tabitha's murderers and to wait patiently for God to dispose of slavery in His own good time.

Her head throbbed so severely from lack of sleep, Caroline feared she was on the brink of a migraine. But she dressed with her usual care and joined

George for the trip to the Capitol to witness Martin Van Buren's inauguration. The crowd was large, but George agreed that most of them were there to get a last glimpse of Andrew Jackson. Once more he thrilled them by bowing to the majesty of the people when he emerged on the portico to watch Van Buren take the oath of office.

The new president's speech was an hour long, and Caroline almost dozed off in the middle of it. What she heard was the expected swarm of evasions and equivocations about every issue before the nation, larded by lavish praise of Andrew Jackson and humble pie about never being able to come close to the zenith of his accomplishments.

The reception at the White House was singularly decorous. The people in their majesty seemed to have no enthusiasm for shaking Little Van's hand. The crowd were almost all politicians and government jobholders. The only entertainment was supplied by the vice president, Colonel Richard Johnson of Kentucky. Another white-haired Western military hero, he claimed to have killed the Indian chief Tecumseh in the 1812 battle of the Thames. His followers had tried to run him as a rival to Van Buren for the nomination with a very Western campaign song.

Rumpsey Dumpsey, Rumpsey Dumpsey
Old Dick Johnson killed Tecumsehy!

Aside from its stupidity, the song had stirred unpleasant memories of her father's death in Caroline's mind, further lowering her enthusiasm for Colonel Johnson. Martin Van Buren shared this negative attitude. He had done everything in his power to keep Johnson off the ticket, but Jackson had insisted on him. Now the vice president stood in the East Room, a big smile on his wide weathered face, his presence advertised by his trademark, a red vest that he had supposedly stripped from Tecumseh's corpse. On his arm was his latest mistress, a tan-skinned mulatto woman about thirty years his junior, who happened to be one of his slaves.

Caroline gravitated to Sarah Polk, who was sipping punch only a few feet from the East Room doors. "Do you think our president, so known for his tolerance, will invite the vice president and his lady friend to the White House?" Sarah asked.

"Mrs. Eaton will insist on it, I'm sure, if she ever returns from Spain," Caroline said.

"Have you heard the latest about her? She's taken to smoking cigars with visiting Frenchmen, while her husband sits in a corner, sodden with brandy."

George and James Polk began discussing Texas. Caroline strolled over to the far corner of the East Room, where John Sladen was chatting with ex-senator William Rives of Virginia and a half dozen congressmen from the Old Dominion. Rives had been Johnson's rival for the vice presidential nomination. Van Buren had sworn to support him at the Democratic Convention and then double-crossed him when Old Hickory proved adamant about Tecumseh's killer.

As Caroline reached the group, Rives, a tall, distinguished man with a lofty senatorial forehead, was saying, "I'm still at a loss to understand why one lucky shot fired at an Indian twenty-five years ago entitles a man to be vice president of the United States."

"You know Mrs. Stapleton, Senator?" John Sladen asked.

"Is there anyone in Washington who doesn't know Mrs. Stapleton?" Rives said. "I've been the grateful recipient of her hospitality many times. How is your fine husband?"

"He's over there, worrying Mr. Polk about Texas," Caroline said. "Obeying a final order from General Jackson, delivered in the White House last night."

"I fear he and Mr. Polk will have to do a lot more worrying in the White House before Texas becomes part of our Union," Rives said. "The new captain of our ship of state is better known for hesitation than navigation."

Senator Calhoun joined them, shaking hands with Rives and the other Virginians. Rives repeated his wry remark about the new vice president. Calhoun chuckled heartily. John Sladen asked if everyone knew the story about the latest mistress. "She's the sister of the girl he turned to last year, after his previous mistress's death. But she found him tiresome and ran off with an Indian. The colonel pursued them down the Mississippi, caught them, and sold the creature to the worst plantation in the Alabama bottomlands. After that, he found her sister remarkably receptive to his addresses."

"Mr. Sladen, please," Rives said. "There's a lady present."

"A Washington hostess can't be shocked at anything she hears, Rives," Calhoun said. "Her profession requires a certain worldliness which I for one find admirable."

"I yield your point, Senator," Rives said. "Lest I be excluded from another sampling of those marvelous quartered oranges glazed with yellow sugar that Mrs. Stapleton serves. But I wonder what the ladies of the South will think of our esteemed vice president and his ménage. They're a good deal less worldly, don't you think?"

"It's one of their outstanding traits," Calhoun said. "But I don't think Mrs. Stapleton approves of the vice president's arrangements, though she can listen to them without blushing. Would you agree, Mrs. Stapleton?"

"I have no plans to invite Colonel Johnson to my home. Or return his mistress's call, if she were imprudent enough to make one," Caroline said.

Caroline looked calmly at John Sladen as she said this. *Does that atone for Mrs. Eaton?* she asked. She was allying her salon with reemerging Southern solidarity. Rives was an invaluable prize for the Calhoun forces. Old Virginia still saw herself as the inevitable leader of the South, ignoring the twin liabilities of depleted soil and mountains of debt. They were extremely reluctant to recognize John C. Calhoun as their natural leader.

That night at the inaugural ball, Colonel Johnson, minus his red vest, displayed himself and his mulatto mistress once more, with the same well-liquored smile on his face. At a nearby table, the new president did his best to pretend the Johnsons did not exist. He was surrounded by his four sons and his close friend and fellow New Yorker, hawk-visaged Benjamin Butler, the U.S. attorney general.

Caroline, seated next to Sarah Polk, filled her in on the amorous history of the president's tall, handsome second son, John Van Buren. The best people in New York locked up their daughters when "Prince John" came to town. Caroline had learned a great deal about him from James Gordon Bennett, editor of the newspaper that was rapidly emerging as everyone's favorite, the *New York Herald*. She had invited the engaging young Scotsman to one of her recent salons. Bennett had rewarded her hospitality by christening her Washington's "premier hostess"—and had given her a minute account of John Van Buren's debts, drinking, and amorous escapades.

"He's currently seeing a certain Maria Ameriga Vespucci, who claims to be a direct descendant of the great navigator. She's hoping for a grant from Congress to reward her ancestor for naming our continent. By promising her his efforts as a lobbyist, he's gained access to heart."

"Do you think she'll guide him to the Temple of Fame?" Sarah asked.

"I fear she lacks a crucial attribute—discretion."

"I thought you were going to say virtue."

"I begin to think virtuosity is more important."

"I sometimes think you may be right."

They were old friends now, capable of joking about their secret profession—yet no less determined to persevere. Sarah began talking about James's problems in the new Congress. He badly wanted to remain Speaker of the House, but many of Senator Calhoun's recent Southern adherents were talking about voting against Polk because of his devotion to General Jackson. The Virginia delegation in particular seemed ripe to support John Bell, a former Speaker and avowed foe of Van Buren's. Bell had played a major role in the president's failure to carry Tennessee.

"I'll talk to John Sladen. I think he can persuade a good number of them to cease and desist. If necessary, I'll risk going to Senator Calhoun himself."

In Washington politics, only a gossamer thread linked personal ties to political necessities. A politician could be persuaded by a personal plea, but not often. Even then, some sort of quid pro quo had to be offered.

"What can James do or say to please Senator Calhoun?"

"He might be able to persuade the Tennessee legislature to vote some money for the Tennessee branch of his railroad."

"I think it should be something congressional."

"One of his people might like the chairmanship of the committee on public lands. That would give them a chance to woo Westerners."

"A very good idea. James might go for that."

Everything was always couched in *might*s and *maybe*s. Nothing was ever certain in the shadowy world of Washington power. So many proud egos had to be stroked, so many hungry or angry interests satisfied.

On the other side of the table, Caroline noticed James Polk and George Stapleton were having a serious conversation with lobbyist Reuben Whitney. His wife, who was as fat as he was, looked around the flag-bedecked hall with an air of bored aplomb. At their mansion a block from Capitol Hill, the Whitneys gave parties far more splendid. Keeping congressmen well fed was vitally important to the banks Whitney represented.

"Mrs. Stapleton. May I have the honor?"

John Sladen stood behind Caroline's chair. They glided out on the floor and passed the vice president's table as he planted a kiss on the cheek of his mistress. "Is there any hope of persuading Clothilde to come to Washington?" Caroline asked.

John shook his head. "We've agreed to disagree on that point."

She switched to James Polk's worries about the Speakership. "He has a right to be worried. I don't think he's going to get it," Congressman Sladen said.

"John, please don't talk to me as if I were a lobbyist. You know Sarah is my dearest friend. I insist on a major effort on your part. And on Senator Calhoun's part. James has proven he's a friend of the South with those endless hours he's spent arguing with that vicious old man, John Quincy Adams, about his abolitionist petitions."

"I suppose so. But he didn't carry his home state for our so-called president. That means the Little Magician will do nothing for him."

"All the more reason for you and Mr. Calhoun to do something. You must convince Mr. Calhoun that if he ever hopes to forge his alliance between the West and the South, Mr. Polk is the man to lead it."

"I fear Mr. Calhoun thinks he's the man."

"He's wrong and you know it. The West adores the Union. Calhoun's loathed there as a secessionist. He'll have to content himself with power behind the scenes."

"You're asking a great deal of me."

"I expect a great deal of you. I always have and always will."

Words sprang to John Sladen's lips. He compressed his mouth into a taut line and did not speak them. Had he been about to reply, *What can I expect of you?* Caroline escaped the question, as she escaped so many things.

"It's time I danced with my husband."

George obediently abandoned Reuben Whitney and led her out on the floor. "You look particularly beautiful tonight."

"Thank you."

She was wearing black, a color she had begun to favor more and more. Did it suit her mood? The gown was taffeta, with great puffed sleeves intricately decorated with black lace. Her dressmaker assured her it was a replica of the gown worn last year at the court of Louis Philippe by none other than the king's mistress. On the bosom was a black taffeta rose, an interesting reminder of the single rose she had worn in her hair at their wedding.

"You've spent most of the night talking to Reuben Whitney. What does he have to say?"

"Plenty. He thinks the roof is about to fall in on everyone in sight. There's too much paper money in circulation, and not nearly enough gold and silver to match it."

"It couldn't happen to a nicer president."

"We're all in the same boat now. I think they call it the ship of state."

"There are more important things to worry about. Do you have the New Jersey delegation lined up to make James Polk the Speaker again?"

Two hours later, the Stapletons rolled home in their crimson-sided carriage. George's hand came out of the darkness to caress the back of her neck. "You've never looked lovelier. Age simply doesn't wither nor custom stale you."

"I'm Cleopatra now?"

"That makes me Mark Antony. Doomed to defeat. Let's try another couple."

"Elizabeth and Essex?"

"Didn't she chop off his head?"

"I fear so. It may be the only way to guarantee a man's respect."

He drew her to him for a rough kiss. "I'll take my chances, Bess."

How could she say no? Josephine Parks drew a warm bath. Caroline floated in the scented water for a half hour and slipped into bed beside him wearing only a negligee. She was willing, warm and willing. But the moment his hand touched her breast, she became a different woman: stubbornly, secretly unyielding, while she seemed to say yes, to return his kisses with mounting fervor. Yes and no, yes and no, the two words became a kind of seesaw in her mind, her soul.

Did he notice? Did he detect behind her eyes the sullen resolution not to yield, to command rather than surrender, to prevail rather than submit? No, no, he was too absorbed in his own pleasure, the sense of his own formidable body, above all that great rod of manhood that she received into her body with sighs and cries worthy of Fanny Kemble at her best. Yes, she was *performing* here as she performed everywhere. Was there anything wrong with that?

Not a thing, not a thing, *not a thing*, not a thing . . .

It was over. A few more sighs, a few more caresses. Then the blessed isolation of darkness, a chance to commune with that lonely girl who prowled Ohio's woods and fields vowing to find a man worthy of her mind and heart. Was it her fault that she had found two, one worthy of the first, the other of the second?

Hours later, sleep still eluded her. Why? George was snoring softly beside her. Hadn't she done her duty? Hadn't she satisfied her husband? What was troubling her? Fear of another pregnancy? She had left the hot water in the bathtub and plunged into it the moment George released her. It was as good as a douche, according to her worldly friend, the wife of the French ambassador, who had been dispensing this Gallic advice around Washington for years.

What was it? Suddenly she knew. The ring on her finger—Hannah Cosway Stapleton's ring. It was too tight again. Twice now she had had it widened—while she and the jeweler puzzled over the mystery. Her other rings still fit her nicely. Why was this one so troublesome? Caroline sat up in bed and tried to pull it off. It would not move. Only after she returned to the bathroom and soaped her hand did it slide off.

By that time she was wide-awake. It took her another hour to get to sleep. The last thing she remembered was a flickering glimpse of Hannah's saintly face in the portrait on Bowood's walls. *Go away*, Caroline told the ghost. Dawn was graying the windows as she slipped into an exhausted doze.

THREE

JEREMY BIDDLE SAT IN THE STAPLETONS' front parlor on Pennsylvania Avenue, trembling from head to foot. "Calm down, Jeremy," George Stapleton said. "It can't be this bad."

"It's worse, infinitely worse," Jeremy said. "We could lose every cent we've got!"

Caroline sat on the couch on the opposite side of the room, as far away from Jeremy as she could get. He had obviously not slept in several days; his eyes were bloodshot, his face had the pallor of a corpse. He looked more like a fugitive from the law than the business leader of New Jersey.

On March 17, 1837, two weeks after Martin Van Buren became president, one of the biggest banks in New York collapsed, sending economic shock waves through the nation. Next came the news that the cotton exchange in New Orleans had closed its doors as the market price of cotton crashed to an all-time low. Now Jeremy was in town with a delegation of Northern businessmen to warn the president and Congress that dozens of other banks were teetering on the brink of collapse and the government had to do something to prevent a huge disaster.

When Andrew Jackson revoked the charter of the Bank of the United States, he set up a new system. The federal government deposited its millions of dollars in revenues from tariffs and the sale of public lands into well-established state banks. Senator George Stapleton had made sure the Merchants Bank of Newark, controlled by the Stapletons, was one of these "pet banks," as the Whigs dubbed them. Almost all of them were in fact controlled by Democrats. But as William Marcy, one of Martin Van Buren's New York lieutenants said, both in war and in politics, "To the victor belongs the spoils."

Like most other bankers, Jeremy had loaned a lot of this found money to investors in Western lands, whose prices seemed to be on a permanent upward spiral. Confident that more government cash was on its way, the Merchants Bank and other banks issued a flood of paper money, which they promised the users could be redeemed at any time in gold or silver ("specie"). The price of cotton cloth and everything else had soared skyward on the same glorious bubble that was kiting real estate values from Aroostook, Maine, to Andalusia, Alabama, and Jeremy had gleefully doubled the size of Principia Mills.

Jeremy had also reluctantly succumbed to George's pressure for loans to Southern enterprises, from railroads in South Carolina and Louisiana to cotton and sugar plantations in Mississippi and Alabama. John Sladen, his brother-in-law Victor Legrand, Andrew Jackson's son, and John C. Calhoun's son were among Jeremy's many grateful borrowers. This was part of Caroline's master plan to make George a Northern senator with a following in the South.

Senator Stapleton had traveled to South Carolina and Louisiana to speak at the groundbreaking ceremonies for the railroads. He was on the committee to celebrate the twenty-fifth anniversary of the Battle of New Orleans in 1840. In the Senate, he repeatedly hailed the economic promise of the South and was hailed in turn as a friend of the region by senators from Alabama and Mississippi—new headquarters of "King Cotton." Now this plan, and much more, seemed to be in danger of vanishing in a whirlwind of panic.

"Next week," Jeremy said. "On May tenth, every bank in New York is going to suspend specie payments. It's the only way they can stave off collapse. They've got millions in outstanding loans from British and French banks that are being called in. The goddamn Limeys and Frogs want hard money. It's going to trigger a tremendous panic. The Merchants Bank doesn't have enough specie to cover a tenth of its obligations."

"Then you'll have to suspend payment too," Caroline said.

"That could lead to riots, revolution. We pay our mill and railroad workers in hard money."

"Tell them to take paper—or else," Caroline said.

"Or else what?" Jeremy said. "Go to jail? Flee the country?"

"What if every other bank in New Jersey, and every bank in Pennsylvania, and Maryland—every bank in the country—suspended payments?" Caroline said. "Maybe then there'd be nothing wrong with it."

George gazed at Caroline with the sort of admiration she had not recently seen. "She may be right," he said.

"But our charter will be revoked," Jeremy said. "The state will shut us down."

"Change the law," Caroline said. "Turn the Camden and Amboy loose on them. Put a thousand workers on special trains to Trenton. Stage your own riot—peaceful, of course—in front of the statehouse."

Jeremy shook his head. "The president has to change the government's policy. He's got to start accepting paper money for Western lands. That's where our hard money's gone. It's all on the other side of the Appalachians."

"He'll never do it," George said. "Not as long as Andrew Jackson's alive. Little Van didn't have the guts to talk the old man out of Tecumseh Johnson for vice president. Do you think he's going to change anything this important? Old Hickory thinks that a hard-money policy is the key to keeping inflation from running wild. It hasn't worked, of course, but who knows how bad things would be without it? You fellows are as much to blame as he is. You didn't have to loan money to every fast talker who came in your door."

"All undoubtedly, or possibly, true," Jeremy said. "But there's no point in blaming anyone. Something has to be done. Andrew Jackson isn't president anymore!"

"He's still running the Democratic Party. That makes him more important than the president," George said. "He's still the voice of the people."

Caroline left the financier and the senator considering alternative strategies and rushed to Sarah Polk's rooms at Gadsby's Hotel. She told Sarah what she had just heard from Jeremy Biddle. Seldom had Caroline seen her friend so dismayed. "This is terrible news. Mr. Polk had a letter from General Jackson today, urging him to begin a campaign for the immediate annexation of Texas. The little coward in the White House will use this for an excuse."

"I fear it may be a perfect excuse. The businessmen are hysterical. They're talking of riots, revolution."

Emily, Sarah's tall, regal black maid, interrupted them. Mr. Sladen was in the hall, most anxious to speak with Mrs. Polk. John rushed into the room, looking almost as frantic as Jeremy Biddle. "Caroline, I didn't expect—"

"You can speak with perfect freedom, Mr. Sladen," Sarah Polk said. "Mrs. Stapleton and I have no secrets from each other."

"I just received a letter from Sam Swartout. He's been told his appointment as collector of the port of New York won't be renewed. Can that be? Is this weasel in the White House declaring war on every Democrat who's ever dared to disagree with him?"

"We know nothing about this, Mr. Sladen," Sarah said.

"As Speaker, Mr. Polk is the third most powerful man in the government. Mr. Swartout has many friends."

"I'll mention it to him. But he has such a press of business from job seekers. Every congressman seems to think he can intercede for his favorites."

Sladen looked more and more desperate. "Is it true what else I learned from New York? Almost every bank is on the point of failure?"

Caroline nodded and told him of Jeremy Biddle's visit. "My God," Sladen said. "Texas will disappear in the maelstrom. Confidentially, Sam Swartout is depending on an immediate annexation to meet some very large obligations. This could have serious implications for the Democratic Party."

"If you're talking about the Galveston Bay and Texas Land Company, Mr. Polk will not lift a finger for that dubious venture," Sarah said. "I hope you don't have any money in it."

Since James Polk had become Speaker of the House, Sarah had acquired an imperious style. She did not hesitate to speak frankly, almost too frankly, to many people. Caroline resolved to warn her friend against letting this tendency go to far.

Or was she especially sensitive to the pain Sarah's candor seemed to be causing John Sladen? "A great many people have money in Texas. Senator Stapleton for one," Caroline said.

"I mean money you can't afford to lose," Sarah said.

Caroline could see John was angry. But he controlled himself and asked— *begged* would be a better word—Sarah to intercede with Mr. Polk to win another four-year appointment for Sam Swartout. "I'd consider it a very large personal favor. With Senator Calhoun's help, we delivered at least thirty votes to Mr. Polk's election as Speaker. We can do even better in the next Congress."

"I fear it's a personal vendetta, John," Caroline said.

"Exactly," Sarah said.

Sarah obviously had no intention of imperiling James Polk's relationship with Martin Van Buren for Sam Swartout's sake. The president controlled far more than thirty votes in the next Congress. Accepting defeat with as much grace as he could muster, John asked Caroline if he could escort her home.

In the Stapleton carriage, he told Caroline far more than he had revealed to Sarah Polk. "Sam is desperate. He's put too much money into Texas. His accounts are short over a million dollars. If he doesn't get reappointed, the new collector's certain to find out about it. The explosion could blow the Democratic Party to pieces. We'll be the laughingstock of the country."

"Shouldn't you have told this to Mrs. Polk? If it came to light, and Mr. Polk was known as his chief backer in the administration . . ."

"I don't consider Mrs. Polk a true friend, as I do you."

"But I consider her one. I must ask your permission to tell her as soon as possible."

John's silence seemed to ask, *When will I be treated as a true friend?* Caroline banished the intuition. It was too painful to consider the probable answer: *Never.*

They passed a coffle of slaves. She heard Hannibal call from the box, "Have patience, brothers. Jesus is on your side. God won't be mocked forever."

"Is that fellow an abolitionist?" John asked.

"He's a Christian."

"You should tell him to shut his Christian mouth!"

"Don't you remember what happened to his wife?"

"You shouldn't bring him to Washington. Leave him in New Jersey."

"I'll talk to George about it. May I tell Sarah Polk?"

"If you insist. My God, what a mess."

He was losing his head, like Jeremy Biddle and George. All these astute males could not deal with defeat. Why was she able to think calmly about it? Were women used to defeat? Or had she learned to accept it in that horrible month after this man retreated to New Orleans? Had she learned that the heart continues to beat, the brain continues to think?

After leaving John at the congressional boardinghouse on I Street where he was living with twenty other Southerners, Caroline ordered Hannibal to take her back to Gadsby's Hotel. She found Sarah dressing for dinner at the White House. "Forgive me for intruding again, but I just learned something about Samuel Swartout that you should know immediately."

"A million dollars!" Sarah said. "That's more money than the entire budget of the State of Tennessee."

"What do you think we should do? Tell the president?"

Sarah adjusted a pale blue turban on her dark head. "We'd get no thanks for it. Mr. Swartout's Southern friends would accuse us of ratting on him."

"No doubt."

Sarah slipped on her engagement ring, reminding Caroline that she had left hers on her bureau. "When and if the great explosion occurs, the real damage will be to the Democratic Party in New York."

How Machiavellian we're becoming. More than a match for the Machiavelli in the White House, Caroline thought. "You see this as damaging a certain politician so badly he might not be renominated?"

"Voters tend to blame a president for the scandals that come to light in his administration. They lose track of when the bad apple was put in the barrel. When you add a huge financial crisis . . ."

"With a buffoon like Tecumseh Johnson as vice president, the next man in line for the nomination should be the Speaker of the House—the third most powerful man in the government."

Sarah smoothed her dress and produced her Mona Lisa smile. "My dearest friend. How marvelously you read my mind."

Delicious delicious delicious. If only she could explain to George Stapleton and John Sladen how infinitely more satisfying a moment like this was, compared to the bliss they imagined themselves bestowing on her with their prowess in the bedroom.

"The best part of it is, the Little Magician will bring it all on himself," Caroline said. "If he weren't a vindictive weasel, he'd let Swartout keep his job, and risk a brawl to bring Texas into the Union, and Sam would make enough money to balance his books."

Sarah's Mona Lisa smile almost became a triumphant Tennessee grin. James Polk bustled into the room and threw up his hands in mock dismay. The Speakership had somehow made him a larger man, without subtracting an iota from his good looks. It had also added not a little to his good humor. "Ye Gods!" he said. "I didn't realize I was interrupting a solemn conclave."

"We've just concluded it, dear," Sarah said.

"What did you decide? Vanny should be impeached as soon as possible for failing to dance with the vice president's lady at the inaugural ball?"

"Something a bit more important than that," Sarah said.

"What was it?"

"Your obnoxious condescension inclines me to think you don't deserve to be told. Do you agree, Mrs. Stapleton?"

"Definitely."

Sarah coolly changed the subject and told Mr. Speaker about the impending financial crunch in New York. He was so distracted, there was no need to tell him what they had decided to do about Samuel Swartout.

Back at the Stapleton residence, Caroline found Jeremy and George in a much more positive frame of mind. "I've convinced him," George said. "He's going back to New Jersey on the first train out of here and pound the legislature into changing the law to let us get away with paper money for a while. He's going to pass the word to the rest of his fellow crooks—I mean bankers—and he thinks they'll all do the same thing in their home states."

Over the next three months, the nation's bankers proceeded to extricate themselves temporarily from their crisis by marching in lockstep to their state legislatures and browbeating or bribing these lawmakers into letting them suspend hard-money payments on their banknotes. The Whigs belabored the mostly Democratic politicians unmercifully. John Quincy Adams was especially cutting. At one of Caroline's salons, he asked George if he could explain the difference between a counterfeiter and a banker.

"The answer, Senator," rasped the old man, "is this. The counterfeiter must have the talent to create illegal money, print it on a decent press, and sign another man's name to it. Whereas the banker prints it legally, signs his own name to the promise to pay in gold and silver, and then reneges on it without the slightest fear of a jail term."

George and his fellow Democrats could only squirm. They did more than squirm over Texas. They agonized, as Andrew Jackson bombarded them with letters from the Hermitage, demanding action. The Texans sent a tall affable gentleman named Memucan Hunt to Washington to negotiate the trifling details of annexation, so he thought. He expected the United States to assume the Republic of Texas's debts and confirm all its land titles, ex post facto, *tout de suite*. Instead, Ambassador Hunt found himself as isolated and adrift in Washington as the sole survivor of a shipwreck.

Three months after he arrived, Hunt held forth at one of Caroline's salons about the perfidy of the man in the White House. He had spoken to the president, who put him off with generalities. He had spoken to the secretary of state and gotten the same treatment. He was returning to Texas to tell Sam Houston that maybe it might be better to do business with the English after all. Caroline's report on this conversation went out to the Hermitage the next day. She and George, and the Polks, had a quiet laugh, imagining the letter that would soon hurtle from Nashville to the White House.

"I hope the General writes it on fireproof paper," Speaker Polk said.

It was amazing the things people were inclined to do to a president they secretly despised. As far as Senator Stapleton and Speaker Polk were concerned, Andrew Jackson was still running the country. It was an easy assumption to make, because Van Buren could not get anything through Congress. A coalition of conservative Democrats, disgusted with his feeble leadership, coalesced with the Whigs to vote down bill after bill.

It was open season on the Little Magician, in and out of Congress. In fall of 1837, John Quincy Adams stumped into Caroline's salon to sip whiskey toddy and describe his recent visit to the White House. "I'd been told the president was looking wretched. But I found no such thing. On the contrary, he grows fat and seems perfectly serene."

"How would you compare him to other presidents you've known?" Caroline asked.

She noticed that John Sladen and stumpy Matthew Davis, close friend of Sam Swartout's and former right-hand man of Aaron Burr, moved noticeably closer as Adams collected his thoughts. Davis now wrote a newspaper column called "The Spy in Washington."

"Mr. Van Buren has many characteristics strongly resembling Mr. Madison's—his calmness, his gentleness of manner, his easy and conciliatory temper," Adams said. "But Madison had none of his obsequiousness, his sycophancy, his profound dissimulation and duplicity. In the last of these, he much more resembles Jefferson, though with very little of his genius. The most disgusting part of his character, his fawning servility, belonged neither to Jefferson or Madison."

The smiles on the faces of Messrs. Sladen and Davis left no doubt that Adams's remarks would be in the New York papers next week. Not a single man in the room, many of them Democrats, said a word in defense of the president. The ladies were equally cold. The widowed Van Buren ran a bachelor's White House, peopled only by two of his sons and his attorney general. There were no balls or teas or receptions.

Meanwhile, Caroline and Sarah waited for the Swartout explosion to wreak havoc in New York. This was their private secret, told to neither husband. Sam Swartout had been replaced as collector of customs and immediately departed for a tour of Europe—a trip, John Sladen muttered to her, that was likely to last for the rest of his life. Early in November the bombshell hit the newspapers. Swartout's accounts were short $1,250,000—and the federal attorney for the southern district of New York, who should have been watching him, had been a sharer in the spoils.

North and South and West, Whig newspapers chortled that the Democrats, in the person of Swartout, had stolen in one swoop more money than all the previous swindlers, defalcators, and miscellaneous crooks employed by the U.S. government since it was launched in 1789, combined! Congressmen rose to demand an immediate investigation. A special committee, put together with only token resistance from Speaker Polk, consisted of three Democrats and six Whigs.

On the night of November 22, 1837, Caroline's salon was in crowded session. John Sladen, morosely drunk, told her once more that Sam Swartout would have paid back every cent of that money if the weasel in the White House had driven the annexation of Texas through the House and Senate. The votes were there. Van Buren was intimidated by the noise the abolitionists were making.

"Talk about gutlessness," Sladen growled. "How many votes did they get in 1836 on their so-called Liberty Ticket? Eight thousand three hundred and eight. Out of one million five hundred thousand."

"Shhh," Caroline said. "I won't have you quarreling with Mr. Adams."

Into the room stumped the ex-president. Henry Orr swiftly served him a mulled wine, and after a hefty swallow the old puritan regarded Mrs. Stapleton with something approaching bonhomie. "Did you hear what I did in the House today? I presented a petition signed by one hundred and forty-eight respectable Boston ladies, praying Congress to abolish slave trading in the District. Do you approve of that, Mrs. Stapleton?"

"I most emphatically approve of women presenting petitions."

"I thought you would. Where's Mrs. Polk? I'm sure she'll say the same thing."

"But I wish the petitions were on a less acrimonious topic."

Before the ex-president could reply, a tremendous crash rattled the windows. Consternation mingled with fear on most faces. The only unruffled person in the parlor was General Winfield Scott, the towering commander of the American army. "I believe that was a cannon," he said.

"Is there any reason for a midnight bombardment, General?" George Stapleton asked.

"None that I know of. Unless the Seminole Indians have marched north and are attacking the White House."

The U.S. Army was fighting an ugly little war with this tribe of Indians in the swamps of Florida.

Another crash and the sound of distant cheering. Had a revolution begun?

The nation was still mired in the economic slump that had begun the last year. There had been food riots in New York and Philadelphia during the winter.

Caroline summoned Hannibal and ordered him to find out what was happening. The big black returned in five minutes, his eyes wide. "They's a crowd of people in front of the president's house, yellin' and cheerin'. They got a big gun and they firin' it and cheerin' some more. Most of'm pretty drunk. They yellin' something about a hundred and twenty-one to twenty-seven."

Into the room charged burly Matthew Davis, the Spy in Washington himself. "Those cannoneers are Whigs," he shouted. "They're telling Van the news about the New York elections. The Whigs have beaten the Democrats silly from Montauk to Buffalo. They've taken over the legislature by a count of a hundred and twenty-one to twenty-seven."

"What a shame!" Sarah Polk said. "To think that President Van Buren has lost his home state!"

Her eyes met Caroline's. The Mona Lisa smile was in them, though her face remained solemn. There was no need to ask the question that Caroline was certain half the room was suddenly pondering. Would the Democratic Party turn to the Speaker of the House for its next presidential candidate? It was amazing what two women could accomplish by keeping their mouths shut.

FOUR

"MISSUS, THIS HERE'S MY MINISTER, THE Reverend Nathan Allen. He's got a power of trouble. I told him you and the senator would help him."

The Reverend Mr. Allen was almost as tall as Hannibal, but much thinner. A large, cranelike old man—austerely dignified. Together the two blacks filled the doorway of the Stapleton bedroom.

Caroline was packing trunks for their summer return to New Jersey. "I'm terribly busy, Hannibal. Can't you see that?"

"But this can't wait, missus. Reverend here's bought his own freedom and his three sons'. But one of his sons married a girl who's still bound to a fellow named Birch. He wants to sell her and her three children, the reverend's grandchildren, south. Reverend's tryin' to raise a thousand dollars by this Friday to free'm, missus."

"Congressman Adams said he was sure you'd help me, ma'am," the Reverend Mr. Allen said.

"How much did he give you?"

"Fifty dollars."

"I'll give a hundred."

"Oh, thank you, missus," Hannibal said. "One of them little girls is a good friend of my Tabitha. She done cry and cry when she heard they might be sold south."

The name Tabitha caused a nerve in Caroline's throat to twitch. "I'll give a hundred and fifty."

It would wreck her household budget for the month, but it was worth it to get these black faces out of her bedroom, out of her sight. More and more, Caroline found the endless quarrel over slavery shredded her nerves. It was doing the same thing to Sarah Polk—to many people.

The dispute had taken a disastrous turn in the Senate last year, when Senator Rives and Senator Calhoun suddenly found themselves on opposite sides. Rives, speaking as a Virginian and a disciple of Thomas Jefferson's, said slavery was evil and he longed for the day when it would disappear. Calhoun vehemently disagreed. He said it was the best solution for both races. Slavery was good for the black race. They could not survive as free men.

John Sladen had followed his leader into this cul-de-sac, and dozens of other Southerners were soon saying the same thing. The abolitionists were goaded to new heights of fury and denunciation. It was male stupidity at its worst. Caroline began to see the necessity of detaching George and John from Calhoun. The man's mind was too logical, too argumentative, for an American politician. He did not know how to ingratiate his enemies; his instinct was to defy them, destroy them.

When she invited Senator Calhoun to her salon, she made sure she omitted John Quincy Adams from the guest list—and vice versa. To cushion the waves of animosity they emanated, Caroline had discovered a far more powerful personage, who radiated benevolence rather than assault and battery: Dolley Madison. The widow of the fourth president had moved back to Washington after his death in 1836. Strapped for cash, Dolley could only afford to give one reception a month. She welcomed as a godsend the chance to shine at Mrs. Stapleton's weekly salons. Her presence invariably guaranteed the bonhomie that the frowning Adams and glowering Calhoun threatened to demolish.

Dressing hastily, running a comb through her hair, Mrs. Stapleton rushed off to the Capitol in her coach. She arrived in time to witness the closing minutes of the House of Representatives' 1838 spring session. She sank into the seat Sarah Polk had been saving for her and whispered an apology for being late. Sarah smiled her understanding.

John Sladen rose to salute Speaker Polk. "I think all the members of the Democratic Party and even a few of those who claim membership in another party will agree, Mr. Speaker, that you have presided over our tumults with a degree of fairness and good humor that this House, taken as a disorderly whole, unquestionably does not deserve. We will miss your talents and your judgment, but we realize that the people of the great state of Tennessee will be the beneficiaries. When we remember who is the First Resident of that state, we're doubly grateful that you are going to bring to Andrew Jackson's lips the sweet taste of Democratic victory this year. I predict that this event will make the people of this whole nation, assembled in their majesty at the polls, insist on your return to federal service in a post even higher than the one you have so ably filled for these past four years."

Sitting beside Sarah were Matthew Davis, the Spy in Washington; Nathaniel Willis, the elegant editor of the *New York Mirror;* and Frank Thomas, the witty Washington correspondent of the *New York Herald*. All three were frequent guests at Caroline's salon. They were industriously scribbling notes on John Sladen's tribute to James Polk. It would be national news before the end of the week.

Sarah had decided that her husband needed to escape the endless warfare of the House of Representatives. He was going home to run for governor of Tennessee, with Andrew Jackson's blessing. As John Sladen's speech, written virtually to Caroline's order, suggested, a larger strategy was at work. If James wrested Old Hickory's state from the grasp of the Whigs, who had held it since Van Buren failed to carry it in 1836, Polk would be a logical candidate for vice president on the Democratic ticket.

Sarah's heady vista of a presidential nomination had been deflated by President Van Buren's grim determination to run again and the Little Magician's iron grip on the party's patronage. Although he was clearly a wounded politician, Vanny was guaranteed the nomination by his ability to handpick the delegates to the Democratic Convention. But everyone was certain he would jettison Richard "Tecumseh" Johnson as his vice president. His lifestyle disgusted Southerners and gave abolitionists a standing target at the very top of the Democratic Party.

Back at Gadsby's Hotel, the Polks held a farewell reception for their many congressional friends. George and Caroline and John Sladen lingered after everyone else had left. Only now did Caroline confront the reality of her separation from Sarah. The habit of controlling her thoughts and feelings had enabled her to keep this dismaying fact at bay.

"Kiss the boys for me," Sarah said.

Caroline nodded mechanically. Pain, a formidable shaft of pain, was cleaving the center of her body. For a decade she and Sarah had spent two-thirds of each year in Washington, seeing each other almost every day. Regret, an emotion Caroline seldom tolerated, burst from her lips.

"This city will be empty without you!"

Tears trickled down Sarah's face. "If I have a single regret, it's the loss of your company—and the fear that I'll never see you again. Life is so uncertain, God's designs are so mysterious . . ."

"I love you so much, I'm almost willing to believe some creator has brought us together for a purpose." Caroline was weeping too. It was wrong, it was inconsiderate, to show such emotion before two men who theoretically loved her. But Caroline did not care. She loved this woman more than she loved either of them. It was a love beyond passion, a true union of souls.

The men stood at a distance, wide-eyed at these protestations. Neither James Polk nor John Sladen seemed to know what to say. Both made a habit of suppressing their emotions. Only George was unintimidated by this outburst of feeling.

"I begin to think you've done the right thing, separating them, Polk," George said. "If they stayed together another year, they'd have taken over the government."

"Unquestionably," James Polk said.

"Poor Vanny would be out of a job," George said.

His contempt for Van Buren had continued to grow. It had been hardened into disgust by the president's refusal to do anything about Texas—and his failure to solve the country's economic crisis.

"Vanny may be out of a job next year, anyway," John Sladen said. "That's the one thing wrong with your master plan. Running on a ticket with that weasel."

Caroline and Sarah had already discussed and discounted this negative possibility. Even if Van Buren lost, Polk would be a prime contender for the nomination the next time around. The race would make him a national figure.

Caroline kissed Sarah violently on the mouth. "We'll see each other again, I'm sure of it. Meanwhile, thank God for the U.S. mail."

Off the Polks clanked on the Baltimore and Ohio (and other railroad lines) to Tennessee. The Stapletons returned to New Jersey by steamboat, which was still faster and safer than "the cars," as everyone called them. Caroline sought refuge at Kemble Manor while George toured the state, doing battle with the growing number of abolitionists. He had worked up a speech that challenged them to solve the problem of what to do with the South's 3 million blacks, if they were freed. None of them had an answer. George then proposed that each Northern state would have to share the burden of educating and supporting the ex-slaves. Everyone in America profited from slavery. The South bought half of New Jersey's leather goods. Principia Mills' looms spun Southern cotton into cloth. At the minimum, George said, New Jersey would have to accept two hundred thousand Africans. At this point, a storm of boos and hisses usually drove the abolitionists from the hall.

Every third or fourth day, the mail brought Caroline a report of James Polk's run for the governorship of Tennessee. It was a hard-fought campaign that took him from one end of the five-hundred-mile-long state to the other, speaking in the brutal subtropical humidity of Memphis and the baking heat of Kingsport. Sarah fretted about his health, but James, glad to be out of the cockpit of the House of Representatives, thrived. At the bottom of one of her letters, he scribbled, *I've never felt better in my life!*

The Stapletons were back in Washington when the glorious news arrived in the newspapers, followed by a triumphant letter from Sarah. James had won by a whisker. A few nights later, the Stapletons were on the White House list for a reception. The president had finally found a hostess for his barren bachelor quarters. His oldest son, Abraham, had married a tall attractive blonde from South Carolina, Angelica Singleton.

Going through the receiving line, Caroline was amused by the way his son and daughter-in-law towered over the president. Van Buren had grown extremely fat, making him look even shorter than he was. As she shook his pudgy hand, she said, "No doubt you've heard the glorious news from Tennessee, Mr. President?"

"I've already congratulated Mr. and Mrs. Polk. I suppose I should congratulate you too—as her partner in crime."

"Crime?"

"Merely an expression. You're looking lovely as usual."

Caroline found herself pondering the partner-in-crime remark. Was the

Little Magician hinting that he knew the game they had played with Samuel Swartout? Who could tell him, except John Sladen? She suddenly remembered John's expression the day she said good-bye to Sarah Polk. The haunted desire had become a deepening bitterness. She would have to do something to show him her love survived—and do it soon. But how could the woman who hid in the icy caverns of her soul speak?

Van Buren began circulating through the crowd. Senator Stapleton brought him to a halt. "Will there be any progress on Texas in this session of Congress, Mr. President?"

Van Buren gazed up at George's formidable bulk. "Remember what I told you about waiting, when we first met? On this question it's true, as they say, in spades. We hold all the cards."

"That's not what I hear from General Jackson."

"General Jackson is getting a great deal of bad advice from his friend Sam Houston."

The president turned to seize the arm of the English ambassador, who equaled him in girth. "Assure this fellow you have no designs on Texas, Sir John."

"None whatsoever," the ambassador said. "Though we believe justice would be best served if they remained affiliated in some way with their parent country, Mexico."

"Mr. Ambassador, I'm sure your grandfather had the same opinion about the United States after the battle of Yorktown," George said. "People who shed blood to win their independence aren't inclined to cut a deal with their oppressors."

"Senator, keep your temper. We're not at the negotiating table," Van Buren said.

Damn you, George, Caroline thought. Why couldn't he wait to bait Vanny about Texas? It was the third or fourth time he had done it this year. As Van Buren retreated, Caroline stepped into his path. "I have a suggestion about Texas, Mr. President. As soon as you win reelection next year, you should send someone at the very top of your government to Mexico with the power to negotiate everything. The one man who would be perfect for this is James Polk. But first you'll have to nominate him for vice president."

"An interesting idea, Mrs. Stapleton. But I already have a vice president with whom I'm completely satisfied."

Caroline found it hard to believe she had heard him correctly. "Completely, Mr. President?"

"Completely. I'm no more inclined to change him for Mr. Polk than I would be for John Sladen."

So that was it. He had never forgiven her and Sladen for the Aaron Burr toast. "Mr. Burr is dead these three years, Mr. President," she said.

"But one of his ex-henchman, Matt Davis, is hawking his biography all over town, with ripe slanders of me in it. I suppose you've bought a copy."

"In fact I have, but I haven't read it," Caroline lied. "I had an interesting conversation with Congressman Adams about it. He says it's a veritable lesson in retributive justice. It describes how Mr. Burr and Mr. Hamilton connived to deprive his father of the presidency after a single term, and they both met miserable ends because of this terrible crime. Do you think it would be a crime to inflict such a fate on you?"

"If it's a crime to inflict political pain, I fear you, or another of my many enemies, might be guilty, Mrs. Stapleton. But knowing your power, I hope to propitiate your support."

"Oh, you have it already, Mr. President. Your name is on my lips constantly."

"But is it in your heart, Mrs. Stapleton?"

"That may be where some propitiation might help, Mr. President."

"For the moment all I can say is, Mrs. Polk ought not to raise her hopes."

This conversation went out verbatim to Nashville, where Governor Polk and Sarah were in residence. Sarah was dismayed to learn Van Buren could be so stupid or vindictive or weak. *Some close friends recently stopped at Vice President Johnson's plantation on their way to Tennessee. He lives in open concubinage with not one but a half dozen of his slaves. The man is repulsive! How can Van Buren renominate him? He has truly lost his sense of direction.*

Renominate Richard Johnson is exactly what Martin Van Buren did, to the almost universal dismay of the Democratic Party. He seemed to think that he needed a Westerner with a military record on his ticket to counter the Whig candidate, General William Henry Harrison of Kentucky. The renomination was managed in Van Buren's usual sneaky style. At the Democratic Convention in Baltimore, George Stapleton nominated James Polk in a vigorous speech as the man who had regained Tennessee for the Democrats. Not a single Van Buren follower said a word for him. Two other names were thrown into the pot, and the convention then announced it would nominate no one. They would let "the people" choose the vice president from the four contenders, in the course of the campaign. The party organization, firmly in Van Buren's control, manufactured petitions and letters to newspapers supporting Johnson, leaving Polk and the other two candidates no choice but humiliating withdrawals.

Sarah Polk was livid. Caroline told George if he made an enthusiastic speech in favor of Van Buren in New Jersey, she would consider divorcing him. Fortunately George needed no encouragement toward tepidity. His efforts on behalf of the incumbent (privately George preferred the word *recumbent*) president were minimal. He concentrated on electing Democrats to state offices and to Congress. Governor Polk went through similar halfhearted motions on the Little Magician's behalf in Tennessee, and John Sladen persuaded his powerful Legrand in-laws to do even less in Louisiana. Their unenthusiasm was widely imitated in other states.

The Whigs nominated the respected former senator from Virginia, John Tyler, for vice president. They had learned from the Democrats how to organize a party, and now they paid them the compliment of imitating their campaigning style. Instead of hickory poles, the Whigs paraded liberty poles through the streets of a thousand towns and cities to an open field, where vast quantities of beer and liquor were consumed and tons of hot air were expelled by speakers on the virtues of "Old Tippecanoe," as General Harrison was called, after the Indiana creek near which he had defeated Tecumseh and 650 Shawnees in 1811.

Everyone then joined in a rousing song:

What has caused this great commotion, motion, motion
Our country through?
It is the ball a-rolling on, on
For Tippecanoe and Tyler too—Tippecanoe and Tyler too
And with them we'll beat little Van Van Van
Van is a used-up man.

Compounding the Democrats' troubles was a remark by the Washington correspondent of a Baltimore newspaper, who sneered that Harrison lacked both the brains and the inclination to be president. He would be perfectly satisfied with a pension of $2,000 a year, leaving him free to spend his days drinking hard cider in his log cabin on the banks of the Ohio.

The Whigs seized on this insult and converted it into another asset. A congressman named Ogle rose to denounce Van Buren for living in luxury in the White House off gold and silver plates, reclining on soft Turkish divans, and walking on Brussels and Wilton carpets deep enough for an honest American to bury his foot in. Little Van's rotund frame, his fondness for flashy clothes, seemed to prove this slander, and the Whigs were soon singing another song:

In the cabin made of logs
By the river side
There the honest farmer lives
Free from sloth and pride
To the gorgeous palace turn
There his rival see
In his robes of regal state
Tinseled finery.

The Whigs roared this ditty while parading log cabins through the streets along with their liberty poles. The drink of choice at all their rallies became hard cider, which did nothing to diminish voters' enthusiasm for Old Tippecanoe and Tyler too. The fact that "Old Tip" was born in a Virginia mansion and lived in an Ohio house that was no more a log cabin than Andrew Jackson's Hermitage swiftly became irrelevant.

At Bowood on election day, George and Caroline held an open house. On previous election days, the event had been called a victory party. Today, the invitations simply called it "a reception for friends, personal and political." The old house was crowded with visitors, among them Sally and Jeremy Biddle. Sally had become almost as fat as her aunt Henrietta Van Rensselaer. Jeremy, on the other hand, was growing lean. Caroline had privately nicknamed them "the Sprats" after the couple in the nursery rhyme. Jeremy apparently ate no fat and Sally certainly ate no lean.

Twelve years in Washington had largely dissipated Caroline's fear of Sally's moral disapproval. The deeper one traveled into the world of politics, the less meaning the word *moral* seemed to have. Peggy O'Neale Eaton was back in Tennessee, watching her ruined husband drink himself to death. Once svelte Sally Stapleton Biddle, growing fatter and more provincial by the hour, was unhappily married to a plodding businessman. The other women of the Golden Horde were going through the motions of vapid gentility in upper-class New York.

Sally still had pretensions, thanks to her image of herself as first lady of Hamilton. She assumed that Caroline was desperately anxious to see Martin Van Buren reelected and spoke to her with oozing condescension about his chances.

"I think you're going to find Little Van is a used-up man before long."

"I *hope* so," Caroline said. "Between us, no one despises him more whole-heartedly than I do."

Sally was astonished and confused. "Why do you say that?"

"I could tell you things about that man, but delicacy prevents me from going into detail."

Sally was reduced to humble murmurs. It was more than adequate revenge for that moment in her drawing room, when she impaled Caroline with that mocking stare ten years ago.

But Sally was not without resources. "How is John Sladen? Do you see much of him when Congress is in session?"

Caroline decided to be bold. "He's in and out of our house constantly. The poor man can't entice his wife to Washington. He and George have become close friends, and political confederates. I take some credit for that."

"I'm sure you do. But I begin to wonder how long *any* moral person can remain a Democrat. I didn't have to change Jeremy. He's a born Whig. But George . . ."

"What do you mean?"

"I mean your alliance with the slave owners. The more I think about it, the more the whole South becomes a blot on our national honor."

"You sound like an abolitionist."

"Oh, no! I have no use for those dreadful people. Yankees, almost every one of them. But I wonder how you tolerate the sight of slavery, of people in chains, right outside your house. I presume you see them every day?"

"I see them often enough."

"And what happened to poor Tabitha . . ."

"Yes. It was terrible. Excuse me. I must attend to my other guests."

Caroline walked swiftly away, looking neither right nor left, until she reached the table where Bowood's black servants were pouring champagne. She picked up a glass and emptied it in one continuous swallow. Very unlady-like.

Looking across the room, she saw Sally was watching her. On her face was a sheen of unmistakable malice. *Damn you*, Caroline thought. *Goddamn you.* She downed another glass, but it did not raise her spirits an iota. Wandering through the lofty rooms, pausing now and then to exchange empty phrases with semistrangers, she found herself in the library. There was the Congressman, gazing down at her from the wall above the fireplace. To the left, lower down, was the painting of the battles of Lundy's Lane and the Thames, with her father and George's father in opposite corners.

A small smile was on the Congressman's face, as if he were saying, *I prevailed.* Only she knew that at the very end, he had not prevailed. The world had slipped beyond his control. So much of life was fate, beyond the reach of the individual will. Would she have been wiser to trust that first primary plunge into the underground river? It would have carried her to another destination in John Sladen's arms. She would be living in Louisiana now, struggling unambiguously in the South's cause instead of living this way, with a divided soul. More and more that river had become synonymous with fate, with all the parts of life that a woman, or a man, inherits. She began to wonder if anyone could resist its remorseless current.

Who could rescue her? *Sarah.* The word whispered in her soul. Yes, yes, yes. Sarah's love, beyond the pull and spin of passion, beyond pleasure and desire, that was her only hope. But Sarah was beyond her reach too, perhaps forever. They had both sensed vibrations of possible pain and disappointment in her withdrawal to Tennessee.

Caroline sank into a chair, filled with intimations of gloom infinitely darker than the political defeat she was anticipating. The next thing she knew was George's kiss on her cheek. The room was deep in shadow. "All sorts of people have been looking for you," he said. "They wanted to say good-bye."

"I'm sorry."

He looked up at Hugh Stapleton's portrait. "I came in here the other night and sat in that chair. I almost said a prayer, asking him for guidance. Was that what you were doing?"

"Perhaps."

Should she tell him what Sally had said about the Democrats and slavery? No. She would not be responsible for planting doubts in his soul. George was not a man who knew how to deal with doubt. Besides, she had pledged her political love to another troubled man. She could not undertake to comfort two lovers. Instead, she would let this lover comfort her.

"Has everyone gone?"

"Yes."

"Why don't we do something romantic? Let the boys eat supper in the kitchen while we have a cold collation—with champagne—in our room?"

"I've already sent the boys off with Jeremy and Sally."

"You schemer—you . . . you politician."

He lifted her out of the chair as if she were a piece of gossamer and kissed her gently on the mouth. Upstairs, she discovered the cold collation, the bottle of champagne, were already waiting. Was George acquiring an ability to read her mind? A disconcerting thought.

They drank the champagne and nibbled on the food and speculated idly on what Washington would be like without President Van Buren. An hour later, as she lay in the bathtub's warm, fragrant water, Caroline realized what George was doing. He was reaffirming their partnership on the edge of the unknown. She was enormously, almost frighteningly touched.

When she slipped into bed beside him, Caroline was closer to the swimmer in the underground river than the married woman balancing choices in her perpetually calculating head. In a haze of champagne and sympathy, she and George exchanged a new sense of partnership. Only when it was over and she sighed in his arms did she realize how little the gift had altered those other pledges—to John Sladen and Sarah Childress Polk.

Somehow this reinforced the ferocity of her final kiss. "Let's never forget this—how much we loved each other tonight."

"How could I?" George said with his incurable blend of romance and optimism.

Caroline could think of a dozen, a hundred things that might make him forget it. But she declined to mar the moment with her doubts. She let Young America's faith in the future rest unquestioning in the arms of La Belle Dame sans Merci. Knowing and not knowing, admitting and denying this stark blend of truth and poetry, Caroline hoped against hope that somehow George's faith would prevail.

FIVE

"WHAT A JOY IT IS, MRS. Stapleton, to find the Adamses now have company in the history books! My father and I, the only presidents to be turned out after a single term, have now been joined by a Democrat—a disciple of Andrew Jackson, no less. Doesn't it reinforce your faith in a just God?"

Old John Quincy Adams blinked cheerfully at Caroline Stapleton over the top of his eyeglasses. The former president was chortling over Martin Van Buren's rout at the polls. Little Van had carried only seven states to William Henry Harrison's twenty. Van had even lost his home state of New York, as well as Tennessee, New Jersey, and Louisiana.

As an avowed Democrat, Caroline could not join the gleeful old Yankee in public jubilation. She turned to gray-haired Dolley Madison, sitting in a nearby chair, her cheeks rouged a merry red. "Mrs. Madison, rescue us, please, from this man's partisan theology."

"Johnny Adams, thee art a blasphemer or worse," Dolley said, the good cheer in her blue eyes making it clear that she was joking. "God has nothing to do with Democrats or Whigs or Federalists or Republicans!"

"Your Quaker faith, my dear Mrs. Madison, prays to an altogether unsatisfying God," Adams said. "He's far too kind for my taste. I prefer New England's deity. A being who cries, 'Vengeance is mine!'"

"God," Mrs. Madison insisted, "is not a politician. Didn't Jesus say He had nothing to do with caesar?"

"I make a motion in favor of Mrs. Madison's theology," rumbled Daniel

Webster, scooping a wing off an ice cream angel and downing it in a single oratorical gulp.

"A new caesar is about to arrive from the West," John Sladen said. "I'll predict this much: he won't be another Andrew Jackson."

"I'll thank any and every god for that," John Quincy Adams said.

"Have you heard from General Jackson, Senator Stapleton?" Senator Henry Clay asked. He was fairly bubbling with ebullience. As he saw it, William Henry Harrison was too old to serve more than one term. That meant the Whig nomination would be his for the asking in 1844.

George nodded cheerfully. "He says the Democrats have been beaten, but not conquered."

That's much better, George, Caroline silently said, keeping her smile intact. Only a severe lecture had persuaded George to pretend to be cheerful for public consumption. The letter from Old Hickory had put Senator Stapleton into a funk. He had beat his breast and wondered if they had done the right thing, letting Van Buren go down to such a crushing defeat. The Whigs had won solid majorities in both houses of Congress. They had done almost as well in the South as in the North.

"Out of respect for his advanced age, I think you should warn the General he may have to alter that tune once Congress assembles," Henry Clay said.

"I'll let you tell him, Senator," George said. "I would advise you to do it by U.S. mail—lest you become one of those messengers who get it in the neck."

Everyone chuckled, but Clay was only half joking. The Kentuckian made no secret of his plans to dismantle Jacksonian-style government. The president was to become the obedient servant of Congress, and Congress was going to vote a new Bank of the United States, a new tariff, and a new internal-improvements program that would pump federal money into roads, canals and railroads.

"I wonder how Tip will deal with the legions of job seekers that are certain to descend on him," John Quincy Adams said. "He was the greatest beggar in my administration. I made him ambassador to Colombia, but he never ceased bombarding me with petitions for better employment."

"Senator Calhoun served with him in Congress," John Sladen said. "He assures me General Harrison is as unconscious as a child of the difficulties the country faces. The man sees his election as a mere affair of personal vanity."

"General Jackson declares him a complete and total imbecile," George Stapleton said.

"Jealousy, patent jealousy," Henry Clay chortled. "General Harrison knows at least as much about government as General Jackson, which is another way of saying nothing whatsoever."

"I had a letter from my friend Ralph Waldo Emerson the other day," Daniel Webster said. "He calls General Harrison 'the Indignation President.' I begin to think even I could have overcome the national loathing for New England men and beaten Little Van."

"A four-year-old child could have beaten Van," John Quincy Adams said. "Which, in terms of the new president's mental capacity, seems to be what has happened."

So went the conversation in Mrs. Stapleton's parlor on March 3, 1841, the eve of President William Henry Harrison's inauguration. Caroline had discovered from the newspapers that Mrs. Harrison had been born in New Jersey. That gave her some faint hope of a favorable reception at the White House. But its very faintness underscored the dreary prospect of four years in the political wilderness.

Complicating Caroline's pessimism was her fifth pregnancy. Her evening with Young America in Bowood had proven more fruitful than she had intended it to be. She hoped for a girl, but not too violently; she sensed fate seemed determined to frustrate her on that score. Perhaps it was just as well. A rebellious daughter—and she was certain a daughter would be a replica of her—would be far more difficult to deal with than a son. Caroline remained supremely confident of her ability to manipulate men.

Her consolation these days was her letters from Sarah Polk. Not that those pages of precise prose cheered her politically. With her usual unblinking honesty, Sarah saw the future in stark terms. If the Whigs succeeded in Washington, the Democrats could become a minority party for a long time. Her only glimmer of hope were the divisions inside the Whig Party. They had more than a few outspoken critics of slavery in their ranks. They could easily be called abolitionists, which spelled political death at the hands of most voters, South and North. The abolitionists had run a candidate on their Liberty Party ticket. He had garnered a pathetic 7,040 votes.

In Tennessee, Texas was the hottest issue. If the Whigs brought that vast expanse of territory into the Union, they would own the state—and the entire South, plus Kentucky and Indiana—for all time. But Sarah was betting the Whigs would be too divided, and "too stupid," to see how important it was. They would concentrate on restoring Henry Clay's American System and let Texas sit there, waiting for the next Democratic candidate to make it the centerpiece of his platform.

> *In fact, talking with General Jackson, I begin to think we can make Texas the basis of a grand movement south and west that will establish us in California and the Texas borderlands. We already have a strong claim to the Oregon territory. The General sees our manifest destiny as continental—a term I rather like, don't you? Think of what a claim on the popular mind that achievement will be, if it is done under a Democratic administration. It will guarantee a succession of Democratic presidents to the end of this century.*

The next day Caroline decided to continue ignoring the rule that pregnant ladies should "retire" until they gave birth. She went to William Henry Harrison's inaugural. It was a cold, windy March day. Hatless and coatless, the big, gray-haired man—at sixty-eight he was the oldest elected president yet—droned through an endless speech that had obviously been written for him by Henry Clay. It announced it was time to eliminate the danger of tyranny from the federal government by making sure its power was distributed the way the Founding Fathers intended it to be—Congress should be in charge of things. As the president nattered on, bored politicians got up and stamped around the platform to restore some circulation to their freezing feet; Caroline was tempted to join them. By the time he finished, her feet, in the thin silk slippers ladies wore to dress occasions, were two blocks of ice.

The inaugural reception at the White House was a model of decorum, making it clear that this Western general had no desire to be a man of the people. But plenty of the people were in the mansion—most of them job seekers. At least a hundred of them did not hesitate to hand the president written pleas on their own behalf. By the time George and Caroline shook Harrison's hand, he had sheaves of paper sticking out of the pockets of his coat.

"Ah, Senator Stapleton. I served in Congress with your grandfather," the president said. "I greatly admired his integrity, his patriotism. I wish we were back in those good old days, when the federal government had fewer jobs to hand out than the state of Delaware. A man could govern with dignity."

He interrupted his lament to unleash an enormous sneeze. Two job seekers rushed forward with handkerchiefs and assured the president he could keep them, along with the petitions inside them.

On the way home, George said, "I'm beginning to wonder why anyone would ever want to be president. It's the most thankless job in the world."

"It's also the most important job in the world," Caroline said.

"More important than the prime minister of England, the czar of Russia?" George said, determined to disagree with her.

"Yes, or it will be soon, when the United States annexes Texas and California and Oregon and becomes a continental power."

"A continental power?"

"Sarah Polk, thanks to her residence in Nashville, has been spending time at the Hermitage. She tells me this is General Jackson's latest vision."

"A continental power. I like the sound of it."

To whom should she give the credit—Andrew Jackson or Sarah Polk? Who was more important, the originator of a vision or the person who sees its potency? For Caroline, that was an easy question to answer. General Jackson was an old man, out of power. Their generation was the one that would implement his vision and win places in the Temple of Fame. And a woman, or two women, would be the secret agents, the hidden creators, of this global transformation.

"It's a beautiful dream," George said. "But I wonder if it will ever happen. Henry Clay told me he has no intention of touching Texas. He calls it a gigantic tar baby. Anyone who goes near it will get smeared. The North won't tolerate it as a slave state and the South won't swallow it as a free state. He plans on making Americans so prosperous, no one will give a damn about acquiring more territory."

"Henry Clay, for all his seeming shrewdness, is a fool," Caroline said. "He's so wrapped up in his ambition to be president, he can't think straight. No matter how prosperous you make Americans, there're always going to be some people who want to get even more prosperous—and what better way to do it than by laying our hands on a few million acres of unclaimed land?"

"I'm inclined to agree with that."

"You should become the Senate's most outspoken advocate for Texas. Go down there and pay Sam Houston a visit. Talk about it, make speeches about it, everywhere you go. Talk about California and Oregon too."

"I might end up sounding like a warmonger. Remember how many Quakers we've got in New Jersey."

"Talk about peaceful purchase. Negotiations with Mexico."

Back home, the Stapletons found twelve-year-old Jonathan and ten-year-old Charlie having an argument with their tutor, a stocky, bullnecked young Virginian named Randolph Cooke. "These young gentleman have gotten their hands on some abolitionist literature. They claim the right to read it. I say no one their age should be permitted to look at such trash," Cooke said.

Jonathan gazed at his mother with John Sladen's rebellious eyes. "I told him Americans—even American boys—should have the right to read what they please."

"Yeah!" said Charlie, who clearly did not care one way or the other. He was enjoying the brawl as a happy alternative to schoolwork.

Swarthy, dark-haired Jonathan was growing taller by the minute, so it seemed to Caroline. Studious, intense, he was always asking her questions about history and politics. By all the laws of logic, he should have been her favorite. But she found him too morose, too humorless, to win her affection. It was freckle-faced Charlie who stirred her heart with his clever pranks and total disinclination to take anything seriously, including his studies. His strong physical resemblance to her father also had something to do with her fondness for him.

Caroline had hired Cooke as a tutor last year, when their shuttles between Washington and New Jersey became more erratic because of the presidential election. Washington's schools were second-rate anyway. George was determined to send his sons to Columbia and was more than willing to spend money to get them ready. Cooke had graduated from the University of Virginia last year at the top of his class.

"Let me see this stuff," George said.

Cooke handed him a copy of William Lloyd Garrison's newspaper, *The Liberator*. The editorial called for Americans to join in a "mighty moral war" to free the South's blacks. The stories from correspondents told of successful British efforts to suppress the slave trade in Africa, of the progress of "reform" in Jamaica and other West Indies islands, where slavery had been abolished seven years ago. Another story told of a mob attacking an abolitionist paper in Indiana and burning down the publisher's house and destroying his printing press.

"Where did you get this?" George asked Jonathan.

"Laura Biddle mailed it to me."

Laura was Sally and Jeremy Biddle's daughter. She was eleven. "Where did she get it?" George asked.

"Her father and mother subscribe to it," Jonathan said.

"I don't see anything wrong with you reading it," George said. "As long as you don't believe everything these fanatics say."

"Their intentions are so dishonorable, Senator, I can't believe you will even tolerate such a piece of offal in your house!" Cooke said.

George grew testy. "Mr. Cooke. I'll decide what I can and cannot tolerate in my house. I think it's better in the long run to read the nonsense these people purvey. Banning them only makes their vaporings more attractive to twelve- and ten-year-old boys."

"If you insist on that stance, sir, I must consider my authority with these young men at an end and respectfully request your permission to resign my contract."

Caroline was appalled by the way the argument was going. Cooke's brother worked as a reporter for the *Washington Telegraph,* a strongly pro-Southern paper. She could see a story appearing in its pages in the next day or two, reporting how a principled young Southern gentleman tutor had resigned his position at Senator Stapleton's home rather than tolerate abolitionist literature in the parlor.

"Mr. Cooke, calm down," Caroline said. "I'll see to it that this paper *never* appears in our house again. While I agree with their father that it does Jonathan and Charles no great harm to read it, I won't tolerate such an offensive publication in my home, where Southern visitors like yourself would be justly offended by it."

"I certainly have no intention of subscribing to this rag," George said.

"Then I take it we may cast it out with the trash?" Cooke said, glaring triumphantly at Jonathan.

"Of course," George said.

Upstairs in their bedroom, Caroline lost her temper. "Really, George. Must I do *all* our thinking? Don't you see what might get into the *Telegraph* if you let that fellow quit over that damn paper?"

"It would be nothing that I couldn't correct with a letter to the editor."

"The *Telegraph*'s not a Jackson paper anymore. They're totally devoted to Calhoun and Southern rights. I don't think your friendship with the senator would stand the test of letting your son read *The Liberator.* I hope you'll write a very stiff letter to Jeremy Biddle and tell him how little use we have for further correspondence between his daughter and Jonathan."

"I'll tell him in a less offensive way that we'd appreciate no more copies of *The Liberator.*"

"George, you don't seem to realize how *serious* this could be. How a seeming trifle like this could destroy your chance to be president."

"Didn't I just finish telling you I didn't particularly want to be president?"

"I didn't take you seriously. I don't take you seriously now."

For a moment George looked as if he were going to say something extremely unpleasant. He let the impulse pass. But Caroline reacted with profound alarm. What a paradox marriage was. The baby swelling in her body was a product of their passionate partnership, but its presence deprived her of a primary sense of control, possession, that was becoming almost as necessary to her as breathing.

Later in the day, Caroline summoned Jonathan to the library and gave him a lecture on his responsibility as his father's older son. "We expect you to set an example to Charlie. Yes, even to represent the family, to a certain degree, before strangers and servants. We're on display here, under scrutiny at all times, even in our homes. That's what it means to be a public man. There's a chance, a very good chance, that someday your father might be called to the highest office in this country. Would you want to be responsible for ruining that chance?"

Jonathan scuffed his toe on the carpet and muttered, "I only did it to get even with Mr. Cooke for his perpetual sermons about the South's superiority to the North."

"You must learn to be more tolerant, more understanding. The South is being attacked with no provocation on their part. They've begun to adopt a defensive mentality. It's important for some of us in the North to assure them that we're still their friends."

"Why can't they free their slaves like the British did?"

"The answer to that is much too complicated for you to understand."

Jonathan stalked out, head down, like a victim of an unjust punishment. For a moment Caroline almost screamed at him. What else could go wrong? An enemy in the White House, enemies in control of Congress, the country careening toward a future in which Senator Stapleton was irrelevant. Was George beginning to think that his domineering wife had given him fatally wrong advice, pushing him into the Democratic Party? Was she herself beginning to wonder if the Democrats had a future? A number of conservative Democrats had switched to the Whigs in the last few years, mostly out of disgust with Martin Van Buren.

Caroline lay down on the bed, the first jagged thrusts of a migraine pulsing through her forehead. For the next week she was miserable. Her pain had one side benefit. George felt so sorry for her, all their arguments, large and small, vanished. John Sladen brought her a bottle of eau-de-vie and sat in the darkened parlor with her (bright light ignited flashes of pain in her eyes), trying to cheer her up. But he was as miserable as she was.

He agreed with her that George should become Texas's spokesman and might well visit the giant republic. But there was an undertone of futility in the discussion. He dropped the subject and tried to amuse her with a word portrait of the hundreds of Whig job seekers swarming through the first floor of the White House, all but marooning the president on the second floor. Mrs. Harrison was wisely staying in Ohio until the jobs were handed out and the administration settled down. Daniel Webster had accepted Harrison's offer to become secretary of state, which should provide Caroline's salon with a steady supply of gossip.

"What about you, John? How do you see your future?"

"I didn't realize you were interested in such minor matters."

"Surely you know how wrong, how cruel, that is."

Dolley Madison, who had grown fond of John, had confided to Caroline rumors about his heavy drinking and his appearance at local taverns and cockpits with women whose reputations were less than sterling. It was not unusual for congressmen to wander in this fashion. There was little diversion in the boardinghouses in which they lived, six, eight, or ten to a "mess," talking politics day and night. But Caroline found John's dissipation poignant. In a sense it was her fault.

A week later, at the first Stapleton salon under the new regime, there was an undercurrent of uneasiness among some of the leading Whigs. Henry Wise, the rambunctious Virginia congressman who usually enlivened every party with outrageous jokes and remarks, was subdued. The president was acting odd; he was declining to fire Democrats from crucial patronage jobs. He had grown testy when Henry Clay started selecting his cabinet, at one point exploding, "Mr. Clay, you forget that I am president!"

Clay was equally exasperated. Wise told of finding him in his hotel room, storming up and down. "I have not influence enough to procure the appointment of a friend to the most humble position!" he had all but shouted. In fact, he was fuming because Harrison had declined to appoint his man to that perennial gold mine, collector of the port of New York. Dolley Madison listened to these intimations of Whig disarray and announced a much more disquieting rumor: the new president was ill. He had gone for a walk to escape the job seekers crowding the White House and had been caught in a sudden rain shower. He was coughing and wheezing like a steam engine and had canceled all his appointments.

A week later, the conversation at the salon had only one topic: the president's illness. Harrison was confined to his bed, surrounded by a dozen doctors. An express messenger had been sent to Ohio to summon Mrs. Harrison. For the first time, people began to think the hitherto unthinkable: what if the president died? Somehow, Andrew Jackson's numerous illnesses and semimiraculous recoveries had lulled everyone into believing God kept a special eye on the resident of the White House.

Dolley Madison confirmed this assumption. She recalled the time when George Washington's life was almost given up by his doctors; a cyst and abscess on his thigh defied healing. But expert nursing by Martha had him on his feet in a matter of weeks. Dolley remembered the way John Adams had brooded for four and five months at a time on his farm in Massachusetts, leading many people to think he was a drunkard or a madman. Mr. Jefferson had regularly been prostrated by his migraines. But death seemed barred from the White House. The very idea somehow contradicted the vitality inherent in the office of president—the summit of national power.

John Sladen noted that General Harrison had called a special session of Congress in May and would not dare be so disrespectful to Henry Clay as to inconvenience him by dying. This got a brief laugh, but Dolley Madison rebuked him for his lack of Christian charity. Caroline reported from "a certain source" that the president's condition was grave. Her secret informant was Hannibal, who attended the same Methodist church as many black members of the White House staff. They talked freely about the chief executive's illness.

Thus it was not a complete shock to the Stapleton circle when the news raced through Washington, D.C., and beyond it to the stunned nation: exactly one month after his inauguration, William Henry Harrison, ninth president of the United States, was dead. While the country mourned, Washington was racked by a question no one had ever expected to ask. What did John Tyler, the new president, or, as some people insisted on calling him, "the vice president acting as president," stand for? His relationship to the Whig Party was suggested by the casual way he had been added to the ticket: "And Tyler too."

In one part of Tennessee there was precious little mourning for Harrison. The new president's funeral was barely over when a letter arrived from the

Hermitage, addressed to Senator and Mrs. Stapleton. *A kind and overruling Providence has interfered to prolong our glorious Union. Tyler will stay the corruption of that clique who have got into power by deluding the people with the grossest slanders and hard cider.*

Most important, wrote Old Hickory, *Tyler will have an open mind on the matter that overrules all others: Texas.*

Caroline smiled triumphantly at George. It was no longer necessary to say *I told you so.* They were of one mind, if not completely of one heart, now.

S I X

Dearest Friend,

By now I hope you have received the news from George that I am a mother again—another boy, blasting once and for all, I suspect, my hopes (and I think, yours) for a girl. We have named him Paul, after George's great-uncle, who died heroically in the American Revolution. He's a rather frail child, caused, I fear, by the awful humidity of our capital in which I all but expired during the two months prior to his birth. I tended at times to curse Mr. Clay and our late president for calling a special session of Congress on May 31. Of course, Sir Harry of the West thought it would only take a week or two at the most to ram through his bank and tariff and improvement bills and then we could all flee to cooler climes. Instead, the statesmen have been sweating for two months now in the fiery furnace created by Beelzebub Tyler. Believe me that is one of the kinder names the Whigs have invented for our accidental president. By vetoing one Clay bill after another, he has created consternation and the most delicious chaos in their ranks. Never have I seen such fury expressed against a president. Not even the most intemperate Nullifiers and Secessionists of 1833 breathed oaths as ferocious on Andrew Jackson.

Last week, only ten days after my confinement, I accepted an invitation to dinner at the White House. The temperature was 95 degrees. George was sure the excitement would be fatal. I finally convinced him that on the contrary, the boredom of sitting home with a squalling baby would more likely demolish me. He submitted, muttering I was part Indian—I'm sure he really meant "politician" (though he would not have added "part" with that word)—and we were soon being received by the mansion's new hostess, Priscilla Cooper Tyler. The President's wife remains totally incapacitated by the stroke she suffered some two years ago. The younger Mrs. Tyler is, as I think I told you several letters back, a former actress, married to the president's eldest son, Robert. Extremely attractive and self-possessed, she gave a superb dinner, replete with fish, venison, the usual desserts, and a number of excellent wines.

Alas, as the desserts were being served, Mrs. Tyler grew deathly pale and slumped in her chair, quite unconscious. (I have since learned she is three or four months pregnant.) She was sitting next to Mr. Webster, our new secretary of state. He leaped up, lifted her from her chair, and began carrying her out of the room. At this point, her husband (who strikes me as a bit of a fool) seized a pitcher of ice water and hurled it all over her and Mr. Webster! I'm sure it totally ruined her beautiful dress, a delicate pink faille, and produced a decided coolness on Mr. Webster's part. The godlike Daniel had to be dried off by a half dozen waiters while our hostess was carried off to her bedroom.

Mr. Clay has made another attempt to pass a bank bill. If it fails for the usual reason, he may personally assassinate "Old Veto," as some are beginning to call Mr. Tyler. I fear the worst—or as a Democrat—hope for the best. Based on a remark in my parlor last night by Robert Tyler, Mr. Clay's prospects are not bright. Mr. Tyler called the latest offering "a humbug compromise."

Have you seen the newspaper squib where some Western farmer remarks, "By gum, Tyler must have found one of Old Andy's pens!"

Be sure to send me all the news of the Governor's run for reelection. With the deliquescence of the Whigs in Washington, victory will unquestionably win him national attention and make him the logical Democratic nominee in 1844.

With deepest affection,
Caroline

Caroline sealed the letter and addressed it to *Mrs. James Polk, The Governor's Mansion, Nashville, Tennessee.* Upstairs, she could hear Paul's whimpers turning into a wail. She summoned Hannibal and asked him to take the letter to the post office immediately.

In spite of the heat, energy was surging in Caroline's veins. President John Tyler was turning into a Democrat before everyone's astonished eyes. The invitations to her salon, canceled for the last months of her pregnancy, had to be distributed with the utmost care. Tempers were being strained, antagonisms stirred, that not even Mrs. Stapleton's beauty, supported by Mrs. Madison's benevolence, could hope to soothe.

Upstairs, Caroline found the wet nurse was answering Paul's needs. She was a big amiable black named Esther Hawkins, with breasts the size of watermelons. The Irishwoman who had nursed Charlie had long since traveled West or South, following her husband to some other construction project. Hovering around the domestic scene were Mercy and eleven-year-old Tabitha, who was on her way to becoming as attractive as her late mother.

"Oh, how I wishes I could do that for him, missus," Mercy said. She was still as thin and small-breasted as the day she arrived in the house.

"Well, I don't!" Tabitha said. "I thinks missus has got the right idea. Let someone else do it!"

Everyone laughed heartily. For a moment they were all simply women. Race did not matter. What a strange business life is, Caroline thought.

Dressing quickly, Caroline was waiting in the hall when Hannibal returned in the gig from his post office errand. She stepped into the seat beside him and said, "The Capitol. Hurry."

They set out at a brisk pace behind Beauty, one of their best trotters. The August sun beat down with almost unbearable intensity, and Caroline took immediate shelter beneath her parasol. The humid air flowed around them with a thickness that soon had sweat pouring down the horse's black flanks.

Not for the first time, Caroline urged Hannibal to marry Mercy. "When I see her doting over little Paul, I realize how much she needs a baby of her own. She's been a mother in all but name to Tabitha, hasn't she?"

"Yes, missus. But the spirit just hasn't spoken in me. Maybe I feels I don't deserve another woman, 'cause of the way I lost Tabitha. I shouldn've never let her go out alone. Should've known what could happen in this perilous city."

"We all should've known, Hannibal."

"Maybe I feels if I 'prive myself, it'll be an offerin' to the Lord God, missus. Like addin' my mite to the sufferin's of our savior Jesus—to redeem my people from bondage. That way helps me, missus, to think Tabitha died for a reason, that it mean somethin'. So hard to think maybe she dyin' means *nothin'*."

The words screeched across Caroline's nerves like a knife on glass. "That's all very fine, Hannibal. But meanwhile poor Mercy is miserable. She loves you so much she can't marry anyone else. It may take a long time—a terribly long time—to free your people."

"I knows that, missus, but—"

"Hannibal, promise me here and now that you'll do it."

Hannibal hung his head. "I promises, missus."

They rode on in silence to the Capitol. There, Caroline hurried to the Senate, where George had reserved a seat for her on one of the couches on the floor. The chamber was almost as humid and airless as the weather outside. George leaned over and murmured, "The president's sent up another veto. Get ready for some fireworks."

Within minutes, Samuel Southard, the Whig senator from New Jersey who was serving as president pro tempore of the Senate, began reading Tyler's veto of Clay's compromise bank bill. The message had an apologetic tone, as if the president knew what a political explosion he was about to ignite. The tone did nothing to silence Whigs in the gallery, who began shouting "Treason" and "Impeach the snake." Democrat Thomas Hart Benton of Missouri leaped to his feet and shouted for the sergeant at arms. "Arrest those ruffians for insulting the president of the United States," he roared.

Henry Clay rose to castigate the president for refusing to obey the will of the nation, as expressed by Congress, the people's representatives. He pointed out that in 1836, when Tyler was a senator, he had been instructed to vote for certain Democratic measures by the Virginia legislature and he had resigned rather than obey them. He should do the same thing now. Clay then introduced a motion to override the veto. The twenty-three Democratic senators voted in a block to sustain it, and the infuriated Kentuckian realized he was far short of a two-thirds majority. He promptly introduced a resolution for a constitutional amendment that would permit Congress to override a presidential veto by a majority vote. Other Whig senators rose to second this idea and the necessity of President Tyler's immediate resignation.

Caroline strolled over to George during this oratory and said, "Let's have a Democratic dinner tonight. I'll have everything ready when you adjourn. Invite Senators Benton, Calhoun, Buchanan, and one or two others. I'll go over to the House and invite John Sladen and a few of his friends."

In the House of Representatives' echoing chamber, Caroline told John about the veto and left him with the task of issuing the additional invitations. Back home, she sent Mercy and the Parks sisters rushing to the markets to purchase the dinner. She made a personal pilgrimage to Henry Orr's house to plead for his assistance. The poor man groaned at the thought of baking anything in the August heat, and they compromised on restricting desserts to ice cream and his famous candied oranges.

The dinner was a sensational success. As the wine flowed and the food—cold crab bisque, cold salmon and lobster salad—won exclamations of delight, Senators Benton and Calhoun, often on opposite sides because of Benton's devotion to Andrew Jackson, grew as cordial as a pair of college roommates. Senator James Buchanan of Pennsylvania, with his goggle eyes and his pompous, old-womanish manner, relaxed and told funny stories about his ambassadorship to Russia. Senator Dixon Lewis of Alabama, all 420 pounds of him, did a marvelous imitation of Senator Clay stamping his feet in indignation—a trait of his. Dixon literally all but brought the house down.

As the coffee and dessert were served, George Stapleton said, "Why don't we call on the president and welcome him back to the Democratic Party?"

"The motion is carried unanimously!" Senator Benton roared.

Hannibal was ordered to produce the carriage. "What of our hostess?" John Sladen said. "Can we leave her behind? This restoration of Democratic happiness was unquestionably her idea."

"We'll take her along," Benton said, "as the personification of the goddess of peace."

Packed in the carriage—Dixon Lewis took up the space of two ordinary riders—they rolled to the White House singing—or better, roaring—the old favorite "Columbia, the Pride of the World."

Oh, there is a region, a realm in the West
To Tyranny's shackles unknown
A country with union and liberty blest
That fairest of lands is our own

At the mansion, the president, tieless and in his slippers, soon greeted them in the front hall. He knew them all from his years in the Senate and invited them into the elliptical salon. He reserved a special greeting for Caroline.

"Mrs. Stapleton. Your presence reassures me that these fellows' intentions are peaceful."

Tyler ordered up a bottle of brandy. Caroline declined a glass but no one else did. Soon the party was as merry as the one that had preceded it. There were numerous toasts to Tyler's courage and patriotism. Finally Benton hefted his bulk forward in his chair and said, "Can we welcome you back into the Democratic Party, Mr. President?"

Tyler, none the worse for several glasses of brandy, said, "Today I resisted the tyrannical power of an individual who thinks he has been divinely ordained to rule the nation. Rid your party of General Jackson, who has similar delusions, and return it to its old respect for the powers and rights of the individual states and you will have my adherence—and even my leadership, if you'll accept it!"

A stunned silence ensued. Finally, Dixon Lewis, in his massive Alabama majesty, spoke. "I think that event is as unlikely as the interruption of the flow of the Mississippi, Mr. President."

"Then we must go our separate ways," Tyler said in a tone more disappointed than angry.

"I believe there is one issue on which we can unite, Mr. President," Senator Stapleton said. "Texas."

A cascade of shouts, drumbeats, bugle calls, and shots erupted outside the White House. Everyone rushed to the windows. A mob of Whigs, some of them no doubt the shouters of insults in the Senate gallery, were at the gates, torches in hand, looking like the reincarnation of the French Revolution.

"Death to the traitor president!" they howled.

"My God!" Tyler said. "Should I call out the army?"

"Are there any guns in the house?" Benton asked.

"A few hunting rifles. A pistol or two."

"Have them sent down, with ammunition," Benton said.

In a few minutes, the president's son Robert Tyler joined them, followed by black servants carrying the guns. They were distributed to the politicians, who grouped themselves around the president at the window. Senator Buchanan looked extremely uncomfortable with his gun. "I favor the army," he quavered.

"Buchanan," Benton said, "for once in your life try not to be a Nancy."

The mob continued to howl, but no one entered the White House grounds. "I begin to think they're harmless," George said.

"My wife is desperately ill upstairs. I shudder to think of what this will do to her nerves," the president said.

A moment later, a figure swayed on a long pole. Someone struck a match and President Tyler watched himself burned in effigy in front of the White House. After more jeers and a final blast of the bugles, the mob dispersed.

"That settles it," George Stapleton said. "I'm going to insist on the creation of a night police force for this city. No president should have to tolerate this sort of treatment."

"I will most earnestly support your motion, Senator," President Tyler said.

"We all will," Senator Calhoun said.

They rode back to their various residences in a subdued mood. "We should never have gone anywhere near him," Senator Benton said.

"I find nothing essentially wrong with telling General Jackson he is no longer the leader of the party," Calhoun said.

"Didn't you hear what Senator Lewis said about the Mississippi?" Benton said. "As long as there's breath in Old Hickory's body, he's going to be our leader."

"Where does this leave Texas?" George Stapleton asked, demonstrating he had no intention of abandoning Andrew Jackson.

"A good question. I wish there were a good answer," Benton said.

"From the look on Tyler's face when Senator Stapleton mentioned it, I predict it will become the president's great whale. The prize that might win him reelection," Calhoun said. "I see no reason why we should let him take the credit when one of us could profit by it far more handsomely."

Caroline saw that John C. Calhoun had not yet given up his hope of becoming president. It was fascinating the way the hunger for this office persisted once it invaded a man's soul. How could she ignite it in George?

Caroline soon sent an account of this White House visit to Tennessee, along with even more sensational political news.

Dearest Friend,

No doubt you've read in the papers the astonishing story of the resignation of the President's entire cabinet, except for Mr. Webster. It was a blow under which Senator Clay hoped President Tyler would fall to pieces and follow them into political oblivion. It was accompanied by a chorus of nationwide abuse that is unparalleled. One mathematically inclined reporter claims Mr. Tyler was burned in effigy at over 100 mass meetings in the past week! But our old friend Webster, whether purchased by some invisible source or motivated, as he occasionally can be, by patriotism, has ruined Harry's plans by staying on as Secretary of State. According to Robert Tyler, when Webster offered to stay, the President seized his hand and exclaimed, "Clay is a doomed man!" Thus bolstered, Mr. Tyler has appointed a new cabinet, half of them Democrats. I hope you've passed on to General Jackson the President's bold attempt to take over the Democratic Party. I'm sure it will amuse him. If there is ever a text written on how to mismanage a president, Mr. Clay's assaults on President Tyler must take first place in the examples. He and his friends insulted and browbeat the man until he had no alternative to a veto, if he wished to retain his self-respect. Imagine how much better a woman would have handled such a contest? Men utterly lack any instinct for conciliation. They are all arm wrestlers at heart. One must always flatten the other and win the whole game. Of course there are times when winning is a necessity. I begin to dislike the tenor of your descriptions of Mr. Polk's opponent. He sounds like a formidable, if thoroughly despicable, adversary.

Yours,
Caroline

Sarah Polk's letters had supplied Caroline with vivid reports on James Polk's struggle for reelection as governor of Tennessee. The Whigs had nominated James "Slim Jimmy" Jones, a politician who had made a close study of the tactics that had elected Tippecanoe and Tyler. To hard cider and empty slogans he added a touch of Davy Crockett. Up and down the state he followed Governor Polk, wearing a coonskin hat and making wicked jokes about how boring Polk was, with his long, earnest speeches on issues such as a national bank and the tariff.

Tennessee still seethed with animosity against Martin Van Buren, some of which spilled over onto his sponsor, Andrew Jackson. Slim Jimmy made artful use of these sentiments, telling voters that Polk had been "Little Van's errand boy" in the House of Representatives, and before that, Andrew Jackson's yes-man. "What's he going to do if old Andy dies?" Slim Jimmy asked. "Run all the way to New York for advice?" George, corresponding with General Jackson about Texas, picked up further intimations of trouble. Old Hickory called Slim Jimmy "an artful demagogue."

In the second week of November, bad news arrived in the Stapleton household from two directions. The *Washington Globe* glumly reported that James Polk had been defeated in Tennessee. But the paper saw rays of a coming Democratic resurrection in the news from New York. Martin Van Buren and his Albany machine had regained control of the state, electing the governor and taking charge of the legislature. "The announcement of Mr. Van Buren's political demise would seem in need of revision," the *Globe* gloated.

The gloom at the Stapleton family's breakfast table was as thick as a London winter fog. "This can mean only one thing," George said. "Little Van will run in 1844."

"Perhaps this time he'll take Mr. Polk as his vice president," Caroline said.

"Not unless he wins back the governorship in 1843. Slim Jimmy will be even tougher to beat as the incumbent."

"Why don't you like Mr. Van Buren?" Jonathan Stapleton asked.

"Because he doesn't like your father," Caroline said.

"He's a lying scheming weasel," Senator Stapleton said.

"How could he get elected president?" Jonathan asked in his solemn way.

"Because most of the voters are lying scheming weasels!" Charlie said with a cheerful grin.

"Really, Father. How could he?" Jonathan persisted.

"He convinced people that he's an honest man."

"If he runs for president again, will you support him?"

"Probably. That's how our system works. You vote with your party, not for the man. As long as you think he'll carry out the party's program."

"How will he do that if he's a lying weasel?"

"Jonathan, shut up! I've told you a dozen times, you're too young to understand politics!" Caroline said.

"Who wants to understand politics?" Charlie said. They're bor—ing."

"You're both excused from the table," Caroline said.

Her head was starting to ache. How could things go so disastrously wrong? Was Sarah Polk's dream of the Temple of Fame nothing but a midnight miasma?

"We'll have a talk later, Jonathan," George said as the boys departed, Jonathan with his head bowed, his mouth drooping.

George waited until they were out of earshot and said, "I wish you weren't so abrupt with Jonathan. He's beginning to think you dislike him."

"He irritates me with his endless questions," Caroline snapped. You all irritate me, no one more than you, she thought. George left her there, brooding. She listened while he called Jonathan and suggested they go for a stroll.

She was still sitting at the table when a letter from John Sladen arrived. His father-in-law, Simon Legrand, was dead, a victim of Mr. Clay's "Dog Day" session of Congress. He had been exhausted since adjournment and had died in a doctor's office in New Orleans. He had left John and Clothilde half his substantial fortune, and a command to seek his seat in the Senate "to carry on the principles of Andrew Jackson."

You irritate me too with your endless worship of a woman who no longer exists, Caroline thought. More and more, the only thing that mattered to her was that vision of Sarah Childress Polk and Caroline Kemble Stapleton in the Temple of Fame.

Sarah Polk's letter arrived a day or two later. She struggled to be philosophic.

Dearest Friend,

I trust you've read the bad news in the Globe. *We lost by 3,000 votes. After such a campaign—three months of incessant speaking in heat and cold and soaking rain, James was so worn down, I almost accepted it as a blessing. I truly feared for his health. His old complaints of the stomach and bowels were coming on in the most rampant form, and I almost dreaded him going back to the Governor's mansion and doing battle with the Whigs who are in control of the legislature. Coupled with the news from New York, about the meaning of which I have no illusions, I fear we must regard ourselves as a sorry pair of prophetesses. But the good thing about politics is its unpredictability. Who would have thought the Democrats could revive anywhere? Perhaps the intervention of another dark angel will work an even greater miracle. Meanwhile we will cheer on the continued ascent of Senator Stapleton. General Jackson sings hosannas to him daily for his championship of Texas.*

With ever deepening affection,
Sarah

Caroline was so discouraged, she could scarcely find the energy to address invitations for her next salon. Like all those who rely on willpower to carry them through life, she reacted with extreme frustration and melancholy when events declined to shape themselves according to her hopes and wishes. It took her days to complete the chore. She did not even look forward to the event, although the guest list included the president himself.

On his card, she wrote in her firm hand:

I know how irregular and presumptuous it is to hope a President will visit a private home—but I feel an obligation to return your impeccable hospitality, especially after your kind remarks the other night. You will find plenty of Democrats here to whom you can send signals of amity—none more so than

Your friend,
Caroline Stapleton

She had no idea this invitation would change the course of American history.

SEVEN

WHILE HANNIBAL WAS DISTRIBUTING THE INVITATIONS, Josephine Parks informed Caroline that two young ladies were at the door. On their engraved cards were the names *Miss Julia Gardiner* and *Miss Margaret Gardiner*. Curious, Caroline greeted them in her front parlor.

The Gardiner sisters were extraordinarily attractive. Julia was dark and shapely, with remarkably expressive eyes and a winning smile. Her older sister, Margaret, was not quite as pretty but she had a sardonic cast to her mouth that made her interesting. Both were wearing the latest Paris style, flaring sleeves over a puff of contrasting fabric, the high necks of their day dresses finished with lingerie collars, the waists tightly laced.

"Our cousin, Fenimore Gardiner, told us we could presume on his acquaintance to introduce ourselves," Julia Gardiner said. "Fenimore insisted our visit to Washington would be utterly wasted if we failed to meet the *famous* Mrs. Stapleton."

"He called you the Madame de Staël of America," Margaret said.

"I hope I don't meet her fate. Wasn't she sent into exile by Napoleon?"

"Yes. But then you might fall in love with someone as romantic as Benjamin Constant!" Julia said.

Benjamin Constant had been the leader of the liberal opposition in the French parliament until his death in 1830.

"Have you read his novel *Adolphe*?" Margaret asked. "I picked it up on our last trip to Paris. The hero is in love with a woman old enough to be his mother. He can't live with her and can't live without her. Very French."

"I see nothing wrong with marrying an older man," Julia said. "They're far more interesting than most young ones I've met."

"My sister is part adventuress," Margaret said. "I can't see marrying for anything but love—don't you agree, Mrs. Stapleton?"

"Absolutely," Caroline said with an inward wince.

"We've become acquainted with a number of politicos who live at our boardinghouse," Julia said. "Margaret's already made a conquest of Congressman Douglas of Illinois. When we visit the House gallery, he all but breaks a leg getting up to see us. But she won't consider him. Among her innumerable requirements for happiness, she insists her husband must be taller than she is. I have only one stipulation. He must be rich—or famous. Preferably both."

Caroline felt her gloom lifting with this onrush of merry chatter. "You must come to my little evening party next Monday night," she said. "Though I fear most of the guests will be old enough to be your grandfathers."

The Gardiners' lovely oval faces were a study in unrestrained dismay. "Can you *possibly* invite some younger people?" Julia said. "Or at least middle-aged—I find men in their thirties extremely interesting."

"I'll see what I can do," Caroline said, realizing these sweet young things classified her with the middle-aged.

"Julia, you're impossibly rude," Margaret said. "Of course we'll be delighted to come."

On the Sunday after Caroline issued this invitation, Hannibal rushed into the dining room as the Stapletons were having breakfast. He knew how eagerly Caroline welcomed news from the White House, and this was news of the largest sort.

"Missus, I done talked to Charles Forten, the president's steward, after church. He say Mrs. Tyler's dyin' for sure. They done send for all d'doctors, but they just shake their heads and say no hope."

The next morning, the *Washington Globe* confirmed the sad news that Mrs. Tyler was sinking fast. The following day she was dead. Caroline canceled her salon and joined the rest of the city in mourning the president's loss. She and George went to the black-draped White House to offer their condolences to President Tyler and his children, who looked truly stricken. The Stapletons listened sympathetically while friends and family recounted Letitia Tyler's Christian virtues.

What would they say about her when she lay dead? Caroline mused. There would be no comments on Christian virtues, that was a certainty. Did she care? No, this was the standard sop to a woman who submitted to being a mere helpmate, bedmate, yes-master slave. She hoped George or her children, or Sarah Childress Polk, would praise her Roman virtues—her courage, her judgment, her candor.

A full month passed before Caroline reconstituted her evening party. She again invited the president, urging him in another deft note not to trouble himself over protocol and to take the opportunity to lift his spirits. She made a point of reinviting the Gardiner sisters and their parents as well. The acceptances poured in at twice the usual rate of speed. Everyone had been reluctant to begin entertaining out of respect for the dead. Mrs. Stapleton's decision to take the lead was clearly welcomed.

Dolley Madison was among the first to arrive, and Caroline set her up in her usual corner, where she could receive her worshipers like the uncrowned queen of Washington. Next came John Quincy Adams, who joined Dolley for some cheerful reminiscences of the days of their youth—a subject Caroline hoped would absorb the old Yankee for the rest of the night. During the past week, he had thrown the House of Representatives into turmoil by introducing a petition from some citizens of Massachusetts asking Congress to dissolve the Union because it was half-slave and half-free. The Southern Democrats, led by John Sladen, had called for a vote of censure, which would have expelled Adams from Congress.

Other guests were soon swarming through the two parlors—Senators Webster, Benton, Calhoun, the first two with their amiable wives. Webster, after a drink or two, began telling everyone about his secret negotiations with British ambassador Lord Ashburton about settling the Maine boundary and putting an end to the British practice of stopping and searching American ships for Royal Navy deserters. Also on the table was an agreement committing the American navy to cooperate with the British navy to end the slave trade once and for all. John Quincy Adams stumped into Webster's corner of the parlor to tell him the slave trade embargo was ten times more important than the Maine boundary. Senator Benton rumbled that he did not agree. "Give the British the idea that they can walk off with even a mile of American territory and they'll try for a hundred or a thousand miles the next time."

"I presume you're talking about the slavocracy's favorite topic, Texas," Adams said.

"Texas, Oregon—all the lands *you* let drift out of our rightful ownership while you were secretary of state, sir," Benton said. "Your craven worship of the English is exceeded only by your malicious desire to destroy this Union."

Heads were turning, eyes were widening. Was even Mrs. Stapleton's salon about to be invaded by the violent emotions that fractured Congress? Was there to be no haven of peace in Washington?

"Mrs. Stapleton?"

In the center of the room were Julia Gardiner and her sister, Margaret, two visions of springtime in dresses of creamy white, hothouse roses in their dark hair. Caroline literally hurled them into the breach that was opening between Congressman Adams and Senator Benton.

"Gentlemen! Here are two lovely young ladies from New York, who've come to Washington to complete their educations by seeing our government in action. Perhaps you've noticed their visits to the Capitol?"

"I've noticed how many congressmen climb the stairs like firemen rushing to a blaze to win a seat beside them in the gallery of the House," John Quincy Adams said. "If I were forty years younger, I'd be on their heels."

"You must honor the Senate with a visit soon," Senator Calhoun said. "We'll show you superior speed to the gallery, as well as superior intelligence on the floor."

Julia Gardiner pronounced Senator Calhoun immensely more handsome face-to-face than any drawing she had seen of him in the newspapers. Margaret agreed—and asked Senator Benton if he minded being compared to a bull, pawing the earth, about to charge his enemies, when he rose to debate a question. "I prefer comparison to the grizzly bear," Benton said, "because he usually wins his fights."

"Mrs. Stapleton," whispered a voice in Caroline's ear. It was Henry Orr, her usually imperturbable caterer. "The president. President Tyler is in the hall!"

Looking more than a little haggard, the chief executive hesitated in the doorway to the front parlor, scouting the room for unwelcome faces. He found none. Caroline, hoping he would accept, had taken the precaution of not inviting Senator Henry Clay or any of his followers.

"Mrs. Stapleton," Tyler said. "Your lovely notes have persuaded me that this is one place in Washington where I can hope for a friendly reception. Will you still countenance the company of a man whom the whole country is burning in effigy?"

"It's a rule of this house, Mr. President, that politics cease at the doorstep."

George was at her side, extending his hand. "What a pleasure, Mr. President. Come meet two of Mrs. Stapleton's most charming discoveries, the Misses Gardiner from New York."

He had towed the Gardiner sisters out of the Webster corner and they occupied the center of the room once more. Julia, by far the more self-confident and flirtatious, greeted Tyler with her brightest smile. "Mr. President. I'm so honored!" she said, performing an elaborate curtsy.

Did she know the impact she might have on this lonely grief-stricken man? Femininity virtually oozed from every pore of her body. Her dress, low-cut in the evening style, revealed more than a little of her lovely breasts when she curtsied. Her eyes radiated an eager wish to please, to tease, and ultimately to satisfy. Woman incarnate, Caroline thought ruefully. It was not a role she ever willingly played. Was thought its enemy?

"My dear Miss Gardiner. The honor, the pleasure, is entirely mine," President Tyler said.

He could not take his eyes off this beautiful creature. He barely managed to summon enough manners to greet Margaret warmly as well. Courtesy required him to circle the room, chatting briefly with many of the guests. But he insisted on Julia accompanying him, arm in arm. Several times he asked people if the mere sight of her did not convince them of the silliness of their political quarrels.

For the next hour, Julia and the president talked elaborate nonsense. He insisted on finding out her favorite colors, her favorite music, her favorite foods, her favorite animals, her favorite books. He wanted to know if she had ever fallen in love with anyone. Caroline realized she was watching courtship, Southern style. Julia Gardiner was being told her tastes, her inclinations, her adventures of the heart, were of overwhelming importance to the president of the United States. She was as dazzled by his attention as he was mesmerized by her beauty.

The president was fifty-two years old, a man without a wife, a politician without a political party. It was easy for him to conclude his life was over. Here in Caroline Stapleton's parlor he was encountering the possibility of rebirth, of new love, new ardor—and this miracle inevitably led him to think it might be replicated in his political life. With Julia still on his arm, he beckoned George Stapleton into a corner and began an intense discussion, in which Caroline heard the word *Texas* at least ten times.

"Does Julia have this effect on other men?" Caroline asked her sister.

"At the moment, she's being pursued by five different congressmen and a justice of the Supreme Court," Margaret said.

John Sladen arrived with an uninvited guest, presuming on Mrs. Stapleton's friendship as usual. This man had a face as dramatically handsome as any Caroline had ever seen. But his head barely reached her shoulder. He looked as if someone had sawed his legs off at the knees. "This is Congressman Douglas from Illinois," John said. "He begged me to bring him here, not for your delicious cakes and pies and ice cream and wine, but because a certain Miss Margaret Gardiner was reported to be on your guest list."

"There she is!" gasped the agitated Douglas. "Mrs. Stapleton, will you excuse me?"

He rushed across the room to present himself to Margaret. She greeted him with a coolness that could only have added to his agitation. She was rather tall for a woman, which probably explained her dislike of short men.

"I fear your friend Douglas is on a lost cause," Caroline said. She told him about Margaret's preference for taller men.

"I'll invite him into the Sans Mercis," John said. "There's a group of us in the House that nurse broken hearts in the best poetic fashion."

He downed a glass of champagne in a gulp.

"John," Caroline said, "isn't it time to stop blaming me for your unhappy marriage? The days of youth are long gone. Are we even the same people who met in New York?"

She wanted to be even more blunt. *Like me you married for money and power. But I don't waste my time in useless regrets.* The pain on his face stopped her. "You're absolutely right as usual," he said. "I hope this wasn't the last of the champagne."

She removed the glass from his hand. "George is over there discussing Texas with the president. Find out what they're saying while I rescue Margaret from Congressman Douglas."

She towed Douglas over to pay obeisance to Dolley Madison and turned her attention to the Gardiner sisters' parents, David Gardiner and his formidable-looking wife, Juliana. They had gravitated to the Webster corner, where Gardiner was holding forth about the eloquence of the New York State Senate, in which he had served. Webster and Calhoun, the two greatest orators in America, could scarcely believe their ears. The man was making a perfect fool of himself, and Caroline suspected from the look on his wife's face that she knew it.

"Your daughter Julia has *conquered* the president," Caroline said to Mrs. Gardiner. "Is she interested in politics?"

"She barely knows the difference between a Whig and a Democrat," her father said. "Which is as it should be, don't you think, Mrs. Stapleton? Politics coarsens a woman."

"Mrs. Stapleton disagrees," John Calhoun said with a sly smile. "But I've seen not the slightest sign of coarsening in the thirteen years I've known her."

"For that compliment, my dear Senator, I'll invite you to join my husband and the president in a conversation that I'm sure will interest you."

She led the smiling Calhoun across the parlor and interrupted George in the middle of quoting Andrew Jackson on the crucial importance of Texas to America's security. "Gentlemen," she said, "here's a man who can't be left out of your discussion."

Three hours later, the guests had departed. The president had taken the Gardiners with him in his coach, expressing horror at the mere thought of Julia being forced to shiver in the March wind while they searched for a hack. As Henry Orr and his team of blacks cleared away the dishes and the ruins of the pies and cakes, Caroline allowed herself her first glass of champagne. John Sladen slumped in a chair, having allowed himself several glasses too many. George was not in much better shape.

"What did you decide?" Caroline asked.

George grinned. "The president of the United States is insanely in love with Miss Julia Gardiner."

"I mean about Texas."

"He's afraid of starting a war. He's going to negotiate with the Mexicans. A waste of time in my opinion," George said. "Jackson tried that for eight years and got nowhere. Texas is independent. The problem is getting an annexation bill through Congress, with Henry Clay opposed to it."

"Harry the Great is terrified of the abolitionists of Massachusetts," John Sladen said.

"What about Secretary of State Webster?" Caroline asked. "Will he negotiate seriously when he knows John Quincy Adams hates the idea?" She told them what Adams had said about the "slavocracy."

"You should stop inviting that vicious old man," John said.

"He's upset about your motion to censure him. Will it carry?"

"No," Sladen said.

"Adams isn't an abolitionist," George said. "He just can't stand the way the South is hiding its head in the sand on slavery."

"George," John said, "I wish you'd come down to Louisiana and visit my sugar plantation. I have one hundred and twenty slaves working there. I have a full-time doctor in attendance. Their food is more wholesome than any Northern mill hand's. They never have to worry about being laid off. They're the healthiest happiest workers in America."

"You're not in the House of Representatives, John," Caroline said. "What did Mr. Calhoun say about Texas?"

"He told the president he might have his support—depending on the treaty. There's talk of the British putting an abolition condition on any treaty. Houston and his crowd might go along—if the British guarantee the treaty against Mexican reprisals. Calhoun will never agree to that."

"Tonight, Secretary of State Webster told Mr. Adams he wouldn't agree to it either. I think we can safely dismiss that worry," Caroline said.

"I told Tyler to settle Oregon at the same time. Oregon will be a new free state, Texas a slave state," George said.

"I'm not sure the South will agree to that," Congressman Sladen said. "More and more, we're tired of apologizing for slavery."

"Johnny, you've obviously had too much champagne," George said. "So have I. I'm going to bed."

"One more glass and I'm gone." John weaved his way across the room to a bottle in a cooler on the serving table. Caroline sensed he was not as drunk as he pretended to be.

"I'll leave you to deal with him, dear," George said, and stamped upstairs. Each heavy step seemed to say, *I am bigger, stronger, more powerful, than Johnny Sladen.*

John poured himself another glass of golden champagne and held it up to the light. "There's much more at stake than Texas," he said. "At the moment that's nothing but a gigantic vacuum which will suck men and money out of the South. But Texas could lead to Mexico. Our agents tell us the Mexicans swear they'll go to war if we annex. On the way back from Louisiana, I traveled through a dozen Southern states. They're forming secret societies that are taking blood oaths to conquer Mexico and keep it, no matter what the Yankees say. Maybe this charmer you've introduced into our play can persuade old Tyler to go along with that idea. It can't be mentioned to anyone, of course. Above all to George."

"I understand," Caroline said.

Congressman Sladen drained his drink. "Aaron Burr's dream is not dead. It is only sleeping. Soon it will awaken on the lips of John C. Calhoun."

"He agrees to this? Taking—keeping Mexico?"

"He will, when I finish persuading him."

"Will this make Tyler president again?"

Sladen shook his head. "Calhoun. That's where your charm girl comes in. She'll ease the pain for Old Veto's inevitable exit."

"Will she marry a man of fifty-two?"

"What do you think?"

Caroline heard Margaret Gardiner say, *My sister is part adventuress.* "I think she will. I think she'll marry him. I'd do the same thing if I were in her shoes."

"Except you'd make him president for two more terms."

Caroline laughed mirthlessly. "Probably."

"When it happens, if it happens, I have another event in mind. The migration of a certain Northern woman to the new Southern nation—beyond the reach of her husband's brainless devotion."

Suddenly, in her mind, Caroline was kissing John Sladen's drunken mouth. His hands were roving her body. "I can promise you nothing on that score."

"I'm simply stating my case."

"Your prophecy has been duly noted. Good night, Congressman."

EIGHT

Dearest Friend,

President Tyler continues to pursue Texas and Julia Gardiner with equal persistence. Both seem determined to elude his grasp. Our charming vixen from New York has been to the White House more often than anyone else in Washington, including members of the President's cabinet. The city abounds with tales of him chasing her from the Elliptical Salon to the Red Room to the Blue Room in pursuit of a kiss while the bewitching creature cries no no no—before yielding it up. Her mother continues to resist the idea of a marriage, and her father would not dream of doing anything to which his wife objects. Would that we had husbands a tenth as obedient as Mr. Gardiner! Julia confides in me as her "second mother"—a title I would gladly forswear—that her heart is exquisitely balanced between yea and nay. Meanwhile she tantalizes the poor man by carrying on simultaneous flirtations with Supreme Court justice McLean and Congressman Pickens. Both have proposed, she confided to me yesterday.

As for Texas, it still looms out there like a gigantic will-o'-the-wisp. The President has jettisoned Daniel Webster as secretary of state and moved a pleasant nonentity named Abel P. Upshur (a boyhood friend) from doing nothing in particular as secretary of the navy to take charge of serious negotiations. In short, Mr. Tyler has become his own secretary of state. The best thing that can be said about Mr. Upshur is, he worships John C. Calhoun and tells him everything that is happening inside the administration. Mr. C. is still running hard for the Democratic nomination.

Mr. Tyler told George he is deeply alarmed by Texas's latest flirtation with the British. Reports from unofficial sources suggest that without some immediate help, the so-called independent republic faces financial collapse—which would invite an early assault from the Mexicans, who still refuse to recognize it.

All this Washington hugger-mugger dwindles to nothing in comparison to my anxiety for you and Mr. Polk in the wake of your latest loss to the insufferable Slim Jimmy Jones. It is dismaying to realize how much power demagoguery can wield in our wonderful republic. I have never been a worshiper of the people, except in the most abstract sense of the term. Are you coming to a similar opinion?

I must close—we're going for a cruise up the Potomac aboard the *new steam frigate USS* Princeton. *It is equipped with a gigantic new gun, the Peacemaker, which is supposedly capable of sinking any warship afloat. George and every other male in Washington cannot wait to see it in action.*

> *As ever,*
> *Caroline*

"Caroline, they're going to sail promptly at noon!" George called from downstairs.

"I'm *ready,*" she said, hastily addressing and sealing the envelope.

Caroline handed the letter to Hannibal as she got into the carriage, with orders to mail it on the way back from the Navy Yard. "How is Polk? Has his health improved?" George asked as they rode through the crowded streets. The exhausting struggle for the Tennessee governorship had triggered a recurrence of his intestinal problems, worsened this time by excruciating cramps and digestive spasms.

"Yes. But not his spirits," Caroline said.

More and more, it began to look as if James Polk was on his way to the political graveyard. Losing two elections in a row in his native state was a mortal blow. Worse, Martin Van Buren was moving inexorably toward the 1844 presidential nomination. State conventions in New York and Pennsylvania had named him their candidate. As long as Andrew Jackson was alive, Little Van did not need a vice president from Tennessee.

"Maybe it's for the best," George said. "Politics doesn't seem to agree with his stomach."

"That's a ridiculous thing to say!" Caroline snapped.

"I'm only saying it to you."

"You shouldn't even think it!"

Again, Caroline's vision of the future had become unhinged by the unpredictability of politics. This time she could not see even a modicum of hope for Sarah Polk's triumphant return to Washington. Without Sarah, John Sladen seemed to be moving into the foreground of her soul. He visited almost every day, telling her about the mounting frenzy for Texas and Mexico sweeping the South.

At the Washington Navy Yard, they boarded the gleaming new man-of-war *Princeton,* which Caroline, as the wife of New Jersey's senior senator, had christened when it slid down the ways in Philadelphia six months ago. The captain, Robert Stockton, gave them an especially warm greeting. He too was a New Jerseyan, from a family as distinguished as the Stapletons. His grandfather had been a signer of the Declaration of Independence.

Faces swirled past. Robert Walker, the short, bald Mississippi senator who had fanned the flames of enthusiasm for Texas's annexation even higher with an open letter arguing it would be good for the whole country, North and South. Rambunctious Congressman Henry Wise of Virginia, the sole member of the Tyler "party" in Congress; he had been pursuing Margaret Gardiner. Although he was no more than forty, she said his wrinkled face made him look as if he had one foot in the grave. Francis Pickens, the South Carolina congressman who had pursued Julia Gardiner, also in vain. She had shown Caroline the poem he had sent her.

> *On! Come to the South*
> *The land of the sun*
> *And dwell in its bower*
> *Sweet beautiful one.*

On the upper deck, Julia Gardiner was chatting with the president. She was wearing a dress of soft rose; her wonderfully expressive face was lifted to his, like a flower to the spring sunshine. Caroline again found herself envying Julia's spontaneity. Or was it her youth?

Julia could be calculating when it suited her. She had allowed Justice McLean, another suitor, to take her autograph album to Capitol Hill to obtain the signatures of the rest of the Supreme Court. In the album was a poem from the president, which Julia had privately shown Caroline. The justices, prone to investigate documents thoroughly like all lawyers, had found it and spread it all over Washington.

> *Shall I again that Harp unstring*
> *Which long hath been a useless thing*
> *Unheard in Lady's bower?*

For another twenty lines the president brooded on his unstrung harp, admitting it was "touch'd with decay." But he still hoped there was a "parting note" left that might stir "a brimy fire" in Julia's eyes.

"Oh, Mrs. Stapleton," Julia called. "Come help me advise the president. He's telling me about his hopes for an early annexation of Texas. But he wonders if Mr. Clay will let his followers vote for it."

"Even so, the Democrats are a majority in Congress again. A little artful politicking on your part at White House dinners can easily detach a few Whigs and give him his two-thirds vote."

"You really think so?" Julia said, her eyes widening with excitement. She pouted prettily. "You could do much more at your salon. You *understand* politics so much better than I do."

"But you, my dear, would be a fresh recruit," President Tyler said. "Mrs. Stapleton and I are like veteran soldiers, hobbled by old wounds, our escutcheons a mixture of victories and defeats. We find it harder and harder to intimidate our enemies."

"Mr. President, that may be an apt description of *you*," Julia said. "But it's grossly unfair to Mrs. Stapleton. I only hope I possess one-half her looks when I reach her age."

"I stand corrected in my aesthetics, but not in my politics," Tyler said, beaming at Caroline. He regarded her as the godmother of his romance.

A chilly February wind was whipping across the Potomac. Julia shivered and remarked that her sister, Margaret, had stayed home, nursing a dreadful cold. The president immediately led them below, where a merry company had assembled to dine and drink their way to Mount Vernon and back. Holding court in a corner of the spacious compartment was Caroline's old friend Dolley Madison. As they got under way, young naval officers led small groups down to the engine rooms to see the gleaming boilers and pistons of the *Princeton*'s steam engines.

Around two o'clock they trooped up on deck for a demonstration of the Peacemaker. Mounted on the bow, it thrust its black snout over the water like a huge ugly animal. A half dozen times, the sailors and the officer in command performed the dance of ramming home the powder and cannonball. Then the officer barked, "Fire!" A sailor thrust a match into the touchhole and the big gun sent the ball hurtling a good mile down the empty river.

The new secretary of the navy, Thomas Gilmer, invited David Gardiner, Julia's father, into the inner circle around the gun. The pudgy little secretary of state, Abel Upshur, proudly joined them. The navy had bought the gun while he was their civilian leader. They stood directly behind the gun's commander, practically inhaling the billowing smoke from the long black muzzle.

Belowdecks again, the guests began enjoying more champagne and a delicious collation that the sailors had laid out on tables. Caroline noticed George and John Sladen were having an intense conversation with Secretary of State Upshur. She joined them in time to hear Upshur say, "I count forty votes in our favor. Do you agree, Senator?"

"With a little greasing of the machinery, yes," George said. "Only one thing worries me. To what extent Mr. Van Buren is committed to annexation. Have you had any contact with his friends?"

Upshur shook his head. "The president is hoping to make this his issue. Why should he give any credit to a man who's spent the last three years in New York?"

"He hasn't spent all his time in New York," George said, making room for Caroline on the bench where he was sitting. "You'll recall he toured the country six months ago. He visited General Jackson—and he also stopped for three days with Henry Clay in Kentucky. In fact, he spent more time there than he did at the Hermitage. Tell us what your friend Sarah Polk heard, my dear."

"Mr. Clay and Mr. Van Buren have jointly agreed not to allow Texas to become a campaign issue," Caroline said. "Their followers in Congress will be told to vote against annexation. Without either of them saying a word."

Upshur was badly shaken. A former Virginia judge, he had no experience in national politics. "I must discuss this with the president," he said.

Elsewhere, the flowing wine was inducing martial songs and poetry. Secretary of the Navy Gilmer, the acting host for the day, decided they were all entitled to another thrill. They would soon be passing Mount Vernon, and he asked Captain Stockton if he would fire the Peacemaker one more time to salute George Washington. The captain was more than agreeable.

By now it was four o'clock. Caroline was not enthusiastic about braving the cold wind on the river and stayed behind. So did most of the women and not a few of the men. George, fascinated by the big cannon, was among the departees. Secretary of State Upshur and Julia's father, David Gardiner, followed him. John Sladen stayed behind to discuss Sarah Polk's rumor about a secret deal between Clay and Van Buren.

"Who told her?" he wanted to know. "These stories should be pinned down."

A young naval officer began reciting a heroic poem to Julia Gardiner. The president, jealous of even the most unlikely suitors, paused near the ladder to the upper deck and called, "Are you coming on deck, Miss Gardiner?" Julia smiled in her flirtatious way but chose to let the young man continue his poem.

"Ten more lines and he'll be on his way to Pago Pago," John Sladen muttered to Caroline.

" 'Eight hundred men lay slain—' " the officer intoned.

A tremendous boom on the deck above their heads shook the ship from bow to stern. The Peacemaker had fired. Everyone burst into applause for the might of the U.S. Navy. Moments later, a dazed powder-streaked lieutenant clattered down the ladder to where the president stood.

"A surgeon," he cried. "For God's sake get a surgeon up on deck. The Peacemaker exploded!"

The president sprang up the ladder. Dozens of people rushed to follow him. Caroline and John Sladen were among the first to reach the deck. A pall of black smoke hung over the ship, which had lost headway. The president and Congressman Henry Wise barred their path to the bow.

"It's not a sight for a lady's eyes!" the president said.

"Are many killed?" John Sladen asked.

"At least a half dozen," Wise said.

"My husband?" Caroline said, horror driving thought from her mind.

"There he is!" John said.

George reeled toward them, blood streaming from his ear. His face was chalky white. With him was Senator Thomas Hart Benton, with the same ghastly coloring. His ear too streamed blood. The explosion had ruptured their eardrums and all but stopped the circulation of their blood. But they were alive.

"Don't let Miss Gardiner come on deck," the president ordered one of the naval officers. "Her father's dead. So is Secretary Upshur and Secretary Gilmer. Make sure their families stay below. Their bodies are badly mangled."

The secretary of state and the secretary of the navy both dead. What a shambles. Was any other president so pursued by the furies? Caroline joined John Sladen in helping George and Senator Benton to seats along the railing, amidships.

"Well, Senator," Benton said, "now we know how it feels to die in the twinkling of God's eye."

"Can anyone get us some brandy?" George said.

"I'll get something," Caroline said.

As she rushed to the companionway, the president took her arm. "Mrs. Stapleton. Would you do what you can for Julia?"

"My husband and Senator Benton desperately need some brandy to revive them."

"They'll have it in an instant from my own hand. Take care of Julia—and you'll have my gratitude compounded infinitely beyond what I already owe you for bringing us together. Only you can rescue me from this disaster."

She knew what he meant. Julia was all too likely to blame him for her father's death. How could she avoid the thought? The scene belowdecks was almost as chaotic as the one above. The wives and families of the dead were sobbing and wailing and flinging themselves into the arms of consolers. Caroline managed to find Dolley Madison in the chaos.

"You must help me with Julia Gardiner. Her father is among the dead," Caroline said.

An instant later, Julia rushed up to them. "Mrs. Stapleton. I want to go to my father. No one will tell me whether—"

Dolley rose to the occasion like the uncrowned queen she was. "Dearest girl. Thy father is in heaven. God has called him home."

"No! Mrs. Stapleton, how could such a thing happen? How could the president—"

"The president is in God's hands, like the rest of us," Dolley said.

"His heart is as broken as yours, as mine," Caroline said.

An instant later, Caroline was supporting a dead weight. Julia had fainted. Caroline managed to half-drag, half-carry her to a nearby bench and hold her erect. John Sladen appeared with some brandy, but he could not force it past Julia's lips. Most of it spilled on her gown.

They sat there holding the unconscious young woman as the *Princeton* steamed up the river to Alexandria. There, a smaller vessel came alongside to take the injured and the survivors ashore. The president came below and lifted Julia in his arms. John Sladen took charge of Dolley Madison, and they mounted to the deck to find their worries were far from over.

The two ships were connected by a narrow gangplank stretched across the swift heaving Potomac. Sailors stood ready to assist everyone, but it was still a tricky business. As the president was halfway across with Julia, she awoke and began thrashing violently in his arms. The chief executive swayed and came within a step of tumbling into the river.

The president told Caroline to take Julia to the White House. He would join them after they removed the bodies of the dead from the *Princeton*. At Alexandria, the navy commandeered carriages and wagons for the distraught fugitives, and in an hour Caroline was helping Julia upstairs to a White House bedroom. She left her there, surrounded by Tyler relatives, and hurried to 3600 Pennsylvania Avenue to see how George was faring. She found him sitting in the parlor sipping brandy with John Sladen. His color had returned. Aside from an earache, he declared himself as good as new.

A chance invitation from Senator Benton had saved his life. George had been standing in the front rank around the gun when Benton suggested he join him on a gun carriage six or seven feet in the rear of the crowd so they could get a better view of the cannonball as it hurtled down the river. They were both knocked off the carriage by the blast, but none of the metal fragments of the gun flew their way.

"It makes a fatalist of you," George said.

"I wonder what it will make of the president?" Sladen said.

"Julia Gardiner's husband," Caroline said.

"I mean as a politician. Who'll be the next secretary of state?"

"Another nobody, probably," Caroline said.

"Not if Tyler wants to push the Texas annexation treaty through the Senate," Sladen said. "He needs a name with real power behind it."

"John C. Calhoun?" George said.

"Who else?" Sladen said.

"I thought he was running for president."

"He was, but Van Buren's sewed up two-thirds of the delegates. I think he'd be amenable. Thanks to Upshur, he's been in close touch with the negotiations."

"Doesn't the president dislike him?"

"He might change his mind if Calhoun announced he was withdrawing as a candidate."

"That can be arranged?" George said.

Sladen nodded. "Simply get us an offer. I promise you the announcement will be forthcoming—before he accepts."

Caroline saw Sladen was trying to arrange a graceful exit for his hero. George was in favor of it because it would significantly increase the chances of pushing the Texas treaty through the Senate. Calhoun had enough prestige to challenge the backstage veto that the two master schemers, Henry Clay and Martin Van Buren, had concocted.

"I'll be going to the White House tomorrow to see Julia Gardiner. I'll speak to the president," Caroline said.

Power. Caroline felt the familiar pleasure pulsing in her blood again. But it was not the mere exercise of influence that stirred her. She sensed that the deadly explosion aboard the *Princeton* had shattered more than the president's cabinet. It had also smashed the political equilibrium that the so-called reasonable men such as Clay and Van Buren were trying to establish, in their own self-interest of course. Out of the upheaval, Senator Calhoun was finding an unexpected political resurrection. Why could not something equally miraculous restore James K. Polk—and Sarah Childress Polk—to the shadowy struggle in the Temple of Fame?

NINE

Dearest Friend,

It is consummated. Mr. Calhoun has arrived in Washington to take up his duties as secretary of state. Before he left South Carolina, he issued a statement, declaring himself out of the presidential race. The President has become reconciled to his presence, after his first strenuous resistance to the idea. Most of his mind is preoccupied with his coming marriage to Julia Gardiner, which I have facilitated not a little on several trips to New York. She has accepted his offer. He will be going to that city for a very private ceremony sometime in the next six weeks. Like all politicians, he is hopelessly superstitious and now regards me as some sort of angelic presence, who will guarantee his political as well as his personal happiness. He consults with me—and occasionally

George—about everything. We have enthusiastically approved his idea of a political convention (composed mostly of officeholders he has appointed) that will nominate him on a third-party ticket with the annexation of Texas as the sole issue. I suggested calling them Democratic-Republicans. This will put pressure on Little Van, who you know has the backbone of a jellyfish, to support the treaty of annexation when it comes before the Senate. He controls at least thirty Democratic votes. Mr. Tyler and Julia entertain fantasies of using success with Texas to dismount the Little Magician and seize the Democratic nomination. It does no harm to encourage these ideas. It will lend zest to their honeymoon. Meanwhile, I am readying the President for a more realistic quest: an insistence, if he withdraws in Little Van's favor, that Albany's favorite weasel accept James Polk as his vice president. I intend to ask this of Mr. Tyler, not only as a personal favor, but as the one hope of stopping Henry Clay, whom he regards as the incarnation of evil, from becoming president. I trust I have your permission to do this.

I am not alone in deploring Little Van's liabilities. Senator Robert Walker, now the chairman of the Democratic Party, has covered his bald head with a black wig and talks incessantly about Van's turpitude. He virtually drove people screaming into the street at my most recent salon with his declamations on the subject.

The other day we went to a fascinating scientific demonstration at the Capitol. An inventor named Samuel Morse has perfected a telegraph and stretched a line between here and Baltimore. The President was in that city, laying the groundwork for his Democratic-Republican Convention. He sent us the message "What hath God wrought!" We had trouble keeping straight faces. Was he talking about a miraculous elevation to a second term? On our end of the line, Mrs. Madison sent a less portentous reply to one of her friends in Baltimore: "Give my love to Mrs. Wethered."

Mr. Morse talks of linking all parts of the Union with telegraph wires. Those of us who wish to create a continental United States, with not only Texas but California and Oregon on our maps, feel the god of progress is confirming our vision. Conservatives grumble that we can barely govern the vast expanse we currently rule, pointing out that it takes ten days for a letter to get from Washington to New Orleans. But if the same letter can be sent in five seconds—what can't Washington rule?

As ever,
Caroline

Downstairs, Caroline heard the front door open and two-year-old Paul running to greet George, calling, "Papa!" The house was so much more peaceful these days without Jonathan and Charlie. Jonathan had been sent to a school in the village of Lawrenceville, near Princeton, to complete his studies before entering Columbia the next year. Charlie had been sent in the opposite direction, to an excellent school in North Carolina that the Polks had recommended. James Polk had attended it before matriculating at that state's university. The two boys were so different in temperament and habits, Caroline thought it best to separate them. George had reluctantly agreed, although it troubled his family feelings.

Descending the stairs, Caroline was dismayed to see Jeremy Biddle beside George in the hall. She should have known he would become a regular visitor, now that he had taken up residence in Washington as a senator from New Jersey. The sudden death of Samuel Southard, the Whig senator Jeremy had helped elect, had given him this opportunity to fill out his term. The New Jersey legislature was still his creature, thanks to the Camden & Amboy's munificence. Between the taxes the railroad paid (amounting to the entire state budget), the jobs he had at his disposal, and the bribes he paid to guarantee the Camden & Amboy's monopoly in New Jersey, the lawmakers would have nominated him for Emperor of the World if he had asked for it.

"Jeremy dear, what an unexpected pleasure," Caroline said, kissing him on the cheek while George beamed. Jeremy had finally grown into his ugly face, which seemed much more appropriate to his jowls and wide thick neck and short bulging body.

Jeremy would be with them for the next four years. Happily, his wife, Sally, chose to remain in New Jersey, realizing there was no hope of challenging Caroline's social supremacy in Washington. There was something to be said for Jeremy's presence in the Senate. George could almost certainly prevail on him for his vote on a close question. The Whig party had been thrown into near total disarray by Tyler's vetoes. Henry Clay had gone back to Kentucky to run for president. Without his leadership, the House and Senate Whigs were splitting into quarrelsome factions.

Settled in the parlor, Caroline demanded the latest news from Capitol Hill. "The administration is big with the child Texas," Jeremy said. "We're told to expect Secretary of State Calhoun's completed treaty tomorrow or the next day at the latest. The midnight oil will begin to burn."

"Surely you're not going to oppose it," Caroline said. "It would be political suicide."

"I cannot disclose the secret deliberations of the Whig caucus," Jeremy said.

He was a bit drunk. So was George. They must have paused at the Hole in the Wall, the infamous saloon on Capitol Hill, or some other watering place, after the Senate adjourned.

"Jeremy says they're waiting for instructions from Henry Clay. Without orders from him, the Whigs have no policy worth mentioning," George said.

"Shall I begin to annotate the quarrels of the Democrats?" Jeremy asked. "North and South, East and West?"

"Don't bother. We know them all too well," George said.

"But we overcome them, thanks to our readiness to listen to the voice of the people," Caroline said.

"Oh, yes, the voice of the people," Jeremy mocked. "Better known as the voice of Andrew Jackson."

It was all good-natured. But it set Caroline's nerves on edge. She suddenly realized how many things could go wrong with the plan she had just outlined to Sarah Polk. President Tyler might not listen very closely to her plea for James K. Polk. Martin Van Buren might not listen very closely to President Tyler. Inflated male egos, narrow self-interests, had to be balanced against the main chance. Would all these touchy men do the right, the sensible thing? Not even George was totally dependable.

"Mr. Sladen, ma'am."

Josephine Parks was at the parlor door. John Sladen slipped past her, assuming he was welcome. He kissed Caroline and shook hands with George—and with Jeremy Biddle. Jeremy was a test of his self-control. John seemed to pass it unscathed. He even managed to smile into Jeremy's complacent conservative face.

"I was hoping I'd find you alone," John said as he sat down. "I have some news—which should only be shared among Democrats."

"Oh, we can trust Jeremy," George said.

"It's *serious* news, George."

Jeremy rose, assuring them he had letters to write. He found his hat in the hall and departed. John waited until the front door closed and resumed the conversation.

"I've come from Calhoun's office at the State Department. He showed me what he's going to submit to the Senate tomorrow. It includes the treaty of annexation with Texas, and this letter to the British negotiator. I'm afraid some Democrats may find the letter exceptional. People like you, George, from states that have a growing abolitionist minority."

George snatched the letter from John's hand and read it in one devouring swoop. He handed it to Caroline and said, "Jesus Christ, Johnny! Is he out of his mind?"

Caroline read it as swiftly and understood George's agitation. The letter told the British ambassador that the annexation of Texas as a slave state was crucial to the future of the South and its role in the Union. The statement annihilated the Democratic Party's argument that annexation was good for all parts of the nation.

Caroline looked from the document into John Sladen's gray eyes. She saw mockery there, and something else. The mockery concerned George. John was handing him this bombshell in advance so she could manipulate him into voting the right way when the time came. But the other shade or shadow in those defiant eyes was telling her something even more important. *I don't care what you think, either.* John was playing his own game, the Southern game, independent of her. If she wanted to come along, well and good. But he no longer cared, in any serious way, if she went elsewhere. Had he somehow divined how much of her heart she had given to Sarah Polk, to their vision of the Temple of Fame?

So be it, Caroline told him in that momentous silence as George thrashed on the couch. She would not, she could not, correct her heart's trajectory. It was her woman's fate, a compound of wish and lifelong thought. She would live without his love, somehow. Without George's love too, if necessary. For a fierce despairing moment she felt invulnerable.

"Johnny, the minute this letter goes to the Senate, someone's going to leak it to the newspapers," George said.

"I know that. I may leak it myself," John said. "I persuaded him to write this letter for only one reason. To destroy Martin Van Buren once and for all."

Aaron Burr's old dream is not dead, it is only sleeping. Now it was no longer sleeping, it was lurching among them like a Frankenstein monster. Of course Caroline had told George nothing about the secret societies in the South who were swearing to conquer Mexico. He was still struggling to preserve the Union. While John Sladen and the men of his generation no longer had much interest in this idea.

But this letter was at best a corollary to their thunderous dreams of Mexico. The letter was pure revenge, on John Sladen's part for Aaron Burr and his lost father, on Calhoun's part for Peggy Eaton, for the eight vacant years as vice president, years that only the presidency could have made meaningful, years that Martin Van Buren had destroyed.

"We've tracked down that rumor Sarah Polk reported," John said. "Van Buren and Clay have cut a deal. They're going to scuttle the treaty, cut Texas loose to wind up God knows where—a British or French protectorate, maybe, or a Mexican province again—with all of Mexico a British-French protectorate. They don't give a damn. They just want to get elected president."

"Maybe you ought to leak it, George," Caroline said.

"I will. But not to a newspaper. I'm sending it to Andrew Jackson, today."

"Send him this, too," John said.

From his pocket he took a newspaper proof. "It's a letter from Van Buren, telling the country he doesn't think it's the right time to annex Texas. It'll be published in the *Globe* tomorrow afternoon. I've been told that Clay's letter, saying the same thing, will be published in the *National Intelligencer* in the morning."

"Johnny, get rid of this letter about Texas and we can make Calhoun president," George said. "Calhoun and Polk for vice president—the South and the West, with New Jersey and Pennsylvania and Maryland—it's a clear majority."

For a moment Caroline's brain whirled. That was a brilliant idea. George Stapleton had learned a lot about politics in the last fifteen years. "Why not try it?" she said to John Sladen.

He shook his head. He could not let go of his revenge, and he hated the thought that Calhoun might be persuaded to abandon his vengeance. "It's too chancy. We've got to rally the South against Van Buren. This letter will do it. Calhoun's already taken himself out of the race."

"Talk to him. I'll talk to him. Where is he?" George said.

He rushed into the hall and summoned Hannibal from the stables. An extremely reluctant John Sladen rode off with him to see John C. Calhoun. Caroline stayed behind and read Van Buren's letter. It was a typical Little Magician production. He talked on all sides of the Texas question, until it was impossible to know where he stood. An even more fatal flaw was the letter's length. It consumed five packed columns in the *Globe*'s small type.

An hour later, George returned with a funereal expression on his face. "Calhoun won't go back in the presidential race and he won't withdraw his letter. He says the letter is necessary to warn the British that we're onto their game of trying to destroy the South's economy to give the world market to their India cotton. He says if some senator leaks the letter, that's his business. As secretary of state, he considered it his duty to write it."

"What did John say?"

"Nothing. He just sat there like the cat that ate the canary. He's got the old man mesmerized."

In two weeks, the Democratic Convention would begin in Baltimore. "If Calhoun won't run and Van Buren can't, who's going to be the nominee?" Caroline asked.

"Who knows? It could go to almost anyone."

"Why not James K. Polk?"

George thought about it for a moment. "Why not?"

"Maybe we ought to take a trip to Tennessee to get General Jackson's opinion."

"I'm ready to leave right now."

By six o'clock they were on the train to Baltimore. The whooping steam engine sent huge cinders flying through the open windows, spreading soot all over their clothes. But it was worth the mess to travel at forty miles an hour. In Baltimore, they caught a night train west to Pittsburgh. Dozing in the seats, the car lit only by the flickering light of the furnace in the engine just ahead of them, they reached the booming Western metropolis in the dawn. A steamboat was departing for Nashville in a half hour. They slept most of the day while the boat churned down the Ohio to the Cumberland River. At noon the following day they were in Nashville—a trip that had taken them a week in 1828.

Although they were honeymooners no more, they could not avoid recollections of their first trip. They were no longer those youthful lovers. Caroline was all too aware that George disliked her imperious ways. Her divided heart had virtually extinguished her capacity for ardor. But they were far more profoundly political partners than they had been in that first fumbling exploration.

They were also still man and wife. In their cabin aboard the steamboat, George hinted that he would like to revive a particular set of memories. But the absence of a bathtub for douching made another pregnancy too risky. Caroline claimed total exhaustion as her excuse.

In another half hour they were debarking at the Hermitage's dock, east of the city. The handsome carriage that carried them up to the mansion was the one in which ex-president Jackson had departed from Washington; it was made from the wood of the famous frigate USS *Constitution*.

At the Hermitage a familiar face greeted them at the door: Andrew Jackson Donelson. He was still functioning as Old Hickory's adviser and secretary. George swiftly explained why they had come and hoped the General's health could tolerate a serious political discussion.

"He's very weak," Donelson said. "But the word *Texas* would bring him out of his coffin. Let me tell him you're here."

A moment later, a shout rattled through the house. "Bring them in! Bring them in!"

They found Andrew Jackson sitting half erect on a settee, a spectral skeleton of the man they had known as president. His cheeks had sunk, his prow of a nose now presided over a skull-like face. As they walked toward him, a spasm of coughing racked his withered body. They saw blood on the hand-kerchief he held to his lips. But life still blazed in his eyes.

"What an unexpected pleasure for a dying man!" he said as he accepted Caroline's kiss and George's handshake.

He settled himself and studied the Stapletons. "Andrew tells me you haven't traveled a thousand miles merely to say good-bye to me."

"Our party is in crisis, General. We've come to you for advice," George said. "The man you've chosen to lead us is betraying you on the last and greatest cause of your life."

He drew from his pocket Martin Van Buren's letter opposing the annex-ation of Texas and handed it to Jackson. He peered at it and pronounced the *Globe*'s type too small for him to read. George summed up the letter—and linked it to the letter Henry Clay published the same day, saying essentially the same thing. Andrew Jackson Donelson scanned the Van Buren letter while they talked and confirmed George's reading.

"Little Van has proven himself a trimmer, once and for all," Donelson said. There was unmistakable triumph in his voice. He was remembering the brawl over Peggy Eaton and the anguish he and his wife Emily had endured over their refusal to recognize her.

Another fit of coughing racked Old Hickory. He wiped more blood from his lips. "I can't believe Van Buren would do such a thing without consulting me."

"He's done it, General. No doubt you'll get a letter from him, trying to explain it away," George said.

"I begin to think you were right about him from the start," Jackson said.

There was a long silence, broken only by Jackson's labored breathing. He looked slowly from Donelson to George to Caroline and said, "We need an-other candidate. Are you here to suggest Calhoun? It might kill me but I'll try to swallow him."

George shook his head and drew Calhoun's letter about Texas and slavery from his pocket. This one Old Hickory managed to read for himself. "Isn't it amazing how an intelligent man can lack ordinary common sense?"

Jackson handed the letter to Donelson and looked into the distance. "Who shall it be?"

"You have a man only a few miles away, in Nashville. A man you trust, who shares every one of your beliefs," Caroline said. "Above all Texas."

"Polk?" Jackson said. "There's no better Democrat alive. But he's got loser stamped on him, thanks to Slim Jimmy Jones. Sarah's persuaded me to push him for vice president."

"He could only manage it with your backing, General," George said. "If you're willing to give me a letter endorsing him, I'll undertake to manage his candidacy at the convention. But first, we're going to need a letter from you, dismissing Van Buren."

"Get me pen and paper. I'll write that one now. It will be in the Nashville papers tonight."

Andrew Jackson Donelson produced pen, ink, and a portable writing desk. For a half hour, Jackson laboriously scrawled a denunciation of the man he had backed for the last fifteen years as his heir apparent.

"Your arrival couldn't be better timed," Andrew Jackson Donelson said. "I'm leaving tonight for Texas. President Tyler has asked me to represent us there. The situation seems to grow more alarming every day. The British are definitely threatening to intervene. They've got a fleet off Cuba. Tyler's ordered Commodore Stockton to take a squadron of our ships to Galveston."

Jackson handed George the letter. It was a thorough repudiation of Martin Van Buren as the leader of the Democratic Party. "As for Polk, maybe we'd better think about him overnight. Why don't you go into Nashville and get his thoughts on the matter?"

In an hour, they were riding through the streets of the Tennessee capital in Old Hickory's carriage. The Polk house was a modest one, on the outskirts of town. He had moved to Nashville to practice law. Sarah had told Caroline he had more clients than he could handle.

The Polks' astonishment at the appearance of the Stapletons on their doorstep was nothing less than total. Sarah almost wept when she embraced Caroline. "I'd begun to think we'd never meet again," Sarah said. It had been five years. She was her same straight-backed dignified self. Her face showed not a wrinkle, but there were flecks of gray in her dark hair.

When the Stapletons told them why they had come, and where they had just been, both Polks were stunned. "Van Buren has finally done it!" Sarah said. "The schemer's outschemed himself. Who'll be the nominee?"

"I hope I'm looking at him," George said, smiling at James Polk.

"James—for president?"

For a moment Sarah was overwhelmed. The whole thing was so far beyond any and all her political calculations a half hour ago. James's reaction was more unexpected. He did not seem especially enthusiastic about the idea.

"The next president won't enjoy his four years in the White House," he said. "He could wind up fighting a war with Mexico and England simultaneously. If the English fly the abolition flag, they could raise hell in New England. It could be a replay of 1812, another Hartford Convention. This time, if they threaten to secede, the South will say good riddance. He could be the last president of the United States."

"James, you have a bad habit of fearing the worst," Sarah said.

"On the other hand," Caroline said, "a winning war would make you the first president of a continental United States. You know what Andrew Jackson really wants—New Mexico, California, Oregon, as well as Texas."

"A winning war in which General George Stapleton, son of a West Point hero of 1812, plays a leading role," Sarah Polk said. "Making him the logical candidate to succeed James K. Polk."

The two men sat there, bemused half-smiles on their faces. "Why don't we try it?" George said. "If it doesn't work, we'll blame it on them—and Old Andy."

He held out his hand to James K. Polk, as he had once extended it to Andrew Jackson. Polk shook it, but there was no enthusiasm in his grasp. Had those two defeats by Slim Jimmy Jones shaken his confidence? Or had he decided that he preferred the tranquil life of a Tennessee lawyer to the raging passions of Washington, D.C.? Did he fear there was a limit to his physical as well as his spiritual strength—a limit that an ordeal in the White House might brutally exceed? If so, why didn't Sarah say something?

Caroline understood as their eyes met. The Temple of Fame. Nothing else mattered.

TEN

TWO WEEKS LATER, CAROLINE PACED HER room at Baltimore's branch of Gadsby's Hotel, waiting for George to return from a foray to the rooms of the New York State delegation to the 1844 Democratic National Convention. She had insisted on coming to this gathering of the party faithful. The thought of sitting home waiting for the latest terse report to reach Washington over Mr. Morse's magical telegraph was intolerable. She wanted to witness, to savor, the details of Martin Van Buren's humiliation—and the transformation of James Knox Polk from forgotten man to presidential candidate.

So far, everything had gone according to plan. Around the corner from Odd Fellows Hall on Gay Street, where the Democrats convened, President John Tyler had staged his own convention of federal officeholders. Every single one of them had been appointed by him or could be dismissed by him with a stroke of his pen. Dispensing generous quantities of rum, gin, and bourbon, surreptitiously paid for by Senator Robert Walker, the chairman of the Democratic National Committee, the president had gotten himself nominated by acclamation on the platform of "Tyler and Texas."

This put unbearable pressure on the Northern Democrats who backed Martin Van Buren. Southerners, notable among them followers of John C. Calhoun, had rammed through a reaffirmation of the two-thirds rule as the convention's first order of business. Who could say no, when such a major issue was dividing them and the nation? From that moment, Martin Van Buren was a dying candidate. His supporters were a clear majority on the first ballot but far from the magical two-thirds.

Over seven more ballots, the Little Magician's totals sank as various states switched to favorite sons and Van Buren supporters and opponents shouted and cursed and groaned around Caroline in the balcony. Ex–vice president Richard Mentor Johnson's Kentucky followers waved Tecumseh's red vest and whooped it up for five minutes. An enormous silence greeted their efforts. James Buchanan of Pennsylvania fluttered aloft, but he too fell back to earth with a thud. Westerners shifted to Lewis Cass, a phlegmatic ex-soldier from Michigan who had served as secretary of war in one of Jackson's later cabinets. He accumulated enough support to alarm George Stapleton. He signaled the chairman of the convention, a firm Jackson-Polk man, to gavel them into recess. Back everyone streamed to the hotels, where a night of furious politicking began. George and a cadre of Tennesseans began visiting state delegations to remind them Jackson was backing Polk.

A knock on the door. "It's your man from Louisiana," John Sladen said.

He was a partner in the intrigue. George had given him a copy of Jackson's letter to show to Southern delegations. At the right moment he had promised to throw Louisiana to Polk when the convention returned to Odd Fellows Hall tomorrow.

"Things are moving along nicely," John said, dropping into a wing chair. "Jackson's letter works like an electric shock, even on the most fervent Van Burenites. They're beginning to see the necessity of giving him up. But they want to make sure they'll get their share of the spoils."

"They will," Caroline said.

"You're delegated to speak for the Polks?"

"Yes."

"We Southerners want to know if we're getting a man we can depend on in other ways."

"You are."

"You're sure he can be managed?"

"Absolutely."

"How much have you told Sarah?"

"Very little so far."

"Then how can you be sure?"

"Because I'm sure of her."

"You mean you're sure you can manage her?"

Caroline was amazed by how much this question disturbed her. Suddenly they were in the basement room again, yielding to incomprehensible needs and desires. She was almost horrified when she said, "Yes."

George burst into the room, a huge smile on his face. "New York's surrendered Little Van! That decides it. They'll announce they're backing Polk before the first ballot tomorrow morning."

"What did you have to promise them?"

"At least two seats in the cabinet. Preferably three."

"That's more than they deserve," Caroline said.

"I know. Polk can keep the promise or not, as far as I'm concerned." George turned to John Sladen. "What's the word from the Land of Cotton?"

"Why, Massa George, we's done committed everything but the honuh of our women to yo cause," John said in a good imitation of a blackface comedian.

"How many *states*?" George said.

"Every one but South Carolina, which has chosen not to attend our historic convention—except for Congressman Pickens."

"Maybe I can persuade him to come forward tomorrow and announce his state is for Polk," Caroline said. "I'll tell him it would please Julia Gardiner to know he played a part in burying the Little Magician."

"A *very* good idea," George said. "A lot of people will think he's speaking for Calhoun."

"He will be," John Sladen said.

"Let's all get some sleep," George said, stifling a gigantic yawn. "It's three A.M."

John Sladen departed. Caroline sat down on the edge of the bed. In the bureau mirror, she saw herself, her combed-out dark hair gleaming on her shoulders in the yellow lamplight. She was wearing a sky blue negligee over her nightdress. *A woman.* A woman surrounded by these power gods, these strutting politicians who imagined they were deciding the nation's destiny. If they ever knew they were performing to a script she had written. They were her puppets. Hers—and Sarah's.

The loose hair added a touch of youth. George was looking at her in that admiring, desiring way that multiplied her elation. Yes, it was the same woman who had sat in Bowood's dining room and realized that her future happiness was entwined with history and power. But the political tyro who had let George put Hannah Stapleton's ring on her finger never dreamt she would help create a president of the United States.

The ring still gleamed on her finger. But she had triumphed over it. She had become a woman infinitely superior to that beatific Quakeress on Bowood's library wall.

Caroline turned to George. "Are you as happy as I am?"

The question seemed to take him by surprise. "I suppose so," he said, sitting down beside her.

"You don't sound it."

"I'm just tired—it's been a lot of work."

"You won't regret it. Sarah meant it when she said George Stapleton would succeed James Polk. She'll do everything in her power to make that promise come true."

"I wish a war wasn't in the plan. I keep remembering something John Calhoun said to me on our trip to South Carolina in 1833. How much he regretted starting the war that killed my father—and your father."

"The Mexicans are going to start the war. Or the British. You won't die in it. You've got a charmed life, like your great-grandfather. Didn't the explosion on the *Princeton* prove that?"

"I'm not just thinking of my own neck. I'm thinking of a lot of kids who'll feel like I felt when I heard my father wasn't coming home."

"I hope you're not saying these things to anyone else."

"Of course not."

"History is full of hard choices, George. There's no room in it for sentiment. Did Andrew Jackson ever stop to think about the men who died under his command?"

"I'm not Andrew Jackson. I'm George Stapleton."

"*President* George Stapleton. Doesn't that stir you? It stirs me—it *arouses* me, George. I'll love that man with a passion, a devotion beyond imagination. I want to help that man lead this nation into a glorious future."

"What if the future turns out to be inglorious? This argument over slavery gets nastier every day. You should hear what some of those New York Democrats are saying about the South. They sound like abolitionists. They sneer at Polk because he owns slaves. If it gets much worse, this country could become ungovernable."

For a moment Caroline almost told him the secret plan, the annexation of Texas and the conquest of California and Oregon—and Mexico. It sat there in her soul like a two-faced god in the Temple of Fame, transcending old-fashioned words such as *union, liberty, the pursuit of happiness*. Could she persuade him to accept it, now? No, George Stapleton would have to be led step by step to its brutal necessity. What he had just told her revealed that the fundamental division in the Stapleton soul was afflicting him, just as she had long ago feared it might. Like too many Americans, the Stapletons wanted to be powerful—and good. More and more, Caroline had concluded Aaron Burr was right—it was impossible.

"I worry about Polk. He's mounting a very large tiger. I hope he doesn't end up minus his arms and legs."

"He has a secret resource. Sarah Childress Polk."

"Her name won't be on what he signs, what he says, what he does. It'll be James Knox Polk's presidency in the history books. That can do terrible things to a man's peace of mind. Not to mention his stomach and intestines."

For a moment she almost told him about the Temple of Fame. "No matter what it says in the history books, for them it will be *their* presidency," she said. "Their chance to live and work together on a scale, with a passion, that no other husband and wife have ever achieved in the history of the world. Then it will be our turn. James trusts in Sarah's love, her intelligence. Why don't you trust in mine?"

"I do. But we're only human, Caroline. We're both . . . human."

"I know that. I know we may fail. The Polks may fail. But if we love each other, even the failure will be glorious."

She flung her arms around his neck and kissed him passionately. For a moment, her left hand was upturned beside his ear. Hannah Stapleton's diamond glinted in the lamplight. I mean what I just said. I mean every word of it, Caroline told herself—and Hannah's hovering spirit—if by some miracle beyond her comprehension such a being existed.

It was unquestionably the beginning of a memorable moment in their marriage. But before George could do more than return her kiss, a fist pounded on the door. A drunken voice shouted, "Senator Stapleton. We've got a new proposition! New York must be heard!"

Caroline slipped under the bedcovers. Three beefy men blundered into the room. She recognized one of them—their old acquaintance Churchill C. Cambreleng, fatter, older, less self-confident. He had been an ex-congressman since the 1837 Democratic rout in New York that had signaled the downfall of Van Buren's presidency.

The sight of Caroline threw Cambreleng and his friends into confusion. They babbled apologies for their bad manners and hastily delivered their proposition to George. For New York to be properly consoled for abandoning Van Buren, they had to have the vice presidency.

"I see no problem with that," George said. "I presume you have Silas Wright in mind?"

"Yes!" all three chorused. Senator Silas Wright had been Van Buren's spokesman in Washington for the last four years. He had a reputation for straight dealing and honest statement that was in ironic contrast to his patron.

Quiet, even shy in mixed company, he often drank too much at Caroline's salons but never lost his dignity. His wife was even more shy and confessed to Caroline that she worried about her husband's drinking.

With more apologies, the New Yorkers stumbled into the hall. "Wright won't accept," Caroline said. "His wife hates Washington. She can't wait to get her husband out of the place. As vice president he'd drink himself to death in a year. You'd better have a substitute in the wings."

George gazed ruefully at Caroline. The moment had passed. "Can I lay your previous motion on the table, Mrs. President? To be taken up at a later date?"

"It can be brought up anytime you please, Mr. President."

The next morning, as the balloting resumed at Odd Fellows Hall, Churchill C. Cambreleng rose to announce that New York's delegation was withdrawing Martin Van Buren's name and switching their support to Polk. Cambreleng made the statement with an absolute minimum of enthusiasm. John Sladen leaped to his feet to shout that Louisiana, which had been supporting Lewis Cass, was also switching to Polk. Francis Pickens marched from the rear of the hall and addressed the chairman: "May I, speaking unofficially for the state of South Carolina, add my voice to this chorus?" The building burst into thunderous cheers; everyone thought he represented John C. Calhoun. At breakfast, Caroline had paused at Pickens's table to urge him to make Julia Gardiner Tyler happy with this declaration.

After casting New Jersey's votes for Polk, Senator George Stapleton asked permission to address the convention. He told them about his visit to Andrew Jackson and the General's unequivocal choice of Polk as his candidate. "Who else but the founder of our party could have made this inspired choice of another man from Tennessee?" George roared. "Our party was born with Old Hickory. It will be reborn with Young Hickory!"

The cheers were even more stupendous. John Sladen made a motion to declare James Knox Polk the candidate of the Democratic Party for president by a unanimous vote. "Polk and Texas!" he howled. "No matter what great power casts its perfidious shadow, the will of the American people will not be thwarted by counsels of caution and timidity!"

Delegates pranced in the aisles. At a signal from George, men in bartender's aprons began handing out bottles of Tennessee bourbon. The band burst into "Hail the Conquering Hero." Other orators ascended the platform to praise "Honest Jim" Polk. Tennesseans made it sound as if he had spent his boyhood at Andrew Jackson's knee. George, making good on his promise, nominated Silas Wright for vice president. It was approved with another unanimous acclamation.

A messenger was rushed to the room in Odd Fellows Hall where Samuel F. B. Morse had set up one of his telegraphs. It was connected to a receiver in the U.S. Capitol. Wright was asked if he accepted the task of becoming a sop to Martin Van Buren's pride. Back whizzed the answer that Caroline had predicted: *No.* The delegates buzzed and swarmed like a hive of agitated bees. Eventually, George mounted the rostrum and nominated ex-senator George Mifflin Dallas of Pennsylvania—another state that Polk had to carry to win. Dallas was accepted with the same enthusiasm that had greeted Wright. By this time the Tennessee bourbon had taken effect and the delegates were ready to cheer anyone—even Henry Clay.

The next order of business was the platform. George and party chairman Robert Walker saw to it that it began with a ringing demand to annex Texas and Oregon. The rest of the document was identical to the statements on which the party had run in 1840. Most important was the call for noninterference by the federal government in any and all "American institutions"—a code term for slavery.

The convention was over. The first stage of the miracle had occurred. Sarah Childress and James Knox Polk were on their way to the White House. Ahead there were still delicate negotiations with President Tyler to persuade him to get out of the race in Polk's favor. But Caroline was confident she and George could handle this problem. Back in Washington, D.C., at their big brick house on Pennsylvania Avenue, she wrote the most important letter of her life to Sarah Polk.

Dearest Friend,

I hardly need congratulate you and James on the nomination. You know my feelings on that score. The newspapers will tell you most of what transpired at the convention. There were reporters swarming everywhere. I want to share something else with you, a vision of the future that I implore you to tell no one—not even your husband. Never have I had such a sense of large events impending since I came to Washington. But thought—true thought—about them is being lost in the welter of arguments about slavery. I believe you and I can think about these events better than any of the distracted males of our acquaintance—including our husbands. I hope that is not too hard a saying for you. I know you love James and I love George. But love does not—or should not—blind a woman to a man's limitations. Do you agree? I know you do, so I will proceed with absolute trust that you will honor the request with which I began this letter.

Together, the Polks and the Stapletons can lay the foundation for the resolution of this immense problem. There is no doubt in my mind or yours that eventually the blacks must be freed. When and how is the question. The Northern states with substantial numbers of blacks—New York, New Jersey, Pennsylvania—abolished slavery in a series of steps, first freeing the children of slaves when they reached maturity and finally ending it altogether. Why were they able to do this without any concern for what terrifies the South—a black insurrection? Because the numbers of slaves in proportion to the white population was relatively small.

As long as the South's 3 million slaves are compacted within its borders, Southerners will regard abolition as an attempt by Northerners to cut the throats of their wives and children. The one hope of persuading the South to accept a gradual manumission of their blacks is diffusion. Only when the Africans are spread over a vastly wider domain, becoming, say, no more than ten or twenty percent of the population in most places, will the fear of a race war subside.

You and James know that the annexation of Texas will almost certainly start a war with Mexico. It will, if you follow Andrew Jackson's vision, inexorably lead to the conquest of New Mexico and California. With an army at your command, it should not be difficult to persuade the British to settle the Oregon border the way General Jackson settled Florida with the Spanish—give us what we want or we'll take it. But that new territory, immense as it is, will not be enough to disperse the blacks to the point where manumission will be permissible. To achieve that we must have Mexico itself.

I know the thought is breathtaking. A politician would recoil at the immense problems the idea suggests. But we who have time to reflect, to plan, to await the moment, should not flinch from what seems unthinkable at first. The advantages would be as immense as the problems. Mexico is already a mixed race, Spanish and Indian. Blacks could be introduced there in large numbers—the country is relatively underpopulated. Grateful to those who gave them freedom, they might even become our legates, or at the worst our helots, to retain control of the country for the foreseeable future. The British have done similar things in India, with armies of native troops under white leadership.

The task of persuading the American people to accept this idea will be large, I admit. But the people worship success. A war that swiftly conquers Mexico will make James K. Polk a national hero. He may well acquire the kind of authority that Andrew Jackson possessed—and the consequent ability to persuade the mass that his vision is inspired by the gods. Waiting in the wings will be General George Stapleton, to second his leadership and assume his power when James lays it aside to the plaudits of a grateful nation.

Does this stir you as it does me? I think it will. I think it will earn us an eternal accolade in the Temple of Fame.

Devotedly,
Caroline

In the nursery, she could hear George romping with little Paul. She had barely kissed the child when they returned from Baltimore. This letter was already burning in her mind. Slowly, Caroline reread it and carefully sealed the envelope. Almost immediately she was assailed by terrific guilt. A voice spoke in her head, her heart, her soul. *How can you leave out the rest of it? Without the whole truth this letter is a lie. Your love for Sarah will become a lie.* But the whole truth was untellable. It was forever sealed in those caves of ice, where the sacred river ran down to the sunless sea.

She would tell her as much as she could—as much, perhaps, as she owed her. She tore open the envelope and added a postscript.

There is a dark alternative to this vision. Throughout the South, men are joining secret societies and swearing solemn oaths to take Mexico and keep it if war breaks out. My friend John Sladen is one of them. They have another purpose—to make the South strong enough to con-

*front the North as an equal, and make demands that the North may
not be able to accept; a complete suppression of abolitionism, for instance, a fugitive slave law with teeth. If the North refuses, the entire
South, puissant with conquest, with Texas and Mexico and California
in its grasp, will secede and dare the North to do something about it.
I think—I hope—this darkness can be averted by inspired leadership.
But if it comes to the worst version of the scenario, is it so terrible if
the two sections go their separate ways? It might be best for both peo-
ples. For the blacks of course there might be a longer wait for freedom.
But their fate is already hard. It is difficult to see how it would be much
worse in a seceded South. The same principle of emancipation by diffusion would, I think, ultimately prevail.*

*Now I have told you everything because I trust you absolutely—as
a woman and as my beloved friend.*

ELEVEN

ON JUNE 24, 1844, GEORGE AND Caroline joined President Tyler, his
sons, Robert and John Jr., and their wives on a voyage to New York aboard
a small steam yacht that George had chartered for the occasion. It was a
cheerful company. The president was on his way to marry Julia Gardner. The
expectation of holding so much loveliness in his arms enabled him to look
serenely on his latest political disappointment.

A week ago, the Senate had rejected Secretary of State Calhoun's treaty
with Texas by a crushing vote. Whigs and disgruntled Van Buren Democrats
combined to provide more nays than yeas—instead of the two-thirds majority
needed to annex the republic. But the president declared himself undaunted.
He was still determined to make Texas the twenty-seventh state, somehow.

Tyler's third-party candidacy was taking on shape and substance. By handing out federal jobs by the dozen, he had persuaded New York's Tammany
Hall, which nursed numerous grievances against Martin Van Buren's Albany
machine, to endorse him for president. Similar tactics had produced endorse-
ments from dissident groups in New Jersey and Pennsylvania. Tyler was going
to be on the ballot in these three key states.

"I haven't heard a word from your friend Polk," Tyler said. "Have you?"

"I'm in touch with him almost every day," George said. "He's very concerned and perplexed by your candidacy, Mr. President. He asked General
Jackson to write me a letter about it—with permission to show it to you."

"You have it with you?"

George took it out of his pocket. Caroline had already read it, of course.
In his unique scrawl, Old Hickory praised Tyler effusively for his efforts on

behalf of Texas. He went on to declare Tyler's withdrawal from the race "would be the certain means of electing Mr. Polk." If Tyler and his followers agreed to this step, the General was sure Polk and his fellow Democrats would look on the president and his followers as "brethren—all former differences forgotten."

"This is what I wanted to see," Tyler said, handing the letter to his sons. "Not for myself, I have no further desire for office, but for my friends, who have risked a great deal for me."

"It's as far as any reasonable man can expect Mr. Polk to go," George said.

"I agree. When I return from my honeymoon, I'll announce my withdrawal from the race."

George summoned the yacht's steward and they soon had glasses of champagne in their hands. "To happiness!" the president said.

Two days later, in the flower-bedecked Church of the Ascension on lower Fifth Avenue, one version of that mystical American word seemed within John Tyler's grasp. The fifty-four-year-old president waited expectantly at the altar as glowing twenty-four-year-old Julia Gardiner came up the aisle on the arm of her brother, Alexander. Not a reporter or a sketch artist was in sight. The president had debarked from their yacht in the dawn and remained unseen in the Gardiners' New York town house until the ceremony.

On the way to the church in the Gardiner carriage, Tyler asked the Stapletons and his two sons to say nothing about his decision to withdraw from the race. "Julia will be disappointed. She honestly believes I can be elected," he said.

"You must focus her energies on Texas, Mr. President," Caroline said. "If Mr. Polk is elected, why can't you convince Congress that they should accept the people's decision as a mandate and vote to annex Texas by a simple majority of both houses before you leave office? You would have the glory of bringing her into the Union—which you richly deserve."

Tyler smiled. "You're not the first person to suggest that idea, Mrs. Stapleton. But few have put it so graciously."

Caroline was acting as Sarah Polk's spokeswoman here. Since Caroline's confessional letter after James Polk was nominated, she and Sarah had been in almost daily communication. As Caroline expected, Sarah did not flinch from the prospect of annexing New Mexico and California as well as Texas— or from the implications of conquering and holding Mexico—but she coolly declined to commit James Polk to such an awesome program. *While it is useful to look far ahead, it is better to go one step at a time,* she wrote. Foreseeing the ferocious opposition to Texas among the Whigs and abolitionists, she urged Caroline and George to use all their influence to persuade Tyler to annex the controversial republic while he was president. James would inherit an accomplished fact—and it would be up to the Mexicans to decide whether they wanted a war. *Let's spread the responsibility around,* Sarah wrote.

The newspapers reacted to the announcement of President Tyler's May-September union with not a little randy humor. The *New York Herald* remarked that the White House had told everyone the president was taking a vacation from his arduous duties. "We rather think the president's arduous duties are only beginning," the reporter chortled. Other papers used the opportunity to make political jokes about Texas. It was, one editor said, a treaty of annexation Tyler could manage without the consent of the Senate.

Whig presidential candidate Henry Clay and his Senate followers who had voted against acquiring Texas soon discovered they had mistaken Washington's hermetic politics for the sentiments of the American people. North, South, East, and West, a hurricane of enthusiasm for bringing the republic into the Union swept the nation. Everyone wanted this immense swath of virtually uninhabited territory to be part of the United States. One reason may have been the announcement that Texas would grant 640 acres to any head of a family who settled there and 320 acres to a single man. For many people, Texas became an instant El Dorado—and James K. Polk's call for annexation won their passionate approval.

Another issue in the election was the disputed territory of Oregon, which both Great Britain and the United States claimed. On this question, candidate Polk announced he was in favor of demanding the entire acreage, from the northern border of California all the way up to the fifty-fourth parallel of latitude, the southern boundary of the Russian possession of Alaska. "Fifty-four forty or fight!" was his motto.

Sarah Polk assured Caroline this was nothing but a campaign slogan. They were using it to portray Polk as a true heir of Andrew Jackson's—who incidentally favored seizing the whole territory from perfidious Albion. Once elected, however, Sarah said they would do the sensible thing and accept the forty-ninth parallel, which had already been established as the American-Canadian border as far west as the Rocky Mountains. *It does no harm to talk big and compromise,* Sarah wrote. *Especially if we are facing a war at the other end of the country.*

Another surprise move was Polk's announcement that he would only serve a single term. "How brilliant," Caroline said to George. "All the disappointed candidates will rally around him now. They can tolerate the thought of waiting four years. Eight would be unbearable."

"But does he mean it?" George said. "Remember Old Hickory swore he was only going to serve one term."

"I think they mean it," Caroline said, remembering the reluctance she had sensed when she and George first told James Polk he would be Jackson's candidate.

"They?" George said. "Do you think people talk about us that way?"

"I doubt it. No one can imagine a mere woman telling a behemoth like you what to do."

In mid-August, back in the White House with Julia, President Tyler announced his withdrawal from the presidential race and his endorsement of James K. Polk as the candidate who would bring Texas into the Union. Alexander Gardiner, Julia's lively brother, immediately began planting stories in the New York newspapers calling for a Texas annexed by John Tyler. He persuaded Tammany Hall to produce a resolution calling for action as soon as "the voice of the people" was heard.

To accelerate his campaign, Gardiner asked George to help a genial Irishman who was looking for money to found a pro-Texas newspaper in New York. John L. O'Sullivan was already editing *The Democratic Review,* which published poems and stories by literary lights such as Nathaniel Hawthorne and John Greenleaf Whittier and resounding essays uniting the future glory of America to the creed of the Democratic Party.

George agreed to lend O'Sullivan ten thousand dollars to start the *New York Morning News,* with the understanding that his spirited editorials and his news stories could be reprinted in the numerous papers controlled by the Stapletons in New Jersey. Senator Stapleton stumped the Garden State telling voters that it was America's "manifest destiny"—an O'Sullivan phrase—to become a continental power. In fact, O'Sullivan was inclined to think there was no limit to America's growth. He told Caroline he saw the southern boundary of the nation as the Isthmus of Panama and the northern one in "the regions of eternal frosts."

In New Jersey, Senator Jeremy Biddle stumped the state for Henry Clay, insisting the annexation of Texas would be viewed by the rest of the world as a blot on America's honor. Caroline turned O'Sullivan loose on him and supplied much of the information for his stories. The result was a portrait etched in Celtic acid.

> *What a contrast the two senators from New Jersey present. They are a virtual paradigm of the two political parties. Senator George Stapleton is a giant of a man, with a heart and mind that more than match his physique. Born rich, he has devoted himself to the service of the common man. That is why he is on the hustings fighting for Texas. He wants every American to have his chance to acquire some wealth. Senator Jeremy Biddle, on the other hand, is a runt. He looks like he was squashed at birth by a steam engine. In his nasal whine, he warns people annexing Texas will make the Mexicans and the English mad. Here is a coward who wants to see no one get rich but his family and their aristocratic friends. To compound the irony, not a penny of the millions in his pocket was earned by his own toil. The son of a bankrupt lawyer from Philadelphia, he married the daughter of one of the richest men in New Jersey. Ever since, Biddle has striven, like a typical Whig, to consolidate every dollar in the state into his bank accounts.*

Caroline saw to it that this and similar abuse of Senator Biddle were faithfully reprinted in every New Jersey newspaper the Stapletons controlled. She was delighted to learn that Sally Stapleton Biddle was livid and had ordered Jeremy to quit politics as soon as possible. Like her aunt Angelica, she now regarded it as no profession for a gentleman.

Angelica Stapleton was still alive, immured in her town house on Beekman Street. George crossed the Hudson to pay her dutiful visits whenever he came to New Jersey, usually taking with him one or two of his sons. Senator Stapleton's growing national fame did not change her mind about his career. She still thought he had made a colossal mistake to go anywhere near the unsavory business of vote-getting.

In mid-September, George pleaded with Caroline to pay Angelica a visit. The pace of the campaign was mounting steadily. The Whigs were pouring in money as usual, and several states, notably Pennsylvania, suddenly looked precarious. Senator Stapleton, the champion of Texas, was being invited to speak there and in New York. His ability to quote General Jackson directly made a huge impact on audiences.

Caroline took three-year-old Paul and journeyed to Beekman Street. Angelica greeted her with frosty politeness. She was growing gaunt but was as regal as ever. Her sister, Henrietta, had eaten herself to death two years ago. Now Angelica played whist against herself and saw no one but a half dozen old friends whose arthritis or gout made it difficult for them to leave their town houses more than once or twice a month.

"Someone told me—I think it was Sally—that you've paid another visit to that border ruffian, General Jackson," Angelica said.

"Yes."

"Is he likely to die soon? That is virtually the only hope I have for this country."

"He's very unwell. But he vows to stay alive until Texas joins the Union."

"No doubt George played a part in recruiting this other ruffian from Tennessee, Polk, to run for the presidency?"

"General Jackson had far more to do with it."

Angelica's stare made it plain that she considered this another of Caroline's lies. She turned to three-year-old Paul. "What will you be when you grow up?"

"I don't know," the little boy said.

"Not a politician, I hope," Angelica said. "I think you should set your sights on a soldier's career. It's an honorable profession, though a dangerous one. Your grandfather—your father's father—was a soldier, you know."

"I know. Papa told me."

"Don't listen to your mother. She'll make you another politician."

"Yes, Grandmother."

For a moment Caroline wondered if the old woman in her brooding loneliness had acquired the power to control the family's destiny. Why did she have these flashes of fear about a spiritual world in which she did not believe? It reminded her of her bouts of anxiety about Hannah Stapleton's hovering specter. For a moment Caroline wished she could talk to Angelica as a member of the family. Perhaps she might convince her that she was adding to the luster of the Stapleton name. Or at least convince her that her motives were unselfish. *You sacrificed your love on the altar of fame. So have I.* But she and Angelica were enemies forever. Such fantasies were pointless.

Finally, the campaign oratory died away and the votes began piling up. First came a dismaying surprise: New Jersey had gone for Henry Clay. Again, it was the South Jersey Quaker voters; they disliked anyone associated with that man of war, Andrew Jackson—and they were equally opposed to annexing Texas because it might start a war. A second shock: Polk had failed to carry Tennessee. But he swept the entire South, except for North Carolina, a state that tended to vote the opposite way to South Carolina on everything. Pennsylvania stayed in the Democratic column, and the entire election soon hinged on New York.

As usual, the Democrats piled up a solid majority in New York City. But the Whigs had an upstate political machine that was as formidable as Martin Van Buren's operation. For three days everyone held their breath as votes from Finger Lakes hamlets and Adirondack villages trickled into Albany. John L. O'Sullivan had a team of express riders mounted and ready to carry the news to New York. At noon on the fourth day, one of these messengers pounded up to Bowood's door with a copy of the *New York Morning News.* "New York Is Polk's by 5,000 Votes!" the headline cried.

A few days later, a letter arrived from Sarah Polk.

Dearest Friend,

I trust you have forgiven me for not answering your extraordinary letter of last May in all its particulars. I thought it best to put my energies into winning the election first. With God's mysterious providence, that has been accomplished. Now the awesome responsibility confronts us. Can we dare to go as far as you suggest? I don't know, James's nature is a barrier. His two defeats by Jimmy Jones were crushing disappointments that make him wary of hoping for the best, of assuming things will go right. When the news that he had won the election was sent to him by a special courier two nights ago, he told no one—not even me. He walked around for an entire day with the news in his pocket, as if he dreaded confronting it as a public fact. Yet the vision you propose is a noble one. I am ready to embrace your analysis of how slavery can ultimately be scoured from our republic by a diffusion of the blacks. But I wonder if the passions already aroused on both sides by that hateful old man, John Quincy Adams, and his counterpart in the South, John C. Calhoun, who is not as hateful but also refuses to yield an inch in the quarrel, have not already become too extreme. That leaves us with your final "dark" alternative, which fills me with sadness. I would not want James Polk—or George Stapleton—to be remembered as men who presided over the breakup of the Union. I am still enough of a Jacksonian to regard that event with dismay. But if we come to that alternative, there will be a host of angry voices in the drama who will bear far more blame. For the time being I want you to know we are allies in heart and mind—as we have been since the day we met.

As ever,
Sarah

Almost immediately, Caroline was stricken by the most excruciating migraine headache she had ever experienced. She lay in her darkened bedroom, asking herself what the pain was trying to tell her, scribbling entries in her diary between bouts of agony. Eventually, she began to see what was tormenting her. Sarah Childress Polk had bared her soul but Caroline Kemble Stapleton's soul still hid in that icy cave above the sunless sea. She could never confess her secret allegiance to John Sladen, her secret hope—which she knew was his hope—that the Union would collapse and the South, where he was rising to power, would pursue its own destiny. In her lost father's name, Aaron Burr's dark dream still had irresistible power in her soul.

George begged Caroline to let him call a doctor. But she shook her head and took nothing for her pain but a little laudanum. On the third night she drifted into a shallow sleep. Suddenly she was on the underground river, drifting past caves of ice on frowning cliffs. In the mouth of each cave there was a woman's face. She did not recognize any of them at first. Then she realized one of them as Catalyntie Van Vorst Stapleton. Beside her was a black woman, who reached out to Caroline with pleading hands. Beside her was Caroline's grandmother, Kate Stapleton Rawdon. "Why don't you understand?" she called as Caroline drifted past. Near her was the face of a woman she had seen in a portrait at Kemble Manor—another Caroline Kemble, Kate's aunt. Finally there was a face Caroline recognized—and feared. Hannah Cosway Stapleton. What was this saint doing in the icy caves of the underground heart? Was she telling Caroline that every woman had a secret love she was forced to surrender? Or a secret wish that she had been forced to abandon? Was this part of woman's fate?

Caroline woke up. Downstairs, the grandfather clock bonged three times. She thought of Hugh Stapleton and wished she had not betrayed him. But it was necessary. Why couldn't people accept the way necessity drove the heart and the head? She got up, threw a wool robe around her shoulders, and descended to the library. She lit a lamp and gazed at Hannah Cosway Stapleton's portrait. Again she noticed the hint of pain in the eyes. But the mouth was so gentle, so serene. Was that the real woman or simply the way the painter, a man, saw her?

The night wind sighed through Bowood's maple trees. Suddenly Caroline heard a voice. *Oh, my dear girl, I fear for thy salvation.* It was a whisper almost as subtle as the wind. But she heard it. Who could have said it? It had to be inside her aching head. *Oh, my dear girl, I fear for thy salvation.* There it was again.

Caroline remembered its source, the Congressman telling the story of Hannah's Quaker mother saying it to her, when she saw her accumulation of fashionable gowns in her New York town house. The Congressman had told it as a joke. But this whisper was no joke.

Caroline fled back to her bedroom. What did that word *salvation* mean? The soul was saved—from what? From damnation? If she did not believe in hell or heaven, was that word irrelevant? Or was there damnation in this world, a fate harsher than her worst fears could foresee? And salvation—could that be a happiness that seemed impossible now?

Caroline knew exactly what that happiness was. The courage to tell Sarah Childress Polk the whole truth. The courage to repudiate the snide question John Sladen had asked: *Is she manageable?* Perhaps the moment would come somewhere in the next four tumultuous years. Sarah had crossed the threshold. She was about to enter the temple of American fame. Caroline would be there too, closer than any other person; yes, closer than James Knox Polk.

Perhaps the whole truth would become a necessity at some point in their journey. Perhaps it would be told with bitterness, anger, despair. Or received with those desolating emotions. Perhaps the truth was Caroline Kemble Stapleton's damnation. What a terrible thought.

T W E L V E

UNQUESTIONABLY, IT WAS THE MOST BRILLIANT party in the forty-five-year history of the White House. Never had the aging mansion contained so many dresses in the latest Paris fashion, or so many diamond and pearl necklaces, pins, bracelets, and earrings. At the center of the whirling throng on the dance floor was Julia Gardiner Tyler in gleaming white satin with a matching cape and headdress embroidered with silver. She gazed adoringly at her dancing partner, stumpy Senator Felix Grundy, of Tennessee, and talked to him about only one topic: Texas.

On the sideline in a gown that was calculatedly less splendid than the first lady's, Caroline Kemble Stapleton gazed with complacent approval on the glittering scene. Beside her, President John Tyler beamed and said, "Now no one can say I'm a man without a party."

Caroline was the invisible manager of this event. It was one of a dozen affairs Julia Gardiner Tyler had staged after consulting with her to assemble the guest lists—always with an eye to sustain the bill to annex Texas, which was working its way through both houses of Congress.

Not since Andrew Jackson's departure had the mansion itself looked so good. Louis Quinze chairs that had not been touched since the Monroe administration had been restored to their original pristine condition. The East Room's walls gleamed with fresh paint. New draperies saluted the eye everywhere. The cash for all this splendor had come, not from Congress, which still collectively loathed John Tyler and his vetoes, but from the Gardiner fortune.

After four years of Martin Van Buren's bachelor's hall and eight previous years in which Andrew Jackson made do with a series of substitute hostesses, and the empty year of mourning following the death of the first Mrs. Tyler, Washington was aching for a first lady who could reign. Caroline had given Julia a motto: "The grand or nothing." Since they had only three months on which to operate on this lame-duck Congress before James Polk's inauguration, it was absolutely necessary to dazzle them.

The grand style suited Julia perfectly. She had the looks and the inclination to reign, dazzle, daze, amaze, astound, awe, and overwhelm. John L. O'Sullivan and Frank W. Thomas of the *New York Herald* were enlisted to supply adjectives. Thomas, hoping for a job for his drunken friend Edgar Allan Poe, all but electrified his own pen. At Julia's New Year's Day reception, the reporter declared her "as beautiful, winning, and rosy as a summer morning on the mountains of Mexico, as admirable as Queen Victoria but far more beautiful and younger and more intelligent—and quite as popular with the people." O'Sullivan repeatedly claimed Julia proved Americans had blended beauty, good taste, and democracy—and it was their manifest destiny to export this heady mixture to the whole world.

Julia surrounded herself with a "court" of female cousins and friends, all of whom wore white and appeared with her when she went to the Navy Yard to christen ships or to the galleries of the House or Senate to cheer on the debate on Texas. All these young ladies were carefully coached to urge their swarms of admirers in and out of Congress to push the all-important topic. At White House dinners, Julia persuaded ex-suitors to swallow their opinions and offer toasts to "Tyler and Texas."

Caroline was pursuing the same policy at her weekly salons. There the atmosphere was somewhat more intellectual and opposition voices were heard. John Quincy Adams maintained that if Congress annexed Texas by a simple majority vote, they might as well scrap the Constitution and become a South American republic, ruled by the latest junta. John C. Calhoun answered him with marvelous rationalizations that argued annexation could precede a treaty or even preclude one. Senator Stapleton and Congressman Sladen stayed out of the argument. They were too busy counting heads in the Senate and House to care what these two great intellects thought.

Dolley Madison opined that she was sure her late husband, who had, after all, written the Constitution, would not object to stretching it a little now and then. After all, Mr. Madison had approved of Mr. Jefferson's Louisiana Purchase, which had been on even shakier ground from a legalistic point of view. The opinion rated a page-one story in John L. O'Sullivan's *New York Morning News*.

All this Caroline reported to Sarah Polk in a stream of daily letters. Sarah returned the favor by telling Caroline about the mail that was pouring into Nashville from job seekers. The Polks had hired two secretaries, but the cresting flood still threatened to overwhelm them. Worse were the obnoxious letters that President-elect Polk was getting from Martin Van Buren, who thought he was entitled to be the invisible prime minister of the new administration, dictating everything from policies to appointments.

> *So far we are keeping Van at arm's length with sweet nothings. He controls enough votes in the lame-duck congress to complicate your push for Texas. You are extremely wise to let Julia Regina do most of the talking. I fear Mr. Van Buren will never forgive you for that Aaron Burr toast. What other woman—or man—can say she/he caused the scaly creature to lose his composure? That should be inserted into a history book, somewhere.*

Sarah's loathing for the ex-president remained intense.

Its path smoothed by feminine wiles and bolstered by vigorous scrawls from the Hermitage, the Texas bill made encouraging progress. The House of Representatives, more responsive to the will of the people, approved it on January 25. But its fate in the Senate remained uncertain until James and Sarah Polk arrived in Washington early in February. Caroline and George visited them at Gadsby's Hotel the night they arrived.

Sarah was radiant. Her embrace, her kiss, her voice, emanated strength and confidence. But Caroline thought the president-elect looked tired, harassed, fretful. There was no trace of the triumph she had imagined every man must feel as he approached the White House. Gone too was the relaxed, genial charm of the young congressman she had known and liked. He let Sarah reiterate their gratitude for all the Stapletons had done to nominate and elect him. His response to an inquiry about General Jackson's health was almost curt. "He's well—and full of advice."

With scarcely a pause, Polk turned to the one topic that interested him. "Where do things stand on Texas?"

George's response was blunt. Out of fear of the abolitionists, Northern Democrats in the Senate would desert the bill unless Polk talked of Texas and nothing but Texas to everyone he met from now until inauguration day. "You've got to convince them you'll push it through eventually if they don't do it now," George said. "That way they can blame you."

"Do you agree, Caroline?" Sarah asked.

Judging from what she had heard at her salon, Caroline reluctantly concurred. She hated to admit their female campaign was faltering. The president-elect was not at all happy to hear this news. "I thought I made it very clear that this was precisely what I did not want to do," he said. "Become responsible for Texas."

He looked at Sarah in an almost unfriendly way as he said this. "Caroline assured me that it could be done," Sarah said. "I don't think she's changed her mind, have you?"

"Not really. Some pressure from you would be more in the nature of insurance, Mr. President." Caroline was using the title playfully, in response to the way he was talking.

"Don't call me that yet. I'm entitled to another month without that noose around my neck." If Polk was trying for gallows humor, he failed. He sounded as if he meant it.

"Everything we've heard from the moment we arrived has been disagreeable," Sarah said, trying to explain her husband's sour mood. "The Van Buren people are more obnoxious in person than their leader has been in the mail. Everyone seems to be claiming credit for getting us here. The election was so close . . ."

In the final count, only thirty-eight thousand votes had separated the two candidates, out of 2 million cast. It was easy to see how almost anyone could boast that his oratory or influence had put James K. Polk in the White House.

"Let me assure you that Mrs. Tyler, and yours truly, have no intention of slackening their efforts for Texas—and we have no interest in any tangible reward," Caroline said.

"Good," Polk said, finally managing a smile.

"Thank God tomorrow is Sunday," Sarah said. "I've decreed—not a single visitor. We'll keep the Sabbath holy—and give James some time to himself."

Riding home in their carriage, the Stapletons were silent at first, though Caroline sensed they were thinking similar thoughts. "He's worn-out from his trip," she said.

"Yes," George said.

"Sarah seems fine."

"Yes."

"He tires so easily."

"Yes."

"I'll see Julia and the president tomorrow. Do you have some suggestions for them?"

"There are three Southern Whig senators who could go either way. Make them guests of honor at something big," George said.

Something big was exactly what Caroline had in mind, and she found a willing collaborator in the first lady. For the next three days, Julia, her sister, Margaret, and Caroline toiled at addressing a staggering two thousand invitations to an ultimate gala on February 18. At the head of the list were the three targeted Southern Whig senators. Among the other guests were the ex-president of the Texas Republic and the commodore of the Texas Navy, who were in Washington lobbying for annexation, plus generals, diplomats, and congressmen by the score.

No less than three thousand people showed up. The White House all but bulged at the seams. While a marine band in scarlet uniforms played waltzes, polkas, and cotillions, Julia concentrated her charms on the three wavering Whigs. They fluttered around her like moths around a flame, and each was forced to drink a private toast to Tyler and Texas. Meanwhile, the rest of the guests were emptying champagne bottles by the dozen and wine by the barrel. Yet decorum was maintained with only a few exceptions.

One of these was John Sladen. He reeled up to Caroline as the band struck up a polka and all but dragged her out on the floor. "What's this I hear about Polk turning pusillanimous on Texas?" he said.

"I've seen or heard nothing to suggest such a thing. I hope you're not spreading the rumor. It has to come from our enemies."

"George hinted at something along that line just now. Why didn't Little Jim and Sarah show up for this ball?"

"They have no desire to identify themselves with a president who's been ridiculed and burned in effigy," Caroline said, growing angrier by the minute. "What the devil is the matter with you?"

"What's the matter with me? Surely you can answer that question."

"I begin to think it's nothing that a temperance lecture couldn't cure. Get out of here before you make a complete fool of yourself."

The polka crashed to a close. Congressman Sladen bowed low before Mrs. Stapleton. "Your wish is my command, madam."

She watched him stagger to the door, wondering at his almost supernatural ability to read her mind. He sensed something was going wrong with their master plan. She had sensed it the moment she looked into James Knox Polk's weary face two weeks ago. The idea had been festering in her mind ever since.

Julia Gardiner floated up to her. "All three of those now somewhat tipsy gentlemen have sworn they'll vote for Texas."

Julia was in white again. John L. O'Sullivan, who was among the guests, had told Caroline that Julia looked like Juno—a line that would undoubtedly appear in the *New York Morning News* tomorrow. But Juno never giggled and glowed like Julia. "Isn't this the most divine fun?" she said. "The president says he's certain no one will dare to vote against Texas now."

Suddenly Caroline saw Julia in the president's arms on the second floor of the White House later tonight. Did he really give a damn about Texas? Was it all a performance to induce this delicious creature to surrender herself to him with total abandon? It had been a long time since Caroline and Senator Stapleton had made love with abandon.

Over the next week, it became apparent that Julia Tyler's influence had severe limits. From one day to the next, George reeled home from the Senate to report that Texas was alternately doomed or saved. Only desperate arm-twisting by him and Senator Robert Walker of Mississippi, who was still chairman of the Democratic Party, rescued the bill. In the deep background, President-elect Polk also played a part. Jobs, favors and committee chairman-ships were promised in all directions.

On February 27, the final vote was taken. The three Southern Whigs re-mained true to their promises to Julia, and George dragged enough Northern Democrats with them to squeak Texas into the Union by a 27–25 vote. With no vice president, if one more senator had voted no, the bill would have died.

On March 1, 1845, in a ceremony at the White House to which the Sta-pletons were naturally invited, President Tyler signed the bill into law and dispatched a messenger to Texas to inform them that if they were still willing to join, they were now part of the United States of America. Tyler gave Julia the small gold pen he had used to sign the measure. She vowed to wear it around her neck as a keepsake for the rest of her life.

The next night, the triumph was celebrated at a cabinet dinner at the White House, to which the Stapletons as well as the Polks and their vice president, George Dallas, were invited. Sarah looked regal in black velvet and a head-dress of ostrich plumes. Caroline wore black blond over white satin, causing Secretary of State John C. Calhoun to abandon his attentions to the first lady and cross the elliptical salon to congratulate her. Portly Vice President–elect Dallas, an old friend of Calhoun's, joined them as the Polks strolled past with President Tyler.

"I fear this will be the last good party in the White House," Dallas said.

"Why do you say that?" Caroline asked.

"Mrs. Polk tells me she doesn't plan to serve any liquor or wine at her dinners or receptions."

How could Sarah commit such a blunder? The policy was certain to start tongues wagging nastily across Washington. "I think it's a health measure, more than anything else, to spare the president the ordeal of endless toasts," Caroline said, concealing her dismay.

"Perhaps," Dallas said. "She offered no explanations or apologies. Un-questionably, she's mistress of herself—and of another I could name."

Caroline's dislike of this big hearty Pennsylvania politician grew every time he opened his mouth. He obviously did not have a shred of loyalty to the Polks. She would warn Sarah against him immediately.

"If I recall correctly, she declined to marry him until he won his first elec-tion," Calhoun said.

"I fear he's won his last one," Dallas said. "The Whigs have already sworn undying enmity to Mr. Polk's policies. The Van Buren Democrats feel no bond to him. If the Mexicans or the English start a war over Texas or Oregon, he'll have a terrible time."

"I agree," Calhoun said. "Wars never go well."

With a pang, Caroline realized Calhoun looked on this possibility without a shred of pity. If the Polk administration collapsed, Calhoun could well emerge from the political wreckage as a presidential candidate in 1848. The years had worn deep grooves in his gaunt cheeks; his hair was iron gray. But his ambition for the ultimate office remained as keen as ever.

Two days later, Caroline huddled beneath George's umbrella on the East Portico of the Capitol listening to James Polk's inaugural address. Rain came down in a steady torrent from the leaden sky. If one believed in omens, the gods seemed to be frowning—or drooling. Solemnly the new president declared to the thin crowd that annexation was a "question that belonged exclusively to the United States and Texas." He assured the world that there was not an iota of military ambition in the American government. How could there be, when the sovereign people have to bear "the burdens and miseries" of a war? He insisted Texas was "the peaceful acquisition of a territory once our own"—words that would delight Old Hickory and infuriate John Quincy Adams because they implied Adams had foolishly signed away America's claim to the territory in the 1819 treaty he had negotiated with Spain.

It was a satisfactory performance, but the postinaugural reception at the White House was another matter. Never did male guests, and even a few female ones, feel more in need of a strong drink to counteract their cold, wet feet and damp clothes. But there was not a trace of alcohol in the punch. More than a few people began muttering under their breath. John Sladen was especially uncomplimentary. "I foresee a huge sale of pocket flasks in this city. Otherwise a visit to the White House will be the equivalent of a trip across the Great Sahara," he loudly informed a circle of disgruntled fellow congressmen and reporters.

The glare he received from Caroline had no visible effect. On the contrary, he extended his attack to her. "I hope you're not going to imitate the first lady's example and serve us nothing but grape juice at Thirty-six Hundred Pennsylvania Avenue, Mrs. Stapleton. That will drive every honest Democrat in town into the Whig Party."

"Rest easy," she said. "We have enough champagne in our cellar to keep you drunk until the next inauguration."

"Who'll be welcoming us here on that great day? President Stapleton?"

The reporters listened with hungry eyes. The moment anyone admitted he was running for president, he was a marked man in Washington, D.C. John knew nothing about what Sarah Polk had said when they exchanged prophecies in Tennessee a year ago. But with his preternatural ability to sense Caroline's inner thoughts, he suspected something or someone was luring her away from her secret allegiance to him.

"Mrs. Polk hopes to establish a truly Democratic style in her White House," Caroline said. "She doesn't think the American people will complain too much if at the end of four years she can say never once was a senator or a congressman disgracefully drunk in these halls. Nor was the people's money squandered to get them that way."

"You don't approve of Mrs. Tyler's entertainments?" asked one of the congressmen, a tall, bucktoothed man from upstate New York. He had been one of Julia's early suitors.

"They were in perfect taste for an administration devoted to the glorification of aristocracy," Caroline said. "But they would be in the worst possible taste for a Democratic president and his first lady."

She did not believe a word of this balderdash. She knew that her criticism of Julia Gardiner Tyler would be in the newspapers tomorrow—and Julia would read it with pain. But it was necessary to defend Sarah against this crew of mindless guzzlers.

At twilight, upstairs in the private quarters, as the rain continued to sluice relentlessly from the darkening sky, Caroline told Sarah what the men were saying about her nonalcoholic White House. "You don't approve either?" she asked.

George and the president were in his study, perusing a map of Texas and Mexico. "It seems likely to cause problems that could be avoided," Caroline said.

"It was James's idea. In that last campaign against Jimmy Jones, he drank so much bad bourbon, his digestion was almost completely ruined. I'm happy to bear the blame. I plan to say it's a religious scruple."

"I suppose that's as good an explanation as any."

"My dearest friend. When I look at the tasks confronting us, I see no time to give many parties. You know I don't particularly enjoy them. They're your forte. What I can't accomplish in the White House at James's side, you must attempt to carry out in your salon. They say the French Revolution started in the salons of Paris. Perhaps they'll say the war that won us a continent started in your parlors."

"You think war is a certainty?"

"We're going to do our best to avoid it. Once we settle the Oregon question, we'll send an ambassador to Mexico who'll offer them thirty million dollars for New Mexico and California. We're practically sure they'll say no. Their government is so weak, the mob rules—and the mob cries no surrender to the Americans."

"Do you have anyone in mind for that mission?"

Sarah shook her head. "Do you have a suggestion?"

"John Sladen. He speaks fluent Spanish. He's a passionate supporter of our—your—policies."

Sarah smiled. "You can call them ours. If he can get California without a war—will he do it? James dreads a war. He remembers what happened to President Madison."

Did that mean Sarah had not told the president-elect about the Southern dream of conquering all of Mexico? Did that mean she secretly agreed with that idea? The answer to both questions was probably yes. For a moment Caroline struggled to breathe. Should she—could she—tell Sarah the whole truth? John Sladen was the worst possible choice, if the real goal was avoiding a war. Did Sarah know that already? If so, there was no harm in not telling her. Once she spoke, Sarah would be forced to reject him. Caroline saw the exquisite balancing act Sarah was performing. She too was trying to be both powerful and good, loyal to her own vision—their vision, now—and loyal to James Knox Polk.

"Yes," Caroline said. "I think you'll have nothing to worry about on that score—if his instructions are carefully spelled out."

"They will be."

"What should George do?"

"Nothing for the moment but support us in the Senate. The minute war begins, James will make him a brigadier general. The rest is up to him—and God."

Caroline felt a shiver of nerves. She never liked Sarah to mention God. It opened a gap between them that drove her back to her secret partner in unbelief, John Sladen. Should she tell Sarah the whole truth now? For a moment it almost burst from her lips. She yearned to confess her involvement with John Sladen—and then repudiate him. But it was neither the time nor the place to speak.

George and the president emerged from the study. "There's no question in my mind that the boundary should be the Rio Grande," George said. "I've studied all the documents. Texas claimed it when they became independent. It was specified in the treaty Santa Anna signed when he was captured. It's the boundary in ancient maps going back to the sixteenth century."

The president explained to Sarah and Caroline. "Calhoun told me the Mexicans are disputing the Texas boundary. They're claiming it should be the Nueces River—a good hundred miles north."

"What would Old Hickory say to that?" Caroline asked with a smile.

"Old Hickory will be in paradise soon," Polk said. "The doctor told me that he can't possibly live more than another month. There are times when I almost envy him."

"James," Sarah said. "Cheer up! The impossible has happened! You're the president of the United States! With friends like the Stapletons and many many others, there's no limit to what we can accomplish."

With a visible effort, the president got a grip on his feelings. "You're right. Let's all join in a prayer."

He held out his hands to Caroline and George. Sarah stepped into the circle. President James Knox Polk bowed his head and prayed, "God of our fathers, we face this task which you have ordained for us with a troubled heart, with doubts about our abilities and our country's good will. Only you can sustain us, only you can direct us according to your purposes. Surround us with your love and support. Without it our frail human love may founder, our courage may falter. With your help we will overcome any and all obstacles and win the victories that will set America's feet on the path to glory."

Caroline suddenly heard Hannibal Flowers saying, *Only God can do it.* What did that mean? She found herself twisting Hannah Stapleton's ring on her finger as if she wanted to tear it off. Why?

"Amen," George Stapleton said. "Amen, amen."

Sarah kissed James Polk. Caroline also pressed her lips to the sallow cheek of this small earnest man whom she had helped make president of the United States. For a moment she saw sadness, even guilt, in Sarah's eyes. The rain drummed on the White House roof. It was an unnerving introduction to the Temple of Fame.

BOOK

SIX

ONE

SOMEWHERE IN THE WHITE HOUSE'S CAVERNOUS halls, a clock
bonged midnight. It was May 11, 1846. Caroline sat with Sarah Polk in the
parlor off the president's study. Through the open door, she could see James
Polk hunched over his desk; beside him loomed Senator George Stapleton.
They were working on a final revision of the president's message to Congress,
asking the lawmakers to declare war on Mexico.

Fourteen turbulent months had passed since James Polk's inauguration.
Caroline had watched the president struggling to cope with the nasty realities
of the Democratic Party without Andrew Jackson. The old warrior had died
on June 8, 1845—leaving a number of large egos in the U.S. Senate and
elsewhere eager to prove they were in charge. It never seemed to occur to any
of them that the logical man was President James K. Polk.

Instead, they all began, in George's words, "kicking sand in his face." The
Calhoun men suddenly joined the Whigs to vote down the appointment of an
obscure Democrat as collector of the port of Bath, Maine. Martin Van Buren
sent his son John to Washington to hold forth in hotel barrooms and finally
in the White House about the president's ingratitude because New Yorkers
were not getting enough good jobs. Senator Thomas Hart Benton of Missouri
descended on the White House at all hours of the day and night with dire
warnings against going to war with Mexico without making him a lieutenant
general in command of the army.

It was how adolescent boys in a schoolyard challenged the authority of
the teacher assigned to keep order. In this case, the schoolmaster, small, anxious James Polk, looked as if he would be easy to bully. That was not the
case—at least, James Polk plus his partner, Sarah Polk, were anything but
easy to bully. But the president had to deal with these formidable characters
and their often obnoxious behavior on his own. Only later in the day or night
could he consult Sarah about how best to dispose of their challenges.

Caroline had reported Vice President Dallas's nasty remark about Sarah
being the real boss, and this had prompted her to withdraw even deeper into
the background of James's presidency. She did not say a political word at her
receptions. Nor did she alter the drab nonalcoholic atmosphere at these events.
Soon she had a nasty nickname in Washington's world of gossip: Sahara
Sarah. An outraged Caroline had no trouble tracing it to John Sladen and his
hard-drinking friends.

Nevertheless, the first lady and the president had pushed ahead with their program. Sarah handed to Caroline the problem of soothing or charming congressional egos. Vice President Dallas became a guest at Mrs. Stapleton's salon. Caroline virtually oozed sweetness every time she saw the man. George was ordered to seek his advice on how to maneuver administration bills through the Senate.

Meanwhile, the British were playing their old game of trying to humble the Americans. They had encouraged the Mexicans to break off diplomatic relations over the annexation of Texas. The president had sent Congressman Sladen to Mexico City with instructions to offer as much as $40 million for New Mexico and California. The Mexicans, changing governments every six months, spurned the proposal and had countered by offering the British the right to colonize California, if they would finance a Mexican war against the United States to regain Texas. The British declined, preferring to threaten the Americans with a war in the Northwest if they did not agree to settle the Oregon boundary on their terms: the forty-ninth parallel and the right to navigate the Columbia River as freely as the Americans navigated the Mississippi.

The secretary of state, goggle-eyed, devious James Buchanan of Pennsylvania, was another Democrat with presidential ambitions. He tended to disagree with everything President Polk said, hoping to create a sort of separate record on which he could run in 1848. He saw nothing wrong with letting British gunboats cruise up and down the Columbia just because the river flowed on both sides of the proposed border. He was terrified at the thought of war with England and was inclined to let the British have anything they wanted, including California. Sarah and Caroline soon coined a private nickname for Mr. Buchanan: the Old Maid.

Buchanan also feared the Mexicans. He was not the only person in the cabinet and out of it who noted Mexico's army numbered thirty-two thousand and most of them were veteran soldiers, hardened by years of fighting in their perpetual revolutions. While the American army numbered seventy-two hundred and had fought no one but a few scattered Indian tribes in the past thirty-one years. This disparity in numbers and training was trumpeted by numerous newspapers when the president decided to order General Zachary Taylor and four thousand men to march to the Rio Grande. The Mexicans had riposted by marching twice that many men to Matamoros, a Mexican town on the river. Critics screamed that Polk had put Taylor and his tiny American army in mortal peril.

Three days ago, a haggard John Sladen had returned from Mexico City to inform the president that the Mexicans were never going to negotiate as long as they thought the British were on their side. Privately, he told Caroline that was the exact truth. There was no need for him to obfuscate negotiations. No Mexican politician could stay in office for twenty-four hours if he agreed to talk peace with the Americans. The country was split into two savagely contending parties: the conservatives, who detested the very idea of democracy, and the republicans, who admired it. Each was ready to accuse the other side of treason if it so much as received an American ambassador.

"We're going to have to beat hell out of them to change their minds," John said. "That may not be as easy as we thought."

"Now is hardly the time to lose your nerve," Caroline said.

In the White House, Sarah Polk shuddered at what the Whigs and abolitionists would say if the United States invaded Mexico. "John Quincy Adams made a vicious speech in the House of Representatives today, denouncing James as a tool of the slavocracy," she said. "Do you still invite that vile old man to your salon?"

"Lately he hasn't come. He wrote me a note saying he was saving his strength to belabor Democrats."

"He and his abolitionist friends are another reason why the Mexicans won't negotiate. They think we're divided. And we are."

"Mrs. Polk?"

A blue-uniformed figure loomed in the doorway. It was Roger Jones, the bulky adjutant general of the U.S. Army. Clutched in his right hand was a sheaf of papers. "Is the president free? I have urgent dispatches from General Taylor on the Rio Grande."

Sarah opened the door to the president's study and announced Jones. Minutes later, Caroline heard the president exclaim, "My God!" He came to the door and said, "A huge force of Mexican cavalry crossed the Rio Grande and attacked a scouting party of sixty American dragoons, killing a dozen and capturing the rest. We're at war."

Sarah embraced him. The gesture was protective, not celebratory. "We knew it might happen," she said.

"They've done us a great favor—firing the first shot," Adjutant General Jones said.

"I hope we can fire the last one as soon as possible," the president said.

Caroline rushed home to tell George. He already knew about it. The news had raced across Washington minutes after Taylor's dispatches arrived at the War Department. "I saw Jeremy Biddle as I was leaving the Capitol," he said. "He asked me if I was happy about the bloodshed."

"I hope you told him to go to hell."

George said nothing. He still disliked the idea of a war. Jeremy was so opposed to it, he had decided not to resign from the Senate, in spite of his wife's demands. It infuriated Caroline to think her old enemy could still influence George on such a crucial matter.

The next day, Caroline returned to the White House, expecting to find the place swarming with soldiers and civilians. Instead Sarah was alone in her sitting room, wearing a doleful face. "James was up most of the night, studying maps of Mexico, planning how to fight the war," she said. "When I begged him to come to bed, he insisted I stay up with him. He said it was my war as much as his. Maybe more."

"I thought we all agreed that it would probably come to blows," Caroline said.

"I fear he never gave up hoping for the success of Mr. Sladen's mission." Sarah sighed. "He doesn't feel qualified to be commander in chief. He's haunted by General Jackson's shadow."

At a cabinet meeting that morning, Secretary of State Buchanan had added to the sleepless president's agitation. He said if the United States declared war, they should combine it with a proclamation that they had no desire for any territory, including New Mexico and California. He had a letter to this effect prepared for circulation to all the U.S. ambassadors abroad. Unless they did this, Buchanan solemnly predicted, England would join the war on Mexico's side. She would seize the moral high ground and declare she was doing it to prevent the spread of American slavery.

This stark prophecy was obviously intended to stampede the cabinet, and the president, into a policy that would satisfy the growing antislavery movement among Pennsylvania Democrats. The president pounded the table and shouted in Buchanan's face that rather than let the English meddle in the affairs of this continent, he would fight them and the Mexicans and the French to the last living American.

"I was listening in the next room," Sarah told Caroline. "Never have I felt so proud of him. But when the meeting ended, James was in a fearful state of nerves. He wondered what to do with Buchanan. He reproached himself for appointing him. General Jackson warned him against it. But the creature carries Pennsylvania in his pocket and it was the only counterweight we had to New York's influence in Congress."

For the next two days, virtually without sleep or rest, President Polk toiled on his war message to Congress. He conferred with the leaders of the Senate, notably John C. Calhoun and Thomas Hart Benton, showing them various drafts. He soon realized this was a mistake. Each had strong opinions on what Polk should and should not say. Calhoun was the most astonishing. He agreed with Buchanan that the United States should renounce any interest in acquiring territory and in general declared himself opposed to the war.

When Caroline heard this, she sent Hannibal to the Capitol with a message summoning John Sladen to her parlor. "What's wrong with your hero Calhoun?" she said as John walked in the door. "Is he losing his mind? He's opposed to the war. Is he trying to put a noose around the president's neck?"

John was drunk. "I can't do anything with him," he said, slurring his words. "He's haunted by the War of 1812. He thinks the same thing will happen here. The war will be a disaster. Anyone who supports it will be ruined."

"Speaking of disasters, when are you going to stop drinking?"

"When you tell me that you still love me."

"Get out of here."

That night at supper, a still panicky Caroline asked Senator Stapleton if he thought the war would be a disaster. He shook his head. "Since the War of 1812, we've graduated a thousand West Pointers. A lot of them are still in the army. Man for man, we've got the best officer corps in the world."

"Doesn't Senator Calhoun know this? He's told the president he's against the war. He thinks we're going to lose it."

"He's been out of touch with the army for a long time."

George gave Caroline a quick summary of his conversation with Calhoun about the War of 1812 on their journey south during the nullification crisis in 1833. "He's a guilt-haunted man. I wonder if I'll feel the same way when I meet some freshman congressman whose father got killed in this war."

"Won't it help that this war will be victorious?"

"Maybe. Anyway, I might not have to worry about it."

"What do you mean?"

"I'm going to Mexico, remember? The president's going to make me a general. That won't make me bulletproof."

Caroline struggled against fresh panic. "Maybe you shouldn't go. I'm beginning to think the president needs you here. He has so few friends."

George shook his head. "I'm going. It's the only way I can square my conscience with voting for the war."

"Haven't the Mexicans fired the first shots? You sound like your insufferable friend Jeremy Biddle."

"Calm down, darling. I agree with your brilliant plan for my life. There's only one thing wrong with it. It's never been my plan. But that's not a fatal flaw. A lot of men get pushed, shoved, or prodded through life by something or someone. You've still got Andrew Jackson on your side—and manifest destiny."

"So you don't hate me?"

"I love you as I loved you when you were sweet seventeen."

What was he telling her? He had become a man who understood a great deal about both of them. But they were still partners. For an incredible moment she loved him more than she had ever loved John Sladen—or Sarah Polk. She loved him as the father of their children, a better parent than she was, by far. She loved him for the years of hard work he had invested in his political career, the tens of thousands of handshakes, the hundreds of speeches.

Caroline was still thinking some of these thoughts as she sat with Sarah Polk in the darkened upstairs parlor on May 11 while George helped the president add some final touches to his war message. "Is George going to volunteer for action?" Sarah asked.

"Yes," Caroline said.

"The sooner the better. James is going to ask Congress to authorize two more major generals and four brigadier generals. You can imagine the competition for those appointments."

"Yes."

"God will watch over him. I'm sure of it. Just as He's watching over James. We've all been led to this task in such a remarkable way. I can't help but believe the rest of the path will be exactly as we foresee it."

"I hope you're right."

"You still feel no impulse, no wish, to believe?"

"No."

There was a painful silence. Did Sarah feel Caroline's atheism was a kind of flaw that God would punish? "I've prayed so hard for God to give you faith. It makes me wonder if He'll listen to my other prayers."

"Perhaps I'm not worthy."

"How can you say that? None of us is truly worthy. But you have so many gifts. Don't you feel grateful for them?"

What have my gifts done but make me unhappy? And you, my beloved. Aren't you unhappy too? Forced to sit in the anteroom, listening to the cabinet blather. When you could settle their stupid arguments in sixty seconds?

What if that wasn't true? What if women discovered, when they achieved great power, that it was as difficult to control, to wield, to retain, as it was for men? Could Caroline Kemble or Sarah Childress make the British negotiate honorably over Oregon or force the Mexicans to be reasonable over Texas and California? Would their husbands be happy, sitting in the parlor while their wives wrote a war message in the president's study? Probably not. Would it improve matters if the wives were in the study correcting this phrase and excising that one? On the contrary, it might make matters worse. Caroline suddenly remembered Sarah's lighthearted observation about men's inability to endure too much correction without reverting to small humiliated boys.

For the first time, Caroline wondered if power and love were incompatible. It was one of the most stunning realizations of her life. Only the discovery of the underground river of the heart compared to it.

President Polk and Senator Stapleton emerged from the study. "I think this message has been tuned to the point where only people with tin ears will hear anything but celestial music," George said.

"I wish there were fewer tin ears in the U.S. Senate," the president said.

"So do I," George said.

The president handed a copy of the message to Sarah. It was full of inserts and scratched out words. She invited Caroline to join her on the couch and read it. *War exists by act of Mexico herself. Mexico has invaded our territory and shed American blood upon American soil.* The president called on Congress to provide money to raise an army of fifty thousand men and begin an immediate expansion of the navy to blockade Mexico's ports.

Sarah pronounced it perfect and Caroline agreed—although she was sure Jeremy Biddle and his fellow Whigs would take exception to the claim that war existed on the basis of a single clash of cavalry. She foresaw the day when they might use the words to accuse James Polk of welcoming the war and even rushing to embrace it. But the exhausted president clearly could not tolerate another round of criticism.

The next day, the House of Representatives took only two hours to vote the president everything he wanted—a declaration of war and the money he needed to fight it. But the Senate was a different story. Senator Benton declared that a war was too important a matter to decide in two hours. Senator Calhoun spoke passionately against the message. He called it a war for territory, which would disgrace America. The Whigs enthusiastically concurred with both Democratic senators. The World's Greatest Deliberative Body had adjourned without making a decision.

At the White House, Caroline found Sarah Polk in agony. James had scarcely slept all night, anticipating the worst in the Senate, which now seemed to be happening. The cabinet was meeting with the president now. From remarks they had made as they gathered in the anteroom, Sarah could see they were pessimistic about the Senate vote.

Caroline confided to Sarah her worries about the war message. "I thought the same thing," Sarah said. "I warned James against it when he showed me an earlier draft. But Mr. Buchanan—or Senator Benton, or both—liked the idea of saying war was already a fact, which would make a vote against it a kind of desertion of our soldiers."

Sarah's voice was so weary, Caroline had to resist an impulse to do or say something extravagantly sympathetic. She struggled to maintain the delicate balance that their silent partnership required.

"This is beginning to be much more difficult than I ever imagined," Sarah said.

" ' 'Tis not in mortals to command success, but we'll do more, Sempronius; we'll deserve it,' " Caroline said.

Sarah managed a wan smile. "I'm afraid I recall *Cato*'s tragic ending more than the sublime opening."

"I begin to think reality, especially political reality, is never sublime."

"The whole thing is so *precarious.*"

The cabinet meeting broke up. They could hear the male voices rumbling in the hall. After a few minutes, the president came into Sarah's sitting room. He looked ghastly. His face seemed to be collapsing into his hollowed cheeks; his eyes were bloodshot with sleeplessness.

"No one thinks the message has a chance," he said, sinking into a chair. "We spent most of the time talking about what we can do if the Senate rejects it."

"What was the conclusion?"

James Polk shook his head. "It's a mare's nest. If I order General Taylor to retaliate for the murder of our soldiers, I can be impeached for making war without a declaration by Congress. If I order him to retreat, we've lost the game. If I order him to stand fast, we risk more loss of life."

"Mr. President?"

Senator Stapleton loomed in the doorway. His face was expressionless. Caroline's heart plummeted. He was bringing bad news. The Senate had rejected the war message. The Polk administration was about to be engulfed by unparalleled humiliation.

"Yes, Senator?"

"I'm here to report that the Senate passed your war message by a vote of forty ayes and two nays."

Life, vigor, joy, surged through James Knox Polk's small frame. He leaped to his feet and pumped George Stapleton's big hand.

"Was there much debate?"

"Plenty. Most of it hot air from the Whigs about how they deplored voting for what my friend Senator Biddle called a mendacious war. But only two men had the nerve to vote no."

"Was one Calhoun?"

"After making another speech against it, he abstained."

President Polk smacked his fist into his palm and turned to Sarah. He seemed to be growing taller by the second. Caroline thought for a moment his head was above George's shoulder. "We've got your war. Now let's see what we can do with it," Polk said.

"We're going to do more than win fame," Sarah said, meeting Caroline's eyes as she spoke. "We're going to deserve it."

Oh, my dear girl, I fear for thy salvation.

Hannah Cosway Stapleton's voice whispered in Caroline's head. She dismissed the specter. Her mind thronged with images of muscular Americans in blue following General George Stapleton in a headlong charge that sent the

Mexican Army fleeing in disarray. She saw the story in the newspapers. She would make sure that John L. O'Sullivan and other reporters hailed the hero senator. There were no limits to the power that throbbed around them in this city now.

"Who knows," Caroline said. "We may end up ruling all of Mexico."

TWO

THREE MONTHS LATER, ON AUGUST 13, 1846, Brigadier General George Stapleton stood on the scorching upper deck of the paddle-wheel steamer USS *Texas* and gazed at the thousands of white tents arrayed in neat military rows for at least three miles on the left bank of the sluggish San Juan River. The sun beat down on the flat arid plain with a ferocity George had never experienced before in his life. Beyond the tents was a collection of white-walled buildings, the Mexican town of Camargo. Beyond that was a vast sunbaked emptiness.

"How many men have we got here now?" he asked stumpy Lieutenant Ulysses S. Grant of Ohio.

"About fifteen thousand. But the volunteers are dying so fast, it may soon be a third of that."

Raising men had been the least of President Polk's worries. When he called for fifty thousand volunteers, the rush to enlist had overwhelmed recruiting offices everywhere. In Tennessee, thirty-six thousand came forward in the first two days, swamping the state's quota of thirty-five hundred men. Similar overflows occurred in Mississippi, Kentucky, and Louisiana. The war was stupendously popular. Huge mass meetings in New York and other cities had pledged all-out support to the president.

Lieutenant Grant had boarded the steamship on the Rio Grande, which met the San Juan about three miles below Camargo. A regimental quartermaster, he had been roving the border in search of pack mules to transport the army's baggage on the advance into Mexico. He was not happy with his assignment. He wondered why he had spent four years at West Point studying mathematics and engineering to become a mule skinner.

"An old sergeant heard me asking that question," Grant said. "He told me there were three ways of doing everything: the right way, the wrong way, and the army way."

George had grown fond of the diffident soft-spoken young lieutenant. They had sat on the top deck last night discussing the war. He was dismayed to learn that Grant and many other members of the regular army disapproved of it. They bought the lies that John Quincy Adams and other Whigs were spouting in Congress that the war was a grab for more territory in which to spread slavery. Grant listened respectfully while George talked about Andrew Jackson's continental vision and President Polk's repeated attempts to negotiate with the Mexicans.

Ashore, George told Hannibal Flowers to guard his baggage while he located the army's commander, Major General Zachary Taylor. Hannibal had volunteered to serve as George's orderly. George suspected the big black was glad to escape his wife, Mercy. He had married her at Caroline's urging, and to give his daughter Tabitha a mother. But in his heart he was still mourning the other Tabitha he had lost in Charleston. Mercy sensed his lack of love and often expressed her discontent with cutting remarks.

Lieutenant Grant said he would be happy to lead George to the general's tent. As they trudged down the dusty camp streets, no less than three funerals passed them, preceded by fifes wailing and drums thudding the march for the dead.

"You see what I mean?" Grant said. "It would be hard to find a more unhealthy place to camp an army. The river is fouled. You can't get clean water anywhere."

The next thing George noticed was the overpowering stench. Grant nodded glumly when George mentioned it. "Fifteen thousand men emptying their bowels and their bladders each day makes for a less than sublime atmosphere, no matter how much quicklime you put in the latrine ditches," the lieutenant said.

At the center of the camp, Grant pointed to a tent with a marquee in front of it. Beneath the marquee was a crude table made by placing a door over two barrels. At the table sat an elderly man in a rumpled civilian coat and a wide-brimmed floppy hat, reading what looked like newspaper clippings. George assumed he was a reporter. Grant had remarked that at least a hundred of them were with the army.

"Excuse me, I'm looking for General Taylor," George said.

"You've found him," the man said with what seemed minimal courtesy.

George introduced himself. Taylor did not produce even the ghost of a smile. "We've been expecting you. I gather you're a close friend of James Knox Polk."

"I've known him almost twenty years."

"What the hell is the matter with the man? Was he behind the door when they passed out the brains?"

General Taylor launched into a tirade against President Polk, his secretary of war, and the Democratic Party. "Look at these slanders," he said, shaking the newspaper clippings. "Every Democratic paper in the country is calling me General Delay. They expect me to win the war overnight. What am I supposed to do when your asshole friend the president sends me fifteen thousand men and not a single wagon to transport their baggage? Or doctors to care for them when they get sick? Or food to feed them? I suppose you've got a pen in your pocket, ready to skewer me in your newspapers. I've been told you own a half dozen in New Jersey and New York—"

"General," George said, "I have no idea what you're talking about. I'm here to fight Mexicans. I'm not in the habit of writing to newspapers about anything."

The general still glowered suspiciously. "Have you had any military experience?"

"I've had a lifelong interest in military matters. I've read Jomini and other writers on strategy and tactics. My father was a West Point graduate. I've served on the military affairs committees in the House and Senate. I can claim some credit for the money that bought the artillery I've heard the army has used to such good effect."

"They're damn good guns," Taylor grudgingly admitted. He drummed his fingers on the table. "See Major Bliss, my chief of staff. He'll tell you where to pitch your tent. Have you brought any men with you?"

"Only a Negro orderly."

"Keep him out of the town of Camargo. That's where the volunteers are catching everything from cholera to the clap. If it weren't for my regulars, we'd have only a ghost of an army here."

George was somewhat astonished by this attitude toward the volunteers. Taylor sounded as if he were talking about two separate armies. "How do you keep the regulars out of there, General?"

"By giving a hundred lashes to anyone found near the place. You can't do that with volunteers. They'd all start writing their mothers and that would be the end of somebody's political career."

George struggled to control his temper. He wanted to say he was not here to further his political career. But that was not entirely true. He had to be satisfied with reiterating, "General, I'm here to fight Mexicans. Also to tell you the president is very anxious for you to begin your advance on Monterrey."

"I'm as anxious as he is!" Taylor snarled. "But I'll be damned if I'll be rushed into a failure so your friend Polk can fire me to make sure I don't run for president."

"If you'll excuse me, General. My orderly is waiting in the hot sun. I'd like to consult Major Bliss."

George found the chief of staff in a nearby tent. A West Pointer, he was as cordial as Zachary Taylor had been rude. He quickly selected a site on the west side of the camp for General Stapleton's tent and summoned a half dozen regular soldiers from the camp guard to help Hannibal set it up. When George expressed a wish to call on the other general officers, Bliss briskly identified the location of their tents. George hurried back to the riverside with the regulars, entrusted Hannibal and his baggage to them, and headed for the tent of Brigadier General Gideon Pillow.

About George's age, Pillow had been James Polk's law partner after Slim Jimmy Jones had temporarily retired him from politics. Handsome, mustachioed, he was a lady-killer who probably reminded Polk of his flamboyant youth, before he met Sarah Childress and got religion. Pillow had been at the Baltimore convention that nominated Polk. He greeted George cordially and ordered his orderly to set out two glasses and a bottle of Tennessee bourbon.

"Have you met Old Zach?" Pillow asked.

"Met is hardly the word," George said. "He practically skinned me alive. I get the feeling he doesn't like Democrats."

"He thinks we're out to get him. He's giving us damn good reason. Why in God's name did Jim Polk put that old Whig curmudgeon in command?"

"He was the ranking officer in this part of the country. We never dreamt he was a politician. He's spent his whole life in the army. Then he won those battles . . ."

Four days before Congress voted for war in Washington, D.C., the Mexican Army had crossed the Rio Grande and attacked Taylor's army. He had beaten them badly in back to back battles and sent them fleeing a hundred miles to Monterrey. The newspapers had christened Taylor "Old Rough and Ready" and made him a national hero. Whigs in Louisiana, where Taylor owned two large plantations, began running him for president.

"Has he got White House fever?" George asked.

"He keeps denying it. But I think the bug has bitten him. His chief of staff, Bliss, keeps whispering it in his ear. He's got a son-in-law down in Corpus Christi who sends him newspaper clippings by the ton."

"What kind of a general is he?"

Pillow sneered. "He hasn't done any real fighting. Our artillery is so much better than the Mexicans', in the first battle, at Palo Alto, the infantry hardly fired a shot. In the second battle, at Resaca de la Palma, it was pretty much the same story. Without the West Pointers operating those guns, Old Zach would have been ruined."

"And he let them run away after he beat them—instead of rounding up every mother's son of'm and ending the war on the spot."

The speaker was gray-haired Major General of Volunteers William O. Butler of Kentucky. His weather-beaten face reminded George of Andrew Jackson. Butler was thoroughly disillusioned with General Taylor. "We've been sitting here for two months with the men dying like dogs," he said. "His regulars are dying too, though he won't admit it."

"How many have we lost?" George asked.

"At least a thousand," Butler said. "Twice that many so sick they'll have to be sent home. I visited a Georgia regiment yesterday. Only three hundred men were fit for duty—out of seven hundred."

Their local bad news exhausted, the two generals wanted good news from Washington. George did his best to supply it. The president was prosecuting the war with vigor. He had ordered a separate expedition commanded by General John E. Wool to march on Chihuahua, another major city in northern Mexico. Colonel Stephen E. Kearney was on his way with another column to take California. A third column under Colonel Alexander Doniphan was marching into New Mexico. "The goal is to occupy all the territory we want by the time the Mexicans sue for peace," George said.

"What has the president heard from Mexico City?" Butler asked.

"Nothing. The only hope on that front is General Santa Anna. He sent a representative from his exile in Havana to tell Polk if he helps him return to Mexico, he'll take over the government and talk peace. The president's ordered the navy to let him pass through the blockade. He should be in Vera Cruz in a few weeks."

General Stapleton did not tell his fellow generals that as Senator Stapleton he had strongly advised the president against trusting General Antonio Santa

Anna, the man who had slaughtered the defenders of the Alamo, signed a peace treaty with Texas and then repudiated it, and been kicked out of Mexico by his own people for his two-faced politics and gross corruption. But Polk was so anxious to end the war quickly, he could not resist the Mexican's offer.

On August 17, General Taylor staged a grand review of his regulars. Wearing a faded old blue uniform, he sat on horseback with his two regular brigadiers, Generals William Worth and David Twiggs. The brigadiers and their staffs were in full dress regimentals, dripping with gold braid. It was obvious that Old Zach was polishing his frontier image for the reporters. George and his fellow volunteer generals—there were now five of them in camp, all Democrats, naturally—were ruefully forced to envy the precision and snap the regular companies displayed as they swung past their commanders. George was even more impressed by the four batteries of artillery, led by West Pointers on prancing horses, with the gunners in red-striped trousers sitting erect on the rumbling caissons.

The next day, Taylor summoned all the general officers in camp and announced his plans for the advance on Monterrey. He was taking only six thousand men. Washington had failed to send the thousand wagons he needed to transport provisions for the whole army. He was being forced to rely on mules. All three thousand regulars were coming with him—and only three thousand volunteers. They would be commanded by Major General William Orlando Butler—and Brigadier General George Stapleton.

That evening at supper in the generals' mess, George noted a distinct coolness emanating from General Pillow. After several drinks of bourbon, Pillow said, "How is it, Stapleton, that the last brigadier to arrive is the first to see action?"

"You'll have to ask General Taylor that," George said.

"It couldn't have anything to do with you owning a lot of newspapers that can hardly wait to write up you—and him—could it?"

"I hope not. I hope you don't think so."

"What if I do think so? What if I thought there was some kind of understanding between you? What would the president think of that? I wonder."

"I doubt if the president will think anything of it—because it isn't true."

"There's something about it that stinks almost as much as this damn camp," Pillow said. He stalked out of the tent. Another brigadier, James Shields of Ohio, followed him, giving George a stony look.

General Butler sat silently through this exchange. "Divide and conquer," he said. "That's Old Zach's policy. Set the Democrats to quarreling with each other."

"It seems to be working beautifully," George said.

"There's not a damn thing anyone can do about it, as long as the old son of a bitch is the commanding general. Why didn't Polk sack him after he let the Mexicans get away from Resaca de la Palma?"

"The Whig newspapers would have crucified him," George said. "He's not Andrew Jackson. He has no military reputation."

Two weeks later, the volunteers selected for the march on Monterrey finally departed from the Camargo camp. General Stapleton and a regiment of

Texas cavalry brought up the rear of the column, which included about four hundred mules. Behind him in camp they left six thousand disgruntled volunteers, who continued to sicken and die at an appalling rate. So far, all General Stapleton had done was preside at funerals. With the army short of wood for coffins, the dead men were simply wrapped in their blankets and buried in shallow unmarked graves in the thick brush and stunted trees the Mexicans called chaparral. Hannibal had been shocked by the way no one even bothered to say a prayer over them.

The march through the dry desert country was hard going. Too many of the men emptied their canteens early and were soon desperately thirsty. They passed through a half dozen white-walled little towns that were completely deserted. "I wonder where the people have gone?" George said as they unpacked the mules and began the tedious process of camping for the night in the desert cold.

"I thinks they figure it's a lot healthier in the desert than it is anywhere near them Texas Rangers," Hannibal said. "Them boys can't wait to start killin' Mexicans. All they talk about is gettin' even for the Alamo."

George was just beginning to get acquainted with the Texans. They were all tough-looking men. Their colonel was Jack Hays, an undersized, boyish-looking officer with a morose beardless face. Like his men, he carried a rifle strapped to his saddle and two Colt revolvers in holsters on his hips plus a wicked-looking fifteen-inch, steel bowie knife on his belt.

The next day, in one of the deserted villages, the Texans dismounted and went through the houses. Out of one they dragged a short, mustachioed Mexican who was shaking with fever—or with fear. Dangling from his waist was a lariat that George assumed he used to round up cattle or sheep. Hays spoke rapidly to the man in Spanish while the Texans crowded around him.

"He says he was sick and couldn't run away," Hays said with a nasty grin.

"Let's give him a runnin' start now, Colonel," one of the men said.

Hays spoke to the Mexican in Spanish again. The man started running for the chaparral. As George watched with disbelief, the Texans hefted their rifles and took aim at him.

"What the hell are you doing?" George said, riding between them and the fugitive.

"What does it look like, General?" Hays said. "Get out of the way."

"That's a civilian. We don't shoot civilians!" George shouted.

"He ain't no civilian," Hays said. "He's a *vaquero.*"

He spurred his horse around George, aimed at the Mexican, and fired. The man was a good two hundred yards away by now. He threw up his hands and toppled to the ground.

"You son of a bitch! I'm going to have you arrested," George said.

"Blow it out your ass, General," Hays said. The Texans laughed uproariously and rode away. George spurred his horse over to the Mexican. He was dead. The bullet had gone through the back of his head. Hannibal hovered anxiously beside him. "Careful, General. Them boys just as soon shoot you."

In a rage, George rode to the head of the column and reported the incident to Major General Butler. He grimaced and wiped his sweaty face and neck with a red bandanna. "Before you got to camp, the army's quartermaster,

Colonel Truman Cross, went out for a ride. They found him two days later with his head bashed in, a lariat around his chest. He'd run into a *vaquero*—one of them rope-slingin' Mexican cowboys. Those fellows can pull you off a horse and kill you in ten seconds."

Butler sighed and gave George a look that made him feel about ten years old. "Fightin' Mexicans is a lot like fightin' Indians, General. They don't play by the rules and that inclines our boys to do the same thing. I fought the Creeks under old Andy Jackson. A lot of bad things was done on both sides. It's better not to think about it."

"I don't agree with you. I'm still going to report Hays to General Taylor."

"Go ahead. Just remember, he fought Indians too."

That night, they camped outside another deserted town. Sentries were posted, latrines were dug. But the volunteers' sentries did not take their jobs seriously. They let men wander into the town and the surrounding chaparral. As the camp bedded down, there was a cry of anguish from the dark tangle of thorny brush and stunted trees. Lighting a torch from a campfire, George led Hannibal and a party of ten Ohioans into the forest. They found two volunteers with their throats cut. They had probably preferred to relieve themselves in the chaparral rather than in the smelly shallow latrines.

One was still alive. He gazed at George and tried to say "Mother." But no sound came from his severed vocal chords as he died.

"Lord have mercy on us," Hannibal muttered.

"Sons of bitches!" one Ohioan shouted. He fired his gun into the surrounding darkness. The others joined him.

"Cease fire!" George said. "You'll have the whole division in here shooting at each other. Carry them back to camp. We'll bury them in the morning."

At the town of Cerraloo, about forty miles from Monterrey, they found the rest of the army waiting for them. George was still inclined to report Hays to General Taylor. But he found himself in a conclave of fellow generals, listening to Taylor predict that there would be no real fighting in Monterrey. He had picked up a rumor that Santa Anna was in Mexico City, taking over the government.

"Doesn't that mean peace, Senator—I mean, General?" Taylor asked George. "I understand the president slipped this fellow into Mexico to cut a deal."

"We hope so," George said.

"Well, just in case Polk's wrong, I want the columns to close up from here to Monterrey. We've had a few brushes with Mexican cavalry. They ran away when our Texas fellows went after them."

The general had another regiment of Texas cavalry at the head of his column. He chuckled and gazed admiringly as a group of them swaggered past. "Those fellows are somethin'. They went through the houses of every town we hit, lookin' for loot. Said they didn't find enough to stick on a single bowie knife. I wish I had another thousand of those boys. I wouldn't worry about the Mexican cavalry."

George decided not to mention the death of the *vaquero*. In close formation, the army slogged uphill through a much more fruitful countryside toward Monterrey. The blasting heat of the desert vanished. Groves of ebony and brazilwood lined the road, interspersed with fields of silk-ripe corn and fat melons. The volunteers did not hesitate to sample this produce, until a messenger from General Taylor curtly ordered them to stop breaking ranks and keep up with the head of the column.

On the fourth day, in the far distance appeared the blue line of the Sierra Madre Mountains, which divided northern Mexico from the rest of the nation. Monterrey nestled in the foothills of these awesome peaks. The next day, September 19, they finally saw the city in the distance—white, flat-roofed houses built in irregular rectangles along narrow streets dominated by a cathedral looming over a central plaza. On the northern edge of the city stood a huge building with weather-blackened walls. As the Americans came down the road, black smoke puffed from this ominous-looking fort. Three cannonballs hurtled toward the intruders. One struck about fifty yards ahead of General Taylor and bounced high over his head. It began to look as if General Santa Anna and his friends were not quite ready to talk peace with the Americans.

Before the end of the day, a dour Taylor called a council of war. Texas ranger scouts and West Point engineers had been reconnoitering. They had come back with grim news. Monterrey was a "perfect Gibraltar" ringed by forts on the north side. The Mexicans had over forty cannon and seven thousand regulars inside the city, supported by another three thousand armed civilians. Suddenly Old Zach's decision to leave half his army at Camargo did not look very brilliant. But he artfully blamed it all on President Polk.

"It looks as if Polk's man, Santa Anna, is pulling one of his standard double crosses," the general said. "He's taken over the government and rushed reinforcements to Monterrey with orders to fight to the death."

Taylor's West Point–trained engineers had found a route around the city. The old Indian fighter proceeded to violate one of the fundamental rules of war. He divided his army in two, gave most of the regulars to General Worth, and ordered him to circle Monterrey by night and attack the city from the south. Taylor and the volunteers would stage a diversion on the north side.

"Aren't you worried about a sortie from the city, General?" George said. "If that Mexican general's any good, he could tear either half of our army to pieces."

"Mexicans don't like to fight in the open," Taylor snapped, making it clear that he was not interested in advice from amateur generals.

The next morning, at eight o'clock, the rattle of muskets and the boom of cannon rolled across Monterrey as Worth's men began their attack. At ten o'clock, Taylor sent his regulars forward with a vague order to "take them little forts down there with the bayonet if you think you can do it." As Brigadier General Stapleton and the rest of the army watched in dismay, the little forts, aided by several larger ones, erupted in a savage cross fire of grapeshot and small arms that left dozens of blue-coated Americans sprawled on the brown earth. As they reached the outlying streets of the town, they were met with blasts of musketry from Mexicans in loopholed houses and on sandbagged roofs.

A rattled Taylor ordered General Stapleton, in command of a brigade of volunteers from Mississippi and Tennessee, to rescue the regulars. As they moved out, George found Hannibal beside him.

"This isn't your fight."

"I volunteered for the whole war, General," Hannibal said. "I done bought these from some Texas fellows." He slapped two Colt pistols on his hips.

Emerging from a cornfield, George ordered his men into line for an assault. A cannonball from a nearby Mexican fort hissed through the Tennessee ranks. It tore off one man's head, another man's arm, disemboweled a third man, and wreaked similar havoc on four others, splattering blood and gore over their companions. A wail of terror rippled through the ranks. "Lord Jesus have mercy on us all," Hannibal said.

"Let's show them how Americans fight a war!" George shouted, pointing his sword toward Monterrey. He felt no fear. Was his father's spirit sustaining him?

The Tennesseans roared a response and surged forward. But more cannon fire and a blizzard of musket balls cut terrible gaps in their ranks. The red-shirted Mississippians on their right did not seem to be suffering as much, and George angled the advance in their direction. By now the battlefield was full of drifting smoke. When George reached the place where he thought the regulars were hanging on, he found they were separated by several streets of well-defended houses, and both brigades were stranded. Muskets and cannon blazed at them from all directions.

Just ahead was a brown-walled building bristling with cannon. Off to its left George saw a company of American regulars on a rooftop, firing at it, forcing the artillerymen to take cover. "Let's take that fort!" George said.

The commander of the Mississippians was an ex–West Pointer around George's age named Jefferson Davis. "Lead the way, General," he said. "Anything's better than standing here getting killed."

George leaped to his feet and lunged into the smoke. The howling Mississippians followed him. Some of the Tennessee regiment came with them. Bullets hissed around General Stapleton, men went down, but they reached the doors of the building, smashed them open with their muskets, and charged inside. A dozen Mexicans on the first floor dropped to their knees and surrendered. The Mississippians surged through the fort; gunshots quickly ended the resistance of a few holdouts. Hannibal appeared with pistols in both hands. "You done captured yourself a fort, General!" he shouted, sweat streaming down his face.

Out of the gunsmoke materialized Zachary Taylor himself leading a brigade of Kentucky and Ohio volunteers. With him was General Butler. Taylor congratulated George for capturing the fort: "This clears the way into the city. Leave a hundred men to hold this and follow me."

George marshaled his battered Tennesseans and Mississippians; they did not look as if they had much fight left in them. But they followed Taylor and Butler into the gunsmoke. In a matter of minutes, they were stopped by sheets of musketry and not a few blasts of grapeshot from barricades across several streets. More bullets came from their rear, where a small fort had been bypassed.

General Butler cried out and went down with blood gushing from a bullet in his thigh. The colonel in command of the Ohio regiment toppled with a bullet in his chest. Taylor exposed himself recklessly to the flying lead, trying to find a way around these new obstacles—in vain. He stood there, cursing, baffled and befuddled.

"This is slow suicide!" Colonel Jefferson Davis said to George. "What the hell does Old Zach think he's doing?"

"It's supposed to be a diversion," George said.

"Maybe he should have brought along a dictionary," Davis said. "Tell him to get us out of here."

Determined to equal Taylor's nonchalance under fire, George strolled through the bullets and suggested a withdrawal. "My men have taken terrible casualties. They're starting to unravel."

Taylor nodded glumly. "We've done all we can for one day. I hope Worth has put our losses to good use."

Carrying General Butler and numerous other wounded, the Americans ingloriously fled the environs of Monterrey. Back at their campgrounds, George found bewildered, shaken soldiers huddling around campfires, exchanging wild rumors. "People sayin' we lost half our army, General. We goin' to retreat?" Hannibal asked.

George visited the wounded Butler. He damned Taylor in sulfurous terms. "He's thrown away a thousand good men in three uncoordinated attacks, without bothering to find out shit about the enemy's defenses," he raged.

As darkness fell, the cries of the wounded echoed across the battlefield. A reporter from the *New York Herald* rushed up to George. "General, I'm Tom Hamer. I've got orders from my editor to keep an eye on you. From what I hear, you're the only man who showed any spunk out there. Capturing that fort . . ."

George had no difficulty making the necessary connections. Caroline's relations with the *New York Herald* were excellent. She fed them a stream of leaks and Washington gossip. This was her quid pro quo. But he found himself filled with loathing for the idea of rising to fame on the bodies of the dead.

"I'm sorry, Tom. I've got work to do. I left a lot of wounded men out there on that battlefield."

Hamer was openmouthed. "General, I just need a few paragraphs . . ."

"Talk to Colonel Davis of the Mississippi Rifles."

George summoned Hannibal and a dozen Tennessee soldiers, and they followed him onto the darkened battlefield. In a few hours, they brought back two dozen wounded men and deposited them at the entrance to the army's dressing station. Outside it in the lamplight, George noticed a pale pile of refuse. What was it?

Looking closer, he realized the pile was severed arms and legs. "The saws'll be goin' all night, for sure," Hannibal said. Amputation was a standard treatment for arm and leg wounds, which easily became infected.

On his third trip into the darkness, George heard someone weeping. He walked toward the sound and in the starlight discovered Lieutenant Ulysses S. Grant sobbing beside the body of a blue-uniformed regular.

"Lieutenant Grant," George said. "Can we help you? I've got a dozen men with me."

Grant shook his head. "Lieutenant Hoskins is dead, General. He was my best friend at the Military Academy. No matter how hard I try, I don't think I'm going to like this war."

"Amen to that," Hannibal said.

THREE

"I'M BEGINNING TO THINK JAMES ALMOST hates me," Sarah Polk said, gazing out at rain-drenched Washington. The Capitol loomed in the gray distance, its stunted wooden dome a kind of reproach to pretensions to grandeur.

"Why do you say such a thing?" Caroline asked.

"Can you blame him, really? I've inflicted this ordeal on him. Oh, my dear friend, if I didn't have you, I think I'd be a madwoman by now. Or an addict to laudanum."

It was March 25, 1847. The city was swirling with rumors that General Zachary Taylor had fought another great battle in Mexico. The war was ten months old and peace seemed as elusive as ever. George's letters from Mexico were a litany of disillusion. Capturing Monterrey after three days of bloody fighting, General Taylor had turned politician and agreed to an eight-week truce with the defeated Mexican general. He had allowed him to march his army out of the city with all their weapons, on a vague promise not to serve again in the war.

Once more, the newspapers had glorified Taylor, portraying him in the front ranks with his men, ignoring enemy bullets, calling for an ax to smash down the door of a Monterrey house. Not a word was said about his horrendous casualties or his assumption of the right to negotiate a truce with the Mexicans instead of defeating them as thoroughly as possible and letting the president and the secretary of state handle the political side of the war.

Taylor had compounded his insubordination by writing a fellow general a long letter full of vicious criticism of President Polk's conduct of the war. He claimed the administration had given him murky and contradictory instructions, and he questioned whether there was any hope of defeating Mexico, a nation of 8 million people, with the ridiculously small number of soldiers the president had given him. His friend had leaked the letter to a New York newspaper, stirring a sensational furor. The president had replied by publishing all the administration's correspondence with General Taylor, demonstrating his failure to request equipment and his repeated refusal to suggest a winning strategy. But few people bothered to plow through the fine print, and Polk had come off a bad second best.

"It's so maddening," Caroline said. "You've captured California and New Mexico. You've settled the Oregon boundary without a war. You've passed a tariff that satisfies the South and most of the rest of the country."

"And what is our reward?" Sarah said bitterly. She picked up a newspaper and read, " 'The president's latest message to Congress was perfectly characteristic of its author: weak, wheedling and sneaking.' "

"Who wrote that?"

"The *Boston Atlas.*" It was Boston's biggest Whig paper. Sarah picked up another paper. " 'Polk takes his ease on sixty-eight dollars per day in the White House, while the soldiers he has driven to the field subsist on fare his very slaves would loathe.' "

"I saw that one in the *New York Tribune.*"

Sarah picked up another paper. " 'I am greatly deceived if we shall not ere long see facts coming to the light which will enable the Congress to charge the President with an impeachable offense for bringing on war in an underhanded and illegal manner.' "

"Daniel Webster," Caroline said.

"Can you imagine what the Mexicans think when they see statements like that? They'll never make peace."

"If only that fool Taylor hadn't let that Mexican army get away . . ."

Sarah nodded gloomily. Both of them knew that General Taylor was not the whole explanation, though his blunders had contributed to the malaise that was spreading through the country. The president's decision to allow General Antonio Santa Anna to return to Mexico from his Cuban exile on the promise that he would make peace was haunting the administration. The double-talking schemer no sooner got to Mexico City than he began rallying the country to drive the hated gringos into the sea. It gave the Whigs an irresistible opportunity to sneer at the president's judgment.

At least as important was the lack of respect his fellow Democrats had for James Knox Polk. The Van Buren men still hated him for depriving their hero of the presidency. Calhoun's Southern followers disliked Polk because he was Andrew Jackson's heir. Many Westerners denounced him because he had compromised on the Oregon boundary. No one rose to defend the president when the Whigs called him Jim Thumb, a cousin of P. T. Barnum's famous midget. Nor did they protest when Senator Jeremy Biddle of New Jersey fastened on him the epithet "Polk the mendacious."

"I don't know who is more infuriating, Taylor or that swine David Wilmot," Sarah Polk said.

The president had asked Congress to vote him $2 million that he could offer the Mexicans as an immediate down payment for a treaty of peace that gave the United States California and New Mexico. Congressman David Wilmot, a Pennsylvania Democrat, was angry because he had risked local obloquy to vote for the lowered tariff, which the Keystone State's manufacturers abhorred, and the president had failed to reward him with government jobs for his relatives and friends. He had attached a rider to the bill stating that slavery would be barred from any territory acquired from Mexico.

John Quincy Adams and his fellow Whigs had all but danced in the aisles with glee. They backed the rider with rhetoric that infuriated the Southern Democrats. After rancorous debate, the rider was finally excised, but a Whig filibuster killed the bill in the Senate, depriving the president of a vital tool for negotiating a quick peace. Worse, Wilmot's so-called Proviso still hovered out there like a vulture, waiting to swoop down and devour Polk's Mexican policy.

Emboldened by this Democratic disarray, the abolitionists in the Whig Party took the offensive. Joshua Giddings, a congressman from Ohio, declared he was in favor of seceding from a government that was conducting this pro-slavery war. "Black Tom" Corwin, a senator from Illinois, declared that he hoped American soldiers in Mexico would be welcomed to "hospitable graves." A Boston newspaper declared the war was so grossly immoral, "if there is a heart worthy of American liberty, its impulse is to join the Mexicans."

"Look at this," Sarah said, handing Caroline a paper in Spanish. "It's the official journal of the Mexican government. They're offering the thanks of the nation to Webster for threatening the president with impeachment."

The president knocked on the open door of Sarah's study. A sheen of sweat was visible on his high forehead, although the temperature outside was in the forties and the White House was not appreciably warmer. He had acquired a slight stoop, as if his shoulders were having trouble bearing the burdens loaded upon them. Sarah said it was from spending too many hours at his desk. Caroline forbore from mentioning that Sarah had acquired one too. She toiled beside him far into the night, scanning reams of paperwork from the War Department and the Navy Department and the State Department, drafting letters to cabinet members and replies to his newspaper critics for anonymous publication in the administration paper, the *Washington Union*.

"You look like a man with some news in your hand," Sarah said. "Or is that just more paperwork?"

"It's bad news, I'm afraid," the president said in a leaden voice. "Taylor reports another victory in Mexico. With a butcher's bill even longer than Monterrey. Our friend Abe Yell is dead at the head of his regiment. Henry Clay's son has been killed. The list goes on and on. It's sickening."

"Abe Yell," Sarah said. "His poor wife—and son. Isn't the boy at Georgetown?"

Polk nodded. Abraham Yell had been a congressman from Arkansas. He was a boyhood friend of the president's. In Zachary Taylor's army, generals and colonels were expected to lead their men from the front.

"George is all right?" Caroline asked, dread seizing her throat. Surely the president would have mentioned him first if he was among the lost. But he might be wounded. Two volunteer generals had returned from Monterrey crippled by bullets.

"A letter from him was included in Taylor's report," the president said with a wry smile. "To my other duties, I may now add the title of postman."

He handed Caroline the letter and began denouncing Taylor. The man had been ordered to remain on the defensive at Monterrey. Instead he had marched his army a hundred miles deeper into northern Mexico, inviting this attack. The president began reading from the *New Orleans Picayune,* one of the most ardently pro-Taylor papers. It described the general, sitting sidesaddle on his horse, facing three lines of charging Mexicans, snarling to an artillery captain named Bragg, "Double-shot your guns and give them hell."

It was the sort of battlefield heroics that Americans adored. "That story could make him president," Sarah said with bitter weariness.

"Excuse me," Caroline said, and began reading George's letter.

> *By the time you get this you may have heard about Buena Vista. It was another glorious victory for Old Zach, the luckiest general on the face of the earth. Two days before the battle, he was dismissing reports of our scouts that Santa Anna was coming after us with 20,000 men— against our 5,000. It was the most desperate fighting I've seen yet. At one point our entire left flank collapsed—men from Indiana and Kentucky ran for the rear. I led Colonel Jefferson Davis and his Mississippians into the gap and we stopped an all-out cavalry charge. Again, it was the West Pointers like Davis and Captain Bragg of the artillery who saved our necks. If Santa Anna had renewed his attack the next day, he would have destroyed us. We had almost 1,000 casualties and another 1,500 had deserted. But his army had run out of food and he had to retreat. What a despicable character he is. At the climax of the battle, we had a brigade of their infantry trapped behind our lines. Santa Anna sent an officer forward with a flag of truce. Old Zach, who still fancies himself a politician, ordered us to cease fire and the brigade escaped. A half hour later their whole army came after us again. I had two horses shot out from under me but once more emerged without a scratch.*
>
> *Please tell the President I don't want to spend another hour with Zachary Taylor. He's an insufferable stupid butcher. I'd appreciate a transfer to General Scott's army.*
>
> *Greet Jonathan, Charlie, and Paul for me and tell them how much I miss them.*
>
> *As ever,*
> *George*

Caroline read the letter aloud and the president nodded grimly. It confirmed his low opinion of Zachary Taylor. "I'll have George transferred to General Scott's army tomorrow. I have good news from him. He's captured Vera Cruz with scarcely the loss of a man."

"Wonderful!" Caroline and Sarah said in unison. In the momentary silence their eyes exchanged their secret understanding. Not for the first time, Caroline wondered how much longer they could sustain it.

"General Santa Anna will soon be dancing to my tune," the president said.

General Winfield Scott represented the Polks' response to Zachary Taylor's glorification—and General Antonio Santa Anna's double-crossing diplomacy. The president had given Scott all of Taylor's regular army regiments and added ten thousand volunteers. Scott had orders to capture Vera Cruz and march to Mexico City, where the Americans would dictate peace at the point of a gun.

Back at her house on Pennsylvania Avenue, Caroline found John Sladen and John L. O'Sullivan waiting for her. She gave them both warm smiles. John had stopped drinking. He was looking more like the shrewd, cocky man she had loved and abandoned in New York. In the fall of 1846, John had become Louisiana's junior senator. It had been one of the most corrupt elections in recent history. John had spent a fortune buying votes in New Orleans. Victory had buoyed his spirits and vastly increased his self-confidence. "What's the latest news from Mr. Polk's war?" he asked.

She told them about Taylor's victory at Buena Vista. They groaned and all but tore their hair. She let them writhe in anguish for a while and then announced Scott's victory at Vera Cruz. Their excitement was unbounded. This was the news they had been hoping to hear.

"Is it time for me to unmask my batteries?" O'Sullivan asked.

"I think so," Caroline said.

"What's the president's mood these days?" John asked.

"You might call it barely controlled rage. At General Taylor and at General Santa Anna."

"The latter is what I want to hear," John said. "We can take care of Taylor."

She gave George's letter to O'Sullivan. He had been extolling General Stapleton in the *New York Morning News* with a flamboyance that New Jersey papers were quick to imitate. "I wish he wasn't so modest," O'Sullivan said, glancing at the text. "He never gives us any vivid details to work with."

"That's where your wonderful imagination comes in," Caroline said.

"I see he's transferring to Scott. We'll use that for a blast at Taylor. Can we quote this stupid old butcher line?"

"You can quote the whole thing."

"It ought to raise a fuss," O'Sullivan said.

"We want more than a fuss. We want a campaign," Senator Sladen said.

"For 'All Mexico'? Don't worry. You'll get it," O'Sullivan said. "We've got the *Public Ledger* in Philadelphia, the *Sun* in Baltimore, the *Crescent City News* in New Orleans, and a dozen other papers lined up to follow our lead."

It was uncanny the way the war was unfolding like a vast drama guided by an unseen hand. So many ifs might have changed the script and rendered this awesome possibility—the conquest of all Mexico and its conversion into an imperial province of the United States, the equivalent of England's India—null and void. If Zachary Taylor had been a better general and destroyed the Mexican armies he had fought, instead of letting them retreat. If General Santa Anna had kept his word and negotiated peace. If General Taylor had not developed White House fever.

Instead, everything was moving relentlessly toward a Caribbean empire—the ultimate expansion of Aaron Burr's dream. But this new domain would not be the febrile creation of a single ambitious man. It would be a major turning point in world history. The more Caroline thought about it, the more convinced she became that it was not only the solution to the South's dilemma, but it would mark the United States' emergence as a world power. The conquest and pacification of Mexico would make them England's political and economic equal.

Sarah saw this too, Caroline was convinced to it. But Sarah was too absorbed in the day-to-day business of the war and the president's relationship with Congress to think about it. More and more, she depended on Caroline to envision the lustrous future that lay beyond the anxious exhausting present.

O'Sullivan departed to catch a train to New York. John Sladen lingered. "It's happening," he said. "I can feel the whole incredible thing heaving, stretching, thrashing—giving birth. It's like watching some mythic giant emerging from the primal mists."

"Yes."

"Who do you love more, now—George . . . or Sarah . . . or me?"

"I love all three of you. I've told you that."

"I asked a quantitative question."

Desire stirred in Caroline's flesh. It had been ten months since George left for Mexico. She had never realized how much he satisfied that subterranean side of her self. Women were not supposed to need sex the way a man needed it. But she was too realistic about herself to believe that myth. Her unblinking intellect—what John erroneously called her man's mind—saw so much.

"As long as George is in Mexico risking his life, I can never be unfaithful to him."

"When he returns, loaded with glory courtesy of O'Sullivan's Irish verbiage, what chance will I have?"

"I don't know. If you're in Mexico, administering a conquered province, will you have time for me?"

"I'll always have time for you."

"John, be realistic. It's impossible. If everything goes as planned, George Stapleton will succeed James Polk as president. Are you suggesting infidelity in the White House? Or in Mexico City, full of leering American reporters? Maybe it's better to face it now. We can only be lovers in our dreams—as long as we both love something else more than any of the other people in our lives."

"What's that?" he said, his voice harsh with pain.

"Fame—as your father and my father and Aaron Burr understood it. Not the cheap version any fool can buy in the newspapers. But the deep ancient kind—the fame of those who change the course of history. That's what we were born to do, to become. Whether we love each other in the routine way is irrelevant."

"You'll never be irrelevant to me!"

"Then I must consider myself your weakness. Perhaps your fatal flaw. I don't love weakness. It's inconsistent with fame."

He snatched up his coat and hat and departed without another word. For the next week, the newspapers boiled with the news of Buena Vista and Vera Cruz. John L. O'Sullivan published George's letter, assailing Zachary Taylor's latest butcher's bill, in the *Morning News*. Whigs dismissed it as Democratic propaganda, and disgusting propaganda at that. Jeremy Biddle made a speech in the Senate, denouncing the very idea of slandering a man who had risked his life for his country. Senator Sladen replied, pointing out that George had risked his life too—and all the risked lives and the lost lives were Taylor's fault.

But there was no mention of All Mexico in the *Morning News* or any other paper. Sarah Polk received at least a hundred newspapers from around the nation, and Caroline spent several hours each day helping her scour them for stories that the president should read. Returning from one of these chores, she was startled to find a copy of the *Morning News* on the side table in her hall. In the right-hand column, beneath a blazing headline, was the story she had been waiting for: "All Mexico Must Be Ours!"

"Hello, Mother," said a familiar voice.

Out of the parlor emerged her son Jonathan, down from Columbia College for spring vacation. At eighteen, he had become a giant almost as tall as his father. But he lacked George's fleshy fame. He was closer to an elongated skeleton. His jet-black hair, the argumentative gray eyes in the gaunt, morose face, sometimes made her feel she was looking at a stretched version of the young John Sladen. But this was a Sladen who thought he was a Stapleton.

"Hello," she said, allowing him to kiss her on the cheek.

"Madam! You're my prisoner!"

Charlie Stapleton seized her from behind, whirled her around, and kissed her on the lips. "Stop it, you silly thing," she said, pushing him away.

"Isn't she incredible?" Charlie said to Jonathan. "She still doesn't look a day over thirty. You'd never think she was sixty-five years old."

Caroline giggled almost girlishly. Charlie was incorrigible. When he was home, the house was always in an uproar. Friends of all ages and social classes thronged the parlor. Raging arguments regularly erupted between him and Jonathan. They agreed on nothing. Charlie's Southern education no doubt had something to do with it. He was now a freshman at the University of North Carolina. But the root of the difference was temperamental.

"I've invited my roommate Ben Dall to join me. I hope you don't mind," Jonathan said. "He's never been to Washington."

"I'm delighted. But you'll have to entertain yourselves. I spend a good deal of time at the White House each day, as I think you know."

"Whoaaaaa," Charlie said. "My mother the stateswoman. Or have you taken a job as steward to make ends meet while Father's shooting Mexicans?"

"Ben—"

A blond, slim, extraordinarily handsome young man came to the parlor door and gave Caroline one of the coolest most appraising stares she had encountered in a long time. "How do you do, Mrs. Stapleton."

"Ben is from Utica. He's at Columbia on a scholarship. He's finishing first in the class in everything this year."

"How nice." Caroline grew almost uncomfortable under Ben Dall's continuing stare. "I see you've brought some New York papers for me to read."

"I knew you'd like to see O'Sullivan's latest effusion," Jonathan said. "I don't think he did Father any favor, printing that letter slamming General Taylor. Where did he get it?"

"I gave it to him."

Jonathan could scarcely conceal his dismay. "I hope you don't agree with this stuff—about taking and keeping all of Mexico."

"It's the first I've heard of it. I must confess I find it intriguing. It's exactly what the Mexicans deserve. I'm sure Father has told you how they've broken promises to negotiate and used flags of truce and armistices in the most dishonorable way."

"I think it's a great idea!" Charlie said. "Think of all these senoritas, Big Brother. Ready to hurl themselves into the arms of their country's conquerors. Women adore conquerors. Don't you agree, Ben?"

"I have too much respect for women to regard them in such a callous way," Ben Dall said.

Charlie staggered back as if he had just been punched in the jaw. "I should have known Big Brother would bring home a roommate like you. Ten bucks say you're also high on the rights of the Negro."

"I'm an abolitionist, if that's what you mean."

"Sure, I can spot one of you crathers at a hundred paces," Charlie said in a perfect imitation of an Irish brogue. He struck a boxer's pose and said, "Shall I throw the fellow into the street, Madam? Surely y'can't allow such a monstroosity in the house of an honest Dimmycrat!"

"Shut up!" Jonathan said, advancing on Charlie with his big fists clenched. "Ben is my guest. I won't have him ridiculed. Surely you can tolerate an intellectual disagreement on the Negro, Mother. I haven't succumbed to Ben's arguments. I've defended the Stapletons' political principles vigorously, I assure you."

"He's almost convinced me once or twice," Ben Dall said in a feeble attempt at jocularity.

"I assure you, Mr. Dall, I'm not likely to let the arguments of a college sophomore change my mind," Caroline said. "Especially when I have an opportunity to see the Democratic Party's principles being applied to the government of the country every day in the White House. I predict James Knox Polk will be considered a great president someday, when history was given us time to appreciate his fame."

"I hope you're right, madam. For our country's sake." An unmistakable sneer was in Dall's voice.

"While we're on the topic or close to it, Mother, why can't I go to Mexico?" Charlie said. "You could change Father's mind in five minutes. The president could get me a commission . . ."

He followed Caroline upstairs, refusing to pay the slightest attention to her vehement refusals. In the upper hall, five-year-old Paul entered the fray. "Mother, Charlie says I could become a powder monkey in the navy. A lot of boys do it. They have great adventures, bombarding forts, capturing enemy ships."

"You must learn never to take seriously anything Charlie says."

In her bedroom, Charlie hurled himself onto Caroline's bed. "Come on, Mother. I'm almost seventeen. Lots of volunteers in Mexico are younger. I have a great military future, Mother. Why are you holding me back?"

"Because I don't want to see you killed by some Mexican peon. Have you noticed how many second lieutenants are on the casualty lists? You have a brilliant future ahead of you as a politician."

Caroline had already chosen careers for her sons. Plodding Jonathan was to take over the Camden & Amboy Railroad and the other family businesses. Flamboyant Charlie, with his good looks and effervescent personality, would be the next politician. Paul was still too young and unformed to decide anything about him.

"A politician doesn't need a college degree, do you think?"

"Not necessarily," Caroline said.

"That's good. Because I don't think I'm going to get one. They've thrown me out of dear old North Carolina U."

"Charlie . . . What did you do?"

"I was flunking all my courses, Mother. But I didn't want to get expelled for stupidity. So I loaded a pound of buckshot into an old cannon on the campus in front of the president's house and aimed it in his general direction around midnight. It blew out every window in sight."

"Your father will be very unhappy with this news."

"Don't tell him about it until he comes home. Senator Sladen says he can get me a job at the Cotton Exchange in New Orleans. I'll be as rich as he is before I'm twenty-five. Meanwhile I'll be enjoying myself. He says he'll introduce me to those beautiful octoroons—"

"Senator Sladen has no business taking charge of your life! I intend to give him a thorough tongue-lashing for encouraging this—this—"

"Mother, face it, I'm not like the rest of the family. I don't want to read every book in the libraries like Jonathan. I don't fret about the future of the country, like Father and you. I'm just Good Time Charlie."

"You have gifts which I'm determined you'll use. You'll enroll in Princeton in the fall."

Charlie groaned in despair and trudged off like a man on his way to his execution. Caroline was changing for dinner when Mercy Flowers knocked on her door. "Missus, you got to help me with Tabitha. That girl is close to losin' her immortal soul. She won't do nothin' I say. If her poor father comes home from Mexico and finds her ruined, he'll blame me."

Tabitha was seventeen but looked twenty. She was fully developed and as beautiful as her mother had been, with the same creamy tan skin and wide liquid eyes. Mercy was training her to replace aging Harriet as their cook. But Tabitha claimed to hate the idea. She was staying out until midnight at dances and parties with "wild friends." Her latest report card from school was a disaster.

Caroline sent for her. The girl stood defiantly in the doorway as Caroline told her sternly that she would not tolerate her behavior.

"What are you going to do about it? Sell me south? I'm not your *slave.*"

"You see what I mean, missus?" Mercy said. "She done take it into her head that she's as good as white folks."

"I am. So are you," Tabitha said. "If you stopped bowing and scraping long enough to think about it."

"Young lady," Caroline said, "while your father is risking his life for our country in Mexico, I consider myself your guardian. You'll do what your mother and I say or I'll whip you personally."

"You lay a hand on me and I'll go to the police. I don't have to live here and learn how to cook to your taste. I met a man who said I could make a hundred dollars a week entertaining congressmen."

"You hear that, missus?" Mercy cried. "Now you know why I fears for her 'mortal soul!"

"This old fool and her God—where was God when my mother got kidnapped and killed?"

For a moment, Caroline was back in Ohio, telling her mother she would never believe in a God who let her father die such a horrible death. What could she say to Tabitha? Caroline groped through old pain and a sudden shuddering sense that the world was an evil place, impossibly beyond anyone's control.

"I can only say this to you, Tabitha. What would your father think if he came home and found you'd become that kind of woman?"

"I don't know," Tabitha said sullenly. "He's so wrapped up in his prayers and his Bible I don't think he gives two damns about me."

"He loves you. I've heard him say that a hundred times. Haven't you, Mercy?"

"He sure do. Why, if he come home and found her a Jezebel, a harlot—it'd kill him as sure as any bullet."

Tabitha's defiance dissolved into tears. "I just miss him so. If he could write to me . . ."

"I'll ask General Stapleton to write a letter for him. Hannibal will tell him what he wants to say."

"Oh, thank you, missus," Tabitha said.

Caroline sank on the bed. Was she some sort of madwoman? How could she believe that she could change the course of American history when she could barely control the chaos in her own family—in her own soul?

Slowly, that steeled will, that relish for power, reasserted itself. It was still possible, as long as she and Sarah controlled that stooped, harassed man in the White House, the president of the United States, James Knox Polk.

FOUR

ON APRIL 17, 1847, BRIGADIER GENERAL George Stapleton sat in his tent not far from a steep ridge called Cerro Gordo. It loomed in the starlit night like a massive wall of absolute darkness. Beyond it stretched a well-paved road through the mountains into the heart of Mexico. The Mexicans had ten thousand men and fifty cannon on Cerro Gordo. They hoped to smash the American army here and send them fleeing back to the humid seacoast, where yellow fever would destroy them.

Around George camped the brigade of Ohio and Kentucky volunteers that he commanded. Men were shouting and laughing, someone was playing "The Girl I Left Behind Me" on a harmonica, dogs were barking. Except for the colonels and majors and captains, they were all in their teens and twenties, mostly big husky young men, bursting with life and confidence. In twelve hours, half of them might be dead. The American army was going to attack Cerro Gordo and its outlying fortifications at dawn.

By the light of a guttering candle, the general was rereading a letter from his wife.

Dear Husband,

I trust this finds you healthy and far happier with General Scott's army. On that force now rests a great deal. All our political hopes, for one thing. If you don't swiftly defeat the Mexicans and extract a peace treaty from them, I shudder to think what may happen in the upcoming congressional elections. The Whigs are becoming ever more vocal critics of the war, in and out of Congress. The Taylor balloon continues to rise and swell. But a swift end to the war by another general (or generals) will send him plummeting to earth. Though I know it troubles your conscience, as you've explained, I hope you'll deign to talk to reporters at least as much as your ex-friend Gideon Pillow, so as to convince voters that not all the President's military appointments are windy idiots.

Enclosed you will find some interesting clippings. They reflect a growing public opinion that if the Mexicans refuse to sign a peace, we should consider taking full possession of their disorganized country for the next fifty years or so, educate them in the fundamentals of democracy, and meanwhile extract from them the full cost of this hideous war, which they have so treacherously prolonged. The result would (or could) be salubrious for both countries in the long run. We would have a docile neighbor to our south, a foreign market for American manufactures—and an occupation for thousands of restless young Americans like our son Charlie. The British have fended off revolutionary upheavals by sending their younger sons and turbulent spirits to India and similar places. But I won't undertake to tell you what to think about it—knowing you will form your own opinion.

Perhaps more important for the moment is the President's decision to send a diplomat to open formal peace negotiations. He is Nicholas Trist, whom I am sure you've met at the State Department or at our house, where he has been an occasional guest at our weekly receptions. How reliable he is, I can't say. The Secretary of State trusts him, but I don't consider that a recommendation, since none of us trust Mr. Buchanan to do anything but promote his own ambitions for president. I would keep an eye on Mr. Trist if possible and report directly to the President if you think he's acting out of channels.

The boys are fine. They send their love. As do I.

Caroline

George Stapleton read this letter with gloomy approval. His attitude toward the war had changed since that slaughterous assault on Monterrey. He had acquired a cold anger at the Mexicans, which was shared by almost everyone in the army. They detested the way Mexican guerrillas preyed on lone dispatch riders or small groups of foragers. They bitterly resented the way the Mexican cavalry murdered wounded Americans without mercy. Above all, they despised the Mexican leader, the one-legged two-faced liar who was opposing them once more at Cerro Gordo, General Antonio Santa Anna. His bombastic proclamations, his readiness to use flags of truce to extricate himself from losing battles, his offers to negotiate peace, followed by pompous repudiations, disgusted the Americans. If any of them had had doubts about the morality or justice of the war, Santa Anna had erased them.

Then there were the dead. With each battle, their voices acquired resonance. In the silences of the night they insisted that they had not died in vain—that this ugly struggle must be resolved in a way that gave meaning to their foundered lives. Their voices pervaded the army. Even doubters like Sam Grant were determined to end it with victory now.

"General Stapleton. Are your men ready?"

Captain Robert E. Lee, one of the engineers on General Winfield Scott's staff, stood in the entrance to the tent. Extraordinarily handsome, with a soft black mustache and high, noble forehead, Lee was the son of Light Horse Harry Lee, one of the cavalry heroes of the American Revolution. George had read the captain's father's memoirs, and his admiration had created a bond between them.

"I think so. I've told them what we have to do. I told them what the Mexican cavalry did to our wounded at Buena Vista. They want to even the score."

Lee nodded. "A little fire in the belly never hurts. I'm happy to report I'm to be your guide."

"I'm happy to learn that. When do we move out?"

"In about an hour."

Four hours later, George and his men found themselves at the base of a smaller hill, La Atalaya, just north of Cerro Gordo. His men waited in the chaparral, under orders to maintain total silence. Brigadier General David Twiggs, pulling on his chest-length white beard, was telling them in his profane way that he needed their help. His men had driven the Mexicans off La Atalaya yesterday. But some of them had kept on going up the slopes of Cerro Gordo and had been badly mauled. They were supposed to drag three huge twenty-four-pound cannon to the top of a La Atalaya for the dawn attack. With their losses, and the exhaustion that followed heavy fighting, they could not do it.

For the next three hours, George and his men undertook this herculean task, under the guidance of Lee and other West Point engineers. It took all the strength of five hundred men, straining on ropes as thick as a wrist, to move the gleaming black monsters one hundred feet up the hill. They had to be replaced by another five hundred men for another hundred feet. George threw aside his general's coat and hauled with the men. By 4 A.M. the big guns were in place.

George had concluded that in the American army, generals needed to do things like hauling on ropes and eating army rations to assure the enlisted men that rank had not changed them into aristocrats. Reporters had taken to calling George "the democratic general" for the way he included these touches in his style of command.

At 7 A.M., as the rising sun streaked the slopes of Cerro Gordo with crimson, the three big guns on La Atalaya opened fire on the startled Mexicans. By this time, Lee had led George and his men deep into the Mexican rear. They were waiting in the chaparral on the edge of the road into the interior of Mexico. It was guarded by a five-gun battery and several regiments of infantry, proof that the Mexicans realized the road's importance. If the Americans cut it, they would have Santa Anna's army trapped.

"There's our objective," Captain Lee said, pointing to the battery. It had a ditch around it and the walls were eight or nine feet high. "Let's wait a few minutes to see how the other attacks go. If they distract the enemy on Cerro Gordo, we should have an easier time of it."

George could see exactly what he meant. Cerro Gordo had gun emplacements on the rear slope that could wreak havoc on his men when they came out in the open.

The artillery thundered and Mexican guns boomed in reply. Then came the rattle of small arms and a swelling cheer from the other side of the hill. Over the top came blue-clad figures. Panicky Mexicans sprang out of their ditches and batteries and began fleeing down the rear slope.

"Now!" Lee said, drawing his sword.

George unsheathed his sword and pulled his Colt revolver from the holster on his hip. "Remember the wounded at Buena Vista!" he shouted.

Out of the chaparral stormed the volunteers, howling like Iroquois. The amazed gunners in the five-gun battery got off a single badly aimed round before General Stapleton, Captain Lee, and the lead companies were in the ditch, firing into the faces of anyone who peered over it, hoisting each other on shoulders to get over the parapet. The first two or three men were shot and toppled back into their comrades' arms. But the number of climbers multiplied along with their bloodcurdling howls, and in five minutes the Mexican gunners and their supporting infantry were fleeing toward Cerro Gordo screaming, "The *yanquis* are in the rear!"

Panic rampaged through the Mexican lines. Off to the right, a handsome vermilion carriage pulled by a dozen white mules lumbered onto the road. "That's Santa Anna's coach!" George shouted. "Don't let him get away."

A hail of bullets riddled the coach, killing the two drivers and most of the mules. But no one was inside it. The drivers were simply trying to rescue the vehicle from the *yanquis*. George led his men past the wreckage toward Cerro Gordo. Hundreds of Mexicans threw down their guns and surrendered, pleading for mercy.

"Should we give them the same treatment they gave our wounded at Buena Vista, General?" one of the men asked. He had his bayonet poised to impale a cowering Mexican.

"No! We don't fight their kind of war," George said.

"That must be Santa Anna's tent!"

George led a surge toward a huge white tent with an elaborate silk-curtained marquee. Inside they found a hot breakfast of tortillas and tamales on gold-rimmed plates. The table service was solid silver. Coffee bubbled in a beautifully engraved silver pot. In a large trunk were a half dozen uniforms, heavy with gold braid. Beside it was one of Santa Anna's wooden legs. He had lost the real leg to a French cannonball, when Paris, irked with Mexico's long-running refusal to pay its bills, sent a fleet to shell Vera Cruz in 1838.

"General, could you come here a moment?" Captain Lee said as the volunteers began stuffing Santa Anna's possessions into their knapsacks.

Outside the tent, George found a remarkably beautiful young Mexican woman standing beside the road, sobbing pathetically. She was wearing little more than a nightgown, her shoulders and arms bare. Her lustrous black hair streamed down both sides of her lovely oval face. "I'm afraid this lady will be abused if we don't offer her some protection," Lee said.

In his seven months in northern Mexico, George had learned enough Spanish to carry on a conversation. "What is your name, madam?" he said.

"Senora Maria Pena de Vega. My husband commanded the heights of Cerro Gordo. I fear he may be among the dead. Excuse my appearance. I fled my tent when shells began exploding near it."

"I'll do my best to find out your husband's fate. In the meantime consider yourself under my protection."

"A thousand thanks, sir. I am happy to learn not all Americans are barbarians."

George seized the first two privates within reach. They were Kentuckians, both in their teens. "Escort this woman back to her tent. If you insult her in any way, I'll have you shot!"

"Yes, sir, General," they said, their eyes wide.

George went back into Santa Anna's tent and commandeered a crimson cloak that a corporal had just pulled out of the dictator's trunk. Outside, George draped it around Maria de Vega's naked shoulders. While the privates escorted her to her tent, George mounted the steep slope of Cerro Gordo. On the summit he found a grisly scene. The shells of the guns on La Atalaya had wreaked havoc on the Mexicans, and the storming parties of infantrymen had only added to the carnage. Dead men lay everywhere. Intermingled with them were a startling number of women. The Mexicans brought their women to war and apparently thought the Americans were going to give them time to depart to the rear before they attacked.

A huddle of surviving Mexicans were being guarded by two husky Irish regulars. Half the men in the regular army regiments were Irish or German born. "Where is General de Vega?" George asked in Spanish.

"You'll find his corpse in the number two battery," said a thick-bodied, swarthy lieutenant.

"Take me to him."

In the wreckage of a three-gun battery, George found a young, hawk-nosed man slumped between two dismounted guns. The front of his gray uniform was soaked with blood. "There is General de Vega," the Mexican lieutenant said. "He was killed by the first of your shells. Without him the men were like so many decapitated chickens."

"His wife asked me to discover his fate."

The lieutenant grimaced. "God never stops smiling on Americans. She's very beautiful."

At the foot of Cerro Gordo, George had no trouble locating Madame de Vega's tent, guarded by his two Kentucky privates. By now she was wearing a pleated, dark red dress, which still left her lovely shoulders bare. "I'm afraid your fears have proven true," George said. "Your husband is dead. Do you want to take charge of his body?"

She shook her head. "Bury him with his men. That's what he would want," she said. Her eyes were red-rimmed but tearless. "It's a fate he foresaw from the day this war began. It would be our punishment."

"Why?"

"We were secret lovers for a year before my father discovered us and put me in a convent. The general stormed the place with his men and carried me away to Yucatán. My father put a curse on us."

"Where is your home?"

"Once it was Mexico City. Since I married it was with General de Vega—with the army. I thought he was the hope of Mexico. Now I begin to think Mexico has no hope."

"You have no relatives in Vera Cruz—anywhere I could send you?"

"None that would risk my father's wrath."

"Then you must stay with our army until we reach Mexico City. Surely when your father sees you face-to-face, he'll forgive you."

"I doubt it. But I have no other choice—except to join my husband. A choice I may yet make."

"Madam, don't say such a thing! Someone so beautiful, so fine . . . It would be a crime against nature!"

"It may be the best answer to my father's cruelty. Someone must bear witness to Mexico's despair."

That night, General Stapleton joined in a boisterous celebration in General Winfield Scott's tent. The majestic, six-foot-five-inch commander of the American army remembered George's father, who had died under his command in that long-ago battle on the Canadian border. Scott was the total opposite of Zachary Taylor—courteous, intelligent, a thinking soldier. He had captured the heavily fortified port of Vera Cruz last month at the cost of less than a dozen lives. He had applied similar professionalism to Cerro Gordo. With the loss of little more than two hundred men, they had captured five thousand Mexicans, forty cannon, seven thousand muskets. Santa Anna was a fugitive. The Mexican army had vanished. There was nothing between them and Mexico City but another 150 miles of hard marching along a good road.

While toasts rang out to General Scott, to General Twiggs, to General Stapleton, to Captain Lee for his daring reconnaissances, which had discovered the route around Cerro Gordo through the chaparral, George's mind drifted to the darkened tent where Maria de Vega sat, listening to their hilarity. Was every shout of triumph, every guffaw of victory, deepening that impulse to bear witness to Mexico's despair?

General Stapleton found himself more and more uncomfortable with the party. Somehow, this beautiful young woman had become his responsibility. He had helped place the batteries that had killed her husband. He had encouraged James Knox Polk to invade her country to teach them a lesson in international behavior. How bizarre, how cruel, those words, that tough policy, seemed when you came face-to-face with the suffering it inflicted on individuals. How little he really knew about Mexico. Why had General de Vega been the hope of the country?

As General Twiggs and General Scott began exchanging war stories from the days of 1812—stories to which George would ordinarily have listened with fascination—he excused himself and walked back to Madame de Vega's tent. A single sentry was guarding it. George had arranged for around-the-clock protection.

"It's George Stapleton," he said, rustling the tent flap. "Are you all right?"

"Yes." Her voice had a dusky timbre.

"Good. I hope our celebration isn't keeping you awake."

"I have no interest in sleep. I prefer my thoughts."

Suddenly George saw this beautiful woman in her nightgown, those sinuous arms, the sculpted shoulders. His mouth was dry with desire. It had been ten months since he touched a woman. He struggled with meaningless words. "Did my servant, Hannibal, bring you dinner?"

"Yes. He was annoyed because I ate nothing."

"I'll see you in the morning."

"Thank you—for everything, General. You have been most kind. I only fear your generosity is being wasted on a woman who no longer has any interest in this life."

Back in his tent, General Stapleton found sleep eluding him for a long time. He too was discovering that part of his soul lived in an underground river of desire. Like the honorable man and faithful husband he was, he rebuked himself. But the memory of Maria de Vega in her nightdress, the dusky timbre of her mournful voice, refused to vanish. It gathered intensity until it became an almost holy image, ringed with light. Somehow, General Stapleton vowed, he would assuage her sorrow. He would right at least one of the wrongs inflicted by this savage war.

FIVE

CAROLINE KEMBLE STAPLETON SAT IN THE gallery of the House of Representatives, looking down on an elongated Illinois scarecrow named Abraham Lincoln, as he declaimed against Mr. Polk's war. "I wunt tew know the eggsact spot where this here blood was spilled that started this here terrible war," he drawled, his thumbs in the buttonholes of his coat. "I got a series of resolutions here, demandin' that James Knox Polk show us the eggsact spot. I am confident, gentlemun, that if he tole us the truth about it, he would be shown to be the wuss liar that ever inhabited that palace on Pennsylvanee Avenoo."

Not a Democrat rose to answer this idiot. A temperature of ninety-six degrees may have had something to do with their torpor. But its real source was political. None of them had any stomach for defending James Knox Polk. The party had lost control of the House of Representatives in the midterm (1846) elections. This arrogant fool Lincoln was one of the Whig winners. Caroline stalked out of the stifling gallery and hurried to the Senate.

A page escorted her to one of the couches on the floor. A half dozen senators, including Daniel Webster and John C. Calhoun, strolled over to pay their respects. Webster was drunk, not an unusual condition for him these days, as the White House receded irrevocably beyond his grasp. Calhoun was obviously a dying man, his chest perpetually choked with catarrh. He too realized the presidency would forever elude him. He croaked an anxious query for George's safety.

"He continues to lead a charmed life," Caroline said.

Senator Edward Hannegan of Indiana had the floor. "I ask you, gentlemen, how much more must we endure from Mexico?" he shouted. "It is a country without a government, without laws, without morality. Remove the firm hand of the United States and she will lapse into anarchy when our victorious troops march home. There is no question in my mind that the president must revise his peace terms. They are much too generous. Moreover, he has placed the negotiations in the hands of a man who is either a scoundrel or a fool. We have a man on the scene who is perfectly capable of taking charge of these negotiations: General George Stapleton. A man who has seen firsthand the treacherous amoral conduct of the Mexican army and government. Who knows what must be done to rescue this people from barbarism."

That was more like it. Caroline scribbled a note and handed it to a page. *What a marvelous speech! Please come to my reception tonight.* The senator had been one of the ultras on Oregon. He had wanted everything up to the border of Russian Alaska. It was easy to convert him into a fervent proponent of conquest in the opposite direction. Everyone in Indiana seemed to want to go elsewhere. The pioneer spirit was in their bones.

Senator Jeremy Biddle of New Jersey rose to answer Hannegan. With a fervor worthy of a Methodist camp meeting, he denounced the idea of conquering all of Mexico. He said it would destroy America as a moral force in the modern world. We would become as venal, as corrupt, as the English and the French, and as tyrannical as the Russians. No one paid much attention to him. The demolition Caroline and her hired character assassin, John L. O'Sullivan, had wreaked on Senator Biddle during the 1844 presidential campaign had reduced him to a political cipher.

Although a reply was superfluous, Senator Sladen of Louisiana could not resist answering his former friend. "We have now heard from a man—and from a mouse. Forgive me for departing from the traditional courtesy the

Senate expects of its members. But the issue is too important to the future of our country to mince words."

Jeremy's desk was only a few feet from Caroline's couch. She felt his eyes on her as she walked past him to the door. She did not bother to notice him. Outside the Capitol, Caroline searched for her carriage. As usual, the new coachman, Judson Diggs, was nowhere to be found. He was a big-bellied lout whom George had hired at Hannibal's recommendation. She finally located Judson shooting craps with several hackmen on the west side of the Capitol. "If I have to walk around the block to find you once more, you're fired," she said.

Judson babbled apologies. He combined all the worst characteristics of the blacks—low cunning and a groveling subservience. Hannibal had recommended him because he was a churchgoer. Like his idol, Senator Stapleton, Hannibal was no judge of character.

"The White House," Caroline said. Waves of humidity shimmered in the blazing noon sun as the open carriage jolted down Pennsylvania Avenue. Judson Diggs continued to apologize. "Shut up," Caroline said.

In fifteen minutes, she was in the private dining room, telling Sarah and James Polk what she had heard in the Capitol. Sarah had the drapes drawn against the sun, trying to keep some of the night's coolness inside the mansion. The dimness gave them both, especially the president, a spectral quality, as if they were dead and merely going through the motions of life in some sort of netherworld.

The president became visibly agitated when she described Senator Hannegan's attack on Nicholas P. Trist, the diplomat he had sent to Mexico to negotiate peace. "Tell me, either of you brilliant intellects, what I am supposed to do with this man? He was selected by the secretary of state as trustworthy and reliable. He's no sooner on the boat than the *New York Herald* prints a full account of his secret instructions. Now I learn he's fallen to feuding with Winfield Scott, who's threatening to resign because of Trist's claims to being his superior."

Caroline let Sarah answer the president. "I think you should get a new secretary of state. There's the traitor in your household. Buchanan leaked those instructions. Or looked the other way while someone else leaked them."

"I can't dismiss him. It would ruin us in Pennsylvania."

"You said that before last fall's elections. What did he do for us in his home state? The Whigs trounced us," Sarah said. "That's where we lost control of the House. We knew Van Buren and his soreheads would sit on their hands in New York."

"Congressman Wilmot is from Pennsylvania," Caroline said. "I don't think it was an accident that his resolution is a first cousin to Mr. Buchanan's ideas about seeking no territory from the war."

"Buchanan has assured me he had nothing to do with Wilmot's proviso," Polk said. "David Wilmot is just a greedy fool who wants me to give his district half the patronage in Pennsylvania. He's one of those Democrats who doesn't give a damn about his party."

Caroline averted her eyes. It was too painful to see the president clinging

to men like Buchanan, who leaked contemptuous stories about him to reporters. The secretary of state was using the war to make sure Polk served
only one term.

"Unless we hold on to what we've got left in Pennsylvania, the Democratic
Party is—"

A fit of coughing shook the president's frame so violently, the dishes rattled
on the table. His skin had acquired a brownish hue. His eyes seemed to have
receded into deep sockets of woe. He constantly moistened his dry lips with
his tongue. More and more, Caroline began to feel she and Sarah were in a
race with time—perhaps with time's grim coadjutor, death. James Polk's
stomach and bowel disorders had returned to torment him as his exhaustion
grew. Bouts of indigestion and diarrhea reduced him to a semi-invalid.

Only victory in Mexico could rescue this beleaguered man, a victory of
extraordinary dimensions, beyond the original vision of the war that he had
inherited from Andrew Jackson. The conquest and occupation of all of Mexico would become James Knox Polk's physical as well as his political salvation. It would restore confidence to his soul and vigor to his body. No longer
would fear and doubt ravage his intestines.

The president did not know this yet. Not with the growing certainty that
held Caroline and Sarah on course. In the president's view, the war was still
tormented by evil spirits. Nothing seemed to go right. After General Taylor
won his bloody and unnecessary battle at Buena Vista in February 1847, he
had screamed for more men. The president rushed him thousands of troops,
which he had originally intended to send to General Scott's army.

That towering egotist, after winning a tremendous victory at Cerro Gordo,
seemed poised to conquer the rest of Mexico within a week. Then he discovered that his volunteers wanted to go home when their twelve-month enlist-
ments expired in May. Patriotic oratory from Scott, from George Stapleton,
and from other generals was ignored. They went home and left the army
stranded in the heart of Mexico, with less than five thousand men. The frantic
president had to persuade a carping Congress to vote money for another ten
thousand men while Scott sat in Puebla, seventy-five miles from Mexico City,
threatening to resign because Polk was not supporting him, a threat he was
now renewing over his quarrel with Nicholas Trist.

In spite of this turmoil, the ultimate goal was far from lost. The Democrats
still controlled the Senate, where the peace treaty would be approved when
the Mexicans finally surrendered. The longer they prolonged the war, the
more they were arousing the same anger and grim resolve in the president
that they had already stirred in George Stapleton.

Picking up Caroline's thoughts, a habit that had grown more frequent and
uncanny over the last several months, Sarah Polk said, "The more I think of
the way things are going, the more I suspect you should revise your peace
terms. Mexico is so chaotic, we may find ourselves dealing with a new government, repudiating a treaty, six months after we sign it. Perhaps it might
be better for both countries if we simply annexed Mexico for the next twenty
or thirty years, brought order out of chaos, created a genuine republic."

"From everything I hear and read in the papers, the All Mexico movement
is growing by leaps and bounds among the voters," Caroline said. "It's es-

pecially appealing to Democrats as a perfect answer to the No Territory Whigs."

A large percentage of the Whig Party, seeking to placate the abolitionists, had taken up this cry. They were ready to accept Texas and a boundary on the Rio Grande. But they piously declaimed that the United States should forswear all interest in California and New Mexico, to prove that the war was not being fought to extend slavery.

"It's a very good answer," Sarah said. "It not only trumps them, it raises them right out of the game."

"Americans like a bold approach," Caroline said.

"It would also be a perfect way of satisfying the Oregon ultras," Sarah said. "Instead of giving them a thousand miles of frozen wilderness, you'd be offering them a country that's enormously prosperous—if it was properly governed."

"I can't dismiss Trist until he makes a serious blunder," the president said. "As long as he's in Mexico with my instructions—"

"Your instructions can be overtaken by events," Sarah said. "Especially since the whole country knows them and has been debating them. Half the Democrats say they're too generous, the Whigs say they're mendacious. What better way to resolve the argument than with a new negotiator, a new departure?"

"Who's the new negotiator?" Polk said.

"George Stapleton," Sarah said. "He's devoted to you personally. From the letters Caroline has shown me, I think he'd support a much stronger approach."

"But I've got obligations to all the volunteer generals. Gideon Pillow, Butler, they'll be infuriated if I give George the privilege of ending the war."

"James, I hate to sound critical," Sarah said, "but isn't it time to admit you can't please people with patronage? How many dozens of hours have you wasted trying to decide who should get a job—and when you decided, what did you accomplish? You made one dubious friend—and twenty offended enemies."

"I must abstain from this argument," Caroline said. "But let me say this much. Whether you appoint George or Senator Benton or some other prominent Democrat, you'd be asserting your leadership of the war, and the country. That's all I care about, Mr. President. Seeing you win the recognition you deserve."

A hall clock bonged 4 P.M. "I'm giving a reception tonight. I must go." Caroline hurried downstairs and along the cavernous central corridor of the White House, thinking, A good day's work. And the night is yet to come. She would make Senator Hannegan her guest of honor tonight. It was a device that years of experience as a hostess enabled her to use subtly, so that no one's ego was irritated. Very important in Washington, where so many egos were large and sensitive. The senator would hold forth on All Mexico in surroundings that added luster to his rustic appearance. Reporters would challenge him, John Quincy Adams would denounce him, and Daniel Webster, who loathed Old Man Eloquent, would confide to her that All Mexico was not a bad idea in his private opinion. His son was fighting in Mexico with a volunteer regiment, and his letters reflected the iron that was growing in the army's soul.

At home she found Senator John Sladen of Louisiana waiting for her. She told him what she had just seen and heard at the White House. "You're marvelous," he said.

"I'm beginning to think you're right. But you deserve as much credit for Senator Hannegan's speech."

"I thought it was better for him to give it. I wrote it for him."

"All we need now is a blunder by Trist."

"He'll make it. He's a perfect idiot. That's why Buchanan picked him for the job. He wants to make the president look like a fool. Then he'll go to Mexico and negotiate a peace of reconciliation. He'll renounce either New Mexico or California—maybe both—and run for president as Saint James the Good, picking up Whig votes in all directions. Poor Polk will be reduced to a spectator."

"Thank God we're a step ahead of him."

"Don't thank God. Thank me."

He was telling her that they alone in this oratorical city, where everyone competed to strike the right note of sanctimony and righteousness, were liberated from such mundane morality. He was also displaying the new sense of power he had acquired since rising to the Senate. Newspapers were calling him the Emperor of Louisiana. He had put together a political machine in New Orleans that more than equaled the power and corruption of New York's Tammany Hall.

She gazed calmly at him, understanding all this, and said, "Thank you." It was mockery. He did not like it.

"Has it occurred to you that there might come a time when grateful words are inadequate?"

"John, I thought we understood each other."

"When are you going to admit that the head has very little influence on the heart, that ultimately the intellect has no control over what's beating in the blood?"

"It beats in my blood sometimes too, but we both have obligations, obligations to history—"

"Damn history."

"You don't mean that, John."

"I do. I mean it absolutely. But I also know you're right. We do have obligations. But when they're fulfilled . . ."

"Then let us see what understanding tells us."

It was cruel, it was devious. She was lying to him, pretending that it was loyalty to George that lay behind her refusal. When it was love—the undefiled love that pulsed between her and Sarah Childress Polk.

S I X

"YOU MARCH TOMORROW?" MARIA DE VEGA said. She already knew the answer.

"Yes," Major General Stapleton said. For his distinguished services at Cerro Gordo, he had been promoted by President Polk with the enthusiastic approval of General Scott.

"You must come to me tonight."

"I can't take advantage—"

She walked toward him with that sinuous, swinging stride, her dark eyes full of anger. "Don't you have ears, General? If you're killed without ever holding me in your arms, I'll be left without the slightest consolation. I'll have no choice but to join you in the shadows." She kissed him softly on the mouth. "You're too good. It's your great flaw."

Never had George known such desire. Had he wanted Caroline this way, twenty years ago? No, that had been a compound of awe and the raw hunger of youth. He could not remember anything that approached the sweet searing exaltation of these weeks of longing for this woman.

"Is it my honor you fear to blemish?" she said. "You read what my father said about me. He had no daughter named Maria. He said you had me confused with a slut who had run off with a mestizo named Vega." She pressed her head against his chest. He breathed the flowery perfume of her hair. "Is it your reputation that worries you? Didn't you tell me last week the whole army assumes we're lovers?"

"We are. But I'm still a married man."

"That man is Senator Stapleton, the politician Caroline Kemble Stapleton created. The man I love is General Stapleton, who loves me—and Mexico."

In a great aching void, George heard himself say, "All that is true, but . . . ."

They were on the shaded rear terrace of the house George had rented for Maria de Vega in Puebla. It was in the hilly outskirts of this beautiful city of seventy-five thousand people. In the near distance loomed the mountains that rimmed the Valley of Mexico. Tomorrow they would march through their passes and descend into the fabled heart of this afflicted nation, in the footsteps of Cortés. George and many other officers had already ridden up there to ponder the maze of causeways and lakes, with Montezuma's great city in the distance.

Winfield Scott had finally received the reinforcements he needed to resume his advance on the capital. For two months the Americans had occupied Puebla with their tiny army of five thousand men. Not a single Mexican had attacked them. Everyone from Lieutenant Sam Grant to General Winfield

Scott had expressed amazement. Only General Stapleton understood what was happening. Thanks to this extraordinary woman, George knew more about this tormented country than anyone else in the army.

For twenty-five years, since Mexico won independence from Spain in 1821, she had experienced nothing but anarchy and revolution. The nation was split into irreconcilable factions, some longing for rapprochement with Spain, others for a king who would create a local version of the ancien régime, others for a radical break with the past that would shatter the grip of the Catholic Church on the hearts and minds of the nation. As a young girl Maria had become a passionate member of this faction, called the Puros. They admired the United States, its secular constitution, its federal system.

But the real arbiter of Mexico's destiny was the army. Without the generals' backing, no one could rule Mexico. That was one of the reasons why she had fallen in love with Arturo de Vega, a man she described as the only general in the Mexican army who was capable of having two consecutive thoughts. Her conservative father had disowned her. She had turned her back on him, on her family, their wealth, and had lived and plotted with Vega to place the Puros in power.

It was all too clear why his death left her bereft. George had struggled to restore hope, even reconciliation, to her life. He had written to her father, explaining her situation, and had received a crushing reply. Such severity was beyond his understanding. What else could he do but offer his companionship, his readiness to learn more about Mexico, as a temporary substitute for hope? He had rented this house, hired a cook, assured her of his devotion. Soon they were taking long horseback rides into the countryside. In the evening on the rear terrace, she sang the haunting melodies of Spain to him and one or two other guests, accompanying herself on a guitar. Alone, she taught him to read Calderón de la Barca and other Spanish poets—above all, Mexico's favorite, Sor Juana.

This extraordinary woman was a Mary Wollstonecraft two hundred years ahead of her time. Beautiful, immensely talented, she had violently resented the low opinion of women that prevailed in Old and New Spain. Rather than marry, she retreated to a convent, where she spent her life composing some of the angriest most erotic love poetry ever written.

> *Hombres necios que acusais*
> *a la mujer sin razón*
> *sin ver que sois la ocasión*
> *de lo mismo que culpas.*

> Ah, stupid men, unreasonable
> In blaming woman's nature
> Oblivious that your acts incite
> The very faults you censure.

> *Cual mayor culpa ha tenido*
> *en una pasión errada.*

Who has the greater sin
When burned by the same lawless fever?

There were days when General Stapleton thought he would go insane if
he did not take this woman in his arms. But wouldn't this convince her all
over again that there was no hope? Only when Gideon Pillow started making
wry remarks, and George saw the knowing smiles in all the other eyes at
General Scott's table, did he realize that everyone assumed he had acquired a
mistress as well as a Spanish teacher.

No one disapproved. Scott said he wished he were twenty-five years
younger. White-bearded General Twiggs heartily seconded that motion. Wise-
cracks about several colonels made it clear that General Stapleton was not
alone in appreciating the senoritas of Puebla. When he tried to protest his
innocence, General Pillow laughed in his face and called him a lousy actor.

Now this—the realization that she had been waiting for him to speak. She
loved him and was telling him that his death—a very real possibility in the
Valley of Mexico—would be the absolute end of hope.

"If you don't come, I'll consider you devoid of courage! A real man never
hesitates to sin for love!"

"What if you have a child?"

"When I was in Yucatán the medicine men of the Mayas gave me herbs
that prevent conception. I've vowed never to bear a child until Mexico is truly
free. Vega and I made love almost every night for five years."

"Can you believe I love you so much—I can't touch you? I want your
reputation to be spotless when we get to Mexico City. So you can speak out
for Mexico, in your husband's name."

She shoved him away with a cry of despair. "Don't you listen to anything
I say, General? No Mexican will listen to a woman without a man at her side.
Didn't I tell you Vega was part Indian? I disgraced my Spanish blood the
moment I let a mestizo into my bed."

Why not now? whispered a voice in George's head. Why not take her in
the bedroom just off this terrace, with flowered curtains rustling in the warm
summer wind. Why wait until tonight? But some nameless force in his head
or his heart paralyzed him. "I'll come tonight. We'll have dinner."

"Come alone. Without a friend to guard you."

Outside his house on the central plaza of Puebla, George encountered President Polk's diplomatic representative, Nicholas Trist. Unkempt as always—
he looked as if he slept in his clothes—with a cheroot in his languid hand,
Trist greeted George with considerable fervor. Part of the reason was probably
General Stapleton's friendship with the president; but Trist also seemed to feel
that George's benevolence toward Maria de Vega suggested he shared with
Trist a sympathy for Mexico—something few officers in the army felt.

"General, I hear you're marching tomorrow. I urged General Scott to give
me another week of negotiations. The British consul in Mexico City, my in-
termediary, as you know, swears we are making progress, even if it is at a
tortoise pace. I fear another harvest of death will exasperate both sides and

turn this war into a permanent state of hostilities. If we destroy the government's reputation, Mexico will collapse into utter anarchy, giving ultras on both sides an excuse to reject any and all accommodations. We could be fighting here for another fifty years. How is your delightful wife? Have you heard from her lately? I'm sure her letters brim with social news. There isn't a scandal in Washington that doesn't dilate through her parlor. My wife says she's the equal of Dolley Madison in her prime."

Trist was a verbal spigot. Once he turned himself on, it was almost impossible to turn him off. "I haven't had much news from Washington lately," George said. "Caroline's spending the summer in New Jersey."

"Ah, mending a few political fences, no doubt. If only I could have persuaded my wife to take an interest in politics, I might be something more than the secretary of state's house slave. But her education at Monticello had amounted to imbibing an absolute detestation for the business. She made me swear I would never run for public office, before she consented to marry me. I thought I could talk her out of it but soon found otherwise."

Trist's wife was a granddaughter of Thomas Jefferson's. Trist had served as the great man's secretary in the closing years of his life. He seldom missed a chance to remind listeners of that fact. It explained to some extent the sudden grandiosity into which he could puff himself—presuming to tell Scott when he should and shouldn't advance, for instance.

"Only time will tell which of us is luckier. Mrs. Stapleton would divorce me in ten seconds if I quit politics."

"I agree with her wholeheartedly, General. You must never even consider it. The Democratic Party needs men like you—with links to the founders. Everywhere I look in my native state, I see a cheapening of our old values. The further south I go, the more I'm appalled by the savagery with which they espouse a permanent state of slavery for the Africans. They don't seem to see how they're playing into the hands of the abolitionists. Don't you agree?"

"I hope President Polk's tariff may temper the wrath of many Southern gentlemen."

"I wish I could believe it. But the slave question is acquiring a momentum of its own, infinitely uglier than the blusterings over the tariff. That quarrel only aroused the upper classes. The slave involves everyone, high and low."

"All this is very fascinating, Mr. Trist. But I must pack. We're marching at dawn."

Trist wandered off across the square in his languid way. Inside the house, George found Hannibal packing his clothes in a small leather trunk. His Colt pistol, oiled and gleaming, hung in a holster on a nearby chair. Hannibal's brow was creased with concern. "Don't much like this march tomorrow, General. We sit here for two months, givin' the Mexicans time to build all sorts of damn forts and barricades."

"I know."

"Lot more men goin' to die before we get to that Mexico City."

"I know."

"All we can do is ask the Lord to keep watchin' over us."

"That's your job, Hannibal."

He studied George for a long moment. "That woman's drivin' you crazy, ain't she, General."

"Pretty close to it."

"Been prayin' for you there too, General. She's got Jezebel and Delilah written all over her. She aims to take you prisoner, General."

"Maybe she does, for her country's sake. She loves her country, Hannibal. Just as much as we love ours."

Hannibal said nothing. It occurred to George that the big black had no reason to love the United States of America. His loyalty was to George Stapleton, the man who had freed him. He could not love a country that kept so many of his people in bondage.

Was there some truth in what Hannibal said about Maria? Maybe she wanted him to be her spokesman when they defeated Santa Anna and entered Mexico City. She wanted him to project her influence in the political vacuum that was almost certain to ensue after Santa Anna fled or finally kept his repeatedly broken promise to die in the ranks with his men.

"Some mail from home, General."

Hannibal handed George two letters. One was from Caroline. The other was from Senator Jeremy Biddle. George and Jeremy had had very little to say to each other since Polk took office and the war began. Under his wife's influence, Jeremy was veering more and more toward abolitionism. It saddened George to think that politics could sour a friendship as close as theirs had once been.

George opened Caroline's letter first. It was thick with newspaper clippings.

Dear George,

> *The political news is all bad. The President is being treated with contempt by everyone, Democrats and Whigs. The war is execrated in New England. It isn't much more popular in New York or New Jersey. Everything depends on your capturing Mexico City soon and dictating a Draconian peace. What do I mean by that? The enclosed clippings will explain it. More and more, the movement to conquer and absorb all of Mexico is gaining momentum in the Democratic Party. It is the only thing that will rescue the President and the party from political oblivion. John Sladen is conducting a masterful campaign in the Senate to make this acceptable to the Democratic majority. Although Calhoun opposes it, John is ready to displace his idol and take charge of the Southern delegation. They're ready to rally around him to a man— because they see it's the South's salvation.*

> *The President is very close to appointing you his chief negotiator, replacing this idiot Nicholas Trist. Are you aware that in one of the preliminary exchanges, he offered terms that left the Texas boundary on the Nueces River? He's playing Buchanan's game; like the old woman he is, Buck thinks the next president will have to be a peace-mongering mollycoddle. He's wrong. The American people want a conqueror. That can be you—the man who fought his way to Mexico City*

and then imposed a peace that will last fifty years, a peace that will pour hundreds of millions into our pockets and make us a world power, with an army that even perfidious Albion will respect. If all goes well, the president will be sending you your instructions in a fortnight. He still has some doubts about this course, but I'm sure they will be resolved shortly. The boys send their love and admiration—as do I.

> *As ever,*
> *Caroline*

Stunning, staggering news. He would have to find out if Trist really did something as stupid as offer to give back a quarter of Texas. He glanced through the clippings, quickly absorbing the basic arguments. They made sense—especially if the Mexicans forced them to fight their way into Mexico City. Another long casualty list would inevitably harden almost every American heart against Mexico.

What would Maria de Vega think of such a peace? Would her admiration for the United States persist when an American viceroy ruled the nation—and the U.S. Army enforced his decrees from Monterrey to Yucatán? Somehow he doubted it. Mournfully, George realized that this letter made it impossible for him to go to her tonight. If he was to become the man who conquered Mexico, he would have to do it as Caroline Kemble Stapleton's husband.

He scribbled a note: *My dearest: General Scott has called a council of war which will probably last until midnight, at least. Perhaps it is better to say good-bye this way, without false pretenses. God willing, I'll see you in Mexico City.*

"Take this to Madame de Vega," he said, handing it to Hannibal.

Now what did pompous old Jeremy Biddle have to say? George tore open the envelope. It too was stuffed with newspaper clippings—almost all of them the same ones Caroline had enclosed, trumpeting the importance of taking and holding all of Mexico.

Dear George,

I write this letter in an agony of trepidation. I have written a dozen versions of it and torn them up. But the love of our country—a love we both share—forces me to try again. You see in the enclosed clippings the creation of a monstrous conspiracy to make Mexico a conquered province. It is a conspiracy that is being conducted by two persons, who have become in my opinion the most malevolent spirits ever to intrude their hellish designs into American politics. The persons are your wife, Caroline, and her lover, John Sladen. Yes, lover. I have not used the word arbitrarily. But I use it with enormous regret. For the past twenty years, I have withheld from you a secret that must now be told. A month before your marriage to Caroline, I found her in flagrante delicto in the basement of Mrs. Burch's brothel with Johnny Sladen. I pounded him into jelly, took her home, and made her vow

*never to see him again. I gave the scum $100 and sent him to New
Orleans. I told you nothing. I did this in the name of our friendship—I
swear it. I acted with a brother's love. But an evil fate reunited them
in Washington, D.C. They may not have become lovers immediately.
But slowly, I am convinced, Sladen gained ascendancy over her and
converted her to his vile scheme to make the South a nation within the
nation. Mexico has always been the centerpiece of this purple dream.
That they are lovers now, as they move toward triumph, I have no
doubt. A private detective I have hired to follow Sladen reports he is
in your house daily, at all hours of the day and night. Through Caroline's almost unnatural friendship with Sarah Polk, they've reduced the
President to a pathetic puppet. You and you alone can prevent them
from winning this evil victory, which will destroy our Union as certainly
as the dark banner of slavery under which it operates.*

*Someday I hope you can forgive me for this. I know it will be im-
possible for many years. Perhaps forever.*

Adieu old friend,
Jeremy

When Hannibal returned from Maria de Vega's house, it was almost dark.
He found George Stapleton sitting in the shadows with Jeremy's letter in his
hand.

"General," he said, lighting an oil lamp, "don't you need some light to
read that?"

"I've read it."

"Good news, I hope?"

"In a way." George heaved himself to his feet.

"You want some supper, General?"

"No. I'm going out."

"Where'll you be, General? In case General Scott wants you for some last-
minute 'mergency meetin'?"

"I'll be at Madame de Vega's house."

SEVEN

IN THE WHITE HOUSE'S MAIN DINING room, Caroline Stapleton sat
at the splendidly appointed dinner table beside General James Corcoran of
Ohio. At the battle of Buena Vista, General Corcoran had been shot in the
head and left for dead on the battlefield. An army doctor had operated on

him, extracting the bullet and saving his life. But General Corcoran was not the same cheerful, loquacious congressman who had gone to Mexico in search of military fame. He walked with a cane and spoke in slow, halting sentences, slurring his words.

Why had Sarah Polk sat her beside Corcoran? Was she trying to warn Caroline that she too might soon find out the bitter truth about the wages of fame? A month ago, they had been told that the American army was descending into the Valley of Mexico, where they were certain to meet the Mexican army again. Across the table, Senator John Sladen of Louisiana gazed hungrily at Caroline. She had made a statement of sorts by retreating to New Jersey for the summer. Only an urgent summons from Sarah Polk had persuaded her to return to Washington for this dinner.

At the head of the table sat President James Polk, looking, if possible, more ghastly than the last time Caroline had seen him. His skin had acquired a permanent shade of brown. His tongue darted ceaselessly around his cracked, bloodless lips. His hand trembled as he raised a water glass to his mouth. His wary eyes roved the oval table, as if he did not really believe in the friendship of his guests, all of whom were in the inner circle of his administration.

The attacks on him in the newspapers and in Congress had reached a new level of ferocity. Ironically, the rhetoric played into the hands of Senator Sladen and his All Mexico campaign. The infuriated Democrats had begun to rally around the president, giving him a semblance of authority. As Senator Thomas Hart Benton said to Caroline at her last salon of the season, "Polk may be a poor thing. But he's our own."

The president was on his feet, a water glass in his hand. "I would like to propose a toast to a hero in our midst. To General James Corcoran, who went to Mexico as a volunteer, not in search of glory, but from a desire to serve our beloved country. This morning, I promoted him to major general. With such men as him, we shall soon conquer a true peace in Mexico."

That was the latest administration slogan, coined by Polk's burly, beetle-browed secretary of war, William Marcy. The United States was in Mexico to conquer a peace. It bespoke the spread of the grim opinion that winning battles was not the answer to peace with Mexico. The Americans had defeated the Mexican army four times and still they refused to negotiate. Santa Anna, with his peg leg and sonorous duplicities, was still in command of the army and the nation.

General Corcoran bowed his head as they drank the president's toast to his heroism. He struggled to his feet with the aid of his cane and responded, wrenching the words from his throat in a series of painful spasms. "Let me respond . . . with a toast to an absent hero . . . the man who saved my life . . . at Buena Vista . . . my friend . . . General George Stapleton. On the chance . . . that I might be . . . alive . . . he risked a thousand Mexican bullets . . . to drag me to safety. It is . . . a privilege to . . . be seated . . . beside . . . his beautiful . . . wife."

"To General Stapleton." The rest of the table saluted George.

"We may soon have more important responsibilities for General Stapleton," growled Secretary of War Marcy, who was sitting on the president's left. "I've urged the president to replace our lamentable chief diplomat, Mr. Trist, with a man who can put some steel in our peace terms."

"I . . . can't think . . . of a better man," General Corcoran said.

Caroline's eyes sought Sarah Polk's. She was sitting at the bottom of the table. They exchanged the silent understanding that had become more and more profound since the ordeal in the White House began. It was tinged with darkness now, but they still clasped hands in the shadows. For a moment, Caroline had to struggle against an impulse to weep.

Secretary of War Marcy began talking about the army's problems with Mexican guerrillas. They were shooting up American supply trains moving up from Vera Cruz and across the deserts from the Rio Grande to the army in northern Mexico. "I've given orders to take none of them prisoners. Any town that harbors them will be put to the torch. We've levied fines on the state of Neuvo León for the cost of every lost or stolen item."

"Mexico seems to be breaking up," the president said. "Yesterday we received a letter from the former mayors of Saltillo and Monterrey. They claim to be part of a movement to set up a separate nation in northern Mexico. They want us to make them a protectorate, to guarantee their independence. It wouldn't be difficult to do. We'll have to maintain an army on the Rio Grande at any event."

"Wouldn't it be far simpler, Mr. President, to make the whole benighted country a protectorate?" Senator Sladen said. "That seems to me the only way we can truly conquer a peace."

"You may have a point, Senator," the president said. "My wife has kept me in close touch with the newspaper campaign for this solution. But I'm not sure it has the approval of the American people."

"Speaking for the South," Sladen said, "I can produce ten thousand letters for you at the touch of a telegraph key. Every man of influence and position I know from Virginia to New Orleans favors it."

"Except John C. Calhoun," the president said.

"Except Mr. Calhoun," Senator Sladen said. "But he has become a party of one, Mr. President."

"I must confess I was a skeptic at first," Secretary of War Marcy said. "But my conversion seems to be approaching. My new faith veritably leaped in my soul when I learned that a certain former great man in New York violently opposes All Mexico. Since his ideas have invariably tended to the ruin of the Democratic Party, I think the law of opposites may prevail here and prove Senator Sladen's case."

Marcy was talking about Martin Van Buren, who was his bitterest political enemy in New York. With Marcy a convert, All Mexico stood a better than even chance to win the backing of the Empire State—especially when Marcy could dangle the thousands of jobs a Mexican protectorate would require. The man at the top of this unparalleled pyramid of patronage would be the American viceroy, General George Stapleton.

Caroline sipped her wine. It was coming together, the whole incredible fabric of empire, Aaron Burr's forfeited dream. Suddenly she was back twenty years in the shabby office off Broadway, sitting beside John Sladen listening to that small elegiac man explain the true meaning of fame. *Father* whispered in her deepest mind, prying open the old grave of grief. This had been his dream too—a dream of empire infinitely beyond the life of a hardscrabble farmer in Twin Forks, Ohio.

But where was the joy? Only irony, a gloating sardonic irony, glittered in Senator Sladen's red-veined eyes. In Sarah Polk's haunted eyes Caroline saw only the slow death of love, expiring day by toilsome day as James Knox Polk bent over his desk and wrote and read and read and wrote from dawn until midnight and beyond, wordlessly asking, *Is this enough? Will only my death prove I loved you?*

Suddenly that familiar, maddening whisper wound through Caroline's head: *Oh, my dear girl, I fear for thy salvation.* It was Hannah Cosway Stapleton speaking to her across the miles from Bowood's library. How had this dead Quaker saint gained access to her soul? It infuriated her every time she thought of it. How could words from a casual conversation almost a hundred years ago, words that had no reference to Caroline Kemble Stapleton's soul, acquire this outrageous meaning?

There were more toasts—to the army, to the navy, to General Winfield Scott, to the president's friend General Pillow, who had been wounded at Cerro Gordo. Defiantly, in a private drama that no one except she understood, Caroline stood up and raised her water glass. "I know women are not supposed to propose toasts. But I have never been a strong observer of all the rules of etiquette. I would like to propose a toast to the man whom history will credit with the conquest of Mexico and New Mexico and California— the man who has already won a harvest of fame worthy of comparison with Andrew Jackson and George Washington—President James Knox Polk."

"I'll second that motion," said Secretary of War Marcy.

"It's unanimous," Senator Sladen said.

A ghost of a smile played across the president's desiccated face. "How nice it is to dine with friends." Tears were on his brown cheeks. He wiped them away. "It will end well—I've always felt it will end well. We're all instruments in a divine plan—for this great country. I didn't seek this task. It sought me. In this house, you see the mysterious workings of destiny. So much becomes clear to you."

How right, how awesomely right he was, Caroline thought, her mind roving back across the last twenty years. So much that seemed pure chance had brought her to this moment in this history-laden house. Her original meeting with Sarah Polk, the visit to Andrew Jackson, the intricate skein of politics and passions, from headstrong Peggy Eaton and slimy slithering Martin Van Buren to John C. Calhoun's lethal mixture of rage and ambition to the death of President William Henry Harrison to the explosion that had catapulted Julia Gardiner into President Tyler's arms to Martin Van Buren's act of self-destruction over Texas—who would attempt to find method, mind, in such a maze? Yet she had guided George Stapleton through it to the doors of the Temple of Fame.

The dinner party was breaking up. General Corcoran was mumbling a final tortured compliment. Sarah walked beside Caroline to the South Portico. "Thank you for that lovely toast," Sarah said. "It will be a shield against tomorrow's newspapers."

"Will Trist be removed soon?"

"Very soon. Do you think George will undertake the task of negotiating a conquered peace?"

"I can guarantee it."

"It won't be a simple task—if things unfold as we suspect they will. George will have to operate without portfolio, so to speak. We're simply going to tell Trist to pack up and come home—and inform the Mexicans that any offers of peace will henceforth have to come from them and should be forwarded to General Scott. We'll instruct Scott to confer with George if, by some miracle, an offer materializes. Far more likely, the Mexican federal government will collapse and disappear. We'll occupy the whole country as our only alternative. Then George will resign from the army and we'll appoint him viceroy."

"I understand. I'll make sure he understands."

They were out on the portico now. The sultry air of Washington in late August engulfed them. The White House's thick walls had kept it at bay. Senator Sladen strolled over to them. "You two ladies look as if you're deciding the fate of the world."

"We are," Caroline said. "Which stirs your male disapproval, I'm sure."

"I've learned to conceal that emotion. The longer an American man lives, the more awe of American women undermines his soul."

He said this in such a weary voice, Caroline felt that old subverter, pity, stir in her blood. But she sternly barred it from her soul. "May I offer you a ride to your hotel, Senator?"

"On such a warm night, I would appreciate that greatly."

The Stapletons' vermilion coach, manned by Judson Diggs, who got fatter every time Caroline looked at him, rumbled to the portico. Caroline kissed Sarah and the president and allowed Senator Sladen to help her into the dark interior.

"So!" he said as they rolled through the gate.

"So," Caroline said.

"Is that all you have to say? Not a murmur of exultation? Not a word of praise?"

"Don't you have any feelings? Can't you see what this is doing to the president—and Sarah?"

"They're paying the price we all have to pay for large ambitions."

"How can you be so complacent?"

"Because I've paid my price. I've passed through my dark night of the soul—a hundred dark nights. Without giving up hope of my reward."

She knew what he was hoping she would say. The house on Pennsylvania Avenue was virtually empty. She had brought only Mercy and Tabitha Flowers with her. They would be sleeping soundly by now. She had left Paul in New Jersey to enjoy the last weeks of summer. Her son Jonathan was in New York arguing about negritude with his abolitionist friend Ben Dall. Charlie was in North Carolina chasing foxes and God knows what else with Southern friends.

But something remarkable and strange was occurring in Caroline Kemble Stapleton's soul. She was discovering the aberrant voice that might or might not belong to Hannah Cosway Stapleton had some meaning after all. She was learning that gratitude and admiration were ingredients in which love could slowly, painfully flower. All the stories she had read and heard about George's courage and competence in Mexico were working a transformation in her soul.

It was a black moonless night. John Sladen was a dark blur on the opposite side of the swaying coach. The sultry air swirled sluggishly through the open windows. It was the perfect place to speak: they might have been in a boat, drifting down the underground river on which they had once embarked—and in their tormented imaginations had spent too much of the rest of their lives. It was time to speak to her fellow voyager in that frozen world—to speak as a traveler in the daylight world of time and chance, of spoken love, of pledged trust, of truth beyond poetry.

"John, the love I once felt for you was real. But like all living things, it's been subject to decay, decline, death. Another man has been in my life, in my arms, for the past twenty years. His generosity, his fidelity, his tenderness, his sense of honor, his modesty, have been visible, ever more visible, to me throughout these years. In response to my ambition, he's risking General Corcoran's fate, or worse, in Mexico at this very moment. It's time for me to tell you that I love him—and I no longer love you."

"There's no gratitude, no admiration, no sympathy—for me?"

"There's a river of it. Only I know what you've sacrificed. You've thrown away Clothilde's love, ignored your children. Only you know what I've sacrificed. My sons dislike me. Other women hate me. I may even have lost George's love—as Sarah's lost James Polk's love. We can't help that hunger. Life, fate, inflicted it on us. But we can make choices, we can still refuse to do certain things that would damn us in this world, no matter what we believe about the next one."

"You're talking idiocy! You can't love one thing without the other. I was with you—you were with me—when Aaron Burr implanted the hunger in our souls. You knew as well as I did that he was speaking in the name of our dead fathers—calling on us to defy the idiocies of conventional morality once and for all. You're succumbing to the ultimate American temptation: you want to be good—and powerful. You'll find out it isn't possible. It will never be possible."

"I'm not talking about goodness, John. I'm talking about love. I can't betray my love for George Stapleton. I'll have to live with that reality, somehow. So will you."

Was she telling the truth? Or was this confession a way of protecting her love for that tormented woman in the White House? At this point in her life, Caroline Kemble Stapleton herself could not be sure. There was no conflict between the two loves. The conflict was between them—and the subterranean love she had once felt for this man.

"Ma'am?" Judson Diggs knocked on the coach door.

"Yes?"

"We's here, ma'am. Been here for a while."

In the darkness loomed the outline of 3600 Pennsylvania Avenue. Diggs had brought Caroline home first. Gadsby's Hotel was another mile from the White House.

Caroline thought of that long-ago journey to Miss Carter's Female Seminary, the way Messrs. Sladen and Biddle and Stapleton had neglected to notice their arrival. "I'm not ashamed of what we did so long ago," she said. "It was a kind of love that I won't forget. But now I'm speaking for a different kind of love. Accept it, John."

"What about Mexico?"

"It should have nothing to do with this."

He kissed her on the mouth for a long bitter moment. She gently extricated herself, without reproaching him.

"Good night," she said.

In the parlor, scene of her triumphs as a hostess, Caroline Kemble Stapleton sat in the darkness, weeping silently. As the tears poured down her cheeks, she twisted Hannah Stapleton's wedding ring on the fourth finger of her left hand. Twisted and twisted and twisted it, as if she wanted to tear it off. But she knew that would be a meaningless gesture now.

EIGHT

IN THE GLOOMY HALF-LIGHT OF A September dawn, Major General George Stapleton led twenty-five hundred men toward a collection of adobe buildings known as the Molino del Rey—the King's Mill. Beside him, Hannibal Flowers muttered, "Don't like the looks of this place, General. I smells trouble here."

General Stapleton paid no attention to Hannibal. He was indifferent to the possibility of sudden death erupting from the roofs and windows of the Molino. He would almost welcome it. Did Hannibal suspect this?

Two weeks before, the American army had smashed another Mexican army at the battles of Contreras and Churubusco, within three miles of the gates of Mexico City. They could have captured the city on the same day. But General Santa Anna had once more played on the American desire for peace by proposing another armistice for further negotiations.

The chief American diplomat, Nicholas P. Trist, had proven himself a total idiot by presenting the Mexicans with the full text of the proposed treaty of peace, giving away his whole hand. Compared to the All Mexico campaign that was being waged by John Sladen and his fellow Southern Democrats, the terms were mild. The Americans were prepared to settle for a Texas boundary on the Rio Grande and the acquisition of New Mexico and California, which Mexico had not a prayer of regaining. Shaving Polk's original offer to reflect the costs of the war, Trist proposed to pay $15 million for New Mexico and California—a sum that would restore order to Mexico's chaotic finances.

It was a generous treaty, considering that Mexico had not won a single battle. But the Mexicans had spent the next two weeks picking holes in the American proposal, while Santa Anna scraped together troops for another battle. The negotiations had collapsed when the Mexicans revealed that their congress had declared anyone who agreed to peace with the United States would be guilty of treason and would be promptly executed.

General Stapleton had distinguished himself at Contreras, leading a charge that swept seven thousand Mexicans out of their entrenched position in seventeen minutes. Reporters were calling him the *beau sabreur* of the American army. General Scott praised him in his dispatches, declaring he had seldom seen an officer display such reckless daring. Neither General Scott nor the reporters had any idea why General Stapleton was so ready to risk his life.

Awaiting him in the nearby village of Tacubaya, where Trist had fecklessly negotiated with the Mexican peace commissioners, was Maria de Vega. They had become lovers on their last night in Puebla. But the general did not tell her why he accepted the gift of her body. His presumed love amounted to a kind of betrayal—his mind, as he enjoyed her, was clotted with only one scarifying thought: revenge. Every thrust, every kiss, was flung in Caroline Kemble Stapleton's imagined face. He saw himself, a Hercules of rage, describing the night to her in exquisite detail.

In the morning, as he rode out of Puebla toward Mexico City with Maria beside him, her lovely face aglow with adoration, he had been appalled by what he had done. He could never explain it to her. He could only continue the charade, telling himself it was necessary now, because when they reached Mexico City, Maria's powerful family might consider her redeemed if she brought a man who was determined to rescue her country from humiliation. But that idea clashed with his own and his fellow Americans' mounting disgust with the dishonorable way the Mexicans were fighting the war. Ultimately even the idea of exquisite revenge foundered on the prospect of divorcing Caroline for adultery and inflicting public disgrace on the Stapleton family and his sons.

In this psychological trap of his own and Jeremy Biddle's devising, death in battle seemed by far the simplest choice for General Stapleton. He had sought it at Contreras. With the irony that the god of history seemed to prefer, he had found glory instead. Maybe the Molino would produce death for him, but he doubted it. They were occupying it to make sure the Mexicans did not seize it to disrupt the assault on the final obstacle between them and Mexico City—the frowning Aztec castle of Chapultepec, which overlooked the main causeway to the capital. The Molino was a quarter of a mile from this fortress, which Santa Anna had crammed with men and cannon for a last-ditch defense.

"Forward the storming party," George said, springing from his horse and drawing his sword. He handed the reins to Hannibal; he had forbidden the big black from following him into the cannon's mouth. There was no reason for him to die, further compounding the ironies of General Stapleton's dreams of glory.

The storming party, five hundred picked men from the regular army's regiments, trotted to the head of the column. The rest of the division peeled off to the left and right, to take up their assigned positions. General Stapleton strode to the head of the storming party. Before them in the gloom, the Molino squatted, silent and seemingly empty.

To the left of the storming party was a battery of six-pounders commanded by a Kentucky-born West Pointer, Captain Robert Anderson. General Stapleton pointed to the Molino's thick wooden gate and said, "Open that for us, Captain."

Anderson's guns boomed. Pieces of wood flew from the gate. "Forward, men," George shouted, and led the storming party on the run. They had covered about half the distance to the gate, which Anderson continued to blast with his guns, when flame erupted from the windows and rooftops of the Molino. Thousands of bullets hissed into and around the storming party. Suddenly the rooftops of the Molino were swarming with Mexicans. From one window a cannon boomed, hurling hundreds of murderous pieces of grapeshot into the ranks.

A terrible groan swept through the storming party. Their line wavered as they stumbled over the bodies of their friends. George turned to call for reinforcements, and something—a bullet or a grapeshot—struck him in the head. He swayed, his sword slipped from his hand, and he toppled to the ground. The storming party turned and fled, leaving at least two hundred men, including General Stapleton, stretched on the brown earth.

With a shout of triumph at least a hundred Mexicans rushed from a doorway not far from the main gate and began stabbing and shooting the Americans who were still alive. This habit of executing the wounded was one of the enemy's least admirable habits. Through a haze of blood, General Stapleton groped for his sword. He wanted to die fighting these bastards.

Shots, groans, cries, swirled around George as the Mexicans continued their slaughter. A blast from Robert Anderson's cannon sent a dozen of them whirling to the earth in agony. As they hesitated, a figure loomed over General Stapleton. It was Hannibal Flowers. Swinging a musket like a club, he demolished a half dozen Mexicans near them. Anderson held his fire while the big black slung George over his shoulder and staggered out of the battle with him.

As Hannibal lowered George to the ground behind Captain Anderson's battery, the rest of the division, recovering from the shock of the surprise attack, rushed forward with a shout of rage to avenge the ambushed storming party. "That's some nigger you got there, General," one of Anderson's gun crew said. "No white man'd gone out there alone against them crazy Mexicans. He figured out the whole thing—got the captain to hold his fire—"

The battery thundered. The gunner rammed home another charge. "One smart nigger," he shouted above the chaos of the erupting battle.

Hannibal asked Captain Anderson to guard General Stapleton while he found a surgeon. George lay propped against a tree, wondering if he was dying, while Anderson's guns continued to crash and the artillerymen shouted news of the battle.

"They're goin' over the walls, General! We'll even the score for you, depend on it. Not one of them little slimy bastards is gonna get out of that place alive!"

"General, so many officers are down," Captain Anderson said, "I'm going to lead a charge on the gate. We've blown a nice hole in it. My sergeant will take good care of you."

A surgeon was crouching beside George, wiping the blood from his eyes. "A nasty graze, General. You'll have a hell of a headache for the next two or three days. But you're not badly hurt."

George's head felt as if someone were shoving knitting needles through it. "I'll worry . . . about that . . . later. My place is with my men."

"You'd only be in the way, General. Let Hannibal here get you on your horse and—"

"Oh, God!"

It was Hannibal. He had been standing beside the surgeon. Bullets from the Molino were still hissing around them, but after a half dozen battles, soldiers got used to the sound. As the army saying went, you only had to worry about the bullet with your name on it. Hannibal's name had been on one of the last shots fired from the Molino del Rey.

The young surgeon turned him over and cut away his shirt to examine the wound. "The lung," he muttered. "He'll be gone before morning."

"Get him to the hospital!" George said.

They had to finish cleaning out the Molino first. It was ugly, brutal fighting; the Mexicans expected no mercy and they got none. Only after the final shots dwindled away did a lieutenant carrying the American flag appear on the roof and signal for the wagons to take the wounded to the hospital in Tacubaya.

George rode in a wagon with Hannibal and a dozen other badly wounded men. A bloody froth kept rising to Hannibal's lips. George wiped it away. Next to him, a man shot in the stomach kept asking George to kill him. The pain was unbearable.

In the hospital, a convent from which the nuns had been exiled, chaos reigned. A frantic surgeon told George there were over five hundred wounded. They had lost seven hundred men at Contreras and Churubusco two weeks ago. "Another victory like this and there won't be much of an army left," the doctor said.

The words clanged around George's skull like an avalanche of carving knives. "What can you do for my friend Hannibal? He saved my life."

The surgeon examined Hannibal's wound, a raw, bleeding gash in his back. A musket ball did terrible things when it struck flesh. "Nothing," the doctor said.

George went looking for Maria de Vega. He found her in Tacubaya's main square. She cried out when she saw his blood-caked forehead. He assured her that he would live and told her about Hannibal. With help from members of Captain Anderson's battery, they carried him to an empty house off the square. Most of Tacubaya's residents had fled to Mexico City.

The surgeon told Maria to give Hannibal a mixture of wine and opium for his pain and gave her a package of opium powder. She wanted George to take some of the potion too, but he refused it. He sat beside the bed as Hannibal drifted in and out of consciousness. At times he seemed to see someone in the shadows on the other side of the room.

"It's Tabitha. She's there waitin' for me, General. I can see her as good as

I see you. She's all in white. Her face is shinin'—she's as beautiful as she ever was."

"If there's one thing in my life I regret, it's her death, Hannibal."

"Wasn't your fault, General. It was God's way of leadin' me to Him. Makin' me ready to go home to her. If you never done nothin' else for me, General, bringin' me to New Jersey so I could meet Tabitha would've been enough."

"I want to do even more for you, Hannibal. For you and little Tabitha—and Mercy."

"You'll be good to 'em, General. I know you will. I got no worries about them. Maybe sometime if you get a chance, you could do even more good—for all the black people in America."

"I'll try, Hannibal. I promise you."

"Maybe you'll be president someday. Then you could do a lot."

The bloody froth was on Hannibal's lips; it gurgled in his throat. "We all . . . in God's hands . . . General. He's a good God . . . He heard my prayers . . . He led me to you . . . and Tabitha."

"I feel God in this room," Maria de Vega said. "There are angels all around us, waiting to take you to Jesus."

"I see them!" Hannibal said, raising himself in the bed. "They're all around Tabitha—smilin' at me."

He fell back on the pillow, drew one more long, shuddering breath, and died. Maria gently closed his eyes. Pain throbbed in George's skull. Maria wiped away his tears. "Now more than ever I know I'm in love with a good man," she said.

Five days later, the American army stormed Chapultepec and, on the same day, thundered down the causeways to the San Cosme and Belén Gates of Mexico City. Once more General Stapleton was in command of a division, leading his men in reckless charges that overwhelmed barricade after barricade until they were close enough to the San Cosme Gate to draw fire from its numerous defenders on the walls and in breastworks around it.

In the late afternoon, George found himself in a ditch beside the causeway with the first soldier he had met en route to Mexico, Lieutenant Ulysses Grant of the Fourth Infantry. Ahead of them were several dozen houses and a small church to the left of the gate. To attack down the causeway in the face of massed cannon and musketry was suicide. "If I had a howitzer," Grant said, "I could work my way around those houses, hoist it to the belfry of that church, and raise hell with those fellows behind that gate."

George scribbled an order and handed it to Grant. "The guns are about a half mile back."

Who should come scrambling into the ditch next but Colonel Jack Hays of the Texas Rangers. "How about using a leaf from our Monterrey book, General. Blast our way through them houses."

In the last day's fighting in Monterrey, the Rangers had combined pickaxes and eight-inch shells to tunnel through dozens of houses and outflank the Mexicans fighting at street barricades. "Get to work," George said.

In an hour, Lieutenant Grant had his howitzer in the belfry of the church. He began dropping shells into the middle of the defenders of the San Cosme

Gate. A half hour later, Hay's Rangers and numerous infantrymen appeared on the rooftops near the gate and swept the already shaken defenders with volleys of pistol and musket fire.

About five o'clock, General Stapleton decided it was time for a frontal assault. He ordered artillery Lieutenant Henry J. Hunt forward to blow a hole through the main gate. Thundering through 150 yards of ferocious Mexican fire, Hunt came within 50 yards of the gate before his horses went down in bloody foaming agony. He and his men leaped off, cut the traces, and proceeded to duel with the massed batteries behind the gate. Already rattled by Grant's howitzer and the Texas Rangers' small arms, the Mexican gunners fled.

General Stapleton led a charge that carried the positions around the gate. But the first Americans to enter the city were shot down by Mexicans fighting from rooftops and windows. George decided his tired men had done enough for one day and brought up reinforcements to solidify their grip on the gate. He sent a messenger back to General Scott telling him San Cosme had been breached. The messenger soon returned with terse orders to stay alert for a counterattack. General John Quitman of Mississippi had captured the Belén Gate and was also being ordered to wait until morning to see whether the Mexicans were going to defend the city street by street.

George's head wound still sent slivers of pain through his skull. Maria had poured some wine with a light dose of opium into his canteen, and he swigged it during the long night, enabling him to get two or three hours of broken sleep. Beyond the San Cosme Gate, Mexico City lay dark and silent. In the dawn, General Stapleton strode among his men, warning them to be ready for more hard fighting. The Mexican cavalry had seen no action in the last six weeks. They might be ordered to make a last desperate charge.

Instead of the clatter of hooves, the shrill bugle calls of attacking lancers, down the empty street plodded a delegation of dispirited civilians carrying a white flag. One of them spoke fairly good English. He informed General Stapleton that General Santa Anna and his remaining troops had fled, and the civilians were here to surrender Mexico City to the Americans.

George accepted the surrender and rushed another messenger back to Tacubaya to tell General Scott this good news. The messenger returned with orders to march the men to the city's Grand Plaza, where they would rendezvous with Quitman's troops, advancing from the Belén Gate. Scott would join them there. With a hundred skirmishers warily moving ahead of his column, George led his men across the great green park known as the Alameda to the vast square, with its immense cathedral and the equally huge National Palace. He and General Quitman went into the National Palace, hoping to find some members of the Mexican federal government. Instead, they found at least two dozen looters going through desks and wardrobes. Most of them fled. But one came at Quitman with a knife, and the Mississippian shot him dead. The knife was gold, with a twisted blade. "Aztec, probably," Quitman said. "Maybe we should use it to cut the heart out of this goddamn country."

Like most of the army, Quitman was bitter about the thousands of Americans who had been killed and wounded thanks to Santa Anna's stalling tactics. He began telling George that he had become a convinced All Mexico man. George nodded noncommittally. Now was not the time to argue with his fellow Democrat.

Outside, they ordered their soldiers to form ranks. George's uniform was splattered with mud. Quitman was minus a shoe. More than half the soldiers were shoeless. Their uniforms, what was left of them, were ragged wrecks. But they had conquered this nation of 8 million people. They were occupying a city of two hundred thousand with a mere six thousand men. The story was an epic, worthy of inclusion in the history books with the exploits of Cortés.

General Stapleton watched the Mexican flag come down and the American flag rise over the National Palace. Was this symbolic ceremony an augury of things to come? In his aching head, a voice suddenly spoke with remarkable clarity. *Not if I have anything to say about it.*

NINE

"HELP! HELP! OH MY GOD!"

THE cry of anguish roiled the humid air of the bedroom overlooking the Avenida St. Francis, where General George Stapleton cradled Maria de Vega in his arms. They had made exquisite elegiac love again and were whispering fragments of joy and regret, longing and transformation, when reality came crashing out of the darkness. They were no longer lovers in some imagined kingdom of romantic desire. They were a wounded man and a damaged woman in a city clotted with violence and rage.

General Stapleton sprang from the bed and flung on his clothes. Pistol in hand, he rushed into the street. On the corner he saw a blue-uniformed body in a patch of moonlight. Two men were bending over him. "Put up your hands!" he shouted in Spanish. The men ran in opposite directions. By the time he reached the corner, they had vanished into alleys off the Avenida St. Francis.

He knelt beside the American. He was a kid—no more than seventeen. They had stabbed him repeatedly in the chest and back. Blood ran in dark rivulets from his body. Out of the darkness clattered a four-man patrol of U.S. Marines. A battalion of these seagoing soldiers had been sent to reinforce the army after the casualties at the Molino del Rey. They had been entrusted with policing the city.

"Jesus!" one of the marines said. "This is the ninth one they got tonight."

"We gotta get tough with these greasers," another marine said, adding a string of expletives to decorate this opinion.

"Two of you go for an ambulance," General Stapleton said. "The other two stay with the body."

He returned to Maria de Vega's apartment. *"Madre de Dios,"* she murmured when he told her what had happened. "Santa Anna will destroy us yet."

The Americans had been in Mexico City for two weeks. The first three days had been a chaos of sniping from rooftops and windows. As he left the city, Santa Anna had opened the prisons and given guns to over two thousand hardened criminals, hoping they would start a popular uprising. The Americans had responded with point-blank artillery fire that soon killed or dispersed most of this impromptu militia. But they, or other Santa Anna operatives in civilian clothes, had continued a haphazard guerrilla war, picking off lone Americans who made the mistake of wandering around the city after dark.

"It doesn't make things easier," George said. "I'm beginning to think we have nothing to rely on but your prayers."

"I fear they don't rise beyond the ceiling of this room, where my heart belongs to no one and nothing but you."

"I feel the same way. But we know it isn't true."

"Yes, the pursuit of happiness is forbidden us."

He had told Maria everything. George Stapleton could not lie to a woman he loved. He had showed her Jeremy Biddle's vicious letter and confessed the mixture of desire and revenge that had brought him to her bed. The truth had been a corrosive elixir that had burned away ambiguities on both sides. Between her love of Mexico and his obligations as a Stapleton, they had established a precarious half-real world where love flourished with transcendent intensity, a wild compound of wish and hope and dream and the rueful knowledge that it was temporary, that there would come a day, an hour, a moment, when the bitter word *good-bye* would have to be spoken.

At first she was able to accept it better than he, with his stubborn American belief that every problem had a solution. Her Spanish fatalism about life and love saw a darker more tragic world. But lately, as the situation in Mexico City and the rest of Mexico oscillated between peace and anarchy, she had become the tormented one.

Maria had introduced George to her uncle, Manuel de la Pena y Pena, the president of Mexico's Supreme Court. He was her father's opposite, a man of grave but compassionate understanding. When Santa Anna abdicated the presidency after his final defeat at the gates of Mexico City, he had designated Judge Pena as the interim president. Reluctantly accepting the office, he had found himself an executive without a government. The federal congress had vanished, afraid that any man who voted for a peace treaty might be signing his death warrant.

Meanwhile, letters from a triumphant Caroline reported that the All Mexico campaign was building up irresistible momentum in the United States. Newspaper after newspaper was taking up the cry, as Mexican guerrilla attacks were described—and frequently magnified—by reporters with the American army.

Last week, George had led a column of fifteen hundred men in pursuit of a fragment of the Mexican Army, operating near Puebla. They had retreated to the town of Humantala. George had sent five hundred Texas Rangers into the town in a headlong charge that had virtually annihilated the Mexicans in a wild orgy of shooting and stabbing. Although the casualties were ten to one in favor of the Americans, the reporters had turned the story into a tragic elegy for Jack Hays, the Ranger colonel, who was killed in the opening volleys. Remembering how Hays had turned the Mexican *vaquero* into a running target on the march into Mexico, George was less inclined to weep. But Hays's death had aroused the Rangers to wild fury, and they had begun massacring every Mexican in Humantala. George had been forced to send in regulars with fixed bayonets to protect the cowering civilians. The experience had convinced him that a long occupation of Mexico would make the two countries irreconcilable enemies forever.

But events seemed to be favoring Caroline and John Sladen. The next morning, George went to a council of war in General Scott's offices at the National Palace. Scott's expression was a study in disillusionment and dismay. He had won his war and he wanted to go home to garner some plaudits—including a possible nomination for the presidency. But it looked as if he would spend the rest of his life in Mexico City.

"Nine more Americans murdered in this city last night," Scott said. "We had twenty killed and a hundred wounded clearing the guerrillas out of Humantala. These people are vastly underestimating our patience. I'm tempted to proclaim martial law, not just in Mexico City but in the entire country."

"Humantala was Santa Anna's last gasp," George said. "Let's not lose our heads. Mexico City is settling down. We've killed or captured most of the thugs they let out of jail."

"Frankly, General," Gideon Pillow said, "I don't think your opinion of these greasers is very objective. You're looking at them through a haze of scented petticoats."

"General Pillow," George said, "I resent that remark—extremely. Unless I hear an immediate apology, my aide will call upon you with a challenge before nightfall."

"I can't officially condone dueling between any officers in this army," Scott said. "But unofficially, I'm tempted to act as your second, General Stapleton."

Pillow's eyes darted around the table, looking for support from one of the other generals. There was none. Several had acquired Mexican mistresses. All of them despised the president's former law partner for writing a letter to the *New Orleans Picayune* trying to claim credit for the strategy that had captured Mexico City.

"I didn't mean to make any reflection on General Stapleton's private life," Pillow said. "But I think I can say with confidence that President Polk is deeply troubled by Mexico's continuing resistance and wants us to conquer a peace that leaves us masters of this country for another fifty years."

"Do you have a letter from him stating this policy?" Scott snapped.

"No. But the twenty thousand reinforcements he's sending us should speak louder than mere words. This is a matter of some political delicacy. If we fail to cooperate with him by publicizing to the fullest Mexico's intransigence—and by reacting to it with maximum force—I think we'll all experience his disapproval."

"I say we should double the marines' night patrols—and warn the soldiers never to go anywhere alone after dark," George said. "I think that will make this city safer than New York."

"I'm inclined to agree," Scott said. "But I'm still at a loss about peace negotiations. There's no trace of a Mexican government—it seems to have evaporated."

"I may have some information on that point in a day or two," General Stapleton said. "Judge Pena y Pena told me there are signs that the federal congress may reassemble in Querétaro. In the meantime, he's dismissed Santa Anna as commander in chief of the army. You'll see it in the newspapers today."

"Please be good enough to pass on to me anything else you learn, General," Scott said with more than a little sarcasm. "Perhaps you could do it before it reaches the newspapers."

"I only learned of it last night, General. I have no desire to interfere with your position as our commander in chief. The fortunes of war have given me this opportunity."

"I understand," Scott said. "You have my full confidence, General. Which is more than I can say for other people at this table."

Scott looked hard at Pillow and then at General William Worth. "Haughty Bill," as he was called, had also persuaded some reporters to give him credit for planning the entire campaign. George was discovering that generals, once the fighting war ends, become as hungry for fame as politicians.

"The regulations of the U.S. Army make it a court-martial offense for an officer to publish anything in a newspaper without the permission of his commanding general," Scott said. "Remember that, gentlemen. We'll meet here at the same time next week. Good day."

On the way down the hall from Scott's offices to the grand staircase, George heard a reedy voice call, "General Stapleton."

It was Nicholas Trist, looking more eccentric than ever. He had let his hair grow to shoulder length. His suit looked as if he had recently worn it in a rainstorm. In his hand was the inevitable cheroot. "I've just received the most dismaying news," he said. "I've been relieved of my duties and ordered to return home."

Caroline had told George this was coming. It was another ominous sign that his duplicitous wife, with Sarah Polk's help, had acquired inordinate influence with the president.

What to do? Trist was the last man George would choose as a negotiator, if he had any freedom of choice. But there was no time for freedom of choice. In the next mail might come a letter formally appointing him viceroy of Mexico with power to make a peace only at the point of a gun. If he refused the appointment, his opposition would be visible—and subject to savage attack in the administration's newspapers. General Gideon Pillow or some other deserving Democrat would be given the job.

"It takes a long time for mail to travel from here to Washington," George said. "A lot of it goes astray. If I were you, I'd tell no one about the letter. Pretend you never got it. Come to my apartment tonight. I'll have Judge Pena y Pena there, ready to listen to your final offer."

Trist looked confused. He had George listed in his head as a devoted president's man. He had just been reprimanded and recalled by James Knox Polk.

Why was General Stapleton telling him to ruin his career completely by defying the White House?

George decided to tell him the truth. "I don't know how closely you've been following American politics. There's a movement building up to occupy all of Mexico indefinitely, the way the British have taken over India. It's being pushed by Senator Sladen of Louisiana and a cadre of other Southern politicians. They see it as a way to make the South, and slavery, invulnerable. They plan to make Mexico a Southern colony. I think that would be a terrible mistake—for Mexico, and the United States."

Trist seemed to recede into himself for a moment. His eyes became opaque. "I'm all too aware of this dream of a slave empire. I was the U.S. consul in Havana for five years. I spent many a drunken hour listening to my fellow Southerners talk about what the South could become if we possessed Cuba and the other Caribbean islands. I suppose Mexico is the ultimate logic of this purple dream."

Trist paced the little office General Scott had assigned to him. "I can remember Mr. Jefferson looking out the window at the slaves working in the fields around Monticello and saying, 'It is written in the book of fate that these people will be free one day.' I thought it was an old man's guilty fantasy. I didn't know then how often he had tried to strike a blow against slavery in the Continental Congress—and when he was president."

Trist stopped and pulled savagely on his cheroot. "I didn't have his kind of courage, General. When I was consul in Havana, I looked the other way and let certain Southerners get rich smuggling slaves from Cuba to New Orleans. They promised to make me secretary of state one day."

He paced again. "I'm not a courageous man, General. I don't have any money, and my wife thinks she should live like Thomas Jefferson's granddaughter."

"Maybe there comes a time in a man's life when he has to do something because he knows it's right, even though he also knows it will probably make him miserable—on a personal level."

George realized he was speaking for himself as well as for pathetic Nicholas Trist. So many lives were meeting here in a bizarre confluence. For a man who was not religious, it was confusing, but somehow reassuring. George sensed a presence, perhaps several presences, in this small, dim room overlooking Mexico City's Grand Plaza.

Heavy footsteps in the hall. General Winfield Scott towered in the doorway, formidable in his gold epaulets and gold-striped trousers. "What's this? A diplomatic tête-à-tête?"

Again, the tone was mildly sarcastic. As commanding general, Winfield Scott did not like to be left out of anything.

Once more George decided honesty was the only policy. "Mr. Trist just received a letter telling him he's been recalled. The president has apparently decided that his mere presence here encourages the Mexicans to think they can somehow better the terms we've offered. The president has decided no more offers should come from us. Future proposals will have to come from the Mexicans."

"Yesterday a delegation of leading citizens of Mexico City called on me," Scott said. "They proposed that I resign from the American army and become dictator of Mexico for six years. They guaranteed me ample funds to raise and equip an army."

"I've just told Mr. Trist I thought he should make one more attempt to get a treaty before he quits the field."

Winfield Scott looked long and hard at General Stapleton. The commander in chief was not a stupid man. He saw all the ramifications of George's words. He was being asked to concur in disobeying, or at least ignoring, the orders of their president. He was being asked, or told, that he should turn his back on becoming dictator of Mexico. Winfield Scott did not like being told to do things. George knew he was risking an explosion.

"I agree," Scott said. "The sooner we get our army out of Mexico on honorable terms, the better it will be for all concerned."

Winfield Scott's sheer size, plus George Stapleton's massive physique, somehow added substance to the wraithlike Trist. "All right," he said. "I'll meet with Judge Pena y Pena one more time. But if there is no progress . . ."

"I think there'll be progress," George said.

TEN

CAROLINE KEMBLE STAPLETON'S HEAD THROBBED. THE mail had just arrived. Once more, there was no letter from George. For two months now, he had not written her a line. She had written him a dozen letters, at first full of confidence that he was ready to become America's first viceroy to Mexico, later questioning his silence, wondering if her previous letters had arrived, finally angrily demanding an answer of some sort. There was no response to any of these missives. Nor had President Polk received an answer to his letter, asking George to assume the duties of American plenipotentiary in Mexico City. Secretary of War William Marcy had chosen this resounding title for the final stage of the campaign to annex all of Mexico.

While these thoughts rampaged through her head, Caroline sat in her Washington parlor, watching her elongated oldest son, Jonathan, pace up and down the room, long arms flailing like some unnatural mixture of bird and beast, denouncing the idea of annexing Mexico. He used the rhetoric of the abolitionists, making him sound like the college junior that he was.

"How can you even *countenance* such an idea, Mother? It's a slavocrat conspiracy—"

"Jonathan, I will not tolerate your use of such terms as *slavocrat* in this house. They're insulting to the Democrats of the South, who are your father's friends and political allies."

"You maintain that the South has not made slavery into an article of faith in their political creed?"

"They've made the safety of their wives and children, their lives and property, into a creed—because the abolitionists have given them no choice."

From a couch where he was sprawled, reading the *New York Morning News*, Charlie Stapleton said, "Mother's right, Big Brother. You're full of hot air. Take a trip South before you shoot off your mouth about slavocrats. It's slavery or a race war—that's our choice."

"*Our* choice?" Jonathan spluttered. "You've become a Southerner, now?"

"Isn't the South part of *our* country?" Charlie said.

"You wouldn't think so, if you listen to the abolitionists," Caroline said.

"Big Brother doesn't listen to anyone else, that's all too clear."

"There's a moral dimension to history, a moral dimension to the destiny of this country," Jonathan said.

"Stuff," Charlie said. "You're a preacher without a collar, Big Brother. Why don't you admit it and join a seminary?"

"Your moral-dimension nonsense is what has prolonged the war in Mexico to the point where we have no choice but to occupy the whole country," Caroline said. "We've been so anxious to be moral, we've allowed scum like Santa Anna to hoodwink us into endless truces and peace negotiations, only to find ourselves confronting a revived Mexican army. If we'd smashed them in a single campaign, the American people would be disposed to a far more generous peace."

" 'The American people,' " Jonathan said. "Mother, we're talking as a family here. We know, or at least I know, the American people have been manipulated by you and your friends in the White House and in the newspapers to the point where they're no more intelligently disposed than a bunch of trained seals in a circus act."

"All the more reason for us to act without idiotic ideals about moral destiny," Charlie said.

In a corner of the parlor, six-year-old Paul Stapleton sat silently on a straight-backed chair, not missing a word. "Paul, go to your room. You're much too young to be listening to such cynical talk," Caroline said.

"I don't agree with either of them, Mother." Paul said. "They're both full of hot air."

"What!" Charlie roared, leaping to his feet. "Suh. Do you realize you've insulted a Suthin' gennlemun? The honuh of the South must be avenged—by no less than ten crampuhs."

"Mother stop him!" Paul screamed, and fled the parlor.

Charlie stamped after him, shouting, "You hear them footsteps, you little no-thun weasul? The honuh of the South is on the march!"

"Charlie, leave that child alone!" Caroline said. "His arms were black-and-blue from your crampers last night."

Men, Caroline thought. They enjoyed inflicting pain on each other. Paul was proud of his black-and-blue arms. A day or two ago, she had overheard Charlie remark to Jonathan, "Little brother has guts. He never goes crying to Momma no matter how much I clobber him." Why was she, of all people, fated to be the mother of three sons?

Alone in the parlor, Jonathan glared at Caroline. "I'm serious about Mexico, Mother. Would you object if I wrote Father a letter telling him what I think?"

"You can write him anything you please!" Caroline was tempted to add, *Maybe you can get an answer from him.* But she had been careful to conceal her anxiety on that score from almost everyone.

Tabitha Flowers came to the door of the parlor. Her face wore its usual mixture of anger and grief. She had become almost unmanageable since she learned of her father's death at the battle of Molino del Rey. George had written a long letter to her, describing Hannibal's heroism. Tabitha had torn it to shreds and said all sorts of extreme things. She had accused George of murdering Hannibal by taking him to Mexico. He had died like a slave in a white man's war.

"Senator Sladen's here to see you, ma'am."

She banished Jonathan and received John Sladen in the parlor, carefully closing the doors behind him. She had shared her bafflement over George's silence with him, hoping he might learn something from New Orleans, where reporters covering the war congregated.

"I have news about George that may upset you," John said. "But I thought you should hear it immediately."

"Tell me."

"General Stapleton has acquired a beautiful Mexican mistress."

"Impossible."

"We of all people should be ready to admit this sort of impossibility can happen."

"I want to know. I want to know *everything*. Who she is, her background. Is she a woman of the street? I think I could understand that. We've been separated over a year."

"I gather every officer down to the rank of lieutenant has enjoyed that sort of liaison. But this woman is from a very distinguished Mexican family."

"Are you suggesting he's in love with her?"

John shrugged. "I can arrange for you to meet the reporter who told me the story."

Caroline saw herself sitting in some tawdry boardinghouse parlor, exposed to the man's condescension. "No. Get me a full account. A written document."

"You'll have it in a week."

His wry smile made no secret of what he was thinking. All those years of fidelity, of lecturing him on the sanctity of her wedding vows—and this was her reward. As infuriating as this mockery was to Caroline, she was even more tormented by another thought. She had no difficulty imagining what this woman was doing with George's body. What was she doing with his mind?

Two days later, as Caroline was finishing breakfast, Tabitha handed her a white envelope. "This come from the White House."

Caroline ripped open the sealed envelope. Sarah Polk had scrawled only two lines. *Dearest Friend: Can you come here without a moment's delay? We have received an extraordinary communication from Mexico City.*

Caroline flung on a fur-lined cloak against the raw December wind and told Jonathan to bring her sulky and her favorite horse, the roan mare, Ginger, to the front door. She would drive herself to the White House without waiting to round up Judson Diggs. The coachman was probably visiting one of his many lady friends in the neighborhood. The man had turned out to be a lothario of extraordinary abilities, considering his spherical shape. She hesitated to fire him because she feared his replacement might be worse. All the coachmen in Washington, D.C., were former hackmen, which meant they had bad habits.

In fifteen minutes she was giving her horse to Ezekiel McCall, the black porter who guarded the South Portico. Inside, a servant led her up the stairs to the second floor and down the hall to the president's study. An anxious-eyed Sarah met her at the door in funereal black. She had taken to wearing that color constantly. They kissed and Sarah waved her to a seat in front of the president's desk. James Polk was in his swivel chair, papers scattered across the broad mahogany desktop. In his hand was a thick document, which he was intently reading. He looked utterly worn. The brown cast to his skin had changed to an alarming gray. Huge pouches sagged beneath his eyes.

"Good morning," he said.

"Good morning, Mr. President." Caroline still preferred to call him that, although they had been on a first-name basis for years before his election.

Sarah sat down on a couch against the wall. "We've been up all night," she said. "Reading and rereading what arrived last night in the valise of a reporter for the *New Orleans Picayune*. It's a treaty of peace with Mexico. Plus a sixty-page letter from our former diplomatic representative, Nicholas Trist, explaining why we should approve it."

"He's negotiated a treaty?" Caroline said. "In defiance of your instructions?"

"Apparently," President Polk said.

"But the most extraordinary thing in the packet is a letter from General Stapleton," Sarah said.

"May I see it?" Caroline said.

"That's why you're here," the president said with a twist of his lips that might have been a tired grin—or a grimace.

He handed her the letter. It was unquestionably in George's large, bold handwriting.

Dear Mr. President:

I write this letter with a mixture of regret and apprehension. You know I went to Mexico determined to do my best to support your policies. I have not changed my mind about the necessity for this war, even though I have seen too many good men die in it. I agree with your conviction, which we both inherited from Andrew Jackson, that Texas, New Mexico, and California belong within our national borders by the nature of their geography and the necessities of our position as a democracy in a hostile world. But I have become more and more alarmed by what I have heard from reporters and from Caroline's letters about the growth of a movement to annex all of Mexico and turn it into a colonial possession, in the style to England's imperial control of India. What I have seen and heard in Mexico convinces me that this would be a disaster for both countries. It would make us eternal enemies and would prove, I think, an inexhaustible source of moral and political corruption that would eventually undermine our government as well as ruin theirs.

Mr. Trist asked me for advice when he received your order to return to the United States. I urged him to try one more time to negotiate a peace based on the proposals he had brought with him. Because the Mexicans—or to be more specific, that lying scumbag Santa Anna—prolonged the war, I advised him to reduce to $15 million the $20 million you were originally prepared to pay for California and New Mexico. Through friendships I have formed with the Mexican family that includes the provisional president, Mr. Pena y Pena, I was able to facilitate these negotiations. The result is the treaty you will find in this pouch, along with Mr. Trist's prolix defense of his actions—which I assured him was superfluous but he insisted on enclosing. To be candid, the man is a bit of a fool, but his intentions are honorable and his devotion to the best interests of our country is genuine.

While Trist was negotiating, I received your letter appointing me as his replacement. I am deeply flattered by the confidence and trust you repose in me as Minister Plenipotentiary. But I did not see how I could execute the responsibilities of that office when I had lost confidence in the policy that my appointment—and Mr. Trist's recall—implied. So I chose to remain silent and let Mr. Trist proceed with his negotiations. The result, in my opinion, is a treaty that will produce a lasting peace.

I hope you will submit this treaty to the Senate for its approval, Mr. President. I plan to return to the United States early in the New Year and resume my seat in that august body. I am prepared to defend the treaty with all the eloquence I can muster. If you decide not to follow this course, I will be in a painful dilemma. I would hate to give aid and comfort to our political enemies. But I fear I would be forced to speak out against an alternative policy—especially an attempt to make all Mexico an American satrapy.

With continuing admiration and friendship.

Sincerely,
George

Caroline placed this letter on President Polk's desk as if it were a ticking time bomb. It might as well have been. Both Polks gazed at her with a tense blend of anxiety and distrust in their eyes. Caroline could almost hear Sarah saying, *How could you have let this happen?* By now she had convinced the president that All Mexico was the only hope of rescuing the administration and the Democratic Party from humiliation. Nothing else would satisfy the Southern wing of the party. Nothing else would defuse the mounting revulsion against the war that the Whigs were gleefully fueling, with the help of the abolitionists.

"Has George revealed any of these sentiments to you?" Sarah said.

"I haven't heard a word from him for almost two months."

"I don't believe you mentioned that to me," Sarah said.

"I didn't think it was significant. The mails are so irregular . . ."

It was bewildering—horrifying. The president was gazing at her as if she were a prisoner in the dock. Sarah was interrogating her like a prosecuting attorney.

"What is he planning to do? Come home and run on my corpse?" The president's voice was half-croak, half-groan. It sounded like a cry from the grave. "The man who rescued Mexico and America from Caesar Polk? I warned Sarah from the beginning that this was what someone might say about this scheme! It was too high a price to pay—to keep the South in the Democratic Party. But I thought the assassin would be a Whig, not a Democrat, not a man I trusted!"

"You have no idea what George plans to do—if we submit to his decree and accept this treaty?" Sarah asked.

"None! I haven't heard from him. I swear it!"

Suddenly Caroline was choking with tears. The pathetic president and his worries about humiliation became irrelevant. She spoke only to Sarah. "Do you really think I could betray you this way? You? The one person in the world I truly love?"

Tears trickled down Sarah's cheeks. "It was the most horrifying thought of my life."

The scrape of the president's chair as he shoved himself away from his desk was almost a human sound. He lurched to his feet, trembling. "Now I know the worst, the very worst—"

"No!" Caroline said. "It isn't what you think. It isn't some mad scheme of two deluded women. It's your fame that we've lived to create. Yours and George's. I love you for your honesty, your devotion to Andrew Jackson, your dedication to this country—as much as Sarah does. I loved George too, for the same reasons, until I read this letter."

The president swayed behind his desk, a man bewildered by this cyclone of emotion and politics swirling around him. Sarah wiped her eyes. "I believe you. We both believe you. Let's try to think calmly about this treaty, this threat of George's."

Polk slumped in his chair. "What choice do we have except surrender—or defiance. Either way it's a debacle."

Into Caroline's head swam John Sladen's anguished face. She heard herself telling him that she loved George Stapleton now. "There may be a middle path between those extremes," she said. "What if you simply sent it to the Senate without any commitment on your part? You might even reveal it was negotiated by a man you had recalled for insubordination and ineptitude. But you thought the Senate should consider it—as proof of your desire for peace. Meanwhile, I'll tell Senator Sladen what has happened. He'll be prepared to denounce the treaty—in the light of the perfidy the Mexicans have displayed since we offered it to them."

"If the Senate rejected it, in spite of George's best efforts, it would leave us with no alternative but All Mexico," Sarah said.

They were together again, their minds, their souls, blended in this no longer beatific place, the Temple of Fame. Now they knew that the temple was more like the anteroom of hell. But they would face the pain, the horror, together.

"It might work," the president said. "But can Senator Sladen match General Stapleton, an authentic war hero?"

"General Stapleton will not say a word against Senator Sladen," Caroline said. "He'll vote against the treaty."

"How can you be sure of that?" Polk asked, new bewilderment on his sagging face.

"He'll have to choose between me—and this treaty."

With no warning, the president began to weep. "James, what's wrong?" Sarah said. "Can you possibly ask more of Caroline?"

Polk shook his head, struggling for breath. "I begin to think . . . we've been fighting . . . the wrong war."

He was looking at Sarah as he said this. What was in his eyes? For a moment, Caroline was sure it was hatred. But she swiftly persuaded herself it was merely a spasm of male bravado. She watched Sarah deal with it.

"James, we've come much too far. We're too close to greatness to turn back now."

James Knox Polk nodded wearily. He was too tired to offer any more than token resistance. He subsided and Sarah walked Caroline down the hall to the grand staircase. At the head of this shadowy descent she took both Caroline's hands but did not kiss her good-bye.

"Have you told us everything?"

"Yes," Caroline said, while in her soul another voice cried No! and begged to be forgiven for the lie. But there was a limit to what even the purest love could demand.

"Will you see Senator Sladen?"

"Immediately."

"Tell him he has the president's support. Let him spread that word as freely as he wishes."

There was a long anguished pause. "You haven't told me everything. I sense it."

"No," Caroline said, avoiding those dark sibyl's eyes. "Someday I will. It doesn't affect my promise."

"I love you anyway." Sarah kissed her on the lips. Then she gripped her hands with a ferocity that almost made Caroline cry out. "But I love James too. Do you understand that?"

"Yes."

Dazedly, Caroline descended the stairs to the first floor of the White House. With each step she felt she was sinking deeper into the underground river that had swirled through all the days of her life. If she could not change George Stapleton's mind about Mexico, she would have to tell John Sladen to destroy him—with the president's heartfelt support, and her approval. What else could that mean to John but the reawakening of his perpetual hope for her love?

Yet Caroline knew, even as Ezekiel McCall, the Negro porter, led her chaise to the South Portico, that there was no possibility of her loving John again. The woman who had given herself to that pitiful boy-man in that New York basement was dead. She had lived too long in those caves of ice above the sunless sea. Her heart had shriveled in the eternal cold to the size of a pumpkin seed, and the winds of chance had long since blown it away.

With George lost, she only loved one thing now. At the gate, Caroline looked back at the white-pillared temple of American fame. A voice whispered:

'Tis not in mortals to command success
But we'll do more, Sempronius; we'll deserve it.

Yes, she thought, yes. She and Sarah would prevail—in spite of the weakness, the stupidity, the cowardice, of men.

ELEVEN

"YOU *MUST* FORGIVE HER. I INSIST on it."

General George Stapleton almost groaned aloud. Dawn was graying his last night in Mexico City. Maria Pena de Vega was lying beside him in his bed, her lips pressed against his throat, telling him that he had to return to Caroline Kemble Stapleton's treacherous arms.

"Even if I find her in bed with John Sladen?"

"Yes. Even if the worst is true. But it may not be so. I have reread your ex-friend Jeremy's letter. He's not a reliable witness. His heart is full of hatred. How strange you Americans are! To hate a whole section of your own country—because they own slaves. It would be like a Mexican hating the people of Yucatán because they have so many Indians living in terrible poverty. We Mexicans only hate individuals—fathers hate daughters and vice versa, brothers loathe sisters and vice versa, wives hate husbands—and we know this hatred is wrong. We know we have to ask God's forgiveness for it eventually. Whereas this abstract hatred of Southerners your abolitionists consider a virtue! Truly appalling. I shudder for the future of your country."

"What about the priests and bishops here in Mexico?"

"Oh, we all hate them—because they want to enslave our souls."

"The South is enslaving souls, and bodies."

"But all this should have nothing to do with your love for your wife! When the political invades the personal, that is the sin against the Holy Spirit, the one that cannot be forgiven."

"I shouldn't hate John Sladen either?"

"That is a more difficult question. If he's conducted an affair with your wife in your own house, he's wounded your honor. You may have to kill him. But you should try to do it without hatred—as an act of duty to your sons."

She was determined to shepherd his soul through the rest of his life so they could meet in paradise. But her insistence on forgiving Caroline went beyond this act of faith. It entered that dark borderland where all women were linked in a perpetual union of sympathy and resentment against the aggrandizing power of men. Again and again Maria had quoted Sor Juana's poem. It whispered now in George's very veins.

Hombres necios que acusais
a la mujer sin razón

Ah, stupid men, unreasonable
In blaming woman's nature

"I love *you,*" George said. "That's the only thing I know right now. If I find Caroline in bed with Johnny Sladen, I'll divorce her and come back here a free man and marry you."

"You wouldn't be happy in Mexico, and I would be miserable in the United States."

"Why?"

"How many times must I tell you? Because I love Mexico and you don't. You love the United States of America, and I don't."

George flung aside the sheet and walked to the window. A four-man marine patrol clumped down the Avenida St. Francis. Mexicans hurried past them, their eyes averted. Maria's words burned in his brain with the bitterness that only history's irony can create. By blocking the All Mexico movement, he was forever separating not only Mexico from the United States, but also George Stapleton from Maria Pena de Vega. As minister plenipotentiary of Mexico, he could make her his wife in everything but name. Caroline and her salon could be left in Washington. His sons could visit him and perhaps find inspiration, or consolation, in their father's fame.

Suddenly George could not breathe. The Avenida St. Francis became a dark blur. A bubble seemed to expand in his chest as if his heart were exploding. But it did not burst. It seemed to be crushing his lungs. "Pray . . . for . . . me," he gasped.

"I will, always," Maria said.

"No . . . now. I—"

He stumbled back to the bed. Maria lit an oil lamp. "*Madre de Dios.* You're so gray. Shall I call a doctor?"

George knew what it was—the same apoplexy that had killed his grandfather. "No. Just hold me. Your arms . . . around me."

Her arms were too short to reach that far. But she pressed herself against him, and for an hour they lay together while she murmured prayers to the Virgin Mary. Slowly, George's breathing became normal. His color returned. In another hour he was able to begin packing for his departure.

That task completed, George went to the residence of Judge Pena y Pena, Maria's uncle, and Mexico's acting president, the man who had negotiated the treaty of peace with Nicholas Trist. "I've come to say good-bye, and to reiterate my intention to do everything I can to support the treaty in our Senate. But there's something even more important I want to discuss. Can you prevail on your brother to accept his daughter into his family again?"

Judge Pena y Pena, a large, solemn man, with a face that emanated aristocracy, shook his head. "My brother is a pharisee to his bones. I can see him in the story Jesus tells, about the man who boasted about his holiness, while the sinner pleaded for forgiveness in the back of the synagogue. But Maria shall have a place in my household. I promise you that as solemnly as anything to which I've pledged Mexico's honor in our treaty."

"Would it help if I spoke to your brother?"

"On the contrary, it might discourage you from saying a word on our behalf in your Senate. He despises our treaty as violently as he condemns his daughter. He accuses me of dishonoring Mexico. He wants everything back—Texas, California, New Mexico—and Louisiana and Mississippi by way of compensation for our dead soldiers."

For a moment George sensed that in his bones Judge Pena y Pena agreed with his brother. Deep inside him there was a Spaniard who snarled, *Death before dishonor*. Negotiating the treaty had been a terrible agony to which he had subjected himself for Mexico's sake.

"It's been an honor to know you, sir," George said.

"Let's hope we can both emerge from this business with a few tatters of that rare ribbon on our escutcheons."

Back at his apartment, George told Maria what Judge Pena y Pena had said about welcoming her into his house. She dismissed the offer. "He'll try to persuade me to crawl on my knees to my father."

Dismayed, George tried to give Maria a draft on Barings, the British bank in Mexico City, for ten thousand dollars. She tore it into shreds and flung it at him, crying, "Can't you imagine what my father would say the moment he heard about this? 'So the whore has received her payment.'"

"How will you live?"

"The way I've always lived. Under Sor Juana's protection. For Mexico."

He tried to kiss her one last time. She refused to let him touch her. "We must begin to deny our love. Starting here and now. Facing each other."

"I'll never do that."

"You must. I was your Mexican whore. You fucked me just as you and the rest of your Yankees fucked Mexico! For money! For glory! For fame!"

For a terrible moment George sensed Maria meant it. Like her uncle, the judge, in a part of her soul she could never forgive the Americans for the humiliation they had inflicted on her country. In another part of her soul she told herself that she was destroying their love for his own good. The revelation of her hatred was the ultimate expression of that love.

"I know exactly what you're trying to do," George said. "It won't work."

Going down the dim stairs to the street, he heard Maria weeping. The sound lingered in his ears for five days, on the highway to Vera Cruz. It dwindled into silence only as Mexico vanished over the horizon and the U.S.

Navy steam frigate *Brandywine* plowed north through wintry seas toward Washington, D.C.

In a few days he would be facing a very different woman. George took Jeremy Biddle's letter out of his wallet and reread it for the hundredth time. Soon Maria's insistence on forgiveness vanished as totally as the sound of her tears. His original rage returned to clog his lungs with a kind of mad pneumonia.

He had deliberately told no one in Washington about his departure from Mexico. He wanted to walk into his house on Pennsylvania Avenue unannounced. He intended to give Caroline no time to prepare a defense. He almost hoped he would find her in flagrante delicto with Senator John Sladen. That would simplify everything. He could send her back to New Jersey in disgrace. He would have a totally free hand politically.

But General Stapleton, now about to become Senator Stapleton again, had no control over the weather and the time of the *Brandywine*'s arrival. He found himself debarking from the frigate in Alexandria in a gloomy December twilight. By the time he located a hack and began the muddy journey to Washington, night had fallen. A cold rain began drooling from the dark sky. In front of 3600 Pennsylvania Avenue, he found a line of waiting carriages and hacks. Yellow light glowed from all the first-floor windows. Caroline's salon was in full swing.

From the steps, a voice called, "Senator—General—is that really you?"

It was Senator Thomas Hart Benton of Missouri and his wife. What could George do but confess his identity and follow them into the house? Benton all but babbled his eagerness to hear the latest news from Mexico. "Is there any hope of a peace treaty?"

"I hope there's one in the White House right now," George said. "If not, I have a copy of it in my trunk."

In the crowded parlor, George's appearance created a sensation. Ancient Dolley Madison was in her usual corner, with Senator Daniel Webster and Congressman John Quincy Adams in attendance. Webster looked old and Adams looked prehistoric. Nearby were two of George's fellow soldiers from Mexico, angular Jefferson Davis of Mississippi and broad-shouldered Franklin Pierce of New Hampshire. Both had recently been elected to the Senate, evidence that the voters were still enthusiastic backers of the war. Caroline was having an intense conversation with diminutive Stephen A. Douglas of Illinois—and Senator John Sladen of Louisiana. She looked, if possible, more beautiful than ever. She was wearing her dark hair high, in a kind of crown. Her classic face had acquired an almost sculpted quality.

Smiling, waving, George kept his eyes on Caroline. Her face registered shock and amazement, but he could see no trace of guilt. But why would there be guilt, if she had been betraying him for twenty years? That vagrant emotion would have long since been banished. "Dearest!" she cried, and rushed across the room to kiss him. "Why didn't you tell me you were coming? I would have had the house decked in flags of triumph!"

"My letter must have gone astray," George said. Did she notice he did not return her kiss? He hoped so.

He had to shake hands with every man in the room, including John Sladen. John bounced upward on the balls of his feet as if he were trying to add a few inches to his height. "I hope you'll give me the honor of nominating you for president at the party's convention next spring, Senator," he said.

"I'm sure there are many more deserving Democrats, Senator. Men more in touch with the party's current opinions and policies," George said.

"Pay no attention to him," Jefferson Davis said. "I saw him in action at Monterrey and Buena Vista. I want the privilege of seconding Senator Sladen."

"He says he has a peace treaty in his trunk—and there's a copy in the White House!" Thomas Hart Benton said.

That got everyone's attention. "I think it's a good treaty," George said, "but I don't feel at liberty to discuss it until I learn what the president thinks. It was negotiated under rather unusual circumstances."

"By whom? You?" Benton said.

"By Nicholas Trist."

"I thought the president recalled that fool. Didn't he try to give Texas back to the Mexicans in his opening gambit?" Benton said.

"He repented of that error—with some help from me," George said.

"Can't you give us at least an idea of what we've gotten—and didn't get?" John Sladen said.

George sensed hostility in his voice. Benton, Webster, and every other man in the room seconded Sladen's motion. "What about the northern provinces of Mexico?" Davis said. "We've conquered them—and pacified them. They want to join the United States."

"Yucatán—I suppose you've heard they've declared their independence of the central government and requested our protection?" Senator Webster said.

John Quincy Adams tottered into the center of the parlor, stooped on his cane. "Tell us the worst, Senator! Tell us what I dread more than the damnation of my own worthless soul!" he cried. "Have we taken all of Mexico? Have we made it into a protectorate that will enable the men of the South to create a slave empire? Has our country turned its back on liberty as totally as the lying hypocrites of London?"

"Mr. President." George and many others still used this title when they addressed the old man. "I wish I could satisfy you. But I'm not free to speak until I learn what the president intends to do. The direction of the country, of the Democratic Party, remains in his hands."

"You've been away from Washington too long, General," John Sladen said. "The president has lost control of the locomotive. The direction of the country is in the hands of everybody—and nobody. If something dramatic isn't done soon, it will be in the hands of the Whigs."

"I'm sorry to hear that." For a moment George wanted to grab Sladen by the throat and throw him across the room. But he mastered the impulse and excused himself, saying, with considerable justification, that he needed a bath and a change of clothes after five days aboard the USS *Brandywine*.

In the upstairs hall, a hoarse voice called, "Father!" It was six-year-old Paul, several inches taller. He rushed into George's arms. "I've kept a scrapbook. I've got every story they printed about you in the Washington and New York and New Jersey papers. Some from New Orleans too that Senator Sladen gave me."

"Good, good. I'll look forward to reading them."

"I prayed for you every night, Father."

"I'm sure that's why I'm here. Nothing else gets a man through a battle in one piece."

In the bedroom, as he pulled off his blue army uniform, George realized that he would probably never wear it again. He was swept by memories of Monterrey, Buena Vista, Cerro Gordo, Molino del Rey. He saw the faces of the dead, he heard the cries of the wounded. He saw Lieutenant Ulysses Grant weeping beside the body of his roommate. He knelt beside the dying Hannibal. He heard Maria de Vega weeping as he descended the stairs for the last time. For their sake, he had to keep his head, he had to play his political cards with a steady hand. If Polk had the treaty of peace in the White House and was concealing it, that was a bad sign. Johnny Sladen was acting like a man who thought he had the winning cards.

George bathed and put on a civilian suit and shirt and tie. He was Senator Stapleton again. From his valise he took Jeremy Biddle's letter. Was it a trump card? He suddenly realized he did not want to play it. Not yet, at any rate. He wanted to settle the treaty with Mexico first and then try to solve his personal dilemma. He wanted to try to judge for himself whether John Sladen and Caroline were still lovers.

Downstairs he found most of the guests had departed. Only old John Quincy Adams, the Bentons, and Webster lingered. They were all obviously determined to learn the whole truth about the treaty. When George stubbornly resisted telling them anything, the two senior senators left displaying more than a little irritation.

Old Adams prepared to follow them. Struggling into his dark blue overcoat, which looked as worn-out as its owner, he turned to George and said, "I knew Hugh Stapleton. I shudder to think his grandson could do anything that would dishonor this country. Can you at least assure me on that point, Senator?"

George was deeply moved. "I can do that much, Mr. President. This treaty will rescue our honor. I hope you'll support it."

"You have my promise—to my last breath."

The old man tottered out the door, taking almost a hundred years of American history with him. He had talked with Washington and Franklin and Hamilton. For a moment George felt strong enough to face anyone and anything. He was sure he was being guided down a path that led to victory and vindication.

Then Caroline spoke. "Shall we talk here, or in the bedroom?" A metallic clang was in her voice, like the clash of sword blades. George saw the anger in her eyes and was no longer sure of anything.

The servants began clearing away the cakes and ice cream and coffee cups. George greeted the Parks sisters and Mercy. He told her how deeply he grieved for Hannibal, and asked for Tabitha. "She's run away," Caroline said.

"Mercy saw her on the street the other day but she wouldn't speak to her. She blames you for her father's death."

"I think I can change her mind if she'll give me a chance."

"I doubt if she will. Why don't we go in the south parlor?"

They crossed the hall and Caroline shut the sliding doors. She drew the drapes on the windows and turned to face him. Never had she looked more goddesslike. Her green velvet gown emphasized the curve of her breasts. Her bare arms and neck gleamed in the lamplight.

"What kind of a game do you think you're playing?"

"The one I just described to John Quincy Adams. The honor game."

"Honor." Caroline virtually spat the word. "You call it honor to betray the man and woman who sent you to Mexico? To cut the ground from under Sarah and the president at the very moment when there's a chance for their vindication? I've always feared you were too stupid to become president. You've fulfilled my worst fears."

"As I see it, I'm rescuing him—and the country—from a blunder that would make his name synonymous with disgrace for the next two hundred years."

"You're not going to rescue anybody. John Sladen has the votes to chase you and your treaty all the way back to Matamoros—or wherever your Mexican slut is waiting to deliver your reward."

For a moment Caroline's face became a blur. The room was clotted with a red mist. George's vows to remain calm, his hesitations about using Jeremy's letter, vanished. "My . . . Mexican . . . slut?"

"We know all about her. John has talked to numerous reporters as they came through New Orleans. They've given us a full and repulsive portrait of your off-the-battlefield activities."

"Fortunately, I've had a correspondent here in Washington who's given me a good picture of your activities."

George took Jeremy Biddle's letter out of his inside coat pocket and handed it to her. At the end of the first page Caroline sank down on the edge of a chair. That sculpted face began to crumple like a papier-mâché mask in soggy weather. "It . . . isn't . . . true," she said.

Dishes clattered faintly in the kitchen. Dark African voices drifted down the hall. "Is Jeremy in town?" George asked.

"I don't know."

"Sladen is. Let's go ask him to affirm or deny it."

"No! I won't let you humiliate him for something that happened twenty years ago."

"Why not?" George roared. "Are you claiming that entitled him to your favors for the next twenty years? Is this some sort of old Ohio custom? First come, first served in perpetuity?"

Caroline glared up at him. "He never touched me again. From that moment of—of disgrace in New York until today he's never touched me. I've been faithful to you. Believe it or not, I realized while you were in Mexico that I loved you more than I ever thought I loved him. Imagine! What a perfect fool I've been. Treasuring up my love to fling it at your feet when you were sitting in Mexico reading this filthy cowardly letter every night and then going to your Mexican slut thinking you were perfectly justified—"

"She wasn't—isn't—a slut. She's a brilliant, compassionate woman who loves Mexico."

"Oh, excuse me. That justifies your infidelity?"

"I loved her. More than I ever loved you. She didn't order me around like a servant!"

"Oh, of course not. She just persuaded you to turn your back on our dead, to ignore her worthless countrymen's repeated betrayals of every standard of honor and good faith between nations, to forgive these scum and reward them with fifteen million dollars and the independence of their excuse for a country. I wouldn't order you around either if I could persuade you to do that!"

George reeled in this blaze of sarcasm. She was outarguing him again. Turning his trump card against him. "Shut up!" he shouted. "Why should I believe what you're telling me about Sladen? The next time I see him I'm going to pound his face to jelly!"

"I hope you do. It will enable him to portray you as the oversized idiot that you are. He'll claim, and I will regretfully confirm him, that the quarrel was about the peace treaty. It will win him a half dozen more votes when the president sends the treaty to the Senate."

"The president is sending it to the Senate? Doesn't that prove I'm right?"

"On the contrary. He's sending it with a message that is as neutral as language can become. He's saying that it was negotiated by a fool, Nicholas Trist, against his president's orders, after he was recalled. But he feels compelled to give the august members of the world's greatest deliberative body a chance to see it. Senator Sladen and a dozen other senators will tear it to shreds before the end of the first day. They'll say it's a meaningless document, in the light of the affronts and betrayals we've endured in Mexico. The only *honorable* alternative has now become the conquest and occupation of all of Mexico."

"It won't work. Because I'm going to stand up and tell the whole truth about why and how it was negotiated."

"John Sladen will make you look like a worse fool than Trist! He'll leak the story of you and compassionate Maria to every newspaper in Washington. It will be reprinted in New Jersey and New York. Your political career will be over!"

"Worse things could happen."

"You're throwing away your chance to be president! You can still rescue it if you say you came home to denounce the treaty! I can fix it with Sarah, and the president. I'll explain that stupid letter you wrote to him as a product of your head wound. He'll send you back to Mexico as minister plenipotentiary. In four years you'll come back and become president!"

George shook his head. "The thing is wrong, Caroline!"

"Wrong, right, how can you be so childish? Can't you see those words mean nothing in the face of history? Can't you see that this is the one chance we have of preventing the South from seceding? Give them Mexico, where they can satisfy their dreams of martial glory and take half of their slaves and reduce their fears of a race war. Give them a future that doesn't fill their nights with horrible dreams."

George shook his head. "Their worries about a race war have nothing to do with this. Occupying all of Mexico is wrong. The end never justifies the means, Caroline. The South will have to deal with slavery where it is, as it is. We'll have to help her, of course. We'll have to be patient."

"You're dreaming. The abolitionists are not going to be patient. They've opened a newspaper here in Washington. Flinging their filthy rhetoric in the very faces of Southern politicians. They're the most vicious, self-righteous people God ever created. Does Jeremy's letter suggest even a hint of a generous spirit?"

"I despise Jeremy Biddle at least as much as I despise Johnny Sladen. But that's personal. I'm prepared to deal with both of them politically."

"Nothing else could explain such delusions but a woman who's made you feel supernatural. Are you going back to her? Is she coming here?"

"No to both questions."

"If you go through with this, you'll never touch me again. You know that?"

For a moment Maria's voice whispered *forgive* in George's throbbing skull. "Caroline, can't we separate these two things, somehow?"

"No. You want to know why? Because you're not just betraying me. You're betraying the president and Sarah. He's dying little by little, day by day, in that house—thanks to this war. She's dying with him, in a way. Now I have to go tell them I've failed to change your mind for an excuse."

"You don't have to do anything. I'll go. I'm not afraid to say what I think. I've seen too many men die for this country—to let it be dishonored."

"They don't want to see you. Sarah wouldn't allow you to subject the president to an argument as stupid as the one we're having."

Caroline twisted away from him to crush her face into the cushions of the chair. "I loved you! I loved you! We could have been so happy!"

George struggled upstairs to their bedroom. He grabbed a nightshirt and blundered down the hall to his son Jonathan's room. He felt dazed, battered—it was not much different from how he felt after the Molino. He stared around the narrow room. The walls were decorated with mementos of Jonathan's years at Columbia. The decades whirled back to the day George Stapleton saw Caroline Kemble on the steamboat dock. Could it be true, what she said about loving him? For a moment Sor Juana flickered in his brain.

Hombres necios que acusais
a la mujer sin razón

Ah, stupid men, unreasonable
In blaming woman's nature

Maria Pena de Vega whispered, *You must forgive her.*

George dismissed them both. Forgiveness would restore Caroline's power over him. Once there was an honorable peace with Mexico, he would think about forgiveness.

Another, harsher voice asked, *But would Caroline?*

George knew the answer: *Never.* But he could not turn back now. Hugh

Stapleton and his shadowy friends, those faceless American fathers he had never met, Washington, Franklin, Hamilton, would not tolerate it. But the voice, unrelenting, refused to let him dodge what his determination meant. Again it snarled, *Never.*

TWELVE

AMERICANS WANT TO BE POWERFUL—AND good. Only a few of us understand we can't be both things. Lying in the canopied bed where she had expected to embrace a triumphant George Stapleton, Caroline listened to Aaron Burr's mordant wisdom. In the morning, without even five minutes of sleep, she arose and faced a haggard husband at the breakfast table. If there was any comfort in their joint insomnia, it was as cold as the weather outside. The rain had turned to sleet overnight, coating trees and buildings with an icy glaze.

In a detached voice, Caroline filled George in on his older sons. "Jonathan is turning into an abolitionist, thanks to his continuing friendship with his roommate, Ben Dall. Charlie is failing all his courses at Princeton. I think we should let him go to New Orleans, where John Sladen assures me he'll flourish on the Cotton Exchange, if you loan him fifty thousand dollars to give him a flying start."

"Where is he now?"

"At Bowood, where I fear he'll ruin some respectable young woman and give us another headache."

She took almost savage pleasure in that *us.* It reminded him that they were still husband and wife, no matter what they thought of each other.

"I'll talk to him. I'll talk to both of them. I'm going up to New Jersey as soon as possible. I intend to run Jeremy Biddle out of the family—and the state."

What did that mean? Was he trying to tell her that he regretted what he had learned from Jeremy? Or was he trying to say he regretted what they had said to each other last night? Probably neither.

"There's no hope of changing your mind about Mexico?"

His face froze into a mask of antagonism. He shook his big head. She shoved aside her coffee cup and told Mercy to order the chaise brought around to the front door.

"Where are you going?"

"To the White House."

She dressed in black, as if she were in mourning. In a way, she was. She was mourning the death of her dream of fame, the death of her dream of love for her husband. Would she also have to face the death of another love? What should she tell Sarah about George's revolt? The thought of confessing every-thing made her shudder.

Walking to the stairs, she passed Jonathan's room, where George had slept last night. On the dresser was Jeremy Biddle's letter. She stuffed it into her purse. What was she doing? Was she going to fling it into the Potomac? Show it to John Sladen? She could not explain the impulse. She only knew the thing belonged to her more than to George or anyone else.

Rolling through the empty ice-glazed streets, Caroline almost hoped the skittish mare that Judson Diggs had chosen for the chaise would stumble or run wild. A fatal accident would be the simplest solution to her dilemma. She composed an obituary in her head: *Mrs. Stapleton's salon at her 3600 Penn-sylvania Avenue home has been one of the adornments of Washington. Ex-pressions of sympathy from everyone of importance in the capital, from the President and First Lady to Daniel Webster to Dolley Madison, have deluged her grieving family.*

"Mornin', Miz Stapleton."

She was at the South Portico of the White House. The smiling Negro porter, Ezekiel, was calming the jumpy horse. The ice glistening on all the White House trees made the place look like a mansion in a fairy tale—or a nightmare. A crack as loud as a cannon shot made the horse—and Caroline—start. "What's that?" she cried.

"Tree limbs breakin' off. Not a good day to go out ridin'. One of them limbs could hurt a body real bad."

She ignored these cautionary words and strode into the White House. Fate apparently had other pains planned for her. Upstairs, a maid said Mrs. Polk was in her study.

Sarah was also in black. She was performing her daily ritual of reading the latest newspapers from New York, Boston, Chicago, and other cities, crowded with the usual sneers against James Knox Polk. The papers were stacked in a neat pile on her worktable.

"Can I interrupt you?" Caroline said.

"You can always interrupt me. Especially from this chore," Sarah said with a tired smile.

They exchanged a kiss and Sarah sank into her chair again. "Wait until you hear the latest news from Mexico," she said. "General Scott has court-martialed General Worth and General Pillow. They in turn are accusing him of all sorts of military misconduct. We were up until three A.M. drafting a letter that reprimands everyone."

Caroline nodded, gripped by an almost overwhelming nausea. How could she tell this exhausted woman more bad news? But it had to be done. "George arrived last night. Without a word of warning. He walked into my Thursday reception. Afterward, we talked. There's—there's no possibility of my chang-ing his mind. He intends to take his seat in the Senate and support the treaty without reservations."

"Is that all you have to tell me?"

Caroline struggled fiercely to suppress her tears. Today if ever she must not, she could not, be weak. But the tears remorselessly trickled down her cheeks. "I don't want to burden you with my . . . my pain. You have more than enough to contend with here."

"When two people love each other, the word *burden* loses its meaning."

"If I told you everything, you . . . might despise me. You would despise me. You couldn't help yourself. It would be the end of our love."

"Try me."

"It concerns an indiscretion, an immoral act, a sin—"

Caroline stopped in utter confusion, unable to believe that she had said that last word. Sins were only committed by believers in God. She was not, she never would be, one of those weak-kneed creatures. But she had said *sin*. Was she trying to anticipate what Sarah would call it?

"A *sin* I committed many years ago."

"Dearest, we're all sinners in God's eyes. He sees through our pretensions, our justifications. Surely you must know that every day I've spent in this house, I've faced my sin, my domineering pride, which has destroyed a good man's love and may yet destroy his life. The only thing that's sustained me is the knowledge that God understands and forgives me—and so do you."

There were tears on Sarah's face now. She wiped them away with the back of her hand, a gesture that somehow underscored her fierce determination to persevere in spite of the way her dream of fame had become a nightmare. A wild hope that love would understand, that love would forgive her, seized Caroline's soul. Wordlessly, she took Jeremy Biddle's letter from her purse and handed it to Sarah Childress Polk.

Caroline watched disbelief, then dismay, then revulsion, play across Sarah's face. When she finished, she slumped in her chair as if someone had struck her a savage blow. "It makes me wish . . . it makes me wish that there was no such thing as a woman."

"But there is," Caroline said. "There always will be."

"There isn't a word of truth in what he says about you and Sladen . . . since?"

"None."

"Has Sladen behaved honorably toward you?"

"Not always. But I've tried to forgive him. Men are tormented by dreams of mythical desire. Men like him, at any rate. With souls full of rage."

Sarah nodded. How much they had learned since they walked down Pennsylvania Avenue on that summer morning in 1828, twenty years ago. "Should we abandon All Mexico?"

"By no means. What George said to me last night has severed all and every bond of love, of loyalty, between us. In a curious way, I feel desolated—but free."

"I know what you mean," Sarah said in low, musing voice. "Love is a burden as well as a joy. We can live without joy."

She was confessing what she had hinted more than once—that her marriage with James Polk was as dead as Caroline's with George Stapleton. Had James snarled atrocious insults at her in the desperate hours between midnight and dawn when he faced the truth about his floundering presidency? Probably. Men have to strike out at something, and who is more convenient than their wives? Especially this wife, who had driven him to this personal Armageddon.

"I think we should proceed with our plan," Caroline said. "The treaty should go to the Senate with a noncommittal message from the president. Senator Sladen and his friends will understand that they have the president's permission to attack and destroy it."

"Have you spoken to Sladen?"

"No. I decided to wait until I saw George. Now I have no alternative—"

"I'm prepared to do it for you."

"No. I think you—above all—should remain aloof from this process. I don't trust Senator Sladen's discretion. He'll have to take my word for your alliance with him."

Sarah gestured to the newspapers. "I just read a letter in the Natchez paper from General John Quitman, endorsing All Mexico. Perhaps we should bring him home and offer to make him our minister plenipotentiary."

"Anyone but General Pillow."

Sarah sighed. "James's infatuation with that man has made me . . ." She let her bitter conclusion go unspoken.

"This will become very ugly before it's over," Caroline said. "There's another woman involved."

She told her about George's affair with Maria Pena de Vega. "John Sladen will use it to vilify George in the newspapers. You may want to use it yourself. A lack of invitations to the White House would say a great deal to insiders."

"I'm not sure I could go even that far."

"You must be prepared to do the *worst*. Don't allow sympathy for me to influence you. I'm prepared to be despised if George sees fit to defend himself with this abominable letter."

She picked up Jeremy Biddle's letter and stuffed it into her purse. She would have to return it to George eventually.

"He won't do that. I'm sure of it," Sarah said.

"I fear that will depend on how the debate on the treaty goes."

"I've never been more certain of our course. Everything I read in the mail and in the newspapers from the South convinces me that All Mexico is the only alternative to the collapse of the Union. The abolitionists have unhinged every politician south of Virginia. Especially since they've opened a newspaper here in Washington."

"George seems to think he can find a middle ground where Democrats can rally. I told him he's dreaming."

"In five years every Whig in the country will be an abolitionist or the first cousin to one. In New York, our old enemy Martin Van Buren is talking of a Democratic version of their creed. That would split the party irrevocably."

They were like priestesses in a secret religion, chanting exhortations to each other. For a soaring moment Caroline felt a thrill of pride, even of exultation. They were no longer mere acolytes in the Temple of Fame. They were mistresses of the establishment. Only their vision could rescue America from dismemberment and collapse.

"I'll go see Sladen now," Caroline said.

"The treaty will go to the Senate as soon as you tell us Sladen and his cohorts are ready. Meanwhile, we'll do what we can to line up support from here."

Out on Pennsylvania Avenue, the bitter wind pummeled Caroline's face. The streets were still glazed with ice. Tree limbs were down everywhere. Negroes, many of them wearing nothing but thin cotton shirts, were hauling the debris to the curbs. Slave traders with rifles and the inevitable whips in their belts shouted orders at them. The District government must have hired some Africans from the Lafayette Square slave market to do this badly needed chore.

Soon she was knocking on the front door of John Sladen's rooming house. It opened to emit a red-haired woman who had slattern written all over her. She even wore a scarlet dress, no doubt left over from last night's party. She shivered in the icy blast whirling down the street and clutched a shawl around her.

"Seen any hacks?"

"No," Caroline said, inhaling the woman's stale perfume as she pushed past her.

Inside, a fat Negress said Senator Sladen had not come down to breakfast. He was probably still in his room. Caroline climbed a stairway that reeked of whiskey and cigars. These bachelor boardinghouses all smelled the same. She knocked on the senator's door. He hastily admitted her, pulling a soiled red bathrobe around his spare frame.

A whiskey bottle was open on the bureau. Coals glowed in the vents of a potbellied stove. The redhead's stale perfume lingered in the warm air. "I'm here on a political errand," Caroline said. "Having seen George arrive last night, you may not be completely surprised by it."

She told him about the Trist treaty and George's support of it—in spite of the president's opposition. She described Jeremy Biddle's letter, but she did not show it to him. Her voice was as matter-of-fact and empty as her heart.

"I'm going to challenge that son of a bitch!" John raged.

"Stop acting like a Southern idiot and start thinking like the intelligent man I hope you still are. You've got the president's backing to destroy this treaty. That will leave us with All Mexico as the only alternative. With proper handling, it will revive the party and guarantee that the next president will be a Democrat."

"But that Democrat won't be George?"

"No."

"Who will it be?"

"I don't think it matters. The crucial thing is to keep the Whigs, and their friends the abolitionists, out of the White House."

"George is formidable. A war hero."

"But you have information that can destroy him. Use it. Put your reporter friends to work telling about his Mexican romance."

"Will you continue to live with him?"

"I suppose so. Our house is big enough to avoid each other most of the time."

"What if I became the Democratic candidate for president?"

"I'd vote for you."

"Is that all you'd do?"

She gazed at Senator Sladen's unshaven face. The man's soul had been shrinking before her eyes all these years, but she had never realized it so graphically until this moment. Was this what unrequited love did to a man? Or was there some other destructive process at work in his spirit?

"That is all I'd do, John. Once and for all, understand that."

"I may still try for it."

"The presidency?"

"Yes."

"Good luck. Let me know how soon you'll be ready to move. The president will wait for word from you before sending in the treaty."

"I understand."

"Rise to the occasion, John. Restrain your impulse to be snide. Speak like a statesman, an American statesman."

"You don't really think I'm one, do you."

You can take the boy out of the gutter, but you can't take the gutter out of the boy. She almost said those appalling words. She drove them from her tongue by an act of the will. "I want you to be one—perhaps for my sake. I'll love that part of you."

"It will be your creation. Like all the rest of me."

He lunged toward her in a blundering attempt at a kiss. She blocked him with her forearm and sent him stumbling back. "No, John. *No.*"

They gazed at each other. Could he really desire this husk of a woman? This inert collection of atoms, drifting in time? Down the fetid stairs to the freezing street Caroline went. She welcomed the savage cold. It could not begin to match the winter in her heart. But it was a tolerable companion. Summer would be the really difficult time. What would she do when the earth opened its warm mouth to the winds of June?

She would worry about that in June. Now, in the midst of winter, she had a country to save. The future of Caroline Kemble Stapleton's soul was irrelevant.

THIRTEEN

"GENTLEMAN, THE PRESIDENT'S ATTITUDE TOWARD THIS treaty speaks for itself. He has sent it to us, along with the sixty-page screed of the fool who negotiated it, simply to protect himself and the Democratic Party from the accusation that we are unnecessarily prolonging the war. Two years ago, we might have welcomed it. Today, with another ten thousand Americans in nameless graves in Mexico, and the government of that so-called country in a state of total disintegration, it is a joke, a joke in bad taste, an insult to the intelligence of every man in this Senate, to suggest we should approve it. Anyone who makes this argument can be identified as a man with an ulterior motive—of party, of ambition, or some even more unsavory stimulus."

Senator George Stapleton hunched forward at his desk, his big body involuntarily coiled to lunge at Senator John Sladen of Louisiana, who was speaking at his desk, only a few feet away from him. George somehow restrained himself. It was better to pretend that none of those sneering words applied to him. In spite of the column that had appeared in the *New York Morning News* yesterday, describing the way a certain senator who had gone to Mexico as a hero had come home as a fancy man. The senator, the reporter declared, was the love slave of a Mexican woman whose family stood to gain a hefty slice of the $15 million Mr. Trist had agreed to pay Mexico for California and New Mexico—territory we already possessed by right of conquest. The column had been reprinted today in the *Washington Union*, the official newspaper of the Democratic Party. The implied message was unmistakable: the president himself was confirming the story.

George gazed around the Senate chamber, remembering other days when history had loomed large here. Daniel Webster annihilating Robert Young Hayne's attempt to argue a state's right to secede; John C. Calhoun denouncing Andrew Jackson's plans to invade South Carolina. Henry Clay lashing Jackson's attack on the Bank of the United States. Now Webster, Clay, and Calhoun were spent men: Webster drunk most of the time, mourning the death of his son Fletcher from typhoid in Mexico; Clay back in Kentucky in the same condition, mourning the death of his son at Buena Vista; Calhoun politically isolated by his refusal to support the war in Mexico. Ultimately, all three of these giants were silenced by the history that had stormed through their days, wreaking havoc on their personal lives and their political ambitions.

How had his grandfather Hugh Stapleton achieved his marvelous serenity? George thought he knew the answer. In the Congressman's marriage, he had found a happiness that transcended the vicissitudes of politics and history. George would never have that consolation. In the lottery of life he had drawn a woman who set preconditions on her love, who only yielded it when a man submitted to her ideas. There she sat, two dozen feet away on one of the couches reserved for special guests, dressed in funereal black, her beautiful face hidden by a veil. The clothes, the veil, were deliberate; she was advertising her grief for the death of her marriage in Mexico. She might as well have dictated that story in the *New York Morning News*.

Rage gathered in George's throat. He might never achieve Hugh Stapleton's serenity. But he would not go to his grave as Caroline Kemble Stapleton's yes-man. George Dallas, the vice president, recognized him as the next speaker.

"Mr. President, the senator from Louisiana and his friends seem to me, in the words of the Bard of Avon, to protest too much. They seem desperately eager to impute to those who recognize this treaty as a more than just compensation for our struggles in Mexico the worst imaginable motives. I will go even further than that: with the help of their hired reporters, they have been willing to stoop to the lowest slanders against me and other senators who support it. My wife, whom all of you know and esteem, is not sitting in this chamber, veiled and in funereal black, by accident. On the contrary, she is making a silent statement of reproach to men who would stoop so low. Their tactics force me to question *their* motives, to wonder if greed has not twisted their judgment, their sense of honor, their commitment to the honor of the United States, which should be the driving force in the heart of every man in this sacred chamber."

George sat down, amused by the fury on Sladen's face. Caroline's expression was withheld from him, but he found a bitter pleasure in imagining it was a fair copy of Sladen's. Before George could savor this small triumph, Senator Jefferson Davis of Mississippi was on his feet. As one of the heroes of Monterrey and Buena Vista, he more than equaled George's military aura. He began talking about the thousands of men he had seen die in northern Mexico. Now, after a year of American occupation, with banditry suppressed and local elections for mayor and other offices conducted democratically, without fear of reprisal from some thug like General Santa Anna, these provinces were clamoring to become part of the United States. "How can we refuse them?" Davis asked. "How can I go back to Mississippi and face the parents, brothers, sisters, wives, of the men who died at Monterrey and Buena Vista and tell them that their loved ones' sacrifices have been ignored? This Trist treaty is a betrayal of American blood!"

Senator Thomas Corwin of Ohio launched a ferocious assault on the treaty from the abolitionist point of view. The war was a James Knox Polk lie, from start to finish, Corwin ranted. "Trist's paper," as he called it, was one more lie. Corwin wanted to see California, New Mexico, even the disputed parts of Texas, returned to Mexico to prove to the world that America had not fought for conquest. He called for an apology from the Senate of the United States to the people of Mexico.

Senator Sam Houston of Texas rose to thunder denunciations against President Polk's "pusillanimity." He could not believe the man Andrew Jackson had chosen to lead the Democratic Party and the nation approved this treaty. Would Jackson accept it? Absolutely not! Houston roared. He would treat Mexican treachery exactly the way he had treated Spanish treachery in Florida. He would exact the full measure of justice that conquest entitled him to demand. He would do so not only to punish Mexico, but to guarantee the safety of Texas. "I ask every Democrat in this chamber to reject this treaty, in the name of the man who stands next to Washington as the father of this country!" Houston shouted.

George looked around him, desperately counting heads. He did not see more than a dozen votes in favor of the treaty. Everyone was allowing personal and particular objections to swell into a chorus of faultfinding. The Whigs were united to a man in favor of rejection. The fools thought it would be President Polk's ultimate humiliation. They were gorging themselves on the bait of party antagonism. They had no intimation of the bombshell the White House was prepared to drop in their laps.

In the House of Representatives, Democrats were orating about the danger of England or France seizing prostrate Mexico, if the United States cut it adrift. Annexation had enormous appeal to the younger members of the party. Bankers and manufacturers backed the idea as a stimulus to business. The army and navy supported it to a man, seeing endless expansion and promotions in a semipermanent state of war. Even some opponents of slavery echoed Caroline's argument that an annexed Mexico would draw off slaves from Tennessee, Kentucky, and Virginia, where the system had become unprofitable, and turn them into free states.

One Whig senator remained silent: Jeremy Biddle. Last week, George had gone to New Jersey with Jeremy's letter. George had thrust it in his face and told him he wanted him out of Principia Industries by the end of the year. George would borrow the money from New York bankers to buy Sally Stapleton Biddle's 50 percent share of the business. Jeremy had wept and begged him to forgive him for the letter. It had been Sally's idea. He had succumbed to it in a moment of weakness. George had slammed him against the wall and told him his moment of weakness began the day he was born.

With the country enjoying an economic boom as a result of the war, the price of Sally Stapleton's shares in Principia Industries would be at least $10 million. Caroline had been appalled. George was risking the loss of the company. The interest on the loan would be five hundred thousand dollars a year. He was bequeathing his children a heritage of debt. George ignored her. He knew it was a bad decision. But he was determined to cleanse his life of everything that had befouled his happiness.

In the Senate doorway stood the stooped withered figure of Congressman John Quincy Adams. George turned his back on Houston's fulminations and took the ex-president by the arm. "Age before beauty, Mr. President," he said. "You must sit at my desk and listen to this nonsense in comfort, at least."

More than a few eyes on the Whig side of the aisle followed Adams as he stumped on his cane to George's desk. Not many Democrats made public appearances with the old man. Every Southern politician hated him for his relentless attacks on slavery.

"I don't much like what I'm hearing," Adams said.

"At the moment, I would say the treaty will be lucky to get twenty votes," George said.

"I have a speech planned for tomorrow. No doubt it will be to an empty House. Every mother's son of them will be over here watching this . . . this obscenity."

"I wish I could offer you some hope, Mr. President."

"What is Polk doing? A president can apply pressure on a few senators, no matter how unpopular he is."

"I fear he's a very sick man. Sick and discouraged and ready to let fate take charge of things."

"Men take charge of things, Senator Stapleton. Fate does very little. When I was president, I drifted into a similar lassitude. I let supposedly more worldly men take charge of my campaign against Jackson in 1828. I found myself forever tarred by those slanders they wrote against Mrs. Jackson. You know Polk. Tell him his days and nights will be haunted by regret if he lets Southern extremists like Sladen take charge of our nation. New England and the Midwest will secede rather than surrender to such an unsavory crew."

"Put that in your speech tomorrow, Mr. President. I promise to be one of the listeners."

The next day, as the Senate began another round of oratory, George went over to the House to hear John Quincy Adams's speech. The old man tottered to his desk looking too feeble for oratory. As he predicted, the House was virtually empty. The members were all following the treaty debate in the Senate. The Speaker of the House recognized the member from Massachusetts. Adams struggled to rise, fell back in his seat, and tried again. A choking sound came from his throat and he toppled sideways onto the floor.

George and several congressmen rushed to his side. They carried him into the Speaker's office and lowered him onto a couch. Pages were sent scurrying to find a doctor. Two or three congressmen had medical degrees. The old man clasped George's hand. "This is the last of earth," he murmured. "Take the notes for my speech—do what you can with them."

A convulsion shook his bulky frame. He lapsed into unconsciousness. For two more days he lingered between life and death and finally slipped into the shadows. The passing of an ex-president, however unpopular he might be to the party in power, was not something official Washington could ignore. The Senate and the House suspended sessions. Adams's body lay in state in the rotunda, and solemn oratory recalled his long service to the nation. Throughout the three days of mourning, George circulated among his fellow senators, telling them what the old man had intended to say in his undelivered speech, and distributing selected quotations from Adams's notes to reinforce his case.

When the Senate reconvened the day after the Adams funeral train left for Massachusetts, George sensed a remarkable change of mood. He rose to deliver a spontaneous speech, without a note to bolster him. "I was not always an admirer of John Quincy Adams," he said. "I felt he sought and even exploited antagonism with the South in the name of his self-righteous New England conscience. But I recognized him as a man who had love of this country implanted in his heart from boyhood—an experience I shared. In the last few days, I have tried to communicate to many of the gentlemen in this chamber the things he hoped to say about the choice we face in accepting or rejecting this treaty with Mexico. He boldly broke with the doctrinaires of his own Whig Party, who are hoping to torpedo this treaty to embarrass the president. He rejected the narrow arguments of the abolitionists, with whom he sometimes seemed to make common cause. Instead, he stood on the lofty heights which age and decades of statesmanship entitled him to hold—and urged us to accept this treaty as honorable to us and ultimately beneficial to Mexico. The fifteen million dollars we are paying them removes the sting of conquest and will enable them to reorganize their government on a sound financial footing. I plead with you, in the name of his years, his association with Washington and Jefferson and Hamilton and Madison, to accept John Quincy Adams's judgment."

To George's amazement, senator after senator rose to support these sentiments. In the three days of mourning, many of them had repented of their hotheaded initial reactions to the treaty. Even Sam Houston, who hated to change his mind about anything, told George during a noon recess that he had decided to take a trip to New Hampshire—withdrawing his formidable presence from the argument and absolving himself from the need to vote either way.

The next day, March 7, 1848, Vice President George Dallas decided it was time to put the treaty to a vote. As the ayes and nays rolled up and down the aisles, George realized no less than a dozen Whigs were voting for the treaty. With them came twenty-six Democrats. Seven Democrats and seven Whigs, all from the South, voted against it. The treaty had won, 38–14, comfortably beyond the needed two-thirds majority.

That night at supper, George Stapleton confronted a sullen wife. They were dining alone. Paul had been sent to visit a friend. The sliding doors of the dining room were shut against the intrusion of everyone except Mercy Flowers, who made a point of knocking before she entered with the next course. They ate in icy silence for a half hour. Finally George spoke. "I didn't do it. Old John Quincy was responsible. If he hadn't died, the vote would have gone the other way by about the same numbers. Sladen had the Democrats stampeded, and the Whigs were going to vote against Polk no matter what anyone said."

"Are you trying to tell me that God is in charge of the foreign policy of the United States?"

"Someone a lot more powerful than you or me seems to have something to do with it now and then."

"You're talking absolute nonsense."

"Maybe."

"I look forward to hearing what you'll say when the South announces it's going to secede. Will you vote for civil war? Will you send your sons to die for your ridiculous opinions?"

"That isn't going to happen."

"It *will* happen. There's nothing you or I can do about it now."

For a moment George felt almost awed by Caroline's passionate certainty. She was like a priestess from some ancient rite, hurling prophecies into history's blank face. A new kind of desire stirred in George's blood. He wanted to subdue this woman, this perpetual other who had challenged and subdued him for so long. Had it all been a performance, a willful determination to conceal her original sin? He had just defeated, even routed, the man she might still love. Now George wanted her surrender, her confession of fault, failure, guilt.

In the same moment George knew that he was wishing for the impossible. *You must forgive her,* Maria Pena de Vega whispered. He could never do that until Caroline Kemble Stapleton asked his forgiveness—and that would never happen.

Caroline's voice, as hard and cold as a gun barrel, broke into this twisting rush of wish and hope and regret. "One thing I will *never* forgive you for is your betrayal of the president. You don't seem to have the slightest idea of how ending the war this way destroys him."

"Caroline, you're wrong. I predict James K. Polk will ride high in the history books. Historians aren't interested in a president's personal agonies. They only measure what he's done, and he's done a great deal. I predict the treaty will be popular with the country, once people calm down and this frenzy about annexing Mexico disappears."

"Frenzy? Is that how you characterize an idea that I presented to you as one of my deepest, most serious convictions?"

"It became a frenzy with a lot of people."

She glared at him, daring him to say what he really thought. Although he avoided her eyes, he accepted her challenge. "It was a bad idea, Caroline. A very bad idea."

"You disgust me. You *repel* me. I think our sleeping arrangements had better become permanent. I don't want you in the same room with me when I'm in a state of undress. The thought of yielding to you on some unwanted impulse horrifies me."

You must forgive her, Maria pleaded. Alas, forgiveness had become a disembodied ghost, receding down a labyrinthine passageway that George could never negotiate. Yet there was the memory of Hugh Stapleton's serenity. Was there no hope of achieving it?

"If you could at least tell me you're sorry," George said.

"Could you tell me that?"

"Yes. I could tell you that now."

"I can't. I doubt if I can ever say it. I may feel it—but I'll never say it."

"So be it," George said.

A knock on the door. Paul stood there, uncertain, earnest, with Jonathan's serious mien and Charlie's good looks. "You're home early," George said.

"Ralph has a lot of homework. So do I." Paul and several other boys his age were being tutored by a graduate of the Jesuit college, Georgetown.

Paul held out a newspaper. "It looks as if you're getting more famous by the minute, Father."

It was a special edition of the *Washington Union*. The story of the treaty's ratification dominated the front page. In the center was a box in bolder type.

> A new leader of the Democratic Party emerged in the Senate today. Senator George Stapleton of New Jersey was the man responsible for ratifying the treaty with Mexico and ending the war on a note of reasonable honorable triumph. His name must be added to the Democratic Party's list of presidential candidates, forthwith. The people will insist on it. The leaders of the Democratic Party should insist on it.

George handed the paper to Caroline. "Do you think the president approved that before it went in?" he asked. Thomas Ritchie, the editor of the *Union,* was often the president's spokesman, but he did not show everything he printed to the White House first.

"I hope Mr. Polk isn't such a fool," Caroline said. "But I've reached the point where I'm ready to believe anything is possible."

She flung the paper on the table, knocking over her water glass, and stalked out of the dining room. Paul was wide-eyed.

"Your mother and I have been having a political disagreement," George said. "Don't let it concern you."

"I thought Mother wanted you to be president. She's told us all you would be, one day."

"She seems to have changed her mind. You'll have to ask her why."

"I will. I think you should be president, Father. Don't listen to that fool Jonathan, with his yammering against the war."

"I've had a long talk with Jonathan. I think he understands a little more about the war now."

Was that true? George wondered, remembering Jonathan's sullen young face, silently refuting every word he said. A desolating loneliness engulfed George. For some reason, life seemed to be stripping him of every human consolation—Jeremy's friendship, his wife's love, his oldest son's loyalty. Could he bear it? He could only hope Maria was praying for him.

At the dark, silent White House, Caroline found Sarah Polk in her study and asked her for an explanation of the story in the *Washington Union*. "We had nothing to do with Ritchie's nomination of George as our next president. But we have no objections to it," Sarah said in a strange monotone.

But I do, Caroline Kemble Stapleton thought. You must know I do. "Surely Ritchie knows what's come out about his private life in Mexico," Caroline said.

"I suppose so. Ritchie's a bit of a fool. I warned James against him."

"But the treaty—by implication you seem to approve its ratification."

"I prayed over the treaty. I asked God to help me accept it. He answered my prayers. It's best for the president. I think it may be best for the country too."

Sarah's voice was lifeless. She sounded as if she were reciting a rote lesson in geography or history, drilled into her head by some fearsome pedagogue. What had happened? Caroline was bewildered—and appalled.

"How can it be best for the president?" Caroline said. "Didn't we agree that only a truly magnificent triumph could rescue his administration from . . . from—"

"We've decided to stop worrying about words like *failure* and *success*. No one knows what they really mean while they're in this house. In a year we'll be out of it. I want to keep James alive. I want to bring him home to Nashville and spend the rest of my life trying to make amends for this nightmare I've imposed on him."

Love, Caroline thought. It was the uncontrollable factor in so many things. Her dearest friend, who had pledged her love to Caroline a thousand times, was confessing there was another love, more needy, more compelling.

"I've prayed for you too," Sarah said. She sat there, still in funereal black, her eyes pleading for forgiveness. On the rose-colored walls of the small study hung a portrait of Dolley Madison in her bejeweled, red-cheeked first-lady prime. She had survived eight years in this house with her serenity intact. What was her secret?

"I'm not withdrawing an iota of my love for you," Sarah said. "Nor do I doubt for a moment the conclusion we reached—that annexing all Mexico could solve the problem of the South and slavery. Another solution will have to be found."

"What if there is no other solution? Can you live with that?"

"In this house, you learn to live with many things you thought would destroy you."

Tears trickled down Sarah's gaunt cheeks. Caroline remained dry-eyed. She was beyond tears, beyond love. She had retreated to her ice cave above the sunless sea. Was that where she would spend the rest of her life?

Perhaps. Because hurtling through her soul were words that would destroy the only love she had left. "You despise me now, why don't you admit it?"

"Despise you?" Sarah said. "How can you even imagine such a thing?"

"You know my secret. You know the disgusting truth about me. In your sanctified soul you can't possibly love a woman who's guilty of such a sin."

"Jesus loved Mary Magdalen."

"Exactly what I mean. You think I'm a whore. You're prepared to love me in Jesus' name. I don't want that kind of love. I want the love we felt when we stood on the West Portico of the Capitol in 1828 and looked down at the White House in the distance. I want that moment or nothing!"

"You have it! I swear to God you have it!"

"No, I don't. If I had it, that obscenity about George Stapleton being our next president would never have appeared in the *Union!* You must know that makes me look like a *fool.* To him, to my sons—to myself!"

Sarah twisted in her chair as if she were strapped into it and desperately trying to escape. Her head drooped. "It was the president's idea. I tried to stop him, but he said George Stapleton had done more for him and this country than I've ever done. He said All Mexico was one more example, the ultimate example, of my arrogance. Then he told me he had sent word to friends in the Senate that he approved the treaty, that he agreed with George. That's why it passed."

Suddenly the stage was barren of players. They were alone, both stripped of love, of pride, of hope. For a long time Caroline heard nothing but Sarah Childress Polk's sobs. Finally Caroline stood up, took her handkerchief out of her purse, and slowly, tenderly wiped away Sarah's tears. Caroline kissed her damp, trembling mouth and walked out of the White House for the last time.

BOOK

SEVEN

ONE

THE DAY AFTER CAROLINE SAID GOOD-BYE to Sarah Polk, she informed George that she was moving back to Bowood. If he wished to continue living in Washington, that was his business. She was sick of the place, sick of politics, sick of trying to save a country that was not worth the effort. George stonily informed her that he not only intended to stay in politics, he planned to seek the Democratic Party's nomination for president. He was sure the story in the *Washington Union* meant he had James Polk's backing.

"What do you think that's worth? Jim Thumb Polk couldn't get elected justice of the peace in any state in the country. How is he going to elect someone like you—with Maria Pena de Vega on his escutcheon?"

"The newspapers said a lot worse about Old Hickory and he got elected," George said.

It was amazing how the mama's boy had changed. George confronted her without the slightest waver in his gaze. He no longer respected her opinions. He no longer feared her disapproval and the implied loss of her love. Caroline decided she did not care. The only thing she wanted now was vindication. She wanted revenge for the monstrous thing George had done to her and Sarah. She wanted the South to secede. She wanted it to happen *tomorrow*.

"You're probably right about Maria. She'll even give you a certain aura with some voters," she said. "But you'll never become president. You'll do something stupid, something I'd never let you do. Even if you get to the White House, you'll find yourself governing only half a country. The South is going to leave this Union sooner or later. Probably sooner."

"I'm going to run as their candidate. I'll get Calhoun's backing. I'll keep them in the Union."

Caroline laughed. "Calhoun is yesterday's hero. He opposed the war. There aren't ten Southerners outside South Carolina who'll listen to him."

He let her go back to New Jersey without another word. She arrived at Bowood after nightfall. She went straight to the library and lit an oil lamp and placed it on a table near Hannah Cosway Stapleton's picture. She sat there for a long time, daring her to say *Oh, my dear girl, I fear for thy salvation*. She wanted to tell her she had no interest in salvation. She only cared about *vindication*. But the voice was silent.

Caroline pulled the wedding ring off her finger. Throw it out the window while those saintly eyes stared into timelessness? Would that make her speak? Eventually, she put the ring back on her finger. Throwing away the ring would be a meaningless gesture. Wearing it until she saw her vindication would be far more satisfying.

She found ink and paper on the desk beneath the Congressman's portrait at the other end of the library and wrote a letter to Sarah Childress Polk, telling her she had left Washington.

> *The love and ambitions we shared have been the most important emotions of my life. They were the compass by which I steered for twenty years. The denouement has been a disappointment so profound, I think it is best to put distance between me and the scene of the tragedy. My love for you remains undiminished and I accept your testimony that your own heart remains undefiled by any taint of diminution. But history, another word for the malice and stupidity of our time, has cut out love's tongue. I fear we have nothing more to say to each other, or the world. I would like to hope I'm wrong. But my mind bars such a possibility. I can only try to accept what has happened and eventually resume a mechanical imitation of life, without its soul. May you and James find a better fate in Nashville.*

Sarah Polk did not reply to this letter. From New Jersey, Caroline watched the rest of the year 1848 unfold in Washington, D.C., like events on a distant planet seen through a telescope. Her lens was John Sladen, who wrote her a stream of letters, reporting on the bizarre twists and turns of the presidential campaign.

George Stapleton's pursuit of the Democratic nomination soon faltered. Senator Calhoun expressed personal support, but as Caroline had predicted, his name was worthless outside South Carolina, and even there they were not inclined to listen to his advice very often. Having declared himself a man of peace, it made no sense for him to back an ex-general such as George Stapleton. *Calhoun is a dead man politically and he will soon be one in all other respects,* John Sladen wrote. It was an epitaph to the hopes he had once flung around this magnetic, tormented man. John's own hopes for the presidency had long since expired. Too many people were repelled by the gross corruption of his Louisiana political machine.

More important than Calhoun's collapse, the Whigs nominated General Zachary Taylor. It was, John Sladen said, a turnabout that should have made the whole country into instant cynics. The party that had excoriated the war with Mexico backed the man who had won it—or so he claimed. The nomination was plausible only because deep in their patriotic hearts Americans approved the victorious war and the treaty of peace. At least they loved the five hundred thousand square miles it had added to the national domain. They could simultaneously salve their consciences by voting for Taylor, implicitly repudiating the president who had gotten the country into the war, supposedly for all the vicious motives the Whigs imputed to him—and then, according to these same inflamed critics, mismanaged the business.

The Whigs are betting that the people believe only the heroism of the American soldier and the genius of General Taylor have rescued us from dis-

grace, John wrote. *If this doesn't stand Jefferson's dictum "The people shall come right in the end" on its head, what does?*

Trapped in this political maze, the Democrats floundered. The only general on the horizon whose fame equaled Taylor's was Winfield Scott, but he was a Whig, on record as despising Democrats in general and James K. Polk in particular. A Southerner was equally out of the question, because Taylor, born in Virginia and living in Louisiana, also held that card.

The Democrats turned to Lewis Cass, the deep-throated, bullnecked senator from Michigan, who had served in Jackson's cabinet and had fluttered aloft at the Democratic Convention that nominated James Polk. Cass gave the party a chance to win the West and the border states, and he was unobjectionable to Democrats in their Eastern strongholds. He could carry the Jackson banner, and he did his best to hoist it high. In Jackson's name he approved the war and the acquisition of Texas and every square inch of the new territories. He said as little as possible about President Polk but damned Congressman Wilmot and his proposal to bar slavery in the new territories as a threat to the solidarity of the Union.

From New York came news that destroyed any chance of a Democrat defeating Taylor. The bitter old fox, Martin Van Buren, announced he was running for president as an antislavery "free soil" Democrat. He backed Wilmot's proviso and insisted that no Democrat with a conscience could vote for Senator Cass. For a vice president, to guarantee his spoiler's role, Van Buren chose Charles Francis Adams, son of John Quincy Adams. John Sladen could only babble Democratic outrage. He told Caroline of trying to persuade the president to denounce Van Buren as a traitor to the party and the country. All he could get from the spent Polk was a sigh: "Mr. Van Buren is the most fallen man I have ever known."

Van Buren and Adams won only 10 percent of the vote nationwide. But they took enough votes away from Cass in New Jersey, Pennsylvania, and New York to give those normally Democratic bastions to General Taylor, making him president by a whiskery thirty-six electoral votes. Caroline could not imagine a worse humiliation for Sarah and James Polk. A majority of the people had swallowed the Whigs' lies and elected the man who had wrecked the president's plan for a swift victory in Mexico and then slandered Polk in the newspapers for failing to support him and his army. The people, an entity in which Caroline had never had much faith, sank to minus zero in her political calculus.

On the morning after the election, Caroline came downstairs to Bowood's breakfast room to find Senator Stapleton reading the newspapers with a cheerful expression on his face. "You look like you're almost glad Senator Cass lost," Caroline said.

"I'm glad that Van Buren lost. He's reduced himself to a cipher, in and out of the Democratic Party. It proves that slavery isn't an issue to most voters. They think the Union is a lot more important."

He pointed to the voter totals in New Jersey, New York, and Pennsylvania. "We'll get a lot of them back in 1852. Taylor is going to be a disaster in the White House. The next president will be a Democrat—if we keep our heads and avoid feuds and fanaticism."

"A rather large if."

"You sound as if you hope I'm wrong."

"What does it matter what I think? I'm a mere woman."

George put down the newspapers. "You'll never be a mere woman to me—or to anyone else who knows you."

George had returned to New Jersey for the 1848 campaign. He had spent many of his nights at Bowood. They had dined together. They had exchanged observations and comments about the candidates. It was impossible not to converse. Especially when Paul returned from his Georgetown school for the summer. They had gone to Kemble Manor for July and August. Caroline could think of no plausible excuse for sweltering in Bowood. The result was more conversation, and disturbing memories of happy summers in that enchanted house.

Was George suggesting they negotiate some sort of truce? Caroline regarded him through the reversed lens of her telescope. It was easily adapted to a personal dimension. He had no idea what she thought or felt, of course. He did not know he was dealing with a creature who had retreated to her cave of ice. The telescope reduced George to the size of a beetle. He even looked a little like one, with the flesh of middle age on his thickening neck. He sat there, looking ready to scuttle for cover if she so much as stamped her foot.

Shoving her telescope aside, what did she see? A presidential candidate. The Democrats, singed twice in eight years by the Whigs' penchant for generals, would likely turn to a general in 1852. George was an authentic hero. Four years of marinating his Mexican exploits in the newspapers and in a book or two could easily convert him into a front-runner. But did it matter? Did she care? He could not prevent the South from seceding. Could she covertly accelerate the process as his supposed helpmate?

She rather liked that idea. It amused her. That was the only way to flavor her life in the ice cave—with the perfume of amusement. "I'm not prepared to let you touch me," she said.

"I understand."

"I have no feeling for you whatsoever."

"I understand."

"Why do you want a zombie as a wife?"

"I want you as a wife, no matter what you say you are. That way we can hope to forgive each other."

"I don't think it will happen. Events . . . are likely to increase the loathing."

"I don't loathe you. I could never even come close to such a thing."

She refused to answer him in kind. The implication was all too clear. Perhaps someday she would explain how he had destroyed not one but two loves in her heart.

"I'll come back to Washington after the Polks leave."

"Why not sooner?"

She shook her head. "After they leave." She was not required to explain anything to him—or anyone else.

They turned to the problem of Charlie. He had just been thrown out of

Princeton for the same reason he had been expelled from North Carolina—a total neglect of his studies. Caroline urged George to consent to sending him to New Orleans with enough money to launch a career as a cotton broker, under John Sladen's supervision. George bristled at the mention of Sladen's name and swore he did not want Charlie exposed to his influence.

"Isn't it time we gave Charlie a chance to become a man on his own terms—not ours?" Caroline said.

Was she conspiring against her husband in the name of Charlie's freedom? She knew exactly what he would do when he got to New Orleans, with its endless procession of available women. Was she trying to give one of her sons—the one she secretly loved the most—a chance to enjoy the wild desire she had denied herself in the name of that spurious goddess, fame?

The questions, which she declined to answer, made Caroline wonder if she too was a tiny insect in someone's eye—perhaps God's.

Jonathan, ever the dutiful oldest son, would soon graduate from Columbia and apparently had no objection to going to work for the Camden & Amboy Railroad. Caroline liked that almost as much as she liked the thought of Charlie in New Orleans. Jonathan was so earnest, so devoted to the Stapleton family's honor and fame. What would he do if she told him he had scarcely an ounce of their sacred patriotic blood in his veins?

Another amusing thought. But she saw no point in disillusioning Jonathan. She was thoroughly in favor of maintaining all their illusions—even Charlie's. Only she, in her airless cave festooned with icy stalactites and failed memories, had no illusions. Only she knew what was going to happen—and she did not care.

"Sarah Polk asks for you every time she sees me," George said.

"Why?" Caroline said.

"She's very fond of you."

"I love her. But we have nothing to say to each other anymore."

"She must be unhappy. Imagine having to smile and shake hands with President-elect Taylor? I don't think I can do it. The man's a charlatan."

"She'll do it."

After all, I'm conversing with you as if I did not loathe you. That's almost as difficult as conversing with Zachary Taylor. Women are resourceful creatures. They have an almost infinite capacity for submission.

"Poor Jim Polk. He never had any luck. Not one stroke of it."

"I never wished him any. I wanted him to deserve his fame."

"What do you mean?"

"It's a line from an old play."

Once more, it was impossible to explain. Once more she was forced to confront how much of her heart had belonged to Sarah Childress Polk.

Caroline stayed in Bowood while George returned to Washington for the final session of Congress in President Polk's administration. Nothing of any consequence transpired, and Zachary Taylor was duly installed as president of the United States on March 5, 1849. The Polks had moved out of the White House the previous night and were staying at the Indian Queen. George skipped the inaugural ball that evening and went to the hotel to say good-bye to them. He found the ex-president extremely agitated and Sarah trying desperately to calm him.

In a letter to Caroline, George described the scene.

> *Polk was lying on a couch, his face as brown as the rug. Sarah was saying, "It's over, James. It's not our responsibility anymore."*
>
> *"It's easy for you to say that," Polk snarled. "They won't mention you in the history books. They won't call you a man who was too small for the job."*
>
> *"Mr. President," I said. "That's not what the historians will say, I'm sure of it."*
>
> *"Oh, no?" Polk said. "Wait until you hear what Taylor said to me today on the way to the inaugural ceremony."*
>
> *Taylor had announced that he supported the Wilmot Proviso and intended to do everything in his power to prevent slavery from spreading to the new territories. He added that he saw no point in trying to rule states as distant as California and Oregon. He thought they should be allowed to become independent! Poor Polk was speechless. I could see why he was still upset. This brainless old faker was going to unravel everything Polk had devoted four agonizing years to achieving.*

Caroline reached Washington a week after the Polks departed. She was instantly deluged with calls and notes from well-wishers, eager to congratulate her on the recovery of her health. George had told everyone she had retreated to New Jersey to recover from some unnamed affliction. The household at 3600 Pennsylvania Avenue welcomed her with equal enthusiasm. Mercy Flowers still presided in the kitchen, and the Parks sisters had kept the rest of the house spotless and gleaming.

"If you have a mind, you could hold one of your salons tonight, mistress," Mercy said.

"I don't think there will be any more salons," Caroline said. "I'm not a politician anymore."

There was one missing face—Tabitha Flowers. Mercy told Caroline that Tabitha had married a free black man named Rhodes. "She still blames the senator for her father's gettin' killed in Mexico," Mercy said.

Caroline studied Mercy and Tabitha through her psychological telescope. Everyone was equal through this magical lens—equally insignificant. They were dust motes, twisting and dancing in the meaningless winds of eternity. But she said all the right things about how sorry she was, how much she wished she could talk to Tabitha.

In the newspapers, Caroline followed the Polks' progress toward Nashville. Sarah had told George they planned to go home via New Orleans, rather than travel west through Pennsylvania and Ohio, states where the Democratic ex-president might have encountered hostile crowds. They journeyed south by train and steamboat, often pausing in places such as Montgomery, Alabama, to be honored at public dinners.

At New Orleans, Polk's 1844 campaign nickname, Young Hickory, was revived by enthusiastic crowds, and for a few days he enjoyed the reflected glow of Andrew Jackson's fame. But Caroline noted signs of trouble in the newspaper accounts. The reporter for the *New York Herald* commented on how easily the ex-president tired and how reluctant he was to eat the rich food served at one of the public banquets. At Memphis, doctors hurried aboard the steamboat to examine Polk, who feared he had contracted cholera. Caroline knew what that meant—the president's "complaint," the diarrhea that had sapped his strength, had returned.

At Nashville, an immense crowd greeted the Polks at the steamboat dock. Again, the *New York Herald*'s reporter noted that the ex-president was visibly exhausted by the brief ceremony. But the next day's story, describing the Polks in the handsome house Sarah had chosen for their retirement, seemed to promise peace and contentment. For the next two months, their names vanished from the newspapers as the new president began the task of governing the divided nation.

Caroline continued her life as a spiritual cave dweller. From an enormous distance she heard George denounce Zachary Taylor's idiotic policies, which were certain to bring on a crisis with the South. George's voice was as tiny as his physique. Everyone she saw in her rare ventures downtown was equally minute. Even the great Daniel Webster was the size of a toy soldier. His voice, lamenting the absence of her salon as Washington's only island of civilization, was a squeak, a comic parody of pride.

On June 16, 1849, when Caroline came down to breakfast, she noticed a peculiar expression on George's face. It was a combination of sorrow and anxiety. "What's wrong?" she asked. "Has something happened to Charlie?" For a moment she actually felt an emotion. She realized love, or some imitation of it, was still alive in her soul.

George handed the *Washington Union* to Caroline as she sat down at the breakfast table. The headline above the story in the center of the front page read, "President Polk Dead." The reporter described how he had visited Polk only two weeks earlier and found him striding across the lawn of his house, directing workmen who were cutting down some dead cedars. He seemed content and healthy. But the next day it rained and he spent it indoors, arranging his library. *The labor of reaching books from the floor and placing them on the shelves brought on fatigue and a slight fever,* wrote the reporter, *which the next day assumed the character of disease in the form of chronic diarrhea, a complaint of many years standing, and easily induced upon his system by any overexertion.*

"Imagine dying from putting a few books on shelves," George said. "It shows how little strength he had left."

"Yes," Caroline said.

"The White House devoured that poor fellow. It makes me wonder if I'm crazy to think about going anywhere near the place."

"Yes."

George's voice and Caroline's own voice echoed in her ears, as if she were standing in a huge temple. That was, in fact, where she was standing—in the Temple of Fame. Through the shadowy light, she saw Sarah beside the empty pedestal reserved for James Knox Polk. She was wearing black. Her face was concealed by a black veil.

"But I think I could handle it better than poor Jim. Somehow, he never seemed big enough for the job. Not just physically but, well, spiritually, for want of a better word. Although I still say he did it well. Damn well for a man who wasn't up to it."

"Yes."

Caroline fled upstairs and summoned Mercy Flowers. "Have one of the servants take this to the Western Union office," she said, simultaneously scribbling the message to Sarah Childress Polk.

THERE ARE NO WORDS
CAROLINE

But in Caroline Kemble Stapleton's icy mind and heart, one word was very much alive. It pulsed like some sort of evil child in her body and blood and brain, waiting for the moment of birth. The word was *vindication.*

T W O

"GOOD MORNING, MRS. STAPLETON. HOW IS General Stapleton today?"

"Very well, General Quitman," Caroline said.

Congressman John A. Quitman of Mississippi shook water from his blue army cloak. A cold April rain sluiced from the gray Washington sky. The general, who lived next door with his wife and two daughters, was taking advantage of George's standing offer of a ride to the Capitol in the Stapleton carriage. Congressmen who came from distant parts of the country lacked the inclination and often the cash to bring horses and a carriage with them.

Quitman had served in Mexico as a major general. Almost as tall as George, the Mississippian had something of an Old Testament prophet in his manner and appearance. Bold blue eyes surmounted a white well-trimmed beard. In Congress he was given to explosive, declamatory speeches, many of them about the failure to annex all of Mexico, the rest about the South's other wrongs and resentments.

"George's speech yesterday was grand. It helps to know one Northern man has the courage to stand up for the South's rights."

"I think his cause is the Union, General."

"Yes. I suppose it is."

The general's lack of enthusiasm for that crucial word was all too apparent. Caroline had become adept at detecting, and eliciting, the secessionists in the Democratic Party. She did or said nothing to encourage them. She was still a mere spectator of events. But by day, she emerged from her ice cave to mingle in the real world of Washington, D.C. Instinct had warned her that she needed the company of fellow humans to preserve her sanity. Too long a sojourn in that shadowy cavern would lead to its grisly counterpart in the real world—a room in an asylum.

Instinct—and Sarah Childress Polk. After months of mutual silence, they had begun to correspond. Caroline told her everything—the cave, her hunger for vindication. Sarah gently chastised her. She did not want to believe that the war she had encouraged James Polk to fight would lead to the collapse of the Union. She urged Caroline to forgive George, as she had forgiven James. She lectured her on the vulnerability of men, their helplessness in the face of the world's cruelty. Caroline read the words and felt nothing. Gradually, she began to pity Sarah. Death had driven her to this aberrant embrace of hope, this desperate exhortation to forgive. She was really trying to forgive herself— to ask her God for this ultimate gift. Caroline, with no need to propitiate a god, refused to forgive George Stapleton, saw no need to forgive herself, and grimly looked forward to vindication.

Boots thumped on the porch. The vestibule door opened to admit their next-door neighbor to the north, Congressman Joshua Giddings of Ohio. George had made a point of also offering him a ride in his coach on rainy days. Caroline greeted him as cordially as she had greeted Quitman. He adjusted the frayed collar of his aging overcoat, glanced sullenly at Quitman, and managed a muffled good-morning.

"Come on, Giddings, cheer up," General Quitman said. "You abolitionists should be used to getting your socks beaten off by now."

He was referring to the abysmal 10 percent of the vote the abolitionists had polled, even with Martin Van Buren at the head of their presidential ticket. In the debates in the House, Giddings violently opposed allowing a single slave in the new territories. But few listened to him. The voters had spoken in 1848 and their collective voice had been clear. They did not care about slavery.

Giddings glowered at Quitman. The Ohioian was one of those rawboned Yankee types, with a face like a peeled onion. He had been ranting and raving against slavery since he came to Congress ten years ago. During the Mexican War he had called on the Northern states to secede rather than permit the South to conquer new territory. Such extremism endeared him only to the voters in his Ohio district, most of whom were fellow migrants from New England.

"What did you think of Senator Stapleton's speech yesterday?" Quitman asked. "I'm planning to read portions of it to the House today."

"I think the senator is misguided about the territories. But we're allies on another matter, which I plan to introduce in the House today. My annual call for the abolition of the slave trade in the District of Columbia."

"I find it hard to believe that the senator supports such a proposal," General Quitman rumbled.

"You can ask him yourself. Last week, another Negro committed suicide rather than accept his sale to a plantation in Mississippi."

"Sir, I own one of the largest plantations in Mississippi. I can assure you that my Negroes are better fed and better clothed than any Northern factory worker. And a great deal happier. If a District Negro did commit suicide for the reason you state, his blood is on your hands—the poor fellow listened to the atrocious lies you abolitionists tell about Southern slavery."

"I've known enslaved District Negroes who have killed their children rather than permit them to be sold south."

"Again, my answer is, I hope you're prepared to face your God with their blood on your conscience—if you have one."

"Gentleman, please," Caroline said.

"Excuse me, Mrs. Stapleton," Quitman said. "Our conduct is particularly appalling in the light of your recent illness. Forgive us both. I doubt if our righteous neighbor can bring himself to apologize to anyone who doesn't cravenly submit to his bizarre creed."

"I sincerely apologize, Mrs. Stapleton," Giddings said.

"Thank you, Congressman," Caroline said.

Tonight, as on other nights, when she retreated to her loveless cave, Caroline would pace for sleepless hours, savoring these signs of coming vindication. Since President Taylor's administration began a year ago, Congress had been locked in a ferocious battle over the future of the southwestern territories acquired from Mexico. The dispute quickly expanded to the vast plains west and north of Missouri. Should Southerners be permitted to take their slaves into either of these regions? When their populations reached the required number, should these expanses of desert and mountain and prairie be organized as slave states or free states? Adding to the turmoil, gold had been discovered in California, leading to a surge in population that had enabled it to apply for immediate statehood with a constitution that barred slavery.

George Stapleton and other Northern Democrats, clinging to the American tradition of majority rule, argued that each territory should vote for or against slavery when its time came. Logically, that meant Southerners were free to bring their slaves into a territory until such a vote was taken. But the growing number of abolitionists like Giddings in the Whig Party and the free-soilers like Van Buren in the Democratic Party denounced this policy as immoral. They were determined to imprison slavery within the confines of the fifteen states in which it was now legal. General Quitman and his friends had an answer to that: secession. Why should Southerners put up with being treated like pariahs in the Congress of the United States? Why should they tolerate abolitionists' repeated attempts to start a slave rebellion? Better to become a separate country, close their borders, and silence the antislavery fanatics with a stroke of the pen.

Down the stairs came Senator Stapleton's heavy tread. George greeted Giddings and Quitman with equal cordiality. Quitman congratulated him for his speech urging free access to the territories. Giddings said nothing. George's eyes clouded briefly. But he chose to act like a presidential candidate and talked about the weather. He kissed Caroline on the cheek and assured her that he would be home for dinner. Her eyes telegraphed: *I don't care.*

In the mail were letters from Charlie in New Orleans and Jonathan in New Jersey. Charlie boasted that he had made fifty thousand dollars on the Cotton Exchange last week. That barely replaced what he had lost the previous week. He was ignoring his father's repeated advice to invest, not to gamble. Everyone gambled on the Cotton Exchange, as the price of the South's principal product gyrated skyward around the world. With 100 million pounds a year shipped from New Orleans and other ports, the South had money to burn. Charlie's politics breathed contempt for abolitionists and free-soilers.

From Jonathan came a report that Jeremy Biddle had accepted a presidential appointment to a federal judgeship in Philadelphia. He and Sally and their daughter, Laura, would soon move to the City of Brotherly Love. Jeremy had not sought reelection to the Senate. His contrition for his letter to George was apparently genuine. This had deepened Sally's contempt for him until it was impossible to conceal from family and friends. Jonathan said he felt sorry for Laura, who was caught between her quarreling parents. He added with studied casualness that he knew "all too well" how she felt. By now their sons had detected the rift between Caroline and George. The younger Stapletons attributed it to politics. They knew nothing about John Sladen or Maria de Vega or Sarah Childress Polk and the Temple of Fame.

"Missus. Senator Sladen's here to see you."

John was looking tanned and fit. He was still drinking moderately if at all. He had seemingly accepted the arrangement that Caroline had decreed for them. He would remain devoted to the memory of their love—without any hope of its renewal. His consolation was the knowledge that she shared his political ambitions for the South—and he shared her hunger for vindication. They were partners again, in a deeper, darker union that both found satisfying.

They discussed George's speech in the Senate and his future in the Democratic Party. "I think there's a very good chance that George could be elected president in 1852," John said. "If the South decided to secede during his administration, it would be vital to persuade him to let us go in peace."

"You mean, I should become his wife again?"

"Whatever gives you the power."

"You men are so stupid. You always pursue the obvious. I have far more power this way, as his public wife and his private enemy. When the crisis comes, I can destroy his self-confidence by saying I told you so. I can reduce him to total dependence on my judgment. Perhaps then I might offer him a reward."

"What a beautiful monster you've become."

"You've done more to create me than anyone else."

In her imagination, Caroline uttered these evil words in front of Hannah Cosway Stapleton's portrait in Bowood's library. She dared her to murmur, *Oh, my dear girl, I fear for thy salvation.* But the voice remained silent. The wedding ring on Caroline's left hand gleamed dully in the gray light. The rain continued to slosh against the windows.

They discussed the probable course of Taylor's administration. The general was still opposed to allowing slavery in the territories. He was threatening to veto any attempt to work out a compromise. "If he does that, the Whig Party will go up in a puff of gunsmoke," John said. "Quitman, even Calhoun, will recommend secession. But cooler, younger heads will prevail, I hope. Taylor has said he'll lead an army against us. That's the last thing we want. The thing has to be done peacefully, so we retain the strength to march elsewhere."

"Into Mexico?"

"Into Mexico, Cuba, Central America. With our stupendous supply of black labor, once we conquer the Isthmus of Panama, we'll build a canal that will give us control of all the trade between Europe and China—and California. We'll detach the Golden State and maybe everything else west of the Mississippi from the Yankees. We've already got Missouri as a base for expansion on that flank."

"How lovely."

Caroline felt ardor stir in her blood. This man knew how to arouse her. He might lure her from her icy refuge yet. She might join him in another Temple of Fame, elsewhere in America. Perhaps in New Orleans. Or in Mexico City.

John sensed her emotion. "I still want you. I want you even more now than I did in 1827. Arrange a visit to New Orleans to see Charlie. Go down the Mississippi by steamboat. I'll be on the boat, traveling incognito."

"Can't you see that's exactly what George would love to hear? It would make him immune to me forever. How often do I have to tell you—only those who sacrifice their private desires change the course of history, John."

She lived on John Sladen's vision of future glory until George returned for dinner. It had been a day of heroic oratory in the Senate. Henry Clay had proposed a four-point compromise to hold the Union together. Admission of California as a free state. Equal access to the territories for slave and free labor. A fugitive-slave law with teeth in it. The abolition of the slave trade in Washington, D.C. "Coming from the man who's run for president twice as the Whigs' candidate, I don't see how they can resist it. Calhoun and Webster are both for it."

"What about the Democrats?"

"As usual, the Southerners don't want to give an inch. But if they don't go along, they're crazy. They've got Texas as a slave state. The territories are wide-open. The slave trade in the District is a disgrace and it always has been."

"Did you speak against it?"

"Not yet. But I intend to."

"Let someone else do it."

"Why?"

"John Sladen came to see me today. He begged me to persuade you to keep a low profile. He says more and more Southerners are turning to you as the party's candidate in '52."

She sat there in the mouth of her cave, watching ambition overwhelm moral indignation in Senator Stapleton's soul. It was amazing what distance and detachment could detect. "Maybe he's right," George said.

"Mistress. Senator. Could you speak to Tabitha? She's in the kitchen." Mercy Flowers's face was wreathed in concern.

"What's wrong?"

"She needs money."

An anxious Tabitha Flowers appeared in the doorway. She was wearing decent clothes. She looked more than respectable. She began by apologizing for not visiting George since he had returned from Mexico. "I couldn't bear to hear the story of how my daddy died. Even if he died a hero like you said."

"I understand," George said. "Why do you need money, Tabitha?"

Tabitha said her husband had an opportunity to move to New York and open a tailor shop. They needed five hundred dollars to lease the shop for a year and buy equipment on the premises. It was a chance to escape Washington, D.C. "You know how much I hate this city, because of what happened to my mother."

There was something fishy about the story—or about the way Tabitha acted while she told it. She rattled it off hastily, as if she were reciting a lesson. She gave no details, such as how the offer had reached her husband. As far as Caroline knew, he was not a tailor. He owned and operated several local hacks. But Caroline knew George would be sympathetic, and she had no reason to be hostile to the young woman. She let George make up his own mind.

"Of course you can have the money, Tabitha. You can pay it back whenever you can afford it. There'll be no hurry."

"Oh, thank you, Senator."

In five minutes, still babbling her gratitude, Tabitha departed into the rainy night with George's check for five hundred dollars in her pocket. "Is she telling the truth?" Caroline asked Mercy Flowers.

"I *hopes* so, mistress."

"You sound like you're not sure."

"I ain't never sure of anything Tabitha says. She like a weather vane, always swingin' one way or another. One day she say she hates all white folks and Senator Stapleton 'specially and wants to go back to Africa. Then she shows up here with this story about goin' to New York. That ain't no promised land from what I hear. All them Irish that come in off the boats lately hate colored people and beats 'em up and kills 'em. Washington's a lot safer, I tole her, but she don't listen to me no more."

"I couldn't say no to her," George said. He told them for the third or fourth time how Hannibal had saved his life at Molino del Rey.

Three mornings later, General Quitman knocked on Caroline's door. The weather had turned fine—spring sunshine filled the streets. Caroline was puzzled. On such days, General Quitman usually walked to the Capitol.

"Mrs. Stapleton, are any of my servants visiting in your house?"

Like most Southerners, General Quitman always called his slaves "servants." He had brought five of them from Mississippi to cook and clean and otherwise run his spacious house for himself, his wife, and two daughters.

"Let me look in the kitchen," Caroline said.

Peering into a room she seldom visited, Caroline found Mercy Flowers scrambling eggs and cooking bacon for George's breakfast. Mercy said she had not seen any of those "Mississippi niggers," as she called General Quitman's servants, for days. She did not like them. She said they tended to steal things.

Caroline told General Quitman there was no sign of backstairs visitors.

"Extraordinary," the general muttered. "They're all gone. Not a speck of breakfast cooked, not a fire lit. It's the damndest thing I've ever seen. I've never whipped a Negro in my life but . . . ."

Across the street, they saw beefy, red-faced Senator Ben Harkins of Florida on his porch, peering up and down the street. "You too?" Quitman called. "They've all run away?"

"It sure looks like it," said Harkins. "I ain't whupped one of 'em in a good month. I can't understand it."

By noon Mercy Flowers had the whole story. No less than seventy-seven slaves—almost 5 percent of the slave population of the District of Columbia, had vanished en masse. All over town Southern families such as the Quitmans and the Harkinses had been reduced to cooking their own food and stoking their own furnaces. Some Southern congressmen demanded that the president issue a general warrant, which would give them the right to search the houses of known abolitionists such as Joshua Giddings. Taylor's attorney general declined to issue such a document, noting it was a British legal weapon that had been discredited well before the Revolution of 1776.

Under General Quitman's leadership, the Washington police marshaled a hundred-man posse to hunt down the runaways. But they did not have a clue in which direction they should ride. They dispersed through the swamps and groves of the District, wearing out men and horses—without finding a trace of the fugitives.

Late that afternoon, Judson Diggs, the Stapleton's fat coachman, came to Caroline with a crafty look in his eyes. "Missus, how much money do you think it'd be worth for General Quitman and his friends to find out where them runaways have gone?"

"A great deal. Do you know?"

"I got a pretty good idea."

Caroline sent Mercy Flowers to General Quitman's house with a note. In an hour or so, the general, his boots and trousers spattered with mud, appeared in their living room. She summoned Judson. The coachman sparred with Quitman until he promised to pay a thousand dollars if Judson helped them catch the fugitives. It was a good bargain on Quitman's part. Each of the runaways was worth at least a thousand dollars at current prices.

The bargain struck, Judson rolled his eyes and announced, "You ain't gonna catch'm with horses, General. You need a boat."

"A boat?"

Judson nodded. "They done left Alexandria last night in a ship called the *Pilgrim*. Tabitha Flowers and her husband hired it for five hundred dollars. Tabitha's been plannin' this for a long time."

"How do you know all this?" Quitman asked.

"Her husband and I is ole friends. I used to drive one of his hacks. He didn't want to do it. But Tabitha, that woman got him so crazy about her, he'd try to walk across the Potomac if she told him that's what she wanted him to do."

Quitman rushed from the house, leaving Caroline alone with Judson and Mercy Flowers. "This nigger is the lowest, most miserable human being on God's earth," Mercy said. "I hopes you fires him, mistress. You know why he done this? He wanted Tabitha for his fancy woman but she wouldn't so much as look at him."

When George returned for dinner, Caroline told him what was happening. "I hope Tabitha gets away with it," he said. "But if she doesn't—"

"You loaned her the money."

A knock on the front door brought Congressman Joshua Giddings into their parlor. "Senator Stapleton, if what I've heard is true, you've done more to drive a stake through the heart of the slave trade in the District of Columbia than I've accomplished with ten years of yammering."

"I don't know what you mean, Congressman."

"Your coachman told my cook all about your part in the flight of the *Pilgrim.*"

"I wish I could claim credit for such a noble deed, Congressman, but—"

"I know you can't admit it. But that won't be necessary. Everyone will know and understand."

The gleeful Giddings departed. Caroline and George sat there, too stunned to speak. "What are you going to do?" Caroline finally asked.

"Fire Judson Diggs." Caroline did not like the set of George's jaw. He was not acting like a presidential candidate. He looked more like a man confronting a harsh fate.

"Wait a moment. Maybe it might be better to give him another thousand dollars to change his story."

"I don't want him to change his story. And I won't tolerate a piece of vermin like him in my household."

Caroline confronted the man who had come back from Mexico confident of his moral course. For the past two and a half years, her icy enmity—and the vagaries of Washington's politics—had slowly eroded that confidence. How could something as ridiculous as this, the recklessness of a twenty-year-old black girl, threaten the restoration of the Temple of Fame?

The following day a triumphant General Quitman was back in Washington. He had hired a steam yacht at Alexandria, and his posse had joined him for a furious all-night dash down the Potomac. They had overtaken the slow-sailing *Pilgrim* in Chesapeake Bay and hauled all seventy-seven runaway slaves, the captain of the ship, and his accomplices, Tabitha Flowers and her husband, Caesar Rhodes, back to Washington. The slaves were in the traders' pens in Lafayette Square, and Tabitha, her husband, and the captain were in the District jail, charged with grand larceny and insurrection.

Inevitably, the *National Era,* the District's abolitionist newspaper, filled its front page with the story. Other papers throughout the nation flooded the capital with reporters. The episode was irresistible. At a time when Southern politicians were confidently demanding the right to export slavery throughout the Union and arrogantly proclaiming that their slaves were happy and contented with their lot, these seventy-seven house servants—blacks who lived comfortable lives in Washington's better homes, wore good clothes, and ate decent food—were willing to risk capture and dire punishment to flee to free soil. The "flight of the *Pilgrim,*" as the story was swiftly dubbed, sent a ripple of panic through the slaveholders of the South and a howl of exultance through the abolitionists of the North.

Judson Diggs soon added a righteous veneer to his version of the story. He claimed that Tabitha had borrowed the five hundred dollars to hire the *Pilgrim* from him. But reporters soon found other blacks who remembered Judson's previous version of the plot. The newsmen crowded the Stapletons' porch, they swarmed in the corridors of the Capitol, shouting questions at George. He was forced to issue a statement admitting he had loaned Tabitha the five hundred dollars. But he denied knowing anything about the *Pilgrim*.

The abolitionists grandly announced they would ransom all the fugitives and hire topflight lawyers to defend Tabitha and her husband and the ship's captain. But it soon became apparent that they had no intention of doing any such thing. The lawyers, former governor of Ohio Salmon P. Chase and former governor of New York William Seward, after volunteering their services and winning headlines, suddenly found themselves too busy to go to Washington. All the runaways were sold by their angry masters to District slave traders, who promptly shipped them to New Orleans for sale to the cotton plantations of Mississippi and Alabama. The abolitionists generated another round of sensational headlines about their harsh fate. But these moralists, many of whom were wealthy, did nothing to help them.

George was totally disgusted with the abolitionists' performance: "These people are the biggest hypocrites that ever existed," he said. He hired one of the best lawyers in the District to defend Tabitha and her husband and the captain of the *Pilgrim*. But there was little the lawyer could do. The evidence against the defendants was overwhelming. The juries were packed with Southerners. The white captain was condemned to life imprisonment. Caesar Rhodes, Tabitha's husband, received a similar sentence.

Tabitha was the last to be tried. On the morning of her trial, George did not join Caroline for breakfast. She went to his room, wondering if he was ill. She found him working on a speech. In spite of their estrangement, he still let her read his speeches before he gave them. "What's this?" she said, walking over to his desk. "I thought everyone's too busy arguing about the *Pilgrim* to worry about affairs of state."

"It's something you won't like," he said, swiftly gathering the pages and shoving them into his inside pocket.

Caroline instantly knew he was planning to testify for Tabitha. "You can't do anything so stupid. Not now, when so much is at stake."

"Is it?"

"John Sladen, General Quitman, have assured me they know Tabitha hoodwinked you. You're still their candidate."

"I'm not sure I want to be."

He rode to the District courthouse, arriving as Tabitha took the witness stand. Her bitter husband had already testified against her. His treachery was superfluous. Tabitha defiantly admitted everything. The jury's guilty verdict was a foregone conclusion.

As the judge prepared to sentence Tabitha, Senator Stapleton asked if he could speak. He proceeded to tell the jurist and the spellbound courtroom the story of her mother's kidnapping, her father's heroic death in Mexico. "Your Honor, this young woman is undoubtedly guilty of breaking our laws. But I must ask you if these laws, in her case, should be tempered with mercy. We might even ask ourselves if these laws deserve to be broken."

The judge was a Virginian. He was visibly shaken by Senator Stapleton's words. But he grimly declared that there was nothing in the statute that gave him the power to alter the jury's verdict. He sentenced Tabitha to life imprisonment. George strode from the courtroom to the floor of the Senate and made a passionate speech, calling for the abolition of the slave trade in the District of Columbia. The story made the front page of every newspaper in the country.

The next morning, another spring rainstorm drenched Washington. Looking out the window, Caroline saw Judson Diggs on a brand-new hack pulled by a fine bay horse that he had bought with his thousand-dollar reward. He stopped in front of General Quitman's house. The Mississippian no longer accepted rides to the Capitol from Senator Stapleton.

"You realize what you've done, don't you?" Caroline said as they sat down to dinner later that day. "You've thrown away the presidency. You couldn't get a Southern vote now if you offered a thousand dollars each for them."

"There are some things more important than being president."

The soldier who had just returned from Mexico confronted Caroline again. Suddenly she understood everything. Her invisible antagonist, Maria de Vega, was still in command of George Stapleton's soul.

Maybe she would take that trip down the Mississippi with John Sladen after all. George's nobility only deepened Caroline's resolve to do anything, to risk everything, in the name of the word that burned in her throat day and night: *vindication.*

THREE

CAROLINE SAT BENEATH HER PARASOL IN the blazing July sun gazing up at the most loathsome sight her eyes had ever encountered in Washington, D.C.—President Zachary Taylor. With over two hundred pounds on his five-foot-eight frame, his torso sat like an overstuffed sack on his short, bowed legs. His jowls bulged over his collar. His belly jutted past his sweat-soaked suit coat. His long, apelike arms dangled almost to his knees. The contented stupidity of his expression completed the picture of an aboriginal imbecile who had wandered by accident into civilization.

The president had just finished giving one of his more moronic speeches, hailing the rise of the idiotic monument to George Washington, a half-built semi-ruin that sat a few hundred yards away, surrounded by wheelbarrows and mounds of sand. It was an emblem of Taylor's haphazard administration—

and might even serve as a symbol of the state of the nation, which was on the brink of becoming a truncated monstrosity.

Caroline's only consolation in this baleful meditation was the knowledge that her noble husband, former presidential candidate Senator George Stapleton, had almost exactly the same opinion of President Zachary Taylor. George did not factor into his disgust Caroline's antipathy for Taylor as the man who had destroyed James Knox Polk's presidency. George saw him in more immediate terms as an incubus that was about to split the Republic in half or perhaps thirds, by starting a civil war.

For two more hours, Caroline and George and the rest of the crowd, which included most of Senate and the House of Representatives, sat in the heat listening to other gaseous orators from the Whig Party extol the virtues of patriotism. On the bare platform, Taylor, sheltered neither by an awning nor an umbrella, repeatedly mopped his streaming forehead with a red-checked handkerchief. But his ugly face retained the complacent self-satisfaction of a circus master who was forcing his trained animals to perform, knowing that at least half of them would take profound pleasure in tearing him to pieces.

All these political gentlemen were sweltering in the capital's atrocious heat and humidity thanks to President Taylor. With any other man in the White House, they would have long since departed to their plantations and villas. Caroline wondered if there was anyone else in the crowd who actually preferred the brutal weather of Washington. She had no desire to go near Kemble Manor, because she stubbornly, ferociously refused to succumb to the faintest possibility of forgiving Senator George Stapleton for his multiple betrayals of her dream of fame.

Finally, the patriotic dithering ended and people milled listlessly in the soupy almost viscous air, exchanging glum smiles and halfhearted hellos. Caroline and George found themselves walking in tandem with the president's daughter, pretty Elizabeth Taylor Bliss and her arrogant husband, William Wallace Bliss, who had been Taylor's chief of staff during the war.

"Oh, Mrs. Stapleton," Mrs. Bliss cooed in her best Southern manner. "I'm so *glad* to see your health is improving. Perhaps we can lure you to the White House for dinner soon."

"Perhaps." Caroline had turned down a dozen invitations. When would this idiot realize Mrs. Stapleton had no intention of going into that house while it was inhabited by her repulsive father?

"Could we tempt you to the reception we're giving today?" Colonel Bliss asked.

"Thank you, no."

Another ten paces and a more welcome voice spoke in Caroline's ear. "What do you think of the chances of Zach succumbing to sunstroke?" Senator John Sladen said.

"I found myself wondering the same thing," Senator Stapleton said. He peered into the distance. "I'll go get our carriage. The police seem to have ordered them to move a good mile away for some stupid reason."

He left Caroline and John Sladen together on the grass. "Do you think a civil war is possible?" she asked.

"Possible? I would say the word is *probable*. It could start in two weeks."

"Does that vile old man mean what he says? He'll march an army into the South? When he only got forty-three percent of the vote?"

"He thinks it will convert him into Andrew Jackson, overnight," Senator Sladen said.

The political tension in Washington and the nation was approaching the volcanic level. Congress had been in session for a record 250 days, roaring, snarling, cursing, over slavery in the territories and the other components of Henry Clay's omnibus compromise. The great obstacle to settling the murderous quarrel was President Zachary Taylor. Although he owned more than a hundred slaves, he persisted in declaring he would veto any bill that allowed slavery in the territories. Senator John C. Calhoun had responded that without access to the territories, the South should secede. Old Zach said he would march the U.S. Army into South Carolina and any other state that tried it and blast them back into the Union.

Hotheads such as General Quitman were inclined to call Taylor's bluff. They pointed out that two-thirds of the army that had fought in Mexico had been Southerners. Now they were being told they had no share in the five-hundred thousand square miles they had conquered. The situation looked more and more like the scenario that John Sladen and cooler heads feared most—a civil war that would desolate the South. Henry Clay's bundle of compromises had enough votes to pass both houses of Congress but not enough to override a presidential veto.

"What is to be done?" Caroline asked.

"I keep asking myself what Aaron Burr would do. Do you think that's impossibly old-fashioned?" John said.

Caroline felt a dark, delicious thrill. It was amazing, the power of that name, forgotten by almost everyone else in American politics. "You're going to challenge Zach to a duel?"

"Hardly. There are other alternatives."

George was calling in the distance. Their carriage was lumbering over the lawn toward them. "You give me hope," Caroline said.

She slipped her arm through John's to keep her balance on the uneven grass. Would George take it amiss? She did not care. They rode home in sodden silence. Dinner was almost as silent. Senator and Mrs. Stapleton did not have much to say to each other these days.

As Mercy Flowers served mounds of vanilla ice cream for dessert, she murmured, "Just heard from that friend who works at the White House. The president's mighty sick."

For a moment, Caroline found it difficult to breathe. The dark thrill was dancing in her flesh again.

"What happened to him?" George asked.

"He come home from that celebration and eat a dish of cherries and drunk four, five glasses of iced milk. Suddenly he was *sick*. Couldn't even sit up. He in bed now with three doctors around him."

"Indigestion," George said. "He'll get over it."

The next day, the news raced through Washington. The president was not getting over it. The doctors hovered by his bed night and day, administering huge doses of calomel and other medicines. But nothing stopped the raging diarrhea and vomiting. On July 9, 1850, at 10:35 P.M., Zachary Taylor died. For the previous four days, Caroline had barely slept. Again and again, the dark thrill raced through her body.

A week later, with Taylor's body barely interred in the Congressional Cemetery, his vice president, Millard Fillmore of New York, announced he would sign Henry Clay's compromises if Clay's name was divested from the bill and other sponsors found for its separate proposals. With lightning speed, the legislation was split into four parts and each was voted and signed into law, permitting Congress to adjourn after 302 wearisome days, still the lawmakers of a united nation.

Among the many who pronounced themselves satisfied was Senator George Stapleton, who had cosponsored the bill to abolish the slave trade in the District of Columbia. In return, he extracted from President Fillmore a promise that he would pardon Tabitha and her husband and the captain of the *Pilgrim* before he left the White House.

"I can hardly wait to get to Kemble Manor," George said to Caroline on the day Congress adjourned.

"You and Paul and Jonathan will have to make a bachelors' hall," Caroline said. "I'm going to New Orleans to visit Charlie."

It was all so innocent, so maternal, how could George object? "I wish I could go with you. But without Jeremy running the business I've got a lot of work to do in New Jersey."

"Poor dear."

A week later, Caroline boarded the SS *Delilah* in St. Louis, Missouri. It was one of the newest steamboats on the river, an immense floating palace driven by two huge paddle wheels. Everything inside gleamed, from the cushions in the salons to the brass fittings on the network of pipes that brought heat from its immense boilers to the luxurious staterooms.

For Caroline it was more than a steamboat. Events in distant Washington, D.C., had transformed it, had transformed everything—the clanking, sooty trains she had ridden to St. Louis, the looming factories of Pittsburgh, the thousands of immigrants swarming across the Mississippi River, the immense river itself—into sinister portents of evil. America had become something different, something darker and more ominous, an almost alien land in which she was a stranger. But not for long, she told herself fiercely. *Not for long.*

Caroline was leaning on the rail on the top deck, watching African roustabouts loading bales of cotton onto *Delilah*'s cavernous bottom deck when Senator John Sladen said, "I like the name of your boat. Did you choose it deliberately?"

"I beg your pardon," Caroline said, "I don't think we've met."

"Nathan Archibald's the name, cotton is my game."

"I'm Amelia Peterson. From Philadelphia."

They descended to the bar, a cool oasis, with broad-bladed fans slowly turning on the dim ceiling, like the wings of enslaved angels. John ordered champagne. Caroline leaned back in her chair, sipped some of the bubbling wine, and said, "Did you kill the president?"

John grimaced, as if he had expected the question and wished she had not asked it. "There are some things I refuse to discuss, even with you."

"You knew I was going to ask you. I was afraid to do it in Washington. I was afraid of how I'd react."

"There are some things it's better not to know."

"Then it's true."

"I prefer to attribute Old Zach's departure to heavenly intervention. It's another sign that the South will achieve her destiny."

"I want to *know*." It was dismaying to realize how much this ultimate inside knowledge meant to her. Those four years she had spent at Sarah Polk's side in the White House had sharpened her appetite for the perquisites of fame. With George Stapleton relegated to the anterooms of the temple, this man was her only hope.

John Sladen clearly enjoyed the power he had over her. "I wish it were true. I wish I could be as daring, as clandestine, as evil, as you want me to be. But I'm afraid it was nothing but a lucky accident."

She studied his crafty face, his mocking eyes. With sudden crushing finality, she realized she no longer loved him and he no longer loved her, no matter what he said. There was not an iota of passion in this voyage south. On a personal level, they were settling scores against George Stapleton. On a political level, they were seeking a redesigned alliance, in which she could resume the role of fame's priestess, without George.

They dined on canvasback duck and desultory conversation as the *Delilah* steamed down the Mississippi. Afterward, they went up on the top deck and gazed out at the shrouded land. Somehow the darkness accentuated America's immensity. Caroline felt it as a gigantic embrace—the East with its crowded millions, the West with its stupendous spaces, meeting here on this surging river. The pounding engines sent vibrations of power through the huge steamboat. The smokestacks left a trail of sparks on the black, gleaming water.

"I almost wish we had been lovers all these years," she said.

"No. You were right. It's better this way. In fact, I'm beginning to think it might be a mistake for us to become lovers now."

Caroline felt a mixture of relief and confusion. She realized she had not been looking forward to his visit to her stateroom. She no longer wanted to simulate emotions she did not feel. But she did not like the suggestion that he felt no need to visit her. She did not want him to escape her.

What was he trying to do? He had become far more devious than she suspected. Hardly surprising after twenty years in Washington, D.C. She reminded herself of how often the newspapers portrayed him as a past master of political corruption, the crafty emperor of Louisiana. Was he waiting for her to protest? She said nothing.

"George can still be very useful to us," he continued. "When the South secedes, he can step forward as the voice of moderation. He can urge the North to let us go in peace. He can speak as a man who has a son in the North and a son in the South. He can personify the nation's anguish."

"Yes."

"He could run for president of the Northern half of the Union on a peace ticket. I could do the same thing on a Southern ticket. You'd be the invisible arbiter, the voice of reason and negotiation, between us. You'd control the fate, the destiny, of the continent. Perhaps two continents."

"Yes!"

She pressed her lips against his mocking mouth. There was only one way to guarantee her devotion, and he knew it. He knew the way to her inner heart, to that lonely cave of ice, better than anyone else in this bedeviled world. She was willing to let his pride, his long cruel years of waiting, make her the supplicant. It was a kind of proof of their equality.

Prudence required them to descend from the upper deck separately. A half hour later, Caroline was in her nightgown when he knocked on the stateroom door. She kissed him again, passionately, angrily, the moment the door closed. She was telling him that she understood, she was ready to be the supplicant. With a heart full of vengeance, she would love her vindicator.

He turned down the oil lamp and undressed. Almost rudely, he pulled off her nightgown and flung it on the floor. "Still as beautiful as ever."

He was lying of course. She no longer studied her body in the mirror. But she knew her flesh had grown soft and flaccid. Her breasts sagged. There was a deep line of worry or woe just above her nose. He was no longer a thing of male beauty. His lean face surmounted an almost gaunt body. The withering process she had noticed years ago continued to shrink his flesh, while George grew more comfortably padded. What was the source of his avoirdupois? A clear conscience?

Or was the body ultimately meaningless, something to lacerate, to torment, for the sake of the soul? Maybe that was the best answer, Caroline thought as he inserted his finger in her vagina and began moving it in and out, in and out, not touching her in any other way. He was telling her that in all their future transactions, he wanted to be the master of their furtive revels—if there were any more.

Eventually he took her with swift savage thrusts. It lasted less than a minute. When it was over, he did not lie beside her as George used to do, fondling her, whispering how much he loved her. He went over to the sink and washed himself, put on his clothes, and sat down at the end of the bed. She put on her nightgown—a defensive gesture. She did not want to lie there naked while he talked to her.

"George should by no means be our only resource when the crisis comes," he said in a crisp dry voice that crackled like pinewood in a fireplace.

"Oh?"

"Julia Tyler is another card you must be ready to play."

"How?"

She hated his voice of authority. It was as flat, as matter-of-fact, as if he were reading stock market quotations.

"I think her husband is already halfway to secession. You and Julia, should bring him the rest of the way. So he can make a resounding statement at the right moment. Ex-presidents can always get attention in the newspapers."

"I see."

"Write to Julia. Invite her to Washington. I gather she's desperate to get off the plantation."

"Yes, massa."

"This is serious business."

"You killed Old Zach, didn't you."

"It was necessary."

Oh, my dear girl, I fear for thy salvation.

For the first time Caroline truly heard those words. Hannah Cosway Stapleton was talking about evil. Hitherto, evil had not worn a face. There had not been a single specific act that reeked of it—except, perhaps, Tabitha's kidnapping and death. But that was just the blind brutality of a system, not much worse than the Stapleton's Northern factories where women and children worked twelve hours a day and often lost fingers, hands, arms, in the whirring machines. That kind of evil was mundane, part of the world's everyday furniture. The evil they confronted now wore a specific human face. It was personal. They were accepting it, perpetuating it in this scented stateroom, with the SS *Delilah*'s engines throbbing *power power power* beneath them. Aaron Burr had told them Americans could not be powerful and good. He had not bothered to take the next step and tell them that power required acts of evil such as the one he had committed the day he killed Alexander Hamilton.

Evil. John Sladen had just loved her the way men loved women in brothels. Caroline knew that with harsh instinctive certainty. He had been having sex in Washington, D.C., brothels for two decades. All those years of loveless love, of the mere conjunction of bodies, had been her fault, Caroline thought. So it was fitting that she should have this loveless fucking, as the Africans called it, for her reward.

Evil. Caroline sensed it flowing through her icy cave, a dark snaking stream. It would be interesting to see where this new reality took her. It was a journey she could only share with this man. That too was more than fitting. It was written in the book of fate since they had embarked on that underground river of desire in New York twenty-five years ago.

"How did you do it?" she asked.

"There are poisons that leave no trace. The voodoo doctors in New Orleans know them all. They brought them from Africa two hundred years ago."

Evil. How fascinating, the way it was woven into America's struggle with the black anaconda of slavery. From the start this thing was coiled around liberty's feet, ready to slowly, inexorably rise higher and higher. Had they found the answer to it in doing evil to fight evil, like fighting fire with fire? Perhaps. Caroline only knew she was ready to defy goodness in the name of vindication—and fame.

FOUR

CAROLINE SPENT THE NIGHT WRITING IT all down in her journal. Sleepless, dazed, she met John Sladen for breakfast. "You've become evil," she said.

"I don't believe the moral law extends south of New England."

"I like it. It adds breadth to your character. Did you act alone?"

"Of course not."

"I wish I could tell Sarah. Zachary Taylor deserved to die. That vicious old man wasted ten thousand lives in Mexico. He destroyed Polk's presidency. He killed Polk as surely as you've killed him."

"I didn't do it to punish him. I did it to save the South and the North from a bloodbath. I did it, ultimately, to rid the South of slavery. Once we have Mexico, Central America, Cuba, we'll be able to begin a process of gradual manumission. It will be carefully administered peonage, at first, slowly graduating over a century to complete freedom in a racially balanced empire."

Caroline almost laughed. He wanted to be good! He wanted to slay the black anaconda. *Oh, my dear boy, I fear for thy salvation.* She almost said it to him. She almost told him about Hannah Cosway Stapleton's voice. But he would think she was mad. Besides, she shared this ultimate noble wish. But she wondered why he did not sense how violently it clashed with their embrace of evil.

"Last night you treated me like a whore. I liked it. Do it again tonight. Do it every night. I want to become as evil as you are."

His eyes glittered with barely suppressed rage. "You want to know everything, don't you."

"Yes."

For the next five nights, he came to the stateroom and fucked her. She made him say the word. She made him tell her the whorehouse names of the positions he ordered her to assume. She obeyed all his commands, however loathsome. Never once did he use the word *love*. Afterward, each night, he sat at the foot of the bed and she lounged, naked, against the headboard while he elaborated his vision of a Southern empire.

The poverty that had enraged the South in the days of the tempests over the tariff was history. In the bottomlands of Alabama and Mississippi and Louisiana and the immensity of Texas, the South had discovered riches beyond the wildest dreams of the California gold rushers. The world's appetite for cotton was apparently insatiable. In 1850, the South produced 100 million pounds. By 1860, it would produce 200 million pounds. All they had to do was put a 5 percent tax on that immense avalanche of fiber and they would have $100 million a year to spend—twice the size of the federal budget for the entire United States. With that money, they would create a navy and an army with the latest weaponry and become one of the great powers of the world.

The empire would be utterly different from the puritanized nation of the North. Its opulent liberties would be based on power and privilege. Its rulers would preside over the lesser races who fought in their armies and toiled on their plantations and in their factories. It would be a new Rome that would eventually destroy the effete rationalizing Yankees of the North and in fifty years rule both Americas. It would give the law to Europe and Asia and India. Allied with England's aristocracy, it would institute a reign of the elect around the globe.

As he spoke, his voice became as shrouded as the room. The *Delilah*'s engines throbbed. Once, her smokestack roared defiance into the night. The river hissed beneath the portholes. Caroline saw the Mississippi on the map, winding through the continent—an image of the black anaconda in America's heart.

"I want to be part of it," Caroline said. "Will you build a statue to me in some secret shrine? Let that be my reward."

"Yes," he said. "There'll be two capitals. One, where the people meet in Congress; the second, where the secret rulers meet, the unelected elect. We'll have statues of our heroes there."

"Heroes—and heroines."

"Yes."

By day they gazed out at proofs of the South's opulence and strength. Mile after mile, the great cotton plantations stretched over the horizon on both sides of the river. White-pillared mansions glistened down avenues of cypress and swamp oak trees. At Memphis and Natchez, where *Delilah* paused to take on more cargo, they hired carriages and rode through the crowded downtown business streets to the splendid houses of the brokers and lawyers and doctors King Cotton enriched. Finally, at noon on the fifth day, John took her up to the top deck and waited while the *Delilah* rounded a huge bend and New Orleans appeared in the distance. He ticked off the principal buildings as they drew closer: the soaring towers of St. Louis Cathedral, the bulky block-long Customs House, and the domed grandeur of the St. Charles Hotel.

On the levee, waving cheerfully, stood Charlie in a cream-colored suit, carrying a huge bouquet of red roses. He looked impossibly handsome in the dense sunshine; his black hair gleamed; the rakish set of his jaw, his reckless smile, were an exact copy of the portrait of her father in his uniform on the wall at Bowood. Caroline felt a leap of saturnine joy, dark faith. This son would help her realize her father's dream of fame.

Charlie gave Caroline a resounding kiss and pumped John Sladen's hand. "Isn't this the nicest coincidence?" Caroline said. "I walked aboard at St. Louis and there stood the senator from Louisiana."

"Wonderful," Charlie agreed. He waved to a waiting hackman and they rumbled past the cotton wagons and oyster peddlers that crowded the huge riverside square named after Andrew Jackson. "I reserved a suite for you at the St. Charles, Mother. You don't want to live with a bachelor. It would start a war that only a Thucydides could adequately describe. Wouldn't you agree, Senator?"

"Emphatically," John Sladen said.

The senator went off to his town house and Charlie escorted her around New Orleans and its environs in a hired gig. Caroline was entranced by the houses of the Vieux Carré, with their long balconies covered with filigreed iron. They drove out to the site of Andrew Jackson's triumph in 1815, and Charlie virtually refought the battle for her. They visited the immense Cotton Exchange, with its tiers of balconies around a central court where brokers and factors shouted bids and made and lost fortunes weekly.

At the end of the day they dined on foie gras and bouillabaisse at a French restaurant whose chef had recently arrived from Paris. Charlie entertained her with tales of John Sladen's political power in Louisiana. Charlie was unbothered by the corruption. Unlike his brother Jonathan, he did not have a reformer's bone in his body. He accepted human nature as it always had been and always would be.

"You're looking contented, Mother," Charlie said. "You don't strike me as the termagant that Brother Jonathan describes, abusing father and him and Paul every time they open their mouths."

"Your father and I have settled our quarrel. It was about Mexico. I thought we should have kept it all. But he prevailed."

"Senator Sladen says if he'd taken the other side—and stayed out of the Tabitha mess—he'd be on his way to the presidency."

"Don't judge your father too harshly at a distance." Defending George as a man with a sensitive conscience, she managed to simultaneously please his son and portray herself as a woman of compassion and understanding. It was remarkable, having embraced evil, how easy it was to impersonate goodness. It was the struggle to remain good that caused so much spiritual anguish—and muddled so many bold enterprises. Sarah Polk was a living example of this melancholy revelatory truth.

The next night there was a dinner in Caroline's honor at the town house of Victor Conte Legrand, son of the senator who had been John Sladen's mentor when he came to New Orleans. Victor was a pompous, oily little man, swollen with self-importance. But he had two attractive daughters and immense political influence inside Louisiana, thanks to his wealth and family connections. The younger of the two daughters, Cynthia, was a beauty, with thick, lustrous, dark hair and green eyes beneath long, seductive lashes, and with an alluring figure. During dinner, Legrand talked jovially of Cynthia marrying Charlie and forming a Stapleton-Legrand alliance that would guarantee peace and prosperity between North and South.

Caroline said she thought that was a wonderful idea. "How old is Cynthia?" she asked.

"She'll be thirteen in January," Legrand said.

"I trust you're not thinking of a June wedding."

Legrand found that amusing. "I think we should wait for a number of things to *mature*. Senator Sladen tells me you're with us, heart and soul."

"I believe in the South's rights—and her wrongs."

"We need more of the latter to convince the trimmers. There are amazing numbers of people who still believe in the Union."

"You'll get wrongs," she said. "The abolitionists are perfect foils. They'll supply you with plenty of ammunition."

"Perfect foils—I like that," Legrand said. "We'll make them perfect fools before we're through."

He had fought in Mexico at the head of a regiment. His voice became choked with rage as he described the feelings of his men when they were told they were going home—abandoning the conquest for which so many of their friends had died. "How I wished Andrew Jackson were still alive. He would never have permitted such a disgrace. As we marched out of Mexico City, women jeered, urchins threw stones . . ."

He gulped champagne. "I told the men, when we discharged them here in New Orleans, that someday I'd lead them back to Mexico. What a cheer they gave me! It shook every window in Jackson Square."

John Sladen was sitting on Caroline's left. He leaned toward Victor Conte Legrand and said, "Before we march on Mexico, we have another matter to settle. If we do it well, we'll rally every adventurous son of the South to our side."

"He's talking about Cuba," Legrand said, gulping more champagne. "It's our answer to California as a free state."

"This devious man hasn't said a word to me about it," Caroline said.

"The Cubans are begging us to ship an army over there and kick the Spaniards into the sea," Legrand said. "We'll introduce you to some of them. They're afraid the Spanish government is going to succumb to English pressure and abolish slavery. Abolition would make them beggars overnight—or corpses. No one has forgotten Santo Domingo."

He was talking about the black revolution that led to a massacre of the whites on the French island of Santo Domingo fifty years ago.

"Old Zach—our late lamented president—opposed the idea. Another reason why his departure was welcomed by every thinking Southerner," Sladen said.

Caroline saw the evil in his mocking eyes. He had done it. He had murdered the president of the United States. A glance at Legrand convinced her that he knew nothing. The Creole aristocrat drank more champagne and said he agreed with Senator Sladen. Old Zach had been a good general but a terrible president.

"What we need for our Cuban adventure is Northern support," John Sladen said. "Someone like Senator Stapleton to sponsor a bill, making Cuba a state, Texas style—as soon as the Cuban provisional government applies for admission to the Union."

"Would the senator consider such a thing?" Legrand asked.

"I think so," Caroline said.

Charlie Stapleton was sitting on the other side of the table, chatting with the two Legrand sisters. He managed to keep one ear to this conversation. He abandoned the young women to lean forward and say, "When Mother makes that kind of promise, Senator Stapleton always delivers."

"Hush, Charlie. It's by no means a sure thing. But I can assure you of *serious* consideration."

"I expect to command at least a company in this expedition," Charlie said.

"You have my promise of a commission, young fellow," Victor Conte Legrand said.

"That should go a long way to persuading Senator Stapleton," John Sladen said.

"I don't know about that. Father hasn't approved of anything I've done since I was about eight years old," Charlie said.

"I saw your father in the field in Mexico. He'll approve a soldier son. I guarantee it," Legrand said.

"Isn't it despicable, Mrs. Stapleton, how men have all the adventures and we women have to sit home worshipin' them?" Cynthia Legrand drawled. She had a sensuous, crooning voice that perfectly matched her lush looks.

"Sometimes we can do more than worship," Caroline said.

"You must teach me how to do that," Cynthia said. "Maybe I can get Charlie to pay some attention to me."

"Wait two or three years, Cyntie darling," Legrand said.

"Then the problem will be how to stop Charlie from paying too much attention," John Sladen said.

"I wish I could believe that," Cynthia said with a pretty pout.

"Take our word for it, little girl," Legrand said.

After dinner, Legrand escorted Caroline on a tour of his town house. On the walls was art from the best painters in France. The halls were filled with Greek and Roman sculpture. The furniture was from Paris, glistening, brilliantly cushioned examples of the sinuous Empire style. The Legrands had been part of Louisiana's ruling class for over a hundred years. He was delighted to invite the Stapletons to share the spoils.

"Where is Mrs. Legrand? I was hoping to meet her," Caroline said.

"She seldom leaves our plantation, Bralston, on the river above Baton Rouge. She comes from nearby Cane River and has so many kin, it's impossible to lure her to New Orleans, no matter how enticing I make the invitation. She's also frequently indisposed. Her health is not of the best. . . ."

There was no need to explain the arrangement. A wife was an inconvenience in New Orleans. Caroline let Legrand lead her to a back parlor, where a half dozen Cubans gazed morosely at a painting of the Spanish royal family by Velázquez, the great court painter of two centuries past. Legrand introduced her as the wife of Senator Stapleton. For a half hour she listened to their assurances that Cuba was ripe for revolution and was eager to join the United States. They reiterated their hatred of the greedy corrupt officials Spain sent to administer the island.

Afterward, in a hack with John Sladen and Charlie, Caroline said she was convinced that Cuba was theirs for the taking. "I'll go with you," she said. "It sounds like it will be more of a pleasure trip than a war."

"Let's see what Madame Leveau tells us," John said.

"She's the voodoo queen of New Orleans," Charlie explained. "Anyone who wants an ex-lover or a husband poisoned, an enemy ruined, his or her future predicted, goes to her."

In ten minutes they were skirting a wide grassy park, splashed with moonlight and shadows. "This is Congo Square," John Sladen said. "Madame Leveau's kingdom."

"Where are the Africans?"

"They all have to be indoors by nine o'clock. It's the law," Charlie said. "To prevent an uprising."

"Just a precaution," Sladen said. "We're perfectly safe."

They climbed to the second floor of a decrepit building. In a large candle-lit room sat a tall, lean black woman with a red turban on her angular head. She wore a necklace of bones that looked suspiciously like human fingers. On the table in front of her was a white cat and a black cat, so real that they seemed about to meow. It took Caroline several minutes to realize they were stuffed. Several human skulls and a large stuffed snake dangled from the walls.

"Greetings, Your Majesty," John Sladen said. "I'm here to report your medicine worked well. My friends have asked me to give you another payment."

"Thank you," Madame Leveau said in a throaty voice. She accepted a fat envelope that John placed before her. Glancing into it, she riffled the banknotes and then handed it to a woman assistant, one of several who stood beside her like ladies-in-waiting around a queen.

"Who are these other people who come to my court?" Madame Leveau said.

"They are people from the North who want to learn to worship your dark god, Your Majesty," Sladen said. "They have money. Will you look into their futures for them?"

Leveau studied Caroline for a long moment. "This woman has powers of her own. Why does she need me?"

"Her power cannot match yours, Majesty," John said, glancing wryly at Caroline.

"Stroke the cats and let me see your hand," Leveau said. "First the white cat, then the black cat."

Caroline obeyed. Madame Leveau seized Caroline's wrist and stared into her hand. She spat on it and rubbed the saliva around and around the palm. An assistant took the snake from the wall and wrapped it around Madame's neck and placed its grinning head in Caroline's hand. The creature twitched as if it were alive. Madame cried out and leaped from her chair. "There are powers here I don't understand."

"What of her future, my queen?" John Sladen asked.

"Her god won't let me see it."

"What if she says she has no god?"

"She is not such a fool," Leveau said, glaring at Caroline.

"What if I said I worshiped your dark god?" Caroline said.

"You can try," Leveau said in a strangely hostile voice. "But there is another god standing between you and him."

"What of the young man?" John asked.

Charlie rubbed the two cats and offered the queen his open hand. Leveau peered at his palm for a moment, then peeled back the lids of Charlie's eyes.

"He will marry a beautiful woman. After that I see nothing but darkness behind his eyes."

"Was that what you saw behind mine?" John asked.

"Behind yours I saw blood. A river of blood."

Somewhere a drum began to beat. It was joined by a half dozen more drums and a wailing flute. "It will soon be midnight. Do you want to stay for the dance?" Leveau said. "You are welcome."

Downstairs, the double doors of the house were open. Across the square came forty or fifty Africans, dancing in a strange contorted way, their bodies jerking and twitching to the drums. Some bent to the waist and walked like chickens, others flung themselves in the grass and slithered like snakes. Into the house they sprang while Madame Leveau greeted them with open arms. The ladies-in-waiting distributed flagons of a dark, fragrant drink to all comers. The drumbeat accelerated. By now the room was packed. The visitors swayed back and forth, their arms twined around each other. "Dance, children, dance. Worship the god who will set you free!" Madame Leveau cried.

One of her court pulled back a screen on the wall. In an alcove hung a crucified black dog with a crown on his head. In his mouth was a white hand. "Dance!" Madame Leveau said.

One of the women flung off her clinging blue dress and stamped it beneath her feet. She had a magnificent body with long legs, coned breasts, slim curving arms. She began dancing before the dog, supplicating, undulating, moving her tapered hands up and down her dark flesh. Soon a half dozen other women joined her in defiant naked ecstasy.

Caroline watched, fascinated, horrified. She understood it all. It was the black anaconda worshiping an evil god, in revenge for the white god's failure to give it freedom. Here in the deepest South, at the mouth of the stupendous river of darkness that flowed through America's heart, was a vision of the evil she and John Sladen were challenging with their dream of fame. Could they prevail? Caroline's heart clotted with doubt.

"Now you can see why I like New Orleans," Charlie said to Caroline. "Can you get more exotic than this?"

"Superstition in action," John Sladen said with a yawn. "Let's get some sleep."

They did not understand. They did not even come close to understanding. Was it because they were men? Trained to think and not feel? While she could do both? Back at the St. Charles Hotel, Caroline was awake until dawn, filling her journal with what she had seen—and understood. Fame in a murderous struggle with evil.

FIVE

"It's the vilest book I've ever read. A slander from cover to cover!"

Julia Gardiner Tyler was seated on the veranda of Sherwood Forest's white-pillared main house in Charles City County, Virginia. She was no longer the slim beauty of her White House reign. Five children had added matronly curves to her figure, but her face was still a worthy subject for any painter's brush. It was the fall of 1853 and a new president was in the White House— Franklin Pierce of New Hampshire. But his pronouncements on the topics of the day won little attention. Everyone in the country was discussing the book that Julia Tyler was denouncing with such vehemence—*Uncle Tom's Cabin,* by a hitherto obscure New England writer named Harriet Beecher Stowe.

"Calm yourself, my dear," said former president Tyler. "No sensible person believes a word of it. Wouldn't you agree, Senator Stapleton?"

"Unquestionably, Mr. President. But I worry about how many sensible people we've got on the voting rolls," George Stapleton said.

"What do you think, Caroline?" Julia asked.

"I think it's a monster that's likely to haunt all our days and nights."

"Why do you say that, Mrs. Stapleton?" Tyler asked.

"Because it casts the quarrel about slavery as a fable of sin within a chosen country and the wrongs permitted by God to prepare us for redemption. For anyone who's religiously inclined, it makes rational argument irrelevant."

Caroline had already read *Uncle Tom's Cabin* twice. She planned to read it again. It was one of the most fascinating books she had ever encountered. No one seemed to see its inner message. Southerners exploded with rage at its crude attack on slavery. Northerners gasped with disbelief at the cruelties the author seemed to expose. Only Caroline saw it was the cry of a tormented soul, trying to understand how a supposedly benevolent God would allow such evil to exist in the world He created.

The Tyler's liveried butler, Daniel, emerged on the porch with another pitcher of ice-filled lemonade. "But anybody who's ever visited a plantation knows there never was an overseer like Simon Legree—or a slave like Uncle Tom," John Tyler said. "Not to mention George, Eliza, and Topsy."

"Unfortunately, only a handful of Northerners have ever visited a plantation," Senator Stapleton said.

Caroline heard the weariness in his voice and felt a stir of pity—mingled with savage triumph. For the senator, the presidential election of 1852 had been an excruciating reminder of his wife's powers of political prophecy. The Democrats had done exactly what Caroline had predicted they would do— they took a leaf from the Whigs' book of election tricks and nominated a former general. But it was not former general George Stapleton. It was former general Franklin Pierce of New Hampshire, a handsome vacuity with a wife who was equally stupid.

"I met Mrs. Stowe at a lecture she gave in New Jersey," Caroline said. "She impressed me as an utterly driven woman, haunted by theological anxiety."

Julia Tyler stared blankly. She had never had a moment of theological anxiety in her self-assured life. Not even her father's violent death had given her more than a spasm of routine grief.

Caroline treasured the six-months-old memory of her encounter with Mrs. Stowe. After her lecture, Caroline had given a reception for Mrs. Stowe at Bowood. As the guests departed and the famous writer was waiting for her carriage, Caroline had said, "I suspect you don't believe in God any more than I do, Mrs. Stowe."

Mrs. Stowe had blanched to the color of a table napkin. "There are times when I doubt Him extensively," she said. "But His saving grace has invariably restored me."

It was another memory Caroline could not share with anyone, neither Sarah Polk nor George Stapleton nor Julia Tyler—nor her partner in the struggle between fame and evil, John Sladen. She was here at Sherwood Forest in pursuit of the fame Sladen had promised her, a wary husband beside her. Caroline had returned to George's bed—or to put it more exactly, permitted George to return to hers. It had been an easy quarrel to resolve, once she realized how readily her evil heart allowed her to impersonate forgiveness and reconciliation.

It had been equally easy to reconstitute her Washington salon and invite Julia Gardiner and her husband to shine at its first evening. Dolley Madison was dead, Sarah Polk was in ignominious silence in Nashville, and Jane Pierce was a recluse who rarely emerged from her bedroom. Julia was delighted to become the first lady of Washington society again.

But always, as Caroline had long since learned, there was the unexpected event, such as *Uncle Tom's Cabin*. It had transformed the slavery quarrel from an argument among political and religious theorists to an earthquake that was shaking hundreds of thousands of households in the North. Three hundred thousand copies of the book had already been sold. A stage version was playing in a thousand theaters. Hatred of slavery and of the South was sweeping the North like an epidemic of some virulent fever that could lead to madness and civil war.

Southerners had responded with anti–*Uncle Tom's Cabin* novels, which no one bothered to read. What was needed was an answer from someone who could attract national attention. That person was sitting only a few feet away from Caroline. "Have you seen the open letter those English noblewomen have sent to the women of the South?" Caroline asked.

"No!" Julia said. "We get only a local paper down here. It has no news worth mentioning in it."

"This is not the sort of news a Southern paper would print," Caroline said.

She produced the clipping from the *New York Tribune* and handed it to Julia, who read it aloud to the company. It was an appeal to Southern women to take the lead in persuading their men to abolish slavery. The authors were the Countess of Derby, the Duchess of Sutherland, the Viscountess Palmerston, and Lady John Russell. Their husbands were all prominent English politicians. To substantiate their case against slavery, they quoted *Uncle Tom's Cabin*.

President Tyler, who had experienced British arrogance firsthand in his attempts to settle the Texas and Oregon disputes, exploded like a Fourth of July rocket. He treated them to ten minutes of fervid oratory on perfidious Albion.

"What we need is some American woman of equal rank to give these ladies a serious reply," Caroline said. "It could also be a response to Mrs. Stowe, without getting into a direct argument with her."

"I'll do it!" Julia Tyler said. "If you'll assist me, Caroline."

"You'll have my assistance—and Senator Stapleton's as well," Tyler said.

"No!" Julia said. "I think this should be written to women—by women."

"Mr. President, I think we've been outvoted, disenfranchised—and dismissed," George said. "This might be a good time to give me a shot at some of those ducks you say are thick on the river at this time of year."

"I agree wholeheartedly, Senator," Tyler said. "Let us make a dignified retreat—before we're routed."

Caroline waited until the men were out of earshot. "I trust you realize the honor of our sex is at stake here, as well as the honor of the South. This must be done well, if it is to be done at all."

"Let's get to work," Julia said.

They retired to Sherwood Forest's library, and soon dozens of pages were covered with Julia's precise penmanship. They worked after supper and after breakfast and dinner the following day, and the day after that, Caroline correcting and suggesting, Julia responding. Finally it was completed, and Julia read it aloud to ex-president Tyler and Senator Stapleton.

Julia began by admitting that slavery was a difficult system to defend. It had "grave political disadvantages" and was "the one subject on which there is a possibility of wrecking the bark of the Union." But she denied that the system was bestiality in the flesh and questioned the right of these upper-class British women to intervene in an American domestic problem. She declared that compared to the white denizens of London's appalling slums, the Southern Negro "lives sumptuously." He had warm clothing, plenty of bread, and meat twice a day. She admitted that slave families were sometimes separated but insisted it was a comparatively rare occurrence. Her husband, who owned more than a hundred slaves, had never separated a family in his fifty years as a master.

She then took the offensive and accused these ladies of mouthing the opinions of their powerful husbands, who had ulterior motives for their abolitionist crusade—the breakup of the American Union, which would guarantee Britain's world power. Julia reminded the titled ladies that the English were the ones who first enslaved the African and brought him to America. She urged them to concentrate their charitable impulses on the destitute and impoverished people of their own country—particularly the Irish, who had recently experienced a famine that had claimed over a million victims.

"Spare from the well-fed Negroes of the United States one drop of your superabounding sympathy to pour into that bitter cup, which is overrunning with sorrow and tears," Julia continued. "Go, my good Duchess of Sutherland, on an embassy of mercy to the poor, the stricken, the hungry, and the naked of your own land—cast in their laps the superflux of your enormous wealth; a single jewel from your hair, a single gem from your dress, would relieve many a poor female of England who is now cold and shivering and destitute."

The ex-president and the senator sat there, dazed. Finally, John Tyler said, "I begin to think those ladies who are agitating for the vote for women may have a point."

"I thought so the first time I heard from them," George said.

"It's magnificent," Tyler said, giving Julia a kiss. "It's beyond anything any male politician in the entire United States and the territories could have composed."

He was right. Caroline sent the finished essay to the *New York Herald,* now the paper with the largest circulation in the United States. They printed it on the front page, and within days it was reprinted in papers across the nation. The *Southern Literary Messenger,* the South's favorite magazine, ran it a month later. Letters poured into Sherwood Forest, many solicited by Caroline. Sarah Polk, Mrs. Webster, and Mrs. Calhoun were among the patrons of the Stapleton salon who joined the chorus of praise. "I verily believe Mrs. Tyler has squashed those English snobs and Harriet Beecher Stowe in one blow," Sarah Polk wrote to Caroline, showing she had not lost any of her political acuity. She knew the real target of the reply.

Caroline was far less optimistic. She accepted John Sladen's congratulations for establishing herself as Julia Tyler's favorite political confidante. But Caroline could only see darkness looming on the political horizon. The Whig Party was in its death throes. Their defeat in 1852 had shattered them so badly, they virtually ceased to function. In the wreckage a kind of political anarchy flourished. For a while, an anti-Catholic, anti-immigrant party called the Know-Nothings won a spate of elections. They even persuaded Andrew Jackson Donelson, Old Hickory's nephew, to become their spokesman in Tennessee, to Sarah Polk's dismay. But they soon split into antislavery and proslavery wings, like the Whigs. Only the Democrats retained a semblance of unity, by holding high the torch of the Union.

From New Orleans came impatient calls for action by Charlie, who was growing bored with making and losing money on the Cotton Exchange. He wanted to help launch that invasion of Cuba, but the chances of persuading President Franklin Pierce to look the other way and tolerate the expedition grew dimmer with every sale of a copy of *Uncle Tom's Cabin.* Complicating the president's problems was a bill that Senator Stephen Douglas of Illinois had persuaded Pierce to back, opening the Kansas and Nebraska Territories to both slave and free-soil settlers. Passed as a Democratic Party measure, it had enabled the abolitionists to whip up a frenzy of criticism against Pierce in the North.

Senator Stapleton, remembering the stubborn resistance that Americans had encountered in Mexico, was lukewarm toward the Cuban expedition. His enthusiasm rose slightly when John Quitman became leader of the project. Quitman had demonstrated military ability in Mexico. George also grudgingly agreed that Charlie was a born soldier, and he ought to be allowed to find out for himself how good he was at it. In the Senate, John Sladen introduced a bill to suspend the neutrality laws, which barred Americans from launching such "filibustering" expeditions, as the newspapers called them. (From the Spanish word for pirate, *filibustero*.) The neutrality laws had never been popular, and the bill easily won the approval of the Foreign Relations Committee.

Caroline was keeping ex-president Tyler in close touch with these developments. She had persuaded Julia Tyler that a well-timed statement from him, supporting Cuba's annexation on the same terms that had brought Texas into the Union, would add luster to Tyler's fame. Julia assured Caroline that the statement would be made when the moment for it came. The abolitionist uproar over the Kansas-Nebraska Act made the ex-president ready and eager to defend the South's right to expand the number of slave states. As the man who had annexed Texas, he was passionately convinced that the South's future depended on its ability to maintain political equality with the North.

On May 25, 1854, Senator John Sladen was one of the first arrivals at Caroline's revived salon. George was still in his room, changing his clothes. She let Sladen kiss her cheek. That was all the familiarity she had permitted him since their voyage to New Orleans. Their liaison had become purely political once more.

"Has the Senate voted on your neutrality bill?" she asked.

"No. Nor is it likely too. Didn't George tell you? We spent the afternoon at the White House."

"I haven't seen him. He came in while I was dressing."

"The President is having kittens over the bill. On top of Kansas-Nebraska, he's afraid it will ruin his chances for a second term. Not only does he want it killed—he's issuing a proclamation against filibustering tomorrow."

"I knew that man was a fool from the moment I saw him," Caroline said. "Didn't George try to stop him?"

As a Northern Democrat and a fellow veteran of Mexico, George had considerable influence with the president. "He didn't say a word," John growled.

Later that night, after the guests had departed, Caroline said several thousand words to George. She told him that he should have challenged the president. By saying nothing, he had tacitly admitted he was as frightened by the abolitionists as the rest of the Northern Democrats. Moreover, he had embarrassed Charlie in New Orleans. Victor Conte Legrand had invested over fifty thousand dollars in the Cuban expedition. Now the guns and ammunition and provisions General Quitman had purchased would have to be sold at a forced auction for next to nothing. Charlie's chances of marrying Cynthia Legrand and forming an alliance with one of the wealthiest families in the South had become less than promising.

"That doesn't worry me," George said. "I'm glad to see the Cuban thing junked. It wasn't a guaranteed success by a long shot. The Spaniards have ten or fifteen thousand troops in Cuba. They could put up a hell of a fight. Quitman only raised about three thousand men. If the Cubans didn't support him, they could have been wiped out."

Caroline declared herself dismayed by George's timidity. When Pierce issued his proclamation, denouncing filibustering as "derogatory to the character" of the nation, she persuaded George to publicly disagree with the president. At her behest, he joined Congressman John Quitman and a half dozen other Southerners who reminded Pierce that the United States could not have won their revolution against England without the aid of filibustering foreign soldiers such as Lafayette.

At Caroline's next salon, exiled Cuban patriots portrayed their countrymen as on fire with a desire for liberty and union with the United States. She produced morose letters from Charlie reporting reproachful remarks from Victor Legrand. Finally George went to see the wavering president and extracted a promise that the government would look the other way if the expedition kept a low profile.

But Pierce could not retract his proclamation, which caused many of the expedition's volunteers to defect. A dismayed Quitman withdrew as the leader and denounced Pierce as an enemy of the South. The president tried to mollify Southerners by offering to buy Cuba from Spain. His diplomacy ran into a stone wall of Spanish intransigence. No Madrid politician could part with this relic of Spain's imperial glory without writing his own death sentence.

While Pierce floundered, another political earthquake shook the country, confirming Caroline's intuition about the power of *Uncle Tom's Cabin*. Ex-Whigs, Know-Nothings, abolitionists, and disgruntled free-soil Democrats coalesced into a new political party, who called themselves Republicans. They proclaimed themselves undying foes of slavery—which meant they did not have a single adherent south of the Mason-Dixon Line. But in the congressional elections of 1854, they swept the North and won a majority in the House of Representatives.

The Democrats retained control of the Senate. That meant the government virtually ground to a dead stop, since the two branches agreed on nothing. When Pierce sent federal troops into Kansas to keep order between pro-slavery and antislavery guerrillas, the Republicans amended an army appropriation bill to deny the president the authority to use the troops to enforce laws passed by the pro-slavery Kansas legislature. The Senate refused to approve the bill, leading to weeks of legislative deadlock and the threat of the U.S. Army's dissolution.

Caroline did not have to say *I told you so*. George said it for her, slumped at the dinner table, worn-out by the endless wrangling between the two sections of the country. He was especially dismayed by reports of Americans killing fellow Americans in Kansas. "It's a civil war out there. Madmen are on the loose. Last week a fellow named John Brown rode into a Southern settlement on Osawatomie Creek and butcherd five men with machetes."

He looked so sad, so discouraged, for a moment Caroline felt an almost irresistible impulse to console him. She was witnessing the pain, the bafflement, of a patriot. Only she knew the fame this man had surrendered in the name of honesty and love of country. Only she understood, thanks to Aaron Burr, the impossibility of his desire to be both powerful and good. She found herself almost wishing she had never met Burr, never heard his bitter wisdom. But that escape into illusion would have required a different father, a different fate.

Evil, Caroline thought. It was seeping across the continent, exactly as she had foreseen it. Had her silence—a kind of complicity—about Zachary Taylor's death made her responsible for it? She pleaded not guilty to that accusation. She did not want to see herself as the cause of George Stapleton's pain. At times, as she watched him trudge off to another day of hate-filled rhetoric in the Senate, she imagined a scenario in which they fled the country to a benevolent exile in Italy or the Greek islands. But she realized she could never persuade him to go, nor could she really persuade herself.

Another night, George came home fuming over a speech by Senator Charles Sumner of Massachusetts. He had accused the South of "the rape" of the "virgin territory" of Kansas—and then turned his invective on individual senators, violating a sacred Senate code of behavior. He had suggested that Senator Andrew Butler of South Carolina had made obscene vows to "the harlot, slavery"—implying he had sex with his female slaves—and added injury to insult by ridiculing the senator's speech impediment. "It was absolutely the most vicious speech I've heard in my twenty-five years in the Senate," George said. "I denounced the self-righteous son of a bitch to his face. He spit at me. Honest to God. On the floor of the U.S. Senate, Charles Sumner spit at me."

Again, there was no need for Caroline to say I told you so. She listened while George morosely described another tormenting problem. After President Millard Fillmore had pardoned Tabitha Flowers and her husband, George sent them to New York with enough money to buy a hack and go into the taxi business. Irish hack drivers had beaten up the husband, wrecked his hack, and cut his horse's throat. The Irish were the underclass of the North, and they were determined not to let blacks take jobs away from them.

That night, although Caroline told herself she was not renouncing her evil heart, she opened her arms to her melancholy husband. "It's not your fault, George. None of it is your fault," she said. He was so grateful, so touched by her sympathy, she grew alarmed. He was seducing her into loving him again!

The next morning John Sladen rescued her with a note: *Don't fail to visit the Senate this afternoon. You'll see something that will thrill you.* That afternoon, Caroline strolled to one of the reserved couches on the Senate floor as the senators wrangled over Sumner's insulting speech. George urged the Yankee, whose skull-like face made him look like a veritable harbinger of evil, to apologize to Butler. John Sladen proposed Sumner's expulsion from the Senate. The vote fell far short of the two-thirds required for such a drastic measure. After some feckless debate on Kansas, the world's greatest deliberative body adjourned. Most departed for the infamous Hole in the Wall or more genteel watering places. A few lingered, chatting to friends. Senator Sumner stayed at his desk, answering mail. Like many senators, he used his desk as an office.

George strolled over to Caroline's couch. "What brings you down this way?" It was her first visit in more than two years. He thought it had something to do with her unexpected sympathy last night.

"I was told something extraordinary was going to happen. But I fear my informant was wrong."

As they spoke, with George's back turned to the rows of desks, Congressman Preston Brooks of South Carolina entered the Senate chamber clutching a thick gutta-percha cane. He strode past them with a grim expression on his handsome face. A moment later there was a thud and a cry. George whirled, Caroline stared aghast. Brooks was smashing Senator Sumner over the head with the cane. A few feet away, Senator John Sladen watched with a sardonic smile.

George rushed to Brooks and tore the splintered cane out of his hand. Sumner toppled to the floor, blood gushing from his head. Butler turned to the handful of senators still on the floor and shouted, "Let the Yankees be warned. The South will not be insulted without retaliation!"

Evil. Caroline's eyes found the resolute face of her fellow conspirator. *Thank you,* she said as the sergeant at arms, the doorkeeper, and Senate pages carried the bleeding Sumner away. *Thank you for giving me another chance to see how serious we are.*

A shaken George took Caroline home in the Stapleton carriage. "I can't believe it," he said. "I can't believe what I just saw."

Caroline said nothing. But her eyes spoke: *I told you so.* Maria de Vega, Mexico, were vanishing in this political maelstrom. Caroline sensed her growing power. "The South has to be given something to soothe their anger," she said. "It can't be Mexico. That would require an army, a war. It will have to be Cuba."

"I'm afraid you're right," George said.

"That means you shouldn't support Franklin Pierce for reelection. He can't retract his idiotic proclamation against filibustering. Not that he deserves your support, anyway. He's done nothing for you or any of our friends. President Tyler wrote to him a half dozen times on behalf of some of his relations and old supporters. He didn't even get the courtesy of a reply."

"Who will it be—the Little Giant?"

He was talking about Senator Stephen Douglas. Caroline shook her head. "A president should be at least five feet eight. I have a personal preference for men over six feet. But that's no longer relevant."

She was talking about their lost presidential hopes. With a sigh she said, "It will have to be Buchanan."

"Old Buck? That decrepit Nancy? I can't believe you're serious. I thought we got rid of him once and for all when we sent him to London to play whist with the Limeys."

Pierce had made James Buchanan ambassador to Great Britain. Everyone thought it was a shrewd move at the time—getting a major rival out of the country. Many people wondered why Buchanan accepted the job. Caroline soon understood why, as Pierce's presidency crumbled around him.

"Buchanan's the only Democrat who can win. Pierce has let Kansas become a tar baby. Douglas is the man who fathered the baby. They're both covered with the stuff—while Old Buck has been prancing around Bucking-ham Palace, spotless. He can run without a speck of tar on him."

"You may be right about that. But what kind of a president will he make?"

For a moment, Caroline almost said what she was thinking: *A weak one. The weakest imaginable president.* But she retained her self-control and re-plied, "One that will let you finance an expedition to Cuba."

George said nothing. His silence was enough. He agreed with her. It was an enormously important moment. Their partnership was being resurrected without Caroline speaking the words of forgiveness that George had once insisted on hearing. She was free to manipulate him with unrenounced evil in her heart.

Or was she? Was pity, the emotion that had lured her into John Sladen's arms, drawing her into a new relationship with her troubled husband? Car-oline vowed she would not make the same mistake twice. But she was vul-nerable to George in ways that infinitely transcended the adolescent emotion that had drawn her to John Sladen. A thousand memories challenged her to be a wife again.

Two nights later, Caroline welcomed Senator Sladen to her salon. "What is the latest news about Congressman Brooks?" she asked. "Will he be ar-rested for his atrocious assault on Senator Sumner?"

She said this in a voice just loud enough to be overheard by several other guests. "I'm afraid not," John said. "The Senate decided today that it had no power to arrest a congressman. The abolitionists voted to expel Mr. Brooks from the House, but they couldn't muster a two-thirds majority."

Congressman Quitman joined them, his prophetic white beard bristling. "I'm planning to buy Mr. Brooks a new cane."

"Please, General," Caroline said, pretending dismay. "I saw the assault."

"Excuse me, but the fellow deserved it."

"My husband agrees entirely," Caroline said.

"That's the best news I've heard about the whole affair," Quitman said.

Quitman strode across the room to interrupt George's conversation with ex-president Tyler. All three were soon in grim agreement on Sumner's fate. "Who are you going to support for the Democratic nomination?" Caroline asked John Sladen in a much lower voice.

"I haven't made up my mind."

"It has to be Buchanan. You should write to him now, making yourself an early backer. That will endear you to him to the point of utter pusillanim-ity. Make him president and what we want to achieve will be infinitely more *simple.*"

John seized a flute of champagne from a passing tray. "I'm beginning to wonder if we can pull it off. There are so many madmen on both sides."

Evil. Why couldn't he understand what they were confronting? "When did you start drinking again?" she said.

"It's one of the few consolations of celibacy."

"No one regrets that more than I do." The words were a lie but her evil heart assured her the truth was no longer relevant. "Some sacrifices are es-sential."

He knew what she meant. They had agreed an affair between two well-known people was impossible in Washington, D.C. She did not tell him that her new sympathy for George made the very idea unpalatable. Even her evil heart recoiled from the idea of adding an unfaithful wife to his woes. But that same malevolent heart was equally determined to keep John Sladen under control.

Caroline decided to demonstrate her renewed power over Senator Stapleton. "George, wait until you hear this. Senator Sladen says a Cuban expedition would be an exact equivalent of the reason my father—and yours—went to war in 1812. To bring liberty to the oppressed."

George said that was a touching thought, although his doleful eyes suggested he was thinking that both of these soldiers of liberty did not survive their war.

A delighted General Quitman declared he was ready to resume command of the expedition tomorrow. Ex-president Tyler proposed a toast: "To a future empire of American liberty, from the north pole to the equator."

Evil, Caroline thought, smiling at General Quitman and Senator Sladen and ex-president Tyler and his beaming wife, Julia, slave owners all. She was weaving them into her wicked triumph. She was going to free them from the grip of the black anaconda, without recourse to law or morality. Suddenly they would find themselves in fame's temple, where she would preside as a goddess of victory. For a little while, Caroline believed it was possible. She was almost happy.

SIX

THE JUNE SUN BEAT DOWN, MAKING Caroline grateful for the blue parasol perched on her shoulder. The mere thought of those scorching rays on her aching head induced shivers of anticipatory pain throughout her whole body. For the past six months, her migraine nemesis had been tormenting her with mounting intensity.

Caroline was standing on the lawn of Bralston, Victor Conte Legrand's Louisiana plantation, watching Cynthia Legrand emerge from the white main house in a wedding dress designed by Worth, Paris's newest couturier. The glowing bride was followed by a half dozen bridesmaids in organdy creations of the same designer. Waiting for Cynthia at the head of a tunnel of flower-bedecked arches was Charlie Stapleton in the blue uniform of the Louisiana Guards. Beside him stood his tall somber brother Jonathan in a gray-striped morning coat.

HOOOOOO-T! A passing steamboat saluted the festivities. The mighty Mississippi flowed only a few hundred feet from Bralston's front door.

"Doesn't she look marvelous?" Caroline said to the plump, plain young woman standing beside her.

"Smashing," murmured Laura Biddle Stapleton, who was making desperate efforts to ingratiate her terrifying mother-in-law.

Standing in their Sunday clothes beyond the seated guests were Bralston's 120 slaves, excited smiles on their faces. They burst into cheers when Cynthia reached the end of the flowery tunnel and her father handed her over to Charlie. The minister cleared his throat and began the ceremony that would create a North-South alliance—and a new state for the Union.

Last night, at a dinner for the wedding party, Victor Conte Legrand and Senator George Stapleton had each given the bridegroom checks for $100,000. Senator John Sladen had contributed another $100,000. Ten other guests had jointly produced $150,000. This remarkable generosity had nothing to do with wanting to give the newlyweds a splendid start in life. Everyone knew that Charlie was going to hand the money over to Los Liberadores de Cuba, the expedition to conquer Cuba. The wedding was a perfect way to collect the money without running afoul of the neutrality laws.

The year was 1858. President James Buchanan was in the White House, thanks to the strenuous backing of Senators Stapleton and Sladen and the still considerable influence of ex-president John Tyler. They had performed the unlikely feat of dumping the incumbent president, Franklin Pierce, and electing another Democrat. Tyler's son Robert had run Buchanan's campaign in Pennsylvania. He could claim with some justice that he had elected Old Buck. Buchanan had won by carrying every Southern state except Maryland but only five Northern states.

If the Republican candidate, John C. Fremont, had carried either Indiana or Illinois and Pennsylvania, he would have become president. Even in Democratic New Jersey, a Republican had won the governorship, although the party's name was too tarred by abolitionism to wear it publicly in such a Democratic stronghold. The winner had run as "the Opposition" candidate.

By the time the campaign ended, John Sladen had become Buchanan's closest confidant. In constant consultation with Caroline, John had virtually selected the new president's cabinet, two-thirds of them Southerners with strong though silent sympathy for secession. John had no difficulty persuading the vain old man that James Buchanan would be the last president of the United States if he did not follow Franklin Pierce's example and promise to look the other way while the South captured Cuba.

Once that task was accomplished, the Cuban provisional government would apply for admission to the Union. The president, having been James Polk's secretary of state, could hardly object to this idea. On the contrary, he was expected to recommend admission by a majority vote of Congress, using Texas as proof that the procedure was perfectly legal. Ex-president John Tyler stood ready to support Buchanan as a spokesman for the South.

The Republicans would be faced with an excruciating choice. Either admit another slave state or give the South a perfect excuse to withdraw from the Union. Driven by their abolitionist wing, the Republicans would almost certainly ignore the president and vote against Cuba in Congress. The South would then secede, with the blessing of a sitting president. Though abolitionists such as Joshua Giddings and Charles Sumner might rant and rave, they would never be able to persuade the people of the North to go to war to prevent the South's departure.

"By the power confided to me by the sovereign state of Louisiana, I now pronounce you man and wife," the minister intoned.

Charlie gave Cynthia Legrand Stapleton an enthusiastic kiss. He was a wholehearted member of their conspiracy—and why not? He was getting one of the most beautiful women in the South for his wife and a new vastly exciting political-military career in the bargain. Caroline gave Charlie a kiss almost as warm as the one Cynthia had given him. His brother Jonathan watched gloomily, knowing his mother preferred Charlie to him—and also knowing the Cuban invasion plans, about which his father had indiscreetly told him on the voyage to Bralston.

Jonathan had forever sealed Caroline's disapproval of his ways and opinions by marrying Laura Biddle, Jeremy Biddle's daughter, last year. Confusing pity and love, like so many people his age, he saw himself rescuing the shy, troubled young woman from her bitter mother and unhappy father. He also saw it as an attempt to bring the two families together on his terms. At the wedding, Jeremy and George had shaken hands and expressed mutual regrets. Caroline, summoning all the power of her formidable will, managed to be polite to the detestable worm and his loathsome wife and affectionate to Laura. His wife's performance had won plaudits from George.

Dozens of guests lined up to congratulate the young couple and kiss the gorgeous bride. John Sladen approached Caroline with his wife, Clothilde, on his arm. She had shriveled into premature old age. Their two daughters had been among the bridesmaids. "How nice to meet you again after all these years," Caroline said.

"I'm surprised you're looking so well," Clothilde said in her no-longer-liquid voice, with its tinge of a French accent.

"Why do you say that?"

"I've hated you so much, I've often practiced juju on you. By now, if it had worked, your eyes would have fallen out, your teeth would have rotted."

She was smiling as she said these atrocious things. John was looking more and more uncomfortable.

"I don't understand," Caroline said.

"Of course you do. My husband is in love with you. But I don't think you love him. In fact, I can see quite clearly you don't. Do you love anyone?"

"My husband."

"Of course," Clothilde said. "God requires us to do that. But whom do you actually love?"

"I'm afraid to tell you. I don't want to expose them to your black magic."

Evil. Caroline sensed it in this woman's mocking antagonism. It reminded her that this marvelous, sun-splashed wedding was surrounded by other intimations of evil. One of them approached her now. Henry Quitman, General John Quitman's slim sad-faced son, had come to the wedding in his father's name, to testify to his family's support for the expedition to Cuba.

"Mrs. Stapleton, on his deathbed my father asked me to tell you how grateful he was for your friendship. He told me how much you had done for the expedition."

"Thank you. If only he were here to say it in person."

"I look forward to a day when I can make that crew of Yankee murderers pay for his death."

In the most recent term of Congress, John Quitman had been a sulfurous spokesman for the South in the House of Representatives. He had repeatedly called on President Buchanan to repeal or modify the neutrality laws. While Buchanan did not dare to do such a thing, with each Quitman blast, the president's cowardly nature flinched at the thought of enforcing these anti-quated statutes, which had been passed in 1818. General Quitman had used his position as head of the Military Affairs Committee to recruit a half dozen talented young officers from the U.S. Army for the Cuban expedition. Soon everyone in Washington knew Quitman was its secret commander in chief.

Suddenly this big robust man became an invalid. Having donated thousands of dollars to the expedition, he had left his wife and family in Mississippi to save money in Washington and was living at the National Hotel, a favorite among Southern congressmen. A dozen other National guests came down with the symptoms that felled Quitman—violent diarrhea, followed by severe swelling of the legs and feet, blurred vision, and acute exhaustion. A doctor diagnosed it as arsenic poisoning. Soon, a great many people were convinced that abolitionists were responsible. Quitman reeled back to Mississippi but never recovered. He had died three months ago.

Caroline had no difficulty believing Quitman had been murdered. Evil was loose on both sides of this obscene struggle. "We'll treasure your father's memory," she told Henry Quitman. "I hope we can soon name a city after him in Cuba. Don't you think that's a good idea, Senator Sladen?"

"Excellent."

"We have two slaves from Cuba on our plantation," Clothilde Sladen said. "They tell me the Cuban blacks will fight the Americans if they try to land. They have hopes of freedom from the Spanish, but none from the Americans."

The woman's hatred was almost palpable. Caroline wondered why John Sladen had brought her here. Was he trying to reveal what he had endured for her sake, all these years? For a moment Caroline was swept by a rush of sympathy. She imagined herself as John Sladen's wife in cosmopolitan New Orleans. Would they have been happy? Or would two such willful souls have clashed unto worse misery than John had endured with Clothilde?

The wedding banquet lasted until darkness fell. At one point, Victor Legrand led the Stapletons down to the plantation's slave quarter, where a separate celebration was in progress. Watching the blacks dancing and singing, Legrand asked Senator Stapleton if he had ever seen a happier, more contented group of workers.

"You never have a runaway?"

"Where would they go? It's five hundred miles to the Ohio River."

"If they're so contented," Jonathan Stapleton said, "why do you have all those guns locked in that cabinet in the main house?"

"I've never had to use one of those guns and doubt if I ever will," Legrand said. "But we're outnumbered five to one in this part of Louisiana."

"The workers in Principia Mills may not like us, but I've never been afraid of them. Have you, Father?"

"Of course not," George said. Uneasily he added, "My oldest son is a free-soil Democrat."

"Why don't you come out and admit you're an abolitionist?" Legrand said.

"Because I'm not. I recognize we can't free all these people overnight. But I can't abide your attitude—that this system is perfect and there's no need to change it."

Jonathan's self-assurance had grown exponentially since he had become president of the Camden & Amboy Railroad. He had begun building branch lines all over New Jersey, giving the railroad a total monopoly on transportation inside and across the state. The Camden & Amboy had become one of the most profitable businesses in the country.

"Master," said a huge black. "Do you think we could open another keg of beer? I guarantee nobody goin' to misbehave."

"Certainly, George," Legrand said. "Here's the key to the icehouse."

He handed George a set of keys, pointing to one of them. "George runs my plantation for me. I trust him with those keys, which include one for my gun cabinet. He's intelligent, brave—I've seen him beat more than one malcontent in a fistfight. As long as men like him are contented with the system, I see no need to change it."

"Have you ever asked him if he's contented?" Jonathan said.

"Why should I even bring up such a topic?"

"Jonathan," Caroline said, "I think you've done more than enough to wound the spirit of this wonderful occasion. Why don't you just shut up?"

Head down, Jonathan stalked into the night, his wife trailing after him, murmuring, "Your mother has a point, Jonathan."

"I'm sure he'll acquire more sense with age," Victor Legrand said.

"If I have anything to say about it, he'll acquire it much sooner," Caroline said.

The migraine suddenly renewed its ratcheting agony in Caroline's skull. Was Jonathan the reason? She almost looked forward to blaming him. But it was not true, and he would not change his opinions for her sake, even if she were on her deathbed. He was determined not to repeat his father's mistakes. As a result, he defied his mother and incidentally tyrannized his hapless wife.

No, the migraines were rooted in the growing division in Caroline's soul between her evil heart and her compassionate head. She had reached the age at which memory suffused the mind with regret and longing. But her unrepentant heart remained armored against these surges of sentiment from the past.

The next day, Charlie cheerfully reported that the "collections" at the wedding had gone over five hundred thousand dollars. This would enable them to hire two armored steamers to deal with Cuban patrol boats and to buy Sharp repeating rifles for the three thousand volunteers. One of John Quitman's regular army recruits, bluff, hearty Colonel Francis Lemoyne, had assumed command of the expedition. Charlie would serve as his aide-de-camp. As the Stapletons boarded the steamboat at Bralston's dock, Charlie assured them, "The next thing you hear from me will be a telegraph from New Orleans: 'Havana is ours!' "

On the way back to New York aboard a coastal steamer from New Orleans, George had numerous conversations with Jonathan. George mournfully informed Caroline that he was unable to change their oldest son's political opinions. Although Jonathan denied it, he was still under the influence of his college roommate, Ben Dall, who had launched an abolitionist newspaper in New York. Caroline suspected Jonathan was a secret backer.

For the next three months, Caroline read letter after letter from Charlie, reporting on the progress—and occasional delays—of the expedition. Colonel Lemoyne's regular-army ways did not sit well with many of the volunteer officers and there had been a spate of resignations. It took time to replace these men. But federal government officials in New Orleans remained quiescent, making no inquiries into the future use of the armored steamers tied up at the Mississippi docks. George and John Sladen made sure President Buchanan knew all about the expedition. The two senators drafted a bill which they planned to submit to Congress the moment Charlie's victorious telegram arrived.

In mid-December 1858 came a final letter from Charlie.

We sail tomorrow with 2,800 men. We plan to land on Christmas Day. We're bringing 5,000 guns to arm the Cubans. Our men in Havana say the Spaniards know nothing. They just shipped two regiments back to Spain.

George fretted that the numbers were too small. He expressed private doubts about the Cubans. Giving men guns was only a first step. They had to be organized and trained. Would the Spanish give them time to do that? The plan was to seize the area around Santiago, Cuba's second city, expand the army there and march on Havana. There were also plans to rush reinforcements from New Orleans and other Southern ports, where volunteers were expected to be numerous as soon as they learned of the expedition's early success.

Caroline lay awake, night after night, seeing the drama unfold like a series of magic lantern slides on the walls of her bedroom. They could not fail. Fame could not, would not be denied her a third time. In the dawn she fingered a telegram delivered several weeks ago to Amelia Peterson, care of Stapleton, urging her to book a stateroom on the steamboat *Delilah* from St. Louis to join the celebration in New Orleans. It was signed Nathan Archibald.

It was John Sladen, of course, urging her to resume their affair. Perhaps she would make the trip. Especially if Charlie returned wounded and needed care. For a moment she was gripped by a near paroxysm of love for him. More than ever, she realized Charlie was the wildness she had suppressed in her own soul for the sake of Sarah Polk's vision of fame. Now she had her own vision and it embodied, it even glorified, American wildness. She saw Charlie in ten years, at the head of the South's army, swaggering into Mexico and Central America, erecting a tropical empire of immense power and wealth.

News from Mexico seemed to add substance to this vision. Civil war had erupted between the liberals and the conservatives and the country was crumbling into chaos again. Caroline said nothing that could be construed as gloating. But she frequently urged George to read the stories of massacres and pitched battles in the *New York Herald* and other newspapers. There was no need to say *I told you so*.

December and the year 1858 trickled away with no word from Cuba. They spent the holidays at Bowood, while George worked on reviving the Democratic Party in New Jersey. The abolitionists' rants over Bleeding Kansas were beginning to offend voters. Backed by a hundred thousand dollars of Stapleton money, the Democrats had regained the governorship and state legislature.

On the morning of January 12, 1859, Caroline remained in her room, waiting for George to depart to make a speech in Trenton. Someone rang the front doorbell. She heard Mercy Flowers answer it. Up the stairs Mercy trudged.

Caroline virtually sprang from her bedroom. "Was that a telegram?"

"Yes. For Senator Stapleton," Mercy said. "From New Orleans."

"Give it to me," Caroline said, snatching it off the tray.

Her hands trembled as she ripped open the yellow envelope. Standing in the dim hall, she read the words:

TERRIBLE NEWS FROM CUBA STOP SPANISH GUNBOATS SANK ONE OF ARMED VESSELS STOP SECOND RAN ASHORE STOP SPANISH TROOPS IN LARGE NUMBERS WAITED FOR THEM STOP SOMEONE HAD BETRAYED THE PLAN STOP EXPEDITION WIPED OUT TO LAST MAN STOP SPANISH EXECUTED WOUNDED AND PRISONERS STOP MY DEEPEST SYMPATHY TO YOU AND CAROLINE STOP SLADEN

"Give that to Senator Stapleton," Caroline said.

She stumbled back into her room, trying to comprehend it. But history was not comprehensible. History was like a huge steamboat lunging through the night, indifferent to human hopes and fears. Things simply happened or failed to happen. Presidents died—or were murdered. Armies won battles— or lost them.

"No!" She heard George's cry as he read the telegram. "Oh, God, no!"

Heavy footsteps in the hall. George swayed in the doorway in his undershirt, tears streaming down his cheeks. "You read it?"

"I read it."

"Oh, Jesus, Caroline. We've murdered our son. As surely as if we put a gun to his head and pulled the trigger. We murdered that poor kid."

"He wasn't a poor kid. He was a brave man—fighting for his country."

"His country? What the hell are you talking about?"

"His country," she hissed. "Don't you remember why we did this? For the sake of the Union? To give the South a reason for staying in it?"

She was amazed to discover that she could continue to lie. In her mangled heart, fame still struggled for life. The dream was not dead. Only Charlie had died. Perhaps his death was part of the evil god's plan. Perhaps he extracted such pain from his servants. Perhaps it was his way of preparing them for their own deaths. She would pay that price too. She would not waver, she would not retreat, no matter how terrible this god became.

For a week, Caroline's migraine tormented her with unparalleled frenzy. George hovered beside her bed. He summoned the doctor at all hours of the day and night. The man could do nothing but increase her dosage of laudanum. She remembered her long-ago conversations with John Sladen about the way suicides used the drug to elude their despair. Was she ready for this final surrender?

Gazing up at George's sorrowful face, Caroline rejected this grim alternative. She clung to this big grieving man and wept and wept and wept. She let herself be a helpless woman, supported by his wounded love. For a little while they were husband and wife again in ways more endearing and intricate than their youthful passion for each other.

President Buchanan issued a pious denunciation of filibustering. The blatant hypocrisy tormented George. But Caroline found it bracing. She credited it with banishing her migraine. With such a fool in the White House, she sensed the redemption of her dark hopes was not only still possible, but probable.

Caroline found additional comfort in the sympathy the Tylers extended to her. The ex-president wrote her a sorrowful note, telling her how he had lost three daughters in childbirth. *The death of a child is like a blow in the face to a parent. But we must soldier on for the sake of the living. Your son died in a noble cause. Let that be your consolation.* Aside from the touching sentiment, it was reassuring proof of how close the two families had become. The ex-president still remained a central figure in the scenario of peaceful secession.

Caroline showed the letter to George. He crumpled it in his big fist and wondered gloomily if they were losing their other two sons. Jonathan was using Charlie's death as proof that anything connected to the South and slavery was odious. Their youngest son, Paul, announced he was applying for West Point. More and more dismayed by the family's divisions, he was reaching back to mythical memories of his heroic grandfather. He told Caroline he wanted a career that had nothing to do with politics. Caroline soothed George by reminding him how often Americans elected soldiers as senators and presidents.

Julia Tyler invited Caroline to Sherwood Forest for weeks at a time. She too was in mourning. Her older sister, Margaret, had died unexpectedly during a visit to the plantation in the spring of 1858. Margaret, who had rejected scores of Washington, D.C., suitors and insisted on marrying only for love, had selected a tall impecunious young New York aristocrat for a husband. He had gone to California during the gold rush of 1849 and was killed when his shotgun accidentally discharged. It took nine tear-drenched years for Margaret's broken heart to kill her.

Wordlessly, Caroline shared her grief for Charlie with Julia, and Julia shared her grief for Margaret with Caroline, affirming at a profound level of silence what they both knew about each other now—they were not like other women. They loved something more elusive and more demanding than other women. Did Julia know it was fame? At times Caroline was tempted to tell her about the vision she had shared with Sarah Polk. But she decided that memory should remain a sacred secret between the two of them.

Caroline was at Sherwood Forest with George in October of 1859 when incredible news from western Virginia swept through the state. Abolitionists had seized the federal arsenal at Harpers Ferry and were calling on the state's Africans to form a black revolutionary army equipped with the thousands of government guns they now controlled. As the telegraph flashed the story throughout the South, the audacity of the raid, the mental picture of a race war it generated, sent shock waves of panic from Richmond to New Orleans.

George rushed back to Washington, D.C., to make sure President Buchanan acted decisively. As chairman of the Senate Committee on Military Affairs, Senator Stapleton knew exactly how many troops were at the president's disposal, and who was the best man to take command in the crisis. George virtually insisted on Buchanan's choosing Colonel Robert E. Lee, who was on leave at his home, just across the river in Arlington, Virginia. Lee's brilliant performance in Mexico had convinced George that he was the outstanding soldier in the American army.

Backed by a presidential proclamation, Lee rushed to Harpers Ferry with a company of U.S. Marines. Four companies of U.S. Army troops were also dispatched from Virginia's Fortress Monroe to support him. Rumors swept Virginia that the insurgents numbered five hundred men. They had seized thirteen prominent Virginians as hostages, among them a grandnephew of George Washington.

Henry Wise, the governor of the state and an old Tyler friend, called out Virginia's militia. Caroline found herself wondering what the slaves thought of it all. The Tylers assured her that Sherwood Forest's Africans posed no danger. But she noticed the ex-president thoroughly approved a decision by a neighbor to organize a cavalry troop of older men to patrol the roads at night, should the younger members of the county's militia be ordered to western Virginia.

Within twenty-four hours the threat of a slave insurrection evaporated. Colonel Lee's marines stormed the Harpers Ferry arsenal and subdued the seven abolitionists who had perpetrated the raid, under the leadership of the Kansas fanatic "Osawatomie" John Brown. The thirteen hostages were freed unharmed. George went to Harpers Ferry with Virginia's Senator James Mason to interrogate Brown. George sent a lengthy letter to John Tyler, reporting his conclusions. Brown was clearly insane. He raved hatred of Southerners and slavery, quoted the Book of Revelation, and saw himself as a latter-day savior. His confederates were a collection of drifters and dimwits, sucked into the vortex of his apocalyptic rhetoric.

I'm telling you this to reassure you that this man and his followers are not typical of the responsible people of the North. They disdain and despise Brown's mad solution to our national dilemma as much as I do, George wrote. He enclosed newspaper clippings reporting that everyone from former Whig congressman Abraham Lincoln, who was campaigning for the Republican nomination for president, to Catholic and Protestant clergymen to all the leaders of the Northern Democratic Party condemned Brown.

Caroline feared few would listen to these reasonable voices. The millions of Northern readers of *Uncle Tom's Cabin* endorsed biblical John Brown in their hearts, even though they flinched from his brutal acts. The abolitionist press became more and more frenzied as Brown was tried for sedition and murder—one of the marines had been killed storming the Harpers Ferry arsenal—and condemned to death. As the day of Brown's execution approached, rumors predicted an abolitionist army would descend on Virginia to rescue him. Governor Wise issued fifty thousand muskets, putting the state on a war footing.

By that time, Caroline was back in Washington, D.C., conferring with Senator John Sladen. She brought with her a statement from ex-president John Tyler: *But one sentiment pervades the South. Security in the Union, or separation. I hope there is conservatism enough in the country to speak peace, and that after all, good may come out of evil.*

Caroline saw it as a call for immediate secession. She wanted to release it to the newspapers. Sladen demurred. "We must save him for the right moment," John insisted. "Give it to George instead. Let him use it as a battle cry to rally unionist sentiment. We'll need them both when the moment comes."

Armed with Tyler's statement, George organized unionist rallies in New Jersey, New York, and Pennsylvania. He spoke at all of them, virtually wearing out his voice. He emerged from this campaign in the spring of 1860 as a major spokesman of moderation in the North. His fervent speeches against the tragedy of a civil war were quoted in hundreds of newspapers. Caroline found herself admiring the senator's growing moral grandeur. For him, the threat to the Union was a personal agony, as acutely painful as the rending of his own flesh. It was fascinating—and terrible—the way her evil god used good men and their noble intentions to achieve her dark purpose.

Julia Tyler sent Caroline an emotional view of the crisis from Virginia. *The Democratic Party is our country's only hope. Everything depends on finding the right candidate. He must be able to win Northern and Southern votes. If a Republican becomes president, the South will secede. They will never let the executive power fall into the hands of men sworn to destroy them.*

Unfortunately, the 1860 Democratic Convention was held in Charleston, South Carolina, headquarters of Southern secession fever. Senator Stapleton was proposed as a candidate, but in the frenzied atmosphere of the Palmetto State, he did not have any hope of winning two-thirds of the delegates. To Robert Barnwell Rhett and other Southern ultras, he was the man who had banished the slave trade from the capital—proof of his hidden animosity to the South. With Northern candidates subjected to this kind of fanatic scrutiny, it soon became apparent that no one was going to win the nomination. Senator Stephen A. Douglas of Illinois was dismissed because he had failed to defend Southerners in Kansas. In his ratchety voice, George took the floor to plead for unity. He was drowned in catcalls.

I told you so, Caroline's eyes said. But her voice spoke sympathy. She listened to George wonder if God was sending him some sort of message. It redoubled his torment, to see the party of Andrew Jackson disintegrate here, where George had struggled beside John C. Calhoun to keep the state in the

Union in 1833. Were they wrong, trying to hold the Union together? Should they let these people secede and leave the problem of slavery to them and their descendants? Was that the lesson of Tabitha's bitter fate?

Caroline's eyes said, *I told you so.* But sympathy continued to flow from her lips. Sympathy and evil wisdom. "I think we should go home, make sure we control New Jersey, and see what happens in the election."

He kissed her and thanked her for listening to him. "Everything you've said and done since Charlie's death has made me ashamed of the way I condemned you for that moment of weakness so long ago. I think I love you more now than I did before I went to Mexico."

"I love you infinitely more."

To her amazement, Caroline was able to say this because it was true—and simultaneously false. She loved the heroic, tragic, wounded figure her husband had become. But that love did not come close to matching her evil heart's passion for fame. She saw the SS *Delilah,* painted black, churning down the Mississippi, that silted artery of America's heartland. She and John Sladen drank the night wind on the hurricane deck. A great fleet awaited them at the mouth of the river, the decks thick with an army of conquest. From a mournful distance, George Stapleton and their sons watched her, calamity on their baffled faces. She would bear their pain and her own pain, she would bear the pain of the whole wounded nation because it was necessary. Only those who understood the remorseless exactions of fame would forgive her. It might take a hundred, perhaps a thousand years. Nevertheless, Caroline Kemble Stapleton told herself she was content.

SEVEN

THE SCREAM CUT THROUGH THE DARK silent house like a flash of lightning. It caught Caroline prowling her room, sleepless as usual. Tabitha Flowers was having another nightmare. George had hired her as a house servant at Bowood. Her husband had disappeared. He blamed her for the *Pilgrim* fiasco. Only after Tabitha arrived did they discover she was a mental mess. During her two years in the District of Columbia's prison after her conviction in the *Pilgrim* affair, she had repeatedly been raped by her white jailers. She often awoke the whole house with her nightmares.

Caroline flung on a robe and hurried to Tabitha's third-floor room. As mistress of Bowood, she considered the troubled woman her responsibility. She was also proving to herself, and to George, that she had genuine compassion for Africans.

As usual, Caroline found Mercy Flowers holding Tabitha in her arms. "You just got to give your pain to Jesus, sweetheart," Mercy said. "Think of what He suffered for our sake. He wants to soothe your misery. Just open your heart to Him. Ain't I right, Mrs. Stapleton?"

"Of course," Caroline said. "But I think some warm whiskey and milk would help too."

Mercy hurried off to get the drink. "I'm so sorry, mistress," Tabitha sobbed. "I can't help it. I see them jail guards comin' toward me like they was real. Here in this very room!"

"My heart breaks for you." With a modest discount for hyperbole, Caroline meant these words. She saw no hope for the blacks in America. In the North they were second-class citizens, forbidden the right to vote in most states, condemned to the lowliest jobs.

Downstairs, Caroline met George in the hall. "Did she wake you?" she asked.

"I was awake. Join me in the library for a drink?"

His voice was a croak. He had been stumping the state trying to make Stephen A. Douglas president. Douglas had been nominated by a rump Democratic convention in Baltimore. Earlier in the night George had addressed a huge torchlight rally that had marched to Bowood's steps. He had called for peace and union.

Caroline followed George downstairs reluctantly. She had been avoiding the library. She found it more and more difficult to confront Hannah Cosway Stapleton's beatific gaze. Caroline could not understand it. Her heart remained resolute, and history was lumbering relentlessly toward her rendezvous with fame. The only explanation was the guilt she felt whenever she gazed into George Stapleton's haunted eyes.

The Democratic Party had come apart. No less than three different candidates were running in its ruins. Meanwhile, the elongated former congressman from Illinois, Abraham Lincoln, had won the Republican nomination. Caroline could not have chosen a better candidate if she had been given divine permission by her evil god. She had seen Abe in action in Washington, and he had impressed her as an egregious ass. At her suggestion, the local Democratic paper had christened him "the brainless bobolink of the prairies." Born in Kentucky, he had an accent so thick, it made Easterners wince—or, if they were Democrats, laugh. He had declared the Union could not continue to exist half-slave and half-free—and when he was in Congress had introduced a bill to abolish slavery in the capital. His election would be an undebatable reason for the South to secede.

George poured himself a half tumbler of bourbon. He had begun drinking hard as the election slid toward disaster. Unless a miracle occurred in the next few days, Lincoln was going to win the presidency. For a while, George and other Democrats, such as ex-president Tyler, had hoped no one would win a majority of the electoral vote. This would throw the election into the House of Representatives, where a compromise president could be chosen, perhaps from one of the border states, and the South would stay in the Union.

"What should we do if Lincoln wins?" George said.

"Go to Washington immediately and do our utmost to prevent the South from seceding."

George shook his head. "They won't listen to me."

"But they'll listen to John Tyler—and he'll listen to you. So will John Sladen, if you give him a chance."

George shook his big head almost truculently. "The last time I talked to John, he wanted me to join him in a call to invade Mexico again to restore law and order."

"He wasn't the only man who suggested it. President Buchanan was half inclined to it. At least a hundred Americans have been killed, millions of dollars' worth of American-owned property destroyed. The French or the British may take over the country if we continue to do nothing."

The Mexican civil war was still raging with incredible fury. The Americans were too involved with their own looming crisis to do anything about it. But Caroline found it worth discussing with George because it was another chance to edge Maria de Vega to the margins of Senator Stapleton's life.

George's eyes drifted to the portrait of his grandfather the Congressman above the fireplace. "I keep asking myself what he would want me to do."

"He's been dead a long time. I doubt if he would have an easy answer—if he were alive."

Caroline's eyes drifted—or were drawn by some malevolent current—to Hannah Cosway Stapleton's portrait. *Oh, my dear girl, I fear for thy salvation,* the saintly lips whispered.

What would you know about salvation, you simpering fool? I'm thinking about America's salvation. Yes, even the salvation of this black race that you in your Quaker goodness supposedly pitied. I'm offering them a chance to become free men and women in a Southern empire a hundred years from now. I'm trying to avoid a war that could kill a million white men. I've already sacrificed a son to the salvation I worship.

Caroline gulped her bourbon, which George had cut with plenty of water. "I sometimes think we should tell Tabitha's story," she said. "It might shut up a few abolitionists. There's no hope for these pathetic people in the United States of America."

"Somehow I can't believe that," George said. "Though God knows the evidence is in your favor."

Caroline was swept by a violent desire to flee Bowood, to escape those faces on the walls of this room, where the Congressman had persuaded her to join the Stapleton family. "I think we should go to Washington now!" Caroline said. "Today. The Republicans are going to carry New Jersey. Why stay around to make humiliating statements to reporters? Better to retain your role as a national spokesman."

George trudged heavily from the room, his big head drooping, massive shoulders slumped. Caroline was shaken by how old he looked. He was fifty-eight; he looked more worn, more weary, than his grandfather had looked at eighty-five. Was it her fault? A quasi answer drifted from Hannah Stapleton's saintly lips. *Oh, my dear girl, I fear for thy salvation.*

Caroline slammed the library door and went upstairs to begin packing. In twenty-four hours she and George were in Washington, D.C., where the magical telegraph soon informed them and the rest of the nation that Abraham Lincoln had won the presidency with only 39.8 percent of the popular vote.

He had carried New Jersey, New York, and sixteen other Northern and Western states, enough to give him a majority in the electoral college. If New York and New Jersey had voted against him, the election would have been thrown into the House of Representatives.

On December 20, 1860, as the Stapleton family gathered for Christmas in Washington, D.C., South Carolina issued an ordinance of secession and called on other Southern states to join her. The abolitionist press immediately demanded President Buchanan declare war on them, à la Andrew Jackson. But Buchanan, his cabinet dominated by Southerners, did nothing but issue a feeble remonstrance, which was all but dictated by John Sladen. The president declared secession was illegal but said that he had no constitutional authority to prevent a state from leaving the Union. As a practical matter, he said it was unthinkable for one part of the Union to make war on another part of it. He went on to denounce abolitionists' attacks on the South as the chief reason for the crisis.

The day after the White House released this statement, a Capitol page delivered an envelope to the Stapleton door. In it was the presidential message in Buchanan's own handwriting, with a note from John Sladen: *I am appointing you the keeper of our archives.*

Caroline's heart pounded. He knew with uncanny skill what aroused her. She thrust the letter and the message into a dresser drawer. It was too soon to celebrate. She had to continue playing the part of loyal wife and dutiful mother. She soon discovered that she had to summon all her resolution to maintain her self-control.

That night at dinner, Jonathan Stapleton glowered at his mother and father and asked them what they thought of South Carolina's departure from the Union. George said he was dismayed and intended to make a peace proposal in the Senate tomorrow. South Carolina had voted to secede once before and retracted it. He thought they could be persuaded again.

"By what? Sweet words?" Jonathan said. "As I recall the story, you said President Jackson's threat to hang every one of them did the trick."

"South Carolina was isolated then," Caroline said. "Now, thanks to *Uncle Tom's Cabin* and John Brown, the South's attitude has been transformed. That kind of threat would stampede every other Southern state to join them."

"I agree completely with Mother," Paul Stapleton said. He was wearing his gray West Point uniform. Rooming with a cadet from Alabama, he had become a strong advocate of compromise. The idea of facing his classmates on the battlefield appalled him.

"So do I, Jonathan," Laura Biddle Stapleton said. Caroline had discovered she had almost supernatural power over her daughter-in-law. Laura despised her mother for her fanatic abolitionism—and her contemptuous treatment of her father.

"You mean we're just going to sit here and let the Union break up?" Jonathan said.

"It hasn't come to that," George said, visibly agitated.

"It's only a step away, Father," Jonathan said.

He was right of course. The year 1860 began with six more Southern states seceding—Alabama, Florida, Georgia, Louisiana, Mississippi, and Texas. Senator Stapleton's peace proposal, which called for the creation of a $20 million dollar fund to begin the purchase of slaves and their repatriation to Africa or Caribbean islands such as Santo Domingo, went nowhere. The seceding states announced plans to form a Southern confederacy and urged other Southern and border states to join them.

"I think it's time for you to bring President Tyler into the picture," Caroline told George. She and Julia Tyler had been exchanging letters almost daily on the mounting crisis. As the ex-president saw it, Virginia was the key to resolving the situation. If the Old Dominion stayed in the Union, the other border states could be persuaded to follow her lead, reducing the Southern confederacy to such a tiny minority of the states, they would almost certainly lose heart and abandon their course.

In mid-January, George and Caroline journeyed to Sherwood Forest. She thought John Tyler looked haggard. He confessed he had been sleeping badly. "It isn't easy to watch the collapse of the Great American Republic," he said. He saw nothing but disaster emerging from secession. The English would immediately foment trouble between the two American nations. Already they had agents in Virginia and other state capitals assuring them of England's support. Each year their textile factories devoured most of the South's 200 million pounds of cotton. They would love to reduce the South to a client state, then manipulate the price of cotton, adding billions to their profits.

Tyler said he admired George's attempt to solve the crisis with money. But he feared many Southerners would reject the idea as a betrayal of their blacks. "I would find it very hard to sell my people and export them to some unknown fate in a foreign land. I consider them my moral responsibility."

For a while Tyler toyed with a novel idea. Maybe Virginia and the other border states, in which he included the Stapletons' New Jersey, ought to join the seceding states, hold a convention in which they would adopt the U.S. Constitution, with additional safeguards against the abolition of slavery, and invite the other states to join them. "It might end up isolating New England, the seedbed of the abolitionist poison," he said.

George shook his head. With New Jersey and New York in Republican hands again, he thought the proposal would be dismissed with scorn. Instead, George suggested a peace conference to meet in Washington. All the states would send delegates, making it a sort of constitutional convention. Tyler doubted that the seceding states would send anyone. That meant Northerners would have a massive majority. Instead, the ex-president suggested limiting the conference to twelve border states: "That would make for a more manageable number of delegates and would involve the states that have the most to lose from a breakup of the Union."

George concurred, and he and Tyler went to work on drafting an open letter to the *Richmond Enquirer* and other newspapers. Caroline took Julia aside and urged her to suggest that the proposal should include a plea for peaceful separation, if the conference failed. Tyler agreed and asked her and Caroline to draft the paragraph. George looked dubious, but he was in no position to object. Between them the two women produced a cry from the heart.

If the Free and Slave states cannot live in harmony together . . . does not the dictate of common sense admonish to a separation in peace? Better so than a perpetual itch of irritation and ill feeling. Far better than an unnatural war between the sections. Grant that one section shall conquer the other, what reward will be reaped by the victor? Ruin and desolation will everywhere prevail. The victor's brow will be encircled with withered and faded leaves bedewed with the blood of the child and its mother and the father and the son. The picture is too horrible to be dwelt upon.

The letter was printed in hundreds of newspapers. Caroline carefully saved the original. It would be another important document in the archives of the Southern confederacy. She saw herself telling John Sladen the story of her secret triumph as the SS *Delilah* churned through the Mississippi darkness.

Almost instantly, a migraine ravaged her composure. In a day and a night of agony, she began to realize that this image was at the root of her desolating guilt. As George hovered beside her bed, she saw it would be impossible to desert him. The *Delilah* would have to sail without her. She would let John Sladen worship her statue in his secret Temple of Fame. But the real woman would not inflict this ultimate betrayal on her husband.

The Virginia legislature acted swiftly on the proposal for a peace conference. But instead of limiting the conclave to the border states, they called for a meeting of delegates from every state still in the Union. John Tyler gloomily predicted this was a recipe for disaster. Nevertheless he agreed to serve as one of Virginia's five delegates to this "peace convention."

A few days later, the legislatures of Pennsylvania and Ohio passed resolutions offering the federal government troops to suppress "the rebellion" of the seceded Southern states. That filled the ex-president and Senator Stapleton with foreboding. These were two of the border states that Tyler had hoped would be inclined to a peaceful settlement.

In Washington, D.C., Caroline urged the Tylers to stay at the Stapleton house. But Julia felt they should assume a posture of complete neutrality and stay at Brown's Hotel, one of the capital's more elegant hostelries. Virginia had not only appointed Tyler a delegate to the peace convention—he was also a special commissioner to the president.

Julia clung desperately to her image of the ex-president as a conciliator: *The seceding states, on hearing that he is conferring with Mr. Buchanan, will stay their proceedings out of respect for him. If the Northern states will only follow up this measure in a conceding spirit, peace will be assured.*

Caroline sent this sad naive letter to John Sladen with the comment *They're ready, I think.* For a moment she felt wistful, remembering the exaltation of her pursuit of fame as Sarah Polk's partner. She felt no such mystical union with Julia Gardiner Tyler. For another moment Caroline yearned to share everything with Sarah, even her pact with her evil god. But Sarah would never approve, even though she agreed wholeheartedly that the South should be permitted to secede in peace. Sarah refused to face the evil at the heart of the great republic—and would never admit evil must be used to eviscerate it.

On January 24, ex-president Tyler and Julia came to the Stapleton house for dinner. Tyler had conferred with President Buchanan that afternoon. He was not encouraged by what he saw. "The man is in a daze," he said. "All he did was whine at me because some of the seceded states had seized federal forts and arsenals. I tried to make him understand that these were no more than minor irritants, the necessary result of popular excitement."

"He's the worst possible man to have in the White House at a time like this," George said. "He doesn't have the backbone of a jellyfish."

"That may be all to the good, George," Caroline said, "if our goal is peace."

"Our goal is to save the Union," George said.

"That can't be done without peace," Caroline said.

"Precisely my view, Mrs. Stapleton." Tyler joined her in agreeing that Buchanan's spinelessness made it easy to put conciliatory words in his mouth. "The president came around to my opinion on the forts and arsenals. He reassured me that he did not plan to undertake any hostile action to prevent other forts, such as the one in Charleston Harbor, from surrendering to their new masters."

Caroline rushed a report of this conversation to John Sladen. Although Louisiana had seceded, he remained in Washington at President Buchanan's request, prepared to conduct negotiations with the peace convention and with the new president, Abraham Lincoln. That gentleman was wending his way to Washington from Illinois, pausing to speak in New York, New Jersey, and other states, each time sounding more and more shaken by the crisis confronting him.

Three days later, when the 132 delegates to the peace convention gathered in the grand hall of the Willard Hotel, they unanimously elected John Tyler their presiding officer. Caroline invited him and Julia and two dozen of the convention's leading figures to her salon the following night. On paper, the peace delegates were impressive. Their numbers included former governors, senators, and congressmen. Six had served in presidential cabinets. But almost all were now old men, no longer active in politics. They limped on canes and complained of rheumatism and bad stomachs. A delegate from Missouri, speaking in a voice choked with phlegm, told Caroline his lungs were so inflamed he was afraid to go outdoors when it rained. None of them seemed to have much hope of rescuing the situation—although all of them deplored the idea of a civil war.

John Sladen arrived as the parlor reached flood tide. Caroline led him to Julia Tyler, who was receiving compliments in Dolley Madison's old corner. She was wearing a pink tulle Worth gown that her husband said with wry bemusement represented half the profits of Sherwood Forest's wheat crop.

John kissed her hand and played the gallant Southern gentleman. "If only more Northern women had married Southern husbands, the two sections would be conducting a love feast, instead of a hate fest. Where is the president? I want to tell him how much I admire his courage, to take on such a responsibility."

"Between the two of us, he has very little hope of success," Julia said.

"Nevertheless, he can be a powerful voice for peace," John said.

"Exactly what I've been telling Julia," Caroline said.

For a moment some negative thought—was it suspicion?—flashed across Julia's lovely face. Had she heard rumors about Mrs. Stapleton and Senator Sladen? "I hate to see him tarred with failure at this point in his life," Julia said.

"Failure to one set of eyes can be success to another onlooker. Perhaps he should aim his policy in a more *southerly* direction," John said. "Why not shape the convention's proposals to draw Virginia and the border states into the new confederacy? If we could persuade Missouri, Tennessee, Kentucky, Indiana, Delaware, Pennsylvania—and New Jersey to join us—the North would never dare to start a war. The odds would be too close to even. The abolitionists, like all bullies, would lose their nerve."

"A very pregnant thought, Senator," Julia said. "I'll discuss it with the president."

Julia gazed up at Caroline, her expression impenetrable. "Do you really think New Jersey could be persuaded?"

"If George can be persuaded, yes. If I have any influence—" Caroline let her voice break. For a moment her emotion was genuine. "I'd consider it a memorial to Charlie."

Julia nodded. "I'll do what I can."

Several Virginia congressmen arrived to pay court to Julia. Caroline led John Sladen to the other side of the room, where George was talking to another delegate to the peace convention—Judge Jeremy Biddle. Pennsylvania had selected him, apparently on the assumption that the convention would have to grapple with constitutional issues. A dozen other judges were among the delegates. Caroline had invited Jeremy to the salon to demonstrate how totally she forgave him and George for the betrayal of All Mexico.

"I thought the brothers three might profit by a reunion," she said.

"I'm not sure how," John Sladen said. "But I'm willing to shake hands."

He extended his hand to Jeremy, who met it with obvious reluctance. "Jeremy's been telling me about this fellow Lincoln," George said. "He met him several times at the Republican Convention. He says he's no abolitionist."

"He'll have to eat quite a few of his public statements to convince me of that," Caroline said.

"He thinks he might be willing to make a public promise not to interfere with slavery wherever it exists."

"I'm quite sure of that," Jeremy said.

Caroline struggled for self-control. Where did this detestable creature get his capacity to frustrate her deepest desires? "I'm quite certain when his abolitionist friends in Congress get through with him, he'll do no such thing," she said.

John Tyler joined them, a glass of bourbon in his hand. George congratulated him for his opening remarks at the peace convention, in which he called for a triumph over party politics in the name of peace and union. George introduced him to Jeremy and recounted his prediction that Lincoln would be willing to compromise.

"I'm afraid the South wants more than a promise of noninterference," the ex-president said. "Speaking as a Virginian, I'm certain we, and the rest of the South, will never consent to have our blacks cribbed and confined within proscribed and specified limits—and thus be involved in all the consequences of a war of the races in some twenty or thirty years. We must have expansion, and if we cannot obtain that expansion in the Union, we may sooner or later look to Mexico, the West India islands, and Central America as the ultimate reservations of the American branch of the African race."

For a moment Caroline was dazed. She could only gaze into John Sladen's hooded eyes and renew her faith in her evil god. Who else could have put those words on this ex-president's lips? There it was, their entire scenario, endorsed, approved, blessed, by the South's premier living politician.

Jeremy Biddle's face grew grave as he listened to John Tyler's recital of the central cause of the crisis. "I doubt very much if Lincoln will agree to such an idea, Mr. President," Jeremy said. "No more slave states has become the bedrock principle of the Republican Party. I think Lincoln wants peace—but not at the price of annihilating the party that's put him in the White House."

"I hope you're wrong, Judge Biddle," Tyler said. "We'll find out in a week's time. I've requested an interview with Mr. Lincoln as soon as he arrives in this city. It's crucial for us to know the limits of his so-called principles."

Tyler turned away to greet an old friend from Tennessee. The brothers three gazed at each other. George and Jeremy looked stricken. Triumph glittered in John Sladen's saturnine eyes. He had never been a true brother to the other two men. In his bitter soul he rejected their overtures because their noblesse oblige somehow suborned his equality. Now he was about to become their superior, a leader of a new nation, a candidate for the Temple of Fame. In spirit if not in fact, Caroline would stand beside him in that shadowy enclave, his clandestine priestess. A rush of passionate happiness filled her soul. It transcended all and every physical pleasure she had ever known. Like her secret lover, she was affirming her soul's destiny before history's graven face.

EIGHT

"THEY'VE MET HIM," JULIA TYLER SAID. Her face was ashen. From the street, her hack driver asked if he should wait for her. It was Judson Diggs, the fat African who had betrayed Tabitha and the slaves who had fled with her on the *Pilgrim*. "My coach will take Mrs. Tyler wherever she wishes to go," Caroline said, barely managing to conceal her loathing for the man.

Fifteen hours had elapsed since Abraham Lincoln had slunk into Washington in disguise, like a foreign agent infiltrating an enemy country. Senator Stapleton and a few other congressional leaders were told that the president-elect had learned of a plot to assassinate him in Baltimore and had decided to travel incognito on a secret train. George promptly asked if Lincoln would receive Tyler and a delegation from the peace convention to discuss ways to defuse the crisis, which was growing more formidable by the hour. The seceded states had created a government, the Confederate States of America, and elected George's good friend and fellow veteran of the war with Mexico, Jefferson Davis, its president.

A week ago, Senator Stapleton and ex-president Tyler had prevented an explosion that would have undoubtedly meant war. South Carolina had sent a spokesman to Washington, Colonel Isaac W. Hayne, the state's attorney general, to demand the surrender of Fort Sumter, the federal fort in Charleston Harbor. By this time, most of the Southerners in President Buchanan's cabinet had resigned to join the new government taking shape in the South. Buchanan, now under the influence of his Northern attorney general, balked. Hayne claimed the manner of the president's refusal had been personally insulting to him. South Carolina, with a hundred cannon aimed at the fort, threatened to take it by force.

The ex-president and Senator Stapleton had rushed to the White House and persuaded Buchanan to assure the South Carolinians that he had not intended to insult Colonel Hayne and was only interested in peace. Tyler had urged Buchanan either to surrender the fort or reduce its garrison to a token six men. Buchanan refused to do this, pointing out the garrison was already so small, the place was indefensible anytime South Carolina wanted to take it. Nevertheless, Tyler managed to calm the angry men in Charleston and a shaky peace was restored.

Now Julia Tyler was here to tell Caroline what Abraham Lincoln had to say about the looming crisis. Julia brushed aside the offer of tea and asked for eau-de-vie. She was deeply shaken by what she had just heard from John Tyler.

"Mr. Lincoln greeted them warmly at first and praised their efforts to find a peaceful solution to the crisis. But his tone changed when James Sedden, one of the Virginia delegation, challenged him to admit he was an abolitionist. He seemed to regard this as an insult and told Sedden that as an intelligent man he shouldn't make such statements.

"Then William Dodge, a businessman from New York, burst out, 'It is for you, sir, to say whether the whole nation shall be plunged into bankruptcy, whether the grass will grow in the streets of our principal cities. Will you or won't you yield to the just demands of the South? Tell us you won't go to war over slavery!'

"Lincoln replied that he was determined as president to live up to his oath to enforce the Constitution of the United States in every part of every one of the United States—let the grass grow where it may.

"The president—my president," Julia continued with a flicker of a smile, "told Mr. Lincoln the peace convention was going to propose a constitutional amendment which would allow new territories to enter the Union as slave states, if the voters approved. Would he, as president, tolerate such an idea?

"Mr. Lincoln scuffed his shoe on the carpet for a moment and said it would be time to consider that question when it arose.

"Then he added, 'In a choice of evils, war may not always be the worst.' "

Somehow, hearing these words from Julia Tyler made them doubly terrible.

She and Caroline had shared so much of the history of the last twenty years. Caroline was flung back to the dream of fame that the admission of Texas had aroused. But Julia knew nothing of the foul taste of failure that Mexico had inflicted on Caroline and Sarah Polk. Julia had escaped the dark illumination Caroline had experienced on the Mississippi and in New Orleans. She was oblivious to the black anaconda of slavery in America's heart. She still denied the evil that had been perpetrated in the South in the name of profits. Caroline had no such illusions. That left her more exposed to the acute possibility of failure.

"The president, my John, says there's no alternative now but secession and preparation for war. Otherwise, Virginia will have an abolitionist army in its midst, freeing and arming our Africans. His one hope now is to take as many border states as possible with us."

"I'll speak to George tonight. We'll be prepared to join you," Caroline said.

"Do you really think you can persuade him?"

"I'll do everything in my power. *Everything.*"

Julia embraced Caroline. "Oh, my friend. I think I know some of what you feel. Not all. Perhaps it's best that I don't know all."

"It is," Caroline said.

Two hours later, Senator George Stapleton came home from his labors on Capitol Hill. Caroline was waiting for him in a sea green Worth gown. An hour before her dressing table mirror had restored the illusion of youth to her face. The dining room table was set with their best silver and blue Wedgwood china. She had drawn her dark hair back to a thick knot on her neck. Greek, she told herself. Speak as if Aeschylus or Sophocles were writing the words.

She sat in the parlor sipping sherry until George changed and joined her. "I have some remarkable news," he said.

"So have I."

"Ladies first," he said, pouring himself a half glass of bourbon. He was still drinking hard.

"John Tyler has seen Lincoln. The meeting convinced him that there's no alternative to secession." She told him what Lincoln had said about war as the lesser evil.

"I know all about it. Tyler was so upset he came up to the Capitol and told me everything. I calmed him down and went to see Lincoln myself."

"And . . . ?"

"He said I was one of the two or three Democrats in Washington he wanted to meet. He'd heard about my proposal to create a federal fund to begin buying slaves and settling them back in Africa or in the Caribbean. He thought it was a brilliant idea and he was planning to propose it to the new Congress."

Caroline struggled for equilibrium. "George—he's toying with you!"

George gulped his bourbon. "What do you mean? We had a long talk. He's not an abolitionist. He considers them a bunch of madmen. He sees the country trapped between extremists on both sides. Exactly the way I see it."

"Why didn't he say something like that to John Tyler? All he had to do was guarantee there would be no war over slavery—all he had to do was say it. But he wouldn't say it. Because he wants the South to crawl back into the Union like whipped dogs. They'll never do that now."

"What are you telling me?"

"I'm telling you not to let that two-faced liar from Illinois make a fool of you. John Tyler is going back to Virginia as soon as this farce of a peace convention ends and call for immediate secession. He's going to invite the border states to join Virginia. If you truly love this country—and me—you'll go back to New Jersey and tell the state legislature that you agree with him. You'll tell them that if New Jersey speaks out on behalf of the South, it will shock New England's fanatics back to reality. It will shock the whole country."

"I don't understand what's happening to you. I don't understand this—this frenzy."

"It isn't frenzy, George. It's vision. Deeply thought—and felt—vision."

He downed the rest of his drink and paced the parlor, staring at the pattern in the Turkish carpet, then at himself in the mirror, as if he were hoping to find some sort of revelation—or escape.

"Look at me, George," Caroline said, rising to her feet. "Remember what I told you after the Mexican peace fiasco? Remember that I predicted we were throwing away our best hope of rescuing this country from civil war? You laughed at me then. Your wonderful Mexican saint, Maria Pena de Vega, was in charge of your soul. Look at what's happening in Mexico now. Look at what's happening here. Doesn't this *compel* you to recognize my intelligence, my prescience?"

"I've always recognized your intelligence. What I worry about is your *motives.*"

A February wind moaned in the street. Were the furies descending on Washington? Caroline invited them into this seemingly peaceful parlor. She knew exactly what he meant by that word *motives*. He was implying that John Sladen still had a lodgment in her soul. It would have been easy to respond to the accusation with righteous fury. But it was better to ignore it.

"My motives? Let's begin with our two surviving sons, both prime cannon fodder. Let's proceed to your political career. Here's a chance to salvage something significant from the wreckage. A chance to win a niche for yourself in American history as the man who prevented the most unnecessary, the most idiotic war in the history of the world. There may be a chance to win an even larger reputation in the future—as the first president of the Northern Confederacy of America."

He stood there absorbing it. Finally grasping the dimensions of her vision of the future—and his place in it. He went over to the tea table and poured himself a full glass of bourbon. "You've never loved me, have you. Not even for one day. You couldn't be saying this to me if you did."

The words had a terrific impact on Caroline's nerves. She felt the migraine heave in her skull. "I told you how much I loved you, before you came home from Mexico and destroyed it. You're doing it again. By refusing to respect my ideas."

She strode from the room and mounted the stairs with slow emphatic steps, waiting for him to call her back. But he said nothing. In her bedroom, she was seized by a paroxysm of weeping. She fell to her knees and prayed to her evil god. *Kill me now. Kill me. I want to die. I can't say another word. I can't breathe another breath.*

After a long silence came that familiar voice: *Oh, my dear girl, I fear for thy salvation.*

Was she going mad? After another hour of mindless weeping, she put on her fur-lined pelisse and fled the house. She paused in the parlor to savor the memories of a thousand salons. She saw John C. Calhoun and Daniel Webster and Henry Clay and John Quincy Adams flinging admiration at her feet. Was she about to become a ghost, as stripped of life as all of those dead worshipers in fame's temple?

On the frigid street she finally found a hack. Before she looked into the driver's black face, she knew who it would be: Judson Diggs, Tabitha's fat betrayer, mocking her with his whining, self-pitying voice. He took her to Senator Sladen's boardinghouse. She mounted the stairs, hoping she would find him in bed with a whore. She was not coming to him for love. She wanted to know if he sensed it too—the mounting flood of evil, swamping the levees of their vision.

"Who is it?" His voice was blurred.

"Open the door and find out."

He stood there blinking at her in his nightshirt. "What's wrong?"

"Everything. I want to hear you say we're doing the right thing. I need to hear you say it. I begin to doubt it in some terrible way at the bottom of my soul. As if there were some sort of jungle creature loose inside me."

He sat her down and poured her a tumbler of brandy. "We are doing the right thing," he said. "But I begin to wonder if we can win the game. Lincoln is tougher, and shrewder, than anyone expected."

He had heard about Lincoln's response to the peace convention delegates. He only nodded grimly when she told him about his wooing of George. "He's done the same thing with Douglas. He has him saying Democrats should be ready to fight to save the Union. He's convinced the drunken slob that he's Andrew goddamned Jackson."

"Can Tyler bring any border states with him?"

"He's a spent bullet. The failure of the peace convention will finish him. He'll be lucky to persuade Virginia."

"Then there's no hope?"

"If one border state came in, it could swing a lot of others. It's time to play the George card. I didn't think you needed any urging—"

"I've played it. But I loathed it. I can't understand why. I thought I passed through that barrier on the *Delilah.*"

"You never pass through that barrier. It's always there, just ahead of you on the path, waiting to torment you again. What's yours like? Mine is a mass of brambles covered with offal."

"Mine is a wall of fire."

"Perhaps we're in hell and don't know it."

"Then there's no cause to fear it, is there."

"Not as long as we have each other."

He kissed her. She held him at arm's length. "No. I didn't come here for that. I came here to find strength, not more shame."

That last word shook him. But he could not contest it. Shame was unquestionably a legacy of their voyage on SS *Delilah*.

Back at 3600 Pennsylvania Avenue, she saw a light under George's door. She knocked.

"Come in." She found him sitting by the window, drinking. "Where did you go?" he said thickly.

"I went to see John Sladen."

"Why?"

"To find out if there was any hope of a peaceful solution. He says it's dwindling fast. But if one Northern Democratic leader—a man like you—spoke out for the South, it could change everything."

"I left my speech on your bed."

She read the scrawled pages swiftly, voraciously. It opened with all the right things. It denounced the abolitionists as warmongers. It listed the South's injuries. Then it urged the citizens of New Jersey to instruct their legislators to declare the state neutral if the Republican Party launched a war on the South. But it said nothing about joining the South in secession. Instead, George Stapleton had written. *I urge my fellow Democrats to join me in this stance, because I believe it is an honest alternative to civil war. I can only hope that enough Democrats in the South will take a similar stance and give men of goodwill—among whom I number President Abraham Lincoln—a chance to solve our terrible differences without bloodshed.*

"It's useless!" Caroline screamed. Clutching the speech, she stormed back into George's bedroom. "It's useless mushy idiocy. Either say you're with the South or against them!"

George was on his feet. His big arm whirled out of the room's shadows and caught Caroline on the check. The blow was like the crash of an explosion inside and outside her skull. She hurtled backward onto the bed and lay there, a high silvery whine racing through her brain. She rubbed the back of her hand across her mouth and tasted blood.

"You're evil. You destroyed Grandfather. You've almost destroyed me. And I know why. Because in your heart you're still fucking John Sladen!"

"That's not true. I made a vow the other day—no matter what happened, I would never leave you."

"You were planning to leave—to go South with him?"

"Yes. But I realized I loved you too much to do such a thing."

"You're a goddamn liar."

Caroline ruefully rubbed her bruised cheek. "I have lied to you more than once. But I'm not lying now. To do good in this world, George, often you must first do evil. When are you going to stop trying to be good? It's the American male's greatest flaw."

"Get out of this room. Before I kill you."

She stumbled into the hall, the whine in her skull deepening to a roar.

"I'm going to make that speech!" George shouted.

"If you do, you'll make a fool of yourself *forever*."

Three days later, the peace convention collapsed in total disarray. Its proposal for a constitutional amendment was rejected by Congress and ignored by every state legislature still in the dwindling Union. Ex-president John Tyler returned to Richmond with Julia and made a speech on the steps of his hotel, urging Virginia to secede immediately and prepare for war. No one paid much attention to him. Union sentiment was strong in Virginia. Voters elected a convention to discuss secession, but it could not reach a decision.

Senator George Stapleton remained silent. His lack of participation in the Senate's debates was noted by several newspapers. A frantic Julia Tyler wrote to Caroline, asking for an explanation. She told Julia that George had decided now was not the time for him to speak. But Caroline assured her that George would speak, in the right time and the right place. She had begun to see a future for George's neutrality speech.

Senator Stapleton said nothing in the Senate because he was more or less drunk, and because the thought of seeing *I told you so* again in Caroline's eyes paralyzed him. History had proven her horrendously right. The South was seceding. The Mexican civil war grew more and more murderous. He stayed drunk for the next month, during which Abraham Lincoln became president and began dealing with the crisis.

Lincoln's inaugural address was a wary mixture of vows to avoid war and veiled threats to enforce the Constitution. But for the next four weeks, he did not show a sign of enforcing anything. In the Senate, Stephen A. Douglas took charge of the remaining Democrats. Bitter about losing the White House, he was as drunk as George most of the time. But he repeatedly assured everyone that the new president wanted peace and urged Lincoln to do nothing to exacerbate the South. John Sladen attacked Douglas for his refusal to renounce the use of force to prevent secession. Douglas mumbled quotations from Andrew Jackson. Senator Stapleton stared at them both as if they were incarnations of a nightmare.

In the White House, Lincoln remained an enigma. Caroline learned from Julia Tyler that he had secretly offered to evacuate Fort Sumter if the Virginia convention called to debate secession agreed to disband. He was trying to isolate the seven seceded states, so they would crumple before the mere threat of force. John Tyler persuaded the Virginia convention to reject Lincoln's proposal. Tyler no longer had the slightest doubt that Lincoln wanted either a war or a political victory that would leave the South demoralized. Caroline told Julia she agreed completely with the ex-president.

Both sides were playing historic poker, trying to make the other side show the first card. If Lincoln called for troops and invaded a South that had not fired a single shot at a federal soldier, he might find himself deserted by the 2 million Democrats of the North. Caroline was almost certain she could persuade George to make his neutrality speech and take charge of that formidable opposition, bringing Lincoln to a dead stop.

In the middle of the first week in April 1861, John Sladen appeared in Caroline's parlor. It was midmorning. Rain drizzled from a gray sky. He looked as gloomy as the weather. "I'm going South," he said. "President Lincoln's ignored my offer to act as a mediator between the two governments. If I stay here any longer, I'll start to look like a trimmer. People in Louisiana haven't forgotten I'm from New York."

In his tormented eyes, Caroline saw other words. *Will you come with me? The* Delilah *is still steaming from St. Louis to New Orleans.*

"You've heard something. Tell me. I thought we had no secrets."

"The ultras, maniacs like Robert Barnwell Rhett, are telling Jefferson Davis he has to act. He has to do something to show the people that the South means business. They want him to open fire on Fort Sumter."

"Can you stop them?"

"I don't know. I'm going to try."

The words he had struggled to hold back burst from his lips. "Come South with me. Give my life some meaning!"

She seized him by the arms. "John Sladen. Your life has meaning. What we've tried to do has meaning. If we fail, someone will tell our story someday. They'll see the depth and breadth of it—the daring."

He stood there, head down, the sullen defeated boy she had loved in New York. But she did not feel an iota of pity for him. Or desire. Why? Caroline realized she was not the same woman. That naive Ohio farm girl Caroline Kemble had become Caroline Kemble *Stapleton*. To flee South with him like an impassioned adolescent would obliterate the meaning of what they were trying to do. It would destroy all the meanings that Caroline Kemble Stapleton had created from her life.

"I can't—and won't—go with you. It would destroy all hope of playing the George card. He can still be played—even if the worst happens in Charleston."

"How? What can he say?"

She shook her head. "You'll find out when it happens. If it happens."

Caroline kissed John Sladen on the cheek and he trudged into the rain. She was totally alone now, face-to-face with history. Somehow she liked that idea.

A week later, Lincoln decided Fort Sumter was the perfect place to test the South's intentions—and nerves. The site could not have been more symbolic. There it sat in the harbor of Charleston, queen city of the state that had invented secession, a piece of federal property that South Carolina insisted now belonged to her. President Lincoln sent a public message to the governor of South Carolina, announcing he intended to resupply the trapped garrison. Lincoln still insisted he did not want war. He was only trying to retain control of federal property and assist starving federal soldiers, as he was constitutionally required to do.

It was, Caroline admitted, an absolutely masterful move. She had been wrong about this elongated prairie lawyer. He had somehow acquired remarkable capacity since he had repeatedly made a fool of himself as a Whig congressman. Lincoln was playing a card that enabled him to say, *Heads I win, tails you lose.* If Confederate president Jefferson Davis permitted Lincoln to assert federal authority this way, Davis would soon find his government looking as isolated and powerless as Andrew Jackson had made the South Carolina nullifiers of 1833.

On the morning of April 12, 1861, Davis ordered Southern guns to bombard Fort Sumter before Lincoln's relief expedition arrived. Instantly, every Republican newspaper in the nation screamed that the South had fired on the flag and attacked defenseless federal soldiers. A wave of war fever swept the North. President Lincoln called for seventy-five thousand volunteers to suppress an armed rebellion. Within days, Virginia voted to secede.

"Now is the time to declare your neutrality," Caroline told George.

"What are you talking about?" George was still drinking a quart of bourbon a day. She had let him stay drunk, once she saw Lincoln's game. There was no point in a declaration of neutrality until the war began. Then would be the perfect moment for a prominent Northern Democrat to decry the rush to bloodshed and call on his fellow Democrats in the border states around the South to declare a similar neutrality. If it worked, it could prevent Northern armies from marching across Maryland, Tennessee, Kentucky, Missouri, to attack the South. It would predispose them to secede the moment a Northern army invaded their neutral soil. If they all seceded, the South would be too strong to conquer.

A passive George allowed Caroline to summon the leaders of New Jersey's legislature to Bowood. Their salaries, and a good deal more than their salaries, were still being paid by the taxes and other emoluments the Camden & Amboy Railroad forwarded to Trenton each year. Thanks to Jeremy Biddle's talent for corruption, few politicians in America could match Senator Stapleton's ability to get the attention of his state's lawmakers. Caroline also invited a dozen reporters from the leading newspapers of New York, New Jersey, and Pennsylvania.

The senator and his wife traveled from Washington, D.C., in the special sleeping car that their son Jonathan had given them for a thirtieth wedding-anniversary present in 1858. George struggled for sobriety while Caroline worked on the speech until she was satisfied with it. They arrived at Bowood at 10 A.M., and Caroline issued orders for the reception. George showed not the slightest sign of hesitation or doubt. She told him he was speaking for Jonathan's sake, for Paul's sake. For millions of parents with sons who would die in this holocaust. He nodded numbly. He had surrendered totally to her judgment.

An hour before the legislative leaders were scheduled to arrive, Jonathan Stapleton strode into Bowood. He was wearing the blue uniform of a U.S. Army colonel. He stared at the servants in their best livery, the trays of sweetmeats, the rows of champagne glasses, and said, "It looks as if there's going to be a party. Am I invited?"

"Of course," Caroline said. "What are you doing in that extraordinary outfit?"

"I'm raising a regiment to support the president's call for volunteers. I'm hoping Father will issue a statement to help my recruiting."

"Your father is planning to issue a statement. But it won't help your recruiting."

"Why not?"

"He's going to declare New Jersey neutral."

Thunder congealed on Jonathan's brow. "Where is he?"

"In the library, reading over his speech. Don't bother him—"

Jonathan was striding down the hall to the library, ignoring her. "Jonathan!" Caroline cried, rushing after him.

In the library, she found her oldest son confronting George at his paper-strewn desk. "Is it true, Father? I can't believe it!" Jonathan roared. "You're going to let these slaveholders break up the Union?"

"Jonathan—it's none of your business!" Caroline said.

Jonathan gazed coldly at her. "None of my business? I'm thirty-two years old, Mother. I have a son. I hope to have more children. Haven't I got a right to think about the future of my country? For my own sake? For my children's sake?"

He whirled on George. "Father, can't you see what this means? If you let these Southern bastards go in peace, they'll be invading Cuba and Mexico in the next five years. They're all drunk on their purple dream of a slave empire. Charlie told me all about it. Eventually they'll attack us. We've got to fight them now—or never."

Senator Stapleton stared numbly at his son. His desperate eyes roved from Jonathan's inflamed face to Caroline's sculpted ferocity. Jonathan flung up his arm and pointed to the portrait of the Congressman on the wall. "What would he think? Your grandfather? Didn't you tell me how he worshiped the Union?"

George Stapleton's breath began coming in ratchety gasps. "He did, he told me that a hundred times. How much Washington, Hamiliton, valued it."

"I know you and Mother consider me an opinionated loudmouth. If not in my name, then in his name you can't do this, Father. You can't turn your back on your family, your country, this way."

Supreme irony. Here was John Sladen's son, oblivious to his bloodline, lecturing his nonfather about his obligations as a Stapleton. Destroying the dream of fame his real father had nurtured with murderous fervor for two decades. Caroline realized she could silence Jonathan, annihilate this whole heartrending scene by revealing the truth of his origin. She let her eyes stray to Hannah Cosway Stapleton's portrait. Why not perform this ultimate act before those saintly eyes? Become a woman who destroyed her own son— and her husband—in pursuit of fame.

But George spoke first. "You're right." Tears streamed down his cheeks. "Oh, Son, you're right. In my heart I know you're right. But once you've seen a war, you're ready to do almost anything to avoid another one."

"Let us younger men worry about the fighting. I have no doubt whatsoever that seventy-five thousand determined Northern men can march from Washington to Charleston in two weeks. Slavery's made the Southerners soft. They have no stomach for a serious contest."

Jonathan was mouthing standard abolitionist propaganda. "You're an ignorant, arrogant fool," Caroline said.

"He's still right." George picked up the neutrality speech and lumbered across the room to the fireplace. "A match," he mumbled. "Where's a match?"

Jonathan handed him a box from the desk. The first one failed to strike. All Caroline had to do was cry *stop!* and begin telling the truth about Jonathan's paternity. But she did not speak. Behind her she felt Hannah Cosway Stapleton's eyes boring into her skull, telling her she was a Stapleton, just as much as these men. Jonathan was one in spite of having scarcely a single drop of Stapleton blood in his veins.

The Stapletons were more than a bloodline. They were a spiritual enterprise, and they had made Caroline Kemble part of it just as they had made Hannah Cosway part of it. The hint of pain Caroline saw in Hannah's saintly eyes was an echo of the same pain she felt now, facing woman's fate, to be forever torn between visions of an independent self and loyalty to primary bonds, those wordless ties of heart and mind and memory that created a family.

There was something else, something deeper, darker, at work here: evil. She was being asked to embrace or repudiate it one more time. Where, why, had she welcomed it into her soul? Was it that primary act thirty-three years ago in that New York cellar? Or was it her refusal to repudiate that act, her reembrace of it in her long collusion with John Sladen? She saw her descent into evil's underground flow, its rush toward ever darker acts and visions, the war with Mexico, the murder of a president, the voyage on the *Delilah,* the black anaconda in America's heart. For a moment Caroline poised on the shore of the sunless sea, finally understanding that tormented poem. One more step and she would vanish into that somber icy immensity. One more word.

But she could not say it, she could not speak, she could not destroy her woman's soul for the sake of this god of hate and horror that slithered and heaved in her flesh. She could not deny that in spite of bitter disappointments and almost intolerable losses she was glad she had chosen to become Caroline Kemble Stapleton, glad—and proud.

In a moment the neutrality speech was a blazing pyre. Caroline could only watch in amazed dismay. A half hour later, when the legislators and reporters gathered, Senator Stapleton was almost sober. He began the festivities with a toast to the Union. Then he asked Jonathan to stand beside him before the mantel in Bowood's spacious drawing room.

"I asked my son to join me here in his uniform to add substance to a statement I want to make. Bitter though it will be to fight a war against our blood brothers, I have reluctantly concluded that it must be done to preserve a gift handed down to us by our fathers, a gift that is more precious than life itself— our Union. I ask all of New Jersey's Democrats to support the president in his attempt to prevent the secession of the Southern states from this great nation."

The politicians and reporters burst into applause. Caroline turned her back on this collection of fools and walked down the darkened central corridor to the library. She sat down in front of Hannah Cosway Stapleton's portrait and whispered, "You've won."

Why was she able to make this surrender? She could not understand it. History would prove she was right about slavery and letting the South go in peace. If the North won the war—and that was by no means a certainty— the South would be a ruin and 4 million Africans would be free—without a clue on either side about what to do with them. The abolitionists' hate-filled dreams of seeing the blacks become masters of the South would never come true. The people of the North would soon lose what little interest they had in these unfortunate victims of history.

If Hannah Cosway Stapleton's God existed, Caroline was repelled by His crude justice. But she was too intelligent to deny that some sort of supernatural hand seemed to be in this afflicted business. What else explained John Quincy Adams's calamitous death when the treaty of peace with Mexico was about to be rejected? Tabitha's involvement with the *Pilgrim,* destroying George's chance to become president? The failure of Charlie's expedition to Cuba? Some mysterious power seemed to have mocked her struggle for fame.

In her woman's soul, she would continue to defy this being, even though she recognized its incomprehensible presence.

Three months later, North and South fought the first battle of the war at Bull Run in northern Virginia. To the amazement of everyone in the North, the Southerners routed the supposedly well-trained Union Army, sending it fleeing back to Washington a disorganized mob. At Bowood, Caroline read the gory details in the newspapers, wondering if Colonel Jonathan Stapleton was among the casualties. She did not wish her son ill. But she did not wish him well, either. There was no mention of him or his regiment.

Grimly, Caroline mounted the stairs to bring the newspapers to George. Still drinking heavily, he had taken to skipping breakfast. Pushing open the bedroom door, she called, "Are you awake? There's all sorts of blood and thunder in the papers today."

No answer. She walked to the bed. It was empty. Then she saw George's body on the floor beside it, his face purple with apoplexy. He had died like his grandfather, silently, without a struggle. Caroline knelt beside him and touched his discolored cheek. "Oh, George."

She realized that she was not surprised. Once he had become a mere bystander in fame's antechamber, George had grown more and more ghostly, more severed from life and events. She suspected this summons was not unwelcome.

Telegrams called Jonathan from Washington and Paul from West Point. Senator Stapleton lay in state in Bowood's drawing room, and newspapers filled columns with eulogies of his heroism in the Mexican War and his patriotic support of the cataclysm that was raging.

At one point Caroline asked Jonathan if he still thought seventy-five thousand Northern men could march to Charleston in two weeks. "We're changing our minds about a lot of things," he said, avoiding her eyes. Paul, still at West Point, talked morosely about how little meaning the war had for him. Everyone at the Military Academy except a few fanatic abolitionists loathed it.

Caroline offered them neither consolation nor advice. She had lost interest in changing the course of history. All that mattered now was purifying her woman's soul. On the night before George's funeral, she lay awake until the hall clock struck 3 A.M. Flinging on a robe, she went downstairs through the silent house to the drawing room and knelt beside George's open coffin. His big face was peaceful—but empty.

"I'm sorry," she whispered.

She paused, although she had no expectation of an answer.

"I loved you," she whispered. "I truly loved you for that little while— before you came home from Mexico."

Candle in hand, she went down the corridor to the library and lit a lamp before Hannah Cosway Stapleton's portrait. She wanted to hear her say those reproachful words again. This time she would not flinch. But Hannah's saintly lips were silent. Could she possibly no longer fear for Caroline Kemble Stapleton's salvation?

AFTERWORD

In the fall of 1867, Jeremy Biddle journeyed to Bowood to visit Caroline Kemble Stapleton. She listened with barely disguised disdain to his proposal to write a book about her and George and John Sladen and the era through which they had lived. "Do you seriously expect me to trust you?" she said.

He told her she had no choice. It was her one chance to tell the story, her final opportunity to win a modicum of fame. The word brought a contemptuous tightening of that proud mouth. She had no use for the petty fame a writer can bestow. Yet she could not entirely resist the lure of the word.

She agreed to work with him, if he promised to let no one see the book until all of her currently living descendants, including her grandsons (Jonathan's sons) Rawdon and George Stapleton (the latter born in 1863), died.

Jeremy agreed to the bargain. What else could he do? It was a test of his avowed devotion to George Stapleton. In retrospect, it was a fortunate agreement. In return Caroline gave him access to her diaries and letters. He felt free to use material that he would never have dared to expose to public view in his prudish century.

The Principia Foundation is proud to publish this volume in its continuing series on the history of the Stapleton family in America.

James Kilpatrick
President
The Principia Foundation